F. PAUL WILSON:

Bestselling Author of THE KEEP, THE TOMB, THE TOUCH, and BLACK WIND, tells an epic story of political intrigu

Praise for

DYDEETOWN WORLD:

"[A] wonderful future-detec

—**Algis Budrys**, *Fantasy & Science Fiction*

"First rate entertainment. . . . Wilson has devoted most of his efforts to horror fiction of late, but he's a delight in either genre." —*Science Fiction Chronicle*

"Full of nuggets of ingenuity, fast action and deft future world-imagining, it belongs in most sf collections."

—Roland Green, *Booklist*

"The dialogue is crisp, the action is fast-paced, and the enjoyment level is high. . . . Recommended."

—*Wilson Library Bulletin*

"Convincing and compelling. . . . Characters you care about, a convoluted plot, interesting extrapolations, and tension enough to make the combination very satisfying." —*Mystery Scene*

"A worthwhile novel . . . full of nuggets of ingenuity, fast action, and deft world-building." —*Chicago Sun-Times*

"F. Paul Wilson, author of suspense horror novels like *The Keep* and *The Tomb*, here offers a fascinating look into the future. . . . It is a sense-of-wonder novel filled with adventure, intrigue, romance and even danger."

—*Rave Reviews*

More Praise for F. Paul Wilson

BLACK WIND:
"A masterful blend of fantasy and reality, science and sorcery." —**Robert Bloch**, Author of *Psycho*

"F. Paul Wilson weaves spells with words, and *Black Wind* is a stunner. Ambitious, unusual, compelling."
—**Dean R. Koontz**

"A superb feast of storytelling, ingeniously and intricately plotted, compellingly told at a pace which never flags. Suspenseful, moving, and at times intensely horrifying." —**Ramsey Campbell**

THE TERY:
"Thought-provoking science fiction adventure."
—*Booklist*

"Wilson's stories are a cut above. . . . He has the knack for developing characters that tug at the reader's heartstrings." —CompuServe

"Good news: The publication of *The Tery* heralds the re-issuing of F. Paul Wilson's books set in the LaNague Federation. These books . . . are some of Wilson's *best* work . . . a welcome delight!"
—*Science Fiction Review*

F. PAUL WILSON

Edited, Sequenced, and with an Introduction by the Author

THE LaNAGUE CHRONICLES

Grateful acknowledgment is made to the authors listed below; excerpts from their work have been used to open the following chapters:

CHAPTER V: from *The Fall* by Albert Camus © 1956 by Librairie Gallimard, Paris.
CHAPTER VIII: *"Affair with a Green Monkey"* which appeared originally in *Venture*, May, 1957. © 1957 by Theodore Sturgeon.
CHAPTER XI: from *Capitalism and Freedom* by Milton Friedman © 1962 by The University of Chicago.
CHAPTER XIII: from *The Plague* by Albert Camus © 1947 by Librairie Gallimard, Paris.
CHAPTER XIV: from *The Devil's Dictionary* by Ambrose Bierce © 1957 by Hill and Wang, Inc.
CHAPTER XXI: from *Dune* by Frank Herbert © 1965 by Frank Herbert.

A Baen Books Original

Baen Publishing Enterprises
P.O. Box 1403
Riverdale, N.Y. 10471

ISBN: 0-671-72139-9

Cover art by Ken Kelly

First printing, October 1992

Distributed by
SIMON & SCHUSTER
1230 Avenue of the Americas
New York, N.Y. 10020

Printed in the United States of America

Contents

One: CONCEPTION

AN ENEMY OF THE STATE 1

Two: EARLY PHASE

HEALER I: Heal Thyself 276
HEALER II: Heal Thy Neighbor 315

Three: MIDDLE PHASE

HEALER III: Hide Thyself 370
WHEELS WITHIN WHEELS 375
HEALER IV: Find Thy Progeny 563

Four: LATE PHASE

HEALER V: Heal Thy Nation 586

INTRODUCTION

Galactic empires are a joke.

At least I've always thought so. So when I started writing science fiction I looked for something different. I wanted to set my stories against a single consistent, coherent background—my own Future History (à la Heinlein and Niven) because even as a novice I recognized the enormous benefits of such an approach to writer and reader as well. After all, half a dozen stories set against a coherent Future History—an interesting one, that is—acquire a scope and sense of depth unattainable by an equal number of unlinked stories.

And besides, I had an ax to grind.

It was the late Sixties, at the height of the New Wave's reign, when I sketched out the LaNague Federation scenario. My world view—*Weltanschauung*, as the literary folks like to say—differed radically from anything being published at the time. I figured I'd be saying something that wasn't being said by anyone else. And even if I was an unknown and a beginner, maybe readers would notice.

In the late sixties (I don't want to wear that out, but it's germane) radicals were in and the *Zeitgeist* was leftward—the New Left was hot, state socialism was the ideal, and communism was okay. None of those SDS types could imagine a future without communism. I used to get a kick out of watching the lefties on campus tie themselves into moral, intellectual, and ideological knots trying to justify the Stalin years and the Berlin wall. Now even the Russians have disowned both.

Even then, barely two decades old, I knew there was something gravely wrong with statism. I was unable to perceive any functional difference between state socialism, communism, and fascism. Different rhetoric, maybe, but the end product was the same: state control of the schools, the media, the means of production, and ultimately the quality of life—all at the expense of the individual.

So I swiveled in the current and swam in a different direction. Not rightward, but *out*ward. I waded ashore from the left-right stream and became my own kind of radical: a reader of Von Mises and Rothbard, a rational anarchist, an advocate of laissez-faire, a radical capitalist. My economic views immediately turned all the lefties against me. Vehemently so. Conversely, my advocacy of the social freedoms that flow so naturally from a free economy—free speech, an end to the draft, legalization of all drugs and of prostitution—scandalized the conservatives. I became a political nut case. An ideological pariah. Nowhere was home.

Believe me, it ain't easy being green. It was lonely. (I didn't know there were other orphans like me. There were. We simply hadn't found each other yet.)

So when it came time to write my future history I decided to base the sociopolitical structure of my interstellar culture on a foundation of laissez-faire economics. On a practical level, the laissez-faire approach makes a lot more sense than an empire. An empire needs absolute control if indeed it is to function in an empirish way. That's all but impossible over interstellar distances, even with an FTL drive. What's needed is a freer, looser sort of government, one dedicated to preserving the diversity of humanity, allowing it to develop along the myriad possible paths open to it, yet carrying a big club to break up the fight when one segment takes a swing at another. And so, in the LaNague Federation, any type of society, no matter how bizarre or crazy the philosophy at its core, is free to develop and follow any -ism it wishes on its own planet. Stalinism, Fabianism, sado-masochism, Taoism, self-mutilationism, Amazonism, tatooism—anything goes. Not only allowed to develop, but *encouraged* to develop.

With a single proviso: free egress must exist at all times. Anyone who wants to opt out of that society must be allowed to do so.

This then shall be the governing principle—the whole of the law, if you will: Go where thou wilt, do what thou wilt, but initiate no force.

So I spent the 1970s writing LaNague Federation novels and stories. They were not politically correct then, and they are not politically correct now. But in 1979 something called the Libertarian Futurist Society honored *Wheels Within Wheels* with the first Prometheus Award. I learned then that there were other radicals like me out there. I was shocked. I was honored. (And the 7.5 oz. of gold coin that went with the award wasn't so bad either.) In 1990, the Libertarian Futurists elected *Healer* to the Prometheus Hall of Fame. They accorded *An Enemy of the State* the same honor the following year. So this entire omnibus is a Prometheus winner.

What's a libertarian futurist? I'm not sure, but I've developed my own definition: A libertarian futurist is someone who, when confronted with the aphorism that nothing is sure but death and taxes, will disagree on both counts. They're an optimistic bunch. They still believe they can change the world. I wish them well.

I'm not so sanguine. One of the last lines in Pete Townshend's "Won't Get Fooled Again" goes, *Meet the new boss—same as the old boss.* It doesn't have to be that way. But you and I know that it probably *will* be that way. Always. At least here on Sol III. True freedom requires taking responsibility for your own life. That frightens the hell out of too many people. They prefer to have Big Brother holding a safety net for them, and they'll sell their own birthright of autonomy and their children's as well to keep it.

That's why I've placed these stories in the future, and set them on far worlds. Out there. Where the gutsy ones go.

The three core novels are here in their entirety (the picaresque *Healer* has been divided up and its component episodes sequenced throughout the text in proper chronological order) and the result is a giant *roman à thèse.* It's been a couple of decades since the first LaNague stories saw print. Some of the props are creaky (especially the references to computers—who would have believed they could get so small and so fast so soon?). But the ideas are what count here, and they remain as fresh and as relevant as ever. Human freedom and personal self-determination are ideals that don't age.

So for those of you who can still dream, here's how it could happen, here's what it could be like. You and I will never see it, but maybe someday . . . somewhere . . .

F. Paul Wilson
The Jersey Shore, 1991

THE COMPLETE LaNAGUE CHRONOLOGY

For those who like to keep track of such things, here is a chronology of all the LaNague Federation fiction (five novels and five short stories) to date. *An Enemy of the State, Wheels Within Wheels,* and all the *Healer* sections are included in this volume. "Lipidleggin'" is on the list because it's philosophically sympatico and because Gurney is an ancestor of Peter LaNague.

"Lipidleggin'" (*Asimov's SF Magazine* 5–6/78)
AN ENEMY OF THE STATE
DYDEETOWN WORLD (Baen Books, 1989)
THE TERY (Baen Books, 1990)
HEALER I
"To Fill The Sea and Air" (*Asimov's SF Magazine* 2/79)
HEALER II
"The Man With The Anteater" (*Analog* 7/71)
HEALER III
"Higher Centers" (*Analog* 4/71)
WHEELS WITHIN WHEELS
"Ratman" (*Analog* 8/71)
HEALER IV
HEALER V

ONE: CONCEPTION

AN ENEMY OF THE STATE

It appears there will always be unanswered questions about the Green Conspiracy, especially since its chief engineer, Peter LaNague, was not available afterward for questioning. The remarkable depth of his conspiracy's penetration into the fabric of Imperial society left many traceable elements in its wake, and so we have a reasonably clear picture of events during the five-year pre-insurrection period.

But what preceded the conspiracy itself? What started it all? What made Peter LaNague decide that the time was ripe for revolution? Scholars diverge at this point, but the single incident theory appears to be coming into favor in recent texts. The arrival of LaNague on Throne and the cessation of attempts to assassinate Metep VII follow closely on the heels of a small anti-militia riot on Neeka. There was one fatality in that riot—a young woman named Liza Kirowicz. But Kirowicz was her married name. Her maiden name was Boedekker. And there's the rub . . .

from LANAGUE: A BIOGRAPHY
by Emmerz Fent

PROLOGUE

". . . and I say we've had just about enough!"

Liza Kirowicz was in the front row with her husband, cheering, stamping her feet, and shouting with the rest of them. There were about two hundred angry people packed into the hall; the air was hot and reeked of sweat, but no one seemed to take much notice. All were tightly enmeshed in the speaker's word-web.

"It's been well over two standard centuries since we kicked the Earthie militia back to Sol System. They were sucking us dry, taking what we produced and shipping it back to Earth. So our great-great-grandparents revolted and set up the Imperium, supposedly to keep us free. But look at us now: are we any better off? The Imperium has been taxing us since it was formed; and if that wasn't bad enough, it later came around and said Neekan currency was no good—we'd have to pay in Imperial marks. Now, instead of Earthie militia, we have the Imperial Guard all over the planet, to 'protect' us from any possible countermoves by Earth! They must think we're all idiots! The Imperial Guard is here for one reason: to make sure we pay our taxes, and to make sure those taxes go into Metep's coffers on Throne! *That's* why they're here! And I for one have had enough of it!"

Again the audience broke into wild cheering. Jugs were being passed and sampled while coats and inhibitions were being shed. Her lips and finger tips were already starting to tingle, so Liza let the jug pass untasted this time and watched with amusement as her husband Frey took a long pull. They had both been born and bred on Earth, a fact impossible to discern from their appearance. Even their parents would have been hard pressed to recognize their children under the layers of grime and callus.

Like many young couples of their generation, and of generations before them, they had been seduced by the call of pioneer life on the outworlds. Farm workers now, they had been such for almost five local years. Soon they would have enough saved to homestead a tract of their own, and that would mean working even harder. But they were where they wanted to be and loving every minute of it.

The economic situation was far from perfect, however. The standard of living was low on Neeka in the best of times; the taxes that went to the Imperium made things worse. If it hadn't been for those taxes, Liza and Frey would probably have their own place by now. It was galling: taxes were withheld from every pay voucher . . . their pay represented time, and time was life . . . little bits of their lives were being snipped off every pay period and sent to Throne . . . little bits of life trailing off into space.

And now a new levy from Throne: a 2 per cent across the board tax hike to defray further the expenses of the Imperial Guard garrisons on Neeka.

That did it. No more. The garrisons would go. This fellow up on the platform said they didn't need the garrisons and, by the Core, he was right!

Liza felt good. There was an exhilarating warmth spreading evenly throughout her body. She looked at Frey and loved him. She looked at all the weathered, impassioned faces around her and loved them, too. These were real people, solid people, people who were grappling with an alien ecology, aided by a minimal amount of technology and a lot of physical effort. No gentleman farmers here—owner and field hand worked side by side.

The hall had begun to empty, not in an aimless, unhurried dribble, but with a direction. The man on the platform must have said something to activate his listeners—something Liza had missed—because they were pulling on their coats and following him out the double rear doors. Frey pulled her into the surge and she trotted along. They were headed for the local garrison.

The cold night air refreshed her and heightened her perceptions. Shielding her blue eyes against the wind that ran through her auburn hair, Liza glanced at the onyx sky and knew she was no longer an Earthie. The stars looked so *right* tonight. There had been such wrongness up there in the early years after her arrival—the sun had been the wrong shade of fire and the wrong size, the day sky was the wrong shade of blue and by night there were two moons. Both of Neeka's satellites were out tonight; the small, playful Mayna swinging after her remote, austere sister, Palo. Both belonged there. Liza was a Neekan now.

The local garrison was a faceless white block at the corner of the landing pad complex. Two shuttles stood by on the pads ready to scramble the troops up to their orbiting cruiser should the need arise—an eventuality that had become increasingly unlikely with each passing decade since the outworlds' break with Earth, and considered an Imperial fantasy for well over a century. Earth still coveted the outworlds and their resources, but the risk and expense of reclaiming them would be prohibitive.

And so the garrison troopers had it easy. They were reasonably well behaved and their major task throughout their hitch on Neeka was the alleviation of boredom. Until tonight. As the crowd approached, the troopers filed out of the single door on the town side of the building and formed an uneasy semi-circle between the locals and Imperial property. The commander had placed a ringer in the meeting hall to give them early warning should the gathering boil over into a confrontation.

Someone in the crowd started chanting, *"Back to Throne, leave us alone! Back to Throne, leave us alone!"* It was quickly picked up by the rest and all began to stamp their feet in time as they marched and chanted.

Liza had become separated from Frey in the press of bodies and had pushed herself to the front rank in search of him. Once there, however, she quickly forgot about her husband. Her stride was long and determined as she was buoyed along on a wave of fraternity and purpose. They were going to send Metep a message: Yes, Neeka counted itself among the outworlds free from Earth; yes, Neeka counted itself as part of the Imperium. But no more tribute to Metep. No more pieces of life shipped to Throne.

An amplified masculine voice blared from the garrison roof: "PLEASE RETURN TO YOUR HOMES BEFORE SOMEONE SAYS OR DOES SOMETHING WE'LL ALL REGRET LATER. YOUR FIGHT IS NOT WITH US. YOU SHOULD CONTACT YOUR REPRESENTATIVE ON THRONE IF YOU HAVE A GRIEVANCE." The message was repeated. "PLEASE RETURN TO YOUR . . ."

The crowd ignored the warning and doubled the volume of its chant: *"Back to Throne, leave us alone!"*

The troopers, edgy and fidgety, held their weapons at ready. Most of them were young, Throners by birth, soldiers by choice due to the sagging job situation on their homeworld. Their training and seasoning to date had consisted of short sessions in holographic simulators. Most of them viewed the locals as stupid dirt-scratchers who spent their lives breaking their backs on reluctant soil because they didn't know any better; but they also knew the locals to be a tough bunch. The troopers had the weapons but the locals had the numbers, and the troopers faced them uneasily.

"COME NO FURTHER!" the voice atop the garrison shouted into the night. "STOP WHERE YOU ARE OR THE GUARD WILL BE FORCED TO FIRE TO PROTECT IMPERIAL PROPERTY!"

The crowd came on. *"Back to Throne, leave us alone!"*

A lieutenant on the ground shouted to his men. "Make certain all weapons are locked onto the stun mode—we don't want any martyrs tonight!" Glancing quickly at the angry mob that was almost upon him, he said, "Fire at will!"

Tight, intense ultrasonic beams began to play against the front ranks of the crowd with immediate effect. Those caught in the wash of inaudible sound began to reel and crumble to the ground as the microvibrations, pitched especially for the human nervous system, wrought havoc on conduction through their neuronal cytoplasm. As the leaders fell twitching and writhing, those being pushed from behind began to trip over their fallen comrades. Soon the entire march was in complete disarray.

With its momentum broken, the crowd backed off to a safe distance and resigned itself to verbal assaults. The troopers turned off their stunners and returned them to the ready position. In a little while, the marchers on the ground began to stir and rise and stagger back to their waiting friends.

All but one.

Liza Kirowicz was not breathing. It would later be discovered that she had been suffering from an unsuspected and, until then, asymptomatic demyelinating disease of the central nervous system. The result was an exaggerated response to the ultrasonic stun beams, resulting in a temporary paralysis of the mid-brain respiratory center. Without oxygen, temporary soon became permanent. Liza Kirowicz was dead.

It was an incident genuinely regretted by both sides as a tragic and unforeseeable accident. But that made little difference to Liza's father when the news finally reached him on Earth a full standard year later. He immediately began searching for a means of retaliating against the Imperium. And when Peter LaNague learned of that search, he knew his time had come round at last.

Lura Kirowicz was not breathing. It would later be discovered that she had been suffering from an unsuspected and, until then, asymptomatic demyelinating disease of the central nervous system. The result was an exaggerated response to the intrusive alien beams, resulting in a temporary paralysis of the mid-brain respiratory center. Without oxygen, temporary soon became permanent. Lura Kirowicz was dead.

It was an incident genuinely regretted by both sides as a tragic and unforeseeable accident. But that made little difference to Lura's father when the news finally reached him on Earth a full standard year later. He immediately began searching for a means of retaliating against the Imperium. And when Peter L. Nagle learned of that search, he knew his time had come round at last.

PART ONE
THE NIHILIST

The Year of the Tortoise

I

"And how about you? What are *you* rebelling against?"
"Whatta ya got?"

The Wild One

A man would die tonight.

The thin blond man sat in the darkness and thought about that. Long before his arrival on Throne, he had known that lives would be lost, but he had promised—*sworn!*—by all he revered that no man would die by his hand or word. And now, tonight, all that had changed.

He had ordered a man's death. No matter that the man was a killer and would be killed before he could kill again. No matter that it was too late to find another way to stop him, or that a life would be saved as a result.

He had ordered a man's death. And that was ugly.

As Kanya and Josef, shadows among shadows, went through their limbering exercises behind him, the blond man sat motionless and gazed out the window before him. It was not a high window. Cities on the outworlds tended to spread out, not up, and the cities on Throne, oldest of the outworlds, were no exception. It was night and glo-globes below limned the streets in pale orange light as they released the sunlight absorbed during the day. People were moving in steady streams toward Freedom Hall for the Insurrection Day ceremonies. He and his two companions would soon join them.

The man inhaled deeply, held the air, then let it out slowly, hoping to ease some of his inner tension. The maneuver failed. His personal *misho*, sitting on the window sill, responded to the tension it sensed coiled like a spring within him and held its trunk straight up from its earthenware container in a rigid *chokkan* configuration. Turning his head toward the twisting, leaping, gyrating shadows behind him, the man opened his mouth to speak but no words came forth. He suddenly wanted out of the whole thing. This was not in the plan. He wanted out. But that was impossible. A course of action had been started, wheels had been set in motion, people had been placed in sensitive and precarious positions. He had to follow through. It would be years before the plan came to fruition, but the actions of a single man tonight could destroy everything. He had to be stopped.

The blond man swallowed and found his throat dry.

"Time to go."

The shadows stopped moving.

Ω

In pre-Imperium days it had been called Earth Hall and the planet on which it sat had been known as Caelum. Came the revolution and "Earth" was replaced by "Freedom," Caelum renamed Throne, seat of the new Outworld Imperium. The hall's vaulted ceiling, however, remained decorated in the original pattern of constellations as seen from the motherworld, and it was toward those constellations that the climate adjusters pulled the hot fetid air generated by the press of bodies below.

Den Broohnin didn't mind the heat, nor the jostling celebrants around him. His mind was occupied with other matters. He kept to the rear of the crowd, an easy thing to do since everyone else in Freedom Hall was pushing toward the front for a better look at Metep VII. It was Insurrection Day, anniversary of the outworlds' break with Earth.

Broohnin blended easily with the crowd. He stood an average one-point-eight meters tall and wore his black hair and beard close-cropped in the current Throne fashion. His build was heavy, tending toward paunchy; his one-piece casual suit had a grimy, worn appearance. A single distinguishing feature was a triangular, thumbnail-sized area of scar tissue on his right cheek, which could have resulted from a burn or a laceration; only Broohnin knew it had resulted from the crude excision of a patch of Nolevatol rot by his father when he was five years old.

The good citizens around him did not notice that his attention, unlike theirs, was not on the dais. Metep VII, "Lord of the Outworlds," was making the annual Insurrection Day speech, the 206th such speech, and Broohnin was certain that this one would be no different from all the others he had suffered through over the years. His attention was riveted instead on one of the ornate columns that lined the sides of Freedom Hall. There was a narrow ledge between the columns and the outer wall, and although he could detect no movement, Broohnin knew that one of his guerrillas was up there preparing to end the career and the life of Metep VII.

Hollowing out the upper section of one of those columns had been no easy task. Constructed of the Throne equivalent of granite, it had taken a high-energy cutting beam three days to carve out a man-sized niche. The huge amphitheater was reserved for rare state occasions and deserted most of the time; still, it had been nerve-wracking to sneak four men and the necessary equipment in and out on a daily basis.

Yesterday morning the chosen assassin had been sealed into the niche, now lined with a thermoreflective epoxy. He had a small supply of food, water, and air. When the Imperial security forces did an infra-red sweep of the hall on Insurrection Day morning, he went unnoticed.

He was out of the niche now, his joints flexing and extending in joyous relief as he assembled his lightweight, long-focus energy rifle. Today had to be the day, he told himself. Metep had been avoiding the public eye lately; and the few times he did appear, he was surrounded by deflectors. But now, on Insurrection Day, he was allowing himself a few minutes out in the open for tradition's sake. And the assassin knew those moments had to be put to use. Metep had to die . . . it was the only way to bring down the Imperium.

He had no worry for himself. It was Broohnin's contention, and he agreed, that the man who killed Metep would have little fear of official reprisals. The whole Imperium would quickly fall apart and he would be acclaimed a hero at best, or lost in the mad scuffle at worst. Either way, he would come out of the whole affair in one piece—*if* he could kill Metep before the guards found him.

He affixed a simple telescopic sight. The weapon was compatible with the most up-to-date autosighter, but the idea had been vetoed because of the remote possibility that even the minute amount of power used by such an attachment might set off a sensor and alert the security force to his presence. Sliding into a prone position, he placed the barrel's bipod brace on the edge of the narrow ledge, Metep stood sixty meters ahead of him. This would be easy—no adjustments for distance, no leading the target. The proton beam would travel straight and true at the speed of light.

The assassin glanced down at the crowd. The forward part of his body was visible—barely so—only to those at the far side of the hall, and they were all looking at the dais. Except for one . . . he had an odd sensation that whenever he glanced at the crowd, someone down there snapped his or her head away. It couldn't be Broohnin—he was at the back of the hall waiting for Metep's death. No, somebody had spotted him. But why no alarm? Perhaps it was a sympathizer down there, or someone who took him for a member of the security force.

Better get the whole thing over with. One shot . . . that was all it would take, all he would get. Alarms would go off as soon as he activated his rifle's energy chamber and scanners would triangulate his position in microseconds; security forces would move in on him immediately. One shot, and then he would have to scramble back into his niche in the column. But Metep would be dead by then, a neat little hole burned through his brain.

Almost against his will, he glanced again to his right, and *again* experienced the uncanny sensation that someone on the fringe of the crowd down there had just turned his head away. But he could not pinpoint the individual. He had a feeling it could be one of the people near the wall . . . male, female, he couldn't say.

Shrugging uncomfortably, he faced forward again and set his right eye into the sight, swiveled ever so slightly . . . there! Metep's face—fixed smile, earnest expression—trapped in the crosshairs. As he lifted his head from the sight for an instant's perspective, he felt a stinging impact on the right side of his throat. Everything was suddenly red . . . his arms, his hands, the weapon . . . all bright red. Vision dimmed as he tried to raise himself from the now slippery ledge, then it brightened into blazing white light, followed by total, eternal darkness.

A woman in the crowd below felt something wet on her left cheek and put a hand up to see what it was. Her index and middle fingers came away sticky and scarlet. Another large drop splattered on her left shoulder, then a steady crimson stream poured over her. The ensuing screams of the woman and others around her brought the ceremony to a halt and sent Metep VII scurrying from the dais.

A telescoping platform was brought in from the maintenance area and raised to the ledge. To the accompaniment of horrified gasps from the onlookers, the exsanguinated corpse of the would-be assassin and his unused weapon were lowered to the floor. The cause of death was obvious to all within view: a hand-sized star-shaped disk edged with five curved blades had whirled into the man's throat and severed the right carotid artery.

As the body was being trucked away, an amplified voice announced that the remainder of the evening's program was canceled. Please clear the hall. Imperial guards, skilled at crowd control, began to herd the onlookers toward the exits.

Broohnin stood fast in the current, his eyes fixed on his fallen fellow guerrilla as the crowd eddied past.

"Who did this?" he muttered softly under his breath. Then louder. *"Who did this!"*

A voice directly to his right startled him. "We don't know who's behind these assassination attempts, sir. But we'll find them, have no fear of that. For now, though, please keep moving."

It was one of the Imperial Guard, a young one, who had overheard and misunderstood him, and was now edging him into the outward flow. Broohnin nodded and averted his face. His underground organization was unnamed and unknown. The Imperium was not at all sure that a unified revolutionary force even existed. The incidents—the bombings, the assassination attempts on Metep—had a certain random quality about them that led the experts to believe that they were the work of unconnected malcontents. The sudden rash of incidents was explained as me-tooism: one terrorist act often engendered others.

Still, he kept his face averted. Never too careful. Breaking from the crowd as soon as he reached the cool dark outside,

Broohnin headed for Imperium Park at a brisk pace. He spat at the sign that indicated the name of the preserve.

Imperium! he thought. *Everything has "Imperium" or "Imperial" before it!* Why wasn't everyone else on the planet as sick of those words as he was?

He found his brooding tree and seated himself under it, back against the bole, legs stretched out before him. He had to sit here and control himself. If he stayed on his feet, he would do something foolish like throwing himself into the lake down at the bottom of the hill. Holding his head back against the firmness of the *keerni* tree behind him, Den Broohnin closed his eyes and fought the despair that was never very far away. His life had been one long desperate fight against that despair and he felt he would lose the battle tonight. The blackness crept in around the edges of his mind as he sat and tried to find some reason to wait around for tomorrow.

He wanted to cry. There was a huge sob trapped in his chest and he could not find a way to release it.

The revolution was finished. Aborted. Dead. His organization was bankrupt. The tools for hollowing out the column had drained their financial reserves; the weapon, purchased through underground channels, had dried them up completely. But every mark would have been well spent were Metep VII dead now.

Footsteps on the path up from the lake caused Broohnin to push back the blackness and part his eyelids just enough for a look. A lone figure strolled aimlessly along, apparently killing time. Broohnin closed his eyes briefly, then snapped them open again when he heard the footsteps stop. The stroller had halted in front of him, waiting to be noticed.

"Den Broohnin, I believe?" the stranger said once he was sure he had Broohnin's attention. His tone was relaxed, assured, the words pronounced with an odd nasal lilt that was familiar yet not readily identifiable. The man was tall—perhaps five or six centimeters taller than Broohnin—slight, with curly, almost kinky blond hair. He had positioned himself in such a manner that the light from the nearest glo-globe shone over his right shoulder, completely obscuring his facial features. A knee-length cloak further blunted his outline.

"How do you know my name?" Broohnin asked, trying to find something familiar about the stranger, something that would identify him. He drew his legs under him and crouched, ready to spring. There was no good reason for this man to accost him in Imperium Park at this hour. Something was very wrong.

"Your name is the very least of my knowledge." Again, that tantalizing accent. "I know you're from Nolevatol. I know you came to Throne twelve standard years ago and have, in the past two, directed a number of assassination attempts against the life of the current Metep. I know the number of men in your little guerrilla band, know their names and where they live. I even know the name of the man who was killed tonight."

"You know who killed him, then?" Broohnin's right hand had slipped toward his ankle as the stranger spoke, and now firmly grasped the handle of his vibe-knife.

The silhouette of the stranger's head nodded. "One of my associates. And the reason for this little meet is to inform you that there will be no more assassination attempts on Metep VII."

In a single swift motion, Broohnin pulled the weapon from its sheath, activated it, and leaped to his feet. The blade, two centimeters wide and six angstroms thick, was a linear haze as it vibrated at 6,000 cycles per second. It had its limitations as a cutting tool, but certainly nothing organic could resist it.

"I wonder what your 'associates' will think," Broohnin said through clenched teeth as he approached the stranger in a half-crouch, waving the weapon before him, "when they find your head at one end of Imperium Park and your body at the other?"

The man shrugged. "I'll let them tell you themselves."

Broohnin suddenly felt himself grabbed by both arms from behind. The vibe-knife was deftly removed from his grasp as he was slammed back against the tree and held there, stunned, shaken, and utterly helpless. He glanced right and left to see two figures, a male and a female, robed in black. The hair of each was knotted at the back and a red circle was painted in the center of each forehead. All sorts of *things* hung from the belts that circled their waists and crossed their chests. He felt a sudden urge to retch. He knew what they were . . . he'd seen holos countless times.

Flinters!

II

There used to be high priests to explain the ways of the king—who *was* the state—to the masses. Religion is gone, and so are kings. But the state remains, as do the high priests in the guise of Advisers, Secretaries of Whatever Bureau, public relations people, and sundry apologists. Nothing changes.

from THE SECOND BOOK OF KYFHO

Metep VII slumped in his high-back chair at the head of the long conference table. Four other silent men sat in similar but smaller chairs here and there along the length of the table, waiting for the fifth and final member of the council of advisers to arrive. The prim, crisp executive image had fallen away from the "Lord of the Outworlds." His white brocade coat was fastened only halfway up, and his dark brown hair, tinged with careful amounts of silver, was sloppily pushed off his forehead. The sharply chiseled facial features sagged now with fatigue as he rubbed the reddened, irritated whites of his blue eyes. He was one very frightened man.

The walls, floor, and ceiling were paneled with *keerni* wood;

the conference table, too, was constructed of that grainy ubiquitous hardwood. Metep II, designer of this particular room, had wanted it that way. To alter it would be to alter history. And so it remained.

Forcing himself to relax, he leaned back and let his gaze drift toward the ceiling where holographic portraits of his six predecessors were suspended in mid-air. It came to rest on Metep I.

Anyone ever try to kill you? he mentally asked the rugged, lifelike face.

Metep I's real name had been Fritz Renders. A farmer by birth, revolutionary by choice, he had led his ragtag forces in a seemingly hopeless assault against the Earth governorship headquartered here on Throne—then called Caelum—and had succeeded. Fritz Renders had then declared the outworlds independent of Earth, and himself "Lord of the Outworlds." That was 206 years ago today, the first Insurrection Day. The rest of the colonials on other planets rose up then and threw out their own overseers. Earth's day of absentee landlordship over her star colonies was over. The Outworld Imperium was born.

It was an empire in no sense of the word, however. The colonials would not stand for such a thing. But the trappings of a monarchy were felt to be of psychological importance when dealing with Earth and the vast economic forces based there. The very name, Outworld Imperium, engendered a sense of permanence and monolithic solidarity. Nominally at least, it was not to be trifled with.

In actuality, however, the Imperium was a simple democratic republic which elected its leader to a lifelong term—with recall option, of course. Each leader took the title of Metep and affixed the proper sequential number, thereby reinforcing the image of power and immutability.

How things had changed, though. The first council meeting such as this had taken place in the immediate post-revolutionary period and had been attended by a crew of hard-bitten, hard-drinking revolutionaries and the radical thinkers who had gravitated to them. And that was the entire government.

Now look at it: in two short centuries the Outworld Imperium had grown from a handful of angry, victorious interstellar colonials into a . . . business. Yes, that's what it was: A business. But one that produced nothing. True, it employed more people than any other business in the outworlds; and its gross income was certainly much larger, though income was not received in free exchange for goods or services, but rather through taxation. A business . . . one that never showed a profit, was always in the red, continually borrowing to make up deficits.

A rueful smile briefly lit Metep VII's handsome middle-aged face as he followed the train of thought to its end: lucky for this business that it controlled the currency machinery or it would have been bankrupt long ago!

His gaze remained fixed on the portrait of Metep I, who in his day had known everyone in the entire government by face and by name. Now . . . the current Metep was lucky if he knew who was in the executive branch alone. It was a big job, being Metep. A high-pressure job, but one with enough power and glory to suit any man. Some said the position had come to hold more power than a good man would want and an evil man would need. But those were the words of the doom-and-gloomers who dogged every great man's heels. He had power, yes, but he didn't make all the decisions. All the civilized outworlds, except for a few oddball societies, sent representatives to the legislature. They had nominal power . . . nuisance value, really. The real power of the outworlds lay with Metep and his advisers on the Council of Five. When Haworth arrived, the true decision-makers of the Imperium would all be in this one room.

All in all, it was a great life, being Metep. At least until recently . . . until the assassination attempts had started. There had been one previous attempt on a Metep—back when the legal tender laws were being enforced by Metep IV—but that had been a freak incident; a clerk in the agriculture bureau had been passed over at promotion time and laid all blame on the presiding Metep.

What was going on here and now was different. Tonight was the third attempt in the past year. The first two had been bombs—one in his private flitter, and then another hidden in the main entrance from the roof pad of the palatial estate occupied by every Metep since III. Both had been found in time, thank the Core. But this third attack, the one tonight . . . this one had unnerved him. The realization that a man had been able to smuggle an energy weapon into Freedom Hall and had actually been in position to fire was bad enough. But add to that the manner in which he was stopped—his throat sliced open by some grotesquely primitive weapon—and the result was one terrified head of state.

Not only was some unknown, unheralded group trying to bring his life to an end, but another person or group, equally unknown and unheralded, was trying to preserve it. He did not know which terrified him more.

Daro Haworth, head of the Council of Five, entered then, bringing the low hum of conversation around the table and Metep VII's reverie to an abrupt halt. Born on Derby, educated on Earth, he was rumored in some quarters to wield as much power on Throne and in the Imperium as the Metep himself. That sort of talk irked Metep VII, whose ego was unsteady of late. But he had to admit that Haworth possessed a deviously brilliant mind. Given any set of rules or regulations, the man could find a loophole of sufficient size to slip through any program the Metep and his council desired. Moved by neither the spirit nor the letter of any constitutional checks and balances, he could find ways to make almost anything legal—or at least give it a patina of legality. And in those rare instances when his efforts were thwarted, he found the legislature more than willing to modify the troublesome law to specification. A remarkable man.

His appearance, too, was remarkable: deeply tanned skin set against hair bleached stark white, a decadent affectation he had picked up during his years on Earth and never lost. It made him instantly indentifiable.

"Afraid I don't have anything new to tell you on that dead assassin, Jek," Haworth said, sliding into the chair directly to the Metep's right. Like all members of the Council of Five, he called Metep VII by the name his parents had given him forty-seven standard years ago: Jek Milian. Other cronies who had known him way back when and had helped him reach his present position used it, too. But only in private. In public he was Metep VII—to everyone.

"Don't call him an 'assassin.' He didn't succeed so he's not an assassin." Metep straightened in his chair. "And there's nothing new on him?"

Haworth shook his head. "We know his name, we know where he lived, we know he was a dolee. Beyond that, it's as if he lived in a vacuum. We have no line on his acquaintances, or how he spent his time."

"Damn dolees!" was muttered somewhere down the table.

"Don't damn them," Haworth said in his cool, cultured tones. "They're a big vote block—keep a little money in their pockets, give them Food Vouchers to fill their bellies, and there'll be no recall . . . ever. But getting back to this would-be assassin. We *will* get a line on him; and when we do, it will be the end of the group behind these assassination attempts."

"What about that thing that killed him?" Metep asked. "Any idea where it came from? I've never seen anything like it."

"Neither have I," Haworth replied. "But we've found out what it is and it's nothing new. Couple of thousand years old, in fact." He hesitated.

"Well?" The entire table was listening intently.

"It's a *shuriken*, used on old Earth before the days of atmospheric flight." A murmur rose among the other four councilors.

"A relic of some sort?" Metep said.

"No. It's new . . . manufactured only a few years ago." Again the hesitation, then: "And it was manufactured on Flint."

Silence, as deep and complete as that of interstellar space, enveloped the table. Krager, a short, crusty, portly old politico, broke it.

"A Flinter? Here?"

"Apparently so," Haworth said, his delicate fingers forming a steeple in front of him on the table. "Or somebody trying to make us think there's a Flinter here. However, judging by the accuracy with which that thing was thrown, I'd say we were dealing with the real thing."

Metep VII was ashen, his face nearly matching the color of his jacket. "Why me? What could a Flinter possibly have against me?"

"No, Jek," Haworth said in soothing tones. "You don't understand. Whoever threw the *shuriken* saved your life. Don't you see that?"

What Metep saw was a colossal reversal of roles. The man who thought himself the gamemaster had suddenly become a pawn on a board between two opposing forces, neither identified and both totally beyond his control. This was what was most disturbing: he had no control over recent events. And that, after all, was why he was Metep—to control events.

He slammed his palm down on the table. "Never mind what I see! There's a concerted effort on out there to kill me! I've been lucky so far, but I'm not supposed to be relying on luck . . . I'm supposed to be relying on skilled security personnel. Yet two bombs were planted—"

"They were found," Haworth reminded him in a low voice.

"Yes, found." Metep VII lowered his voice to match the level of his chief adviser's. "But they shouldn't have been planted in the first place! And tonight tops everything!" His voice began to rise. "There should have been no way for anyone to get an energy weapon into Freedom Hall tonight—but someone did. There should have been no way for him to set up that weapon and sight in on me—but he did. And who stopped him before he could kill me?" His eyes ranged the table. "*Not* one of my security people, but someone, I'm now told, from Flint! *From Flint!* And there shouldn't even *be* a Flinter on Throne without my knowing about it! My entire security setup has become a farce and I want to know why!"

His voice had risen to a scream by the time he finished and the Council of Five demonstrated concerned respect for his tantrum by pausing briefly in absolute silence.

Haworth was the first to speak, his tone conciliatory, concerned. "Look, Jek. This has us frightened as much as you. And we're as confused as you. We're doing our best to strengthen security and whip it into shape, but it takes time. And let's face it: we're simply not accustomed to this type of threat. It's never been a problem before."

"Why is it a problem now? Why me? That's what I want to know!"

"I can't answer that. At least not yet. In the past, we've always been able to funnel off any discontent in the direction of Earth, always been able to point to Sol System and say, 'There's the enemy.' It used to work beautifully. Now, I'm not so sure."

"It still works." Metep VII had regained his composure now and was again leaning back in his chair.

"To a certain extent, of course it does. But apparently there's someone out there who isn't listening." Haworth paused and glanced at the other members of the council. "Somebody out there thinks *you're* the enemy."

III

> Never initiate force against another. That should be the underlying principle of your life. But should someone do violence to you, retaliate without hesitation, without reservation, without quarter, until you are sure that he will never wish to harm—or never be capable of harming—you or yours again.
>
> from THE SECOND BOOK OF KYFHO
> *(Revised Eastern Sect Edition)*

Nimble fingers ran through his hair, probed his clothes and shoes. Finding him void of further weaponry, they released him.

"That's Josef to your right"—the male figure bowed almost imperceptibly at the waist—"and Kanya to your left"—another bow. "Kanya is personally responsible for the death of your assassin back there in Freedom Hall. I'm told her skill with the *shuriken is without parallel.*"

It's over was the only thought Broohnin's mind could hold at that moment. If Metep was able to hire protection of this caliber, then all hope of killing him was gone.

"How did he do it?" Broohnin said when he was finally able to speak. "What did he have to pay to get Flinters here to do his dirty work for him?"

The blond man laughed—Broohnin still could not make out any facial features—and there was genuine amusement in the sound.

"Poor Den Broohnin! Can't quite accept the fact that there are people other than himself who do not have a price!" The voice took on a sterner tone after a brief pause. "No, my petty revolutionary, we are not here at Metep's bidding. We are here to destroy him. And by 'him' I do not mean the man, but everything he represents."

"Lies!" Broohnin said as loudly as he dared. "If that was true you wouldn't have interfered tonight!"

"How can a man who has built up such an efficient little terrorist group right under the noses of the Imperial Guard be so naïve about the Imperium itself? You're not dealing with a monarchy, my friend, despite all the showy trappings. The Outworld Imperium is a republic. There's no royal bloodline. Metep VII's term is for life, granted, but when he's gone his successor will be elected, just as he was. And should Metep VII be assassinated, a temporary successor will be in his place before the day is out."

"No! The Imperium will collapse! The people—"

"The people will be terrified!" the stranger said in harsh, clipped tones. "Your ill-conceived terrorism only serves to frighten them into clamoring for sterner laws and harsher measures against dissent. You only end up strengthening the very structure you wish to pull down. *And it must cease immediately!*"

The stranger paused to allow his words to penetrate. Then: "The only reason you remain alive at this point is because I have some small use for certain members of your organization. I am therefore giving you a choice: you may fit yourself into my plan or you may return to Nolevatol. Should you choose the former, you will meet me in the rearmost booth of the White Hart Tavern on Rocklynne Boulevard tomorrow night; should you choose the latter, you will be on an orbital shuttle by that time. Choose to oppose me and you will not survive one standard day."

He gave a short, quick bow and strolled back the way he had come. The Flinters disappeared into the darkness with a whisper of sound and Broohnin was suddenly alone once more under his tree. It was as if nothing had happened. As if the entire exchange had been a hallucination.

He had a sudden urge to move, to get where the lights were bright and there were lots of people around. Thoughts swirled through his consciousness in a confused scramble as his pace graduated from a walk to a loping run from the park. There were Flinters on Throne . . . they were here to bring down the Imperium . . . that should have been a cause for rejoicing but it wasn't. Reinforcements had arrived but they might as well be aliens from another galaxy as Flinters.

No one knew anything for sure about Flinters beyond the fact that every member of their culture went about heavily armed and was skilled in the use of virtually every weapon devised by man throughout recorded history. They kept to themselves on their own little world and were rumored to hire out occasionally as mercenaries. But no one could ever document where or when. No traders were allowed to land on Flint—all commerce was conducted from orbit. The Flinters had no relations with Earth and did not recognize the Imperium as the legitimate government of anything. A sick society, by all accepted standards, but one that had proven viable and surprisingly unaggressive.

Broohnin slowed his pace as he reached the well-lit commercial district. Only a few people dawdled about. Even here in Primus, seat of the Imperium and capital of the most cosmopolitan of the outworlds, people went to bed early. News of an attempted assassination of Metep had driven them off the streets even sooner. Dolees were an exception, of course. Excitement of any sort stimulated them, and since they had nothing ahead of them the next day, they could stay out to all hours if they wished. Sometimes that meant trouble. Violent trouble. An unfortunate outsider, or even one of their own, could be beaten, vibed, or blasted for a few marks or just to alleviate the bleakness of their everyday existence.

On any other night Broohnin would have felt uneasy to be weaponless as he passed through knots of bored young dolees. The possibility that a Flinter might be watching him from the shadows erased all other fears, however. The youths ignored him, anyway. He was on the dole himself, sheltered and warmed by rent and clothing allowances, fed via Food Vouchers. And he was scruffy enough to pass for one of them. When he finally reached his side-street, one-room flat, he sealed the door behind him and flopped on the thin pneumatic mattress in the corner. And began to shake.

He was no longer faceless. Playing the guerrilla, the unseen terrorist, striking from the shadows and running and striking again was exciting, exhilarating. He could remain a shadow, an anonymous symbol of revolt. He could go down to the public vid areas and mingle with the watchers as reports of his latest terrorist acts were replayed in all their holographic splendor.

But that was over now. Someone knew his name, where he came from, and all he had done. And what one man could learn, so could others.

Flinters! He couldn't get over it. Why was Flint involving itself in the overthrow of the Imperium? Its attitude toward interplanetary matters had always been strict non-involvement. Earth and the rest of Occupied Space could fall into the galactic core for all Flint cared. Why were Flinters here now?

And that other one . . . the blond man. He was no Flinter. His accent hovered on the brink of recognition, ready to fall into place. But not yet. That was not what was bothering Broohnin, however. The most deeply disturbing aspect of the scene back in Imperium Park was the realization that the blond man seemed to be in command of the Flinters. And nobody tells Flinters what to do. They have utter contempt for all would-be rulers and barely recognize the existence of the rest of humanity . . . with the possible exception of the residents of the planet Tolive—

Tolive! Broohnin rose to a sitting position. *That* was the blond man's accent—he was a Tolivian! And that was the connection between him and the Flinters. Outworld history lessons from his primary education trickled back to him as the associations multiplied.

The key was Kyfho, a staunchly individualistic, anarcho-capitalist philosophy born on Earth before the union of the Eastern and Western Alliances. Its adherents became outcasts on the crowded collectivist motherworld, forming tight, tiny enclaves in an attempt to wall out the rest of the world. An impossible task. The all-pervasive world government seeped through every chink in their defenses and brought the movement to near extinction.

The interstellar colonization program saved it. Any sufficiently large group of prospective colonists meeting the given requirements of average age and rudimentary skills was given free transportation one way to an Earth-class planet. It was understood that there would be no further contact with Earth and no rescue should the colony run into trouble. A sink-or-swim proposition. Earth had its hands full managing the awesome mass of its own population, the solar system colonies, and its own official star colonies. It could afford neither the talent nor the expense of playing guardian to a host of fledgling interstellar settlements.

The response was overwhelming. The followers of every utopian philosophy on Earth sent delegations to the stars to form the perfect society. Splinter colonies, as they came to be known, were sent off in every direction. Wherever an exploration team had discovered an Earth-class planet, a splinter group was landed. Tragically and predictably, many failed to survive a single turn around the primary. But a significant percentage hung on and kept on, making mankind an interstellar race in the truest sense.

The program served two purposes. It gave divergent philosophies a chance to test their mettle . . . if they thought they had the answers to humanity's social ills, why not form a colonial group, migrate to a splinter world, and prove it? The program's second purpose directly benefited the newly unified Earth state by unloading a host of dissidents on the stars, thereby giving it some time to consolidate its global reach. The plan worked beautifully. The troublemakers found the offer irresistible and Earth once more became a nice place for bureaucrats to live. It was such an easy and efficient solution . . . but one that Earth would pay for dearly in the future.

By the time the splinter colony program was getting started, the Kyfho adherents had mitosed into two distinct but cordial factions. Each applied separately for splinter colony status and each was approved. The first group, composed of rationalists and intellectual purists, was a quiet, introspective lot, and named its planet Tolive. The second group wound up on a harsh, rocky planet called Flint. Its members had been raised for the most part in the Eastern Alliance and had somehow blended Kyfho with remnants of old Asian cultures; each adherent had become an army unto him- or herself.

Like most splinter colonies, both groups had major problems and upheavals during their first century of existence, but both survived with their own form of the Kyfho philosophy intact. It had been that philosophy which kept both planets aloof when the rest of the splinter colonies joined Earth in the establishment of an outworld trade network, and subsequently spared them the necessity of joining in the revolution that broke Earth's resultant economic stranglehold on those very same outworlds. Neither Tolive nor Flint had taken any part in the formation of the Outworld Imperium and had ignored it during its two centuries of existence.

But they were not ignoring it now, as Den Broohnin was well aware. Flint and Tolive were actively involved in bringing down the Imperium. Why? There would always be a philosophical link between the two cultures, a bond that the rest of the outworlds could neither share nor understand. Perhaps it was something in that very philosophy which was bringing them into the fray. Broohnin knew nothing about Kyfho . . . did not even know what the word meant.

Or was it something else? The blond stranger seemed to have eyes everywhere. Perhaps he knew some secret plans of Metep and his Council of Five that would explain the sudden appearance of Flinters and Tolivians on Throne. Something big must be in the wind to make them reverse their centuries-old policy on non-involvement.

Broohnin dimmed the light and lay back on the mattress. He was not going to leave Throne, that was certain. Not after all the effort he had invested in Metep's downfall. Nor was he going to risk being killed by some bizarre Flinter weapon.

No, he was going to be at the White Hart tomorrow night and he was going to be all ears. He was going to agree to any conditions the blond man wanted and was going to play along as long as it seemed to suit his own purposes. For if nothing else, Den Broohnin was a survivor.

VOLUME 1  NUMBER 1

THE ROBIN HOOD READER

Look to the Skies!

A
TAX
REFUND
IS
COMING

Look to the Skies!

The Economic Weather Eye

PRICE INDEX (using the 115th year of the Imperium—when the Imperial mark became mandatory legal tender—as base year of 100)	154.6
MONEY SUPPLY (M3)	949.4
UNEMPLOYMENT LEVEL	7.6%

	Imperial Marks	Solar Credits
GOLD (Troy ounce)	226.2	131.7
SILVER (Troy ounce)	10.3	5.9
Bread (1 kg. loaf)	.62	1.81

IV

No state shall . . . make anything but gold and silver coin a tender in payment of debts. . . .

The Constitution of the United States

"What *are* these things?"

"Flyers. Nobody seems to know where they came from but they're all over the city. I thought they'd amuse you."

After Metep had the courtesy of first look, Haworth passed other copies of the flyer across the table to the rest of the Council of Five. The mood around the table had relaxed considerably since Metep's outburst. Expressions of deep concern for his safety had mollified the leader and it was decided to lower further his already low public profile.

"Robin Hood, eh?" Krager said, smiling sardonically as he glanced over the flyer. He looked to Haworth. "Wasn't he . . . ?"

"An old Earth myth, right," Haworth replied with a nod. "He robbed from the rich and gave to the poor."

"I wonder which of the rich he plans to rob?"

"Not from me, I hope," Bede, the slim Minister of Transportation said with a laugh. "And what's this little insignia top and bottom? Looks like an omega with a star in it. That supposed to mean something?"

Haworth shrugged. "Omega is the last letter in the Greek alphabet. If this is some revolutionary group, it might mean the Last Revolution or something equally dramatic. 'The Last Revolution of the Star Colonies.' How does that sound?"

"It doesn't sound good," Metep said. "Especially when they appear on the night of an assassination attempt."

"Oh, I doubt there's a link," Haworth said slowly. "If there were, the flyers would have been printed up in advance proclaiming your death. This mentions nothing about death or disaster. Probably a bunch of Zem addicts, but I'm having security check it out anyway."

Bede's brow was furrowed. "Isn't omega also the ohm, symbol for resistance? Electrical resistance?"

"I believe it is," Krager said. "Perhaps this Robin Hood group—it may be one man for all we know—considers itself some sort of resistance or revolutionary group, but the message in this flyer is totally economic. And well informed, too. Look at that price index. Sad but true. It takes 150 current marks to buy now what 100 marks bought back in the 115th year. That's a lot of inflation in eighty years."

"Not really," Haworth said, looking up from the notes before him on the table.

"That's Earthie talk," Krager said, an ill-concealed trace of annoyance in his tone. "The Earthies are used to inflation by now—"

"Earth has recently brought her economy under control and—"

"—but we outworlders are still suspicious of it." The older man had raised his voice to cut off Haworth's interjection and had perhaps put unnecessary emphasis on the word "we." Haworth's Earth-gained education still raised hackles in certain quarters of the Imperium.

"Well, we'd all better *get* used to it," Haworth said, oblivious to any implied slur, "because we're all going to be living with it for a long time to come."

Amid the mutterings up and down the table, Metep VII's voice broke through. "I take it, then, the new economic projections are in and that they're not good."

"Not good at all," Haworth said. "This downtrend is not one of the cyclic episodes the outworld economy has experienced from time to time in the past half dozen decades. We are in a slow, steady decline in exports to Earth with no slackening of our import growth rate. I don't have to tell any of you how serious that is."

They all knew. Knew too well.

"Any bright ideas on how we can turn it around—besides more inflation?" It was Krager speaking, and his tone had yet to return to neutral.

"Yes, as a matter of fact. But I'll get to that later. Those of you who have kept up to date know that we're caught in the middle of two ongoing trends. Earth's rigid population controls are paying off at last; their demand for grain and ore is decreasing, and at a faster rate than anyone expected. Outworld populations, on the other hand, are expanding beyond our ability to keep up technologically. So our demand for Sol System hardware keeps growing."

"The answer is pretty obvious, I think," Metep VII said with bland assurance. "We've got to pump a lot more money into our own technical companies and make them more competitive with Earth's."

"How about an outright subsidy?" someone suggested.

"Or an import tax on Earth goods?" from another.

Haworth held up his hands. "This has to be a backdoor affair, gentlemen. A subsidy will have other industries wailing for some of the same. And an import tax will upset the whole economy by sending technical hardware prices into orbit. Jek's right, however. We have to pump money into the right industries, but discreetly. Very discreetly."

Krager again: "And where do we get it?"

"There are ways."

"Not by another tax, I hope. We're taking an average of one out of every three marks now—seven out of ten in the higher brackets. You saw what happened on Neeka when we announced that surcharge. Riots. And that dead girl. Not here on Throne, thank you!"

Haworth smiled condescendingly. "Taxes are useful, but crude. As you all know, I prefer adjustments in the money supply. The net result is the same—more revenue for us, less buying power for them—but the process is virtually undetectable."

"And dangerous."

"Not if handled right. Especially now while the Imperial mark still has some strength in the interstellar currency markets, we can shove a lot more currency out into the economy and reap the benefits before anyone notices. The good citizens will be happy because they'll see their incomes go up. Of course prices will go up faster, but we can always blame that on unreasonable wage demands from the guilds, or corporate profiteering. Or we can blame it on Earth—outworlders are always more than ready to blame Earth for anything that goes wrong. We have to be careful, of course. We have to prime the pump precisely to keep inflation at a tolerable level."

"It's at 6 per cent now," Krager said, irritated by Haworth's didactic tone.

"We can push it to 10."

"Too dangerous!"

"Stop your nonsensical objections, old man!" Haworth snarled. "You've been living with 6 per cent inflation—causing it, in fact!—for years. Now you balk at 10! Who are you play-acting for?"

"How dare—" Krager was turning red and sputtering.

"Ten per cent is absolutely necessary. Any less and the economy won't even notice the stimulus."

Metep VII and the rest of the Council of Five mulled this dictum. They had all become masters of economic manipulation under Haworth's tutelage, but 10 per cent . . . that marked the unseen border of monetary no-man's land. It was double-digit inflation, and there was something inherently terrifying about it.

"We can do it," Haworth said confidently. "Of course, we have Metep IV to thank for the opportunity. If he hadn't rammed through the legal tender laws eighty years ago, each outworld would still be operating on its own currency instead of the Imperial mark and we'd be helpless. Which brings me to my next topic . . ."

He opened the folder before him, removed a sheaf of one-mark notes, and dropped them on the table.

"I'd like to take the legal tender laws one step further."

Metep VII picked up one of the marks and examined it. The note was pristine, bright orange and fresh out of the duplicator, with the satin gloss imparted by the specially treated *keerni* wood pulp used to make it still unmarred by fingerprints and creases. Intricate scrollwork was printed around the perimeter on both sides; a bust of Metep I graced the obverse while a large, blunt *1* dominated the reverse. Different polymer sheets had been tried and discarded when the legal tender laws were introduced during the last days of Metep IV's reign, but the *keerni* paper held up almost as well and was far cheaper. He lifted the bill to his nose—smelled better, too.

"You're not thinking of going totally electronic like Earth, I hope," he asked Haworth.

"Exactly what I'm thinking. It's the only way to truly fine-tune the economy. Think of it: not a single financial transaction will be executed without the central computer knowing about it. We talk of subsidizing certain industries? With a totally electronic monetary system we can allot so much here, pull away just enough there . . . it's the only way to go when you're working with interstellar distances as we are. And it's worked for Earth."

Metep VII shook his head with deliberate, measured slowness. Here was one area of economic knowledge in which he knew he excelled over Haworth.

"You spent all that time on Earth, Daro," he said, "and got all that fine training in economic administration. But you've forgotten the people you're dealing with here. Outworlders are simple folk the most part. They used to barter exclusively for their needs until someone started hammering coins out of gold or silver or whatever else was considered valuable on that particular colony. Metep IV damn near had a full-scale revolt on his hands when he started to enforce the legal tender laws and make the Imperial mark the one and only acceptable currency in the outworlds."

He held up a one-mark note. "Now you want to take even this away and change it to a little blip in some computer's memory bank? You intend to tell these people that they will no longer be allowed to have money they can hold and count and pass back and forth and maybe bury in the ground somewhere?" Metep VII smiled briefly, grimly, and shook his head again. "Oh no. There's already a maniac fringe group out there trying to do away with me. That's more than enough, thank you. If we even hinted at what you suggest, I'd have every man and woman on the outworlds who owns a blaster coming after me." He lifted a copy of *The Robin Hood Reader* in his other hand. "The author of this would be predicting my death rather than a tax refund. No, my friend. I have no intention of being the only Metep overthrown by a revolution."

He rose from his seat and his eyes came level with Haworth's. "Consider that idea vetoed."

Haworth looked away and glanced around the table for a hint of support. He found none. Metep had veto power at council meetings. He also knew outworld mentality—that was how he became Metep. The matter was, for all intents and purposes, closed. He looked back to Metep VII, ready to frame a graceful concession, and noticed a puzzled expression on the leader's face. He was holding the two sheets of paper—the mark note in his left hand, *The Robin Hood Reader* in his right—staring at them, rubbing his thumbs over the surface of each.

"Something wrong, Jek?" Haworth asked.

The Metep raised each sheet in turn to his nose and sniffed. "Have there been any thefts of currency paper?" he asked, looking up and fixing Krager with his stare.

"No, of course not. We guard the blank paper as well as we guard the printed slips."

"This flyer is printed on currency paper," Metep VII stated. "Impossible!" Krager, who was Minister of the Treasury, reached for one of the flyers on the table. He rubbed it, sniffed it, held it up to gauge the glare of light off its surface.

"Well?"

The old man nodded and leaned back in his form-fitting chair, a dumbfounded expression troubling his features. "It's currency paper all right."

Nothing was said for a long time. All present now realized that the author of the flyer that had been so easily dismissed earlier in the meeting was no fevered radical sweating in a filthy basement somewhere in Primus City, but rather a man or a group of men who could steal currency paper without anyone knowing. And who showed utter disdain for the Imperial mark.

V

> I sometimes think of what future historians will say of us. A single sentence will suffice for modern man: he fornicated and read the papers.
>
> *J. B. Clammence*

The White Hart had changed drastically. The thin blond man whose name was Peter LaNague noticed it as soon as he entered. The décor was the same: the rich paneling remained, the solid *keerni* bar, the planked flooring . . . these were as inviolate as the prohibition against women customers. During the five standard years since he had last visited Throne and had supped and drunk in the White Hart, there had been no physical alterations or renovations.

The difference was in the mood and in the level of sound. The regulars didn't realize it, but there was less talk around the bar these days. No one except LaNague, after a five-year hiatus, noticed. The diminution of chatter, the lengthening of pauses, both had progressed by tiny increments over the years. It was not just that the group's mean age had progressed and that familiarity had lessened what they had left to say to one another. New faces had joined the ranks while some of the older ones had faded away. And yet the silence had crept along on its inexorable course.

The process was less evident in the non-restricted bars. The presence of women seemed to lift the mood and add a certain buoyancy to the room. The men wore different faces then, responding to the opposite sex, playing the game of being men, of being secure and confident, of having everything under control.

But when men got together in places where women could not go, places like the White Hart, they left the masks at home. There was little sense in trying to fool each other. And so a pall would seep through the air, intangible at first, but palpable by evening's end. Not gloom. No, certainly not gloom. These were not bad times. One could hardly call them good times, but they certainly weren't bad.

It was the future that was wrong. Tomorrow was no longer something to be approached with the idea of meeting it head on, of conquering it, making the most of it, using it to add to one's life. Tomorrow had become a struggle to hold one's own, or if that were not possible, to give up as little as possible as grudgingly as possible with as tough a fight as possible.

All men have dreams; there are first-order dreams, second-order dreams, and so on. For the men at the bar of the White Hart, the dreams were dying. Not with howls of pain in the night, but by slow alterations in aspiration, by a gradual lowering of sights. First-order dreams had been completely discarded, second-order dreams were on the way . . . maybe a few in the third-order could be preserved, at least for a little while.

There was the unvoiced conviction that a huge piece of machinery feeding on hope and will and self-determination, ceaselessly grinding them into useless powder, had been levered into motion and that no one knew how to turn it off. And if they were quiet they could, on occasion, actually hear the gears turning.

LaNague took a booth in a far corner of the room and sat alone, waiting. He had been a regular at the bar for a brief period five years ago, spending most of his time listening. All the intelligence gathered by the investigators Tolive had sent to Throne over the years could not equal the insight into the local social system, its mood, its politics, gathered in one night spent leaning against the bar with these men. Some of the regulars with long tenures gave him a searching look tonight, sensing something familiar about him, and sensing too that he wanted to be alone.

If LaNague had judged the man correctly—and he hoped he had—Den Broohnin would walk through the front door momentarily. He would have to be handled carefully. Reason would be useless. Fear was the key: Just the right amount would bring him into line; too much and he would either run or attack like a cornered animal. A dangerous man, an explosive man, his co-operation was imperative if the plan was to maintain its schedule. But could his berserker tendencies be controlled? LaNague didn't know for sure, and that bothered him.

He reviewed what he knew about Broohnin. A native of Nolevatol's great farm lands, he had grown up with little education, spending most of his daylight hours trying to pull a crop from the alien soil of his family's farm. Friction between the boy and his father began and grew and culminated in young Den Broohnin fleeing the family farm—but only after beating his father senseless. He somehow made it to Throne where years on the streets of Primus toughened and seasoned him in the ways of city life.

Somewhere along the line he had come to the conclusion that the Imperium must fall and that he was the one to bring it down—by any means. For Broohnin the murder of the reigning Metep seemed the most direct way to accomplish this. That course of action had to be stopped, for it threatened to ruin all of LaNague's plans.

Ω

When Broohnin entered, the already low level of chatter at the bar lowered further as it does when any outsider ventures near an insular group such as this. He knew his uneasiness showed. His lips were tight behind his beard as his eyes scanned the room. He spotted a blond stranger waving from the corner. Conversation gradually returned to its previous level.

With every muscle in his body tense and ready to spring at the first sign of danger, Broohnin stalked warily to the booth and slid in opposite LaNague.

He was now truly seeing the stranger for the first time. He had spoken to a shadowy wraith last night; the figure before him now was flesh and blood . . . and not exactly an imposing figure. A thin, angular face with an aquiline nose dividing two green eyes, intense, unwavering, all framed with unruly, almost kinky, blond hair. Long neck, long limbs, long tapered fingers, almost delicate. Alarmingly thin now without the bulk of last night's cloak, and dressed only in a one-piece shirtsuit and a vest, all dark green.

"Where are your friends?" Broohnin asked as his eyes roamed the room.

"Outside." The stranger, who already held a dark ale, signaled the barman, who brought the tray he had been holding aside. He placed before Broohnin a small glass of the colorless, potent liquor made from hybrid Throne corn with a water chaser beside it.

Broohnin ran the back of his hand across his mouth in an attempt to conceal his shock: this was what he drank, just the way he drank it. Any hope he had held of dealing with this man on an equal footing had been crushed beyond repair by that one little maneuver. He was completely outclassed and he knew it.

"Am I supposed to be impressed?"

"I certainly hope so. I want you to be in such complete and total awe of my organization and my approach to a . . . change . . . that you'll drop your own plans and join me."

"I don't see that I have much choice."

"You can go back to Nolevatol."

"That's hardly a choice. Neither is dealing with your Flinter friends." He lifted his glass. "To a new order, or whatever you have in mind."

The stranger hoisted his ale mug by the handle, but did not drink. He waited instead until Broohnin had swallowed his sip of liquor, then made his own toast.

"To *no* order."

"I'll drink to that," Broohnin said, and took another burning pull from his glass while the other quaffed half a mugful. That particular toast appealed to him. Perhaps this wouldn't turn out too badly after all.

"LaNague is the name," the stranger said. "Peter LaNague." He brought out a small cube and laid it on the table. "The Flinters gave me this. It creates a spheroid shell that distorts all sound waves passing through its perimeter. Radius of about a meter. It's quite unlikely that anyone here would be much interested in our conversation, but we'll be discussing some sensitive matters, and with all the assassination attempts lately"—a pause here, a disapproving twist of the thin lips—"I don't want some overzealous citizen accusing us of sedition."

He pressed the top of the cube and suddenly the chatter from the bar was muted and garbled. Not a single word was intelligible.

"Very handy," Broohnin said with an appreciative nod. He could think of dozens of uses immediately.

"Yes, well, the Flinter society is obsessed with the preservation of personal privacy. Nothing really new technologically. Only the pocket size is innovative. Now . . ."

"When does the Imperium fall?" Broohnin's interjected question was half facetious, half deadly earnest. He had to know.

LaNague answered with a straight face. "Not for years."

"Too long! My men won't wait!"

"They had better wait." The words hung in the air like a beckoning noose. Broohnin said nothing and kept his eyes on his glass as he swirled the colorless fluid within. The moment passed and LaNague spoke again.

"Most of your men are Throners, I believe."

"All but myself and one other."

"A very important part of my plan will require a group such as yours. It will help if they're natives. Will they co-operate?"

"Of course . . . especially if they have no other choice."

LaNague's head moved in a single, quick, emphatic shake. "I'm not looking for that kind of co-operation. I called you here because you seem to be an intelligent man and because we are both commited to bringing the Outworld Imperium to an end. You've developed an underground of sorts—an infrastructure of dedicated people and I don't think they should be denied the chance to play a part. But you and they must play according to my plan. I want to *enlist* your aid. The plan requires informed, enthusiastic participation. If that is beyond you and your cohorts, then you'll not participate at all."

Something was wrong here. Broohnin sensed it. Too much was being withheld. Something did not ring true, but he could not say where. And there was an air of—was it urgency?—about the slight man across the table from him. Under different circumstances he would have played coy and probed until he had learned exactly what was going on. But this fellow had Flinters at his beck and call. Broohnin wanted no part of any games with them.

"And just what is this plan of yours? What brings a Tolivian to Throne as a revolutionary?"

LaNague smiled. "I'm glad to see I didn't underestimate your quickness. The accent gave me away, I suppose?"

"That, and the Flinters. But answer the question."

"I'm afraid you're not in a position of confidence at this point. Be secure in the knowledge that the stage is being set to bring down the Imperium with a resounding crash—but without slaughter."

"Then you're a dreamer and a fool! You can't smash the Imperium without taking Metep and the Council of Five out of the picture. And the only way those fecaliths will be moved is to burn a few holes in their brain pans. *Then* see how fast things fall apart! Anything else is wasted time! Wasted effort! Futility!"

As he spoke, Broohnin's face had become contorted with rage, saliva collecting at the corners of his mouth and threatening to fly in all directions. His voice rose progressively in volume and by the end of his brief outburst he was shouting and pounding on the table. He caught himself with an effort, suddenly glad LaNague had brought the damper box along.

The Tolivian shook his head with deliberate slowness. "That will accomplish nothing but a changing of the guard. Nothing will be substantially different, just as nothing is substantially different now from the pre-Imperium days when Earth controlled the outworlds."

"You forget the people!" Broohnin said, knowing he sounded as if he were invoking an ancient god. "They know that everything's gone wrong. The Imperium's only two centuries old and already you can smell the rot! The people will rise up in the confusion following Metep's death and—"

"The people will do nothing! The Imperium has effectively insulated itself against a popular revolution on Throne—and only on Throne would a revolution be of any real significance. Insurgency on other worlds amounts to a mere inconvenience. They're light years away and no threat to the seat of power."

"There's no such thing as a revolution-proof government."

"I couldn't agree more. But think: more than half—*half!*—the people on Throne receive all or a good part of their income from the Imperium."

Broohnin snorted and drained his glass. "Ridiculous!"

"Ridiculous—but true." He began ticking off points on the fingers of his left hand: "Dolees, retirees, teachers, police and ancillary personnel, everyone in or connected to the armed forces"—then switched to his right—"Sanit workers, utility workers, tax enforcers/collectors, prison officials and all who work for them, all the countless bureaucratic program shufflers . . ." He ran out of fingers. "The list goes on to nauseating length. The watershed was quietly reached and quietly passed eleven standard years ago when 50 per cent of Throne's population became financially dependent on the Imperium. A quiet celebration was held. The public was not invited."

Broohnin sat motionless, the rim of his glass still touching his lower lip, a slack expression on his face as LaNague watched him intently. Finally, he set the glass down.

"By the Core!" The Tolivian was right!

"Ah! The light!" LaNague said with a satisfied smile. "You now see what I meant by insulation: the state protects itself from being bitten by becoming the hand that feeds. It insinuates itself into the lives of as many of its citizens as possible, always dressed in the role of helper and benefactor but always leaving them dependent on it for their standard of living. They may not wind up loving the state, but they do wind up relying on it to increasing degrees. And chains of economic need are far harder to break than those of actual physical slavery."

Broohnin's voice was hoarse. "Incredible! I never thought—"

"The process is not at all original with the Outworld Imperium, however. States throughout history have been doing it with varying degrees of success. This one's been slyer than most in effecting it."

As he turned off the sound damper and signaled the waiter for another round, the conversation drifting over from the bar became mildly intelligible. After the drinks had been delivered and the shield was operating again, LaNague continued.

"The Imperium has concentrated its benefits on the citizenry of Throne to keep them in bovine somnolence. The other outworlds, with Flint and Tolive as notable exceptions, get nothing but an occupation force—pardon me, 'defense garrison' is what it's called, I believe. And why this disparity? Because outraged citizens on other planets can be ignored; outraged Throners could bring down the Imperium. The logical conclusion: to bring down the Imperium, you must incite the citizens of Throne to outrage against the state. Against *the state!* Not against a madman who murders elected officials and thus creates sympathy for the state. *He* then becomes the enemy instead of the state."

Broohnin slumped back in his seat, his second drink untouched before him, a *danse macabre* of conflicting emotions whirling across his mind. He knew this was obviously a crucial moment. LaNague was watching him intently, waiting to see if he would accept an indirect approach to felling the Imperium. If he still insisted on a frontal assault, there would be trouble.

"Have I made myself clear?" LaNague asked, after allowing a suitable period of brooding silence. "Do you still think killing Metep will bring down the Imperium?"

Broohnin took a long slow sip of his drink, his eyes fixed on the glass in his hand, and hedged. "I'm not sure what I think right now."

"Answer honestly, please. This is too important a matter to cloud with face-saving maneuvers."

Broohnin's head shot up and his gaze held LaNague's. "All right—no. Killing Metep will not end the Imperium. But I still want him dead!"

"Why? Something personal?" LaNague appeared struck by Broohnin's vehemence.

"No . . . something very general. He's there!"

"And is that why you want the Imperium overthrown? Because it's there?"

"Yes!" Silence followed.

"I'll accept that," LaNague said after a moment's consideration. "And I can almost understand it."

"What about you?" Broohnin asked, leaning forward intently. "Why are you here? And don't tell me it's something personal—you've got money, power, and Flinters behind you. The Gnomes of Tolive wouldn't get involved in something like this unless there was some sort of profit to be made. What's their stake? And how, by the Core, are we going to pull this off?"

LaNague inclined his head slightly in acknowledgment of the "we" from Broohnin, then reached into his vest and withdrew three five-mark notes.

"Here is the Imperium's insulation. We will show the higher-ups and all who depend on it just how thin and worthless it really is. Part of the work has already been done for me by the Imperium itself." He separated the oldest bill and handed it to Broohnin. "Read the legend in the lower right corner there."

Broohnin squinted and read stiltedly: "'*Redeemable in gold on demand at the Imperial Treasury.*'"

"Look at the date. How old is it?"

He glanced down, then up again. "Twenty-two years."

Broohnin felt bewildered, and simultaneously annoyed at being bewildered.

LaNague handed over the second bill. "This one's only ten years old. Read *its* legend."

" '*This note is legal tender for all debts, public and private, and is redeemable in lawful money at the Imperial Treasury.*' " Broohnin still had no idea where the demonstration was leading.

The third bill was handed over. "I picked this one up today—it's the latest model."

Broohnin read without being prompted. " '*This note is legal tender for all debts, public and private.*' " He shrugged and handed back all three mark notes. "So what?"

"I'm afraid that's all I can tell you now." LaNague held up the oldest note. "But just think: a little over two standard decades ago this was, for all intents and purposes, *gold.* This"—he held up the new bill—"is just paper."

"And *that's* why you're trying to topple the Imperium?" Broohnin shook his head in disbelief. "You're crazier than I am!"

"I'll explain everything to you once we're aboard ship."

"Ship? What ship? I'm not going anywhere!"

"We're going to Earth. That is, if you want to come."

Broohnin stared as the truth hit him. "You're not joking, are you?"

"Of course not." The tone was testy. "There's nothing humorous about going to Earth."

"But why would—" He stopped short and drew in a breath, narrowing his eyes. "You'd better not be bringing Earthies into this! If you are, I'll wring your neck here and now and not an army of Flinters will save you!"

LaNague's face reflected disgust at the thought of complicity with Earth. "Don't be obscene. There's a man on Earth I must see personally. On his response to a certain proposal may well hinge the entire success or failure of my plan."

"Who is he? Chief Administrator or some other overgrown fecalith?"

"No. He's well known, but has nothing to do with the government. And he doesn't know I'm coming."

"Who is he?"

"I'll tell you when we get there. Coming?"

Broohnin shrugged. "I don't know . . . I just don't know. I've got to meet with my associates tonight and we'll discuss it."

He leaned forward. "But you've got to tell me where all this is leading. I need something more than a few hints."

Broohnin had noted that LaNague's expression had been carefully controlled since the moment he had entered the tavern. A small repertoire of bland, casual expressions had played across his face, displayed for calculated effect. But true emotion came through now. His eyes ignited and his mouth became set in a fierce, tight line.

"Revolution, my dear Broohnin. I propose a quiet revolution, one without blood and thunder, but one which will shake this world and the entire outworld mentality such as no storm of violence ever shall. History is filled with cosmetic revolutions wherein a little paint is daubed on an old face or, in the more violent and destructive examples, a new head set on an old body. Mine will be different. Truly radical . . . which means it will strike at the root. I'm going to teach the outworlds a lesson they will never forget. When I'm through with the Imperium and everything connected with it, the people of the outworlds will swear to never again allow matters to reach the state they are in now. Never again!"

"But how, damn you?"

"By destroying these"—LaNague threw the mark notes on the table—"and substituting this." He reached into another pocket of his vest and produced a round metal disk, yellow, big enough to cover a dead man's eye, and heavy—very heavy. It was stamped on both sides with a star inside an ohm.

Ω

The circle was to meet at the usual place tonight. Broohnin always referred aloud to the members of his tiny revolutionist cadre as "my associates." But in his mind and in his heart they were always called "the Broohnin circle." It was a varied group—Professor Zachariah Brophy from Outworld U.; Radmon Sayers, an up-and-coming vidcaster; Seph Wolverton with the communications center; Gram Hootre in the Treasury Department; Erv Singh at one of the Regional Revenue Centers. There were a few fringe members who were in and out as the spirit moved them. The first two, Zack and Sayers, had been out lately, protesting murder as a method; the rest seemed to be going along, although reluctantly. But then, who else did they have?

There was only one man on the rooftop: Seph Wolverton.

"Where are the others?"

"Not coming," Seph said. He was a big-boned, hard-muscled man; a fine computer technician. "No one's coming."

"Why not? I called everyone. Left messages. I told them this was going to be an important meeting."

"You've lost them, Den. After last night, they're all convinced you're crazy. I've known you a long time now, and I'm not so sure they're wrong. You took all our money and hired that assassin without telling us, without asking our approval. It's over, Den."

"No, it's not! I started this group! You can't push me out—"

"Nobody's pushing. We're just walking away." There was regret in Seph's voice, but a note of unbending finality, too.

"Listen. I may be able to work a new deal. Something completely different." Broohnin's mind was racing to stay ahead of his tongue. "I made a contact tonight who may be able to put a whole new slant on this. A new approach to stopping the Imperium. Even Zack and Sayers won't want to miss out."

Seph was shaking his head. "I doubt it. They're—"

"Tell them to give it a chance!"

"It'll have to be *awfully* good before they'll trust you again."

"It will be. I guarantee it."

"Give me an idea what you're talking about."

"Not yet. Got to take a trip first."

Seph shrugged. "All right. We've got plenty of time. I don't think the Imperium's going anywhere." He turned without saying good-by and stepped into the drop chute, leaving Broohnin alone on the roof. He didn't like Seph's attitude. He would have much preferred angry shouts and raised fists. Seph looked at him as if he had done something disgusting. He didn't like that look.

Broohnin looked up at the stars. Whether he wanted to or not, it appeared he would be going to Earth with LaNague. There was no other choice left to him, no other way to hold on to the tattered remnants of "the Broohnin circle." He would use LaNague to pull everyone back together, and then take up again where he had left off. Once he got a feel for LaNague he was sure he could find ways to maneuver him into a useful position.

Off to Earth . . . and why not? Who could pass up a free trip like that anyway? Few outworlders ever got there. And right now he was curious enough about what was going on in that Tolivian head to go just about anywhere to find out.

VOLUME I  NUMBER 2

THE ROBIN HOOD READER

A Shot in the Arm

The duplicators at the Imperial Mint are working overtime these days, turning out new mark notes at an alarming rate. The idea is to give our sagging economy a "shot in the arm," which is what deliberate inflation of the money supply is called in Bureaucratese. The theory holds that the extra marks in circulation will increase consumer buying power, which will in turn increase production, which will lead to greater employment, resulting in a further increase in buying power, and so on.

Sounds good, but it doesn't work that way. With more marks suddenly available to buy existing goods, the prices of those goods go up. And stay up. Which means more marks are needed.

Let's continue the medical analogy: it's like treating a steadily weakening patient who's bleeding internally by giving him a shot of Zemmelar and nothing else. True, he feels better for a while, but he's still bleeding. After the Zemmelar wears off, he's weaker than before. So you give him another jolt of Zem and he feels better again, but for a briefer period this time. He continues to weaken. Before long, he's lost. Even if the internal bleeding halts spontaneously, he's too weak to respond . . . and he's now a hopeless Zemmelar addict anyway.

The Economic Weather Eye

PRICE INDEX (using the 115th year of the Imperium—when the Imperial mark became mandatory legal tender—as base year of 100)		155.2
MONEY SUPPLY (M3)		942.6
UNEMPLOYMENT LEVEL		7.6%

	Imperial Marks	Solar Credits
GOLD (Troy ounce)	227.0	131.6
Silver (Troy ounce)	10.4	5.9
Bread (1 kg. loaf)	.62	1.83

VI

Nor law, nor duty bade me fight.
Nor public men nor cheering crowds.
A lonely impulse of delight
Drove to this tumult . . .

Yeats

Vincen Stafford hung lazily suspended alongside the *Lucky Teela* with only a slim cord restraining him from eternity. As Second Assistant Navigator, the fascinating but unenviable duty of checking out all the control module's external navigation equipment fell to him. The job required a certain amount of working familiarity with the devices, more than the regular maintainance crew possessed. Only someone in the Navigator Guild would do. And since Stafford had the least seniority imaginable—this was his first assignment from the guild—he was elected.

Although finished with the checklist, he made no move to return to the lock where he could remove his gear and regain his weight. Instead he floated free and motionless, his eyes fixed on the ring of cargo pods encircling the control module

. . . a gently curving necklace of random, oddly shaped stones connected by an invisible thread, reflecting distant fire.

The outworld-Earth grain run was ready to move. The area here at the critical point in the gravity well of Throne's star was used as a depot for Earth-bound exports from many of the agricultural worlds. The cargo pods were dropped off and linked to each other by intersecting hemispheres of force. When the daisy chain was long enough to assure sufficient profit from the run, the control module and its crew were linked up and all was set to go.

This run would not be completely typical, however. There were two passengers bound for Earth aboard. Unusual. Few if any outworlders outside the diplomatic service had contact with Earth. The diplomats traveled in official crusiers, all others traveled any way they could. The two passengers within had to be wealthy—passage to Earth, even on a grain run, was not booked cheaply. They didn't look rich, those two . . . one dark of clothing, beard, and mood, the other blond and intense and clutching a small potted tree under his arm. An odd pair. Stafford wondered—

He realized he was wasting time. This was his maiden voyage in a navigational capacity and he had to be in top form. It had taken a long time for the guild to find him this post. After spending the required six standard years in intense encephaloaugmented study until he had become facile in every aspect of interstellar flight—from cosmology to subspace physics, from the intricacies of the proton-proton drive to the fail-safe aspects of the command module's thermostat—he was ready for the interstellar void. Unfortunately the void was not ready for him. The runs were not as frequent as they used to be and he had spent an unconscionably long time at the head of the list of applicants waiting for an assignment.

Vincen Stafford did not ask much of life. All he wanted was a chance to get in between the stars and earn enough to support himself and his wife. Perhaps to put away enough to eventually afford a home of their own and a family. No dreams of riches, no pot of gold.

When he had almost despaired of ever being assigned, word had come; he was now officially a spacer. His career had begun. He laughed inside the helmet as his cord reeled him toward the *Teela*'s lock. Life was good. He had never realized how good it could be.

Ω

"Why the bush? You carry it around like you're related to it."

"It's not a bush," LaNague said. "It's a tree. And one of my best friends."

If the remark was meant to be amusing, Broohnin did not find it so. He was edgy, fidgety, feeling mean. The *Lucky Teela* had dropped in and out of subspace three times in its course toward Earth, accompanied by the curious, much-investigated but little-explained wrenching nausea each time.

LaNague did not seem to mind, at least outwardly, but for Broohnin, who had not set foot on an interstellar ship since fleeing Nolevatol, each drop was an unnerving physical trial, causing the sweat to pour off him as his intestines tried to reach the outside world through both available routes simultaneously. In fact, the entire trip was a trial for Broohnin. It reminded him of that farmhouse on Nolevatol where he grew up, a tiny island of wood in the middle of a sea of grain, no one around but his mother, his brother, and that idiot who pretended to be a father. He had often felt like this on the farm . . . trapped, confined, with nothing outside the walls. He found himself wandering the corridors of the control ship incessantly, his palms continually moist, his fingers twitching endlessly as if possessed of a life of their own. At times the walls seemed to be closing in on him, threatening to crush him to currant jelly.

When his mental state reached that stage—when he could swear that if he looked quickly, without warning, to his right or left he could actually catch a trace of movement at the edges of the walls, always toward him, never away—he popped a couple of Torportal tablets under his tongue, closed his eyes, and waited. They dissolved rapidly, absorbed through the sublingual mucosa and into the venous circulation almost immediately. A few good pumps of his heart and the active metabolite was in his brain and at work on the limbic system, easing the tension, pushing back the walls, allowing him to sit still and actually carry on a coherent conversation . . . as he was doing now.

He wondered how LaNague could sit so calmly across the narrow expanse of the tight little cabin. Space was precious on these freight runs: the chairs on which they sat, the table on which LaNague's tree stood, all had sprung from the floor at the touch of an activator plate; the bed folded down from the wall when needed; all identical to Broohnin's quarters across the hall. A commom-use toilet and washroom were located down the corridor. Everything was planned for maximal usage of available space, which meant that everything was cramped to a maddening degree. Yet LaNague seemed unperturbed, a fact which would have infuriated Broohnin to violence were he not presently in a drugged state. He wondered if LaNague used any psychotropics.

"That's Pierrot," LaNague was saying, indicating the tree which stood almost within Broohnin's reach on the table aftward and between them. "He started as a *misho* many years ago and is now a stunted version of the Tolivian equivalent of the flowering mimosa. He shows he's comfortable and at ease now by assuming the *bankan* position."

"You talk like it's a member of the family or something."

"Well . . ." LaNague paused and a hint of a mischievous smile twisted his lips upward. "You might say he *is* a member of my family: my great-grandfather."

Not sure of just how he should take that, Broohnin glanced from LaNague to the tree. In its rich brown, intricately carved *fukuro-shiki-bachi* earthenware container, it stood no taller than the distance from the tip of a man's middle finger to the tip of his elbow. The foliage consisted of narrow, five-fingered fronds, spread wide and lined with tiny leaves, all displayed in a soft umbrella of green over its container. The trunk was gently curved to give an over-all picture of peace and serenity.

A thought occurred to Broohnin, a particularly nasty one that he found himself relishing more and more as it lingered in his mind. He knew he was physically superior to LaNague, and knew they were no Flinters aboard. There was no further reason to fear the Tolivian.

"What would you do if I uprooted your precious little tree and broke it into a pile of splinters?"

LaNague started half out of his chair, his face white. When he saw that Broohnin had not yet made an actual move toward Pierrot, he resumed his seat.

"I would mourn," he said in a voice that was dry and vibrated with—what? Was it fear or rage? Broohnin couldn't tell. "I might even weep. I would burn the remains, and then . . . I don't know. I'd want to kill you, but I don't know if I would do it."

"You won't allow Metep to be killed, but you'd kill me

because of a stinking little tree?" Broohnin wanted to laugh in the other man's face, but the coldness in LaNague's voice gave him pause. "You could get another."

"No. I couldn't. There is only one Pierrot."

Broohnin glanced over to the tree and was startled by the change in its appearance. The finger-like fronds had pulled close together and the trunk was now laser-beam straight.

"You've startled Pierrot into the *chokkan* configuration," LaNague said reproachfully.

"Perhaps I'll break *you* into splinters," Broohnin replied, turning away from the disturbing little tree that changed shape as mood dictated, and focusing again on LaNague. "You've no Flinters to do your dirty work now . . . I could do it easily . . . break your back . . . I'd enjoy that."

He was not saying this merely to frighten LaNague. It would feel *good* to hurt him, damage him, kill him. There were times when Broohnin felt he must destroy something, anything. Pressure built up inside him and fought madly for release. Back on Throne, he would wander through the dimmest areas of the dolee zones when the pressure reached unbearable levels, and woe to the poor Zeemelar addict who tried to assault him for the few marks he had. The ensuing scuffle would be brief, vicious, and unreported. And Broohnin would feel better afterward. Only the Torportal in his system now kept him from leaping at LaNague.

"Yes, I believe you would," LaNague said, totally at ease. "But it might be a good idea to wait until the return trip. We're on our way to Sol System, don't forget. You'd be taken into custody here and turned over to the Crime Authority once we reached the disengagement point. And the Crime Authority on Earth is very big on psycho-rehabilitation."

The inner rage abruptly dissolved within Broohnin, replaced by shuddering cold. Psycho-rehab started with a mindwipe and ended with a reconstructed personality.

"Then I'll wait," he said, hoping the remark did not sound as lame as he felt. There followed a protracted, uncomfortable pause—uncomfortable, it seemed, only for Broohnin.

"What's our first step once we get to Earth?" he asked, forcing himself to break the silence. The whole idea of a trip to Earth to lay groundwork for a revolution in the outworlds bothered him. Bothered him very much.

"We'll take a quick trip to the southern pole to confirm personally a few reports I've had from contacts on Earth. If those prove true—and I'll have to see with my own eyes before I believe—then I'll arrange a meeting with the third richest man in Sol System."

"Who's that?"

"You'll find out when we meet him."

"I want to know *now!*" Broohnin shouted and sprang from his chair. He wanted to pace the floor but there was no room for more than two steps in any direction. "Every time I ask a question you put me off! Am I to be a part of this or not?"

"In time you will be privy to everything. But you must proceed in stages. A certain basic education must be acquired before you can fully understand and effectively participate in the workings of my plan."

"I'm as educated as I need to be!"

"Are you? What do you know about outworld-Sol System trade?"

"Enough. I know the outworlds are the bread basket for Sol System. It's grain runs like the one we're on right now that keep Earth from starving."

"*Kept* Earth from starving," LaNague said. "The need for an extraterrestrial protein source is rapidly diminishing. She'll soon be able to feed her own and these grain runs will become a thing of the past before too long. The outworlds will no longer be Earth's bread basket."

Broohnin shrugged. "So? That'll just leave more for the rest of us to eat."

LaNague's laugh was irritating in its condescension. "You've a lot to learn . . . a *lot* to learn." He leaned forward in his chair, his long-fingered hands slicing the air before him as he spoke. "Look at it this way: think of a country or a planet or a system of planets as a factory. The people within work to produce something to sell to other people outside the factory. Their market is in constant flux. They find new customers, lose old ones, and generally keep production and profits on an even keel. But every once in a while a factory makes the mistake of selling too much of its production to one customer. It's convenient, yes, and certainly profitable. But after a while it comes to depend on that customer too much. And should that customer find a better deal elsewhere, what do you think happens to the factory?"

"Trouble."

"Trouble," LaNague said, nodding. "Big trouble. Perhaps even backruptcy. That's what's happening to the outworlds.

You—I exclude Tolive and Flint because neither of those two planets joined the outworld trade network when Earth was in command, preferring to become self-supporting and thus sparing ourselves dependency on Sol-System trade—you members of the Outworld Imperium are a large factory with one product and one customer. And that customer is learning how to live without you. Before too long you'll all be up to your ears in grain which everyone is growing but no one will be buying. You won't be able to eat it fast enough!"

"Just how long is 'before long'?"

"Eighteen to twenty standard years."

"I think you're wrong," Broohnin said. Although he found the idea of a chaotic economic collapse strangely appealing, he could not buy it. "Sol System has always depended on the outworlds for food. They can't produce enough of their own, so where else can they get it?"

"They've developed a new protein source . . . and they're not feeding as many," LaNague said, leaning back in his chair now.

The pollution in the seas of Earth had long ago excluded them from ever being a source of food. What could be grown on land and in the multilevel warehouse farms was what humanity would eat. Yet as the population curve had continued on its ever-steepening upward climb, slowing briefly now and then, but moving ever upward, available land space for agriculture shrank. As the number of hungry mouths increased and took up more and more living space, Earth's Bureau of Farms was strained to its utmost to squeeze greater and greater yields out of fewer and fewer acres. The orbiting oneils helped somewhat, but the crush of people and the weight of their hunger surpassed all projections. Synthetic foods that could be processed in abundance were violently rejected; palatable staples could not be supplied in sufficient quantities.

And so the outworld trade network was formed. The colonies were recruited and made over into huge farms. Since a whole ring of grain pods could be dropped in and out of subspace almost as cheaply as one, the outworld-Sol System grain runs were begun and it appeared that a satisfactory solution had at last been found.

For a while, it worked. Came the outworld revolution and everything changed. Sol System still received grain from the outworlds, but at a fair market price. Too broke to start settling and developing new farm colonies, Earth turned inward and began setting its own house in order.

First step was genetic registry. Anyone discovered to have a defective, or even potentially defective, genotype—this included myriad recessive traits—was sterilized. Howls and threats of domestic revolution arose, but the Earth government was not to be moved this time. It gave the newly formed Bureau of Population Control police powers and expected it to use them.

An example was made of Arna Miffler: a woman with a genotype previously declared free of dangerous traits. She was young, childless, single, and idealistic. She began a campaign of protest against the BPC and its policies, a successful one in its early stages, one that was quickly gathering momentum. At that time, the BPC re-examined Arna Miffler's genotype and discovered a definite trait for one of the rare mucopolysaccharide disorders. She was arrested at her home one night and led off to a BPC clinic. When released the next morning, she was sterile.

Lawyers, geneticists, activists who came to her aid soon learned that their own genotypes, and those of their families, were undergoing scrutiny. As some of Arna's supporters here and there were dragged off to BPC clinics and sterilized, the protest movement faltered, then stalled, then died. It was quite clear that the Bureau of Population Control had muscle and was not afraid to use it. Resistance was reduced to a whisper.

It rose to a scream again when the next step was announced: reproduction was to be limited to the status quo. Two people were only allowed to engender two more new people. A male was allowed to father two children and no more; a female was allowed to deliver or supply ova for two children and no more. After the live birth of the second child, each was to report for voluntary sterilization.

The option for sterilization after fathering or mothering a second child was about as voluntary as Earth's voluntary tax system: comply or else. The genotype of every newborn was entered into a computer which cross-analyzed each parent's genetic contribution. Once the analysis indicated the existence of a second child derived from a certain genotype, that individual's number was registered and he or she was immediately located and escorted to the nearest BPC clinic, where a single injection eliminated forever the possibility of producing another viable gamete.

The BPC looked on this approach as a masterful compromise. Each citizen was still allowed to replace himself or herself via a child, something many—too many—considered an inalienable right. But no more than self-replacement was permitted. Fathering or mothering a third child was a capital offense, the male or the female parent being chosen for death by lot in order to "make room" for the newborn child.

The population thus decreased by attrition. Death from disease, although rare, still whittled away at the numbers. Accidential deaths did the same at a faster rate. Children who died after birth—even if they were only seconds old—could not be replaced. The one-person/one-child rule was adhered to dogmatically. Special tax incentives were offered to those who would submit to sterilization before giving rise to new life, higher taxes levied on those who insisted on reproduction.

It worked. After two centuries of harsh controls, the motherworld's population was well into an accelerating decline. There were still food riots now and again in a megalopolis, but nowhere near as frequently as before. There was breathing space again; not much, but after what the planet had been through, it seemed like wide open spaces.

"Sol System is rapidly approaching a break-even point," LaNague was saying, "where its population will be such that the existing farm land, the oneils, and the new protein source will be sufficient to feed everyone. That's when it will stop importing grain from the outworlds. That's when the Imperium will fall apart. What we do in the next few days, weeks, and years will decide whether anything is to be saved at all."

Broohnin said nothing as he stood by his chair and considered what he had been told. LaNague made sense, much as he hated to admit it. Everything was going to fall apart one way or another. That seemed certain now. The two men could at least agree on that point.

But as for saving something? He and LaNague would be at odds on that score. Broohnin wanted nothing spared in the final collapse.

VII

You can see it in their eyes as they sit and move the levers that work the gears of the State. They look at you and know there really is a free lunch. And when they reach to tear off a piece of your flesh, do you bite the hand that feeds on you? Or do you, like so many of your fellows, ask if the maggot likes you rare, medium, or well done?

from THE SECOND BOOK OF KYFHO

A drop of blood formed at the puncture site after the needle was removed from LaNague's thumb. The technician dabbed it away and smeared the area with stat-gel to halt any further bleeding.

"That should do it, sir. But let's just run a little check to make sure." She tapped a few numbers into the console on her left, then pointed to a small funnel-like opening at the front of the console. "Put your thumb in there."

LaNague complied and a green light flashed on the counter. "Works?"

The technician nodded. "Perfectly. You are now an official part of the Sol-System credit network."

"I may not appear so on the surface," LaNague said with a wry twist to his mouth, "but inside I am filled with boundless ecstasy."

Broohnin watched the technician smile. It was a nice smile; she was a pretty girl. And LaNague's remark went right by her. Broohnin turned back to the huge transparent plate that made up the greater part of the outer wall of the way station. Earth hung outside.

The *Lucky Teela* had completed its last subspace jump ahead of schedule and had emerged north of the rotating disk of planets, gas giants, and debris that made up Sol System. The grain pods were deposited in orbit around Earth and the two passengers transferred to the *Bernardo de la Paz,* an orbiting depot for people and freight run by the Lunarians. People seemed to be scarce at the moment: except for a group of vacationers outward bound for Woolaville on the winter border of Mars' northern ice cap, Broohnin and LaNague had most of the way station to themselves.

LaNague's first step had been to establish credit for himself before their descent to the planet below. He had given a pile of Tolivian ags to the station's exchequer official in order to establish a balance in Earth's electronic monetary system. The silver coins had been eagerly accepted, converted into Solar credits, and entered into the computer network. A coded signature device had been implanted into the subcutaneous fat pad of his right thumb with an eighteen-gauge needle. As long as his balance lasted, he could buy anything legally available on Earth. A light on consoles similiar to the one beside the pretty technician would flash red when he exhausted it.

"Ingenious little device, wouldn't you say?" LaNague remarked, admiring his thumb as he joined Broohnin at the viewing wall. "I can't even feel it in there."

Broohnin tore his eyes away from the planet below. "What's so ingenious? All I have to do is cut off your thumb and I'm suddenly as rich as you are."

"They're ahead of you there, I'm afraid. The little device is sensitive to extreme alterations in blood flow . . . I imagine that's why they asked me if I had Raynard's disease. Even a tourniquet left in place too long will deactivate it."

Broohnin returned his attention to the view wall. As ever, LaNague was unflappable: he had already considered and discarded the possibility of someone cutting his thumb off. Someday, Broohnin promised himself, he would find a way to break that man. The only time he had been able to pierce the Tolivian's shield was when he had threatened his damned miniature tree. And even that was out of reach now in the quarantine section of the way station. But someday he would get through. Someday . . .

Right now he stood transfixed by the motherworld whirling outside the window.

"Think of it," LaNague said at his shoulder. "Down there is where humanity first crawled out of the slime and started on its trek to the stars."

Broohnin looked and saw something like a blue Nolevatol thornberry, mottled brown with rot and streaked with white mold. He wanted to jump.

Ω

LaNague's thumb was quickly put to good use after they shuttled down to the Cape Horn spaceport. Their luggage was stored, a two-man flitter rented. It was only after they were airborne and headed further south that Broohnin realized the precariousness of his position.

"Think you're pretty smart, don't you?" he told LaNague.

"What's that supposed to mean?"

"Your thumb. It makes you rich and me penniless. You're free to move, I have to follow. You wanted it that way." He felt rage growing within him even as he spoke.

"Never thought of it, actually." LaNague's face was guileless. "I just couldn't see opening two accounts when we're only going to be here for a day or so. Besides"—he held up his right thumb—"this is not freedom. It's the exact opposite. The Earth government has used these implants and the electronic credit network to enslave its population more effectively than any regime in human history."

"Don't try to change the subject—"

"I'm not. Just think what that implant does to me. Every time I use it—to rent this flitter, to buy a meal, to rent a room—my name, the amount of money I spent, what I spent it on, the place of purchase, the time of purchase, all go into the network!" He thrust his thumb toward Broohnin's face. "And this is the only legal money on the entire planet! Coins and paper money have been outlawed—to use any leftovers is illegal. Even barter is illegal. Do you know what that means?"

Surprised by LaNague's vehemence, Broohnin fumbled for an answer. "I—"

"It means your life is one big holovid recording to anyone who wants to know and has connections. It means that somewhere there's a record of every move you make every day of your life. Your entertainment tastes can be deduced from where you spend your leisure time, your sexual preferences from any devices you might buy, your taste in clothes, your favorite drink, your confidences, your infidelities!"

LaNague withdrew his hand and lay his head back into the upper portion of the padded seat. His eyes closed as he visibly relaxed. After a while he exhaled slowly but kept his lids shut, basking in the dying rays of the sinking sun as they played off the sharp planes of his face.

Finally: "If you really want, I'll set up a small credit balance for you when we get to the peninsula."

"Forget it," Broohnin replied, hating the meekness he heard in his voice. "Where are we going?"

LaNague opened his eyes. "I punched in a course for the South Pole, but we'll never reach it. They'll stop us long before we get near it."

The flitter took them across Drake Passage, over the tip of the Antarctic Peninsula, and along the western shore of the Weddell Sea. The concepts of "east" and "west" steadily lost meaning as they traveled toward the point where even "south" held no meaning, where every way was north.

Darkness swallowed them as they cut through the cold air above the monotonous white wastes of the Edith Ronne Ice Shelf. When all around him had become featureless darkness, Broohnin finally admitted to himself that he was frightened. He doubted either of them could survive an hour down there in that cold and wind if the flitter went down.

"This was a stupid idea," he muttered.

"What was?" LaNague, as usual, seemed unperturbed.

"Renting this flitter. We should have taken a commercial flight. What if we have a power failure?"

"A commercial flight wouldn't take us where we have to go. I told you before—I have to see this new protein source myself before I'll really believe it."

"What protein are you going to find on an ice cap? Everything's frozen!" This trip was becoming more idiotic by the minute.

"Not everything, I'll bet," LaNague said, craning his neck forward as he scanned the sky through the observation bubble.

He pointed upward and fifteen degrees off the flitter's port bow. "Look. What do you think those are?"

Broohnin saw them almost immediately. Three long, narrow ellipses of intensely bright light hung in the black of the sky, motionless, eerie.

"How high you think they are?" LaNague asked.

Broohnin squinted. They looked *very* high, almost fixed in the sky. "I'd say they were in orbit."

"You're right. They're in a tight polar orbit."

"Orbiting lights?"

"That's sunlight."

"By the Core!" Broohnin said in a breathy voice. He knew what they were now—mirrors. Orbiting solar reflectors were almost as old in practice as they were in concept. They had been used by wealthy snow belt cities in the pre-interstellar days to reduce the severity of their winter storms. But the advent of weather modification technology had made them obsolete and most of them had been junked or forgotten.

"I've got it!" he said. "Someone's melted enough ice to be able to plant crops at the South Pole!"

LaNague shook his head. "Close, but not quite. I doubt if there's enough arable soil under the ice to plant a crop. And if there were, I certainly wouldn't feel impelled to see it with my own eyes. What I've—"

The traffic control comm indicator on the console flashed red as a voice came through the speaker.

"Restricted zone! Restricted zone! Turn back unless you have authorized clearance! Restricted zone! Restricted—"

"We going to do it?" Broohnin asked.

"No."

He fumbled with the knobs on the console. "Can't we turn it off then?" The repetitious monotone on the recorded warning was getting on his nerves. When the volume control on the vid panel did nothing to lessen the droning voice, Broohnin raised his hand to strike at the speaker. LaNague stopped him.

"We'll need that later. Don't break anything."

Broohnin leaned back and bottled his growing irritation. Covering his ears with his hands, he watched the solar mirrors fatten in the middle, growing more circular, less ellipsoid. As the flitter continued southward, they became almost too bright to look at.

The cabin was suddenly filled with intolerably bright light, but not from the mirrors. A police cutter was directly above them, matching their air speed. The voice from the traffic control comm finally cut off and a new one spoke.

"You have violated restricted air space. Proceed 11.2 kilometers due south and dock in the lighted area to the sentry post. Deviation from that course will force me to disable your craft."

LaNague cleared the pre-programmed course and took manual control of the flitter. "Let's do what the man says."

"You don't seem surprised."

"I'm not. This is the only way to get to the South Polar Plateau without getting blasted out of the air."

The cutter stayed above them all the way to the sentry station and remained hovering over their observation bubble even after they had docked.

"Debark and enter the sentry station," the voice said from the speaker. Without protest, LaNague and Broohnin broke the seal on the bubble, stumbled to the ground, and made a mad dash through the icy wind to the door of the station. The sentry joined them a moment later. He was young, personable, and alone. Broohnin considered the odds to be in their favor, but LaNague no doubt had other ideas.

Ω

It was much roomier in the cab of the sentry's cutter. Broohnin stretched out his legs and started to doze.

"Keep awake!" LaNague said, nudging him. "I want you to see this, too."

Broohnin struggled to a more upright sitting position and glared at the Tolivian. He felt tired, more irritable than usual, and didn't like anyone nudging him for any reason. But his annoyance faded quickly as he remembered LaNague's masterful handling of the sentry.

"Are all Earthies that easy to bribe?" he asked.

There was no humor in LaNague's smile. "I wouldn't be surprised if they were. Those two coin tubes I gave him were full of Tolivian ags, and each ag contains one troy ounce of .999 fine silver. With silver coins, that sentry can operate outside the electronic currency system. The official exchange rate is about six solar credits per ag, but the coins are each worth ten times that in the black market. And believe me, Earth's black market is second to none in size and diversity."

Broohnin remembered the way the sentry's eyes had widened at the sight of the silver coins. The man had looked as if he were about to lick his lips in anticipation. He had hardly seemed to hear LaNague as he explained what he wanted in return for the coins.

"Black market prices are higher," Broohnin said. "Why bother with it?"

"Of course they're higher. That's because they've got something to sell. Look: all prices and wages are fixed on Earth, all goods are rationed. Whatever makes it to the market at the official price disappears in an instant, usually into the hands of friends and relatives of the people with political connections. These people sell it to black marketeers, who sell it to everyday people; the price goes up at each stop along the way."

"That's my point—"

"No. You've *missed* the point. The price of a three-dimensional display module for a home computer is 'X' Solar credits in the government-controlled store; it's a fixed bargain price, but the store never has any. So what good is a fixed price? The black marketeer, however, has plenty of them, only he wants 'double-X' Solar credits for each. It's an axiom of Kyfhon economics: the more rigidly controlled the economy, the bigger and better the black market. Earth's economy is run completely from the top, therefore there's hardly a thing you cannot buy in Earth's black market. It's the biggest and best there is!

"The black market here also means freedom from surveillance. You can buy anything you want without leaving a record of what, where, and when. Of *course* the sentry was easy to bribe! It costs him nothing to let us take this ride, and look what he got in return!"

The sentry had not come along. There was no need to. He had searched them for weapons and cameras; finding none, he had sealed them into the cutter and programmed a low-level reconnaissance flight into the craft's computer. The two outworlders would get a slow fly-by of the area that interested them, with no stops. Anyone monitoring the flight would detect nothing out of the ordinary—a routine fence ride. The chance of the cutter's being stopped with the outworlders aboard was virtually nil. The sentry was risking nothing and gaining a pocketful of silver.

The solar mirrors were now almost perfect circles in the night sky, intolerably bright. LaNague pointed to a soft glow ahead of the horizon.

"That's it. That's got to be it!"

The glow grew and spread left and right until most of the

horizon ahead of them was suffused with a soft yellow haze. Suddenly they were upon it and in it and sinking through wispy clouds of bright mist. When those cleared, they could see huge fields of green far below them. A sheer wall of ice was behind them, swinging away to each side in a huge crystal arc.

"By the Core!" Broohnin said softly. "It's a huge valley cut right out of the ice!"

LaNague was nodding excitedly. "Yes! A huge circular cut measuring thirty kilometers across if my reports are correct—and they haven't failed me yet. But the real surprise is below."

Broohnin watched as their slow descent brought them toward the floor of the valley. The fine mist that layered over the top of the huge man-made depression in the South Polar Plateau diffused the light from the solar mirrors, spreading it evenly through the air. Acting as a translucent screen, it retained most of the radiant heat. The valley was one huge greenhouse. Looking down, Broohnin saw that what had initially appeared to be a solid carpet of green on the valley floor was actually a tight grove of some sort of huge, single-leafed plants. Then he saw that the plants had legs. And some were walking.

"It's true!" LaNague whispered in a voice full of wonder. "The first experiments were begun centuries ago, but now they've finally done it!"

"What? Walking plants?"

"No. Photosynthetic cattle!"

They were like no cattle Broohnin had ever seen. A vivid bice green all over, eight-legged, and blind, they were constantly bumping into and rubbing against each other. He could discern no nose, and the small mouth seemed suited only to sucking water from the countless rivulets that crisscrossed the valley floor. The body of each was a long tapered cylinder topped by a huge, green, rear-slanting rhomboidal vane averaging two meters on a side. All the vanes, all the countless thousands of them, were angled so their broad surfaces presented toward the solar mirrors for maximum exposure to the light . . . like an endless becalmed regatta of green-sailed ships.

"Welcome to Emerald City," LaNague said in a low voice.

"Hmmmm?"

"Nothing."

They watched in silence as the sentry's cutter completed its low, slow circuit of the valley, passing at the end over herds of smaller green calves penned off from the rest of the herd, held aside until they were large enough to hold their own with the adults. The cutter rose gently, leaving the valley hidden beneath its lid of bright mist.

"Didn't look to me like one of those skinny things could feed too many people," Broohnin remarked as the wonder of what they had seen ebbed away.

"You'd be surprised. The official reports say that even the bones are edible. And there are more hidden valleys like that one down here."

"But what's the advantage?"

"They don't graze! Do you realize what that means? They don't take up land that can be used for growing food for people; they don't eat grains that can be fed to people. All they need is water, sunlight, and an ambient temperature of 15 to 20 degrees."

"But they're so thin!"

"They have to be if they're going to be photosynthetic. They need a high surface-area-to-mass ratio to feed themselves via their chlorophyll. And don't forget, there's virtually no fat on those things—what you see is what you eat. As each green herd reaches maturity, they're slaughtered, the derived protein is mixed with extenders and marketed as some sort of meat. New ones are cloned and started on their way."

Broohnin nodded his understanding, but the puzzled expression remained on his face. "I still don't understand why it's being kept a secret, though. This is the kind of breakthrough I'd expect Earth to be beating its chest about all over Occupied Space."

"It doesn't want the outworlds to know yet. Earth realizes that those green cows down there could spell economic ruin for the outworlds. And the longer they keep the outworlds in the dark about them, the worse shape they'll all be in when grain imports are completely cut off."

"But why—?"

"Because I don't think Earth has ever given up hope of getting the outworlds under its wing again."

"You going to break the news?"

"No."

They flew in silence through the polar darkness for a while, each man digesting what he had just seen.

"I imagine that once the word gets out," LaNague said finally, "and it should leak within a few standard years, the Earthies will move the herds into the less hospitable desert areas where they can probably expect a faster growth rate. Of course, the water requirement will be higher because of increased evaporation. But that's when Earth's need for imported grain will really begin to drop . . . she'll be fast on her way to feeding all her billions on her own."

The lights of the sentry station appeared ahead.

"Speaking of all these billions," Broohnin said, "where are they? The spaceport wasn't crowded, and there's nothing below but snow. I thought you told me every available centimeter of living space on Earth was being used. Looks like there's a whole continent below with no one on it. What kind of residue you been giving me?"

"The coast of the South Polar continent is settled all around, and the Antarctic Peninsula is crowded with people. But from what I understand, inland settlements have been discouraged. It's possible to live down there," he said, glancing at the featureless wastes racing by below the cutter. "The technology exists to make it habitable, but not without extensive melting of the ice layers."

Broohnin shrugged. He managed to make it a hostile gesture."So?"

"So, a significant ice melt means significant lowland flooding, and there are millions upon millions of people inhabiting lowlands. A few thousand square kilometers of living space down here could result in the loss of millions elsewhere in the world. Not a good trade-off. Also, 80 per cent of Earth's fresh water is down there. So Antarctica remains untouched."

The cutter slowed to a hover over the sentry station, then descended. As they prepared to debark, LaNague turned to Broohnin.

"You want to see billions of people, my friend? I'll show you more than you ever imagined. Our next stop is the Eastern Megalopolis of North America. By the time we're through there, you'll *crave* the solitude of the cabin you occupied on the trip from the outworlds."

VIII

> . . . human beings cease to be human when they congregate and a mob is a monster. If you think of a mob as a living thing and you want to get its I.Q., take the average intelligence of the people there and divide it by the number of people there. Which means that a mob of fifty has somewhat less intelligence than an earthworm.
>
> *Theodore Sturgeon*

"You sure you know where you're going?"

"Exactly. Why?"

"It's not the type of neighborhood I'd expect to see the 'third richest man in Sol System' in."

"You're right. This is a side trip."

The press of people was beyond anything Broohnin had ever imagined. They were everywhere under the bleary eye of the noonday sun, lining the streets, crowding onto the pavement until only the hardiest ground-effect vehicles dared to push their way through. There were no fat people to be seen, and the streets themselves were immaculate, all a part of the ethics of starvation wherein everything must be recycled. The air was thick with the noise, the smell, the *presence* of packed humanity. And even behind the high, cheap, quickly poured apartment walls that canyonized the street, Broohnin was sure he could feel unseen millions.

"I don't like it here," he told LaNague.

"I told you you wouldn't."

"I don't mean that. There's something wrong here. I can feel it."

"It's just the crowds. Ignore it."

"Something is *wrong!*" he said, grabbing LaNague's arm and spinning him around.

LaNague looked at him carefully, searchingly. "What's bothering you?"

"I can't explain it," Broohnin said, rubbing his damp palms in fearful frustration. There was sweat clinging to his armpits, his mouth felt dry, and the skin at the back of his neck was tight. "Something's going to happen here. These people are building toward something."

LaNague gave him another long look, then nodded abruptly. "All right. I know better than to ignore the instincts of a former street urchin. We'll make this quick, then we'll get out of here." He looked down at the locus indicator disk in his palm, and pointed to the right. "This way."

They had returned to the tip of the South American continent and dropped off their flitter at the Cape Town Spaceport. From there a stratospheric rammer had shot them north to the Bosyorkington Spaceport, which occupied the far end of Long Island, formerly called the Hamptons. Three hundred kilometers west northwest from there by flitter brought them to the putrescent trickle that was still called the Delaware River, but only after carrying them over an endless, unbroken grid of clogged streets with apartments stretching skyward from the interstices. Everything looked so carefully planned, so well thought-out and laid out . . . why then had Broohnin felt as if he were descending into the first ring of Hell when their flitter lowered toward the roof of one of the municipal garages?

LaNague had purchased a locus indicator at the spaceport. They were big sellers to tourists and people trying to find their roots. It was a fad on Earth to locate the exact spot where a relative had lived or a famous man had been born or had died, or a historical event had occurred. One could either pay homage, or relive that moment of history with the aid of holograms or a sensory-cognitive button for those who were wired.

"What are we looking for if not your rich man?" Broohnin asked impatiently. The tension in the air was making if difficult to breathe.

LaNague did not look up from his locus indicator. "An ancient ancestor of mine—man named Gurney—used to live in this area in the pre-stellar days. He was a rebel of sorts, the earliest one on record in my family. A lipidlegger. He defied his government—and there were many governments then, not just one for all Earth as there is now—out of sheer stubbornness and belligerence." He smiled at a private thought. "Quite a character."

They walked a short distance further to the north. There seemed to be fewer people about, but no less tension. LaNague didn't seem to notice.

"Here we are!" he said, his smile turning to dismay as he looked around, faced with the same monotonous façades of people-choked apartments that had oppressed them since leaving the municipal garage.

"Good. You found it. Let's go," Broohnin said, glancing about anxiously.

"This used to be a beautiful rural area," LaNague was saying, "with trees and wildlife and mist and rain. Now look at it: solid synthestone. According to my co-ordinates, Gurney's general store used to be right here in the middle of the street. This whole area used to be the Delaware Water Gap. How—"

A sound stopped him. It was a human sound, made by human voices, but so garbled by the overlapping of so many voices that no words were distinguishable. Its source was untraceable . . . it came from everywhere, seamlessly enveloping them. But the emotion behind the sound came through with unmistakable clarity: rage.

All around them, people began to flee for their homes. Children were pulled off the street and into apartment complex doorways that slid shut behind them. LaNague dove for the door of a clothing store to their left but it zipped closed before he could reach it and would not open despite his insistent pounding. As Broohnin watched, the storefront disappeared, fading rapidly to a blank surface identical to the synthestone of the apartment walls around it. LaNague appeared to be trying to gain entry to a solid wall.

"What's going on?" Broohnin yelled as the din of human voices grew progressively louder. He could now localize the source to the north of them, approaching rapidly.

"Food riot," LaNague said, returning to Broohnin's side. "Sounds like a big one. We've got to get out of here." He pulled a reference tablet the size of a playing card from his vest pocket and tapped in a code. "The garage is too far, but there's a Kyfhon neighborhood near here, I believe." The surface of the tablet lit with the information he had requested. "Yes! We can make it if we run."

"Why there?"

"Because nobody else will be able to help us."

They ran south, stopping at every intersection while LaNague checked his locus indicator. The bustling stores they had passed only moments before had disappeared, glazed over with holograms of blank synthestone walls to hide them from the approaching mob. Only a rioter intimately familiar with this particular neighborhood would be able to locate them now.

"They're gaining!" Broohnin said breathlessly as they stopped again for LaNague to check their co-ordinates. After nearly two decades of living on Throne, his muscles had become acclimated to a gravitational pull approximately 5 per cent less than Earth's. The difference had been inconsequential until now because his activity had been limited to sitting, dozing, and strolling. Now he had to run. And he felt it.

LaNague, who weighed about seven kilos less on Earth than he did on Tolive, found the going easy. "Not much further. We should be—"

The mob rounded the corner behind them then and rushed forward with a roar. An empty, hapless g-e vehicle parked at the side of the street slowed their momentum for a moment as a number of rioters paused to tear it to pieces. The strips of metal pulled from the vehicle were used to assault any store windows they could find behind their holographic camouflage. The windows were tough, rubbery, and shatterproof. They had to be pierced and torn before entry could be gained.

LaNague and Broohnin stood transfixed with fascination as they watched a clutch of rioters attack what seemed to be a synthestone wall, their makeshift battering rams and pikes disappearing into it as if no wall existed. And none did. With a sudden shout, those in the forefront pushed their way into the wall image and disappeared. They must have found the hologram projector controls immediately because the camouflage evaporated and the crowd cheered as the wall became a storefront again . . . a furniture outlet. Its contents were passed out to the street bucket-brigade style and smashed with roars of approval.

"That's not food!" Broohnin said. "I thought you called this a food riot."

"Just a generic term. Nobody riots for food any more. They just riot. Theories have it that the crowding makes a certain type of person go temporarily berserk every so often."

And then the crowd began to move again. Blind, voracious, swift, deadly.

Broohnin found his fear gone, replaced by a strange exhilaration. "Let's join them!" The carnage, the howling ferocity of the scene had excited him. He wanted a chance to break something, too. He always felt better when he did.

"They'll tear you to pieces!" LaNague said, shoving him into motion away from the mob.

"No, they won't! I'll be one of them!"

"You're an outworlder, you fool! They'll see that immediately. And when they're through with you, nobody'll be able to put you back together again. Now run!"

They ran. The mob was not after them in particular, but it followed them. Nor was the riot confined to a single street. As they passed various intersections, LaNague and Broohnin could see extensions of the crowd to the right and left. Fires had been set and smoke began to thicken in the air.

"Faster!" LaNague shouted. "We could get ringed in! We're dead if that happens!"

It was unnecessary advice. Broohnin was running at maximum effort. His muscles screaming in protest as the smoke put an extra burden on his already laboring lungs. LaNague had slowed his pace to stay with him and yell encouragement. Broohnin resented the ease with which the skinny Tolivian loped beside him. If worse came to worse, he would throw LaNague to the mob which was now only a scant hundred meters behind them, and gaining.

"Not much further!" LaNague said. "Don't quit now!" He glanced down at the indicator in his palm. "That should be it straight ahead!"

Broohnin saw nothing different at first, then noticed that the street after the next intersection was a different color . . . yellow . . . and there were still people in the street . . . children . . . playing. There were men on the corners. Women, too. And they were all armed.

The Kyfhons stood in small placid groups, watching the two fleeing outworlders with mild interest. Except for the long-range blasters slung across their shoulders and the hand blasters on their hips, they looked like all the other Earthies seen since landfall. It was only when it became obvious that LaNague and Broohnin were going to cross onto the yellow-colored pavement that they sprang to life.

A dozen blasters were suddenly pointed in their direction.

Broohnin glanced at the children who had stopped playing—some of the older ones had small hand blasters drawn and ready, too. LaNague swung out his arm and slowed Broohnin to a walk, then trotted ahead of him. The Tolivian held his hands in front of him, out of Broohnin's sight. He seemed to be signaling to the group of Kyfhons on the right-hand corner. They glanced at each other and lowered their weapons. One stepped forward to have a quick conversation. There were brief nods, then LaNague turned to Broohnin.

"Hurry! They'll give us sanctuary."

Broohnin quickly followed LaNague onto the yellow pavement. "Where do we hide?" His words were barely audible between gasping respirations.

"We don't. We just lean against the wall over here in the shade and catch our breath."

"We're not getting off the street?"

LaNague shook his head. "That would mean entering someone's home. And that's asking too much."

The mob surged forward, its momentum constant, irresistible, spilling out of the confines of the narrow street and into the intersection. The Kyfhons had reslung or reholstered their weapons and now stood in clusters, eying the onrushing wave of humanity in attitudes of quiet readiness.

Although LaNague seemed calm beside him, Broohnin was unable to relax. He leaned back with his palms flat against the wall, panting, ready to spring away when he had to. And he was sure he'd have to soon. That mob was rolling and it wasn't going to be stopped by a few adults and kids with blasters. It was going to tear through here, yellow pavement or no, and destroy everything in its path.

As it happened, Broohnin was only half right. The mob did not stop, but neither did it pour into the Kyfhon street. It split. After filling the intersection, half of the rioters turned to the right, half to the left. Not a single foot crossed onto the yellow pavement.

Den Broohnin could only stare.

"Told you we'd be safe," LaNague said with a smug air.

"But why? There's not enough firepower in this street to even nick a mob like that, let alone stop it!"

LaNague looked up at the overhanging buildings. "Oh, I wouldn't say that."

Broohnin followed his gaze. The roofs, and every window at every level, were lined with Kyfhons, and each of them was armed. Looking back to the mob that was still surging and dividing at the end of the street, he saw not the slightest hint of reluctance or hesitation in the rioters as they skirted the yellow pavement. It seemed to be taken for granted that this neighborhood was untouchable. But how—?

"Over the years, I imagine a lot of rioters died before people got the message," LaNague said, answering the unspoken question. "It's called 'a sense of community'—something that's been long forgotten on Earth, and even on the outworlds. We Kyfhons are set apart from others by our attitudes and values. We form a close-knit family . . . even to the point of having secret hand signals so we can recognize each other. I used one to gain sanctuary today." He gestured toward the mob that was finally beginning to thin. "We're not interested in traffic with people who don't share our values, and so we're driven together into neighborhoods like this one, or to planets like Tolive and Flint. But it's a self-imposed exile. Our ghetto walls are built from the inside."

"But does the Crime Authority allow—"

"The Crime Authority is *not* allowed in here! The motto of Eastern Sect Kyfhons is 'A weapon in every hand, freedom on every side.' They police their own streets, and have let it be known for centuries that they protect their own. Public temper tantrums like the one that almost ran us over are not tolerated on their streets. The word has long been out: Do what you will to your own community, but risk death if you harm ours."

Broohnin had finally caught his breath and now pushed himself away from the wall. "In other words, they get away with murder."

"It's called self-defense. But there are other reasons they're left alone. For instance: didn't you wonder why there were no Crime Authority patrols in the air trying to quell the riot? It's because life is still a surplus here. If a few rioters get killed, that's fewer mouths to feed. The same logic applies to any rioters foolish enough to invade neighborhoods like this.

"As for criminals who might belong to the Kyfhon communities, the justice meted out here against their own kind is swifter and often harsher than anything that goes on in the Crime Authority prisons. And finally, from a purely pragmatic viewpoint, you must remember that these people grow up learning how to fight with every part of their body and with every weapon known to man." LaNague smiled grimly. "Would you want to walk in here and try to arrest someone?"

"They're like a bunch of Flinters," Broohnin muttered,

glancing around and feeling the same uneasiness he had experienced in Throne's Imperium Park steal over him again.

"They are!" LaNague said, laughing. "They just never moved to Flint. After all, Flinters are just Eastern Sect purists in ceremonial garb who have a planet all to themselves. Just as Tolivians are Western Sect Kyfhons with their own planet."

"Where do these Western Sect types keep themselves on Earth?"

LaNague's smile faltered. "Most of them are gone. We—they never took to violence too well . . . gobbled up . . . destroyed. Tolive is just about the only place left where Western Sect Kyfho is practiced." He turned away. "Let's go."

After speaking briefly to a small knot of the adults on the corner, obviously thanking them, he moved toward the now deserted street, motioning Broohnin to follow.

"Come. Time to see the rich man."

Ω

They were three kilometers up in the cloud-cluttered sky, heading southeast to full throttle. The Bosyorkington megalopolis had been left behind, as had the coastal pile-dwelling communities and the houseboat fleets. Nothing below now but the green algae soup they still called the Atlantic Ocean.

"He live on a boat?"

LaNague shook his head.

"Then where're you taking us?" Broohnin demanded, his gaze flicking between the map projected on the flitter's vid screen and the rows of altocumulus clouds they were stringing like a needle through pearls. "There's nothing out here but water. And we'll never reach the other side."

LaNague checked the controls. "Watch up ahead."

Broohnin looked down toward the ocean.

"No," LaNague told him. "Ahead. *Straight* ahead."

There was nothing straight ahead but clouds. No . . . there was something . . . they speared into a patch of open air, and there it was, straight ahead as LaNague had said: a sprawling Tudor mansion with a perfect lawn and rows of English hedges cut two meters high and planted in devious, maze-like patterns. All floating three kilometers in the sky.

"Ah!" LaNague said softly at Broohnin's side. "The humble abode of Eric Boedekker."

IX

Competition is a sin.
John D. Rockefeller, Sr.

Eric Boedekker's home sat in a shallow, oblong, six-acre dish rimmed with batteries of anti-aircraft weapons. The general public looked on the skisland estates as mere toys for the obscenely rich, totally devoid of any practical value. The general public was wrong, as usual.

"Looks like a fort," Broohnin said as they glided toward it.

"It is."

Members of the uppermost layers of Earth's upper-upper class had long ago become regular targets of organized criminal cartels, political terrorists, and ordinary people who were simply hungry. Open season was declared on the rich and they were kidnaped and held for ransom at an alarming rate. The electronic currency system, of course, eliminated the possibility of monetary ransom, and so loved ones were held captive and returned in exchange for commodities useful in the black market, such as gold, silver, beef.

Huge, low-floating skislands had long been in use as vacation resorts, guaranteeing the best weather at all times, always staying ahead of storms and winter's chill. Seeing the plight of the very rich, an enterprising company began constructing smaller skislands as new homes for them, offering unparalleled security. The skisland estates could be approached only by air, and were easily defensible against assault.

There were a few drawbacks, the major one being the restriction from populated areas, which meant any land mass on the planet. Huge gravity-negating fields were at work below the skislands and no one knew the effects of prolonged exposure to the fields on human physiology. No one was volunteering, either. And so the skislands were all to be found hovering over the open sea.

A holographic message was suddenly projected in front of LaNague's flitter. Solid-looking block letters told them to approach no further, or risk being shot from the sky. A vid communication frequency was given if the occupants wished to announce themselves. LaNague tapped in the frequency and spoke.

"This is Peter LaNague. I desire a personal meeting with Eric Boedekker on a matter of mutual interest."

There was no visual reply, only a blank screen and a curt male voice. "One moment." After a brief pause, the voice spoke again. "Audience denied."

"Tell him I bring word from Flint!" LaNague said quickly before the connection could be broken, then turned to Broohnin with a sour expression. " '*Audience* denied'! If it weren't so vital that I see him, I'd—"

A bright crimson light began blinking on and off from the roof of the squat square structure to the left of the main buildings. The male voice returned, this time with a screen image to go with it . . . a young man, slightly puzzled, if his expression was a true indicator.

"You may land by the red flasher. Remain in your flitter until the escort arrives to take you inside."

Ω

They walked idly about the great hall of the reconstructed Tudor mansion, waiting for Boedekker to appear. After being carefully scanned for anything that might conceivably be used as a weapon, they had been deposited here to await the great man's pleasure.

"He doesn't appear to be in much of a hurry to see you,"

Broohnin said, staring at the paintings framed in the gold leaf ceiling, the richly paneled walls, the fireplace that was functional but unused—nobody on Earth burned real wood any more.

LaNague appeared unconcerned. "Oh, he is. He's just trying hard not to show it." He ambled around the hall, thin arms folded across his chest, studying the collection of paintings which seemed to favor examples of the satyr-and-nymph school of art.

"Boedekker's probably one of your heroes, isn't he?" Broohnin said, watching LaNague closely for a reaction. He saw one he least expected.

LaNague's head snapped around; his thin lips were drawn into an even thinner line by anger. "Why do you say that? Are you trying to insult me? If you are—"

"Even *I've* heard of Eric Boedekker," Broohnin said. "He single-handedly controls the asteroid mining industry in Sol System. He's rich, he's powerful, he's big business . . . everything you Tolivians admire!"

"Oh. That." LaNague cooled rapidly. He wasn't even going to bother to reply. Broohnin decided to push him further.

"Isn't he the end product of all the things you Tolivians yammer about—free trade, free economy, no restrictions whatsoever? Isn't he the perfect capitalist? The perfect Tolivian?"

LaNague sighed and spoke slowly, as if explaining the obvious to a dim-witted child. It irked Broohnin, but he listened.

"Eric Boedekker never participated in a free market in his life. He used graft, extortion, and violence to have certain laws passed giving him and his companies special options and rights of way in the field of asteroid mineral rights. He used the Earth government to squash most of the independent rock jumpers by making it virtually impossible for them to sell their ore except through a Boedekker company. Nothing you see around you was earned in a free market. He doesn't eliminate his challengers in the market place by innovations or improvements; he has his friends in the government bureaus find ways to put them out of business. He's a corruptor of everything a Tolivian holds dear! He's an economic royalist, not a capitalist!"

LaNague paused to catch his breath, then smiled. "But there's one Earth law even he hasn't been able to circumvent, despite every conceivable scheme to do so: the one person/one child law."

"I would think that'd be the easiest to get around."

"No. That's the one law that can have no exceptions. Because it affects everyone, applies to everyone the same. It has been held as an absolute for as long as any living human can remember. If you allowed one person to have one extra child—no matter what the circumstances—the entire carefully structured, rigidly enforced population control program would fall apart once word got out."

"But he has two children . . . doesn't he? What's he want another for?"

"His first born was a son, another Eric, by his second wife. When they were in the process of dissolving their marriage, they fought over custody of the child. With Boedekker pulling the strings, there was no chance that the wife would keep the boy, even though by Earth law he was rightfully hers because she had him by intrauterine gestation. In a fit of depression, the woman poisoned herself and the child.

"He fathered a second child, a girl named Liza, by his third wife. Liza was gestated by extrauterine means to avoid potential legal problems should the third marriage break up—which it did. She grew to be the pride of his life as he groomed her to take over his mining empire—"

"A girl?" Broohnin said, surprise evident on his face. "In charge of Boedekker Industries?"

"The pioneer aspects of outworld life have pushed women back into the incubator/nest-keeper role, and it'll be a while before they break out of it again. But on Earth it's different. Anyway, Liza met a man named Frey Kirowicz and they decided to become outworlders. It was only after they were safely on Neeka that she sent her father a message telling him what he could do with Boedekker Industries. Eric tried everything short of abducting her to get her back. And eventually he might have tried that had she not been accidentally killed in a near-riot at one of the Imperial garrisons on Neeka."

"I remember that!" Broohnin said. "Almost two years ago!"

"Right. That was Eric Boedekker's daughter. And now he has no heir. He's been trying for an exemption from the one person/one child rule ever since Liza ran off, but this is something his money and power can't buy him. And he can't go to the outworlds and father a child because the child will then be considered an outworlder and thus forbidden to own property in Sol System. Which leaves him only one avenue to save his pride."

Eric Boedekker entered at the far end of the room. "And what avenue is that, may I ask?" he said.

"Revenge."

Like most Earthies, Eric Boedekker was clean-shaven. Broohnin judged his age to be sixty or seventy standards, yet he moved like a much younger man. His attire and attitude were typical of anyone they had seen since their arrival from the outworlds. Only his girth set him apart. The asteroid mining magnate's appetite for food apparently equaled his appetite for power and money. He took up fully half of an antique love seat when he sat down, and gestured to two other chairs before the cold fireplace.

"Neither of you appears to be a Flinter," he said when Broohnin and LaNague were seated across from him.

"Neither of us is," LaNague replied. "I happen to be a Tolivian and have been in contact with representatives from Flint."

"May I assume that Flint has changed its mind in regard to my offer last year?"

"No."

"Then we have nothing further to discuss." He began to rise from the seat.

"You wanted the Outworld Imperium crushed and destroyed, did you not?" LaNague said quickly. "And you offered the inhabitants of Flint an astonishingly large sum if they would accomplish this for you, did you not?"

Boedekker sat down again, his expression concerned, anxious. "That was priviledged information."

"The Flinters brought the offer to a group with which I am connected," LaNague said with a shrug. "And I'm bringing it back to you. I can do it for you, but I don't want your money. I only want to know if you still wish to see the Outworld Imperium in ruins."

Boedekker nodded twice, slowly. "I do. More than anything I can think of. The Imperium robbed me of my only surviving child. Because of it, I have no heir, no way to continue my line and the work I've begun."

"Is that all? You want to bring down a two-hundred-year-old government because of an accident?"

"Yes!"

"Why didn't you try to bring down the Earth government when your first child died?"

Boedekker's eyes narrowed. "I blamed my wife for that. And besides, no one will ever bring the Earth bureaucracy down

. . . one would have to use a planetary bomb to unravel that knot."

"There must be more to it than that. I'll have to know if I'm to risk my men and my own resources—a lot of my plan depends on you."

"You wouldn't understand."

"Try me."

"Do you have any children?"

"One. A daughter."

Boedekker's expression showed that he was as surprised as Broohnin. "I didn't think revolutionaries had families. But never mind . . . you should then be able to understand what it's like to groom a child all her life for a position and then have her run off to be a farmer on the edge of nowhere!"

"A daughter isn't a possession. You disowned her?"

"She didn't care! She kept saying . . ." His voice drifted off.

"She tried for a reconciliation?"

Boedekker nodded. "She wanted me to come out and visit her as soon as they had a place of their own." Tears began to well in his eyes. "I told her she'd be dead and buried out there before I ever came to visit."

"I see," LaNague said softly.

"I want to see that pompous ass, Metep, and his rotten Imperium dead and forgotten! Buried like my Liza!"

Broohnin watched and marveled at how LaNague had turned the conversation to his advantage. He was the guest of an extraordinarily powerful man, yet he was in complete control of the encounter.

"Then it shall be done," LaNague replied with startling offhandedness. "But I'll need your co-operation if I'm to succeed. And I mean your *full* co-operation. It may cost you everything you own."

It was Boedekker's turn to shrug. "I have no one I wish to leave anything to. When I die, my relations will war over Boedekker Industries, break it up and run home with whatever pieces they can carry. I'll be just as happy to leave them nothing at all. BI was to be my monument. It was to live long after I was gone. Now . . ."

"I'm offering you the downfall of the Imperium as your monument. Interested?"

"Possibly." He scrutinized LaNague. "But I'll need more than grandiose promises before I start turning my holdings over to you. Much, *much* more."

"I don't want your holdings. I don't want a single Solar credit from you. All you'll have to do is make certain adjustments in the nature of your assets, which need never leave your possession."

"Intriguing. Just what kind of adjustments do you have in mind?"

"I'll be glad to discuss them in detail in private," LaNague said with a glance at Broohnin. "I don't wish to be rude, but you haven't reached the point yet where you can be privy to this information."

Broohnin shot to his feet. "In other words, you don't trust me!"

"If you wish," LaNague replied in his maddeningly impassive voice.

It was all Broohnin could do to keep from reaching for the Tolivian's skinny throat and squeezing it until his eyes bulged out of their sockets. But he managed to turn and walk away. "I'll find my own way out!"

He didn't have to. An armed security woman was waiting on the other side of the door to the great hall. She showed him out to the grounds and left him to himself, although he knew he was constantly watched from the windows.

It was cold, windy, and clear outside the house, but Broohnin found his lungs laboring in the rarefied air. Yet he refused to go back inside. He had to think, and it was so hard to think through a haze of rage.

Walking as close to the edge as the meshed perimeter fence would allow, he looked out and down at the clouds around the skisland. Every once in a while he could catch a glimpse of the ocean below through a break. Far off toward the westering sun he could see a smudge that had to be land, where people like him were jammed so close together they had to go on periodic sprees of violence—short bursts of insanity that allowed them to act sane again for a while afterward. Broohnin understood. Understood perfectly.

He looked back at the mansion and its grounds, trying to imagine the incomprehensible wealth it represented. He hated the rich for having so much more than he did. Another glance in the direction of the megalopolis that had so recently endangered his life and he realized he hated the poor, too . . . because he had always found losers intolerable, had always felt an urge to put them out of their misery.

Most of all, he hated LaNague. He would kill that smug

Tolivian on the way back. Only one of them would return to the outworlds alive. When they made their first subspace jump he'd—

No, he wouldn't. The Flinters would be awaiting LaNague's return. He had no desire to try to explain the Tolivian's death at his hands to them!

He cooled, and realized he didn't trust LaNague. There were too many unanswered questions. If Tolive and Flint were going to be spared in the coming economic collapse as LaNague said they would, why were they involved in the revolution? Why didn't they just sit back and refuse to get involved as they had in the past, and just let things take their course?

And then there was the feeling that LaNague was maneuvering him toward something. It was all so subtle that he had no idea in which direction he was being nudged . . . but he felt the nudge. If LaNague was in such complete control of everything, why was he spending so much time with Broohnin? What did he have in mind for him?

"Mr. LaNague awaits you at the flitter dock."

Broohnin spun sharply at the sound of the voice behind him. It was the same female guard who had led him out.

"Something wrong?" she asked.

He ignored her and began walking toward the dock.

Ω

"You'll be taking the *Penton & Blake* back alone," LaNague told him.

Broohnin was immediately suspicious. "What about you?"

"I'm taking the *Adzel* back to Tolive. I've business to attend to there before I return to Throne."

Both men sat staring out the view wall of the *Bernardo de la Paz* way station as the globe of Earth passed above them. LaNague had retrieved his tree from the quarantine section and sat with it on his lap.

"And what am I to do until then?"

"You'll be contacted shortly after your return."

"By Flinters?"

LaNague smiled at Broohnin's concern, but it was not a jeering grimace. He seemed relaxed, at ease, almost likable. The thought of returning to his homeworld seemed to have changed him into a different person.

"Flinters made up only a small part of my force on Throne. And they must stay out of sight." He turned toward Broohnin and spoke in a low voice. "Have you ever heard of Robin Hood?"

"Does he live in Primus City?"

LaNague's laughter was gentle and full of good humor. "In a way, yes! You'll become intimate friends, I think. And if all goes well, people will come to think of you and he as one and the same."

"What's that supposed to mean?" Broohnin found this new, easygoing side of LaNague disconcerting, and harder to deal with than the dour, reserved, omniscient conspiratorial mastermind he had been traveling with since their departure from Throne. Which was real?

"All in good time." He rose to his feet. "My ship leaves before yours. Have a good trip. I'll see you again on Throne."

Broohnin watched the Tolivian stroll away with his damned tree under his arm. It was obvious that LaNague thought he was going to use him. That was okay. Broohnin would be quite happy to play along for a while and wait for his chance. He'd let LaNague live as long as he was useful. When the time was right, Broohnin would step in and take over again. And then he would settle with LaNague once and for all.

PART TWO
THE ANARCHIST

The Year of the Tiller

X

> The world little knows or cares the storm through which you have had to pass. It asks only if you brought the ship safely to port.
>
> *Joseph Conrad*

The first time had been a frantic headlong dive to ease a mutual hunger of desperate dimensions, begun and ended so quickly that it had already become a dim memory. The second was more exploratory, a fruitful search for familiar responses, familiar patterns of give and take. And the third was a loving, leisurely welcome home that left them both drained and content.

"Been too long, Peter," Mora said.

"Much."

They huddled in deep-breathing silence for a while, then Peter spoke. "You haven't asked me about the trip."

"I know. I thought it could wait."

"Afraid we'd fight again?"

Peter could feel her head nodding in the dark next to him.

"I was sure of it. With the new year beginning, I wanted us to enter it *in* arms instead of *at* arms."

He smiled and held his wife closer. "Well, it's here and so are we. And this is the only way to start a new year."

"You were gone when the Year of the Tortoise began. That was a lonely time. And you won't be here for the Year of the Malak either."

"But I'm here now and we can discuss the rest in the morning. No talk now."

Mora fell asleep first, her head on his shoulder. Peter, despite his fatigue, lay awake awhile longer, listening to the rumble of the storm-whipped surf outside. It was so good to be home. So comfortable. So safe. He knew he could not bring himself to leave again. Let someone else take care of things on Throne from now on. He'd had enough. Next Year Day and every other day in between would find him here in his little house on the dunes. Then the dream would stop.

That decision made, he drifted off to sleep.

The first one was a woman. She slipped through the open bedroom door and slinked across the room toward the bed, a large cloth-wrapped bundle in her arms. After peering carefully at his face to be sure that it was him, her eyes lit with maniacal rage and she dumped the contents of her bundle over him. Thousands of orange and white Imperial mark notes fell like a poisonous snow. She turned and called soundlessly over her shoulder, and soon a steady stream of strangers trailed through the door, all with hate-filled eyes, all with bundles and bushels of mark notes that they emptied over him. He could only move his head back and forth. Mora was gone. He had been left alone to face this silent, murderous crowd. And still they came, and the pile of mark notes covered his face, and he could no longer breathe, and he was dying, dying, suffocated by Imperial marks . . .

Peter awoke in a sitting position, drenched with sweat. It had happened again. The dream had pursued him across half of Occupied Space. That did it! He was through. Tomorrow he'd tell the Trustees to find someone else to handle the revolution.

Ω

"Come *on*, Daddy! Hurry, please!"

Children, he thought, trudging up the celadon dune in the wake of his seven-year-old daughter. You go away for a year and a half and you don't recognize them when you come back, they've grown so. And they're a little shy with you at first. But by the next day, they treat you like you were never away.

"I'm coming, Laina." She stood at the top of the dune, slim and sleek and straight and fair, staring seaward, her blond hair streaming in the stiff onshore breeze. Something began to squeeze his larynx and knot the muscles of his jaw as he watched her. *She's growing up without me.* He continued up the dune, not daring to stop.

The wind slapped at him when he reached the top. The weather did nothing to lighten his mood . . . one of those gray days with a slippery slate sky dissolving into a molten lead sea, small white clouds like steam obscuring the junction. Another two steps and he could see the beach: Laina hadn't been exaggerating.

"Daddy, it's really a malak, isn't it?"

"So it is!" Peter muttered, staring at the huge blunt-headed mass of fish flesh, inert and lifeless on the sand near the high water mark. "Last time this happened was when I was about your age. Must be at least thirty meters long! Let's go down for a closer look."

As Laina leaped to run down the dune, Peter scooped her up and swung her to his shoulders, her bare legs straddling the back of his neck. She liked to ride up there—at least she had before he left—and he liked the contact. Needed it.

Sea wind buffeted their ears and salt mist stung their eyes as they approached the decaying form.

"A sieve malak, leviathan class," he told her, then sniffed the air. "And starting to stink already. Before they were all killed off, there used to be creatures like this on Earth called baleen whales. But whales weren't fish. Our malaks are true fish."

Laina was almost speechless with awe at the immensity of the creature. "It's so big! What killed it?"

"Could've died of old age out at sea and drifted in, but I don't see much evidence of the scavengers having been at it. Probably got confused by the storm last night and wound up beached. I read somewhere that all the insides get crushed when a malak is beached . . . killed by its own weight."

"Must eat a whole lotta other fish to make it grow so big."

"Actually it doesn't eat other fish at all." He walked her

closer to the huge mouth that split the head, their approach stirring up a flight of scale-winged keendars from their feast on the remains. "See those big plates of hairy bone along the upper jaw . . . looks like a comb? That's the sieve. As they swim along, these malaks strain sea water through their sieve and eat all the tiny animals they trap in the hairs. Mostly it's stuff called plankton."

He let Laina down on the sand so she could run up for a closer look. She wasn't long—the stench from the cavernous maw was too strong to allow a leisurely inspection.

"What's plankton?" she asked as she returned to his side. "I never heard of that before."

"Let's go back up on the dune where the smell isn't so bad and I'll tell you all about it."

Hand in hand they plodded through the damp, yielding blue granules to a point overlooking the waterline, yet beyond the carcass' fulsome stench, and watched the screaming, circling keendars for a quiet moment.

"Still interested in plankton?" Receiving a nod, Peter spoke in a slow, almost reminiscent manner, gearing his explanation to a child's mind, yet keeping it up at a level where Laina would have to reach a bit.

"Plankton is the basic food of the sea. It's billions of tiny little creatures, some plants, some animals, but all very, very tiny. They gather in huge batches out at sea, some just drifting, others wiggling a little whip-like arm called a flagellum to push them here and there.

"All they really do is live and die and provide food for most of the ocean. They probably think they know just where they're going, never realizing that all the time the entire plankton patch is being pushed about at the whim of wind and current. They get gobbled up by huge sieve malaks that can't see what they're eating, and the plankton don't even know they've been eaten till it's over and done with."

"Poor plankton!" Laina said, concern showing in her face.

"Oh, they're happy in their own way, I suppose. And while the malaks are cutting huge swaths out of their ranks, they just go on whipping the old flagella about and having a grand time. Even if you tried to tell them of the malaks and other sea creatures that constantly feed off them, they wouldn't believe you."

"How come you know so much about plankton?"

"I've studied it up close," Peter said, thoughts of Earth flashing through his mind.

Laina eyed the long baleen combs on the malak's jaw. "Glad I'm not a plankton."

"If I have my way," Peter said, putting his arm protectively around his daughter, "you never will be." He stood up and gave the inert leviathan one last look. "But it's nice to know that malaks die, too. Let's go. Your mother'll have the morning soup ready and we don't want cold soup."

Backs to the ocean, they walked along the blue dune toward the house, wind spasms allowing a murmur or two of small talk to drift back to the beach where keendars were crying the sound that had given them their name and pecking morsels from the malak's landward eye, glazed and forever sightless.

Ω

"You're going back, aren't you," Mora said as they sat in the Ancestor Grove under Peter's great-grandfather tree. He hadn't told her of his pre-dawn resolution to stay, and was glad. The light of day quickly revealed the many flaws in plans that had seemed so simple and forthright in the darkness. He had to go back. There was no other way.

"I must." Leaning against the tree, a much larger version of Pierrot, gave him the strength to say it. On the day of his great-grandfather's death, a hole had been dug into the root ball of this tree and the coffinless remains interred there. Throughout the remainder of the following year, the tree had absorbed nutrients from the decomposing body, incorporating them into itself, growing taller on the unique organic fertilizer. The seeds that formed on the tree's branches the following spring were saved until the birth of the next LaNague child. And on that day, the day of Peter LaNague's birth, two of those seeds were planted—one in the Ancestor Grove, and one in an earthenware pot that would remain cribside as the child grew.

The Tolivian mimosa, it had been learned, possessed a unique ability to imprint on a human being. A seedling—called a *misho*—in constant exposure to a growing child will become attuned to that particular child, sensitive to and reflective of his or her moods. The art of branch and root pruning, necessary to limit the tree's size, is carefully taught as the child grows. Raising a child with a personal *misho* was a common practice on Tolive, but hardly universal. Mora's family considered it a silly custom and so she was never given her own tree, and now could never have once since codevelopment was necessary for imprinting. She could never understand the indefinable bond between her husband and Pierrot, nor the growing bond between Laina and her own *misho,* but she could see that it seemed to add an extra dimension to each of them and felt poorer for never having experienced it herself.

Peter looked at his wife in the midday light. She hadn't changed, not in the least. The deep, shining, earthy brown of her hair caught the gold of the Tolivian sun and flung it back. The simple shift she wore did little to hide the mature curves enclosed within. She appeared at ease as she reclined against him, but he knew that was a façade.

"The gloves ready?" he asked, making small talk.

"A hundred pairs. They've been ready for a long time." She looked away as she spoke.

"And the coins?"

"Being minted as fast as possible. But you know that."

Peter nodded silently. He knew. He had seen the reports around the house. Mora was a supervisor at the mint. The star-in-the-ohm design was hers, in fact.

"You could still get out of it," she said abruptly, twisting toward him.

"I could. But would you want to live with me if I did?"

"Yes!"

"I don't think I'd be good company."

"I don't care! You know how I feel. This revolution is all a huge mistake. We should just sit back and let them all rot. We've no obligation to them. They built the fire—let them burn!" Mora was not alone in her opinion; quite a few Tolivians were uncomfortable with the idea of fomenting a revolution.

"But we'll burn, too, Mora. And you know that. We've been over this a thousand times, at least. When the Imperium economy crumbles—and it's already started to—they'll go looking for ways to bolster the mark. The only way for a bankrupt economy to do that is to find a huge new market, or to confiscate a hoard of gold and silver and use it to make its currency good again. Tolive is known to be the largest hoarder of precious metals in Occupied Space. They'll come to us and they won't be asking, they'll be demanding—with the full force of the Imperial Guard ready to back up any threat they care to make."

"With Flint on our side we could hold them off!" Mora said

eagerly. "And then the Imperium will fall apart on its own. All we have to do is hold them off long enough!"

"And then what? With the Imperium gone, Earth will step in and take over the outworlds without a single energy bolt being fired. With everything in chaos, Earth will act as if it's doing everyone a favor. But this time they'll make sure none of the outworlds get free again. This time they'll not allow maverick planets like Tolive and Flint to remain aloof. And with our own resources already drained by a drawn-out battle with the Imperium, we'll have no chance at all against the forces Earth will array against us. There *must* be a revolution now if there's to be a free Tolive for Laina."

"You don't know that Earth'll take us over!" Mora said, warming to their habitual argument. "You want to cut all the outworlds free of the Imperium so they can go their own ways. But do you have the right to do that? Do you have the right to cut people free like that? A lot of them won't want it, you know. A lot of people are scared to death of freedom. They *want* somebody hanging over them all the time, wiping their noses when they're sad, paddling their rumps when they diverge from the norm."

"They can have it, if they wish! They can set up their own little authoritarian enclaves and live that way if it pleases them. I don't care. Just don't include me, my family, my planet, or anybody else who thinks that's no way to live! We have a right to try to preserve a place for the safety and growth of the people, ideas, and things we value!"

Despite her anguish, Mora could not bring herself to disagree with him then, for she believed what he believed, and valued what he valued. Tears came to her eyes as she pounded her small fists futilely against the ground at the base of the tree.

"But it doesn't have to be you! Somebody else can go! It doesn't have to be *you!*"

Wrapping his arms around her, Peter held her close, his lips to her ear, aching to tell her what she wanted to hear, but unable to. "It has to be me. The Charter, the Sedition Trust, they've all been LaNague family projects for generations. And it so happens that the destruction of the Imperium, which we all knew would someday be necessary, has fallen to me."

He rose and pulled her gently to her feet, keeping his arm around her. "I'll walk you home. Then I've got to go see the Trustees."

Mora was quiet for a while as they walked through the sun-dappled tranquillity of the Ancestor Grove. Then: "You should stop by the Ama Co-operative on your way to the Trustees. Adrynna's been sick."

Sudden fear jolted him. "She's dying?"

"No. She recovered. But still, she's old and who knows . . . ? She may not be here when you get back."

"I'll stop in first thing this afternoon."

Ω

Peter was consistently struck by the smallness of the Ama Co-operative whenever he visited it, probably because all his impressions of the asymmetrical collection of squat buildings where the teachers of Kyfho dwelt were gathered during his childhood. He was announced via intercom from the courtyard and granted immediate entry. Everyone knew who he was and knew his time on the planet was short. He found his ama, his lifelong intellectual guide and philosophical mentor, in her room, gazing out the window from her low chair.

"Good day, Ama Adrynna," he said from the doorway.

She swiveled at the sound of his voice, squinting in his direction. "Come into the light where I can have a good look at you." Peter obliged, moving toward the window, where he squatted on his haunches next to her. She smiled, cocking her head left, then right. "So it's you after all. You've come to say good-by to your old ama."

"No. Just hello. I'm on my way to the Trustees and thought I'd stop in and see you. Heard you've been sick or something like that."

She nodded. "Something like that." She had aged considerably but had changed little. Her hair, completely white now, was still parted in the middle and pulled down each side of her face in two severe lines. The face was tightly wrinkled, the mouth a mobile gash, the body painfully lean. Yet her eyes were still the beacons of reason and unshakable integrity that had inspired him throughout his youth and continued to fuel him to this day.

He had seen little of her in the past decade. As a member of the amae, Adrynna spent her days teaching and defining the Kyfho philosophy, and he had progressed beyond the stage where he relied on her counsel. He had taken what she had taught him and put it to use. Yet a large part of whatever he was and whatever he would be derived from the years he had spent at her knee. Tolive, the outworlds, humanity, and Peter LaNague would be so much poorer when she was gone.

"The Trustees, eh?" Adrynna continued, her eyes narrowing. "The Sedition Trust is now your plaything, Peter. Whatever the Trustees think or say or do means nothing now that the revolution mechanism has been set in motion. Only the man in charge on Throne has the final say. And that man is you, Peter. For many generations, countless Tolivians have denied their heirs a single ag by willing all their possessions to the Sedition Trust upon their deaths. Their beliefs, their fortune, the products of their lives ride to Throne with you, Peter LaNague."

"I know." No one had to tell him. The burden of that knowledge weighed on him every day. "I won't fail them, Adrynna."

"What you mean by failure and what I mean by failure may be two different things. You know the quote by that old Earthie writer, Conrad, about bringing ships to port? Then you know that he was not talking about Tolive. *This* world cares about the storms through which you'll have to pass. Our concern for your mission is not limited to its success. We will want to know *how* you succeeded. We will want to know what moral corners you had to cut, and will want 'None' for an answer."

"You taught me well. You must know that."

"I only know one thing," the old woman said in a voice ringing with her fierce conviction, "and that is that the revolution must be conducted in accordance with the principles of Kyfho if it is to have any real meaning. There must be no bloodshed, no violence unless it is defensive, *no* coercion! We must do it our way and our way alone! To do otherwise is to betray centuries of hardship and struggle. Above all else: Kyfho. Forget Kyfho in your pursuit of victory over the enemy, and you will become the enemy . . . worse than the enemy, for he doesn't know he is capable of anything better."

"I know, Adrynna. I know all too well."

"And beware the Flinters. They may be Kyfhons, but they follow a degraded version of the philosophy. They have embraced violence too tightly and may overreact. Watch them, as we will watch you."

He nodded, rose, and kissed her forehead. It was hardly a comforting thought to know that his actions would be under such close scrutiny. But it was hardly a new thought, either—it had come with the territory.

The Trustees were his next stop: three people who, like

many before them, had been elected guardians of the fund begun by the LaNague family in the early days of the colony. There being no government to speak of on Tolive, the matter of undermining a totalitarian state had been left to the efforts of individuals, and would be backed by that fund: the Sedition Trust. No one had envisioned an Outworld Imperium then—it had always been assumed that Earth would be the target of the Trust. And until recently, the job of Trustee—decided by votes from all contributors—had been a simple bookkeeping task. Now it was different. Now they held the purse strings on the revolution.

Yet Adrynna, in her offhanded manner that cut as quick and true as a vibe-knife, had pointed out something Peter had overlooked. The revolution as it was set up was really a one-man operation. Peter LaNague would make the moment-to-moment decisions and adjust its course as he went along. With the Trustees light years away, Peter LaNague was the revolution.

Adrynna must have had the most say in his being chosen as the agent provocateur—an ama knew her student better than a parent knew a child. Of course, out of deference to the founding family of the Sedition Trust, the same family that had spent generations honing a charter for a new organization which would rise from the ashes of the revolution, a LaNague would always have first consideration for the task if he or she was willing . . . and capable . . . and of the necessary fiber. The task was rife with possibilities for abuse—from simple malfeasance to outright betrayal of the cause—and could not be entrusted to someone merely because of lineage.

Peter LaNague had apparently met all the criteria. And when offered the job, had accepted. He had been working as a landscaper, a task that kept his hands busy but had allowed his mind long periods in which to roam free. He had known the call was coming and had developed myriad ideas on how to assault the Imperium's weak points. Circumstances, the Neeka incident, and Boedekker's subsequent proposal to the Flinters had narrowed him down to a devious strategy that would strike at the heart of the Imperium. It had all been so clean and simple then, so exciting in the planning stage. Now, in the midst of the sordid details of actually bringing the plan to fruition, he found he had lost all of his former enthusiasm. He wanted it over and done with.

All three Trustees were waiting for him when he arrived at the two-story structure that sat alone on the great northwestern plain of Tolive's second-largest continent, the building people called "Sedition Central." It was to these men and this building that the Flinters had come with news of what Eric Boedekker had offered them in exchange for the Imperium's demise. Peter LaNague's life had been radically altered by that information.

After greetings and drink-pouring, Peter and the Trustees seated themselves in an open square. Waters, senior Trustee, brought the talk around to business.

"We've all heard your report and agree that the killing of the assassin was justified and unavoidable."

"If there had been another way, I would have tried it," Peter said. "But if we hadn't moved immediately, he would have murdered Metep. It was a life for a life."

"And the agreement with Boedekker? He's actually staking his fortune on you?"

Peter nodded. "He's risking little. The necessary conversions merely change the nature of his assets. They never leave his control."

"But if you're successful, he'll be ruined," said Connors, the most erudite of the Trustees. "He must know that! He certainly didn't reach his present position by taking this kind of risk!"

"He doesn't care about his present position. He wanted to build a monolithic financial empire and center it around his family. But he's lost his family, and the Earth government won't let him start another. My plan gives him the opportunity to use his own empire to destroy another empire, the one that destroyed the last hope of his dream becoming reality. He agreed."

"Then that's it!" Waters said. "It's all set!"

"Yes . . . yes, I think so."

"What about this Broohnin you mention?" It was Silvera, youngest of the three and an eminent architect before she became a Trustee. "He worries me."

"Worries me, too," Peter said. "But I think—I hope—I've dazzled him enough to keep him off balance for a while."

"He does sound dangerous," Connors added. "Violent, too."

"He's a wild card—as dangerous as they come and as unpredictable. But I can't bring the revolution through in the necessary time period without his contacts. I don't like him, I don't trust him, but without his co-operation there can be no revolution."

The three Trustees considered this in silence. Only Connors had further comment.

"Is your five-year limit that strict? Can't we afford a year or two extra to slip our own people into sensitive positions?"

"Absolutely not!" Peter replied, shaking his head vigorously. "The economic situation is going to deteriorate rapidly on its own. If we allow seven, or even six years before we bring the house down, there may be nothing left to salvage. We figure that twenty years from now the Imperium, even if left alone, will be in such disarray that Earth could move in unchallenged. What we need is quick collapse and quick reconstruction before Earth is able to make its move. We can do it on a five-year schedule. On a seven-year schedule, I doubt we could move fast enough to keep the Earthies out." He held up the fingers of his right hand. "Five years. No more. And only four are left."

Connors persisted: "Couldn't we use Broohnin's organization without him?"

"Possibly. But that could be risky. We might be suspected of collusion with the Imperium. If that happened, we'd get no co-operation at all. Broohnin has valuable contacts in most of the trade guilds, in the Imperial communications centers, in the Treasury itself. Plus, there's a minor vid personality and a professor at the University of the Outworlds who might prove useful. They're peripherally associated with Broohnin's group, not necessarily out of approval of his methods, but because he's the only resistance they've got. I need Broohnin to reach them."

"I see then we have no choice," Connors said resignedly. "But it *feels* wrong, and that bothers me."

"You're not alone."

Ω

Despite her best efforts to stanch them, tears were brimming and spilling over Mora's lower eyelids. She faced away from the smooth, flat expanse of the spaceport grid and the orbital shuttle patiently waiting on it.

"I don't want you to go," she said against her husband's chest. "Something's going to happen, I know it."

"The Imperium's going to come crashing down," Peter said with all the confidence he could muster. "That's what's going to happen."

"No. To you. Something bad. I can feel it. Let somebody else go."

"I can't."

"You can!" She lifted her head and looked at him. "You've done your share—more! All the groundwork is laid. It's just a matter of time from now on. Let somebody else finish it!"

Peter shook his head sadly. There was nothing in Occupied Space he wanted more than to stay right where he was. But that couldn't be.

"It has to be me, Mora. It's my plan. I've got to handle it, I've got to be there myself."

"There must be some other person you can trust!" Mora's tears were drying in the heat of growing anger. "Surely you don't think you're the only one capable of overseeing the revolution. You can't tell me that!"

"I must know! I can't sit light years away and entrust this to someone else. It's too delicate. The future of everything we've worked for is at stake. I can't walk away. I want to—but I cannot!"

"But you can walk away from me! And from Laina! Is that so much easier?"

"Mora, please! That's not fair!"

"Of course it's not fair! And it's not fair that your daughter won't see you for years now! Maybe never again! She was so upset about your leaving again that she wouldn't even come down to the spaceport! And as for my having a husband—" She pulled free of his arms.

"Mora!"

"Maybe Laina had the right idea!" She was backing away from him as she spoke. "Maybe we both should have stayed home and let you come here all by yourself. We're both second place in your life now anyway!" She swung around and began walking away.

"Mora!" Peter heard his voice break as he called after his wife. He started to follow her but stopped after two steps. She was beyond gentle reasoning now. They were two stubborn people who shared a life as fierce in its discord as in its lovemaking. He knew from long experience that it would be hours before the two of them could carry on a civil conversation . . . and there were no hours left to him on Tolive. There were complex interstellar travel connections to be made and he had to leave now. If he tarried too long, his arrival on Throne could be delayed as long as a standard month.

He watched her until she rounded a bend in the corridor, hoping she would look back, just once. She never did.

Peter LaNague entered the boarding tube that would drop

him at the waiting shuttle. Dealing with Den Broohnin, keeping the Flinters in line, masterminding a revolution that still hinged on too many variables, that if successful would significantly alter the course of human history . . . none of these disturbed his *wah* as much as an argument with that stubborn, hot-tempered, and occasionally obnoxious creature called Mora, who could make his life so miserable at times, and yet make it all so worth while. He would never understand it.

It helped somewhat when he glimpsed her standing on the observation tower, gripping the railing with what he knew must be painful intensity, watching the shuttle, waiting for lift-off. It helped, but it failed to loosen the knot that had tightened to the fraying point in the center of his chest, nor did it lighten the lead cast that sat where his stomach had been.

He could not allow himself to dwell on Mora, nor on Laina. They were a part of his life that had to be completely walled off if he were to function effectively on Throne. As the shuttle rose toward the stars, he cast Mora as Fortunato, played Montresor himself, and began the brickwork.

It hurt.

VOLUME II NUMBER 2

THE ROBIN HOOD READER

Good News

Average wages increased a full five per cent (5%) in the past standard year. More outworlders are earning more than ever before.

Bad News

Inflation hit a full eight per cent (8%) last year. Subtract this from the five per cent (5%) average increase in wages and you're left with a bit of a deficit. In other words, despite an increase in wages, your buying power is now three per cent (3%) less than last year. Sorry.

Worse

Because the schedule of progressive tax rates has not been corrected for inflation, more and more outworlders are moving into the upper income brackets and paying upper bracket taxes. Now, if you've read the above, you know that increased income no longer means increased buying power. And now that tax time is here, you'll find your buying power further diminished by the fact that you will be giving more of those hard-earned marks to the Imperial Tax Service.

The Economic Weather Eye

PRICE INDEX (using the 115th year of the Imperium—when the Imperial mark became mandatory legal tender—as base year of 100)	160.2
MONEY SUPPLY (M3)	995.7
UNEMPLOYMENT LEVEL	7.9%

	Imperial Marks	Solar Credits
GOLD (Troy ounce)	244.3	130.5
Silver (Troy ounce)	11.2	6.0
Bread (1 kg. loaf)	.69	1.80

XI

The free man will ask neither what his country can do for him nor what he can do for his country.

Milton Friedman

It was just another warehouse on the outskirts of Primus City, no different from the dozens of others surrounding it. The name across the front wall, ANGUS BLACK IMPORTS, told the passer-by nothing about the company or what lay within. It could house crates of vid sets, racks of open-seamed clothing ready for autofitting, or seafood delicacies from planets like Friendly or Gelk. Just another warehouse. LaNague wanted it that way.

Tonight was the first step in the active phase, the first blow against the empire, the first physical act of sedition. The principals were all present, along with a few extraneous characters who were there to see them off and wish them well. Faces that had been new three months ago could be seen here and there across the wide, empty interior of the warehouse . . . LaNague had come to know them all intimately since his return from Tolive, gaining their confidence, and they gaining his.

Singly, then in pairs, then in a group, they approached him as he entered the warehouse carrying a box under his arm.

Zachariah Brophy, professor of economics at the University of Outworlds, was the first. Very tall, bony, knobby, and sixtyish, he raised a knotted fist toward LaNague's face.

"Either you let me go along or I flatten you right here and now!"

LaNague laughed. "Sorry, Doc, but we don't have a holosuit to fit you, and I'm afraid some of your former students would recognize you even if we did."

"Aahh!" he sighed with exaggerated despondency, unfolding his fist and laying the open hand on the younger man's thin shoulder. "You've been telling me no all along. I guess now I'll have to believe you."

LaNague had developed a genuine affection for the older man, loved his wit, his intelligence, his integrity. And Doc Zack, as his students had called him for years, reciprocated warmly. Apparently he saw many things he liked in LaNague, the same things he had sought and found lacking in Broohnin. He made no secret of his relief at the fact that LaNague had superseded him.

"Why don't you try your hand at one of the flyers," LaNague suggested. "We've fallen behind schedule because of all the calling cards we've been duplicating for tonight. You can draft up the next *Robin Hood Reader* while we're out playing the part."

"Fair enough. At least I'll get to be one of the Merry Men one way or another." He squeezed LaNague's shoulder where his hand rested. "Good luck tonight." He turned and made his way toward the bank of duplicators against the rear wall.

Radmon Sayers was next, stopping briefly on his way out. He was portrait handsome with the perfect features and meticulous grooming that befitted a vid personality. His sleek black hair reflected the ceiling lights as it lay plastered against his scalp in the latest fashion. His eyes were less calculating and more genuinely lively tonight.

"It's really going to happen, isn't it!" he said, rubbing gloved hands together in barely suppressed glee.

"Did you think all these preparations were for some elaborate hoax?" LaNague replied evenly, trying to keep annoyance out of his voice. He had found Sayers aloof and hard to like. He gave news reports on one of the smaller independent vid systems on Throne. He was good—able to project sincerity, objectivity, and concern as well as anybody else in the business, but was condemned to relative obscurity by the fact that most of Throne's population watched the Imperial Vid System, which had long ago commandeered the best wavelengths and transmitted with the strongest signal. His obscurity, however, was destined to be short-lived if LaNague had his way.

"No, of course not," Sayers said. "But still, it's hard to believe that tonight I've been involved in making some news instead of just reading it. That'll be nice for a change. Very nice."

"You've got your diversion set?"

Sayers nodded. "We'll monitor the official channels, as usual. When we hear them talking about the hijack, I'll delay the remote crew until it starts to rain."

"Good. Just watch the time."

There were further words of encouragement to say to the tense men who were gathered around the large, enclosed flitter lorry sitting in the middle of the warehouse floor. Computer experts, communciation technicians, Flinters, street toughs, all gravitated toward the one who would make them into wanted men tonight. Only Broohnin hung back, conspicuous by his lack of enthusiasm.

"All right," LaNague said after a while. "It's full dark outside by now and time to go. But first, I want you all to wear these."

He opened the box he had been carrying under his arm and began handing out pairs of transparent, gossamer-light gloves.

"What're these?" someone asked.

"They serve two purposes. First of all, they protect all of you from any chance of leaving epidermic clues behind. All the Imperial investigators have to do is find one of your skin cells when they go over the hijacked ships tomorrow—and believe me, they'll go over them as they've never been gone over before—and they'll have your genotype, which they'll try to match against every type on record. Some of you had to have a genotype recording made when you applied for the sensitive jobs you're in. If one of your cells is identified, you're as good as caught.

"The second reason for wearing these gloves has to do with the fine little pattern of whorls you'll notice on the palmar surface. The gloves are made of a micropore material that will let sweat and skin oils through . . . enough to leave good fingerprints."

A sudden murmur of protest arose from the group, but LaNague quelled it by raising his hand.

"Don't worry. They won't be your fingerprints. They'll be my great-grandfather's. He knew the revolution would come someday, and knew he wouldn't be around to see it. So his dying request was that someone wear gloves like these at some time during the revolution, just so he could say he had a hand in the downfall of the Imperium."

The ensuing laughter lightened the mood as the men, fifteen of them, filed quickly and spiritedly into the flitter. LaNague felt no lightness, however. His palms were moist and he had a pain crawling up the back of his head from his neck—this was the first overt move and everything had to be just right. But he hid his fears well, pretending to have everything under control, exuding confidence and competence he did not feel.

Josef acted as pilot on the way out; another would return the ship after the Merry Men were dropped off. The wide warehouse doors opened and allowed the flitter to slide out into the night. It flew low and slow until past the Primus City limits, then rose to thirty meters where it could pick up speed and be safe from interfering treetops.

"Everyone have their projectors secured?" LaNague asked once they had reached cruising speed. There was a murmured assent from the group crowded into the cargo area. "All right. Let's try them."

The holosuit was a whimsical concoction, designed for imaginative types who found stimulation in role-playing. The most popular models were sexual in nature, but those to be employed tonight had been specially modified. They were the standard six-piece models consisting of two wrist bands, two ankle bands, a belt, and a skull cap. When activated, they formed a holographic sheath around the wearer, a costume of light that could make him appear to be anything he chose—a male, a female, a demon, a lover. Anything, depending on what had been programmed into the unit.

The suits flickered to life one by one, causing their wearers to fade from view, replaced by lean and wolfish outlaws garbed in leather and Lincoln green, topped by jaunty, feathered caps. To any of their contemporaries, the men in the command flitter would be as alien in appearance as creatures from another galaxy. A few adjustments had to be made, especially on one man's skull cap which failed to activate, leaving his own head and shoulders exposed. This was quickly remedied, bringing his appearance into line with his companions'.

"This is stupid!"

It was Broohnin. He had already doused his holosuit and leaned sullenly against the wall opposite LaNague, scowling through his beard.

"I expected that from you," LaNague replied without missing a beat. "Care to give us grounds for your opinion? We've got time to listen."

Broohnin swaggered into the middle of the group. It was obvious that he still considered himself the unacknowledged leader, despite the fact that LaNague was giving the orders. He was keeping to his role of the tough, hard-hitting, no-quarter revolutionary. It had worked before, and there was no reason why it shouldn't work now.

"We're just playing games with these funnysuits! This is no masquerade ball—this is the real thing! We're not going to get prizes for how good we look; we're just going to get stunned and maybe even blasted into a couple of pieces by the fecaliths guarding this shipment. We have to hit them *hard!* Make them remember us! Let them know we mean business! Make them leave the lights on at night when they go to sleep! Never let them forget we're out here, ready to strike at any time, without warning!"

"Then you think we should forget disguise and mount a frontal assault?" LaNague said, unmoved by the oratory.

"Absolutely!"

"What about the multiple cameras in each of the ships we're going after tonight? Our images will be transmitted to the Imperial Guard the instant we board the first currency ship. We'll all be marked men after that!"

"Don't board!" Broohnin snarled. "Blow them to bits! *Then* let the cameras try to take our pictures!"

"There are men on board each of those ships. They'll be killed."

"They're Imperial lackies—they take the pay, they take the chances. This time they lose."

"And what of your own man on board the second ship. You intend to blow him up, too?"

"Of course not! We'll get him off first, then blow the rest."

The momentum of the argument was swinging toward Broohnin. He offered easy solutions, hard and fast victory. But he had left an opening for LaNague.

"You realize, don't you, that as the only survivor, your man will become an instant fugitive. Every Imperial Guardsman on Throne will be hunting him as an accomplice in the slaughter of their comrades. Do you wish that on him?"

Broohnin paused for an instant, and in that instant he lost his audience. LaNague had shown that he had considered the problem from more sides than his burlier counterpart; and while it might be said that he seemed to be overly concerned for the well-being of the men guarding the targeted currency shipment, it was also obvious that he was equally concerned about the men who would be at his side during tonight's raid.

But LaNague would not let it go at that. He had to win these men firmly to his side. So firmly, that if it came to a choice between Peter LaNague and Den Broohnin, the men would choose LaNague.

"There's more to these holosuits than a mere masquerade ball, I assure you," he said, ostensibly speaking to Broohnin, but letting his gaze rest in turn on each and every man in the flitter. "We need to protect our identities—that's our primary requirement for success. If we can't move about freely on Throne, we've lost our usefulness. Another thing: there's always a chance that one or even all of us might someday be captured; how we're treated then will depend a lot on how we treat the crews of the transports tonight, and how we treat all Imperial Guardsmen in the future. Remember that. So—if we intend to leave live witnesses behind, we need disguises. And if we intend to use disguises, *why not make a point with them!*"

He paused to let this sink in. He was marking a trail of logic and he wanted no one to lose his way. All eyes were on him. Even Broohnin's.

"The Robin Hood motif was not chosen capriciously. As most of you remember, he was a mythical do-gooder on Old Earth who supposedly robbed from the rich and gave to the poor. But that's the sanitized, government-approved version of the legend. Anyone reading between the lines will see that Robin Hood was the archetypical tax rebel. He robbed from the rich, yes—but those rich happened to be King John's tax collectors. And he gave to the poor—but his beneficiaries were those who had been looted by the tax collectors. He merely returned their own property.

"So what we're going to do tonight," he said, lowering his voice to a conspiratorial undertone, "is replay history. Metep is King John, we're Robin Hood and his Merry Men, and tonight we rob from the very rich—the Imperial Treasury. By the end of tonight, the poor—the public, that is—will be the recipients of our good deed." He smiled. "I doubt the message will be lost on them."

LaNague's smile was returned by the faces around him. He debated whether or not to delve into the other reason for his resurrection of Robin Hood. This was probably not the time or place for it . . .

Josef's voice cut through his thoughts and made the decision for him: *"We're over the drop-off spot. Going down."*

Ω

It was tax time on Throne. For two months, the good citizens would be required to figure out how much they owed the Imperium for the preceding year, subtract from that what they had already given over in withholding taxes, and remit the difference. The Imperium called it "a voluntary tax system." Those who refused to pay, however, were fined or jailed.

Throne's population was clustered on a single large land mass, with Primus City occupying the central plateau, four thousand kilometers from each coast. Inhabitants of the central regions sent their taxes directly to Primus City. Regional Revenue Centers collected the extorted marks on the coasts and shipped them inland to the Treasury Bureau for culling and replacement of old currency. From there it disappeared into the insatiable maw of the Imperium bureaucracy.

A three-ship convoy was on its way now from the west coast Regional Revenue Center, laden with currency as it flew over the barren hinterlands between the coast and the central plateau. The transports were well armed and manned with members of the Imperial Guard. This was purely routine, however, since no one had ever even attempted to hijack a currency transport since the runs began.

Ω

Erv Singh waited for the lurch. If he had timed everything right, the circuits would be overloading just about now. He waited, and it came. A gentle tug, imperceptible to someone who wasn't looking for it. But it was there, and it meant that Mother Gravity was firming up her grip on the ship. He watched the altimeter start to slip, gave the anti-grav generator a little more juice to no avail. The warning light flashed red. They were sinking. Right on schedule.

"Ship Two to Leader," he said into the communicator panel. "We're getting heavy here. No a-g response. I think we've got an overload."

"Hit the auxiliary, Ship Two," came the calm reply.

"Will do." He phased in the backup a-g generator, but there was no boost in altitude. After a sufficient trial: "Sorry, Leader, but we're still getting heavier. Up to zero-point-four-five normal mass now and sinking, I think we'd better turn back."

"You'll never make it, Two. Not at the rate you're putting on mass. Better look for a place to put down and see what's wrong."

"Right. Shouldn't be too hard to find." Erv Singh knew it wouldn't be too hard at all. He had the place all picked out. He just hoped everybody below was insulated by now. "Looks like a good clearing half a kilomeeter ahead. How does she scan?"

The reply was delayed for a few prolonged heartbeats. *"Nothing but big rocks and bush. No movement, no major heat sources, not even any minor lifeforms. Looks safe. You go down and we'll keep cover overhead."*

"What's up?" One of the guards had come up from the rear. "Why we going down?"

"No life. We're almost to normal mass," Erv told him.

"Hey, Singh—you mean you can't even fly from the back burgs to Primus without a breakdown? Some pilot!"

Erv looked suitably annoyed. "You want to take over? I'd take baby-sitting all that money any day to trying to fly this piece of junk!"

"Don't get excited, Erv," the guard said. "There's nothing to look at back there anyway. It's all crated and it's all very dull."

"Then get back there before it runs away."

Singh overrode the guidance cassette and took manual control of Ship Two, settling it gently into a clearing ringed by the deciduous, red-leafed brush indigenous to Throne's hinterlands. The two companion ships in the convoy circled warily overhead. After releasing the safety locks on the a-g generator inspection ports from his command center, Singh opened the hatch and strolled out for a look. After shining a hand lamp into two of the ports, he turned and hurried back inside.

"I'm down to stay, Leader," Erv said, returning to his communicator.

"That bad?"

"Everything's burned up."

"Look like sabotage?"

"I wouldn't know sabotage if I saw it. All I know is I can't fix it." There was silence at the other end. Erv allowed sufficient time for thought, then made his own suggestion, a preplanned red herring. "Why don't you guys stay up there and keep watch while we wait for another ship from the center. I can transfer my cargo over and then you can all be on your way."

"No!" came the reply after a brief pause. *"Take too long."* Erv knew what was going through the convoy leader's head: it was to have been a quick and simple run tonight: leave early, get to the Primus Treasury, unload, and spend a night on the town. If they wasted half the night waiting for a replacement ship, there'd be no fun and games in Primus City. *"We're coming down."*

"You think that's wise?"

"Let me worry about that. The area scans clean. We'll offload your consignment and divide it up between Ships One and Three. Then we'll head for the Treasury while you wait for a lift."

"Thanks a lot, Leader." Erv refrained from showing the relief he felt, knowing that his every move was being recorded. The bait had been taken.

"Sorry, Ship Two, but somebody's got to stay with her."

Erv waited at the hatch until the other two cargo flitters were down. In strict compliance with regulations, he ordered one of the three guards in the cargo bay to man the external weapons control panel, then opened the rear of the ship, letting the loading ramp slide toward the ground. The same procedure began on the other ships and soon the men were transferring the cargo from Ship Two to the other two, pushing float-dollies down the ramps, across the dirt and grass, and into the waiting holds.

The men moved warily at first, on guard against any would-be hijackers. But as the work progressed and the scanners picked up no suspicious activity in the surrounding area, they relaxed and talked and joked among themselves. The talk concerned the near-superhuman feats they would perform tonight once they were let loose in Primus; the jokes were mostly at the expense of Erv and his crew, teasing them about what they were going to miss.

Ship Two was soon emptied of her cargo of currency, every

last crate of it squeezed into the companion ships. As his own crew sat inside the barren hold, grousing about being left behind, Erv stood at his boarding hatch, watching, listening. He saw the other crews begin to board their own ships, and heard a shout from the man at the weapons console behind him:

"We've got activity outside, Erv! Lifeforms! A whole bunch of them coming out of nowhere! Almost on top of us!"

"Close up quick!" Erv yelled in reply. "But whatever you do, don't fire—you'll hit the other ships!"

The boarding hatch started to slide closed, but not before a running figure darted by and threw something. There were metallic pings as a number of tiny silver balls danced along the ship's deck and bounced off the walls. Erv knew what was next. His hands went involuntarily to his ears, but no matter how tightly he pressed against them, he could not shut out the sound that started as a dull whine and grew in pitch until he could no longer hear it. But he could feel it growing, expanding, pressing against the inside of his skull until he was sure his head would explode. And then it did.

Ω

The heat inside the thermoreflective dome had quickly reached a stifling level. Its rough, irregular outer surface would scan cold and inert—no heat, no movement, no life. Inside was another matter. The respiratory heat of fifteen bodies had nowhere to go. The men sat still and silent in the dark while LaNague watched the clearing through a peep lens in the wall. He saw the first ship, Ship Two, the one with their man aboard, land jarringly a few meters away, saw the pilot step outside and go through the motions of peering into the inspection ports, saw him return to the cabin of his ship.

The remaining two ships soon joined their companion on the ground and the unloading process began. It had been decided to let the employees of the Imperium do the heavy work; that would allow the Merry Men more time before reinforcements arrived from Primus. When Ship Two was empty, LaNague split a handful of pea-sized metallic globes between Kanya and Josef.

"Whatever you do," he whispered, "don't drop them."

The warning was superfluous. LaNague and the two Flinters had practiced short sprints for the past week in preparation for this moment, and all three were aware that the sonibombs in their hands were impact-activated—one good bump and they went off.

"Holosuits on," he said to the others. "Check the man on your right, making sure his gloves are on and his holosuit is fully functional."

A vague glow lit the interior of the dome as the holosuits came on. When everyone was checked out, LaNague split the seam and the "rock" opened. The next few moments were a blur of tense, feverish activity. He and the Flinters ran full tilt into the center of the triangle formed by the three ships. Surprise was on their side, as was the fact that the ships were so situated that each was in the other's line of fire. They were all set to defend against attacks from the air and from the ground, but not from within their own perimeter. Each runner reached his assigned ship and hurled a handful of sonibombs through the hatchway before it could be closed off, then dove for the ground. All before a shot could be fired.

The transports were shielded from any external ultrasonic barrage. But a single thirty-second sonibomb going off within the small confines of the ship was enough to render anyone on board unconscious. Handfuls of the little weapons were used to reduce the chance of a miss-throw, and all went off on impact with the deck or rear wall. The Merry Men outside remained unaffected because the bombs weren't focused and the sound waves dissipated rapidly in the open air. None of the crewmen managed to escape his ship, but in case one did, a few of the Merry Men stood ready with stun rifles.

As soon as it was evident that there would be no resistance, the Merry Men divided up into pre-arranged work groups. Some began hauling the unconscious crewmen out of Ships One and Three, dragging them to Ship Two and stretching them out on the deck there. Others carried sacks of small leaflets from the "rock" to the cargo holds of the two operable ships. Still others went to the control areas and began blasting the monitoring equipment. LaNague had assigned Broohnin to the last group, realizing that the man must be allowed to destroy something or else he would go berserk. One of the Merry Men passed, carrying a blaster rifle. LaNague recognized Broohnin's gait and followed him into Ship Three.

Broohnin went to the main communications console and waved into the receiver. There he lifted his blaster and melted the panel with a tight proton beam. The last thing seen by the communications hand on the other end of that monitor was an oddly dressed man raising a blaster toward his face. The alarm would go out immediately and flitterfuls of Imperial Guardsmen would be mobilized and sent careening in their direction. Although no expression could be read through the holomask, LaNague could see that Broohnin was thoroughly enjoying himself as he stalked the length of the ship destroying the monitor eyes. LaNague was content to let him vent his fury as he wished until one of the crewmen rolled over at Broohnin's feet and started to rise to his hands and knees.

"Don't!" LaNague shouted as he saw Broohnin lower the blaster muzzle toward the man's head. He leaped over and pushed his arm aside.

No words passed between the two men as they stood in position over the wavering form of the crewman. Broohin could not see the face of the man who had interfered with him, but there could be no doubt in his mind as to who it was. Further conflict was made moot by the crewman's abrupt collapse into unconsciousness again. LaNague did not release Broohnin's wrist until the inert form had been dragged from the ship.

"If I ever see anything like that again," he said, "you'll spend the rest of the revolution locked in a back room of the warehouse. I will *not* tolerate murder!"

Broohnin's voice trembled with rage as he replied in kind. "If you ever touch me again, I'll kill you!"

Peter LaNague did what he then considered the bravest act of his life. He turned his back on Broohnin and walked away.

After all the unconscious crewmen had been stretched out in Ship Two, the hatches were closed and locked, but not before a steel-tipped longbow arrow, with "Greetings from Robin Hood" emblazoned on the shaft, had been driven into the cushion on the pilot's seat. The Merry Men then hurriedly boarded the two functional transports and took to the air. After inserting a pre-programmed flight cassette into the control console, the new pilot of each ship sat back and watched the instruments.

The two Treasury Transports took separate courses, one to the northeast, another to the southeast. The flight cassettes, which had been carefully programmed meter by meter the previous week, would keep the ships moving as low and as fast as possible, each taking a divergent route to Primus. They could be traced and located, but not with any great ease or accuracy. And no one would be expecting them to head to Primus, the very seat of the planet's major police and militia garrisons.

"All right," LaNague said, now that Ship One was underway, "let's get to work."

Most of the men had turned their holosuits off by now; all leaped to the task of tearing open the crates of orange currency ships and dumping the contents onto the floor of the cargo hold. The flattened, empty crates were passed to a man at the boarding hatch who threw them out toward the darkened grasslands not far below. To the north on Ship Three, Broohnin, Kanya, and Josef were directing a similar task.

When all the currency had been dumped into a huge pile in the center of the hold, the men stood back and surveyed the mass of wealth.

"How much do you think?" someone said in an awed voice to anyone who was listening.

"About thirty million marks," LaNague replied. "And about the same amount in the other ship." He bent and lifted one of the sacks that had been loaded earlier. "Time to add the calling cards."

The men each grabbed a sack and emptied the thousands of tiny white slips of paper within onto the pile of marks, creating a mound of orange cake with white icing. Then they began kicking at the mound and throwing handfuls of it into the air until currency and calling cards were evenly mixed.

LaNague looked at the time. "Sayers ought to have his remote crew just about ready to move out now." The first dump was designated for the neighborhood outside the vid studio. He hoped Sayers had been able to stall long enough.

Eternities passed before the ship began to rise and the control panel buzzed warning that the flight cassette was coming to its end. They were at Primus City limits, and the pilot took manual control.

"Open the loading hatch," LaNague said.

Slowly, the rear wall of the cargo bay began to rise. When the opening was a meter high, LaNague called a stop and it held that aperture. A cool wind began to whirl through the hold as the men awaited word from the pilot. Then it came:

"First target below!"

Reluctantly at first, and then with mounting enthusiasm, they began kicking piles of mark notes mixed with their own private calling cards out the opening.

It began to rain orange and white.

Ω

His first thought was that he had finally cracked . . . the boredom had finally worn away his sanity until he was now beginning to hallucinate.

Well, why not? Vincen Stafford thought uneasily. *After all, here I am in the dead of night, standing in the middle of my vegetable patch.*

The little garden had become an important part of Stafford's life lately. He had been getting fewer and fewer assignments on the grain runs, and had actually been bumped off the last one. Two small orders had been consolidated into one and he had been left hanging due to lack of seniority. The runs seemed to be coming fewer and farther between . . . hard to believe, but that was the way it was.

At least he had the house. After navigating six consecutive runs, he had applied to a bank for a mortgage and had been approved. The single-level cottage on a synthestone slab behind him was the result. Not much, but it was a place to start, and it was home.

Then the runs had slowed up. Good thing his wife had that part-time night job, or things really would have been tight. He hadn't wanted Salli to take it at first, but she'd said she needed something to do while he was shuttling between the stars. She didn't want to sit home alone. But look who was staying home alone now! Very alone, since he had yet to make any fast friends in the neighborhood. That was why the garden had become so important. The loneliness and the boredom of waiting for an assignment had driven him to try his hand at growing a few vegetables, especially with produce prices being what they were. He had planted a few legumes and tubers last week and they had just started to sprout.

So here he was, out in the dark, standing over his newborn vegetable plants like an overprotective parent. But the garden gave him peace, eased that empty gnawing feeling that followed him around like a shadow. It sounded crazy, so he kept to himself. Just as he would have to keep this hallucination to himself . . . he could swear it was raining mark notes.

He turned around. By the light pouring from the rear windows of his house he could see that there was money all over the back yard. He bent over to see if it just might be real . . . if it could be touched. It could. It was real—old bills, new bills, ones, fives, ten-mark notes were spilling from the sky. And something else . . .

He reached down and picked up one of the small white slips of paper that fell with the currency.

YOUR TAX REFUND
AS PROMISED.
ROBIN HOOD AND HIS MERRY MEN

Stafford looked up and saw nothing. The rain of money had stopped. He had never heard of Robin Hood . . . or had he? Wasn't there an old story about someone with that name? He'd have to ask Salli when she got home.

As he walked about the yard, picking up what later totaled one hundred and fifty-six marks, he idly wondered if it might be stolen money. They weren't in any dire financial trouble, but the extra cash would certainly come in handy, especially with a new house to care for.

Even if he never spent it, Stafford thanked Robin Hood, whoever he might be, for brightening up a dull evening.

VOLUME II NUMBER 3

THE ROBIN HOOD READER

You Can't Afford to Own Money!

Inflation for the past ten-month standard year has now been officially rated at 8% (which means that the *real* rate of inflation is at least 11%). DUMP YOUR MONEY, FOLKS! That 100 marks you put in the savings account last year is now worth significantly less. What's that you say—what about the interest?

Let's give Metep's mob the benefit of the doubt and assume that the inflation rate really was 8% last year. This means that the 100 marks you put in the savings account ten months ago is now worth only 9.2. But you collected 6 mark's interest. Harrah! Of course, you realize that you owe around 25% of that in taxes, leaving you a net of 4.5 marks interest.

To sum up: that 100 marks you put away in hopes of watching it grow into a fortune in an interest-bearing account has now shrunk to 96.5 marks. There's only one solution. Get your money and . . .

BUY! BUY! BUY! BUY!

The Economic Weather Eye

PRICE INDEX (using the 115th year of the Imperium—when the Imperial mark became mandatory legal tender—as base year of 100)	165.7
MONEY SUPPLY (M3)	1032.3
UNEMPLOYMENT LEVEL	8.1%

	Imperial Marks	Solar Credits
GOLD (Troy ounce)	262.1	130.3
Silver (Troy ounce)	12.9	5.9
Bread (1 kg. loaf)	.74	1.78

XII

Pity the poor, diseased politician. Imagine: to spend your days and expend your efforts making rules for others to live by, thinking up ways to run other lives. Actually to strive for the opportunity to do so! What a hideous affliction!

from THE SECOND BOOK OF KYFHO

"How many times are they going to show that sequence?" Metep VII catapulted himself out of his seat as he spoke and stalked about the small, darkened room, irritation evident in every move.

Daro Haworth's reply was languid, distracted. "As long as they can get an audience for it." His eyes were intent on the large, sharply focused vid globe in the center of the room. "Don't forget, they have an exclusive on this: they were the only ones on the street with a remote crew when the rains came."

"Which is just a little too pat, don't you think?"

"We had security look into it. There's a logical explanation. They monitor the official frequencies just like the other two vid services, and heard the hijack alarm along with everybody else. But they've got a small budget with no remote crew on stand-by, so they were way behind their competition in getting to the scene. It so happened they were just about to take to the air when the money started to fall. A good example of how inefficiency can pay off once in a while."

Radmon Sayers' familiar face filled the vid globe. Orange mark notes fluttered all around him, interspersed occasionally with flashes of white, all so real and seemingly solid that a viewer with a large holo set would be tempted to reach out and grab a handful. Sayers' expression was a mixture of ecstatic delight and barely suppressed jubilation.

"Ladies and gentlemen," he said from within the globe, "if someone had told me about this, I'd have called him a liar. But here I am in the street outside our studio, and it's raining money! No, this is not a stunt and it's not a joke. There's money falling from the sky!"

The camera panned up the side of a building to the dark sky yielding orange and white slips of paper out of its otherwise featureless blackness, then jumped to a wider angle on Sayers. He was holding one of the white slips. Behind and around him, people could be seen scurrying about, snatching up money from the street.

"Do you remember those crazy little flyers we've been seeing around town for the past half-year or so? *The Robin Hood Reader?* One of the early ones promised a tax refund—'Look to the skies,' it said, if I remember correctly. Well . . . I think I may be standing in the middle of that tax refund right now."

He held up the white piece of paper and the camera angle closed in on it, virtually thrusting his magnified hand into the room. The printing on the slip was clear: "*Your tax rebate as promised. Robin Hood and his Merry Men.*" For those who could not read or whose reception might be poor, Sayers read the inscription.

"So it looks like this Robin Hood fellow kept his promise," he said as the rain of paper tapered off to nothing. "There was an unconfirmed report of one of the Imperial Treasury convoys being hijacked this evening. If that's true, and this is the stolen money, then I fear Mr. Hood and his Merry Men are in big trouble."

The camera angle widened to a full-length shot of Sayers and the street. People could be seen standing here and there around him, faces upward, expectantly watching the sky, wads of bills clutched tightly in their hands. He went over to a middle-aged woman and put his arm around her shoulder. She obviously recognized him and smiled at the camera.

"Let's ask this woman what she thinks of this whole affair."

"Oh, I think it's just wonderful!" she cooed. "I don't know who this Robin Hood fellow is, but he's welcome in my neighborhood any time!"

"But the money may be stolen."

Her smile faltered. "From who?"

"From the government, perhaps."

"Oh, that would be too bad. Too bad."

"What if the government confirmed that it was the same money that was hijacked from the Imperial Treasury ships and asked that all good citizens turn in the money they had picked up tonight . . . would you comply?"

"You mean would I give it back?"

"Yes."

"Of course I would!" Her expression was utterly deadpan as she spoke; then she smiled; then she began to giggle.

"Of course." Sayers, too, allowed a smile to play about his lips. He stepped away from the woman and faced the camera. "Well, it looks as if the monetary monsoon is over. This is Radmon Sayers saying good night from a scene that neither these people around me nor the Imperial Treasury officials are likely to forget for a long time. By the way, it might not be a bad idea to take a look outside your own window. Perhaps Robin Hood is delivering *your* tax refund right now."

The globe faded to gray and then the head of another vidcaster appeared. Haworth touched a groove in the arm of his chair and the globe went dark.

"We all look like fools!" Metep said, still wandering the room. "We'll have to make a real example of these do-gooders when we catch them!"

"That won't be too easy, I'm afraid."

"And why not?"

"Because they didn't leave a single clue to their identities behind. A sweep of those ships turned up countless sets of fingerprints—all identical, all unregistered, all obviously phony—but not a single epidermis cell other than the crews'. And of course their use of holosuits during the entire affair precludes visual identification."

"Identifying them shouldn't be the problem!" Metep shouted. "We should have them in custody!"

"Well, we don't, and there's no use ranting and raving about it. They pulled some very tricky maneuvers last night, the trickiest being the finale when they had everyone pursuing empty transports halfway back to the west coast."

"Idiots! We all look like idiots!"

"Yes, I'm afraid we do," Haworth said, rising to his feet and rubbing both hands up over his eyes and through the stark white of his hair. "But not as idiotic as we're going to look when the results of Krager's programs for voluntary return of the money are in. A 'patriotic gesture,' he called it! The old fool!"

"Why? I think it's a good idea. We may even get a few million back."

"We'll get nothing back except a few token marks, and then we'll really look like idiots!"

"I think you're wrong."

"Really? What would you do if you just found a tax-free bonus lying in your back yard, and knew it was stolen from the same people who had recently taken a sizable piece of your income in taxes? How would you respond when those people asked for their money back, and they didn't know exactly who had it? What would you do?"

Metep considered this. "I see what you mean. What'll we do?"

"Lie. What else? We'll announce that more than 90 per cent of the money has been returned and that only a greedy, disloyal few have failed to return the money that rightfully belongs to their fellow citizens."

"Sounds good. A little guilt is always good for the common man."

Haworth's smile was sardonic. "Assuming they'll feel guilty." The smile faded. "But there's a lot about this Robin Hood character—if he's actually an individual at all—that bothers me. What's he up to? He doesn't call for your death or violent overthrow of the Imperium. He just talks about money. There's no heated rhetoric, no obvious ideology. Just money."

"That bothers you? Not me! I prefer what he's doing to threatening my life. After all, he could have robbed a military base and been dropping neutrons on us."

"It bothers me because I don't know where he's heading. And I sense there's method to his madness. He's got a goal in mind and I can't see what it is. Perhaps he'll let us know in his newsletter."

"Which we've already outlawed, naturally. Anyone caught in possession of a *Robin Hood Reader* from now on will be arrested and interrogated."

"And that's another thing that bothers me. We lend Robin Hood a certain mystique by officially declaring him and his silly little flyers illegal."

"But we have no choice. He's committed armed robbery. We can't ignore that!"

Haworth didn't appear to be listening. He had walked to the wall and turned it to maximum transparency. The northern half of Primus City lay spread out before him.

"How many people do you think got a handful or two of money last night?" he asked Metep.

"Well, with two ships and sixty million marks . . . has to be thousands. Many thousands."

"And only a tiny fraction of those giving the money back." He turned to Metep VII. "Do you know what that means, Jek? Do you know what he's done?"

Metep could only shrug. "He's robbed us."

"Robbed us?" Haworth's expression could not disguise his contempt for his superior's obtuseness. "He's turned thousands of those people out there into accomplices!"

Ω

"My compliments to you, sir!" Doc Zack said, raising a glass of iced grain alcohol toward LaNague as they sat alone in one of the small offices that lined the rear of the Angus Black warehouse. "You have not only thumbed your nose at the Imperium, you've also succeeded in extracting joyful complicity from the public. A master stroke. Long live Robin Hood!"

LaNague raised his own glass in response. "I'll drink to that!" But he only sipped lightly, finding the native Throne liquors harsh and bitter. He preferred Tolive's dry white wines, but importing them in quantity would be a foolish extravagence. He didn't need any ethanol now anyway. He was already high. *He had done it!* He had actually done it! The first overt act of sedition had come off flawlessly, without a single casualty on either side. Everyone was intact and free.

There had been a few tense moments, especially after they had made the money drops over the various sectors of Primus City and the Imperial Guard cruisers were closing in. Dropping them down to street level, the pilots had run a zigzag course toward the city limits. At a pre-determined point, the transports were halted in the dolee section of the city, all the crew poised at the cargo and boarding hatches. With touchdown, everyone jumped out and scattered. The pilots were the last to leave, having been assigned the duty of plugging in a final flight cassette designed to take the pursuing cruisers on a merry chase. LaNague's pilot must have been delayed inside, because Ship One was a full three meters off the ground before he appeared at the boarding hatch. But without a second's hesitation, he leaped into the air and hit the street running. Everyone melted away—into alleys, into doorways, into waiting ground cars. Within the space of a few heartbeats, the hijacked transports had arrived, discharged their human cargo, and departed, leaving the streets as they had been before, with no trace of their passing.

And now all were safe. Yes, he had done it. It was an exhilarating feeling. And an immense relief.

"But what happens to Broohnin now that Robin Hood has arrived?"

"He remains a part of the revolution," LaNague replied. "I promised him that."

"You always keep your promises?"

"Always. I promised Broohnin a front row seat at the Imperium's demise if he would turn over his Throne contacts to me, and if he didn't interfere in my plans. I intend to keep that promise."

"Den is a sick man, I'm afraid."

"Then why were you a member of his group?"

Doc Zack laughed. "A member of his group? Please, sir, you insult me! He contacted me after a few of my critical remarks about the Imperium's shortsighted policies reached the public. We met a few times and had a few disjointed conversations. It was refreshing to talk to someone who was as anti-Imperium as myself—the halls of academe on Throne are filled with yea-sayers who fear for their positions, and who thus follow the safest course by mouthing the proper attitudes and platitudes. But I could see that violence was just a hair's breadth away from Broohnin's surface and so I kept my distance."

"And Radmon Sayers? How did he and Broohnin make contact?"

"That I don't know, but I get the impression they knew each other in their younger days, before Broohnin became obsessed with overthrowing the Imperium and Sayers became a public face. But enough of Broohnin and Sayers and myself. Tell me, my friend," Zack said, leaning back in his chair and luxuriating in the mellow mood induced by his third glass of spirits. "Isn't there a lot more to this Robin Hood pose than meets the eye? I mean, I can see drawing on archetypes and so on, but this goes beyond that."

"Just what do you mean? Specifically." LaNague was quite willing to tell the professor, but wanted to see if the man could draw an accurate conclusion on his own.

"As I see it, the Robin Hood gambit provides the average outworlder with a flesh and blood human being as a focus, a conduit for his discontent. Through the persona of Robin Hood he can conceptualize his aggressions and vicariously act them out. Isn't that what you have in mind?"

LaNague laughed. "Maybe. I don't think in those terms, Doc. My initial idea was to provide something concrete for the outworlder to respond to. He lives a tough life and doesn't have much room left in the hours of his day for abstractions. He won't respond to an idea anywhere near as quickly as he'll respond to another man. Robin Hood will hopefully provide him with that man."

"But what of the final act? You're going to have to set things up so the outworlder—at least the ones here on Throne—will have to make a choice between Metep and Robin Hood. How are you going to arrange that?"

"I'm not sure yet," LaNague said slowly. "I'll have to see how things develop. Any definite plans I make now will undoubtedly have to be altered later on . . . so I'm not making any."

"And me—when do I get to play my part?"

"Not for a while yet. We first have to build Radmon Sayers' reputation up a little, to make sure you get the kind of coverage your part will deserve." He glanced at the glowing figures on the wall clock. "His ratings will begin a long and steady climb as of tonight."

"You going to feed him some exclusives, or what?"

"No . . . he's going to find a very loyal friend in the central ratings computer."

Doc Zack nodded with gleeful insight. "Ah, yes! So you're putting Seph to work tonight."

"He should be at it right now."

Ω

He had a clearance for the building, but without an official work requisition, he'd have a tough time explaining his presence in this particular section. Viewer preferences were tabulated here, and adjustments made accordingly. Every vid set manufactured on Throne contained a tiny monitoring device that informed the rating computer when the set was on and to which program it was tuned. The presence of the device was no secret, and it was quite legal to have it removed after purchase of the set. But few people bothered. The Imperium said it was there to better tune programming to the current tastes of the public, so why not leave it in the set and forego the trouble and expense of having it removed?

Everyone knew the value of the vid as a propaganda weapon; that was self-evident, and so any attempts at overt propaganda would be routinely ignored. Since it licensed every transmitter, it would be a simple matter for the Imperium to impose its will directly and forcefully on the vid companies. But this was not necessary. The Imperium had many friends in all the media, seen and unseen, who liked to be considered part of the inner circle, who liked to help in any way they could in molding and mobilizing public opinion. Certain themes would begin to recur in dramas, or even comedies; certain catchwords and catch phrases would be mouthed by popular newsreaders and personalities. Soon public opinion would begin to shift; imperceptibly at first, then by slow degrees, then in a giant leap, after which it would never occur to anyone that he had ever thought any differently. Vid addicts were totally unaware of the process; only those who ignored the pervasive entertainment machine could see what was happening, but their cries of warning went unheeded. No one liked to admit that he or she could be so easily manipulated.

Seph Wolverton locked himself in with the central ratings computer and began removing a plate over an inspection port. Here was the starting point for all public influence operations. This particular section of the central computer tallied the number of sets tuned to a given program at a given time. A crucially important operation, since the best way to reach people through the vid was to reach them via the programs they liked best.

Seph laid a small black box in the palm of his hand. It popped open at a touch and revealed two compartments. One was empty; the other held a tiny sphere, onyx black. He had spent weeks programming that little sphere. Now it was time to put it to work.

He attached a light plate to his forehead and turned it on. A world of tiny geometric shapes, arranged in seemingly incomprehensible patterns and matrices, opened up before his eyes as he thrust the upper half of his body into the inspection port. Using an insulated, socket-tipped tool in his right hand, he removed a black sphere from the matrix of spheres and replaced it with the one he had brought with him. The old one was placed in the box for safekeeping and the inspection port closed. Soon he was back in the corridor and on his way to a section of the building in which he belonged.

The new chip would soon be at work, subtly altering the delicate magnetic fields the computer used to store new information and retrieve old. Seph had formed a crossover in the matrix that would funnel a percentage of the impulses from "*Sugar! Sugar!*"—a popular late-night comedy about a praline-crazed dwarf and his misadventures on and between the outworlds—over to the Radmon Sayers news report. Sayers would be experiencing an expected boost in ratings now anyway, due to his coverage of "the money monsoon." That would be short-lived, however, since no news program could normally hold out against "*Sugar! Sugar!*" for long. What Seph Wolverton had done tonight would convince the people who monitored such things that perhaps Radmon Sayers was on his way to becoming the new fair-haired boy of the newsreaders, and that perhaps it might be wise if one of the larger networks offered him a spot in a better time slot, one that would take full advantage of the man's obvious drawing powers.

Seph glanced at the row of vids in the monitoring station as he passed. Yes, there was Sayers now, halfway through his show.

". . . and on the business scene: The Solar Stock Exchange experienced a mild selling panic today when it was learned that Eric Boedekker, the wealthy asteroid mining magnate, has dumped every single share of stock, common and preferred, in every one of his many portfolios. He has been doing it gradually for the past few months through numerous brokers, and he has been selling the stocks for cash. This amounts to billions of Solar credits! No one knows if he's reinvesting it elsewhere. But fearing that the notoriously shrewd and ruthless Boedekker might know something they do not, a large number of smaller investors sold their own holdings today, causing a precipitous dip in many stock prices. The situation seems to have stabilized at this time, however, after numerous assurances from many investment councilors and brokerage houses that investor concern is unwarranted, that Earth's economy is sounder than it has ever been. Eric Boedekker has remained steadfastly unavailable for comment throughout the entire affair.

"On the home front: Throne . . . authorities have yet to track down any of the culprits in last night's daring hijack of an Imperial Treasury currency shipment, and the subsequent dumping of that shipment into the air over Primus City. Police say they have some good leads as to the identity of Robin Hood and his Merry Men, as the hijackers call themselves, but are not commenting yet on the nature of those leads.

"Last night, this reporter was an eyewitness to the now infamous 'money monsoon,' and for those of you who may have missed that particular vidcast, and its various replays during the course of today's programming, here it is again . . ."

VOLUME II  NUMBER 4

THE ROBIN HOOD READER

The Rule of 72

This is a handy little pearl to carry around in your head while trying to find your way through an inflation-ridden economy like ours. It instantly gives you an idea as to when the money in your pocket is going to lose half of its present value, and allows you to play accordingly.

Example: if inflation is constant at 3%, you merely divide 72 by three and get 24. This means that 24 years of 3% inflation will cut the spending power of that 100 marks in your pocket to 50. It means the price of everything will *double* every 24 years.

Not so bad, you say? Let's try 6%. That rate of inflation will double prices (or cut your money's spending power, however you wish to look at it) every dozen years.

You can live with that, you say? All right, try this: the new official inflation rate (remember, they lie) is now 12%. That's TWELVE PER CENT! It means that all the ridiculously high prices you see around you now will double in six (6) years! And I foresee 24% in the near future. Mull that . . .

The Economic Weather Eye

PRICE INDEX (using the 115th year of the Imperium—when the Imperial mark became mandatory legal tender—as base year of 100)	171.3
MONEY SUPPLY (M3)	2002.7
UNEMPLOYMENT LEVEL	8.5%

	Imperial Marks	Solar Credits
GOLD (Troy ounce)	275.9	130.4
Silver (Troy ounce)	13.8	6.0
Bread (1 kg. loaf)	.78	1.77

XIII

"... when you see the misery it brings, you'd need to be a madman, or a coward, or stone blind to give in to the plague."

Dr. Rieux

LaNague sat silent and unmoving, listening to dissension brewing ... and so soon. But the deaths of four good men could do that.

"Retaliate!" Broohnin said, standing in the center of the office. "We've got to retaliate!"

For once, LaNague found himself ready to agree. Perhaps it was what he had seen a few hours ago, perhaps it was the long day and the sleepless night that lay behind him. Whatever the cause, something dark within him was demanding revenge and he was listening.

No ... he couldn't allow himself the luxury of giving in to that seductive siren call. But four lives! Gone! And so early on. They were only three quarters through the Year of the Tiller and already four lives lost. All his fault, too.

Everything had been going according to plan during the

three months since the first hijack. Robin Hood had been keeping a low profile, with only the *Reader* to keep him in the public consciousness. Distribution of the *Reader* had been going well, too, experiencing a dramatic increase in interest and circulation since being outlawed after the "money monsoon." Metep and the Council of Five were making all the expected moves as the economy picked up speed in its downward spiral, right on schedule. The time finally arrived when the Imperium needed another jolt to its complacency. Another raid by Robin Hood and his Merry Men. Another "money monsoon."

It wasn't going to be quite so easy this time, of course. Currency shipments to and from the Central Treasury were now escorted by heavily armed cruisers. There would be no simple way to relieve the Imperium of its fiat money in route. So the obvious conclusion was to hit the currency transports before they linked up to their escorts and became an armed convoy. Hit them before they ever left the ground.

The East Coast Regional Revenue Center was chosen as target this time. It was located in the port city of Paramer, and handled smaller volumes of currency due to the fact that most of the population and industry on Throne were concentrated around and to the west of Primus City. But the amounts funneled through it were more than adequate for the purposes of Robin Hood and his Merry Men.

The tax depot was hit with precise timing—the strike had to occur immediately after the transports were loaded and before the escort cruisers arrived. Sonic weapons were again used, then the two loaded transports were manned with four Merry Men each and programmed with flight cassettes that would take one ship over Paramer itself, and the other north to the smaller Echoville. LaNague would have preferred to make another run over Primus City, but it was too far away . . . they never could have flown the transports from Paramer to the center of the continent without being intercepted. It was probably just as well; it wouldn't do to have the east coast towns feel slighted.

While the transports made their deliveries into the air over the two target towns, LaNague, Broohnin, and the Flinters manned four speedy little sport flitters, ready to act as interceptors if the escort crusiers happened to appear ahead of schedule. They had been scheduled to arrive from the Imperial garrison to the south, but unknown to LaNague and the rest, an unexpected change had been made in the plans: they had been routed to a repair station in Paramer itself. They would depart from the repair station directly to the tax depot.

And so it was with growing concern that LaNague and his lieutenants awaited the arrival of the cruisers, ready to fly into their faces and lead them away from the transports. It would be dangerous, but their smaller craft had speed and maneuverability on their side and could outrun anything in the sky. They didn't know that while they were waiting, the escort happened upon the transport assigned to Paramer just as it was making its final pass over the center of the town. The chase was short, the battle brief, the transport a ball of flaming wreckage by the time it slammed into the sea.

"They were only doing their duty, Den," Radmon Sayers said, watching Broohnin carefully.

"And it's our duty to even the score! If we don't, they'll know they can kill as many of us as they want whenever they get the chance. We owe it to ourselves and to those four dead men!"

"We all knew what we were risking when we started out last night," LaNague said, fatigue putting an edge on his voice. "We all knew there was a chance some of us might not come back one of these times. This happened to be the night. It was just bad luck—rotten, stinking, lousy luck that the tight routine the escort cruisers have followed for months was altered last night."

"Luck?" Broohnin sneered. "Tell those dead men about luck!" He turned to Doc Zack and Sayers. "I say we retaliate! I want a vote on it right now!"

"Forget it, Den," Doc said in a low voice. "That's not what we're about here."

"Then what *are* we about?" Broohnin asked, piercing them with his fierce gaze. "Where's all this leading us? What have we done so far besides play a few games and lose a few lives? Are we any closer to ending the Imperium? If we are, show me how and where and I'll shut up!"

"That was not your original demand," Doc Zack said softly, maintaining his professional cool. "You want us to turn killer. We decline. I'd like to be sure you understand that before we go on to other topics."

Broohnin's beard hid most of his expression, but what could be seen of his mouth was a thin, tight line. "And I just want *you* to understand," he said, stabbing his fingers at Sayers and

Doc, "that I'm not going to die for *him!*" The finger went toward LaNague on the last word. After a final glare at all present, he wheeled and strode from the room.

"He's right," LaNague said after he was gone. "I *am* responsible for those deaths. Those men were following my orders when they died. If I had checked just a little more carefully last night, they'd be out on the warehouse floor celebrating now." He rose from his seat and walked over to where Pierrot sat on a shelf, its drooping leaves reflecting his master's mood. "If I hadn't come here and started this whole thing, they'd still be alive. Maybe I should have stayed on Tolive."

He was speaking more to himself than to anyone else. The other two occupants of the cubicle realized this and allowed him a few moments of silence.

"Den did have a point at the last there," Zack said finally. "Where is all this leading? It's all very dramatic and great copy for guys like Radmon, but where is it taking us?"

"To the end of the Imperium."

"But how? I'd like to know. I'd like to go to bed at night and know that something I've done that day has pushed us closer to getting this very weighty piece of government off our backs. But that's not happening. I mean, I seem to be doing a lot, and it's all antigovernment, but I don't see any dents in the Imperium. I see no cracks in the foundation, no place to drive a wedge in. We're winning psychological victories, but every morning I wake up and find we're still at square one."

"Fair question," Sayers said. "We're big boys, and we can be trusted. I think we deserve to know where you're leading us."

LaNague turned and faced them. He wanted to tell them, wanted to unburden himself to someone. He desperately wished Mora were at his side at that very moment. He had a pounding in both his temples and a pain at the back of his head that felt like a muscular hand had arisen from his neck and clamped the back of his skull in a death grip. Tension headaches were no strangers, but this one was one of the worst he could remember. He almost felt he could chase it away if he could tell these two good men what he had in mind for their world. But he couldn't risk it. Not yet. Not even Josef and Kanya knew.

"You're right, both of you," he said. "But you'll have to trust me. I know that's a lot to ask," he said quickly, sensing the objections forming on their lips, "it's the way I have to work it. The fewer people who know exactly where all this is heading, the less chance of someone telling all when and if one of us is captured. And don't kid yourselves—a simple intravenous injection and any one of us, no matter how strong-willed he thinks he is, will answer any question without the slightest hesitation."

"But there's no sign of progress!" Zack said. "Not the slightest indication that we're getting anywhere!"

"That's because the real work is going on behind the scenes. You don't see any progress because that's the way I want it. I don't want anyone getting tipped off too soon. Everything's going to happen at once. And when it does, believe me, you'll know it. Trust me."

There was silence again, and again Zack broke it. "If you weren't a Tolivian, and if I didn't know what I know about the Kyfho philosophy's code of honor, I'd say you were asking too much. But frankly, my friend, you're all we've got at the moment. We *have* to trust you."

"Well, *I* don't know all that much about the Kyfho philosophy," Sayers said, "but I agree you're all we've got." He looked past LaNague to Pierrot. "You've always got that tree around. Does that have something to do with Kyfho?"

LaNague shook his head. "No. Just an old friend."

"Well, it looks like he needs water." Sayers didn't understand why LaNague seemed to think this was funny, and so he continued speaking over the Tolivian's laughter. "What does Kyfho mean, anyway? It's not a word with any meaning in Interstellar."

"It's not a word, really," LaNague said, marveling inwardly at how much a little laughter could lighten his mood. "It's an acronym from one of the Anglo tongues on Old Earth. The philosophy was first synthesized on pre-unification Earth by a group of people in the Western Alliance. It could only have been formed in the Western Alliance, but as it experienced slow and limited growth, it was picked up and modified by people in the Eastern Alliance. Modern Kyfho is now a mixture of both variants. The acronym was derived from the title of the first book—a pamphlet, really—in which Kyfho was expounded, a supposedly scatalogical phrase that meant 'Don't touch.' Does either of you understand Anglo?"

Sayers shook his head. "Not a word."

"I used to know a little when I was in the university," Doc said, "but I remember almost nothing. Try me anyway."

"All right. The title was KEEP YOUR FUCKING HANDS OFF. Mean anything to you?"

"Not a thing."

"Nor to me. But it supposedly summed up the philosophy pretty well at the time."

"The important thing," Zack said, "is that we trust you. The next question is, when do I get to do my bit?"

"Very soon. Especially now that our public personality here," he indicated Sayers, "has been moved into the limelight. I forgot to congratulate you, by the way, Radmon."

"Nothing more than I deserve," Sayers said, beaming. His ratings had risen steadily thanks to the computer fix and to the follow-the-leader phenomenon that causes people who hear that lots of other people are watching a certain program to start watching it too, thus inducing still more people to start watching it, and so on in a geometric progression. The result was an offer of a spot on the early evening news show of one of the larger vid services, thereby assuring him a huge audience. The ratings computer would now have to be returned to its untampered state.

"I'm all set to go," Zack said. "Have been for months on end now. Just give me the word."

"Take the first step."

"You mean change the course name?"

"Right. But don't show them your lesson plans until they're good and mad. Hit them with those when they're in the wrong mood and the regents will be sure to cancel your course."

"And then will they be sorry!"

"I don't care if the regents are sorry or not. I want Metep to be sorry."

Sayers stood up and walked toward the door of the cubicle. "And I'll be sorry if I don't get home and get some sleep. Tonight's my first appearance on the new show and I need my beauty rest. Good luck to us all."

Ω

". . . and the big news of the day remains the story from Paramer concerning an aborted attempt to repeat the famous Robin Hood caper of three months ago. The end result this time, however, was death, with an Imperial cruiser intercepting and shooting down the hijacked Treasury transport in the air over the port city. But not before the Merry Men had completed their mission—an estimated twenty-five million marks hurled into the sky over Paramer, with the same Robin Hood calling cards as the last time. Four bodies were found in the transport wreckage, burned beyond recognition. The Imperial Guard, it appears, takes its work seriously. Let all would-be tax rebels take a lesson from that.

"More news from Earth tonight on the strange behavior of Eric Boedekker, the wealthy asteroid mining magnate. It seems he has just sold the mineral rights to half of his asteroid holdings to his largest competitor, Merrit Metals, for a sum that probably exceeds the gross planetary product of some of our brother outworlds. The mineral rights to the rest of the Boedekker asteroids are reportedly up for sale, too. Anyone interested in buying a flying mountain . . . ?"

VOLUME II NUMBER 5

THE ROBIN HOOD READER

HIT THE BANKS!

Notice how many banks are encouraging second mortgages lately? How they're telling you to borrow on your current home and use the money for renovations or added conveniences or vacations? Suspicious? Do you feel that the bankers must know a whole lot more about money than you do and there must be a catch?

Well, you're right—there is a catch, only this time the bankers will get caught. With construction at a virtual standstill, they've got all this money lying around in the savings accounts of people who have either not been reading these flyers, or ignoring them. (They'll learn!) The banks want to lend it out. So do yourself a favor: borrow it. Sure, they'll charge you 11%, but with inflation officially running at 14% now, every 100 marks you pay back next year will only be worth 86 of the marks you borrow today. You thus get the spending power of this year's marks and pay back the bank with impaired marks in subsequent years. (Remember the Rule of 72!) And as inflation worsens, you'll be paying the bank back with increasingly worthless paper. Ah, but what to do with this borrowed money? Watch this space, and . . .

BORROW! BORROW! BORROW!

The Economic Weather Eye

PRICE INDEX (using the 115th year of the Imperium—when the Imperial mark became mandatory legal tender—as base year of 100)		179.7
MONEY SUPPLY (M3)		2061.7
UNEMPLOYMENT LEVEL		9.0%
	Imperial Marks	Solar Credits
GOLD (Troy ounce)	282.1	130.8
Silver (Troy ounce)	14.6	5.9
Bread (1 kg. loaf)	.83	1.74

The Year of the Malak

XIV

BRAIN: In our civilization, and under our republican form of government, brain is so highly honored that it is rewarded by exemption from the cares of office.

Ambrose Bierce

The confrontation had been considerably delayed by a computer programmer who either meant well or didn't pay too much attention to what she was doing. Any aware and upright programmer, conscious of job security, would have immediately reported Dr. Zachariah Brophy's change in the title of his first-year economics course from *Economics: The Basics* to *Economics: Our Enemy, the State.*

And so it was not until the printed course booklet was issued to all the students at the University of the Outworlds that Doc Zack's little act of provocation came to light. Reaction was mixed. The course was immediately booked solid, but that only meant that fifty students were interested; it hardly reflected the view of the campus at large. The university was state-supported—grounds, buildings, materials, and a full 75 per cent of tuition was paid for by the Imperium. Even room and board at the university dorms was state-funded. This could have resulted in a free, open forum for ideas, where no point of view was proscribed. Could have, but did not.

There was a long waiting list for seats in the University of the Outworlds; students who made the slightest ripple, such as objecting too loudly to course content and narrow viewpoints among the faculty, soon found it most difficult to obtain passing grades in key courses. And without those passing grades, their educational support was withdrawn. They had to drop out and join the great unwashed, monitoring the courses and taking examinations via the vid. It always happened within the first months of a term to the few free spirits who had managed to slip in with the new class. And it only took the academic demise of a couple of those to enlighten the survivors to the facts of life at the University of the Outworlds: co-operate and graduate.

Doc Zack's move was something else. This was not a questioning voice speaking out of order; this was no mere breach of academic etiquette. This was a red handkerchief fluttering in the faces of the regents and those to whom they had to answer. And what was worse, the offending course title was now in the hands of every student at the university. The semester was about to begin. Something had to be done, and quickly!

They canceled the course. A message was sent to each student who had possessed the temerity to enroll in a course entitled *Economics: Our Enemy, the State* informing him or her that a new course would have to be chosen to fill the time spot. The names on the class list were placed in a special file of students who would bear watching.

But Doc Zack had his own list and he sent word to the students who had signed up for his class, and to favored students from past years, that he would be giving the first lecture as scheduled in the course catalogue. Anyone who was interested was welcome to come and listen. Radmon Sayers was also informed of the time and location of the lecture, but by a more circuitous route. He would see to it that Dr. Zachariah Brophy's first and last lecture of the new semester would have a much larger audience than the regents or anyone else anticipated.

Ω

"I'm not exactly overwhelmed by the turnout this morning,"

Doc Zack said, strolling back and forth across the front of the classroom in his usual speaking manner, looking as cadaverous as ever. "But I guess it would be hoping too much to see a standing-room-only crowd before me. I know that the prices of everything are keeping two jumps ahead of salary increases, and that many of you here are risking your places in this glorious institution just by being here. For that I thank you, and commend your courage."

He craned his neck and looked around the room. "I see some familiar faces here and some new ones, too. That's good." One of the new faces sat in the last row. He was young enough to pass for a student, but the square black vid recorder plate he held in the air, its flat surface following Zack wherever he went, gave him away as something more. This would be Sayers' man, recording the lecture. Zack took a deep breath . . . time to take the plunge.

"What we're going to discuss here today may not seem like economics at first. It will concern the government—our government, the Imperium. It's a monster story in the truest, Frankensteinian sense, of a man-made creature running amuck across the countryside, blindly destroying everything it touches. But this is not some hideous creature of sewn-together cadavers; this creature is handsome and graceful and professes only to have our best interests at heart, desiring only to help us.

"Where most of its power lies is in the economy of our land. It creates the money, controls its supply, controls the interest rates that can be charged for borrowing it, controls, in fact, the very value of that money. And the hand that controls the economy controls you—each and every one of you. For your everyday lives depend on the economy: your job, the salary you receive for working that job, the price of your home, the clothes on your back, the food you eat. You can no more divorce a functioning human being from his or her ambient economy than from his or her ambient air. It's an integral part of life. Control a being's economic environment and, friend, you control that being.

"Here on the outworlds, we live in a carefully controlled economy. That's bad enough. But what's worse is that the controlling hand belongs to an idiot."

He paused a moment to let that sink in, glancing at the recorder plate held aloft at the rear of the room, noting that it was aimed in such a way that if it happened to include any of the students in its frame, only backs of heads would be visible.

"Let's take a look at this handsome, ostensibly well-meaning, idiotic monster we've created and see what it's doing to us. I think you'll soon see why I've subtitled this course, *Our Enemy, the State.* Let's see what it does to help those of us who can't seem to make ends meet. I won't start in on the Imperial Dole Program—you all know what a horrendous mess that is. Everybody has somcthing bad to say about the dole. No . . . I think I'll start with the program that's been most praised by the people within the government and press: the Food Voucher Program.

"As it stands now, a man with a family of four earning 12,000 marks a year is eligible for 1,000 marks' worth of food vouchers to supplement his income and help feed his family. That's okay, you say? You don't mind some of your taxes going to help some poor working stiff make ends meet? That's lucky for you, because nobody asked you anyway. Whether you like it or not, approve of it or not, he's going to get the 1,000 marks.

"But putting that aside, did you realize that the Imperium taxes this man 2,200 marks a year? That's right. It takes 2,200 marks out of his pocket in little bits and pieces via withholding taxes during each pay period. And the withholding tax is a very important concept as far as the government is concerned. It is thereby allowed to extract the income tax almost painlessly, and to force the employer to do all the accounting for the withholding tax free of charge, despite the fact that slavery has never been allowed in the outworlds. It needs the withholding tax, because if the Imperium tried to extract all the year's income taxes at once it would have the entire citizenry out in the streets with armfuls of rocks . . . it wouldn't last a standard year.

"But back to our food voucher recipient: his 2,200 marks are collected each year, sent to the Regional Revenue Center, and from there shipped to the Central Treasury in Primus City—if Robin Hood doesn't get it first." This brought a laugh and a smattering of applause from the class. "Now don't forget that everybody who handles it along the way gets paid something for his time—from the lowliest programmer to the Minister of the Treasury, everyone takes a chunk. Then the money has to be appropriated by the legislature into the Bureau of Food Subsidization, and the case workers have to decide who's eligible, and how much the eligibles should get, and somebody has to print up the vouchers, and somebody has to run the maintenance machinery to keep the floors of the Bureau of Food Subsidization clean and so on, ad nauseam. Everybody along the line gets paid something for his or her efforts.

"In the end, our lowly citizen gets his thousand marks' worth of food vouchers, but in the process, not only has his 2,200 marks in taxes been consumed by the bureaucracy, but an additional 830 marks of *your* taxes as well! A total of 3,030 marks! That's right: it costs 3.03 marks in taxes for our enemy, the Imperium, to give a single mark's worth of benefits. And has anyone along the line suggested that we just cut this poor citizen's taxes by a thousand marks? Of course not! That would save us all a net of 2,000 marks, but it would also mean cutting appropriations, and fewer do-nothings in the Revenue Service and the Bureau of Food Subsidization, and who knows where else. The men who run these bureaus and run these outworlds don't want that. And they have the say and we don't. And that's why the Imperium is our enemy, because it is filled with these men."

Zack paused briefly here for breath and to allow himself to cool. He always got worked up talking about the excesses and idiocy of the Imperium, and had to be careful not to say more than he meant to.

"And so you can see why you have to understand the working of a large and powerful government if you are to understand modern economics. The Food Voucher System is only a very obvious example. There are economic machinations going on within the Imperium which are far more subtle and far more sinister than the buffoonery of the Bureau of Food Subsidization, and we shall delve into those at a later date. But first we must teach you all some of the rudiments of free market economics, a realm of economic theory that has been the victim of de facto censorship in teaching centers from here to Earth for centuries. We'll begin with von Mises, then—"

Noting alarmed expressions on the faces of some of the students, and sensing that the focus of their attention had suddenly shifted to a point somewhere behind him, Zack turned around. Two university security men stood in the doorway.

"We have a report of an unauthorized class being conducted here," the burly one on the right said. "Are you a member of the faculty, sir?"

"Of course I am!"

"And what course is this?"

"Economics 10037: *Our Enemy, the State.*"

The guard on the left, taller but equally well muscled, frowned disapproval and scanned the readout on his pocket directory. "Didn't think so," he said, glancing at his partner. "There's no such course."

"What's your name?" said the burly one.

"Zachariah Brophy, Ph.D."

Again the pocket directory was scanned. Again a negative readout. "No one on the faculty by that name."

"Now wait just a minute! I've been teaching here for twenty years! I'll have you know—"

"Save it, pal," the burly one said, taking Zack's elbow. "We're going to escort you to the gate and you can find yourself somewhere else to play school."

Zack pulled his arm away. "You'll do no such thing! I demand that you call the regents' office and check that."

"This is a direct link to the regents' computer," the taller guard said, holding up his pocket directory. "The information out of here is up to the minute—and it says you don't belong here. So make it easy for all of us and come quietly."

"No! I won't go anywhere quietly! This is supposed to be a university, where all points of view can be heard, where inquiring minds can pick and choose among a variety of ideas. I won't be stifled!" He turned to the class. "Now, as I was saying—"

The two guards behind him could be seen glancing at each other and shrugging. Each stepped forward and, grabbing an elbow and an armpit, dragged Doc Zack backward from the classroom.

"Let me go!" Zack shouted. He dug his heels into the floor, struggled to free his arms but to no avail. As a last desperate hope, he turned to the class. "Some of you help me, please! Don't let them take me away like this!"

But as they dragged him out through the door and around the corner and down the hall, no one moved, and that was what hurt most of all.

Ω

". . . now I think you all know that it's not my policy to editorialize. I merely report the news the way it happens. But I believe that what we've just seen is so extraordinary that I must comment upon it. The exclusive eyewitness recording of the expulsion of Professor Zachariah Brophy from the campus of the University of the Outworlds that was just replayed was obtained because I had heard that this renegade professor was determined to give his treasonous course despite the fact that his superiors had canceled it. I sent a recorder technician to the classroom to see just how the regents would handle such an incident, and you have seen the results yourselves tonight.

"I must say that I, as a citizen of the Imperium, am proud of what I have just seen. Enormous amounts of our tax marks are spent yearly to keep the University of the Outworlds one of the top institutions of learning in Occupied Space. We cannot allow a few malcontents to decide that they are wiser than the board of regents and to teach whatever they see fit, regardless of academic merit. We especially cannot allow someone like Professor Zachariah Brophy, impressive as his credentials might be, to denigrate the Imperium, which supports the university, and therefore denigrate the university itself by his unfounded and inflammatory criticism!

"I support freedom of speech to the fullest, but when it's being done on my time and being supported by my tax dollars, then I want some control over what's being said. Otherwise, let Professor Brophy take his podium to Imperium Park and give his message to whoever wishes to gather and listen. And to anyone else who tries to waste the taxpayers' money by trying to besmirch the Imperium at their expense, let this be a warning."

The final segment of the recording, wherein Doc Zack was dragged kicking and pleading from the classroom, was rerun, and then Radmon Sayers' face filled the screen again.

"And now, new word from Earth on the mysterious behavior of Eric Boedekker, the wealthy asteroid mining magnate, who has just sold the remainder of his asteroid mineral rights to a consortium of prospectors for an undisclosed but undoubtedly enormous sum. Still no hint as to what he's doing or plans to do with all that credit.

"And on Neeka—"

Metep VII touched a stud on the armrest of his chair and the holovid globe went dark. "That Sayers is a good man," he told Haworth, who sat an arm's length away to his left.

"Think so?"

"Sure. Look how he defended the regents. That could have been a very embarrassing recording. It would take nothing to exploit it into an example of repression of academic freedom, freedom of speech, creeping fascism, or whatever other nonsense you want. But Sayers turned it into a testimonial to the way the regents and the Imperium are ever on guard against misuse and abuse of educational taxes. He turned it into a plus for us and kept Brophy a miscreant instead of elevating him to a martyr."

"You think he's on our side, then?"

"Definitely. Don't you?"

"I don't know." Haworth was pensive. "I really don't know. If he were really on our side, I don't think he would have shown that recording at all."

"Come now! He's a newsman! He couldn't pass up a story like that!"

"Yes, that's very obvious. But it all seems too pat. I mean, how did he happen to know that Brophy would be giving that lecture against the orders of the regents?"

"Probably one of the students told him."

"Possible. But do you realize that even if the regents had left Brophy to his own devices and let him give his course as originally scheduled with no interference, only a few thousand would have heard him over the closed-circuit vid? And if it weren't for Sayers, only twenty or thirty would have heard him today. But now, after showing that recording on the prime time news, Professor Brophy's message has reached millions. Millions!"

"Yes, but it was a silly message. There are a dozen stories like that going around every month about waste in government. Nobody pays them too much mind."

"But the contempt in his voice," Haworth said, frowning. "The utter contempt . . . it came across so strongly."

"But it doesn't matter, Daro. Sayers negated any points that old bird managed to score by painting him as a tax waster and a disloyal employee."

"Did he? I hope so. Maybe he made Brophy look silly to you and me, but what about all those sentimental slobs out there? How did Brophy look to them? Are they going to remember what Radmon Sayers said about him, or is the one thing that sticks in their minds going to be the image of a skinny old man being forcibly dragged from view by a couple of young, husky, uniformed guards?"

Ω

"And what was all that supposed to prove?" Broohnin asked as Radmon Sayers' face faded from the globe.

"It proves nothing," LaNague replied. "Its purpose was

merely to plant a seed in the backlot of the public mind to let it know what kind of power the Imperium has."

"I'm not impressed. Not a bit. We could have had a full-scale riot on the campus if we had planned it right. The Imperial Guard would have been called out and then Sayers would have really had something to show on his news show!"

"But the effect wouldn't have been the same, Den," Zack said from his seat in the corner. "There's big competition for on-campus placement at U. of O., and people seeing the students out on the grounds rioting would only resent the sight of rare opportunity being wasted. They'd want the Imperial Guard to step in; they'd cheer them on. And people would get hurt, which is what we're trying to avoid."

"We could see to it that a lot of the Guard got hurt!" Broohnin said with a grin. "And if a few students got banged up, all the better. I mean, after all, you wanted to show the oppressive powers of the Imperium. What better evidence than a few battered skulls!"

Zach shook his head in exasperated dismay and looked at LaNague. "I give up. You try."

LaNague didn't relish the task. He was beginning to think of Broohnin as more and more of a lost cause. "Look at it this way: the Imperium is not an overtly oppressive regime. It controls the populace in a more devious manner by controlling the economy. And it controls life within its boundaries as effectively via the economy as with a club. The indirection of the Imperium's controls makes us forget that it still has the club and is holding it in reserve. The only reason we don't see the club is because the Imperium has found ways to get what it wants without it. But as soon as necessity dictates, out it will come. And it will be used without hesitation. We didn't want the club brought out today, because that would mean bloodshed. We just wanted the public to get a peek into the sack where it's kept . . . just a reminder that it's there."

"And it was relatively painless," Zack said, rubbing his axillae. "The worst I got out of it was a couple of sore armpits."

"But what the public saw," LaNague continued, "was an elderly man—"

"Not so elderly!"

"—who is a renowned professor, being pulled from the classroom by force. He wasn't destroying the campus or disrupting the educational process. All he was doing was standing and talking—teaching!—a group of students. And for that he was dragged away by two uniformed men. And believe me, there's something in the sight of uniformed henchmen laying their hands on a peaceful civilian that raises the hackles of outworlders."

"But what did they do? There've been no protests, no cries of outrage, no taking to the streets! Nothing!"

"Right!" LaNague said. "And there won't be, because it was a minor incident. Doc Zack wasn't arrested and he wasn't beaten to a pulp. But he was silenced and he was dragged away by force. And I think people will remember that."

"And so what if they do?" Broohnin said, as belligerent as ever. "The Imperium isn't weakened one erg."

"But its image is. And that's enough for now."

"Well, it's not enough for me!" Broohnin rose and wandered aimlessly around the room, pulling something from his pocket as he moved. LaNague watched him pop whatever it was under his tongue—he guessed it to be a mood elevator—and stand and wait for it to take effect. Yes, Broohnin was definitely on the brink. He would have to be watched closely.

"Hear about the meeting?" Zack said into the tension-filled silence.

"What meeting?" LaNague said.

"Metep and the Council of Five. Word's come down that they've called a special hush-hush, super-secret enclave next week. Even Krager's cutting his vacation short and coming back for it."

"Sounds important. Anybody know what it's about?"

Zack shrugged. "Ask Den . . . One of his people picked it up."

Broohnin turned and faced them. The anger lines in his face had smoothed slightly. His voice was calm, even. "Nobody's sure exactly what it's about, but Haworth's behind it. He wants the meeting and he wants it soon."

That troubled LaNague. "Haworth, eh?"

"Something wrong with that?" Zack asked.

"It's probably nothing of any real importance, but there's always the chance that Haworth has come up with some sort of brainstorm to temporarily pull them out of the current crunch . . ."

"I thought you had all exits covered," Broohnin said, barely hiding a sneer. "Afraid Haworth'll slip something past you?"

"With a man like Haworth around, it doesn't pay to get over-confident. He's shrewd, he's sly, he's smart, and he's ruthless. I'll be anxious to see what comes out of this meeting."

"I'd worry along with you if I could," Zack said. "But since you're the only one who knows where all this is taking us, I'm afraid you're going to have to sleep with those worries alone." He paused, watching LaNague closely. "I do have a few ideas about your plan, however, gathered from what I've seen and heard during the past year."

"Keep them to yourself, please."

"I will. But do you actually think there's any way Haworth or anybody else can turn this whole thing around?"

LaNague shook his head. "No. The Imperium has started its descent and only magic can save it."

"Well, let's just hope Haworth doesn't know any magic," Zack said.

"He might. But just in case they run dry of things to say at the meeting, I think Robin Hood should be able to find a way to keep the conversation going."

VOLUME III  NUMBER 2

THE ROBIN HOOD READER

The Lesson of the Gold Outie

You don't see them in circulation any more—Gresham's Law took care of that—but just sixty years ago, real gold coins were used for money. Exempt from the Legal Tender Laws because it was a symbol of our independence from Earth, each gold outie contained one Troy ounce of gold and was worth about 25 Imperial marks.

A one-ounce gold coin for 25 marks? The price is now 279!

Which brings us to the subject of price vs. value. The Metep mob is trying to confuse the two so you won't know that it is solely to blame for the current inflationary spiral.

Consider: A good quality, natural fiber business jumper cost about 25 marks six decades ago. Today, although there's no fabric shortage and they're certainly not better made, suits of comparable quality cost 250 marks. That's *PRICE.*

Sixty years ago all you needed to buy a business suit was a single gold outie. Today, you can still buy a high quality suit for a single gold outie. That's *VALUE.*

The Lesson: MONEY SHOULD HAVE VALUE.

Now, you should no longer have to ask what to do with any cash you can scrape up or borrow. Buy gold, silver, platinum, etc!

The Economic Weather Eye

PRICE INDEX (using the 115th year of the Imperium—when the Imperial mark became mandatory legal tender—as base year of 100)	200.3
MONEY SUPPLY (M3)	2195.5
UNEMPLOYMENT LEVEL	9.6%

	Imperial Marks	Solar Credits
GOLD (Troy ounce)	309.3	131.3
Silver (Troy ounce)	18.0	6.1
Bread (1 kg. loaf)	.88	1.70

XV

Heroes don't take money! They work on a government subsidy!

Roger Ramjet

"It's no good, Vin. He's not coming."

"Yes, he is. He's *got* to come!"

As persistent and patient and straight as a tree rooted in the soil, Vincen Stafford stood with his arm around his wife's shoulders and waited in the back yard of what had once been their house. It stood locked, barred, and empty behind him as he watched the sky. Better to stare into the empty blackness above them than to stare into the empty bleakness of the structure behind. The house had become the symbol of all his failures and of all the things that had failed him. He couldn't bear to look at it.

The drop-off in grain runs to Sol System had started it all, causing him to be bumped from one scheduled flight after another due to his lack of seniority. Finally, he had been laid off. The Imperial Grain Export Authority had let him down—promising him full-time employment when he signed on, and then leaving him grounded. That was bad, but he knew he could make it through on his unemployment benefits from the Spacers Guild. Salli had a part-time job and they had a little money in the bank. It would be tight, but they could squeak through until something broke loose for him.

But the only things that broke loose were prices. Everything except grain seemed to cost more—food, clothing, transportation, everything. Only his mortgage payment had remained fixed. The bank had tried to get him to refinance at a higher interest rate but he had resisted, despite the advice of the *Robin Hood Reader* to borrow all he could and invest it in gold and silver. That, he now realized, had been his biggest blunder. As daily living expenses went up, he and Salli had found it harder to scrape together the mortgage payments each month. Their savings were soon gone and the bank was soon penalizing them for late payments.

Then catastrophe: the Spacers Guild cut his benefits in half due to the drain put on its finances by heavy layoffs. Then the benefits stopped all together; the Spacers Guild had arbitrarily cut him off in order to concentrate benefits on the senior members. Even his union had let him down.

Vin and Salli had immediately tried to refinance the house, but the bank was no longer interested. Mortgage money had dried up and there was none to spare for an out-of-work interstellar navigator. They put the house on the market, but with so little mortgage money around, nobody was buying at the current inflated prices. They missed payments; the bank foreclosed. They were locked out of their own home.

Vincen Stafford was now at the lowest point of his entire life. He and Salli lived in a shabby one-room apartment in the dolee section of town . . . and why not? He was on the dole. When they weren't screaming at each other, they sat in stony silence across the room from each other. Only tonight had brought them together. Robin Hood was coming.

"He's not going to show, Vin," Salli said. "Now let's go home."

"Home? We have no home. It was taken from us. And he *is* coming. Just wait a little longer. You'll see."

Robin Hood was just about the only thing on this world or any other that Vincen Stafford had left to hold onto. When the first "money monsoon" had come, he had turned in the money he had collected. At that time it seemed like the right thing to do . . . after all, the money belonged to the Imperium. And when he analyzed it to any depth, he admitted that he had hoped his name would show up somewhere on a list of exemplary citizens and he would have a crack at the next grain run out, seniority or no. But that hadn't happened. He hadn't made a single run since. His friends had laughed at his naïveté then, and he cursed himself for it now. What he wouldn't give to have those mark notes in his hand right now. A year and a half could make a lot of changes in a man.

If only he'd listened to that newsletter and followed its advice. He knew a couple of men his age who had done just that—refinanced their homes, borrowed to the limit of their credit, and invested it all in gold and silver and other precious metals. One had used the profits from the soaring prices of the commodities to supplement his income and keep him in the black and in his home. Another had let the bank repossess his home and had moved into an apartment. He was now sitting on a pile of gold coins that was growing more and more valuable every day while the bank was stuck with a house it couldn't sell.

Vincen Stafford wasn't going to get caught looking the other way this time. Robin Hood and his Merry Men had robbed a currency shipment this morning; if they held true to form, there'd be money raining down soon.

"This is ridiculous!" Salli said. "I'm going back to the apartment. You heard what they said on the vid. He's not coming."

Stafford nodded in the darkness. "I heard what they said. But I don't believe it." Police authorities had been on the air all day telling the public that Robin Hood and his Merry Men were now robbing tax collections and keeping the money for personal uses, showing themselves for the common thieves and renegades they really were. Anyone waiting for another "money monsoon" would be bitterly disappointed! But Stafford didn't believe it. Couldn't—wouldn't believe it.

One of the stars winked out overhead, then another to its left. Then the original star came on again.

"Wait!" he told Salli, reaching for her arm. "Something's up there!"

"Where? I don't see anything."

"That's the whole idea."

When the first mark notes began slipping down into sight, a great cheer was heard all over the neighborhood . . . Stafford and his wife were not alone in their nocturnal vigil.

"Look, Vin!" Salli said excitedly. "It's really happening. I can't believe it! It's money!" She began scrambling around the yard, picking up the mark notes, disregarding the white calling cards. "Come on, Vin! Help!"

Vincen Stafford found himself unable to move just yet. He merely stood with his face tilted upward, tears streaming down his cheeks, silent sobs wracking his chest.

At least there was still *somebody* left you could count on.

Ω

". . . and it appears that Robin Hood and his Merry Men have lowered their sights, physically and figuratively. After more than seven months of inaction since the costly east coast caper, with only the caustic, omnipresent *Robin Hood Reader* as evidence of his continued presence among us, Robin Hood has struck again. A ground effect vehicle, carrying a large shipment of fresh currency from the Central Treasury to the North Sector branch of the First Outworld Bank of Primus, was waylaid on the streets of the city early this morning.

"The death of four of his Merry Men last year should have made Robin Hood more cautious, but he appears to be as daring as ever. The vehicle was stopped and its guards overpowered in the bright light of morning before a crowd of onlookers. The shipment of currency was quickly transferred to two sport flitters which took off in different directions. No one was hurt, no witnesses could identify any of the perpetrators due to the holosuits they wore, and no evidence was left behind other than the customary arrow with the inscribed shaft.

"As news of the robbery spread, people rushed out into their streets and yards, anticipating a rain of mark notes. But none came; the authorities began to suspect that either Robin Hood was now stealing taxpayer money for personal gain, or that the caper was the work of clever imitators.

"People steadfastly waited all day. So did the Imperial Guard. But alas! No Robin. The majority of hopefuls went home, but a large number of the faithful hung on into the dark. However, it began to look like the police were right. There would be no money monsoon tonight.

"And then it happened. After a year-and-a-half-long drought, the skies of Primus City opened up at 17.5 tonight and began to pour marks down on the parched populace. The fall was much lighter than on the previous occasion—sixty million had been hurled into the air then; tonight's precipitation amounted to approximately one fourth of that. But from the cheers and shouts of joy that arose from every quarter of the city, it is evident that anything was welcomed by the citizens of Primus City.

"If this reporter might be permitted a comment or two: I find it reprehensible that so many of our fellow citizens demean themselves by standing and waiting to receive stolen money from this Robin Hood charlatan. There are no solutions to be found in thievery and cheap showmanship. The real solutions lie with the Imperium's leaders. We should seek solutions there, not in the dark skies of night.

"And now to other news:

"Word from Earth shows that Eric Boedekker, the wealthy asteroid mining magnate, is still at it. Having disposed of his extraterrestrial holdings, he has now sold all of his Earthside property—millions of square meters' worth of land on all of the planet's five continents. And if you think land is getting expensive here on the outworlds, you should look into the prices on Earth! Eric Boedekker has now amassed a liquid fortune that must be unparalleled in the financial history of the human race. No indication as yet as to just what he's doing with it. Is he reinvesting it or just keeping it in a huge account? The entire interstellar financial community is buzzing with curiosity.

"And speaking of buzzing, insiders here on Throne are doing a little of their own as they speculate on the sudden premature return of Treasury Minister Krager from his Southland vacation. Is something afoot in the inner circles of the Imperium? We'll see . . ."

Ω

"Gentlemen," Haworth said, standing behind his chair to the right of Metep VII, "we are in trouble. *Big* trouble."

There were no groans of protest or resignation. The Council of Five knew the Imperium was in trouble, and each member knew that he didn't have a single idea as to how to remedy the situation. All they could come up with as a group were the same things they had been doing all along, only more so. All looked to Haworth now for some glimmer of hope.

"You've all read the report I sent to each of you by special courier last night—at least I hope you have. You all know now why our grain imports have been falling off. My sources on Earth are reliable. If they say the Earthies have developed photosynthetic cattle, then, believe me, it's true."

"All right," said Cumberland of the Bureau of Agrarian Resources. "I read the report and I'll grant that it's possible. And I can see how it affects my department and all the farmers under me. But I don't see why it's such bad news for everybody else."

"Domino effect," Haworth replied. "If we export less and less grain, which is just about all the outworlds have that Sol System wants, then we cut a significant chunk out of total outworld productivity. Which means there's less profit going to the agrarian worlds, which means less income for us to tax. The result is that the Imperium has less money to work with.

"But it doesn't stop there. The drop in profits to the agrarian worlds means that they're going to start cutting their work forces. That means an increase in unemployment roles, which inevitably leads to an increase in the number of former workers going on the dole where they become tax consumers instead of taxpayers.

"Which means that the Imperium's expenses are going up while its income is going down. Naturally, we just increase the money supply to meet our needs. But our needs have been such that the money supply has increased too rapidly and we're caught in a period of steep inflation. This increases the viciousness of the circle: inflation wipes out savings, so people don't save. That leaves the banks with no money to lend, and that means no construction, no growth. Which leads to more unemployment and more people on the dole. Which means we have to spend more money. Inflation is also allowing more and more people to meet criteria for participation in other programs such as Food Vouchers." He shook his head. "The Food Voucher Program is chewing up marks as fast as we can turn them out. Which adds to the inflation which adds to . . . well, you get the idea."

Cumberland nodded. "I see. Then we'll just have to control the rate of inflation."

Haworth smiled and Krager laughed aloud from the far end of the table. "That would be nice. We just hit a 21 per cent annual rate, although publicly of course, we're only admitting to 15. To slow inflation, the Imperium has to stop spending more than it takes in in taxes. We either have to increase taxes, which is out of the question, or we have to start cutting the Imperial budget." He turned his smirking visage toward Cumberland. "Shall we start with the farm subsidies?"

"Impossible!" Cumberland blustered and blanched simultaneously. "Those subsidies are depended on by many small farmers!"

"Well? Where shall we start cutting? The dole? Food Vouchers? With more people than ever on public assistance, we'd be risking wide-scale food riots. And it's because I fear there may be some civil disorder in the near future that I don't advise cutting defense budgets."

"I suggest we freeze the money supply for the next half year," Krager said. "There'll be some fallout, naturally, but we've got to do it sometime, and it might as well be now."

"Oh no, you don't!" It was Metep VII speaking. He had bolted upright in his chair at Krager's suggestion. "A freeze would swing us into a depression!" He looked to Haworth for confirmation.

The younger man nodded his white-haired head. "A deep one, and a long one. Longer and deeper than any of us would care to contemplate."

"There! You see?" Metep said. "A depression. And during *my* term of office. Well, let me tell you, gentlemen, that as much as I desire a prominent place in the annals of human history, I do not wish to be known as the Metep whose administration ushered in the first great outworld depression. No, thank you! There'll be no freeze on the money supply and no depression as long as *I* sit in the chair. There has to be another way and we have to find it!"

"I don't think another way exists," Krager said. "As a matter of fact, we're now getting to the point over at Treasury where we're seriously talking about changing the ratio of small bills to large bills. Maybe even dropping the one-mark note altogether. We may even get to the point of issuing 'New Marks,' trading them one to ten for 'old marks.' That would at least cut duplicating expenses, which gives you a pretty good idea of how fast the money supply is expanding."

"There's no way out if we persist in limiting ourselves to simple and obvious solutions," Haworth said into the ensuing verbal commotion. "If we freeze, or even signficantly slow, the growth of the money supply, we face mass bankruptcy filings and soaring unemployment. If we keep going at this pace, something's bound to give somewhere along the line."

Metep VII slumped in his chair. "That means I'm to be 'the Depression Metep' for the rest of history, I guess. Either way, I lose."

"Maybe not." Haworth's voice was not raised when he said

it, but it cut cleanly through the undertone of conversational pairs around the table and brought all talk to an abrupt halt.

"You've got an idea? A way out?"

"Only a chance, Jek. No guarantees, and it will take lots of guts on all our parts. But with some luck, we may get a reprieve." He began strolling around the conference table as he spoke. "The first thing we do is start to inform the police about Earth's new protein source, playing it up not as a great biological advance, but as a sinister move to try and ruin the outworld economy. We'll create a siege mentality, ask everyone to sacrifice to fight the inflation that Earth is causing. As a stopgap, we'll impose wage-price controls and enforce them rigidly. Anyone trying to circumvent them will be portrayed as an Earthie-lover. If legal penalties don't scare them into compliance, social pressure will. And we'll play the unions off against the businessmen as usual."

"That's not a reprieve!" Krager said, turning in his seat as Haworth passed behind him. "That's not even a new trial—it's just a stay of execution, and a short one at that! It's all been tried before and it's never solved anything!"

"Kindly let me finish, won't you?" Haworth said as calmly as he could. The latent hostility between the Chief Adviser and the Minister of the Treasury was surfacing again. "What I'm proposing has never been attempted before. If we succeed, we will be heroes not only in the outworld history spools, but in the recorded history of humanity. I'm calling it Project Perseus."

He scanned the table. All eyes were on him, watching him with unwavering attention. He continued strolling and speaking.

"We've been monitoring multiple radio sources concentrated in the neighboring arm of this galaxy. We've been at it ever since our ancestors settled out here. There's no doubt that their origin is intelligent and technologically sophisticated. We've sent a few probe ships into the region but they were lost. It's cold, black, and lonely out there and a single probe ship hunting for life is like loosing a single member of a hymenoptera species into the atmosphere of a planet which supports a single flower on its surface, and waiting to see if the bug can find the flower. But if a whole hiveful of the insects is freed into the air at carefully calculated locations, chances of success are immeasurably better. So that's what we're going to do: build a fleet of probe ships and contact whoever or whatever is out there."

They all must have thought he was crazy by the looks on their faces. But Daro Haworth had expected that. He waited for the first question, knowing ahead of time what it would be and knowing that either Cumberland or Bede would ask it.

It was Cumberland. "Are you crazy? How's that going to get us out of this?"

"Through trade," Haworth replied. "By opening new markets to us out there. The latest calculations show that there's another interstellar race in the Perseus arm, outward from here. It lives a damnable number of light years away, but if we try, we can reach it. And then we'll have billions of new customers!"

"Customers for what?" Metep said. "The only thing we've got to trade in any quantity is grain. What if they don't eat grain? Or even if they do—and that's unlikely, I'm sure—what makes you think they'll want to buy ours?"

"Well, we've got plenty of grain at the moment," Cumberland said. "Let me tell you—"

"Forget about grain!" Haworth shouted, his face livid. "Who am I talking to—the most powerful men in the outworlds or a group of children? Where is your vision? Think of it! An entire interstellar race! There has to be a million things we can exchange—from art to hardware, from Leason crystals to chispen filets! And if we don't have it, we can ship it out from Earth. We could arrange trade agreements and be sole agents for whatever alien technology is found to have industrial uses. We could corner any number of markets! The outworlds could enter a golden age of prosperity! And"—he smiled here—"I don't think I have to remind you gentlemen what that could mean to each of us in the area of political clout and personal finances, do I?"

The undertone began again as each man muttered cautiously at first to his neighbor, then with growing enthusiasm. Only Krager had a sour note to sing.

"How are we going to pay for all this? To build and equip a fleet of probe ships will take an enormous sum of money. Billions and billions of marks. Where are we supposed to get them?"

"The same place we get all the other billions of marks we spend but don't have—the duplicators!"

Krager began to sputter. "But that will send inflation into warp! It'll go totally out of control! The mark is already weakened beyond repair. Why it's still holding up in the Interstellar

Currency Exchange, I can't fathom. Maybe the speculators haven't figured out how bad off we are yet. But this probe ship idea will completely ruin us!"

"That's why we've got to act now!" Haworth said. "While the mark still has some credibility on the Exchange. If we wait too long, we'll never be able to get enough credit to purchase the drive tubes and warp units necessary for the probe fleet. The mark has been holding up better than any of us ever expected. That indicates to me that the people active in the Interstellar Currency Exchange have faith in us and think we can pull ourselves out of this."

"Then they're dumber than I thought they were," Krager muttered.

"Not funny," Haworth said. "And not fair. You forget that Project Perseus will also create jobs and temporarily stabilize the tax base in the interim." He walked back to his place at Metep's side. "Look: it's a gamble. I told you that before I broached the subject. It's probably the biggest gamble in human history. The future of the entire Imperium and all our political careers is riding on it. If I thought there was another way out, believe me, I'd try it. Personally, I don't give a damn about getting in touch with the aliens in the Perseus arm. But right now, it's our only hope. If we succeed, then all the extra inflation caused by Project Perseus will be worth while and eventually compensated by the new avenues of trade we'll establish."

"Suppose we fail?" Metep said. "Suppose there's something out there that gobbles up probe ships. Suppose they find nothing but the ruins of a dead civilization!"

Daro Haworth shrugged with elaborate nonchalance. "If we fail, every outworlder will spit when he hears our names five years from now. And in perhaps a dozen years, Earth will reinstate her claim to the outworlds."

"And if we do nothing?" Metep asked, afraid of the answer.

"The same, only the spitting stage won't be reached for perhaps ten years, and the return of Earthie control won't occur for twenty. Face it, gentlemen: this is our only chance. It may not work, but I see no other alternative. We're all to blame; we've all—"

"I won't take the blame for this mess!" Krager shouted. "I've warned you all along, all of you, that someday—"

"And you went right along, too, old man." Haworth's lips twisted into a sneer. "You okayed all the increases in the money supply. You made noises, but you went along. If your objections had had any real conviction behind them, you would have resigned years ago. You flew with us, and if we go down, you'll crash with us!" He turned to the others. "Shall we vote, gentlemen?"

Ω

It was the first time LaNague could remember being happy to see Broohnin. He and Doc Zack and Radmon Sayers had waited in the warehouse office into the hours toward dawn. The money drop earlier in the evening had gone off as smoothly as the heist that morning. Things were looking up all over, at least as far as his plans for the revolution were concerned. Everything was going according to schedule, and going smoothly. Too smoothly. He kept waiting for a kink to develop somewhere along the line, waiting and hoping that when it appeared he would be able to handle it. The meeting tonight between Metep and his Council of Five could possibly produce a kink, but that was unlikely. There was no way out for the Imperium now. No matter what they did, no matter what they tried, they were unaware of the purpose of Boedekker's activities on Earth. The Imperium was going to crumble, that was for certain. The Boedekker aspect of the plan would enable LaNague to control the exact moment of its fall, its rate of descent, and its force of impact. The Boedekker aspect would ensure an impact of such force that no trace of the cadaver would remain.

"What's the word from the meeting?" LaNague asked as Broohnin entered the office.

"Nothing!" Broohnin said, scowling through his beard. "A complete waste of time. You wouldn't believe what they wound up deciding to do after hours in hush-hush conference."

"Spend more money, of course," Zack said.

Sayers nodded. "Of course. But on what?"

"Probe ships!" Broohnin looked around at the uncomprehending faces. "That's right—probe ships. I told you you wouldn't believe it."

"What in the name of the Core for?" Sayers asked.

"To find aliens. Haworth wants to jump over to the next arm of the galaxy and sell stuff to aliens. He says they're over there and they can save the Imperium."

As Zack and Sayers began to laugh, Broohnin joined in. The three of them whooped and roared and pounded the arms of their chairs until they noticed that LaNague was not even smiling. Instead, he was frowning with concern.

"What's the matter, Peter?" Sayers said, gasping for breath. "Have you ever heard of a more ridiculous idea?"

LaNague shook his head. "No. Never. But it may ruin everything."

"But how could—"

LaNague turned away from the vidcaster toward Broohnin. "When does construction start?"

"Immediately, from what I can gather."

"Is it going to be a military or civil project?"

"Civil. They're going to run it through the Grain Export Authority."

"And monitoring?"

Broohnin looked at him questioningly. LaNague's intensity was alarming. "I don't—"

"Communications! The probes have to have a place to report back to, a nerve center of some sort that'll co-ordinate their movements."

"That'll be the CEA comm center, I guess. That's where all the grain pods reported to as they assembled for a run. It's got all the necessary equipment."

LaNague was up and pacing the room. "Have you got any contacts in there?" Seeing Broohnin nod, he went on. "How many?"

"One."

"Get more! Slip our people onto the duty roster in the communications area. We need people on our side in there."

"That's not going to be easy. With the grain runs falling off, they've cut the common staff. Not enough work to go around."

"If we have to, we'll bribe our way onto the staff. Beg, plead, threaten . . . I don't care what you do, but get us enough people in that comm center to keep it covered at all times!"

"But why?" Sayers asked.

"Because I want to be the first to know what those probe ships find. And if I don't like what they find, I'm going to see to it that the information takes an awful long time getting to the Council of Five."

Doc Zack spoke from his seat. "You don't really think finding aliens to trade with could open up a large enough market to offset what the Imperium's already done to the economy, and what the cost of this probe ship program will do on top of that, do you? Let me say as an authority on economics that there isn't the slightest chance of success."

"I realize that," LaNague said from the middle of the room.

"Then why the sudden panic? Why tell us that it could ruin everything when you know it can't."

"I'm not worried about them trading with whatever aliens are out there. I'm worried about them stumbling into something else—the one thing that might turn everything we've worked for around; the one thing that's always helped the Meteps and the Imperiums of history out of slumps. And you of all people, Doc, should know what I'm talking about."

Doc Zack's brow furrowed momentarily, then his eyes widened and his face blanched.

"Oh, my!"

VOLUME IV  NUMBER 1

THE ROBIN HOOD READER

THE THREE LAWS OF POSITRONIC CITIZENSHIP

1) A citizen may not injure the State, or, through inaction, allow the State to come to harm.

2) A citizen must obey orders given it by the State except when such orders conflict with the First Law.

3) A citizen must protect its own existence as long as such protection does not conflict with the First or Second Law.

If you do not respond positively to all of the above, report immediately to your local public library for rewriting.

Library? Yes, library. More on them next time.

The Economic Weather Eye

PRICE INDEX (using the 115th year of the Imperium—when the Imperial mark became mandatory legal tender—as base year of 100)	219.7
MONEY SUPPLY (M3)	2612.4
UNEMPLOYMENT LEVEL	14.9%

	Imperial Marks	Solar Credits
GOLD (Troy ounce)	502.1	133.2
Silver (Troy ounce)	29.6	6.3
Bread (1 kg. loaf)	1.08	1.71

PART THREE
"ABOVE ALL ELSE: KYFHO"

The Year of the Sickle

XVI

Do you wish to become invisible? Have no thought of yourself for two years and no one will notice you.

Old Spanish Saying

"Meat?" Salli cried, her gaze shifting back and forth between the roast on the table and her husband. "How did you get it?"

"Bought it." Vincen Stafford was smiling. For the first time in two years he was feeling some pride in himself.

"But how? You just can't get meat any more, except in—"

He nodded. "Yeah. The black market."

"But they don't accept Food Vouchers. And we don't have any money."

"Yes, we do. I signed up as a pilot for Project Perseus today."

"You mean that probe ship thing? Oh no, Vin! You can't mean it! It's too dangerous!"

"It's the only thing I know how to do, Salli. And it pays thirty thousand marks a year. They gave me half in advance for signing."

"But you'll be out there all alone . . . nobody's ever been out there before."

"That's why I got such a premium for signing. It's nothing to pilot those one-man ships. All the skill's in the navigation. And that's what I do best. It was made for me! I've got to take it." The light in his face faded slightly. "Please understand. We need the money . . . but more than that, I need this job."

Salli looked up at her husband. She knew he needed the job to feel useful again, to feel he had control over something in his life again, even if it was just a tiny probe ship in the uncharted blackness between the galactic arms. And she knew it would be useless to argue with him. He had signed, he had taken the money, he was going. Make the best of it.

She rose and kissed him.

"Let's get this roast cooking."

Ω

". . . and once again there's news from Earth about Eric Boedekker, the wealthy asteroid mining magnate. It seems that he has now sold his fabulous skisland estate to high bidder in one of the most fantastic auctions in memory. As far as anyone can tell, the estate was the last of the Boedekker holdings to be liquidated, and the former owner is now living in seclusion, address unknown.

"Thus, one of the largest fortunes in human history has been completely liquidated. Whether it sits in an account for future use or has been surreptitiously reinvested remains a tantalizing question. Only Eric Boedekker knows, and no one can find him.

"And here on the outworlds, Project Perseus is proceeding on schedule. A crew for the fleet of ships has been picked from the host of heroic applicants—most of whom were underqualified—and all that is necessary now is completion of the tiny probe ships themselves . . ."

Ω

It was the same old argument, over and over again. Broohnin was sick of it. So was everyone else. LaNague still refused to let them know where it was all heading. He was promising them the full story by the end of the year, but Broohnin wanted it now. So did Sayers and Doc Zack. Even the Flinters looked a little uncertain.

"But what have we *done*?" Broohnin said. "The Imperium's inflating itself out of business. But Doc says that'll take another ten years. We can't wait that long!"

"The Imperium will be out of business in two," LaNague said, calmly, adamantly. "There won't be a trace of it left on Throne or on any other outworld."

"Doc says that's impossible." Broohnin turned to Zack. "Right, Doc?" Zack nodded reluctantly. "And Doc's the expert. I'll take his word over yours."

"With all due respect," LaNague said, "Doc doesn't know certain things that I know, and without that information, he can't make an accurate projection. If he had it, he'd concur with two years or less as a projected time of collapse."

"Well, give it to me, then!" Zack said. "This is frustrating as hell to sit around and be in the dark all the time."

"At the end of this year, you'll know. I promise you."

From the look on Doc Zack's face, that wasn't what he wanted to hear. Broohnin stepped back and surveyed the group, withholding a smile of approval. He saw LaNague's hold on the movement slipping. His rigid rules of conduct, his refusal to let anyone know the exact nature of his plan for revolution, all were causing dissension in the ranks. Which meant that Broohnin had a chance to get back into the front of everything and run this show the way it should be run.

"We fear Earthie involvement, LaNague." One of the Flinters had spoken. Broohnin had to squint to see whether it was the male or the female. With the bunned hair and red circles on their foreheads, and their robes and weapons belts, they looked like twins. He noticed the swell of the speaker's chest. It had been Kanya.

"Yes," Sayers said. "I'm sure Earth's planning right now when and how to move in and take over."

"I'm sure it is," LaNague said, concentrating his reply on the silent, standing forms of Josef and Kanya. "But Earth will also be projecting a ten- to twelve-year period before the Imperium smothers in its own mark notes. When it crumbles two years from now, they'll be caught off guard. By the time they get organized, their chance will be gone."

Doc Zack was speaking through clenched teeth. "But what can you do that will cause it to crumble so quickly?"

"You'll know at the end of the year."

The meeting broke up then, with the frustrated participants leaving separately, at intervals, via different exits. All that had been decided was that the next Robin Hood robbery should be put off for a while until a new device the Flinters had ordered from their homeworld could be smuggled in. The

Flinters had made their own arrangements for delivery, which was expected any day. It would give the Merry Men a totally new approach to robbery. Conventional methods were out now, due to the heavy guard that had been placed on anything that even looked like a currency shipment. The Imperial Guard had been caught looking the other way due to the long interval between the second and third heists. It appeared they did not intend to be caught again.

Broohnin watched the two Flinters as they stood by the front exit, waiting for their turn to depart. For all the fear they inspired in him, Broohnin found the Flinters infinitely fascinating. He saw them not as people but as weapons, beautifully honed and crafted, staggeringly efficient. They were killing machines. He wished he could own one. Pulling his courage together, he sauntered over to where they stood.

"You two have any plans for the evening?" They looked at him but made no reply. "If not, maybe we could get together over a few drinks. I've got some things I'd like to discuss with you both."

"It was previously agreed," Josef said, "that we would not allow ourselves to be seen together outside the warehouse unless we lived together."

"Oh, that was LaNague's idea. You know what an old woman he is! Why not come down to the—"

"I'm sorry," Josef said, "but we have other plans for the evening. Sorry." He touched his belt and activated a holosuit that covered his Flinter garb with the image of a nondescript middle-aged man. Kanya did the same. They turned and left without so much as a "Next time, perhaps."

Broohnin watched them stroll down the darkening street. There were no other pedestrians about. At night the streets had become the property of the barbarians of Primus City—the hungry, broke, and desperate, who jumped and stole and ran because there was nothing else left to them, were bad enough; but then there were those who had found themselves beaten down, humbled, and debased by life, who had retreated once too often and now needed proof that they were better than somebody—anybody. They needed to force someone to his or her knees and for just a moment or two see another human being cringe in fear and pain before them. To taste power over another life before they snuffed it out was, in some twisted way, proof that they still had control over their own. Which they didn't.

Broohin shook his head as he watched the two bland, weak-looking figures walk into the darkness, looking like so much fresh meat for anyone hungry for a bite. Pity the jumper who landed on those two.

On an impulse, he decided to follow them. What did Flinters do in their spare time? Where did they live? He was not long in finding out. Kanya and Josef entered a low-rent apartment building not far from the warehouse district. He watched for a while, saw a third floor window on the east wall fill with light before it was opaqued. Fantasizing for a moment, he idly wondered if weaponry and combat were as much a part of their sex play as the rest of their daily life. He cut off further elaboration on the theme when he noticed a standard size flitter lift off from the roof of the apartment building. As it banked to the right, he could see two figures within, neither one identifiable, but definitely a pair. He wondered . . .

With no flitter at his disposal, Broohnin was forced to stand helplessly and watch them go. They were probably off to pick up that new device for the next Robin Hood heist. He would have liked to have seen how they smuggled things onto Throne so easily. It was a technique that could prove useful to him some time in the future. As it was, he was stuck here on the street. It was all LaNague's fault, as usual. He should have seen to it that they were all provided with their own personal flitters. But no. Broohnin wasn't allowed to have one because Broohnin was on the dole and, as far as the records showed, could not afford a personal flitter. To be seen riding around in one all the time would attract unwanted attention.

One thing he could do, though, was go into the apartment building and see if Kanya and Josef were still there. He crossed the street, entered, and took the float-chute up to the third floor. From where he had seen the lighted window earlier, he deduced the location of their apartment. Steeling himself, he approached the door and pressed the entry panel. The indicator remained dark, meaning either that no one was within, or that whoever was in did not want to be disturbed.

With a sigh of relief, he turned away and headed for the float-chute. An unanswered door was hardly evidence that Kanya and Josef had been in that flitter, but at least it didn't negate the possibility. The next thing to do was to go up to the flitter pad on the roof and wait. If they returned tonight, perhaps he could get some idea as to where they had been. What he intended to do with the information, he didn't know.

Nothing, most likely. But he had no place to go, no one waiting for him anywhere, no one he wanted to be with, and knew no one who wanted to be with him. He might as well spend the night here on the roof as within the four walls of his room on the other side of town.

The wait was not a long one. He had found himself a comfortable huddling place in the corner of the roof behind the building's own solar batteries, discharging now to light the apartments below, and had just settled in for his vigil when landing lights lit the roof pad from above. It was the flitter he had seen earlier, and after it had locked into its slot, the figures of two familiar middle-aged men emerged.

The first one looked carefully around him. Satisfied that there was no one else on the roof, he nodded to the other and they removed two boxes from their craft, one large and rectangular, the other small and cubical. Carrying the larger box between them with the smaller resting atop it, they pushed through the door to the drop-chute and disappeared.

And that was that. Broohnin sat and bitterly questioned what in the name of the Core he was doing there alone on a roof watching two disguised Flinters unload a couple of boxes from their flitter. He knew no more now about their smuggling procedure than he did before. Bored and disgusted, he waited until he was sure the Flinters were safely behind the door to their apartment, then took the drop-chute directly to street level and headed for the nearest monorail stop.

Ω

The wracking total-body parasthesia that enveloped him during the lift into real space as his nervous system was assaulted from all sides was an almost welcome sensation. Vincen Stafford had made the first long jump in his probe ship. The nausea that usually attended entering and leaving subspace passed unnoticed, smothered by a wave of exultation. He was alive again. He was free. He was master of reality itself.

After a few moments of silent revelry, he shook himself and got to work, taking his readings, preparing the beacon to be released and activated. It would send out an oscillating subspace laser pulse in the direction of the radio sources in the Perseus arm; in real space it would send a measured radio beep. Stafford considered the latter mode useless since his subspace jumps would take him far ahead of the radio pulses, but if that was the way the people running the brand-new

Imperial Bureau of Interstellar Exploration and Alien Contact wanted it, that's the way they would get it.

The subspace laser beacon was a good idea, however. If the target radio sources really did belong to another interstellar race, and that race was advanced enough to have developed subspace technology, the beacons he and his fellow probe pilots would be dropping off in a predictable zigzag pattern would blaze an unmistakable trail through the heavens for anyone with the equipment to follow. Hopefully, some member of that race would plot out the course of one of the probes and send a welcoming party to wait for it when it lifted into real space at the end of one of the jumps.

Stafford thought about that. If the aliens happened to choose his ship to contact, the responsibility would be awesome. The entire future of the relationship between humankind and the aliens could be marred or permanently estranged by some inadvertent bungle on the part of a hapless probe pilot. He didn't want to be that pilot. He could do without the glory of first contact. All he wanted was to do his job, do it well, and get back to Throne and Salli in one piece.

In one piece. That was the crux of the matter. He would be making a lot of jumps . . . far more in the following months than he would during years as a navigator on the grain runs. Warping down was always a hazard, even for the most experienced spacer. He was tearing open the very fabric of reality, accentuating the natural curve of space to an acute angle, and leaping across the foreshortened interval, reappearing again light years away from his starting point. Probe ships were small, fragile. Sometimes they didn't come out of subspace; sometimes they became lost under the curve of space, trapped forever in featureless, two-dimensional grayness.

Stafford shuddered. That wouldn't happen to him. Other probes had traveled out here between the arms and not come back. But he would. He had to. Salli was waiting.

Ω

"The old 'little black box' ploy, ay?" Doc Zack said from the corner seat that had become unofficially his whenever they met in the warehouse office.

"Yes," said LaNague, smiling, "but like no little black box you've ever seen."

"What's it do?" Sayers asked.

"It's a time machine."

"Now just a minute," Zack said. "The Barsky experiments proved time travel impossible!"

"Not impossible—impractical. Barsky and his associates found they could send things back in time, but they couldn't correct for planetary motion in the cosmos. Therefore, the object displaced past-ward invariably wound up somewhere else in space."

Sayers shook his head as if to clear it. "I remember reporting on that at one time or another, but I can't say I ever fully understood it."

Broohnin was paying little attention to the conversation. He was more interested in the whereabouts of the larger box the Flinters had unloaded from their flitter last night. They had brought the small one in with them, and that was what had triggered this meaningless discussion of time travel. But where was the big one?

"Let me put it this way," LaNague was saying. "Everything occupies a locus in time and space, correct? I think we can take that as given. What the Barsky apparatus does is change only the temporal locus; the spatial locus remains fixed."

Sayers' eyebrows lifted. "Ah! I see. That's why it ends up in interstellar space."

"Well, *I* don't see," Broohnin snapped, annoyed that his wandering thoughts had left him out. "Why should sending something back in time send it off the planet?"

LaNague spoke as patiently as he could. "Because at any given instant, you occupy a 'here' and a 'now' along the space/time continuum. The Barsky device changes only the 'now.' If we used it to send you back ten years into the past, your 'now' would be altered to 'then,' but you'd still be 'here' in space. And ten years ago, Throne was billions of kilometers away from here. Ten years ago, it hadn't reached this point in space. That's why they could never bring any of the temporally displaced objects back. Barsky theorized that this was what was happening, but it wasn't until the Slippery Miller escape that he could finally prove it."

Broohnin vaguely remembered the name Slippery Miller, but could not recall any of the details. Everyone else in the room apparently could, however, by the way they were nodding and smiling. He decided not to look like an idiot by asking about it.

"Well, if you've got any idea of sending me or anyone else back into time with that thing, you can just forget it." He consciously tried to make it sound as if he were standing up for the group against LaNague. "We're not taking any chances like that for you or anybody!"

LaNague laughed in his face, and there was genuine amusement in the sound rather than derision, but that didn't blunt its sting. "No, we're not planning to send any people back in time. Just some of the Imperium's money."

Ω

It was strictly understood that after Broohnin had completed his little mission, he was to return the flitter to LaNague. No joy-riding. If he broke one of the air regs, he'd be hauled in, and not only would he have to answer a lot of questions about how a dolee came to be in possession of a nice new sporty flitter, but he might also be linked with LaNague. That was something to be avoided at all costs.

But Broohnin didn't consider this a joy ride. And even if he had, the displeasure of Peter LaNague was hardly a deterrent. He had delivered the Barsky temporal displacer in the tiny black box to Erv Singh on the west coast, and had passed on LaNague's instructions. Erv's next currency run wasn't until the following week; he'd have to wait until that time before he could place the box according to plan. He'd contact Broohnin as soon as everything was set. That done, the rest of the night lay free ahead of Broohnin. He had been approaching the Angus Black Imports warehouse when the idea struck him that now was a perfect time to check up on the Flinters. The nature of the other box they had unloaded that night on the roof of their apartment still nagged at him. Something about the way they had handled it pestered him, like an itchy patch of skin out of reach in the middle of his back.

He had a little trouble finding their apartment building from the air, but after following the streets as he had walked them, he reached a familiar-looking roof. And yes, the Flinters' flitter was still there. Broohnin circled around in the darkness until he found a resting place for his craft on a neighboring roof. He'd give it an hour. If there was no sign of the Flinters by then, he'd call it a night. No use making LaNague wait too long.

He waited the full hour, and then a little bit longer. The extra time spent in watch had not been a conscious decision. He had popped a torportal under his tongue to ease his restlessness in the cramped flitter seat and had nodded off. Only the stimulus of flickering light seeping through the slits between his eyelids roused him to full consciousness. A flitter was rising off the neighboring roof. It was the same one the Flinters had used last night. As it moved away into the darkness, its running lights winked off. Now Broohnin was really interested.

Leaving his own running lights off, he lifted his craft into the air and climbed quickly to a higher altitude than he thought the Flinters would be using. Without their running lights to follow, Broohnin would lose them before they had traveled a few kilometers. His only hope was to get above and keep them silhouetted against the illumination given off by Primus City's ubiquitous glo-globes. As long as they stayed over the urban areas, he could follow above and behind them without being seen. If they moved over open country, he would have to think of something else.

They stayed over the city, however, and headed directly for Imperium Park at its center. Broohnin began to have some trouble over the park since its level of illumination was drastically less than the dwelling areas. It was only by chance that he noticed them setting down in a particularly dense stand of trees. Broohnin chose a less challenging landing site perhaps two hundred meters east of them and sat quietly after grounding his craft, unsure of what to do next.

He desperately wanted to see what two Flinters could be up to in the middle of Imperium Park in the dead of night, but he didn't want to leave the safety of the flitter. If the streets of Primus City were on their way to becoming nighttime hunting grounds, Imperium Park was already far into the jungle stage. Once he stepped out onto the ground, he was fair game for whoever was walking about. Not that Broohnin couldn't handle himself in a fight with one or even two assailants. He carried a vibe-knife and knew how to use it to damaging effect. It was just that nowadays the jumpers hunted in packs in the park, and he had no illusions about his fate should he stumble onto one of those.

He only hesitated briefly, then he was out in the night air, locking the flitter behind him. All things considered, the odds were probably in his favor for coming through this jaunt unscathed. The section of the park in which he had landed was on high ground where the underbrush was the thickest. There were no natural paths through here and it would not be considered prime hunting area for any of the packs.

He pushed his way carefully through the brush until he felt he had traveled half the distance to the Flinters, then he got down on his belly and crawled. And crawled. His chest and abdomen were bruised and scratched, and he was about to turn back, thinking he had wandered off course, when his right hand reached out and came in contact with nothing but air. Further tactile exploration brought his surroundings into clearer focus; he was on the edge of a low rocky bluff. Below him and to the right he heard grunting and groaning. Craning his head over the edge, he spied the Flinters' craft.

A hooded lamp provided faint illumination for the scene, but enough for Broohnin to discern two figures pushing and pulling at a huge slab of rock. With a prolonged agonized chorus of guttural noises from two bodies straining to the limits of their strength, the rock began to move. Intensifying their efforts, the Flinters rolled it up on its edge in one final heave, revealing a rectangular hole. After a panting, laughing pause as they leaned against the up-ended stone; they returned to the flitter and the large box that lay on the ground beside it . . . the same box Broohnin had seen them unload on the roof the other night.

Each of them removed a small white disk from his or her belt—even with their holosuits deactivated, Broohnin could not tell Kanya from Josef at this distance—and pressed it into a slotted opening in the side of the crate in turn. Then the white disks went back into the weapons belts. Carefully, almost gingerly, they carried the crate to the hole under the rock, placed it within and covered it with a thin layer of dirt. With less effort and fewer sound effects, they toppled the stone back over the hole.

Then the two Flinters did something very strange—glancing once at each other, they stepped away from the rock and stood staring at it. From their postures, Broohnin could not be sure whether he was reading guilt or grief or both. He almost slipped from the bluff in a vain attempt to get a glimpse of their faces. What was going on down there anyway? What was in that crate and why was it being buried in Imperium Park? If security was all they were looking for, there were certainly better places to hide it out on the moors. And why was LaNague having all this done without telling the group?

The questions plagued Broohnin as he returned through the brush to his flitter, and left the front of his mind only long enough for him to make the dash from cover to the flitter and to get into the air as quickly as possible. As he rose into the night, a thought occurred to him: what if LaNague didn't know about that box either?

Ω

LaNague stopped at the door to his apartment and rubbed his temples with both hands. Another headache, but a mild one this time. As the plan reached the ignition point, they seemed to be bothering him less frequently, and were less severe when they struck. And the dream . . . months had passed since it had troubled his sleep. Everything seemed to be falling into line as predicted, everything coming under control.

There were still variables, however. Boedekker was the biggest. What if he balked? LaNague grimaced in annoyance at the thought as he placed his palm against the entry plate which was keyed to him, Kanya, and Josef. The door slid open and he stepped through. Boedekker so far had followed his instructions to the letter, at least as far as LaNague could tell. He had liquidated anything of value that he owned, and other indicators showed that he was following through with the secondary aspects of his part in the play. Boedekker could still go his own way, and that bothered LaNague. The man was out of reach. He didn't want to trust him, but he had no choice.

He let the door slide closed behind him but did not move into the room just yet. He felt good, despite the headache. This buoyancy of mood was a fairly recent development, a slow process over the past year. At first the knowledge that the fate of the outworlds was falling more and more completely into his hands had weighed on him like half a dozen G's. Billions of people were going to be affected to varying degrees across the light years of Occupied Space. Even Earth would not escape unscathed. The agrarian outworlds were already on their way into a deep depression, and by the time the Imperium came apart, they'd be back to a barter economy and would hardly notice its demise. But the people on Throne . . . their entire social structure would be destroyed almost overnight.

Mora's angry words came back to him—what right did he have to do this? The question used to trouble him fiercely, despite his standard answer: self-preservation. But it troubled him no more. It was all a moot point now, anyway. The plan was virtually to the point of no return. Even if Mora could show up and convince him that he had been in error all along, it would be too late. The juggernaut had begun to roll and could not be stopped. Its course could be altered, modified to a degree, its moment of impact adjusted—that was the purpose of LaNague's continued presence on Throne—but no one, not even LaNague, could stop it now. The realization had a strangely exhilarating effect on him.

Odd he should think of Mora now. He had been managing to keep her at the far end of his mind except when making a holo for her or viewing one from her. The communications were too brief, too few, and too long in coming. He missed her. Not as much as he had at first, though. Perhaps he was getting used to life without her . . . something he had once considered impossible.

Walking over to where Pierrot sat on the window sill, he touched the moss at the tree's base and noted that it felt dry. Due for some water soon, probably a root-pruning, too. Soon . . . he'd get to it soon. The trunk was halfway between *chokkan* and *bankan,* which was neutral, but the leaves seemed duller than usual. Closer inspection revealed a few bare inner branches with peeling bark—a sure sign of localized death.

Was something wrong with Pierrot? Or was the tree reflecting some sort of inner rot afflicting LaNague himself? That was one of the drawbacks of having an imprinted *misho*—there was always a tendency to read too much into its configuration, its color, its state of health. It did prompt introspection, though, and a little of that was never bad. But not now. There were too many other things on his mind.

He broke off the dead wood and threw it into the molecular dissociator that stood in the corner. The appliance was not the extravagance it seemed. LaNague made a point of disintegrating everything that was not part of a normal household's garbage. There was another dissociator at the warehouse in wihch all debris from production of *The Robin Hood Reader* and other sundry subversive activities was eventually destroyed. He would not have the revolution tripped up by a wayward piece of refuse.

He turned toward the sink for Pierrot's water and froze as he caught a glimpse of movement in the doorway that led to the bedroom.

"Peter, it's me."

"Mora!" Conflicting emotions rooted him to the spot. He should have been overjoyed to see her, should have leaped across the room to embrace her. But he wasn't and he didn't. Instead, he felt resentment at her presence. She had no right showing up like this . . . she was going to interfere . . .

"But how?" he said when he found his voice.

"I came on a student visa. I'm supposedly going to do research at the U. of O. library. Kanya let me in this morning." Her brow furrowed. "Is something wrong?"

"No."

"I was watching you with Pierrot. He's your only friend here, isn't he?"

"Not really."

"You look older, Peter."

"I am."

"Much older." Her frown turned into a smile that failed to mask her hurt and concern at his remoteness. "You almost look your age."

"Where's Laina?"

She drifted toward him, cautiously, as if fearing he'd bolt from her. "With your mother. She's too young to join the Merry Men."

It took a while for the implications of what she had said to filter through to LaNague's befuddled brain. But when it did: "Oh no! Don't even consider it!"

"I've been considering it since you left." She moved closer, gently touching his arms with her hands, sending shock waves through him, cracking the paralysis that held him immobile. "I was wrong . . . this is the only way out for Tolive . . . for Laina . . . for our way of life . . . and the minting's done . . . the coins are ready to be shipped . . ."

"No! There's chaos coming to Throne. I don't want you here when everything comes apart. Too dangerous!" He wouldn't want her here even if it were safe.

Mora kissed him gently, tentatively, on the lips. "I'm staying. Now, are we going to stand here and argue, or are we going to catch up on two and a half years of deprivation?"

LaNague replied by lifting her up and carrying her into the adjoining room. He could no longer deny his hunger for her. He'd send her home later.

Ω

Vincen Stafford prepared to eject another beacon into the starry void. How many was this, now? He'd have to check his records to be exactly sure. It was all becoming so mechanical and routinized—jump, release a beacon, jump, release a beacon, jump . . . even the jumps themselves seemed to be less traumatic. Was there such a thing as acclimation? He shrugged.

He'd never heard of it, but maybe it happened. And if it did or didn't, so what? He was more than halfway to the Perseus arm. If he reached it without being contacted, he could turn back and go home. So far, so good.

There was a buzz behind him. He turned and saw his communicator light flashing. Someone—or something—was trying to contact him. Opening the circuit gave rise to no audio or visual signal. That meant the incoming message was not on the standard frequency. Stafford was liking this less and less every second. Reluctantly, he activated the search mechanism. It would lock in on the frequency of the incoming signal when it located it.

It didn't take long. The vidscreen suddenly lit with a face like nothing Stafford had ever seen. No, wait . . . there was something vaguely familiar there . . . the snout, the sharp yellow teeth, the bristly patches of fur around the ears . . . canine. Yes, that was it. The creature was definitely dog-faced. But not like any dog he ever wanted in the same room with him. He was glad the probe ship was equipped with only flat-screen reception. A holograph of that thing would be downright frightening. No torso features were visible but that was okay.

"Greetings," the image said in Interstellar that was garbled and gutturalized far beyond the capability of a human throat.

"Who—who are you?" Stafford blurted inanely. "Where are you?"

"I am an emissary of the Tark nation"—at least it sounded like "Tark," a barking sound with a harsh initial consonant—"and my craft is approximately two of your kilometers aft of you."

"You speak our language." Stafford was reaching for the aft monitor. He wanted to see what kind of welcoming party had been sent to intercept him. An intensified image of a bulky ovoid filled the screen. At first he thought the emissary had understated the distance, but the readout showed a large mass two kilometers aft. Stafford took another look. That was no peaceful envoy ship. He had no idea what alien weaponry might look like, but he saw all sorts of tubes pointed in his direction and there was a definite feeling about the ship that said it wasn't built for mere information-gathering duties. It reminded him of a Sol-System dreadnought. But then, maybe they were just being careful. In their position, he'd probably come armed to the teeth, too.

"Of course," the Tark replied. "We've been keeping watch

on your race for quite some time. We are not so timid as you: as soon as we had sufficient evidence of an interstellar race in your arm of the galaxy, we investigated."

"Why didn't you contact us?"

"We saw no need. Your race is obviously no threat to the Tark nation, and you are much too far away to be of any practical use to us."

"What about trade?"

"Trade? I am not familiar with the term." He looked down and seemed to be keying a reference into a console to his right.

Stafford couldn't resist prompting him. "An exchange of goods . . . and knowledge."

"Yes, I see now." He—for no good reason, Stafford had automatically ascribed a male gender to the creature—looked up. "Once again, we do not see purpose in that. Your race does not appear to have anything that interests us sufficiently at this point." The subject of trade apparently bored the Tark and he turned to another. "Why do you invade Tarkan space? You made certain that we would intercept you. Why?"

"To offer trade with us."

The Tark gave a sharp, high-pitched yelp. Laughter? Annoyance? "You must understand—we do not trade with anyone. That would involve an exchange, requiring Tarks to give up one thing in order to gain another."

"Of course. That's what trade is all about."

"But Tarks are not weak. We do not surrender what we have. If you had something we truly desired, we would take it."

"You don't understand . . ." Stafford began to say, but heard his voice trail off into silence. Perspiration had been collecting in his axillae since the comm indicator had buzzed; it was now running down over his ribs. They didn't understand, not at all. And to think that he had dreaded being in the contact ship for fear of unintentionally offending the aliens. This was worse. These creatures seemed devoid of anything approaching a concept of give and take. They were beyond offending.

The face on the screen had apparently come to a decision. "You will shut down your drive mechanism and prepare to be boarded."

"Boarded! Why?"

"We must be assured that you are not armed and that you pose no threat to the Tark nation."

"How could I threaten that monstrosity you're riding?"

Stafford said, glancing at the aft monitor. "You could swallow me whole!"

"Shut down your drive and prepare for boarding! We will—"

Stafford switched off the volume. He was frightened now and needed to think, something he couldn't do with that growling voice filling the cabin. He felt a sharp tug on the ship and knew that a tractor beam or something very similar had been focused on him. He was being drawn toward the Tark dreadnought. In a brief moment of panic, he stood frozen in the middle of his tiny cabin, unable to act, unable to decide what to do next.

He was trapped. His real space propulsion system was the standard proton-proton drive through a Leason crystal tube. But small. Too small to break free of the tractor beam. Activating it now would only serve to move him through space pulling the dreadnought behind him, and that futile gesture would last only as long as his fuel or the Tark commander's patience. If the latter ran out first, his probe ship might become a target for those banks of weapons which could easily reduce it to motes of spiraling rubble.

There was the warp capacity, of course. It could be used for escape, but not now . . . not when he was in the thrall of a tractor beam and in such close proximity to a mass as large as the Tark ship. The thought of attempting a subspace drop under those circumstances was almost as frightening as the thought of placing himself at the mercy of the Tarks.

No, it wasn't. A quick look at the canine face that still filled his comm screen convinced him of that. Better to die trying to escape than to place his life in that creature's hands.

He threw himself into the control seat and reached for the warp activator. If the tractor beam and the dreadnought's mass sufficiently disturbed the integrity of the probe ship's warp field, it would be caught between real space and subspace. The experts were still arguing over just what happened then, but the prevailing theory held that the atomic structure of that part of the ship impinging on subspace would reverse polarity. And that, of course, would result in a cataclysmic explosion. It was a fact of life for every spacer. That was why the capacity of the warp unit had to be carefully matched to the mass of the ship; that was why no one ever tried to initiate a subspace jump within the critical point in a star system's gravity well.

He released the safety lock and placed his finger on the activator switch. A cascade of thoughts washed across his mind as he closed his eyes and held his breath . . . *Salli* . . . if the ship blew, at least he'd take the Tarks with him . . . *Salli* . . . was this what had happened to the few probe ships that had been sent this way in the past and were never heard from again? . . . *Salli* . . .

He threw the switch.

VOLUME IV NUMBER 3

THE ROBIN HOOD READER

YOU CAN DEPEND ON THE IMPERIAL LIBRARY LIKE YOU DEPEND ON THE IMPERIUM!

For the real truth, go straight to the source: go down to the local library branch and peruse the spools you require on the premises, or have them keyed to your home vid. You can depend on the Imperial Library system.

Really? Take a look at this excerpt from an old memo sent to all the librarians in the Imperial Bureau of Libraries:

RE: THE WIZARD OF OZ. Only the specially revised edition of L. Frank Baum's classic fantasy is recommended for purchase by regional and school branches of the Imperial Library. The reason should be obvious to anyone reading the original closely. The state, in the person of the Wizard, is portrayed as fraudulent, incompetent, ineffectual, and impotent. The Lion, the Scarecrow, and the Tin Woodsman [citizens] are seen on a pilgrimage to the Wizard [the state] in quest of qualities they already possess in abundance. Conclusion: the state is supercilious.

We don't want our children exposed to that kind of thinking! In the revised version, the Wizard imbues them with Courage, Intelligence, and Heart *before* they tackle the Evil Witch, thus enabling them to succeed.

YOU CAN DEPEND ON THE IMPERIAL LIBRARY LIKE YOU DEPEND ON THE IMPERIUM!

The Economic Weather Eye

PRICE INDEX (using the 115th year of the Imperium—when the Imperial mark became mandatory legal tender—as base year of 100)	257.6
MONEY SUPPLY (M3)	3103.4
UNEMPLOYMENT LEVEL	171.1%

	Imperial Marks	Solar Credits
GOLD (Troy ounce)	933.3	134.0
Silver (Troy ounce)	41.1	6.2
Bread (1 kg. loaf)	1.15	1.70

XVII

When two coins are equal in debt-paying value but unequal in intrinsic value, the one having the lesser intrinsic value tends to remain in circulation and the other to be hoarded or exported.

Gresham's Law (original version)

Bad money drives out good.

Gresham's Law (popular version)

Mora not only refused to return to Tolive, she insisted on coming along on the next Robin Hood caper.

"Give me one good reason," she said, looking from her husband to Zack, to the Flinters, to Broohnin. "One good reason why I shouldn't go to the mint with you."

None of them wanted her along, but the non-Kyfhons objected to her presence solely on the basis that she was a woman. They had all come to know Mora well during the past week, and she had charmed every one of them, including Sayers, who was absent today. Even Broohnin's sourness mellowed when she was around. But this was man's work, and although neither Zack nor Broohnin verbalized it internally or externally, each felt that the significance of their mission was somehow diminished if a woman joined them.

The Flinters objected because she was a non-combatant, no more, no less.

LaNague's objection rested on different grounds. Her presence made him feel uncomfortable in some vague way that he found impossible to define. He felt as if he were being scrutinized, monitored, judged. Mora made him feel . . . guilty somehow. But of what?

"I'm a big girl, you know," she said when no one accepted her challenge. "And as long as firing a weapon or damaging another person is not involved, I can keep up with the best of you."

Zack and Broohnin glanced at each other. With the exception of Flint and Tolive, sexual equality was an alien concept on most outworlds. Men and women had reached the stars as equals, but women had become nest-keepers again as the overall technological level regressed on the pioneer worlds. They would soon be demanding parity with men, but there was no movement as yet. Mora knew this. She obviously chose her words to goad Zack and Broohnin, and to remind the Flinters and her husband of their heritage.

"You'll fly with me," LaNague said, bringing the dispute to a close. He knew his wife as she knew him. By now each could recognize when the other had reached an intransigent position.

"Good. When do we leave?"

"Now. We've already wasted too much time arguing. And timing is everything today."

Erv Singh had called Broohnin the day before to report that he had finally been able to place the Barsky box in a vault filled with old currency waiting to be destroyed. He mentioned that the vault was unusually full. LaNague explained the reason for that to his wife as their flitter rose into the air over Primus City.

"The one-mark note has finally been rendered obsolete by inflation; the Treasury Bureau is trying to cut expenses by phasing it out. Supply of the larger denomination bills is being upped. When the good coins started disappearing, that was an early warning sign. But now, even the most obtuse Throner should get the message that something is seriously wrong when small bills are no longer produced."

They flew toward the dying orange glow of the sun as it leaned heavily on Throne's horizon, over Imperium Park and the surrounding structures that housed the bureaucratic entrails of the Imperium itself, and then over the city's dolee zone, a sector that was expanding at an alarming rate, on to a huge clearing fifty kilometers beyond the limits of Primus City. An impregnable block of reinforced synthestone occupied the middle of that cleaning, like an iceberg floating still in a calm sea, nine tenths of its structure below the surface.

LaNague brought his craft to rest in a stand of trees on a hill overlooking the site; the second flitter followed him down. Broohnin emerged first, followed by Zack and the two Flinters. Kanya was carrying an electronic timer of Flinter design, unequaled in precision. She set it on the deck of LaNague's flitter and removed a round white disk from her belt.

"What's that?" Broohnin asked. Something in the man's voice made LaNague turn and look at him. He had worn a bored and dour expression all day. Now he was suddenly full of life and interest. Why?

"A timer," Kanya said. She did not look up, but concentrated on fitting the disk, which could now be seen to have a red button in its center, into the circular depression atop the timer.

"No . . . that." He pointed to the disk.

"That's the trigger for the Barsky box."

"Do they all look like that? The triggers, I mean."

"Yes." Kanya looked up at him. "Why do you ask?"

Broohnin suddenly realized that he was under close scrutiny from a number of sources and shrugged nervously. "Just curious, that's all." With visible effort, he pulled his eyes away from the trigger and looked at LaNague. "I still don't understand what's going to happen here. Go over it again."

"For me, too," Mora said.

"All right." LaNague complied for his wife's benefit more than Broohnin's, who he was sure knew exactly what was going to happen. He wondered what was cooking in that bright but twisted mind now. "When activated, the Barsky box in the vault will form an unfocused temporal displacement field in a rough globe around itself. Anything encompassed by that field will be displaced exactly 1.37 nanoseconds into the past."

"That's all?" Mora said.

"That's enough. Don't forget that Throne is not only revolving on its axis and traveling around its primary; it's also moving around the galactic core along with the other star systems in this arm, while the galaxy itself is moving away from the location of the Big Bang. So it doesn't take too long for Throne to move the distance from here to Primus City."

Mora frowned briefly and chewed on her lower lip. "I'd hate to even begin the necessary calculations."

"The Flinters have formulae for it. They've been experimenting with the Barsky apparatus as a means of transportation." LaNague smiled. "Imagine listing an ETA at point B *before* the time of departure from point A. Unfortunately, they've been unable to bring anything through alive. But they're working on it."

"But why the timer?" Mora asked.

"Because the box has to be activated at the precise nanosecond that Throne's axial and rotational attitudes come into proper alignment. The Flinters have it pin-pointed at sometime between 15.27 and 15.28 today. No human reflex can be trusted to send the signal at just the right instant, so an electronic counter is employed."

Mora still looked dubious. She pulled her husband away from the flitter.

"It'll work," LaNague told her, glancing back over his shoulder as he moved and watching Broohnin, whose eyes were fixed again on the white trigger mechanism.

"What if there's someone in the vault?" Mora asked when they were out of earshot.

"There won't be," LaNague assured her. "The workday is over down there. Everybody's gone."

"No guards?"

"A few."

"How do you know where they'll be when you activate the Barsky device? What if one of them gets sucked into the field?"

"Mora," LaNague said, trying to keep his tone even, "we've only got one device and it has to be activated soon . . . tonight."

"Why? Why can't we wait until we're sure no one's going to get killed down there?"

"Because the money in that vault is tagged for destruction. And when they burn it, they're going to burn the Barsky box along with it. We only have one Barsky box!"

"Then let's wait until later . . . just to be sure."

"We'll never be sure!" Impatience had passed into exasperation. "We can't see inside the vault, so we can't be sure it's unoccupied. And the device has to be activated between 15.27 and 15.28 tonight or not at all, because proper alignment won't occur again for another three days!"

"Is it so important then? Do you have to get this money out? Why not just forget about it this time."

LaNague shook his head. "I need one more Robin Hood episode to keep his reputation up and his name before the public eye. And with all currency shipments so heavily guarded now, this is the only way I can make one last big strike."

Mora's voice rose to a shout. *"But somebody could be in that vault!"* The others by the flitter turned to look at her.

"Then that's too bad," LaNague said, keeping his own voice low. "But there's nothing I can do about it." He turned and strode back toward the flitter. It had happened as he knew it would—Mora was interfering in his work. It hadn't taken her long to get involved. For a while it had actually seemed that she would keep to herself and stay out of his way. But no—that would have been too much to ask! The more he thought about it, the more it enraged him. What right did she—?

He was half the distance to the flitter when he realized that there was a sick cold sphere centered in the heat of his anger, and it was screaming for him to stop. Reluctantly—very reluctantly—he listened. Perhaps there was another way after all.

As he approached Broohnin and the Flinters, he said, "I want you to take the other flitter and strafe the entrance to the mint."

"With hand blasters?" Broohnin asked, startled.

LaNague nodded. "You're not out to cause damage, but to create a diversion—to pull the inside guards toward the entrance and away from the vaults. One pass is all you should need, then head for Primus as fast as you can. By the time they can mobilize pursuit, you should be lost in the dolee sector."

"Count me out," Broohnin said. "That's crazy!"

LaNague put on what he felt was his nastiest sneer. "That figures," he said in a goading tone. "You rant and rave about how everything in my plan is too soft and too gentle, but when we give you a chance for some action, you balk. I should have known. I'll ask the Doc. Maybe he'll—"

Broohnin grabbed LaNague's arm. "No you don't! You don't replace me with a teacher!" He turned to the Flinters. "Let's go."

As the flitter rose and made a wide circle to the far side of the mint, LaNague felt an arm slip around his back. "Thank you," Mora said.

"We'll see if this works," he said, not looking at her.

"It will."

"It had better." He felt utterly cold toward Mora. Perhaps she had been right, but that did not lessen his resentment of her interference.

The flitter with Broohnin and the Flinters was out of sight now on the other side of the mint, gaining momentum in full throttle. Suddenly, it flashed into view, a silver dot careening over the barracks straight toward the squat target structure. Alarms were already going off down there, LaNague knew, sending Imperial Guardsmen to their defense positions, and the mint guards into the corridors as the vaults within began to cycle closed automatically. There were small flashes briefly brightening the entranceway to the mint, and then the flitter was gone, racing toward Primus City and anonymity.

LaNague checked the time—it was 15.26. He pressed the trigger in the center of the white disk, arming it. The timer would do the rest.

When the precise nanosecond for firing arrived, the timer pulsed the trigger, which in turn sent a signal to the Barsky box in the vault, activating it. The money in the vault, along with small amounts of synthestone from the walls and floors, abruptly disappeared. The package traveled 1.37 nanoseconds into the past and appeared in the air over Primus City at the exact locus the treasury vault was destined to occupy 1.37 nanoseconds from then.

Ω

". . . although officials are more tight-lipped than usual, it does appear that the 'money monsoon' that occurred earlier this evening consisted of obsolete currency stolen from the vaults of the mint itself. From what we can determine, the mint was briefly harassed by a lone flitter in the early evening hours; guards reported that the money was in the vault before the incident, and discovered to be missing when the vaults were reopened approximately an hour after the flitter had escaped. The particular vault in question is thirty meters underground. The walls were not breached and no tunnel has been found. The rain of one-mark notes carried no white calling cards this time, but there is no doubt in anyone's mind that Robin Hood has struck again. The Bureau of the Treasury has promised a full and thorough investigation of the matter . . ."

Ω

"Money, money, money!" Mora was saying as they sat in the apartment, watching Radmon Sayers on the vid. "That's all you seem to care about in this revolution. There's more to a government—good or bad—than money!"

"Not much. In any government, dictatorial or representational, the politicos spend 95 per cent of their time taking money from one place and shuttling it to another. They extort money from the citizenry and then go about the tasks of passing bills to appropriate to this group, grant to that group, build here, renovate there."

"But legislation for freedom, rights—"

"That's all decided at the outset, when the government is formed. That's when there's the most freedom; from then on it's a continuous process of whittling down the individual's franchise and increasing the state's. There are exceptions, of course, but they're rare enough to qualify as aberrations. Look back in the Imperium: one, perhaps two, pieces of legislation a year are involved purely with extension or abridgment—usually the latter—of freedom. What the public never realizes is that it really loses its freedoms in the countless appropriations passed every day to create or continue the countless committees and bureaus that monitor human activities, to make countless rules to protect us from ourselves. And they all require funding."

"Money again."

"Correct! Keep a government poor and you'll keep it off your back. Without the necessary funds, it can't afford to harass you. Give it lots of money and it will find ways to spend it, invariably to your eventual detriment. Let it control the money supply and all the stops are out: it will soon control you! I shouldn't have to tell you this."

"But what of culture?" Mora spread her fingers in a gesture of frustration. "Whatever culture the outworlds were beginning to develop is dying now. What are you going to do about that? How does that fit into your plan? How're you going to tie that into economics?"

"I'm not even going to try. I don't want an outworld culture! That connotes homogenization, something the Imperium has been attempting to do. If everyone is the same, it's much easier for a central government to make rules for its subjects. I don't want one outworld culture—I want many. I want human beings to stretch themselves to the limit in every direction. I don't want anyone telling anyone else how to live, how to think, what to wear. I want diversity. It's the only way we'll keep from stagnating as a race. It almost happened to us on Earth. If we had remained on that one little planet, we'd be a sorry lot by now, if any humans at all still existed. But you can't have diversity in a controlled society. If you control the economy, you control lives; you have to bring everyone down to the lowest common denominator. You have to weed out the oddballs, stifle the innovators. Do that on all the outworlds and pretty soon you'll have your 'outworld culture.' But would you want to participate?"

Mora hesitated before answering, and in the interval the vidphone chimed. LaNague took the call in the next room. He recognized Seph Wolverton's face as it filled the screen.

"News from the probe fleet," he said without salutation. "Contact made halfway to the Perseus arm. Hostile. Very hostile from the report."

LaNague felt his stomach lurch. "Who knows?"

"Nobody except you, me, and the man who decoded the subspace call, and he's with us."

LaNague sighed with minimal relief. It was a bad situation, but it could have been much worse. "All right. Send a message back as pre-arranged. He's to return directly to Throne, with no further contact until he's in the star system, and even then he's only to identify his craft and answer no questions until he is picked up by an orbital shuttle and brought down for debriefing. See that the probe's message is erased from the com computer. No one is to know the contents of that message. Clear?"

Wolverton nodded. "Clear."

LaNague cut the connection and turned to see Mora staring at him from the doorway.

"Peter, what's the matter? I've never seen you so upset."

"The probes have made contact with a hostile alien culture out toward the Perseus arm."

"So?"

"If word of this gets to Metep and Haworth and the others, they'll have the one lever they need to keep themselves in power and maybe even save their skins: war."

"You're not serious!"

"Of course I am! Look through history—it's a tried and true method for economically beleaguered regimes to save themselves. It works! Hostile aliens would push humans together out of fear."

"But hostile aliens are not a war."

LaNague smiled grimly. "That could be arranged. Again: not the first time it's happened. All Metep and the Council of Five would have to do is send a 'trade envoy' with a half-dozen cargo ships out toward the Perseus arm, ostensibly to open peaceful relations. If these aliens are as aggressive as the contact probe pilot seems to think, they'll either try to take possession of whatever enters their sphere of influence, or will feel directly threatened by the approach of human craft—either way, there's bound to be bloodshed. And that's all you need. 'The monsters are coming! They ambushed unarmed cargo ships in interstellar space. Guard your wives and children.' All of a sudden we've got to put aside our petty differences, close ranks, and defend humanity. The Imperium may be rotten and teetering, but it's the only government we've got right now, so let's not switch horses in midstream . . . And so on." He shut off the torrent of words with visible effort.

Mora stared at her husband. "I've never seen you so bitter, Peter. What's happened to you these past three years?"

"A lot, I suppose." He sighed. "Sometimes I wonder if I'm still me. But it's opposition to the men who are the Imperium—and after all, the Imperium doesn't have a life of its own; it's just people—that lets you see that there's not much beneath their reach. They'll go to any lengths, including interstellar war, just to save their careers and their places in history. The lives lost, the trauma to future generations, the chaos that would follow . . . they wouldn't care. It would all fall on the shoulders of the next generation. They'd be out of it by then."

He lapsed briefly into silence, and finally came to a decision. "I'm going to send Boedekker his signal. It's a little earlier in the game than I had planned, but I really don't have much choice. I want things in pieces by the time that pilot gets back. And even then, I must see to it that no one connected with the Imperium learns about the aliens in the Perseus arm."

"It's almost Year Day," Mora said softly.

"For Tolivians, yes. The Year of the Dragon begins in a few days. I suppose it will be a Dragon year for Throners, too . . . they'll be feeling his fiery breath soon. Very soon."

The Year of the Dragon

XVIII

> . . . no government, so called, can reasonably be trusted for a moment, or reasonably supposed to have honest purposes in view, any longer than it depends wholly on voluntary support.
>
> from NO TREASON by *Lysander Spooner*

"Good evening, this is Radmon Sayers. It does not seem possible that there could be anyone watching right now who is not already aware of the catastrophic events that have rocked the length and breadth of Occupied Space today. But just in case someone has been unconscious since the early hours of the morning, I will recap:

"The Imperial mark has crashed. After holding fairly steady for years at an exchange rate of two marks per Solar credit, the Imperial mark began a steady decline at 5.7 hours Throne time. As most of you know, the Interstellar Currency Exchange never closes, but all this trading in Imperial marks was suspended at 17.2 hours Throne time this evening when it hit a terrifying low of eighty marks per Solar credit. There is no telling how far its official trade value would have fallen had not trade been suspended.

"The precipitating factors in the selling panic have not yet been pin-pointed. All that is known at this time is that virtually every brokerage firm involved with the Exchange received calls this morning from multiple clients, all with sizable accounts in Imperial marks, informing them to sell every mark they possessed, no matter what the going rate happened to be. And so billions of marks were dumped on the market at once. The brokers say that their clients were quite insistent: they wanted no further Imperial marks in their portfolio and were willing to take losses to divest themselves of them. The Exchange authorities have promised a prompt and thorough investigation into the possibility that a conspiracy has been afoot to manipulate the exchange rate for profit. So far, however, no one has been found who has made a windfall profit from the crash.

"In an extemporaneous speech on the vid networks, Metep VII assured the people of Throne and all the other outworlds that there is nothing to fear. That all we can do is keep calm and have faith in ourselves and in our continued independence from Earth. 'We've had hard times before and have weathered them,' Metep said. 'We shall weather them again . . .' "

Ω

"Was Eric Boedekker behind all this?" Doc Zack asked as LaNague darkened the holovid and Sayers' face faded from the globe. The inner circle was seated around the vid set in LaNague's apartment.

"Yes. He's been selling everything he owns for the past three years or so, and converting the credit to marks. Thousands of accounts under thousands of names were started during that period, with instructions to the brokers to buy Imperial marks every time their value dipped."

"And thereby creating an artificial floor on their value!" Zack said.

"Exactly."

"But for all Eric Boedekker's legendary wealth," Zack said, "I don't see how even he could buy enough Imperial marks to cause today's crash. I mean, there were hundreds of billions of marks sold today, and as many more waiting to be disposed of as soon as trading on them opens again. He's rich, but nobody's *that* rich."

"He had help, although the people involved didn't know they were helping him. You see, Boedekker made sure to call public attention every time he sold off one of his major assets. His financial peers thought he was crazy, but they kept a close eye on him. He had pulled off some major coups in the past and they wanted to know exactly what he was doing with all that accumulated credit. And they found out. You can't keep too many things secret down there on Earth, and the ones who really wanted to know found out that he was quietly, anonymously, buying up Imperial marks whenever he could. So they started buying up marks, too . . . just to be safe. Maybe Boedekker knew something they didn't; maybe something was cooking in the outworlds that would bring the Imperial mark up to trading parity with the Solar credit. I sent him the 'sell' signal last week and he's been getting ready ever since."

"Ah, I see!" Zack said. "And when *he* dumped—"

"—*they* dumped. From there it was a cascade effect. Everybody who was holding Imperial marks wanted to get rid of them. But nobody wanted to buy them. The Imperial mark is now worth one fortieth of its value yesterday, and would probably be less than a hundredth if trading had not been suspended. It's still overpriced."

"Brilliant!" Doc Zack was shaking his head in admiration. "Absolutely brilliant!"

"What's so brilliant?" Broohnin said from his reclining position on the floor. For a change, he had been listening intently to the conversation. "Is this the spectacular move you've promised us? So what? What's it done for us?"

Zack held up a hand as LaNague started to reply. "Let me answer him. I think I see the whole picture now, but correct me if I'm wrong." He turned to Broohnin. "What our friend from Tolive has done, Den, is turn every inhabitant of Throne into a potential revolutionary. All the people who have come to the conclusion that the Imperium is inimical to their own interests and the interests of future generations of outworlders have been constrained to go on supporting the Imperium because their incomes, either wholly or in part, have depended on the Imperium. That is no longer a consideration. The money the Imperium has been buying their loyalty with has now been reduced to its true value: nothing. The velvet coverings are off; the cold steel of the chains is now evident."

"But is that fair?" Mora said. She and the Flinters had been silent until now. "It's like cutting off a flitter's power in mid-air. People are going to be hurt."

"It would have happened with or without us," LaNague told her brusquely. "If not now, then later. Boedekker has only allowed me to say when; he didn't really change the eventual outcome."

"And don't forget," Zack said more gently, "that the people getting hurt bear a great deal of the blame. They've allowed this to go on for decades. The people of Throne are especially guilty—they've allowed the Imperium to make too many decisions for them, run too much of their lives, buy them off with more and more worthless fiat money. Now the bill's come due. And they've got to pay."

"Right," LaNague said. "This could not have happened if outworlders had refused to allow the Imperium to debase the Imperial mark. If the mark had had something real backing it up—if it had represented a given amount of precious metal or another commodity, and had been redeemable for that, if it had been something more than fancy printed *keerni* paper, then there would have been no crash, no matter how many Imperial marks Eric Boedekker bought and dumped on the Interstellar Currency Exchange."

"Why not?" Broohnin said.

"Because they would have real value, intrinsic value. And that's not subject to much speculation. People have been speculating in the mark for years now, watching for fluctuations in exchange rates, taking a little profit here and there, but knowing all the time that it really had no intrinsic value, only what had been decided on by the money lenders and traders."

"But what does Boedekker get out of all this?" Zack asked. "He doesn't seem like the type to give up his fortune just to ruin the Imperial mark."

"He gets revenge," LaNague said, and explained about Liza Kirowicz. "With no direct descendant to hand his fortune to, he lost all desire to keep adding to it. And don't worry—I'm sure he's got plenty of credit left in his Earth accounts, plus I'm sure he probably sold a good number of marks short before the crash."

"But I still don't see where all the Robin Hood business ties in," Broohnin said, combing his fingers through the coiled blackness of his beard. "One doesn't lead to the other."

"There's an indirect connection," LaNague replied. "We'll let the people of Throne find out what's really happened to them, and then we'll offer them a choice: Metep or Robin Hood."

Ω

"What are you going to *do*?" Metep VII wandered in a reverberating semi-circle around the east end of the conference table, alternately wringing his hands and rubbing them together. His perfect face framed eyes that were red-rimmed and hunted-looking. "I'm ruined! I'm not only broke, I'm now destined to go down in history as the Metep who killed the mark! What are we going to do?"

"I don't know," Haworth said softly from his seat. Metep stopped his pacing and stared at him, as did everyone else in the room. It was the first time they could remember Daro Haworth without a contingency plan.

"You don't know?" Metep said, stumbling toward him, panic flattening and spreading his facial features. "How can you say that? You're *supposed* to know!"

Haworth held Metep's gaze. "I never imagined anything like this happening. Neither did anyone else here." His eyes scanned the room, finding no sympathy, but no protest either. "It was a future possibility, a probability within a decade if we found no new markets for outworld goods. But no one could have predicted this. No one!"

"The Earthies did it," Krager said. "They're trying to take over the outworlds again."

Haworth glanced at the elderly head of the Treasury and nodded. "Yes, I think that's the approach we'll have to take. We'll blame it on Earth. Should work . . . after all, the Exchange is based on Earth. We can say the Imperial mark has been the victim of a vicious manipulation in a cynical, calculated attempt by Sol System to reassert control over us. Yes. That will help get the anger flowing in some direction other than ours."

"All right," Cumberland said, shifting his bulk uneasily in his chair. "That's the official posture. But what really happened? I think that's important to know. Did Earth do this to us?"

Haworth's head shake was emphatic. "No. First of all, the outworlds have fallen into debt to Earth over the past few years, and the credit has always been tallied in marks—which means that our debt to them today is only 2 or 3 per cent of what it was yesterday. Earth lost badly on the crash. And second, I don't think anyone in the Sol System government has the ingenuity to dream up something like this, or the courage to carry it through."

"You think it was just a freak occurrence?"

"I'm not sure *what* I think. It's all so far beyond the worst nightmare I've ever had . . ." Haworth's voice trailed off.

"In the meantime," Krager said sarcastically, "while you sit there in a blue funk, what about the outworlds—Throne in particular? All credit has been withdrawn from us. There's been no formal announcement, but the Imperium is now considered bankrupt throughout Occupied Space."

"The first thing to do is get more marks into circulation," Haworth said. "Immediately. Push the duplicators to the limit. Big denominations. We've got to keep some sort of commerce going."

"Prices will soar!" Krager said.

"Prices are soaring as we talk! Anyone holding any sort of useful commodity now isn't going to part with it for Imperial marks unless he's offered a lot of them, or unless he's offered something equally valuable in trade. So unless you want Throne back on a barter economy by week's end, you'd better start pouring out the currency."

"The agrarian worlds are practically on barter now," Cumberland said. "They'll want no part—"

"Let the agrarian worlds fall into the Galactic Core for all I care!" Haworth shouted, showing emotion for the first time since the meeting had begun. "They're useless to us now. There's only one planet we have to worry about, and that's Throne. Forget all the other outworlds! They can't reach us, and the sooner we put them out of our minds and concentrate our salvage efforts on Throne, the better we'll be! Let the farmers out there go on scratching their dirt. They can't hurt us. But the people here on Throne, and in Primus City especially . . . they can cause us real trouble."

"Civil disorder," Metep said, nodding knowingly, almost thankfully. Riots he could understand, cope with. But all this economics talk . . . "You expect major disturbances?"

"I expect disturbances—just how major they'll be depends on what we do in the next few weeks. I want to try to defuse any riots before they start; but once they start, I want plenty of manpower at our disposal." He turned to Metep. "We'll need an executive order from you, Jek, ordering withdrawal of all Imperial garrisons from all the other outworlds. We can't afford to keep them supplied out there anyway, and I want them all gathered tight around us if things get nasty."

There was a chorus of agreement from all present.

Haworth glanced up and down the table. "It's going to be a long, hot summer, gentlemen. Let's try to hold things together until one of the probe ships makes contact with the aliens in the Perseus arm. That could be our only hope."

"Any word yet?" Metep said.

"None."

"What if we never hear anything from them?" Cumberland asked. "What if they never come back?"

"That could be useful, too."

Ω

"Fifty marks for a loaf of bread? That's outrageous!"

"Wait until tomorrow if you think fifty's too much," the man said laconically. He stood with his back against a blank synthestone wall, a hand blaster at his hip, his wares—unwrapped loaves of bread—spread on a folding table before him. "Probably be fifty-five by then."

Salli Stafford felt utterly helpless, and frightened. No one had heard from Vin or any of the other probe pilots; no one at Project Perseus knew when they were coming back. Or *if* they were coming back. She was alone in Primus City and could daily see signs of decay: lengthening, widening cracks in its social foundations. She needed Vin around to tell her that everything would be all right, that he would protect her.

She needed money, too. She had read in one of *The Robin Hood Readers* that came out just after the bottom had dropped out of the mark that she should immediately pull all her money out of the bank and spend every bit of it. She didn't hesitate. Vin had grown to have unwavering faith in whoever was behind those flyers, and Salli had finally come around to believing in him, too. Especially after that long wait in their old back yard, when she had laughed at Vin's almost childish faith, and then the money had come down. She wasn't going to waste time laughing this time; she was down at the bank first thing the next morning, withdrawing everything that was left from Vin's advance for joining the probe fleet.

That had been a month ago, and it was the smartest thing she had ever done in her life. Within the first three days after the crash of the Imperial mark, fully half the banks in Primus had closed. They didn't fail—the Imperium prevented that by seeing to it that every depositor was paid the full amount of his or her account in nice, freshly minted paper marks—they simply ran out of depositors.

Salli followed up her foresight with shortsightedness that now seemed incredibly stupid. Instead of spending the entire ten thousand marks she had withdrawn on commodities, as *The Robin Hood Reader* had suggested, she waffled and spent only half. The rest she hid in the apartment. She now saw the error of that—prices had risen anywhere between 1,000 and 2,000 per cent in the intervening weeks. Steri-packed vegetables and staples she could have picked up for five marks then—and she had considered that exorbitant—were now going for fifty or sixty, with people thankful they could find them. It was crazy! The four thousand marks she had hidden away then would have bought her fifty thousand marks' worth of food at today's prices. She cursed herself for not following Robin Hood's advice to the letter. Everyone in Primus now knew from personal experience what he had said back then. Nobody held onto cash any more; it was spent as soon as it was in hand. The only things worth less were Food Vouchers . . . retailers laughed when you brought them in.

Salli was afraid. What was going to happen when her money ran out? She had called Project Perseus but they had said they could not release Vin's second fiften thousand until he had returned. She shrugged as she stood there on the street. What was fifteen thousand any more? Nothing!

"You gonna buy, lady?" the man asked, his eyes constantly shifting up and down the street. His legs straddled a large box of currency and he mentally took the measure of every passer-by.

"Will you take anything else?"

His eyes narrowed. "Gold, silver, platinum if you've got any. I can let you take it out in trade or I can give you a good bundle of marks depending on what you've got."

"I—don't have any." She didn't know what had made her ask. She didn't really want bread. It was being made out in the hinterlands on isolated farms and there were no preservatives being used because there were none to be had. Bread like that went stale too fast to be worth fifty marks to a woman living alone.

He looked her up and down, his gaze seeming to penetrate her clothing. "Don't bother to offer me anything else you've got," he sneered. "I've got more offers for that every day than I could handle in a lifetime."

Tears sprang into Salli's eyes as she felt her face redden. "I didn't mean that!"

"Then why did you ask?"

Salli couldn't answer. She had been thinking about the future—the near future, when her money ran out. How was she to get by then? Her employer had told her he couldn't give her a raise, that his business had fallen off to the point where he might have to close up shop and go home.

As she turned away, the man called after her. "Hey, look, I'm sorry, but I've got a family of my own to feed. I've got to fly out and pick this up on my own. The freight unions aren't running till they get more money, you know that."

Salli knew all that. The vid was full of it—bad news and more bad news. Shipping of goods was at a standstill. Employers were unable to raise wages quickly enough to keep their employees at subsistence level. Salli glanced back over her shoulder and saw that the bread seller had already forgotten her, and was now busy dickering with a man holding up a handful of fresh vegetables.

What was she going to do? Nothing in her life had prepared her for anything like this—she was slowly coming to the realization that her life had prepared her for little more than child rearing. No skill beyond rudimentary mathematics was required of her in the part-time job she was barely holding onto; she could be replaced in minutes. All her childhood had been spent learning to be dependent on men—her father, her brothers, and then Vin. Which was fine until now, when everything was falling apart, and her father and brothers were on the other side of the planet with no way to get to her or she to them. She was suddenly on her own, scared to death, and helpless.

Why am I like this? she thought, then snorted cynically. Why is the world like this? Why isn't Vin's money worth anything?

Vin—the name conjured up a vision of her husband's earnest face, and the worry lines that seemed to have become a part of his features over the past few years. She had never understood what had been plaguing him all this time. He had always acted as a buffer between her and the real world, taking the blows, absorbing them, and allowing only a few vibrations to disturb her. Now he was gone, and so was her insulation. And now she knew first hand the malaise of impotency that had so afflicted his psyche. She felt trapped in a world she had not made. On the surface it was physically similar, but everything had changed. Neither she nor anyone in the street around her had any control over what was happening to them. Powerless, all of them.

And yet, we're to blame, she thought. No one out here made this world, but they all sat around idly or looked the other way while it was being made for them. It could have been stopped way back when, before things got too pushed out of shape, too far out of line. But it was too late now. Salli had an eerie feeling that giant forces were swinging back into balance again, impervious now to whatever was thrown up to block their return.

But she would cope. Anger would help her. Anger at the Imperium for causing this. Anger at herself and her society for leaving her so ill-equipped to cope with this or any other challenge outside the security of the nest. How many other women were caught in her situation right now? How many were losing the fight?

Salli wouldn't lose. She was learning fast. Today she would spend every last one of the remaining four thousand marks before they depreciated further. But not all at once. A little here, a little there, with frequent trips back to the apartment, hiding the purchases within her garments while in transit. It wouldn't do to have someone get the idea that she was stocking up on food; that was a sure way of inviting robbery. No, she would buy whatever was available, whatever was the least perishable, and then keep to her apartment, venturing out only for work and for absolute necessities. Yes, Salli would survive and hold out until things got better and Vin got back . . . she was somehow sure the latter would lead to the former.

And if things ever did get better—she set her mouth in a determined line—something would have to be done to see that this never happened again. She wanted a family, but no child deserved to grow up and face something like this.

Never again! she thought. This must never happen again!

Ω

LaNague held his position until the recorder cycled off, then rose and stretched. "There. That ought to do it." He glanced at Radmon Sayers, who said nothing as he dismantled the vid recorder. The warehouse was empty except for the two of them. "What's the matter, Rad?"

"Nothing," Sayers replied, removing the recorded spool and

handing it to LaNague. "It's just that I don't think this will work."

"And why not?" LaNague snapped. "They have to be presented with a choice, and in order to make that choice they've got to know what their alternatives are."

"I still think you could go about this differently. You're placing too much emphasis on these recordings. And frankly, I'm not impressed."

LaNague bit back a terse reply. It angered him to be questioned at this point. With effort he kept his tone measured. "Do you still doubt me? I had to put up with enough of that from you and the rest before the floor fell out from under the mark. And then all of a sudden I was 'brilliant,' a 'genius.' When are you going to learn that I have been planning this, preparing it for years. I've had a lot more time to think things out than you or Zack or Metep or anyone on the Council of Five. I've out-thought them all. I know what I'm doing."

"I don't doubt that," Sayers replied. "You've proved it over and over again. But that doesn't make you infallible. That doesn't mean you're immune to an error of judgment, a miscalculation, just like the rest of us. Are you beyond a second opinion?"

"Of course I'm—"

"Then here's mine: I think the final phase of your plan is too personally dangerous to you, is subject to too many variables, and rests precariously on the persuasive power of these recordings . . . which, in my opinion as a professional in this area, is slight."

"I appreciate your concern," LaNague said softly after a short pause.

Sayers read his expression. "But you're not going to modify your plans, are you?"

LaNague shook his head. "I'm going to have to go with my record, and that's been too accurate so far to ignore." He reached within his vest and withdrew a fifty-mark note. "Look at that!" he said, handing it to Sayers.

"What about it?" He glanced down at the face and could see nothing of any great significance.

"Turn it over."

The reverse side was blank. "Counterfeit!" Sayers cried.

"No. That's the way the mint is releasing them. Not only is the supply of *keerni* paper getting short, but so's the dye. It's the ultimate ignominy. And fifty marks is now the lowest denomination. It's a mere three months since the crash and already the mark is approximately its true value: that of the paper it's printed on! Three months! None of you believed me when I told you things would happen this fast, so I don't expect any of you to believe me now." He held up a vid spool. "But this will work—I guarantee it!"

"And if not?"

"It will! That's the end of discussion on the matter. And remember: Mora and the others are to know nothing of this next step until it's past the point of no return. Especially Mora!"

Sayers was about to add further comment when Broohnin's abrupt entry through a side door cut him off.

"Just heard from Seph Wolverton over at the Project Perseus Comm Center," Broohnin said as soon as he caught sight of them. "That probe ship just popped into the system and is heading for Throne. Seems to be following instructions to the letter."

LaNague cursed silently. If only he had another month! The Imperium would be gone by then and there would be no one left in power to manipulate the hostile aliens in Perseus into a war threat. But that wasn't to be, and it was probably just as well that the probe returned now when he was able to deal with it personally, rather than leave it to the others. Their narrow vision was disconcerting, their lack of faith discouraging. If left to handle the probe pilot alone, they'd probably botch it.

"All right," LaNague said through a sigh. "Tell Wolverton to do all he can to keep the ship's presence in the system a secret. It can't remain a secret forever. The closer it moves, the more monitors it will alert. But we, at least, will have the most time to prepare."

"Why don't we just find a way to blow it out of the sky?" Broohnin said with a grin. "That'll solve the problem very nicely, I think."

LaNague paused for an instant, horrified by the realization that the very same solution had already occurred to him. He had discarded it, naturally, but the idea that his mind might even briefly follow a line of thought similar to Den Broohnin's was chilling.

"We have to get to him first," LaNague said, ostensibly deaf to Broohnin's suggestion. "We have to meet him, spirit him away, and see to it that nobody from the Imperium knows where to find him. After there's no more Imperium, he can tell all of Occupied Space what he found out toward the Perseus arm."

"That sounds like a tall order," Sayers said.

"Don't worry," LaNague told him. "I'll see that it's done. Just leave it to me. I'll take care of everything. As usual."

Wafting briefly through his mind as he spoke was the thought that he sounded like a stranger to himself. He was acting like a pompous ass, impatient, intolerant of any challenge to his notions, of any opinion that deviated from his own. The thought became a question: were these symptoms of some occult malignancy devouring him from within, endangering not only himself, but the revolution and all who had worked for it? He brushed it away like an annoying insect. Nonsense. The revolution was secure. Victory was at hand. Nothing could stop him now. Nothing!

FINAL ISSUE

THE ROBIN HOOD READER

Don't Recall Metep!

There is talk all over Throne of organizing a recall of Metep and his mob. Don't participate! Petitions are being passed. Don't sign them!

The "free election" resulting from a successful recall movement will offer you three or four clones of Metep VII. They'll have different names, different faces, different genotypes, but once in office they'll follow the same stupid, irresponsible, reckless policies that have brought the outworlds to their present state.

DO NOT VOTE!!! As presently set up, it's a meaningless franchise even if the votes are counted with scrupulous accuracy. Because nowhere on the ballot is there a place for you to indicate your dissatisfaction with *all* the candidates. A ballot means nothing, is an utter fraud, unless you can say "None of the above."

Don't recall Metep . . .

Recall the Imperium!

The Economic Weather Eye

PRICE INDEX (using the 115th year of the Imperium—when the Imperial mark became mandatory legal tender—as base year of 100)	12,792.4
MONEY SUPPLY (M3)	167,322.1
UNEMPLOYMENT LEVEL	31.0%

	Imperial Marks	Solar Credits
GOLD (Troy ounce)	21,500.2	133.3
Silver (Troy ounce)	1,320.7	6.2
Bread (1 kg. loaf)	51.0	1.71

XIX

The Paternalistic State does give its people a sense of security. But a snug, secure populace tends to resist movement—especially *forward* movement.

from THE SECOND BOOK OF KYFHO

From this far out, Throne looked like any other Earth-class planet: blue, brown, swirled with white. Not too impressive, but it was home. And Salli was there. Vincen Stafford wondered what was going on planetside. Something was wrong, that was certain. He didn't know what it was, and he didn't know how big it was, but something tricky was going on. How else to explain the crazy orders he had received?

Part one of the instructions had been logical—return directly to Throne at top speed, stop for nothing; use tight beam to signal comm center immediately upon arrival in Throne System. No problem. That's what he had expected to be told, and was exactly what he wanted to do. One encounter with the Tarks was quite enough, thank you.

The remaining instructions were the crazy ones. After notifying the comm center of his presence in the system, he was to proceed with all haste to Throne and establish an orbit that would pass over Throne latitude eighty degrees north and longitude ninety degrees east. At no time—this was repeated and doubly emphasized—was he to have further contact with anyone. *Anyone.* No matter who tried to contact him, he was neither to answer nor to listen. He was not to identify himself to anyone else. The Project Perseus Comm Center knew who he was and that was all that mattered. He would be met in orbit by a shuttle and taken down for debriefing.

Something was up, but he couldn't imagine what. Were they afraid he'd cause a panic down below by telling scare stories about the Tarks? They should know him better than that! Maybe they were just being careful, but the precautions seemed extraordinary. Why?

He shrugged. The orders had come from Project Perseus Comm Center . . . his boss. Not his worry. Not his to reason why. He just wanted to get his feet planted firmly on Throne, find Salli, and celebrate the bonus due him for being the contact ship . . . an extra twenty thousand marks. They could do a lot of living on that.

It would be good just to be home again.

He slipped into Throne's gravitational field on a flat trajectory early the next morning, ship's time. The retros slowed him enough to allow the delicate but intractable fingers of the planet's gravity to wrap around the ship and hold it at arm's length. He had plotted the approach carefully during the three days since his arrival in the system, and now he smiled as he made the final minor course adjustments. Perfect! The probe ship's orbit would pass right over the desired co-ordinates with hardly a second's drift. He hadn't spent all those years in navigation school for nothing!

A small blip showed on his screen. He cued the image intensifier to home in on it and . . . there it was. An orbital shuttle, rising to meet him. He upped the intensity. Funny . . . no Imperial markings. But that sort of went with all the other craziness. If the Project Perseus heads were being so secretive about his return, it wasn't all that strange to bring him down to the surface in an unmarked craft.

The comm indicator flashed again. It had been doing that repeatedly for the past day and a half. But like a good soldier, he had followed orders and steadfastly ignored it. At first there had been a strong temptation to disconnect the light, but he had decided against it. Let it flash. Who cared. He was going home.

Ω

"Still no answer from that ship?" Haworth asked.

The tiny face on the vidscreen in his hand wagged back and forth. "None, sir."

"Is there any sign that the ship may be out of control? Is the flight pattern erratic? Could the pilot be hurt?"

"If he's hurt, sir, I'd love to see him fly when he's well. The ship seems to have a definite course in mind. His communicator console could be malfunctioning, but with all the fail-safes built in, it seems unlikely, unless there's major damage. And the ship handles like an undamaged craft. I don't know what to tell you, sir."

"Why weren't we aware of his presence in the system sooner?"

"I don't know, sir."

"You're paid to know!" Haworth gritted. "What good are you if you don't know!"

The insolence in the shrug was apparent even on the minuscule screen. "Not much, I guess." His smile was insolent, too. No one seemed to have any respect any more.

"We'll find out soon enough," Haworth said, passing over the veiled insult—he'd deal with the man later. His name was Wolverton. He wouldn't forget. "Send a shuttle up there immediately and bring that pilot directly to me. I'll debrief him personally. And then we'll get to the bottom of all this."

"There's already a shuttle on the way. You should know that, sir."

Haworth felt a brief, deep chill. "Why? How should I know?"

"You sent it yourself." The man glanced down at something off screen. "I've got the message right here from the shuttle. Said it was under direct orders from you to intercept the probe in orbit and bring the pilot to you."

"I gave no such order! Stop that shuttle!"

"I don't know if we can do that, sir. It looks like it's already made contact."

"Then intercept it before it lands!" He looked at the man's laconic expression and suddenly came to a decision. "No. Never mind. I'll arrange that myself." With no warning, he broke the circuit and began punching in the code for the commander-in-chief of the Imperial Guard. If he had to scramble a fleet of interceptors, he'd do it. He had to interrogate that probe pilot!

Ω

The man who came through the lock was not with the Imperial Guard. He was dressed in Lincoln green hose, a leather jerkin, and a feathered cap. And he held a blaster.

"Quick! Through there. We're taking you down!" He spoke without moving his lips.

Stafford hesitated. "What's going—"

"Move!"

It was suddenly clear to Stafford just whom he was dealing with. The drawings had been flashed on the vid often enough: this was either Robin Hood himself or one of his Merry Men. A closer look revealed a barely perceptible shimmer along the edges of the man's form, a sure sign of a holographic disguise.

"Are you Robin Hood?" he asked, already moving toward the hatch. Despite the menacing presence of the blaster, he did not feel threatened. In fact, the blaster gave him good excuse to go along.

"You'll find out later. Hurry!"

Stafford ducked through the lock and was propelled along a narrow corridor into an even narrower cubicle with a single seat.

"Strap yourself in," the figure said. "We may have a rough ride ahead." The door slid shut and Stafford knew he was locked in. There was a jolt that signaled release of the probe from the shuttle, and increasing drag toward the rear of the cubicle as the craft picked up speed. Stafford decided to strap himself in. He had ridden many a shuttle, but could not remember any that could accelerate like this one.

Ω

"We lost them," Commander-in-chief Tinmer said flatly. There was enough of an edge of anger in his tone to warn Haworth against too much abuse. The man was looking for someone to lash out at, someone to trip his hammer. Haworth decided to let him save his wrath for the interceptor pilots who had evidently flubbed their mission. And besides, Haworth wanted the commander on his side.

"How is that possible?" he said, employing concerned disappointment to mask his growing rage at the incompetence that confronted him at every turn.

"For one thing, that shuttle was not exactly a standard model. It must have had a special drive or something because it pulled a few tricks that left our men sitting up there like hovercraft. Some of the men think it's the same craft we've chased before on suspicion of smuggling—they were never able to catch that one either. Anyway, the ship went down in the western hinterlands and we've got search teams out now. But even if we find it, there'll be no one on board."

Haworth closed his eyes in a moment of silent agony. How could this be happening to him? Everything was going wrong! He opened his eyes.

"Find that pilot! It is absolutely imperative that we contact him and find out what he knows. Get the identification number of the probe, check with the Project Perseus center to get the pilot's name and address. Track him down, bring him to me, and no more mistakes! I don't care if you have to mobilize every Imperial Guardsman under your command and send them all out beating bushes and going door to door. That man must be found!"

The commander stiffened visibly. "Everything that can be done will be done."

"See to it, Tinmer."

Daro Haworth stared at the screen after it had gone dark. He knew they would never find the pilot. The guardsmen who would be used for the search were worse than useless. Primus City and the surrounding garrisons were swollen with them; they were bored, inactive, and the less duty they were given, the less they wanted. At least they were assured of shelter and food and clothing, more than could be said for most of the civilian population now. It was costing a fortune to support them, but they had to be kept on ready . . . martial law was no longer an if, but a when. And that when was drawing nigh.

He had thought that time had come yesterday when the dolee section of Primus had its first food riot. By the Core, that had been frightening! It took him back to his student days on Earth when he had almost been caught in one of those frequent outpourings of unfocused rage. If the fellow student with him hadn't been an Earthie, and hadn't developed a sixth sense for the riots, and hadn't pulled him into a building . . . he didn't allow his imagination to venture into the possibilities of what would have happened to a well-dressed outworlder trapped in the middle of that frenzied torrent of humanity. But yesterday's riot had been broken up by a few low-flying troop transports from the garrison out by the mint, and by a few well-placed warning blasts.

Next time would not be so easy. With Food Vouchers being refused everywhere, the dolees were starving. The legislative machinery couldn't raise their allotments fast enough to keep up with prices. And with all the people on the dole now, the mint was hard-pressed to put out currency fast enough to meet the demand. Haworth had heard of runaway inflation but had never thought he'd see it. Nothing he had read could even come close to the reality, however. Nothing. It was like a grossly obese dog chasing its tail . . . futility leading to fatality.

That's why the guardsmen had to take priority. The dolees had been the big power block before with their votes, but votes were no longer important. Blasters were going to be the legislature soon, and Haworth wanted to keep the men who had them happy. Keep them happy, keep them fed, keep them ready to run around and shoot their toys to keep the mobs in line. They weren't good for much else.

They'd certainly never find that pilot. The brazenness of the abduction—if in fact it really was an abduction—along with the perfect timing and daring escape maneuvers . . . all pointed to Robin Hood. It fit his *modus operandi*. And it was clear now that Robin Hood was more than an economic gadfly and tax rebel; he was steadily revealing himself as a full-fledged revolutionary. No mere wild-eyed bomb-thrower, but a crafty conspirator who had anticipated all the ills that had befallen the Imperium and had taken advantage of them. How had he seen it coming? How had he known? Unless . . .

Ridiculous! No one man could kill the Imperial mark! Not even Robin Hood!

If only they could capture *him!* That would be a boon to the Imperium's cause! Take Robin Hood out of the picture—or even better, keep him in the picture and turn him to the Imperium's advantage—and perhaps something could be salvaged. Haworth knew he'd like to sit down and have a long discussion with Robin Hood, whoever he was . . . find out where he was getting his funds, what his final goals were. It would be the most fascinating conversation he had ever had in his life, he was certain. And after it was over, it would be an even greater pleasure to kill Robin Hood.

Ω

"Are you Robin Hood? I mean, *the* Robin Hood?"

LaNague smiled, warmed by the glow of awe and open admiration in the other man's face. "We never really decided who was actually Robin Hood. It's been a group effort, really."

"But you seem to be in charge. Was the Robin Hood idea yours?"

"Well, yes."

"Then you're him." The pilot thrust out his hand. "I'm proud to meet you."

LaNague grasped and shook the proffered hand in the age-old ceremony of greeting and good will, then watched the probe pilot as he walked around in a tight circle, taking in the interior details of the Angus Black warehouse. The man was short, slight, and dark, with an appealing boyish face, now filled with wonder.

"So this is the center of operations . . . this is where you plan all those raids and put out *The Robin Hood Reader* . . . never thought I'd ever see it." He turned to LaNague. "But why am I here?"

LaNague put a hand on his shoulder and guided him toward the back office. "To keep you out of Haworth's hands. Once he gets hold of you he'll turn your information into a war scare to keep the out-worlds in line behind the Imperium. And especially to keep the people of Throne looking to the Imperium as protector from whatever might be coming out of the sky, rather than as culprit for all the misery they're suffering. We can't allow that to happen. Things are too close to the end point."

Stafford's mouth opened to reply as he entered the back office ahead of LaNague, and remained open but silent when he saw the occupants of the room. The two Merry Men who had shuttled him down from his probe ship had retreated to this office soon after depositing him in the warehouse. They were gone now, replaced by two black-robed figures.

"Flinters!" Stafford squinted his eyes to detect a telltale shimmer along their outlines.

"Those aren't holosuits," LaNague told him. He was watching Stafford's reactions closely. "Does it bother you that Robin Hood is associated with Flinters?"

Stafford hesitated, then: "Not really. It shows you mean business . . . that you aren't just playing games and looking for attention." He finally tore his eyes from Kanya and Josef and looked at LaNague. "Does this mean that I'm a prisoner?"

"A guest," LaNague said. "You'll be kept comfortable and well treated for the next few weeks, but we must keep you out of Haworth's hands."

Stafford's features slackened. "But I won't tell him anything! If you say he's going to use the information to keep himself in power, I'll see that he doesn't get it."

"I'm afraid you can't guarantee that," LaNague said with a weary smile. "Haworth knows you know *something*, and a simple injection is all it will take to have you answering in minute detail every question he asks. I know you may mean well, but Haworth is quite ruthless."

"But my wife—"

"We'll bring her here and set up quarters for the two of you. We'll do anything we can to make your stay as pleasant as possible."

"But I *must* stay," Stafford said. There seemed to be a catch in his voice. He turned away and slumped into a chair, staring at the floor.

"You all right?" LaNague asked.

Stafford's voice was low. "For some reason, I thought things were going to be different. When I saw Merry Men operating the shuttle, I figured Metep and all the rest were on the way out, that things were going to be different now. Better. But they're not. And they never will be, will they?"

"I don't understand."

"I mean, you're going to set yourself up as another Metep, aren't you?"

"Of course not!"

"Then let me go home."

"I can't. You don't seem to understand that I—"

"All I understand," Stafford said, rising to his feet and gesturing angrily, "is that I had it better under Metep VII! I could walk the streets. I could sleep in my home. I can't do that now!"

"You wouldn't be able to do it if Haworth found you, either," LaNague replied. "Think of that."

"The only thing I'm thinking is that I'm a prisoner and you're my jail keeper. Which makes you no better than anyone else in the Imperium. In fact, it makes you worse!"

The words struck LaNague like so many blows. He mentally fought the implications, but finally had to accept them: he had put aside everything he believed in, his entire heritage, in order to further the revolution.

Above all else: Kyfho . . . Adrynna's words came back to him . . . *forget Kyfho in your pursuit of victory over the enemy, and you will become the enemy . . . worse than the enemy, for he doesn't know he is capable of anything better.*

"The enemy . . . me," he muttered, feeling weak and sick. Stafford looked at him questioningly. "You wouldn't understand," he told him. He glanced at Kanya and Josef and saw sympathy there, but no help. It was his battle, one that could only be won alone.

So close . . . so close to victory that victory itself had become his cause. How had he let that happen? Was this what power did to you? It was horrifying. He had always felt himself immune to that sort of lure . . . above it. Instead, he had placed himself above all others, ready and willing to subject their personal desires to his ultimate vision—the very reason for which he so loathed the Imperium!

When had he begun to yield? He couldn't say. The onset had been so insidious he had never noticed the subtle changes in perspective. But he should have realized something was wrong that day by the mint when he had been willing to risk the lives of some of the guards inside rather than delay activating the Barsky box. Since when had a Robin Hood caper meant more than a human life? He should have known then. He was embracing the "can't make an omelet without breaking eggs" attitude that had brought the outworlds to the brink of ruin. Ends had never justified means for him in the past. Why had he let them do so now?

If not for Mora that day, he might have killed someone. And life was what his whole revolution was about . . . letting life grow, allowing it to expand unhindered, keeping it free. The revolution he had originally envisioned was for everyone on all the outworlds, not just a few. And if his revolution was to be everyone's, it had to be for the men in the Imperial Guard, too. They had to have their chance for a new future along with everybody else. But dead men weren't free; neither was a probe pilot locked up in a warehouse.

He wanted to run, to kick down the doors, and flee into the night. But not to Mora—anywhere but to Mora. He felt so ashamed of himself now, especially after the way he had been treating her, that he couldn't bear the thought of facing her . . . not until he had made things right.

"You can leave," he said, his voice barely audible as he leaned back against the office doorframe.

Stafford took an uncertain step forward. "What? You mean that?"

LaNague nodded, not looking at him. "Go ahead. But be warned: Primus City is not as you left it. It's night out there now, and the streets belong to whoever feels strong enough or desperate enough to venture onto them. You won't like it."

"I've got to get to my wife."

LaNague nodded again, stepping away from the doorway. "Find her. Bring her back here if you wish, or take your chances out there. I leave the choice up to you. But remember two things: the Imperium is looking everywhere for you, and we offer you and your wife safety here."

"Thank you," Stafford said, glancing between LaNague and the two Flinters. Hesitantly at first, and then with growing confidence, he walked past LaNague, across the warehouse floor, and out the side door. He only looked back three times before he was out of sight.

LaNague was silent for a while, gathering his thoughts. The next steps would have to be moved up, the schedule accelerated. "Follow him," he told Kanya and Josef. "Make sure he's left with a choice. If a few Imperial Guardsmen should get hold of him, let him go with them if that's what he wants. But if he decides he'd prefer to stay with us, then see to it that they don't get in his way."

The Flinters nodded, glad for an opportunity to do something besides sit and wait. They adjusted their holosuits to the middle-aged male images, and started for the door.

"One thing," LaNague said as they were leaving. "Don't bring him back here. Take him and his wife to my apartment. Under no circumstances bring him back here."

LaNague could see no expression through the enveloping holograms, but knew the Flinters must have looked puzzled.

"Trust me," he said. The words tasted stale on his tongue.

They were not gone long when Broohnin entered. "Where's the probe pilot?" he asked, his head swiveling back and forth in search of Stafford.

"Gone." LaNague had taken over the seat Stafford had vacated.

"Where'd you hide him?"

"I let him go."

It took a moment for the truth of that statement to register on Broohnin. At first he reacted as if to an obvious and rather silly attempt at humor, then he looked closely into LaNague's face.

"You *what?*"

"I don't believe in imprisoning a man completely innocent of any wrongdoing."

The small amounts of facial skin visible above Broohnin's beard and below his hairline had turned crimson. "You fool! You idiot! Are you insane? What he knows could ruin everything—you said so yourself!"

"I realize that," LaNague said. An icy calm had slipped over him. "I also realize that I cannot allow one unpleasant fact to overcome a lifetime's belief."

"Belief?" Broohnin stormed across the office. "We're talking about revolution here, not belief!" He went to the desk and started rifling through the drawers.

"What *do* you believe in, Broohnin? Anything?"

Pulling a hand blaster from a drawer, Broohnin wheeled and pointed the lens directly at LaNague's face. "I believe in revolution," he said, his breathing ragged. "And I believe in eliminating anyone who gets in the way of that belief!"

LaNague willed his exterior to complete serenity. "Without me, there is no revolution, only a new, stronger Imperium."

After a breathless pause that seemed to go on forever, Broohnin finally lowered the blaster. Without a word, he stalked to the far exit and passed through to the street.

LaNague lifted his left hand and held it before his eyes. It was trembling. He could not remember being exposed to the raw edge of such violent fury before. He let the hand fall back to his lap and sighed. It would not be the last. Before this thing was over, he might well come closer to even greater physical danger. He might even die. But there was no other way.

He heaved himself out of the chair and toward the disheveled desk. Time to move.

Ω

"Why don't you calm down?" Metep VII said from his form-fitting lounger as he watched Daro Haworth pace the floor. There was an air of barely suppressed excitement about the younger man that had grown continually during the few moments he had been present in the room.

"I can't! We've just heard from the municipal police commissioner. They've had a tip on the whereabouts of Robin Hood."

"We've been getting those ever since the first currency heist. They've all been phony. Usually someone with a grudge on somebody else, or a prankster."

"The commissioner seems to think this is the real thing," Haworth said. "The caller gave the location of a warehouse he says is the center of all the Robin Hood activities. Says we'll find Robin Hood himself there along with enough evidence to convince a dead man that he's the genuine article." Haworth's hands rubbed together as if of their own will. "If only it's true! If *only* it's true!"

Metep coughed as he inhaled a yellow vapor from the vial in his hand. He had always liked the euphorogenic gases, but appeared to be using them with greater frequency and in greater quantities lately, especially since the recall talk had started. The calls for votes of confidence in the legislature recently had only compounded his depression. "I'm not so sure the commissioner is the right man to oversee such a project. After all, the municipal police lately have been—"

"I know that!" Haworth snapped. "That's why I've told them to wait until Tinmer, our illustrious commander-in-chief of the Imperial Guard, can arrive with reinforcements and redeem himself after bungling the capture of that orbital shuttle this morning."

"Let's hope so," Metep said. "Speaking of the shuttle incident, you still have men out looking for that pilot?"

"Of course. I've also got them waiting at his apartment here in the city just in case he shows up looking for his wife." Haworth smiled. "Wouldn't that be nice: Robin Hood himself, and our elusive probe pilot in hand before daybreak. That would change everything!"

Ω

Vincen Stafford had never seen the streets of Primus dark before. Glo-globes had always kept the shadows small and scarce. But someone had decided to smash every globe up and down the street, and no one had bothered to replace them. As he walked on, the intersections he crossed gave dark testimony to the fact that this was not the only street to be victimized so. Every street was dark, lined with useless pedestals supporting dim, shattered, useless fragments.

He was not alone on the street. There were dark forms

huddled in doorways and skulking in the deeper shadows. He was also aware of other pedestrians ahead of him and behind; not many, but enough to make him feel that he could at least count on some help should there be any trouble.

As Stafford walked on, he had the distinct impression that he was under scrutiny. But by whom? He could detect no one following him. Soon the sensation passed, replaced by a gnawing fear.

Robin Hood had been right. This was not the Primus City he had left a year ago. That city had been bright and lively—dingy on the edges, true, but nothing like this. The streets were choked with litter; ground-effect vehicles were virtually absent from view, and only one or two flitters crossed the night sky. After walking two kilometers, he gave up hope of ever seeing a taxi. He'd have to try the monorail.

As he entered the business district of town, he was in for an even greater shock. A number of the stores stood dark and empty, their fronts smashed open, their insides either stripped of their contents or gutted by fire. The ones that were intact but closed had left their lights on. Stafford peered into the window of one and saw a man sitting conspicuously under a light in a chair against the rear wall of the store. A short-range, wide-beam blaster rifle rested across his knees. When he noticed that Stafford did not move on immediately, he lifted the weapon and cradled it in his arms. Stafford moved on.

Only one store on this street was open. Before he had left on his probe ship mission, every store would be open and busy this early in the evening. Tonight the lights from the front of the open store—a food store—shone out on the street like a beacon. People were clustered around the front of it, waiting to get in. Some carried luggage cases, others shopping bags, some nothing.

Drawn by the light and by other people, Stafford decided to take a quick look to see what the attraction was. As he approached, he noticed armed guards on either side of the doorway, and more inside. On closer inspection, he could see that many of the customers were armed, too.

Since he was not interested in getting through the door, he found it easy to push through the press to the window. A careful, squinting inspection revealed only one product for sale in the market: flour. The center of the floor was stacked with transparent cylinders of it. Stafford gauged their probable weight at fifty kilos each. One by one, people were being allowed to go to the pile, heft a cylinder to a shoulder, and exit through the rear.

But first they had to pay. At a counter to the left, an armed man was counting bundles of currency, stacking it, then dumping it into a bin behind him when the proper amount was reached. The bin was half full; another toward the rear was completely full, and an empty one waited. An armed guard stood over them. Customers were allowed into the store one at a time; a guard frisked them, removed their weapons at the door, and returned them at the exit. There was a strong family resemblance between the guards and the storekeeper—father and sons, most likely.

Fascinated, Stafford watched the strange procession for a while, watched the customers empty sacks and satchels of currency onto the counter, watched the second bin behind the man grow full. And then two men were allowed to enter at once. Both were empty-handed. The first caused a stir at the counting table when he produced a handful of what looked like old silver marks, extinct from general circulation for half a generation. The storekeeper studied them, weighed them on a scale, and placed them in an autoanalyzer one at a time. Apparently satisfied with their metal content, he nodded to the two men. Each claimed a cylinder and exited through the rear.

"Nice what a little silver can do these days," said a man beside him at the window. Stafford stepped back for a better look at the speaker. He saw a shabbily dressed man of average build with greasy hair who was giving his flight jumper an appraising glance. There was a bulge under the man's coat that probably meant a weapon, and an overloaded suitcase in his left hand from which a few stray marks protruded at the seam.

"What are they charging for that flour in there?" Stafford asked.

The man shrugged and glanced through the window. "Around ten thousand marks, I'm told." He saw Stafford's jaw swing open. "A bit expensive, I know—a whole day's pay—but I'll be glad to get it at all, what with the surface and air transport unions on strike again."

"Strike? *Again?*"

"I don't blame them though," the man said, seeming to look right through Stafford as he continued speaking in a tremulous monotone. "I wouldn't want to get paid by the week, either. They say they're going to stay out until they get daily pay. Otherwise, it's not worth working." Without warning, tears began to slip down his cheeks and he began to cry. "It's not really worth working, anyway. The money loses value faster than you can spend it . . . and nobody cares any more . . . we're all just putting in our time . . . used to like my job at the bureau . . . used to like my house . . . and my family . . . nothing matters now 'cause I don't know how much longer I'm going to be able to keep any of them . . ."

Embarrassed by the display of naked despair, Stafford pushed away from the window and out to the open sidewalk with a single worrisome thought in his mind: *Salli!* Where was she? How could she have survived this insanity on her own? She could be dead of starvation by now! His only hope was that she had somehow got to her family, or they to her. He never should have left her on her own! He broke into a run. He had to get back to the apartment.

There was a monorail station at the next intersection. The glo-globes that usually surrounded it were shattered like all the rest he had passed, but he did see a light at the top of the platform where the ticket booth would be. On his way to the float-chute, he passed half a dozen loitering men who eyed him with little interest. He quickened his pace and was about to hop into the chute when something stopped him. Pausing at the threshold, he thrust out a hand—no breeze. There was supposed to be an updraft. The sound of derisive laughter made him turn.

"Almost got him!" The loiterers had known the chute wasn't operating but had chosen to wait and see if he fell down the shaft. Stafford took the stairs two at a time up to the platform and gave a crosstown station as his destination to the man in the ticket booth.

"Fifteen hundred," a voice rasped from atop the blasterproof compartment.

Stafford gulped. "Marks?"

"No, rocks!" the man within snarled.

Stafford turned and walked slowly down the stairs. He had a grand total of forty marks in his pocket. He'd have to walk. It would be a long trek, and he was already weary—a year in a probe ship, despite artificial gravity and a conscientious exercise program, had left him out of condition and short on stamina—but it was the only way.

First, however, he would have to pass through the knot of six or seven idle men blocking the end of the stairway.

"Nice suit you've got there," said the one in front. "I rather think it would fit me better than you." He smiled, but there was nothing friendly about the grimace.

Stafford said nothing. He glanced around and saw no one he could call upon for help.

"Come on, now. Just take it off and give it to us—and whatever money you've got on you, too—and we'll only rough you up a little. Make us chase you and we'll have to hurt you." He glanced up to the monorail platform ten meters above. "We may try and see if you can really fly in that fancy flight suit."

"I—I have no money," Stafford said in as stern a voice as he could manage. "I didn't even have enough for a ticket."

The man's smile faded. "No one who runs around in that sort of outfit is broke." He started up the steps toward Stafford. "Looks like you want to do this the hard way."

Stafford vaulted over the railing and landed on the ground running—and collided head-on with a darkened glo-globe pedestal. Before he could regain his feet, they were upon him, fists and feet jabbing at his face, his groin, his kidneys.

Suddenly the weight on him lessened, the blows became less frequent, and then stopped. Using the pedestal for support, he struggled to his feet, gasping. When the agony caused by the brutal pummeling subsided to a bearable level, he opened his eyes and looked around.

It was as if there had been an explosion during the assault on him and he had been ground zero. His attackers were strewn in all directions, either sprawled flat on the pavement, slumped on piles of debris, or slung over the stairway railing. Someone or something had pulled them off him and hurled them in all directions, battering them unmercifully in the process. No one was moving—wait—the one who had done all the talking was slowly lifting his head from the ground. Stafford limped over to see if there was to be more trouble. No . . . apparently not. The man grunted something unintelligible through a bloody, ruined mouth, then slumped down again, unconscious.

Stafford turned and lurched away, gradually forcing his headlong gait into some semblance of a trot. He could only guess at what had happened, but after seeing two Flinters back at Robin Hood's warehouse and knowing of Robin Hood's concern for his safety, it seemed reasonable to assume that he had acquired two incredibly efficient bodyguards. He just hoped that they stuck with him past Imperial Park and to his apartment.

After that, he'd no longer need them. He hoped.

The journey through the city became a blur of surreal confusion as his legs and arms became leaden and the very air seared his lungs. But he persisted despite the physical agony, for the mental agony of not knowing what he might find at home was greater. He moved through a city that had lost all resemblance to the place where he had dwelt for years, past people who were not like any he had ever known. There were times when he wondered through the haze of his oxygen-starved brain if he had landed on the wrong planet.

Finally, he found himself before the entrance to his own apartment building, gasping, weak, nauseated. The door was still keyed to his palm, for it opened when he pushed against it. Inside was an oasis of light and warmth, shelter from the dark, silent storm raging behind him. As he trudged to the float-chute, he thought he caught a hint of movement behind him, but saw nothing when he turned, only the entry door slowly sliding closed.

The chute was operating, further testimony to the wisdom of some ancient designer's insistence on decentralized power; each building had its own solar energy collectors and amplifiers. The anti-grav field was a physical joy for Stafford at this moment—he would have spent the rest of the night in the chute if he had not been so frightened for Salli. The fifth floor was his. He grasped a rung and hauled himself out into the real world of weight and inertia.

The door to his apartment was to the right and slid open when it recognized his palm. He saw Salli sitting in a chair straight ahead of him, watching the vid. She gasped and rose to her feet when she saw him, but did not come forward. So Stafford went to her.

"You're all right?" he asked, slipping his arms slowly, hesitantly around her. Her coolness puzzled him. "How did you possibly survive all this alone?"

"I managed." Her eyes kept straying away from his.

"What's the matter?"

Salli's gaze had come to rest at a point over his right shoulder. He turned. Two members of the Imperial Guard were approaching from the inner corner of the room, weapons drawn.

"Vincen Stafford?" said the one in the lead. "We've been waiting for you. You're under arrest for crimes against the Imperium."

Ω

"We've got the pilot, sir."

It was all Haworth could do to keep from shouting with joy. But he had to maintain his bearing. After all, this was just a callow trooper on the screen. "Very good. Where is he?"

"Here at his apartment with us."

"You mean you haven't brought him to the Complex yet?" He heard his voice rising.

"We were told to call you directly as soon as he was in custody, sir."

True—he had demanded that. "All right. How many with you now?"

"Just one other."

"Did he resist at all?"

"No, sir. He just walked in and we arrested him."

Haworth considered the situation. As much as he wanted to interrogate that pilot, he doubted the wisdom of allowing a pair of unseasoned Imperial Guards to escort him in. Who'd have ever thought he'd be stupid enough to return to his own apartment?

"Wait there until I send an extra squad to back you up. I don't want any slip-ups."

"Very well, sir." The guardsman didn't seem to mind. He didn't want any slip-ups either.

Haworth arranged for the extra squad to go to Stafford's apartment, then he turned to Metep and clapped his hands.

"This is the night! We've already got the pilot, and within the hour Robin Hood will be in custody, too!"

"What's taking so long with Robin Hood?" Metep asked. His words were slurred from the excess inhalant in his system.

"I'm not leaving a single thing to chance with him. All the city maps have been combed for any possible underground escape route. Every building around the warehouse is being taken over by Imperial Guards; every street is being blocked; even the air space over that building is being sealed off. When we finally close the trap, not even an insect will get through unless we let it! This is it, Jek! Tonight we start getting things under control again!"

Metep VII smiled foggily and put the open end of the vial to his nose again. "That's nice."

Ω

The door chimed and one of the two Imperial Guardsmen approached it warily. It was much too early for the backup squad to arrive. The viewer set in the door revealed two rather plain-looking middle-aged men on the other side. They kept shuffling around, turning their heads back and forth.

"We know you're in there, Mr. Stafford, and we want our money." The guardsman wasn't sure which one of them spoke. They kept wandering in and out of the range of the viewer.

"Go away! Stafford is under arrest."

There was laughter on the other side. "Now *that's* a new one!"

"It's true. This is a member of the Imperial Guard speaking."

More laughter. "We'll have to see that to believe it!"

The guard angrily cycled the door open. "Now do you—"

He was suddenly on the floor and a figure was vaulting through the door, a stunner aimed at the other guard's head. There was no sound from the attacker, the guard, or the weapon, but the guard closed his eyes and joined his comrade on the floor.

"If you wish to go with them, you may," said the bland-looking male invader in a female voice as the pistol was holstered. "We are only here to give you a choice. Someone is offering you and your mate a safe place if you want it. Otherwise, you may wait until they regain consciousness."

"We'll go with you," Stafford said without hesitation.

"Vin!" It was Salli.

He turned to her. "It's all right. We'll be safer with them than with anybody else. I know who they are."

Salli made no reply. She merely clung to him, looking physically exhausted and emotionally drained. She watched as the two newcomers closed the apartment door and arranged the two guardsmen neatly on the floor.

Ω

Broohnin floated in the chute, holding his position with a foot and a hand each hooked into a safety rung. Popping his head into the hall, he took a quick look up and down, then arched back into the chute. He had no idea what lay on the other side of Stafford's apartment door, but he had to go through. He had to be sure Stafford had not told what he knew—would never tell what he knew.

As he prepared to thrust himself into the hall, he heard the whisper of a door cycling open . . . it came from the direction of Stafford's apartment. Broohnin had two options: he could let go of the rungs and float up to the next floor, or he could step out and confront whoever it was.

He chose the latter. If nothing else, he'd have surprise and a drawn weapon on his side. Placing his right foot flat against the rear wall of the chute, he gave a kick and catapulted himself into the hall.

Broohnin almost vomited when he saw Stafford's escort. The holosuit images were all too familiar to him. But it was too late to do anything but act.

"Stop right there!" he said, pointing the blaster at the middle of the pilot's chest. "Another step and he dies!"

They stopped. All four of them—the pilot, a woman, and the two Flinters flanking them. "What is wrong with you, Broohnin?" said a male voice that appeared to be coming from the left: Josef's voice. "There's a squad of Imperial Guard on its way here now. Let us by without any further trouble."

"I'll let three of you by," Broohnin said warily, watching the Flinters for any sign of movement. He was far enough away that no one could reach him before he fired, and he was too close to miss if he did. He had to play this scene very carefully. There would be time for only one blast; the Flinters would be on him after that. The blast would have to kill the pilot, and then Broohnin would have to drop his weapon immediately. There was a chance they'd let him live then, and return him to LaNague, who would do nothing, as usual. But at least the pilot would be dead. The thing he had to be absolutely sure *not* to do was to hit one of the Flinters with the blast, because there was no telling what the other one would do when he or she got hold of him.

"What do you mean, 'three'?" It was Kanya's voice.

"The pilot's got to die."

"You don't have to worry about that," Josef said. "He's decided to stay with us. We're taking him back to LaNague."

"I don't care what he's decided or where you're taking him. He could change his mind and walk out again . . . or Metep could publicly offer him a huge reward if he turns himself in." Broohnin shook his head. "No . . . can't risk it. He could ruin everything. You know that."

Broohnin didn't realize what had happened until it was too late. While he was talking, the Flinters had edged closer and closer to Stafford and his wife. Then, with one quick sideward step from each, they had placed themselves in front of the couple, completely eclipsing Broohnin's intended target.

"Don't do that! Move aside!"

"Best to give us the weapon, Broohnin," Kanya said. Moving in unison, they began to approach him, one slow step after another.

"I'll fire!" he said, aching to retreat but finding himself rooted to the floor. "I'll kill you both, and then him!"

"You might kill one of us," Josef said. "But that would be the last thing you would do. Ever."

The blaster was suddenly snatched out of his hand. He saw it in Kanya's, but the exchange had been a complete blur. He hadn't seen her move.

"Quickly, now," Josef said, turning to Stafford and his wife and motioning them toward the drop-chute. "The backup squad will be here any time now."

As Stafford passed, Kanya handed him Broohnin's blaster. "Put this in your waistband and forget about it unless we tell you to use it."

"What about me?" Broohnin asked, fearing the answer more than he had feared anything in his life.

Kanya and Josef merely glanced his way with their expressionless holosuit faces, then followed the pilot and his wife down the chute. Broohnin hurried after them. If Imperial Guardsmen were on their way, he didn't want to be caught here and have to explain the pilot's empty apartment. He was right behind them when they all pushed their way out to the street and came face to face with the backup squad as it debarked from a lorry flitter. The squad leader recognized Stafford immediately—no doubt his features had been drummed into their brains since his escape earlier in the day.

"What's going on here?" he yelled and readied the blaster rifle he had been cradling in his arms. "Where are the others? Who are these?"

Kanya and Josef edged toward the front of their group. Josef's voice was low but audible to the rest of the civilians. "Be calm, stand quiet, let us handle everything. There's only six of them."

"I asked you a question!" the squad leader said to anyone who would listen. "Where are the two Imperial Guardsmen who are supposed to be with you?"

"I assure you we don't know what you mean," Josef said. "We are not with these others."

The squad leader leveled his blaster at Josef as the other five members of his squad arrayed themselves behind him. "Show me some identification. It had better be perfect or we're all going upstairs to find out what's going on here."

Broohnin felt panic welling up within him, shutting off his air, choking him. This was it—they were either going to be killed or wind up Metep's prisoners. One was as bad as the other. He had to do something. He saw Stafford standing just ahead and to his left, his arms folded cautiously across his chest. His wife was clinging to his left arm and his attention was on her. Peeking out from under his right elbow was the butt of Broohnin's confiscated blaster.

Without thinking, without a conscious effort on his part, Broohnin's hand reached out and snatched at the weapon. He had to have it. It was floating debris on a storm-tossed sea, a chance for survival. No guarantee that it would carry him to safety, but it seemed to be all he had right now.

Stafford spun reflexively as he felt the weapon pulled from his waistband and grabbed for it. "Hey!"

Now was as good a time as any to get rid of the damn pilot, so Broohnin squeezed the trigger as soon as his finger found it. But Stafford's reflexes were faster. He thrust Broohnin's arm upward and Salli screamed as the beam flashed upward, striking no one.

Josef was not so lucky. At the sound of the scream and the sight of a blaster held high and firing, the squad leader responded by pressing his own trigger. There was a brief glare between the guardsman and Josef, illuminating the features of the former, briefly washing away the holosuit effect of the latter. Josef fell without a sound, a few of the accouterments on his weapons belt detaching with the impact, seeming to pop right out of his body as they passed through the holosuit image and landed on the pavement.

Everyone dropped then, including Broohnin. Kanya was the exception. She dove into the midst of the squad of guardsmen and began to wreak incredible havoc—punching, kicking, swirling, dodging, making it impossible for them to fire at her for fear of blasting a fellow guardsman. Broohnin found himself in sole possession of his blaster again. Stafford had rolled on top of his wife and both had their hands clasped protectively and uselessly over their heads. He was about to put an end to the pilot's threat once and for all when something on the pavement caught his eye.

A white disc with a small red button at its center lay beside Josef's inert form. Broohnin could not tell how badly the Flinter was hurt, or even if he were still alive, because of the camouflaging effect of the holosuit. There was no pool of blood around him, but then there seldom was much bleeding from a blaster wound due to the cauterizing effect of the heat. Deciding to risk it, he crawled over to Josef on his belly, reached for the disc, then began to crawl away. A glance over his shoulder revealed that Kanya had just about disposed of the entire squad, so he rose to his feet and sprinted in the other direction, into the safety of the darkness down the street.

With the disc in his left hand and the blaster in his right, Broohnin ran as fast as his pumping legs would carry him, through back alleys, across vacant lots, changing streets, altering direction, but always heading away from the center of town, away from Imperium Park and the Imperium Complex that surrounded it. He no longer needed LaNague or the Flinters or anyone else. The destruction of the Imperium was clutched in his left hand.

XX

> In the constant sociability of our age people shudder at solitude to such a degree that they do not know of any other use to put it to but . . . as a punishment for criminals.
>
> *Søfren Kierkegaard*

"Josef dead?"

LaNague wanted to scream. The quiet, pensive man who had been with him for nearly five years, who was walking death down to his finger tips and yet so gentle and peace-loving at heart, was dead. It was easy to think of Flinters as nothing more than killing machines, living weapons with no personalities, no identities. Yet they were all individuals, philosophically sophisticated, profoundly moral in their own way, human, mortal . . .

"How?"

Calmly, briefly, Kanya explained it to him, her face on the vid-screen displaying no trace of emotion. Flinters were like that: emotions were not for public display; she would suffer her grief in private later.

"I tried to bring his body back to the warehouse for storage until it could be returned home," she concluded, "but there was no access. They have the building surrounded—on the street level and in the air, with infra-red monitors every twenty meters. I could not approach without being detected."

"Poor Josef," LaNague said, his mind still rebelling at the news of his death. "I'm so sorry, Kanya." He watched her on the screen. How do you comfort a Flinter? He wished he could put an arm around her, knew there would be no steel or stone beneath his hand, but soft, yielding flesh. He sensed her grief. He wanted to pull her head down to his shoulder and let her cry it out. But that would never happen, even if she were standing next to him. Absolute emotional control was an integral part of Flinter rearing. A being skilled in a hundred, a thousand, ways of killing could not allow emotions to rule, ever.

Kanya was demonstrating that control now as she spoke. "Didn't you hear me? You're trapped. We've got to get you out."

LaNague shook his head. "I know what's going on outside. I've been watching. I'll wait for them here . . . no resistance. How's the pilot?"

"He and his wife are safe with Mora."

"And Broohnin? Is he safe where he can cause no more trouble?"

Kanya's face darkened for an instant; lightning flashed in her eyes. "Not yet. But he will be soon."

LaNague stiffened involuntarily. "What aren't you telling me, Kanya?"

"Josef is dead because of Broohnin," she said flatly. "If he had not delayed us at the pilot's apartment, we would have been gone before the squad of Imperial Guard arrived. Even after we were halted in front of the building, if he had followed directions and stood quietly, there would have been no shooting. Josef would be alive and beside me now."

"Let him go, Kanya. He can only harm himself now. You can settle with him later when your grief is not so fresh."

"No."

"Kanya, you pledged yourself to my service until the revolution was over."

"He must be found immediately."

LaNague had an uneasy feeling that Kanya was still not telling him everything. "Why? Why immediately?"

"We dishonored ourselves," she said, her eyes no longer

meeting his. "We circumvented your authority by planting a fail-safe device in Imperium Park."

LaNague closed his eyes. He didn't need this. "What sort of device?" He had a sinking feeling that he already knew the answer.

"A Barsky box."

Just what he had feared. "How big? What's the radius of the displacement field?"

"Three kilometers."

"Oh no!" LaNague's eyes were open again, and he could see that Kanya's were once more ready to meet them. "Didn't you trust me?"

"There was always the chance that you might fail, that the Imperium would reassert control, or that Earth would move in faster than anyone anticipated. We had to have a means to ensure final destruction."

"But a radius that size could possibly disrupt Throne's crust to the point where there'd be global cataclysm!"

"Either way, the Imperium or the Earthie conquerors who replaced it would no longer be a threat."

"But at a cost of millions of lives! The whole purpose of this revolution is to *save* lives!"

"And we've co-operated! The device was only to be used in the event of your failure. A new Imperium or an Earth takeover would inevitably lead to an invasion of Flint as well as Tolive. I do not know about your planet, but no one on Flint will ever submit to outside rule. Every single one of us would die defending our planet. *That* would be a cost of millions of lives! *Flinter* lives! We prefer to see millions die on Throne. We will never allow anything to threaten our way of life. *Never!*"

LaNague held up his hands to stop her. "All right! We'll have this out later. What's it all got to do with Broohnin?"

"There were two triggers to the device. Broohnin now has one of them."

LaNague sat for a long, silent moment. Then: "Find him."

"I will."

"But how? He could be anywhere."

"All the triggers are equipped with tracers in the event they're lost. No matter where he goes, I'll be able to locate him."

"He's crazy, Kanya. He'll set that thing off just for the fun of it. He's got to be stopped!" After another silence, shorter this time: "Why couldn't you have trusted me?"

"No plan, no matter how carefully wrought, is infallible. You *have* made miscalculations."

LaNague's heated response was reflexive. "Where? When? Aren't we right on schedule? Isn't everything going according to plan?"

"Was Josef's death in the plan?"

"If you had trusted me a little more," he said, hiding the searing pain those words caused him, "we wouldn't have this threat hanging over our heads now!"

"If you hadn't insisted on keeping Broohnin around against the advice of everyone else concerned—"

"We needed him at first. And . . . and I thought I could change him . . . bring him around."

"You failed. And Josef is dead because of it."

"I'm sorry, Kanya."

"So am I," the Flinter woman replied coldly. "But I'll see to it that he causes no further harm." Her shoulders angled as she reached for the control switch on her vid.

"Don't kill him," LaNague said. "He's been through a lot with us . . . helped us. And after all, he didn't actually fire the blast that killed Josef."

Kanya's face flashed up briefly, inscrutably, then her image faded. LaNague slumped back in his chair. She had a right to hate him as much as she did Broohnin. He was responsible, ultimately, for Josef's death. He was responsible for all of Broohnin's folly, and for his eventual demise at Kanya's hands should she decide to kill him. She could certainly feel justified in exacting her vengeance . . . Broohnin seemed to be acting like a mad dog.

All his fault, really. All of it. How had he managed to be so stupid? He and Broohnin had shared a common goal—the downfall of the Imperium. He had thought that could lead to greater common ground. Yet it hadn't, and it was too clear now that there had never been the slimmest hope of that happening. There was no true common ground. Never had been. Never could be.

At first he had likened the differences between Broohnin and himself to the differences between Flinters and Tolivians. Both cultures had started out with a common philosophy, Kyfho, and had a common goal, absolute individual sovereignty. Yet the differences were now so great. Tolivians preferred to back away from a threat, to withdraw to a safer place, to fight only when absolutely necessary: *leave us alone or we'll move away*. The Flinters had a bolder approach; although threatening no one, they were willing to do battle at the first sign of aggression against them: *leave us alone or else*. Yet the two cultures had worked well together, now that Tolive had finally decided to fight.

He had once thought a similar rapprochement possible with Broohnin; had at one point actually considered the possibility of convincing Broohnin to surrender himself to the Imperium as Robin Hood, just as LaNague was about to do.

He smiled ruefully to himself. Had he been a fool, or had he deluded himself into believing what was safest and most convenient to believe? In truth, he wished someone—*anyone*—else were sitting here now in this empty warehouse waiting for the Imperial Guard to break in and arrest him. The thought of giving himself over to the Imperium, of prison, locked in a cell, trapped . . . it made him shake. Yet it had to be done . . . one more thing that had to be done . . . Another part of the plan, the most important part. And he could ask no one else to take his place.

Wouldn't be long now. He slid his chair into the middle of the bare expanse of the warehouse floor and sat down, his hands folded calmly before him, presenting an image of utter peace and tranquility. The officers in charge of the search-and-seizure force would be doing their best to whip their men up to a fever pitch. After all, they were assaulting the stronghold of the notorious Robin Hood, and there was no telling what lay in store for them within.

LaNague sat motionless and waited, assuming a completely nonthreatening pose. He didn't want anyone to do anything rash.

Ω

"It is utterly imperative that he be taken alive! Is that clear? Every task assigned to the Imperial Guard today has been a catastrophic failure! This is a final chance for the Guard to prove its worth. If you fail this time, there may not be another chance—for any of us!"

Haworth paused in his tirade, hoping he was striking the right chord. He had threatened, he had cajoled; if he had thought tears would work, he'd have somehow dredged them up. He had to get across to Commander Tinmer the crucial nature of what they were about to do.

"If the man inside is truly Robin Hood, and the warehouse

is his base of operations—and all indications are that it may very well be—he must be taken alive, and every scrap of evidence that links him with Robin Hood must be collected and brought in with him. I cannot emphasize this strongly enough: he must be taken alive, even at the risk of Guard lives."

Lacking anything more to say, or a clearer, more forceful way of saying it, Haworth let Tinmer, who had taken personal command of the Robin Hood capture mission, fade from the screen. He turned to Metep and found him deep in drugged sleep in his chair, an empty gas vial on the floor beside him.

Haworth shook his head in disgust as he found his own chair and sank into it. Metep VII, elected leader of the Outworld Imperium, was falling apart faster than his domain. And with good reason. He, Haworth, and the other powers within the Imperium had spent their lives trying to mold outworld society along the lines of their own vision, no matter how the clay protested. And had been largely successful. After establishing a firm power base, they had been on the verge of achieving a level of control at which they could influence virtually every facet of outworld life. It was a heady brew, that kind of power. One taste led to a craving for more . . . and more.

Now it was all being taken away. And Jek Milian, so at home in his powerful role as Metep, was suffering acute withdrawal. The Imperium had gradually stolen control of the outworlds from the people who lived on them, and now that control was, in turn, being stolen from it. Everything was going crazy. Why? Had it all been circumstance, or had it been planned this way? Haworth bristled at the idea that some individual or some group had been able to disrupt so completely everything he had striven to build. He wanted to believe that it had all been circumstance—*needed* to believe it.

And yet . . . there was a feather-light sensation at the far end of his mind, an ugly worm of an idea crawling around in the dark back there that whispered *conspiracy* . . . events had followed too direct a pattern . . . *conspiracy* . . . situations that should have taken years to gestate were coming to term in weeks or months . . . *conspiracy* . . . and every damaging event or detrimental situation consistently occurring at the worst possible time, always synergistically potentiating the ill effects of the previous event . . . *conspiracy* . . .

If it were conspiracy, there was only one possible agent: the man who had mocked the Imperium, derided it, made it look foolish time after time, and eluded capture at every turn—Robin Hood.

And it was possible—just possible—that the man or men known as Robin Hood would be in custody tonight. That bothered him a little. Why now? Why, when it looked as if all was lost, did they get a tip on the whereabouts of Robin Hood? Was this yet another part of the conspiracy against the Imperium?

He slammed his hand against the armrest of his chair. That was not a healthy thought trend. That sort of thinking left you afraid to act. If you began to see everything as conspiracy, if you thought every event was planned and calculated to manipulate you, you wound up in a state of paralysis. No . . . Robin Hood had finally made a mistake. One of his minions had had a falling out with him or had become otherwise disaffected and had betrayed him. That was it.

Tonight, if all went right, if the Imperial Guard didn't make fools of themselves again—he shook his head here, still unwilling to believe that the probe pilot had slipped through their fingers twice in one day—he would face Robin Hood. And then he would know if it had all been planned. If true, that very fact could be turned to the Imperium's advantage. He would not only know whom and what he was fighting against and how they had managed to get the best of him, but he would have undeniable proof that the blame for the current chaos did not lie with the Imperium. He would have a scapegoat—the Imperium badly needed one.

Robin Hood was his last chance to turn aside the tide of rage welling up around the Imperium. He had apparently lost the probe pilot as a possible source of distraction. Only Robin Hood was left to save them all from drowning. And only if taken alive. Dead, he was a martyr . . . useless.

Ω

The doors blew open with a roar that reverberated through the empty warehouse. Imperial Guardsmen charged in through the clouds of settling dust and fanned out efficiently in all directions. So intent were they on finding snipers and booby traps that LaNague went temporarily unnoticed. It wasn't long before he became the center of attention, however.

"Who are you?" said someone who appeared to be an officer. He aimed his hand weapon at the middle of LaNague's forehead as he spoke, making this the second time in one day he had been at the wrong end of a blaster.

"The name is LaNague. Peter LaNague. And I'm alone here." He held his palms flat against his thighs to keep his hands from shaking, and worked at keeping his voice steady. He refused to show the terror that gnawed at him from within.

"This your place?"

"Not exactly. I lease it."

An excited young guardsman ran up to the first. "This is the place, sir! No doubt about it!"

"What've you found?"

"High speed duplicators, stacks of various issues of *The Robin Hood Reader*, and boxes full of those little cards that were dropped with the money. Plus a dozen or so holosuits. Should we try one on to see what kind of image we get?"

"I doubt that will be necessary," the officer said, then turned to LaNague. The other members of the unduly large assault force were slowly clustering around as their commander asked the question that was on everyone's mind: "Are you Robin Hood?"

LaNague nodded. His throat was tight, as if unwilling to admit it. Finally: "I go by that name now and then."

An awed murmur rustled through the ranks of the guardsmen like wind through a forest. The officer silenced his command with a quick, angry glare.

"You are under arrest for crimes against the Imperium," he told LaNague. "Where are the rest of your followers?"

LaNague looked directly into the officer's eyes. "Look around you."

He did, and saw only his own troops, each struggling to peek over the other's shoulder or to push his way to the front for a glimpse of the man who was Robin Hood. And suddenly the meaning was clear.

"To your posts!" the commander barked. "Start packing up the evidence immediately!"

After the duty assignments were given, the officer turned the task of overseeing the warehouse end of the operation to a subordinate while he took personal command of a squad of Guard to lead LaNague back to the Imperium Complex.

In a state of self-induced emotional anesthesia, LaNague allowed himself to be led away. Fighting off a sudden awful feeling that he would never return, he cast a final backward glance and saw that every guardsman in the building had stopped what he was doing to watch Robin Hood's exit.

Ω

Finally! Finally something had gone right!

"And there's proof?" Haworth said. "Incontestable proof?"

Tinmer beamed as he spoke. "Ten times more than any jury could want."

"He'll never see a jury. But how do we know he's *the* Robin Hood, not just one of his lackeys? I'm sure he gave you a good story as to why he happened to be there."

"Not at all. He admitted it. Said straight out he was Robin Hood."

The elated tingle of victory that had been coursing along every nerve fiber in Haworth's body suddenly slowed, faltered.

"Freely?"

"Yes! Said his name was Peter LaNague and that he had authored the flyers and planned the raids. According to the census computer, though, he doesn't exist. None of his identity factors match with anyone on Throne."

"Which means he's from one of the other outworlds."

"Or Earth."

Haworth doubted that, especially now that he remembered a certain weapon used to save Metep VII's life almost five years ago, about the same time *The Robin Hood Reader* began to appear. A weapon made on Flint. Things were fitting together at last.

"Check with the other planets—the ones still speaking to us. And with Earth." Haworth knew the replies would all be negative, but decided to keep Tinmer busy.

"You going to interrogate him now?"

Haworth hesitated here. The prisoner probably expected to be hustled into the Complex and immediately filled with drugs to make him talk. Let him wait instead, Haworth thought. Let him spend the night in one of those claustrophobic cells wondering when the interrogation would begin. He'd lie awake wondering while Haworth caught up on some much needed rest.

"Throw him in maximum security and tell your men not to be too rough on him. I want him able to talk in the morning."

"That won't be a problem." Tinmer's expression was grim and dour. "They've been treating him like a visiting dignitary, like a V.I.P., like . . . like an officer!"

Haworth again felt a twinge of anxiety, a chill, as if someone had briefly opened and closed a door to the night air. It wasn't right for the Guard to give the man who had outrun and outfoxed them all these years such treatment. They should hate him, they should want to get even. Apparently they didn't. Inappropriate behavior, to be sure. But why did it bother him so? He broke the connection and slowly turned away from the set.

Haworth didn't bother attempting to rouse Metep to tell him the news. Tomorrow he'd be in much better shape to comprehend it, and Haworth would be in better shape to deal with it. He was tired. It had been a long, harrowing day and fatigue was beginning to get the best of him. There was no chance for Robin Hood . . . no . . . stop calling him that. He was Peter LaNague now. He had a name just like everybody else; time to start de-mythifying this character. There was no chance for Peter LaNague to escape from the max-sec area. What Haworth needed now was sleep. A dose of one of the stims would keep him going, but beyond cosmetics he didn't approve of artificial means to anything where his body was concerned. The closest he got to a drug was the alpha cap he wore at night. It guaranteed him whatever length of restful slumber he desired, taking him up and down through the various levels of sleep during the set period, allowing him to awaken on schedule, ready to function at his peak.

Despite his fatigue, Daro Haworth's step was light as he strode toward his temporary quarters in the Imperium Complex. Members of the Council of Five and other higher-ups had been moved into the Complex last month, ostensibly to devote all their efforts to curing the ills that afflicted the Imperium, but in reality to escape the marauding bands wandering the countryside, laying siege to the luxury homes and estates occupied by the Imperium's top-level bureaucrats. He would not mind the cramped quarters at all tonight. For tomorrow morning, after six hours under the cap, he'd be fresh and ready to face Ro—*No!* Peter LaNague.

Ω

After an hour in the cell, LaNague had to admit that it really wasn't so bad. Perhaps his quaking terror at the thought of prison had been an overreaction. Everything had been routine: the trip to the Imperium Complex and the walk to the maximum security section had been uneventful; the recording of his fingerprints, retinal patterns, and the taking of skin and blood samples for genotyping had all gone smoothly. Only his entry into the max-sec cell block had held a surprise.

The prison grapevine was obviously better informed than even the established news media. The public was as yet completely unaware of his capture, but as soon as he set foot on the central walkway between the three tiers of cells, a loud, prolonged, raucous cheer arose from the inmates. They thrust their arms through the bars on their cages, stretching to the limit to touch him, to grab his hand, to slap him on the back. Most could not reach him, but the meaning was clear: even in the maximum security section of the Imperium Complex, the area on Throne most isolated from the daily events of the world outside, Robin Hood was known . . . and loved.

Not exactly the segment of Throne society I've been aiming at, LaNague thought as he took his place in a bottom tier solo cell, watching the bars rise from the floor and ooze down from the ceiling, mechanical stalagmites and stalactites in a man-made cave. They met and locked together in front of him at chest level.

After his escort departed, LaNague was bombarded with questions from all directions. He answered a few, evaded most, remaining completely unambiguous only about identifying himself as Robin Hood, which he freely admitted to anyone who asked. Feigning fatigue, he retired to the rear of his cell and lay in the wall recess with his eyes closed.

Silence soon returned to the max-sec block as the celebrity's arrival was quickly accepted and digested. Conversation was not an easy thing here. Max-sec was reserved for psychopaths, killers, rapists, and habitually violent criminals . . . and now for enemies of the state. These breeds of criminal had to be isolated, separated from the rest of the prisoners as well as the rest of society. Each was given a solitary cell, a synthestone box with five unbroken surfaces, open only at the front where bars closed from above and below like a gap-tooth grin, separating them from the central walkway and from each other.

There was no chance of escape, no hope of rescue. LaNague had known that when he called in the tip that led to his arrest. The walls were too thick to be blown without killing those inside. There was only one exit from the section and it was protected by a close mesh of extremely tight ultrasonic beams. No human going through one bank of those beams could maintain consciousness long enough to take two steps. And there were five banks. Should there be any general disturbance in the max-sec block, another system would bathe the entire area with inaudible, consciousness-robbing sound, forcing a half-hour nap on everyone.

LaNague didn't want to get out just yet anyway. He had to sit and hope that Metep and the Council of Five would play into his hands . . . and hope that Sayers would be able to play one of those recordings on the air . . . and hope that the populace would respond. So many variables. Too many, perhaps. He had shredded the outworlder's confidence in the Imperium, now he had to mend it, but in a different weave, a different cut, a radical style. Could he do it?

Somewhere inside of him was a cold knot of fear and doubt that said no one could do it.

LaNague had almost dozed off—he had a talent for that, no matter what the circumstances—when he heard footsteps on the walkway. They stopped outside his cell and he peered cautiously out of his recess toward the bars. One of the prison guards stood there, a flat, square container balanced on his upturned palm. LaNague gently eased his left hand into his right axilla, probing until he found the tiny lump under the skin. He desperately hoped he would not have to squeeze it now.

"You hungry?" the guard said as he caught sight of LaNague's face in the darkness of the recess.

Sliding to the floor and warily approaching the front of the cell, LaNague said, "A little."

"Good." The guard tapped a code into the box attached to his waist, a code LaNague knew was changed three times a day. The central bar at the front of his cell suddenly snapped in two at its middle, the top half rising, the bottom sinking until about twenty centimeters separated the ends. After passing the container through the opening, the guard tapped his box again and the two bars approximated and merged again.

It was a food tray. LaNague activated the heating element and set it aside. "I would have thought the kitchen was closed."

"It is." The guard smiled. He was tall, lean, his uniform ill-fitting. "But not for you."

"Why's that?" LaNague was immediately suspicious. "Orders from on high?"

The guard grunted. "Not likely! No, we were all sitting around thinking what a dirty thing it was to put someone like you in with these guys—I mean, most of them have killed at least one person; and if not, it wasn't for not trying. They'd kill again, too, given the chance. We can't even let them near each other, let alone decent people. A guy like you just doesn't belong here. I mean, you didn't kill anybody—or even hurt anybody—all these years. All you did was make the big boys look stupid and spread the money around afterwards so everybody could have a good time. We don't think you belong here, Mr. Robin Hood, and although we can't do much about getting you out of max-sec, we'll make sure nobody gives you any trouble while you're in here."

"Thank you," LaNague said, touched. "Do you always second-guess your superiors this way?"

After a moment of thought: "No, come to think of it. You're the first prisoner I ever gave a second thought to. I always figured you—you know, Robin Hood—were crazy. I mean, dropping that money and all. I never got any. My sister did once, but I work the night shift so I never had a chance. Did read that flyer of yours though . . . that *really* seemed crazy at the time, but from what I've seen lately, I know you're not crazy. Never were. It's everybody else that's crazy."

He seemed surprised and somewhat abashed at what he had just said. He gestured to the tray, which had started to steam. "Better eat that while it's hot." As LaNague turned away, the guard moved closer to the bars and spoke again. "One more thing . . . I'm not supposed to do this, but—" He thrust his open right hand between the bars.

LaNague grasped it and shook it firmly. "What's your name?"

"Steen. Chars Steen."

"Glad to know you, Steen."

"Not as glad as I am to know you!" He turned and quickly strode toward the exit at the end of the walkway.

LaNague stood and looked at the tray for a while, moved by the small but significant gesture of solidarity from the guards. Perhaps he had touched people more deeply than he realized. Sitting down before the tray, he lifted the lid. He really wasn't hungry, but made himself eat. After all, it was a gift.

He managed to swallow a few bites, but had to stop when Mora drifted through his mind. Since his arrest he had been doing his best to fend off the thought of her, but lost the battle now. She would be learning of his capture soon, hopefully not from the vid. Telling her beforehand would have been impossible. Mora would have done everything in her power to stop him; failing that, she would have tried to be arrested along with him, despite the way he had been treating her.

A short spool had been left explaining everything . . . a rotten way to do it, but the only way. With his appetite gone, he scraped the remaining contents of the tray into the commode and watched them swirl away, then crawled back into the recess and forced himself to sleep. It was better than thinking about what Mora was going through.

Ω

"How could you let him do it?" Mora's voice was shrill, her gestures frantic as she twisted in her seat trying to find a comfortable position. There was none. Her mind had been reeling from the news about Josef—now this!

"How could I stop him?" Random Sayers said defensively as he stood before her in the LaNague apartment. He had waited until the pilot and his wife had fallen asleep in the other room, then had put on the spool and let LaNague explain it himself.

"Someone else could have gone! One of his *loyal*"—she hated herself for the way she snarled the word—"followers could have taken his place! No one in the Imperium knows what Robin Hood looks like!"

"He didn't feel he could allow anyone else to be placed in custody as the most wanted man in the outworlds. And frankly, I respect that decision."

Mora sank back in her chair and nodded reluctantly. It was unfair of her to castigate Sayers, or to call into question the courage of any of the Merry Men. She knew Peter—although with the way he had been behaving since her arrival on Throne, perhaps not as well as she had thought. But he had never been good at asking favors of anyone, even a simple favor that was due him. He preferred to take care of it himself and get it out of the way rather than impose on anyone. So the idea of asking someone else to risk his life posing as Robin Hood would have been completely beyond him.

"I'm sorry," she mumbled through a sigh. "It's just that I had the distinct impression he had someone else in mind as the public's Robin Hood."

"That may have been a calculated effect for your benefit."

"Maybe. What are we supposed to do now?"

Sayers fished in his pocket and came up with three vid spools. "We wait for an opportunity to play one of these over the air."

"What's on them?" Mora asked, rising from her seat.

"Your husband . . . making an appeal to the people of Throne to choose between Metep and Robin Hood."

"Are they any good? Will they convince anyone?" She didn't like the expression on Sayers' face.

"I can't say." He kept his eyes on the spools in his hand. "A lot of the public's acceptance will depend on the fact that he's been identified as Robin Hood. The news bulletins should be breaking just about now, although hardly anybody's watching. But all of Throne will know by breakfast."

"Play one for me."

"There's three, one for each of the contingencies he thought possible."

"Play them all."

Sayers plugged them into the apartment holovid set, one after another. Mora watched with growing dismay, an invisible hand making a fist with her heart in the middle, gripping it tighter and tighter until she was sure it must stop beating. Peter's messages to the people of Throne were beautifully precise and well reasoned. They pointed out the velvet-gloved tyranny of the Imperium, and the inevitable consequences. No one living in the economic holocaust engulfing Throne could deny the truth of what he said. He appealed on the grounds of principle and pragmatism. But there was some vital element missing.

"He's doomed," Mora said in a voice that sounded as hollow as she felt. The third spool had just finished throwing out its holographic image of Peter LaNague, alias Robin Hood, sitting at a desk and calmly telling whoever might be listening to rise up and put an end to the Outworld Imperium once and for all.

Sayers puffed out his cheeks and exhaled slowly. "That's what I told him when we recorded these. But he wouldn't listen."

"No . . . of course he wouldn't. He expects everyone in the galaxy to respond to pure reason, now that he's finally got their attention." She gestured toward the vid set. "A Tolivian or a Flinter would understand and respond fiercely to any one of those spools. But the people of Throne?"

She went to the window. Pierrot sat on the sill, drooping heavily over the edge of his pot in the morose *kengai* configuration. She had watered the tree, spoken to it, but nothing she did brought it upright again. She looked beyond to the dark empty streets awaiting dawn, and thought about Peter. He had become a different man since leaving Tolive—cold, distant, preoccupied, even ruthless. But those spools . . . they were the work of a fool!

"Why didn't he listen to you, or check with me, or take *some*body's advice? Those spools are dry, pedantic, didactic, and emotionally flat! They may get a good number of people nodding their heads and agreeing in the safety of their homes, but they won't get them out in the street, running and shaking their fists in the air and screaming at the tops of their lungs for an end to Metep and his rotten Imperium!" She whirled and faced Sayers. *"They won't work!"*

"They're all we've got."

Mora saw the three spools sitting in a row beside the vid set. With one swift motion she snatched them up, hurled them into the dissociator in the corner, and activated it.

Sayers leaped forward, but too late. *"No!"* He stared at her in disbelief. "Do you realize what you've done? Those were the only copies!"

"Good! Now we'll have to think of something else." She paused. It had been necessary to destroy the spools. As long as they remained intact, Sayers would have felt duty-bound to find a way to broadcast them. But with them now gone beyond any hope of retrieval, he was free to act on his own—and to listen to her. Mora had already concocted a variation on Peter's basic plan. But she would need help—Flinter help. With Josef dead and Kanya gone she knew not where, Mora would have to turn to other Flinters. They were available, filtering down in a steady stream over the past few weeks, setting up isolated enclaves, waiting for the time when their services would be needed. Mora knew where to find them.

Ω

He was almost there. Gasping for breath, Broohnin stopped on a rise and looked back at the dim glow that was Primus City. Last year it would have lit up half the sky at this distance, but with glo-globes fast becoming an endangered species on its streets, the city was a faint ghost of its former self. He sat down for a moment and scanned the terrain behind him, watching for any sign of movement as his lungs caught up to his body.

After a long moment of intense scrutiny, he was satisfied. His eyes were adjusted to the darkness and he saw no one on his trail, not even an animal. He had come a long way; his muscles were protesting as much now as they had on the Earth jaunt. He had allowed himself to get soft again . . . but he had to push on. A little farther out from the city and he'd feel safe.

The trigger was still in his hand, although the activating button was locked. No problem there . . . not many small locks could stand for long against his years of experience in bypassing them. He bet it wasn't even a true lock . . . the trigger was most likely protected by a simple safety mechanism. When he reached a spot he considered safe, he was sure he could release it with a minimum of ado.

Heaving himself again to his feet, he forced his protesting muscles onward. Not far now. Not too much longer. Then it was good-bye Imperium. He had originally planned to hold the trigger back, use it as a trump card in his continuing battle with LaNague. But that was out of the question now. Somewhere along the path of his flight from Primus he had stopped to rest in an all-night tavern near the city limits. He could have used an ale but there was none to be had. As it was, nearly all of his cash went for a small wedge of cheese anyway. It was in the tavern that he learned of Robin Hood's arrest.

At first he thought it was a hoax or a mistake, but the face that filled the projection field of the tavern's holovid was LaNague's. Caught him red-handed, they said, and were holding him under heavy guard in the Imperium Complex. Broohnin had rushed out of the tavern then, continuing his flight from Primus at full speed.

The revolution was over. Without LaNague to direct things, it would sputter and stall and die. Broohnin hated to admit it, but the ugly truth wouldn't go away: only LaNague had the power to marshal the various forces necessary to bring the tottering Imperium all the way down. Only he had the authority to command the Flinters and who-knew-what-other resources. Only he knew what the final phase of the revolution was to be.

Broohnin had nothing except the trigger for the giant Barsky box he had seen buried in Imperium Park. That would be enough to literally decapitate the Imperium by sending Imperium Park and the entire Imperium Complex surrounding it to some unspecified point in time and space. Wherever it ended up, Broohnin was sure it would be far from Throne. Everyone within the Complex—Metep, the entire Council of Five, all the myriad petty bureaucrats—along with a few early risers in the park, would vanish without a trace, without warning.

He had an urge to stop where he was, find the way to release the trigger, and activate the box *now*. But that might mean a less than completely satisfactory result. He had to wait until mid-morning when the Complex was acrawl with all the lice that kept the huge bureaucracy functioning. To destroy the Imperium Complex before then was to risk missing a key person, perhaps Metep himself.

He'd have to wait, and wait out here, far from the city. Much as he would have loved to see the Complex and all it represented flash from view and existence, he preferred to keep a safe distance between himself and the event, and stroll into Primus later to see the open pit where the Imperium had been.

He smiled as he thought of something else: he would also be looking at the spot where Peter LaNague had been.

Ω

Haworth awakened with a start. The vidphone had activated the auto shut-off in his alpha cap, thrusting him immediately up to consciousness. He pulled it off and leaned over to activate the receiver. He would accept the call once he saw who was on the other end.

"Daro!" It was Jek. Metep VII had finally come out of his stupor. "Daro, you there?"

Haworth keyed in his transmitter so Metep could see and hear his chief adviser. "Yes, Jek, I'm here. What is it?"

"Why wasn't I told of the Robin Hood capture immediately?" His manner was haughty, his voice cold. He was in one of his Why-wasn't-I-consulted-first moods, a recurrent state whenever he felt that Haworth and the council were making too many independent decisions. Fortunately, they were short-lived.

"You were sitting not two meters away from me when the word came." He kept his tone light but drove his point home quickly and cleanly: "Trouble was, you weren't conscious."

"I should have been awakened! It had been a long day and I was dozing, waiting for the news. I should have been told immediately!"

Haworth looked closely at Metep's image. This was not the anticipated reaction. A quick comment about Jek's overindulgence in one gas or another was usually sufficient to deflate him, eliciting a nervous laugh and a change of subject. But this was something new. He seemed to have puffed up his self-importance beyond the usual level, to a point where he was impervious to casual barbs. That worried Haworth.

"Well, that's not important," he said easily. "What really matters is—"

"It *is* important. It is of paramount importance that Metep be kept apprized of all developments, especially where enemies of the state are concerned. I should have been awakened immediately. Precious time has already been wasted."

"I'm sorry, Jek. It won't happen again." *What's he been sniffing now?* Haworth wondered. *Acts like he thinks he's really running things!* "I'm going to get the interrogation procedures started as soon as I've had some breakfast. After we've learned all we can from him, we'll have a quiet little trial and have done with him."

"We can't wait that long!" Metep said, his vocal pitch rising, his lips twitching. "He must be tried and convicted *today!* And in public. I've already made arrangements for proceedings in Freedom Hall this afternoon."

The same odd sensation that Haworth had experienced last night upon learning that the prisoner had freely admitted to being Robin Hood, and again when told of the deferrential treatment given him by the Guard, came over him again. He could almost hear the crash, feel the vibrations as giant tumblers within some huge, unseen cosmic lock fell into place one by one.

"No! That's the worst thing you could do! This man has already become some sort of folk hero. Don't give him the extra exposure!"

Metep sneered. "Ridiculous! He's a common criminal and his own notoriety will be used against him." His face suddenly softened and he was the old Jek Milian again. "Don't you see, Daro? He's my last chance to save my reputation! We have evidence aplenty that he's Robin Hood; we just have to manufacture a little more to link him to Earth and blame him for this runaway inflation that's ruining everything. He'll get us all off the hook!"

"I'm calling a meeting of the council," Haworth said. "I can't let you do this!"

"I thought you'd say that!" Hard lines formed in Metep's features once more. "So I did that myself. If you think you can get enough votes to override me, you're wrong!" His face faded away.

Ω

Broohnin awoke cold and stiff with the light. After an instant of disorientation, he remembered his circumstances. He had been running on stims the past few days, and had left the city with none on him. The crash had come before dawn, and now the sun glowered hazily from its mid-morning perch in the sky.

Pulling himself erect, he immediately reached for the trigger. Wouldn't be long now. Everything had gone wrong and got pushed off the track. But now everything was going to be set right. A brief inspection in the light of day showed the safety mechanism to be of rudimentary construction, geared more toward the prevention of accidental firing than determined tampering. Easy to circumvent it. He'd just have to—

The trigger disappeared from his hands in a blur of motion. Broohnin whirled around as best he could from a sitting position, pulling his blaster out as he moved. That too was torn from his grasp as soon as it cleared his belt. When he saw who was behind him, all his sphincters let go in an uncontrolled rush.

Kanya dropped the trigger device and blaster at her feet and struck him across the face, sending him reeling into the dirt. As he tried to scramble to his feet and run away, she tripped him and knocked him sprawling again. Each time Broohnin caught a glimpse of her face it was the same: expressionless, emotionless, with neither anger nor mercy in her eyes, only cold, intense concentration. And silent. She uttered no sound as she hovered over him like an avenging angel of death.

With each attempt to rise, she would knock him flat again, bruising a new area of his body with unerring accuracy. He pleaded with her at first, but she might as well have been deaf. He gave that up soon. And when he gave up trying to escape her, she began to lift him up and hurl him against the ground or a boulder or a tree trunk. Always hurting him, always damaging him, always increasing the agony a little more each time. Yet never enough to cause him to lose consciousness. He became a broken-stringed marionette in the hands of a mad puppeteer, hurled limply from stage right to stage left.

Soon his eyes were swollen shut, and even if he had wanted to look at Kanya, he would have been unable to. And still the systematic beating continued. When he had seen her drop the blaster before she hit him the first time, Broohnin had been afraid Kanya intended to beat him to death. Now he was afraid she wouldn't.

XXI

A leader . . . is one of the things that distinguishes a mob from a people. He maintains the level of individuals. Too few individuals and a people reverts to a mob.

Stilgar

One look at the expressions on the faces around the table and Haworth knew he was wasting his time. The members of the council were disposed toward Jek in the first place, not only because he was the current Metep, but because they considered him one of their own. Haworth had always been an outsider. They were as frightened and confused as Jek, and he had their ear. So the Council of Five—*sans* Daro Haworth—was squarely behind Metep VII. He considered turning at the doorway and leaving them to approve Metep's proposal blindly, but forced himself to enter. He had to try. He had spent too many years clawing his way up to his present position to let everything go without a fight.

"Now that we're all here," Metep said as soon as Haworth had crossed the threshold, "the question will be brought to a vote." He wasn't even going to wait until Haworth was seated.

"Isn't there going to be any discussion?"

"We *have* discussed it," Metep said, "and we've decided, all of us, that a speedy public trial is the only sensible course. Documents are at this moment being prepared to show incontrovertible proof of Robin Hood's link with Earth. We'll show that Earth hired him and financed him, and even show that it was his theft of millions upon millions of Imperial marks that sparked the whole inflation spiral. And to demonstrate to the people that I am still their leader—a strong leader—*I* will personally conduct the trial."

Haworth sat down before answering. "Did it ever occur to any of you that this may be exactly what he wants you to do?"

Over rumbling comments of "Ridiculous!" and "Absurd!" Metep said, "No man in his right mind would turn himself over to us for trial. And I think you'll have to admit that this Robin Hood fellow—LaNague, isn't it?—is hardly insane. Nor is he stupid."

"Nor is he Robin Hood." The chatter stopped. Haworth had their attention now.

"He admits to it!"

Haworth smiled. "Very well: *I'll* admit to it, too. But that doesn't mean I'm Robin Hood. Any one of Robin Hood's so-called Merry Men could have volunteered to stand in for him. Remember, we don't have a single physical characteristic by which to identify Robin Hood. I'm willing to bet this man Peter LaNague is a fraud. I'm willing to bet he's been planted here just to make fools of us, to make us convict him and sentence him in public; and then he'll come up with evidence to prove that he wasn't even on Throne when the raids occurred. Keep in mind that there's no verifiable identity for the prisoner. We can't even prove he's someone called Peter LaNague, let alone Robin Hood!"

He watched their faces as they considered his words. He had been speaking calmly, softly, hiding his inner tension. He didn't believe a word of what he had just said, but he knew he had to stop the public trial and was throwing out every suspicious thought that popped into his head, anything that would muddy the water and keep the council members confused. He personally believed the man who called himself LaNague to be Robin Hood, and for that reason wanted him kept out of the public eye.

"But we *need* him to be Robin Hood!" Metep said into the ensuing silence. "He *must* be Robin Hood! It's the only way we can salvage *anything!*" His tone became plaintive. "The trial will draw attention from us to him. Discontent will focus on him and Earth. That will give us time—"

"No trial," Haworth said firmly. "Interrogate him quietly, execute him secretly, then announce that he has been released due to conflicting evidence and that the search for the real Robin Hood continues. No public trial is going to give us breathing room of any consequence."

"But that leaves us where we are now!" Metep said through quivering lips. "Don't you understand? They're out there getting ready to recall me! And when they kick me out, you'll all go with me!"

"You can declare martial law due to the economic crisis," Haworth said into Metep's growing hysteria. "They can't recall you then."

"But I don't want to be known as the only Metep who had to call out the Guard to stay in office! If I have to, I will, certainly. But the trial—"

"The trial is a trap!" Haworth was on his feet, shouting. It was a release of the pressure that had been building within him since Metep had awakened him this morning. It was also a last resort. "Can't you get it through those neutronium skulls of yours that we're dealing with a genius here? I know for certain in my mind that Robin Hood—whoever he is—is responsible for everything bad that has happened to us. I don't know how he did it, I don't know why, I don't know what his next move is, but I am certain a public trial is just what he expects of us. *Don't do it!* Let me interrogate him for a few days. The right combination of drugs will start him talking and then we'll know everything—perhaps even the identity of the real Robin Hood."

He paused for breath, watching their impassive faces. "Look . . . I'll compromise: when I'm done with him you can have your little show if you still want it. But let me break him first!"

"It must be now. Today." From Metep's tone, Haworth knew he was beyond persuasion. "All in favor?" Metep said, raising his right hand and not bothering to look around the table. The other four members of the council raised their hands.

Haworth wheeled and stalked toward the door. "Then it's on your heads! I'll have no part of it!"

"Where do you think you're going?" Metep asked in a flat, cold voice.

"Off this planet before you send it up in smoke!"

"Earth, perhaps?" Krager said, his lined face beaming gleefully in the wake of Haworth's defeat.

"You are under house arrest," Metep said. "You will be confined to your Complex quarters until the trial, at which time you will be escorted to Freedom Hall with the rest of us. I knew you'd try to run out on us and cannot allow it. It is crucial that we keep up appearances of unity."

"You can't do that!"

Metep smiled wanly as he pressed a stud on the table top. "Can't I?" The outer door cycled open and two guardsmen entered. "Take him."

Ω

By the time the guard stopped in front of the cell, LaNague had the lump in his right axilla trapped between his thumb and forefinger, ready to squeeze.

"Well," the guard said—this one was as portly as Steen had been lean, "the fecaliths on top must want to get you out of the way real bad, Mr. Robin Hood."

LaNague's fingers tightened on the lump. "What makes you say that?"

"They scheduled your trial for this afternoon . . . in Freedom Hall. It's all over the vid."

"Is that so?" LaNague released the lump, actually a pea-sized wad of jelly encased in an impermeable membrane, and relaxed. It was all he could do to keep from laughing aloud and doing a jig around the cell. He had dreaded the thought of squeezing that little packet, and now it looked as if he wouldn't have to. It contained a neuroleptic substance that would leak out into the surrounding subcutaneous fat when the membrane was ruptured. From there via the bloodstream it would eventually find the way to its only active site in the body, the Broca area in the right hemisphere of his brain, where it would cause a membrane dysfunction in the neurons there, effectively paralyzing his language function for two weeks. He would be incapable of verbalizing any of his thoughts; any questions asked verbally would be perceived as incoherent sound; written questions would be seen as a meaningless jumble of marks, beyond comprehension; anything he tried to write would come out the same way. The condition was known as total receptive and expressive aphasia. LaNague would be rendered incapable of giving his interrogators truth or fiction, no matter what drugs they pumped into him.

"I swear by the Core, it's the truth!" the guard said. "Never seen anybody brought to trial so fast. They're really going to make an example of you, I'm sorry to say."

"You don't think they should?"

The guard shook his head. "You had the right idea all along, from what I can tell. But how'd you know all this was going to happen?"

"History," LaNague said, refraining with an effort from quoting Santayana. "This has all happened before on Earth. Most of the time it ended in ruin and temporary stagnation. Occasionally it gave rise to monstrous evil. I was hoping we'd avoid both those roads this time."

"Looks like you're not going to be around to have much say either way," the guard said resignedly.

"What's your name?"

"Boucher. Why?"

"You could help me."

Boucher shook his head. "Don't ask me to get you out, because I couldn't, even if I decided to risk it. It's just not possible." He smiled. "You know, I could lose this job just for talking to you about it. Not that it would matter much. The money I get doesn't buy enough food for me to feed my kids. If it wasn't for the stuff I sneak out of the kitchen a couple of times a week, we'd starve. Imagine that! I'm getting paid a thousand marks an hour and I'm losing weight! And they missed paying us yesterday. If that happens again, we're going to start demanding twice-a-day pay periods or we'll walk. *Then* there'll be trouble! But no, I can't get you out. Even if I gave you my blaster, they'd stop you. They'd let you kill me before they'd let you out."

"I don't want that kind of help. I just want you to see that I get to the trial alive."

Boucher laughed. "No one's going to kill you, at least not until they give you the death sentence!" He sobered abruptly. "Look, I'm sorry I said that. I didn't mean—"

"I know you didn't. But I'm quite serious about that. Someone may try to see that I don't get to trial . . . ever."

"That's—"

"Just do this one favor for me. Get some of the other guards you know and trust, and keep careful watch. After all, I'm not asking anything more than what the Imperium pays you to do: guard a prisoner."

Boucher's eyes narrowed. "All right. If it'll make you feel better, I'll see to it." He walked away, glancing back over his shoulder every few paces and shaking his head as if he thought the infamous Robin Hood might be crazy after all.

LaNague wandered the perimeter of his cell. Adrenalin was pounding through his system, causing his heart to race, his underarms and palms to drip perspiration. Why? Everything was going according to plan. Why this feeling of impending doom? Why this shapeless fear that something was going to go terribly wrong? That he was going to die?

He stopped and breathed slowly and deeply, telling himself that everything was all right, that it was a stress reaction due to the swift approach of the trial. Everything would come to a head at the trial once Sayers played the designated tape sometime today, beaming Robin Hood's pre-recorded message out to the people. LaNague would then know if he had wasted the last five years. If he had, the Imperium would see to it that he had no further years left to waste.

Ω

Twelve ought to be enough, Mora thought. Even if the building down there were loaded with armed guards on full alert, twelve Flinters would be more than enough. As it was, according to Sayers, only a few unarmed and unsuspecting security personnel would be scattered throughout the three floors of the broadcasting station. No problem taking over.

That wasn't what filled her with dread. It was her own part in the little escapade about to be launched. Could she measure up? Maybe she shouldn't have destroyed Peter's spools. Maybe she had been overly critical of them. After all, Peter had been so right all along, why shouldn't he be right now? Mora clenched her teeth and closed her eyes in silent determination. *Don't think like that!* She had to follow through with this. She had burned her bridges, and the only way left was straight ahead. Peter *had* been wrong about those tapes and only she had had the courage to do something about them.

She glanced around at the impassive faces of the six robed figures crowded into the tiny flitter cabin with her. Six more hovered in the flitter behind. All were in full ceremonial battle dress, fully aware that their appearance alone was a most effective weapon.

The tension was making her ill. She wasn't used to this. Why did everyone else look so calm? Come to think of it, she looked calm, too. All her turmoil was sealed under her skin. She wondered if the Flinters beside her were equally knotted up inside. Probably not. No one could feel like this and be a Flinter.

It was time. The two craft swooped down to the roof of the broadcast station and the Flinters poured out of their flitters and through the upper entrance Sayers had arranged to leave open. They all had their assignments and would make certain that Mora had a clear path to her destination.

Sayers himself was in his studio on the second floor doing a well-publicized news special on Robin Hood. He had given her specific directions on how to reach his studio. The Flinters had cleared the way and no one questioned her presence in the building. She swung out of a drop-chute, turned left. There was a Flinter at the door to the studio, motioning her forward. This was it. Sayers was inside waiting to put her before millions of Throners. Her mind was suddenly blank. What was she going to say? Peter's very life depended on what she would be doing in the next few minutes.

I'm doing this for you, Peter, she thought as she crossed the threshold. *Neither of us is the same person we were when this began, but right or wrong, this is my way of saying I still believe in you.*

Ω

It was midday when Boucher returned, hurrying down the walkway, carrying something in his hand.

"You married?" he shouted from half the length of the corridor.

Filled with an unstable mixture of curiosity and dread, LaNague hesitated. "Yes," he finally managed to say. "Why?"

"Because somebody who says she's your wife is on the vid!" Boucher said, urging his bulky frame into a trot. "And is *she* going to be in trouble!" He puffed up to LaNague's cell and held out a hand-sized vid set. It was a flat screen model and Mora's face filled the viewplate.

LaNague watched with growing dismay as Mora sent out a plea for all those who had come to believe in Robin Hood to come to his aid. She was saying essentially what LaNague himself had said on the second pre-recorded spool—the one to be played for the trial contingency—but not the way he had said it. Her appeal was rambling, unfocused, obviously unrehearsed. She was ruining everything!

Or was she?

As LaNague listened, he realized that although Mora was speaking emotionally, the emotion was clearly genuine. She was afraid for her man and was making an appeal to any of his friends who might be listening to help him now when he needed them. Her eyes shone as she spoke, blazing with conviction. She was reaching for the heart as well as the mind, and risking her life to do it. Her message was for all Throners; but most of all, for her husband.

As she paused briefly before beginning her appeal again, Boucher glanced at LaNague, his voice thick. "That's some woman you've got there."

LaNague nodded, unable to speak. Turning his face away, he walked to the far corner of his cell and stood there, remembering how he had so bitterly resented Mora's very presence on Throne, his cold rejection of the warmth, love, and support she had offered. Through the thousand tiny insults and affronts he had heaped on her during the past few months, she had remained true to him, and truer than he to the cause they shared. He remained in the corner until he could breathe evenly again, until the muscles in his throat were relaxed enough to permit coherent speech, until the moisture welling in his eyes had receded to a normal level. Then he returned to the bars to watch and listen to the rest of Mora's appeal.

"Yes," he told Boucher. "Some woman."

Ω

They may have confined him to quarters, but at least he wasn't incommunicado. He had turned on the vid to see what Sayers would be saying to the public on his Robin Hood news special; but instead of the vidcaster's familiar face in the holofield, there was a strange woman calling herself Robin Hood's wife, pleading for revolution. He immediately tried to contact the studio, but no calls were being taken through the central circuits at the building. Checking a special directory, he found a security code to make the computer patch him through to the control booth in Sayers' studio.

A technician took the call. He did not look well. Although he recognized Daro Haworth immediately, it seemed to have little effect on him.

"What is going *on* over there? I want that transmission cut immediately! *Immediately!* Do you hear?"

"I can't do that, sir."

"Unless you want this to be the last free day of your life," Haworth screamed, "you will cut that transmission!"

"Sir . . ." The technician adjusted the angle on his visual pickup to maximum width, revealing a number of black-cloaked figures with red circles painted on their foreheads and weapons belts across their chests arrayed behind him. "Do you see my predicament?"

Flinters! Was Robin Hood a Flinter? "How did they get in?"

The technician shrugged. "All of a sudden they were here with the woman. Radmon seemed to be expecting them."

Sayers! Of course he'd be involved! "What about security? Didn't anyone try to stop them?"

The technician glanced over his shoulder, then back to Haworth. "Would you? We got an alarm off immediately but no one's showed up yet."

At that point, one of the Flinters leaned over and broke the connection. Shaken, but still functioning, Haworth immediately stabbed in the code to Commander Tinmer over at the Imperial Guard garrison. The commander answered the chime himself, and his expression was far from encouraging.

"Don't say it!" he said as soon as he recognized Haworth. "I've been personally trying to muster a force big enough to retake the broadcast station ever since we received the alarm."

"You've had plenty of time!"

"We're having some minor discipline problems here. The men are letting us know how unhappy they are with the way their pay has been handled recently. There's been a delay here and there in the currency shipments due to breakdowns in machinery over at Treasury, and the men seem to think that if the pay can be late, *they* can be late." His sudden smile was totally devoid of humor. "Don't worry. The problem's really not that serious. Just some flip talk and sloganeering. You know . . . 'No pay, no fight' . . . that sort of thing."

"What are they doing instead of obeying orders?"

Tinmer's smile died. "Instead of scrambling to their transports as ordered, most of them are still in their barracks watching that whore on the vid. But don't worry. We'll straighten everything out. Just need a little more time, is all. I—"

Haworth slammed his fist viciously against the power plate, severing the connection. He now saw the whole plan. The final pieces had just angled into place. But there was no attendant rush of triumph, only crushing depression. For he could see no way of salvaging the Imperium and his place within it. No way at all, except . . .

He pushed *that* thought away. It wasn't for him.

Gloom settled heavily. Haworth had devoted his life to the Imperium, or rather to increasing its power and making that power his own. And now it was all slipping away from him. By the end of the day he would be a political nonentity, a nobody, all his efforts of the past two decades negated by that man down in max-sec, that man who called himself Robin Hood.

It no longer mattered whether or not he was actually Robin Hood. The Imperium itself had identified him as such and that was good enough for the public. They were ready to follow him—Haworth could sense it. No matter if he were the true mastermind behind the colossal conspiracy that had brought the Imperium to its present state, or just a stand-in, the public knew his face and he would live in the battered and angry minds of all outworlders as Robin Hood.

Or die . . .

The previously rejected thought crept back into focus. Yes, that was a possible way out. If the proclaimed messiah were dead, the rabble would have no one to follow, no rallying point, no alternative to Metep and the Imperium. They would be enraged at his death, true, but they would be leaderless . . . and once again malleable.

It just might work. It *had* to work. But who to do it? Haworth could think of no one he could trust who could get close enough, and no one close enough he could trust to do it. Which left Haworth himself. The thought was repugnant—not the idea of killing, *per se*, but actually doing it himself. He was used to giving orders, to having others take care of unpleasant details. Trouble was, he had run out of others.

He went to a locked compartment in the wall and tapped in a code to open it. After the briefest hesitation, he withdrew a small blaster, palm-sized with a wrist clamp. He had bought it when civil disorder had threatened, when street gangs had moved out to the more affluent neighborhoods, oblivious to the prestige and position of their victims. He never dreamed it would be used for something like this.

Hefting the lightweight weapon in his hand, Haworth almost returned it to the compartment. He'd never get away with it.

Still . . . with an abrupt motion, he slammed the door shut and clamped the blaster to his right wrist.

As far as he could see, there was no choice. Robin Hood had to die if Haworth's life was to retain any meaning, and an opportunity to kill without being seen might come along. The tiny blaster could be angled in such a way that he could appear to be scratching the side of his face while sighting in on the target. With caution, and a great deal of luck, he could get away with it.

If he didn't get away with it—if he killed LaNague but was identified as the assassin, he would no doubt be torn to pieces on the spot. Haworth shrugged to no one but himself. It was worth the risk. If Robin Hood lived, the goals Haworth had pursued throughout his life would be placed far beyond his reach; if he killed him and was discovered, Haworth's very life would be taken from him. He could not decide which was worse.

Allowed to run to its conclusion, the Robin Hood plan would mean the end of everything Haworth had worked for. He would lose the power to shape the future of outworld civilization as he saw fit. He would be reduced from a maker of history to a footnote in history. Without ever standing for election, he had become a major guiding power within the Imperium . . . and perhaps should take some blame for guiding it into its current state. But he could fix everything—he was sure of it! All he needed was a little more time, a little more control, and a lot less Robin Hood.

Ω

There were fully a dozen guards escorting LaNague to Freedom Hall. He noticed Boucher in the lead and Steen among them, even though it wasn't his shift. The prisoners on max-sec all shouted encouragement as he was led away. So did the remaining guards.

"Boucher told me what you said about someone trying to kill you," Steen whispered as they marched through the tunnel that passed under the Complex and surfaced at the private entrance to Freedom Hall. "I think you're crazy but decided to come along anyway. Lots of crazy people around these days."

LaNague could only nod. The eerie feeling that he would never leave Freedom Hall alive was stealing over him again. Attributing it to last-minute panic didn't work. Nothing shook it loose, not even his fervent disbelief in premonitions of any sort.

His escort stopped in a small antechamber that opened onto

the dais at the end of the immense hall. The traditional elevated throne for Metep, a diadem-like structure with a central pedestal six meters high, had been set up center stage with five seats in a semi-circle around it at floor level. To the right of it, closer to LaNague, a makeshift dock had been constructed, looking like a gallows.

All for me, he thought.

Although he could catch only meager glimpses of it between the heads of his escort, it was the crowd that caught and held LaNague's attention. There were people out there. *Lots* of them. More people than he ever thought could possibly squeeze into Freedom Hall. A sea of humanity lapping at the dais. And from what he could gather, there were thousands more outside the building, trying to push their way in. All were chanting steadily, the various pitches and timbres and accents merging into a non-descript roar, repeating over and over:

". . . FREE ROBIN! . . . FREE ROBIN! . . . FREE ROBIN! . . ."

When the Council of Five finally made its appearance, its members looked distinctly uneasy as they glanced at the unruly crowd surging against the bulkhead of Imperial Guard, three men deep at all points and fully armed, that separated them from their loyal subjects. Haworth came in last, and LaNague had the impression that he was under some sort of guard himself. Had the chief adviser been threatened, or had he decided to skip the public trial and been overruled? Interesting.

The noise from the crowd doubled at sight of the council, the two words of the chant ricocheting off the walls, permeating the air. And it trebled when Metep VII, dressed in his ceremonial finest for the vid cameras sending his image to the millions of Throners who could not be here, was led in and rode his throne up the pedestal to the top of the diadem.

All six of the Imperium's leaders appeared disturbed by the chant, but in different ways. The council members were overtly fearful and looked as if nothing would please them more than to be somewhere else, the farther away the better. Metep VII, however, looked annoyed, angry, suitably imperious. He was taking the chant as a personal affront. Which, of course, it was.

When his seat had reached the top of the diadem's central pedestal, Metep spoke. Directional microphones focused automatically on him and boomed his amplified voice over the immense crowd within, and out to the throngs surrounding Freedom Hall and choking the streets leading to it.

"There will be silence during these proceedings," he said in a voice that carried such confidence and authority that the crowd quieted to hear what he had to say. "Any observers who cannot conduct themselves in a manner suitable to the gravity of the matter at hand will be ejected." He looked to his left. "Bring out the prisoner."

As LaNague was led to the dock, the crowd rustled and rippled and surged like the waters of a bay raised to a chop by a sudden blast of wind. People were pushing forward, craning their necks, climbing on each other's shoulders for a look at the man who had made it rain money. The Imperial Guardsmen assigned to crowd control had their hands full, but even they managed a peek over their shoulders at the dock.

There were a few cheers, a few short-lived, disorganized chants of "Free Robin!" but mostly a hushed awe. LaNague looked out on the sea of faces and felt a horrific ecstasy jolt through him. They were for him—he could feel it. But they were so strong, so labile . . . they could wreak terrible damage if they got out of control. Much would depend on pure luck from here on in.

"The prisoner's name is Peter LaNague, and he has freely admitted to being the criminal known as Robin Hood. He is to be tried today for armed robbery, sedition, and other grievous crimes against the state."

The crowd's reaction was spontaneous: multiple cries of "No!" merged smoothly and quickly into a single, prolonged, deafening, "*NOOOOO!*"

Metep was overtly taken aback by the response, but with a contemptuous toss of his head he pressed on, fumbling only on the first word when he spoke again.

"Due to the extraordinary nature of the crimes involved, the trial will be held before a tribunal consisting of Metep and the Council of Five, rather than the traditional jury. This is in accordance with the special emergency powers available to the Imperium during times of crisis such as these."

"*NOOOOO!*" Clenched fists shot into the air.

Metep rose in his seat. From the docket, LaNague could see that the man was clearly furious, his regal mien chipping, cracking, flaking off.

"You admire Robin Hood?" he said to the crowd in a voice that shook with anger. "Wait! Just wait! Before we are through here today, we will have presented irrefutable evidence that this man who calls himself Robin Hood is in truth an agent of Earth, and an enemy of all loyal outworlders!"

The "Nooooo!" that rose from the audience then was somewhat diminished in its resonance and volume, due not to a lessening of conviction in the crowd, but to the fact that many people in the hall had begun to laugh.

"And the penalty for this"—there was a touch of hysteria in Metep's voice as it climbed toward a scream; sensing it, the crowd quieted momentarily—"is death!"

If Metep VII had expected utter silence to follow his pronouncement, he was to be bitterly disappointed. The responding *"NOOOOOOO!"* was louder and longer than any preceding it. But the crowd was not going to limit itself to a merely verbal outburst this time. Like a single Gargantuan mass of protoplasm leaving the primordial sea for the first time, it flowed toward the dais shouting, "FREE ROBIN! FREE ROBIN!" The Imperial Guardsmen could do no more than give ground gracefully, pushing with the sides of their blaster rifles against the incredible mass of humanity that faced them, retreating steadily rearward despite their best efforts.

"Order!" Metep shrieked from his pedestal. "Order! I will have the Guard shoot to kill the first man to set foot on the dais!"

On hearing this, one of the guardsmen backed up toward the diadem throne and looked up at Metep, then back to the crowd. With obvious disgust, he raised his blaster rifle over his head, held it there momentarily, then hurled it to the floor in front of him.

That did it. That was the chink in the dam. Within the span of a single heartbeat, the rest of the guardsmen threw down their own weapons, leaving nothing between the crowd and the dais. Most of them joined in the forward rush, shouting "FREE ROBIN!" along with everybody else.

The crowd divided spontaneously, part surging toward Metep's throne, the rest rushing in LaNague's direction. He knew their intent was to rescue him, but he was frightened all the same. Their movements were so wild and frantic that he feared they would unintentionally wash over and trample him to death.

They didn't. Their laughing faces surrounded the dock, calling his name, tearing the side railings away with bare hands, pulling him from the platform and hoisting him onto their shoulders.

A much grimmer scene was being played at center stage as the other half of the crowd—the angry half—stormed the diadem throne. The members of the Council of Five on the lower level were completely ignored as they scattered in all directions. The crowd wanted only one man, the man who represented the Imperium itself: Metep VII. Seeing his angry subjects approaching him, Metep had wisely locked his seat into position at the top of the pedestal. All attempts to start his descent failed until someone thought of shaking him loose.

The diadem throne was a huge, gaudy structure with considerable mass. But the crowd, too, was huge and considerably determined. At first the throne moved imperceptibly as the group on one side pushed while the other pulled, both quickly reversing their efforts. Soon the entire structure was swaying back and forth, with Metep VII, bereft of every shred of dignity, clutching desperately to his seat to the accompaniment of wild laughter from below. And when he finally decided to start his seat back down the pedestal, it was too late. He suddenly lost his grip and tumbled screaming to the waiting crowd below. The roar of human voices that arose then was deafening.

LaNague's immediate concern was that the crowd would beat Metep without mercy. Fortunately, that was not to be. Metep's scrambling efforts to maintain purchase on the rocking throne had been comedic enough to raise the general mood of his tormentors, averting a potentially ugly confrontation. He was hauled by his arms and his legs like so much baggage to the dock that had just been vacated by his former prisoner, while LaNague was carried shouldertop to the now empty throne. The seat had reached floor level by this time and LaNague was thrust into it. Someone reversed the controls and it began to ascend the pedestal again, this time with a new occupant. As he rode toward the top of the diadem, a new chant arose from below:

"METEP EIGHT! *METEP EIGHT*! METEP EIGHT! . . ."

LaNague ignored it, expecting this kind of response. It was naïve, it was shortsighted, it was all too typical. It was why history repeated itself, over and over. What he had not expected was to be raised on this idiotic throne. He felt ridiculous and naked, like an oversized blaster target. For that feeling was back; the feeling that he was going to die.

He brushed it off again. It was just that he hadn't heard from Kanya, which meant that Broohnin could still be loose with the trigger to the big Barsky box. If activated, it would mean instant death for LaNague and everyone in sight.

He looked around at the undulating mass of upturned faces, all joyous, all filled with unhoped for hope, all sensing that they were midwives at the birth of something new. Just what it might be, they didn't know, but it had to be better than what they had been living through recently.

Not all faces were smiling, however. He spotted Haworth looking up at him, his right hand pressed against his forehead—injured, perhaps?—a look of utter concentration on his face, his left eye squinted closed. The crowd seemed to be ignoring him despite his outlandish appearance. Metep had held the title and was therefore the power in the Imperium as far as the public was concerned. Only a few knew Haworth as the real decision-maker.

LaNague looked away from the chief adviser, back toward the huge expanse of the crowd stretching to the far end of Freedom Hall and out into the growing darkness beyond. As his head moved, however, he caught a glint at Haworth's wrist out of the corner of his eye, and realized what the man was doing.

Pointing below, LaNague rose to his feet and shouted, "Daro Haworth!" The remote directional microphones, automatically trained on the seat's occupant, Metep or not, amplified it to a "*DARO HAWORTH!*" that shook the walls.

Silence descended on Freedom Hall like a muffling cloak as Haworth was immediately grabbed and his arms pinned to his sides by a familiar middle-aged male figure.

"Release him," LaNague said, his voice still amplified, but not to such a degree now that he was speaking in a more subdued tone. "And give him room."

The crowd either would not or could not move away from Haworth. They kept pawing at him, shoving him.

"Give him room, please," LaNague said from almost directly above the scene. When the crowd around Haworth still did not move back, he nodded to the middle-aged man who then touched a hand to his belt. The holosuit flickered off and suddenly there was a Flinter female in full battle regalia beside Haworth. And just as suddenly there was a circle of empty space around Haworth as people backed away. Kanya had returned.

"Go ahead, Mr. Haworth," LaNague said in a soft voice audible to the end of Freedom Hall. "Kill me. That's what you were about to do, wasn't it? Do it. But bring your blaster out into the open so everyone can watch. When this mock trial was over and I was found guilty—the verdict was never in doubt, was it?—I was to be executed. But you were going to let someone else do the actual deed. Now that won't be necessary. The pleasure is yours alone. Do it."

LaNague felt dizzy standing there six meters in the air, watching a man with artificially darkened skin and artificially whitened hair pull a blaster from his sleeve and point it in his direction. But he had to stand fast, hoping Haworth would miss if he fired, that Kanya would be able to ruin his aim. Hoping above all that he would be able to face Haworth down. The scene was being played to every operating vid set on the planet, and being recorded for replay on all the other outworlds. Metep, slumped useless and ruined in the prisoner's dock, had already been made to look like a fool. All that was left now was Haworth, who had to be faced and disgraced, otherwise he might become a rallying point for the few royalists who would remain active in the wake of the revolution.

Haworth looked as frightened as LaNague felt. And although the weapon was pointed upward, he was not sighting on his target. Instead, his head swiveled back and forth, oscillating between the flesh and blood Flinter beside him, to the silent, fearful, hostile ring of faces that enclosed him.

LaNague's voice became a booming whisper. "*Now*, Mr. Haworth. Now, or drop it."

With an agonized groan of equal parts fear and frustration, Haworth swung the blaster away from LaNague and placed the lens at the end of the barrel against his forehead. Members of the crowd behind him winced and ducked, fully expecting the back of his head to explode over them. Haworth glanced quickly about and saw that only Kanya was standing within reach of him. She had the ability to snatch the weapon from his hand before he could fire, but she did not move.

Neither did Haworth. Even the perfunctory courtesy of forcible restraint from committing suicide was to be denied him. He was on his own, completely. No one was going to pull the trigger for him, no one was going to prevent him from pulling it himself. It was all up to him. As centerpiece in the grim tableau, with all Throne—and soon all of the outworlds—watching, he stood naked, stripped of all pretense, split from throat to pubes with all his innards steaming and reeking in the air for everyone to see.

An utterly miserable and despairing sob broke from his lips as he let his arm slump to his side and the blaster fall unused to the floor. Kanya scooped it up immediately. As she led him away, the chant began again.

"METEP EIGHT! METEP EIGHT! METEP EIGHT!"

LaNague sat down heavily in the chair to take the weight

off his suddenly wobbly knees. As he gathered his thoughts, gathered his strength, and hoped that he had been looking death in the eye for the last time that day, he heard the chant falter. Looking up, he saw the crowd dividing down the middle. Like a vibe-knife through a haunch of raw meat, a wedge of a dozen or so Flinters was cleaving a path toward the dais. Watching the group move closer, he saw that someone was shielded within that wedge: Mora.

As soon as he recognized her, LaNague started his seat into descent. By the time it reached the floor of the diadem, Mora was standing there, waiting for him. She leaped to his side in the chair, and as they embraced, the chair began to climb the pedestal again.

At that point, the crowd within and without Freedom Hall dissolved into a veritable frenzy of jubilation. None of LaNague's carefully calculated ploys to win support from the people of Throne could even approach the impact of seeing him and his wife embrace on the diadem throne. All present had seen Mora on the vid; most were there in response to her plea. And now they saw her together with her man and felt they had played a part in reuniting the couple. They were cheering for themselves as well as for Robin Hood and his gutsy wife.

"I love you," LaNague whispered close to Mora's ear. "I never stopped. I just . . . went away for a while."

"I know," she said in a voice as soft as the body he clutched against him. "And it's good to have you back."

Gradually, the cheers organized into the bothersome chant: "METEP EIGHT! METEP EIGHT! METEP EIGHT!"

Would they never tire of calling for a new Metep? As he looked down into the thousands of hopeful eyes, the thousands of happy, trusting faces, he knew that the past five years had all been a prelude. Now the *real* work began. He had to take all the horrors these people had experienced and wash them away; he had to convince them that although it could happen again, it need not; that there was another way . . . a better way. Doing that might prove more difficult than the revolution itself.

He had to convince all these good people that he was not the new Metep. More, he had to convince them that they did not want another Metep. Ever again.

Epilogue

> Still one more thing, fellow citizens: a wise and frugal government, which shall refrain men from injuring one another, which shall leave them otherwise free to regulate their own pursuits of industry and improvement, and shall not take from the mouth of labor the bread it has earned. This is the sum of good government.
>
> *Thomas Jefferson*

He threw the clothes into the shipping canister with sharp, angry motions. Had they been objects made of something less pliant than cloth they would have shattered or bounced off to the other side of the room. A full standard year ago he had been brought to the Imperium Complex a prisoner; he had remained within the Complex after the revolution of his own accord. Now he was leaving. Leaving Throne altogether, in fact. For good.

By the window, Pierrot's trunk was in a constant state of slow, confused flux. The tree appeared healthy, with new growth a lighter green against the dark of the old. The trunk was now held in a neutral position, balancing LaNague's joyous anticipation of returning to Tolive against his anger at the piece of news he had just received.

A long year, this last one, and ultimately frustrating. It had begun so well in Freedom Hall, telling the assembled multitudes there and all the millions watching on the vid that a new Metep was not the answer, that the Imperium was dead and should gratefully be allowed to remain so. The enthusiastic cheers that greeted this were repeated when LaNague broached his idea that the outworlds band together within a totally new structure, one of unique design, with many-doored walls and no roof—an alliance that would allow each member planet to pursue its own course in whatever direction its inhabitants desired, and yet still feel a part of the whole of humanity. In the bright afterglow of Metep's downfall, anything and everything seemed possible.

A call was sent to all the sibling outworlds: the Imperium is dead . . . send us someone you trust to help form a new organization, a new alliance—a Federation. And while the people of Throne awaited the arrival of the representatives, the task of restoring social and economic stability was begun.

Muscle was provided by the planet Flint. For the first—and doubtlessly the last—time in outworld history, Flinters became a common sight on the streets of another planet. They were especially visible on the streets of Primus City. And when there were none in view, it was highly possible that an innocent-looking civilian was actually a holographic patina under which lurked an armed Flinter, ready to strike if attacked.

Such tactics were necessary. Too many street gangs had formed during the holocaust; too many had come to think of the streets they roamed as their own private preserves, had become accustomed to taking whatever they wanted, whenever they wanted it. They had to be dealt with . . . sometimes harshly. Gang members either learned that violence was no longer a means to anything on Throne, or died trying to prove otherwise. The word was out: peace or else.

Soon, there was peace.

Coincident with the Flinter efforts, Tolive took on the massive task of correcting the economic chaos that was the underlying cause of the social upheaval. Freighterloads of gold and silver coins, minted on Tolive and stamped with the now familiar star-in-the-ohm insignia that had become so intimately associated with Robin Hood, were delivered to Throne. Exchange rates were established for trading the new coins for the worthless paper marks glutting the economy. Someday the Tolivians hoped to be paid back, at least partially. There was no hope of full reimbursement, ever. But this was the price they were willing to pay. They were, in effect, buying a secure future for their way of life. To their minds, it was money well spent.

The effect of a new, stable medium of exchange was almost miraculous. Within days, the transport unions were back to work, raw materials were reaching manufacturers, staple commodities were flowing into the cities. Gone were demands for daily and twice-daily pay periods, gone was the fearful drive to spend whatever one had as soon as it was in hand, gone the urge to hoard. Old businesses reopened, and a few new ones started up, all looking for workers. During the holocaust it had been futile to manufacture or offer a product for sale—if it wasn't stolen first, the money received in exchange would be depreciating in buying power so rapidly that it became a losing proposition even to consider any sort of commerce. Now, it was different.

The hope and feeling of security engendered by the hard currency went a long way toward restoring a sense of normalcy. Tomorrow was no longer feared, but eagerly anticipated. Myriad problems needed attending, however. Despite the resurgence of industrial activity, there remained a huge body of unemployed, many of them former employees of the Imperium. The dole was temporarily maintained for their sake, and those able were put to work cleaning up the debris of the breakdown. As new businesses sprung up to tend to the tasks no longer being done by the Imperium's endless arrays of bureaus, the former government workers gradually found places for themselves.

Throne was undergoing an amazing transformation. Someone had answers; someone was in charge again and everything was going to be all right. The people were ready to follow Robin Hood anywhere, do anything he said, just as long as they didn't have to go through *that* again. LaNague found no comfort in their blind devotion. Had he been a different sort of man, he could have forged the outworlds into a totalitarian regime the likes of which human history had never seen. Throners especially were so vulnerable during the aftermath that they would have done anything he asked as long as he kept food on the shelves and the monorails on schedule. It was sad. It was terrifying.

The representatives from the other outworlds finally began arriving, in an uncertain trickle at first, then in a steady stream. LaNague gathered them all together in Freedom Hall and presented them with a blueprint for a new alliance, a charter for a commonality of planets that would provide a nucleus for defining the goals and common interests of the member worlds, yet would stay out of all planetary and interplanetary affairs as long as aggression was not involved. The Outworld Federation, as LaNague called it, would serve mainly as a peace-keeping force and would be strictly bound by the limits of the charter, a document written, rewritten, and refined by generations of the LaNague family.

No planet could initiate force against another planet without risking immediate reprisals by the Federation Defense Force. The Federation would be a voluntaristic organization; member planets would pay dues and would have a voice in Federation policy—a tiny voice, for the charter put strict limits on what the organization could do; in turn, they would receive the full protection of the Defense Force. Planets not wishing to join could go it alone, but could not expect any aid from the Federation at any time.

Only one internal requirement was mandated of every planet: all inhabitants of said planet, who were not fugitives from justice, must be free to emigrate at will. A planet could place whatever restrictions it wished on ingress, but free egress with all legally acquired possessions was an absolute necessity for membership. Penalties for infringement of this rule ranged from fines to expulsion.

Beyond containing the aggressive tendencies of its more acquisitive members, and protecting the free movement of trade between all the planets in its jurisdiction, the charter left the Federation with little to do. Unless someone somewhere initiated force against a member planet or its citizens, the Federation merely stood by and watched humanity go about its business. Many of the representatives found this sort of radical noninterventionism profoundly disturbing. It was something completely beyond their experience, beyond their education, as alien as the Tarks had seemed when news of their existence was announced. In the minds of many representatives, the form of government envisioned in the LaNague Charter was simply not enough. It didn't really . . . govern.

And that's when the trouble began.

LaNague realized now that he should have seen it coming.

Even Broohnin foresaw it when LaNague had visited him in the hospital where he was recovering from the not-quite fatal beating Kanya had administered to him. After reading through the charter, Broohnin had laughed derisively.

"I always said you were a dreamer, LaNague! They'll cut this thing to pieces the minute you turn your back! They'll hack away at it, bit by bit by bit until you won't recognize it. They won't be able to keep their hands off it!"

LaNague hadn't believed him then; he was sure the outworlds had learned their lesson. He was wrong. A significant percentage of the representatives who appeared intelligent turned out to be ineducable in certain areas of life. There followed a battle that took up the remainder of the year, between the purists who wanted the charter accepted as it was, reactionaries who wanted significant changes, and centrists who proposed a compromise—leave the charter as is, but attach an emergency clause to be activated only in times of crisis to give the Federation special powers to deal with an unexpected and grave threat to the member planets.

Despite LaNague's months of pleading, cajoling, threatening, warning, and begging, word had just come through that the charter had been accepted *in toto*—with the emergency clause firmly attached by an overwhelming majority of the representatives. The Outworld Federation, which many were now calling the LaNague Federation, had been born. Throne was to be renamed Federation Central, and a new era was beginning for the outworlds.

Pete LaNague's anger was fading to despondence now as he continued to pack. He had sent word to the representatives that he wanted his name completely expunged from the violated version of the charter. He disowned it and the Federation itself, and would have no further contact with anyone connected with the organization. The new president of the General Council sent his regrets, but said that as far as everyone was concerned, it was still the LaNague Charter.

Privately, LaNague knew he might one day change his mind, but for now he was too angry, too discouraged. All those years . . . all that work . . . had it all been for nothing? He saw the emergency clause as a ticking bomb sitting under the charter and the organization it guided, a constant temptation to all the Daro Haworths and would-be Meteps of the future.

The vidphone chimed. It was Broohnin. With his beard gone, he looked almost handsome, his features marred only by the triangular scar on his cheek and the leering smile twisting his lips.

"Just heard the news. Looks like they've already started tearing up your little dream. What're you going to do now?"

"Leave. Right behind you."

"Oh, I'm leaving all right," he said, his eyes squinting in anger. "But don't think I'm just going to sit around and get fat on Nolevatol. I'll be getting together a few people who think like me, and when your *Federation*"—he spat the word—"steps out of line, I'll be ready to make life miserable for it!"

"Good," LaNague said tiredly. "Because I won't. I'm through." He cut the transmission.

Broohnin had been allowed to remain on Throne to recuperate as long as LaNague and Flinters remained to watch him. Kanya had broken nearly every bone in his body, and although fully mended now, he would have aches and pains and stiffness as lifetime reminders. With LaNague's departure, Broohnin was being deported to Nolevatol, his homeworld.

LaNague's own homeworld, and all it held, awaited him. He and Mora had returned to Tolive shortly after the revolution. He still could not get over how Laina had grown and changed. After a few weeks of getting to know both his wife and his daughter again, he had returned to Throne, leaving them behind. His next homecoming was to be his last.

He went to the window and looked out at the quiet, green expanse of Imperium Park, wondering what they were going to rename it . . . not LaNague Park, he hoped. The sunlight, the sight of children playing, of couples walking slowly along, leaning together, making plans, lightened his mood.

Perhaps he was being too hard on his fellow outworlders. Perhaps it was possible the emergency clause would never be invoked. Perhaps the outworlds had truly learned their lesson. He hoped so. He had given them their chance. The rest was up to them and their children.

Peter LaNague was going home.

triangular scar on his cheek and the leering smile twisting his lips.

"Just avoid the news. Looks like they've already started tearing up your little dream. What're you going to do now?"

"Leave. Right behind you."

"Oh, I'm leaving all right," he said, his eyes squinting in anger. "But don't think I'm just going to sit around and get fat on Nokovatol. I'll be putting together a few people who think like me, and when your Federation—hope I got the word—steps out of line, I'll be ready to make life miserable for it."

"Good," LaNague said dryly. "Because I won't. I'm through." He cut the transmission.

Brodhun had been allowed to remain on Throne to recuperate as long as LaNague and Flinters remained to watch him. Kanya had broken nearly every bone in his body, and although fully mended now, he would have aches and pains and stiffness as lifetime reminders. With LaNague's departure, Brodhun was being deported to Nokovatol, his homeworld.

LaNague's own homeworld, and all it held, awaited him. He and Mora had returned to Tolive shortly after the revolution. He still could not get over how Lana had grown and changed. After a few weeks of getting to know both his wife and his daughter again, he had returned to Throne, leaving them behind. His next homecoming was to be his last.

He went to the window and looked out at the quiet, green expanse of Imperium Park, wondering what they were going to rename it ... not LaNague Park, he hoped. The sunlight, the sight of children playing, of couples walking slowly along, leaning together, making plans, softened his mood.

Perhaps he was being too hard on his fellow outworlders. Perhaps it was possible the emergency clause would never be invoked. Perhaps the Outworlds had truly learned their lesson. He hoped so. He had given them their chance. The rest was up to them and their children.

Peter LaNague was going home.

TWO:
EARLY PHASE

HEALER I

(age 36)

Heal Thyself

The Healer was a striking, extraordinary man whose identity was possibly the best-kept secret in human history. To this date, after hundreds of thousands of research hours by countless scholars, it remains an enigma. There can be no doubt that he led a double existence much like that of the romantic fictional heros of yore. Considering the hysterical adulation that came to focus on him, an alter ego was an absolute necessity if he was to have any privacy at all.

For some inexplicable reason, however, the concept of a double identity became subject to mythification and evolved into one of the prime canons of The Healer liturgy: that this man had two *minds,* two *distinct areas of consciousness, and was thereby able to perform his miraculous cures.*

This, of course, is preposterous.

from *The Healer: Man & Myth*
by Emmerz Fent

I

The orbital survey had indicated this clearing as the probable site of the crash, but long-range observation had turned up no signs of wreckage. Steven Dalt was doing no better at close range. Something had landed here with tremendous impact not too long ago: There was a deep furrow, a few of the trees were charred, and the grass had not yet been able to fully cover the earth-scar. So far, so good. But where was the wreckage? He had made a careful search of the trees around the clearing and there was nothing of interest there. It was obvious now that there would be no quick, easy solution to the problem, as he had originally hoped, so he started the half-kilometer trek back to his concealed shuttle-craft.

Topping a leafy rise, he heard a shout off to his left and turned to see a small party of mounted colonists. Tependians by their garb. The oddity of the sight struck him. They were well inside the Duchy of Bendelema, and that shouldn't be: Bendelema and Tependia had been at war for generations. Dalt shrugged and started walking again. He'd been away for years and it was very possible that something could have happened in that time to soften relations between the two duchies. Change was the rule on a splinter world.

One of the colonists pointed an unwieldy apparatus at Dalt

and something went *thip* past his head. Dalt went into a crouch and ran to his right. There had been at least one change since his departure: Someone had reinvented the crossbow.

The hooves of the Tependian mounts thudded in pursuit as he raced down the slope into a dank, twilit grotto, and Dalt redoubled his speed as he realized how simple it would be for his pursuers to surround and trap him in this sunken area. He had to gain the high ground on the other side before he was encircled. Halfway up the far slope, he was halted by the sound of hooves ahead of him. They had succeeded in cutting him off.

Dalt turned and made his way carefully down the slope. If he could just keep out of sight, they might think he had escaped the ring they had thrown around the grotto. Then, when it got dark—

A bolt smashed against a stone by his foot. "There he is!" someone cried, and Dalt was on the run again.

He began to weigh the situation in his mind. If he kept on running, they were bound to keep on shooting at him, and one of them just might put a bolt through him. If he stopped running, he might have a chance. They might let him off with his life. Then he remembered that he was dressed in serf's clothing and serfs who ran from anyone in uniform were usually put to the sword. Dalt kept running.

Another bolt flashed by, this one ripping some bark off a nearby tree. They were closing in—they were obviously experienced at this sort of work—and it wouldn't be long before Dalt was trapped at the lowest point of the grotto, with nowhere else to go.

Then he saw the cave mouth, a wide, low arch of darkness just above him on the slope. It was about a meter and a half high at its central point. With a shower of crossbow bolts raining around him, Dalt quickly ducked inside.

It wasn't much of a cave. In the dark and dampness Dalt soon found that it rapidly narrowed to a tunnel too slender for his shoulders to pass. There was nothing else for him to do but stay as far back as possible and hope for the best . . . which wasn't much no matter how he looked at it. If his pursuers didn't feel like coming in to drag him out, they could just sit back and fill the cave with bolts. Sooner or later one would have to strike him. Dalt peered out the opening to see which it would be.

But his five pursuers were doing nothing. They sat astride

their mounts and stared dumbly at the cave mouth. One of the party unstrung his crossbow and began to strap it to his back. Dalt had no time to wonder at their behavior, for in that instant he realized he had made a fatal error. He was in a cave on Kwashi, and there was hardly a cave on Kwashi that didn't house a colony of alarets.

He jumped into a crouch and sprinted for the outside. He'd gladly take his chances against crossbows rather than alarets any day. But a warm furry oval fell from the cave ceiling and landed on his head as he began to move. As his ears roared and his vision turned orange and green and yellow, Steve Dalt screamed in agony and fell to the cave floor.

Hearing that scream, the five Tependian scouts shook their heads and turned and rode away.

Ω

It was dark when he awoke and he was cold and alone . . . and alive. That last part surprised him when he remembered his situation, and he lost no time in crawling out of the cave and into the clean air under the open stars. Hesitantly, he reached up and peeled from his scalp the shrunken, desiccated remains of one dead alaret. He marveled at the thing in his hand. Nowhere in the history of Kwashi, neither in the records of its long-extinct native race nor in the memory of anyone in its degenerated splinter colony, had there ever been mention of someone surviving the attack of an alaret.

The original splinter colonists had found artifacts of an ancient native race soon after their arrival. The culture had reached preindustrial levels before it was unaccountably wiped out; a natural cataclysm of some sort was given the blame. But among the artifacts were found some samples of symbolic writing, and one of these samples—evidently aimed at the children of the race—strongly warned against entering any cave. It seemed that a creature described as the *killing-thing-on-the-ceilings-of-caves* would attack anything that entered. The writing warned: "Of every thousand struck down, nine hundred and ninety-nine will die."

William Alaret, a settler with some zoological training, had heard the translation and decided to find out just what it was all about. He went into the first cave he could find and emerged seconds later, screaming and clawing at the furry little thing on his head. He became the first of many fatalities attributed to the *killing-thing-on-the-ceilings-of-caves*, which were named "alarets" in his honor.

Dalt threw the alaret husk aside, got his bearings, and headed for his hidden shuttlecraft. He anticipated little trouble this time. No scouting party, if any were abroad at this hour, would be likely to spot him, and Kwashi had few large carnivores.

The ship was as he had left it. He lifted slowly to fifty thousand meters and then cut in the orbital thrust. That was when he first heard the voice.

("Hello, Steve.")

If it hadn't been for the G-forces against him at that moment, Dalt would have leaped out of his chair in surprise.

("This pressure is quite uncomfortable, isn't it?") the voice said, and Dalt realized that it was coming from inside his head. The thrust automatically cut off as orbit was reached and his stomach gave its familiar free-fall lurch.

("Ah! this is much better.")

"What's going on?" Dalt cried aloud as he glanced frantically about. "Is this someone's idea of a joke?"

("No joke, Steve. I'm what's left of the alaret that landed on your head back in that cave. You're quite lucky, you know. Mutual death is a sure result—most of the time, at least—whenever a creature of high-level intelligence is a target for pairing.")

I'm going mad! Dalt thought.

("No, you're not, at least not yet. But it is a possibility if you don't sit back and relax and accept what's happened to you.")

Dalt leaned back and rested his eyes on the growing metal cone that was the Star Ways Corporation mothership, on the forward viewer. The glowing signal on the console indicated that the bigger ship had him in traction and was reeling him in.

"Okay, then. Just what *has* happened to me?" He felt a little ridiculous speaking out loud in an empty cabin.

("Well, to put it in a nutshell: You've got yourself a roommate, Steve. From now on, you and I will be sharing your body.")

"In other words, I've been invaded!"

("That's a loaded term, Steve, and not quite accurate. I'm not really taking anything from you except some of your privacy, and that shouldn't really matter since the two of us will be so intimately associated.")

"And just what gives you the right to invade my mind?" Dalt asked quickly, then added: "*—and* my privacy?"

("Nothing gives me the right to do so, but there are extenuating circumstances. You see, a few hours ago I was a furry, lichen-eating cave slug with no intelligence to speak of—")

"For a slug you have a pretty good command of the language!" Dalt interrupted.

("No better and no worse than yours, for I derive whatever intelligence I have from you. You see, we alarets, as you call us, invade the nervous system of any creature of sufficient size that comes near enough. It's an instinct with us. If the creature is a dog, then we wind up with the intelligence of a dog—that *particular* dog. If it's a human and if he survives, as you have done, the invading alaret finds himself possessing a very high degree of intelligence.")

"You used the word 'invade' yourself just then."

("Just an innocent slip, I assure you. I have no intention of taking over. That would be quite immoral.")

Dalt laughed grimly. "What would an ex-slug know about morality?"

("With the aid of your faculties I can reason now, can I not? And if I can reason, why can't I arrive at a moral code? This is your body and I am here only because of blind instinct. I have the ability to take control—not without a struggle, of course—but it would be immoral to attempt to do so. I couldn't vacate your mind if I wanted to, so you're stuck with me, Steve. Might as well make the best of it.")

"We'll see how 'stuck' I am when I get back to the ship," Dalt muttered. "But I'd like to know how you got into my brain."

("I'm not exactly sure of that myself. I know the path I followed to penetrate your skull—if you had the anatomical vocabulary I could describe it to you, but my vocabulary is your vocabulary and yours is very limited in that area.")

"What do you expect? I was educated in cultural studies, not medicine!"

("It's not important anyway. I remember almost nothing of my existence before entering your skull, for it wasn't until then that I first became truly aware.")

Dalt glanced at the console and straightened up in his seat. "Well, whatever you do, go away for now. I'm ready to dock and I don't want to be distracted."

("Gladly. You have a most fascinating organism and I have

much exploring to do before I become fully acquainted with it. So long for now, Steve. It's nice knowing you.")

A thought drifted through Dalt's head: If I'm going nuts, at least I'm not doing it halfheartedly!

II

Barre was there to meet him at the dock. "No luck, Steve?"

Dalt shook his head and was about to add a comment when he noticed Barre staring at him with a strange expression.

"What's the matter?"

"You won't believe me if I tell you," Barre replied. He took Dalt's arm and led him into a nearby men's room and stood him in front of a mirror.

Dalt saw what he expected to see: a tall, muscular man in the garb of a Kwashi serf. Tanned face, short, glossy brown hair . . . Dalt suddenly flexed his neck to get a better look at the top of his head. Tufts of hair were missing in a roughly oval patch on his scalp. He ran his hand over it and a light rain of brown hair showered past his eyes. With successive strokes, the oval patch became completely denuded and a shiny expanse of scalp reflected the ceiling lights into the mirror.

"Well, I'll be damned! A bald spot!"

("Don't worry, Steve,") said the voice in his head, ("the roots aren't dead. The hair will grow back.")

"It damn well better!" Dalt said aloud.

"It damn well better what?" Barre asked puzzledly.

"Nothing," Dalt replied. "Something dropped onto my head in a cave down there and it looks like it's given me a bald spot." He realized then that he would have to be very careful about talking to his invader; otherwise, even if he really wasn't crazy, he'd soon have everyone on the ship believing he was.

"Maybe you'd better see the doc," Barre suggested.

"I intend to, believe me. But first I've got to report to Clarkson. I'm sure he's waiting."

"You can bet on it." Barre had been a research head on the brain project and was well acquainted with Dirval Clarkson's notorious impatience.

The pair walked briskly toward Clarkson's office. The rotation of the huge conical ship gave the effect of one-G.

"Hi, Jean," Dalt said with a smile as he and Barre entered the anteroom of Clarkson's office. Jean was Clarkson's secretary-receptionist and she and Dalt had entertained each other on the trip out . . . the more interesting games had been played during the sleep-time hours.

She returned his smile. "Glad you're back in one piece." Dalt realized that from her seated position she couldn't see the bald spot. Just as well for the moment. He'd explain it to her later.

Jean spoke into the intercom: "Mr. Dalt is here."

"Well, send him in!" squawked a voice. "Send him in!"

Dalt grinned and pushed through the door to Clarkson's office, with Barre trailing behind. A huge, graying man leaped from behind a desk and stalked forward at a precarious angle.

"Dalt! Where the hell have you been? You were supposed to go down, take a look, and then come back up. You could have done the procedure three times in the period you took. And what happened to your head?" Clarkson's speech was in its usual rapidfire form.

"Well, this—"

"Never mind that now! What's the story? I can tell right now that you didn't find anything, because Barre is with you. If you'd found the brain he'd be off in some corner now nursing it like a misplaced infant! Well, tell me! How does it look?"

Dalt hesitated, not quite sure whether the barrage had come to an end. "It doesn't look good," he said finally.

"And why not?"

"Because I couldn't find a trace of the ship itself. Oh, there's evidence of some sort of craft having been there a while back, but it must have gotten off-planet again, because there's not a trace of wreckage to be found."

Clarkson looked puzzled. "Not even a trace?"

"Nothing."

The project director pondered this a moment, then shrugged. "We'll have to figure that one out later. But right now you should know that we picked up another signal from the brain's life-support system while you were off on your joy-ride—"

"It wasn't a joyride," Dalt declared. A few moments with Clarkson always managed to rub his nerves raw. "I ran into a pack of unfriendly locals and had to hide in a cave."

"Be that as it may," Clarkson said, returning to his desk chair, "we're now certain that the brain, or what's left of it, is on Kwashi."

"Yes, but where on Kwashi? It's not exactly an asteroid, you know."

"We've almost pinpointed its location," Barre broke in excitedly. "Very close to the side you inspected."

"It's in Bendelema, I hope," Dalt said.

"Why?" Clarkson asked.

"Because when I was on cultural survey down there I posed as a soldier of fortune—a mercenary of sorts—and Duke Kile of Bendelema was a former employer. I'm known and liked in Bendelema. I'm not at all popular in Tependia because they're the ones I fought against. I repeat: It's in Bendelema, I hope."

Clarkson nodded. "It's in Bendelema."

"Good!" Dalt exhaled with relief. "That makes everything much simpler. I've got an identity in Bendelema: Rasco the mercenary. At least that's a starting place."

"And you'll start tomorrow," Clarkson said. "We've wasted too much time as it is. If we don't get that prototype back and start coming up with some pretty good reasons for the malfunction, Star Ways just might cancel the project. There's a lot riding on you, Dalt. Remember that."

Dalt turned toward the door. "Who'll let me forget?" he remarked with a grim smile. "I'll check in with you before I leave."

"Good enough," Clarkson said with a curt nod, then turned to Barre. "Hold on a minute, Barre. I want to go over a few things with you." Dalt gladly closed the door on the pair.

"It's almost lunchtime," said a feminine voice behind him. "How about it?"

In a single motion, Dalt spun, leaned over Jean's desk, and gave her a peck on the lips. "Sorry, can't. It may be noon to all of you on ship-time, but it's some hellish hour of the morning to me. I've got to drop in on the doc, then I've got to get some sleep."

But Jean wasn't listening. Instead, she was staring fixedly at the bald spot on Dalt's head. "Steve!" she cried. "What happened?"

Dalt straightened up abruptly. "Nothing much. Something landed on it while I was below and the hair fell out. It'll grow back, don't worry."

"I'm not worried about that," she said, standing up and trying to get another look. But Dalt kept his head high. "Did it hurt?"

"Not at all. Look, I hate to run off like this, but I've got to get some sleep. I'm going back down tomorrow."

Her face fell. "So soon?"

"I'm afraid so. Why don't we make it for dinner tonight. I'll drop by your room and we'll go from there. The caf isn't exactly a restaurant, but if we get there late we can probably have a table all to ourselves."

"And after that?" she asked coyly.

"I'll be damned if we're going to spend my last night on ship for who-knows-how-long in the vid theater!"

Jean smiled. "I was hoping you'd say that."

Ω

("What odd physiological rumblings that female stirs in you!") the voice said as Dalt walked down the corridor to the medical offices. He momentarily broke stride at the sound of it. He'd almost forgotten that he had company.

"That's none of your business!" he muttered through tight lips.

("I'm afraid much of what you do is my business. I'm not directly connected with you emotionally, but physically . . . what you feel, I feel; what you see, I see; what you taste—")

"Okay! Okay!"

("You're holding up rather well, actually. Better than I would have expected.")

"Probably my cultural-survey training. They taught me how to keep my reactions under control when faced with an unusual situation."

("Glad to hear it. We may well have a long relationship ahead of us if you don't go the way of most high-order intelligences and suicidally reject me. We can look on your body as a small business and the two of us as partners.")

"Partners!" Dalt said, somewhat louder than he wished. Luckily, the halls were deserted. "This is *my* body!"

("If it will make you happier, I'll revise my analogy: You're the founder of the company and I've just bought my way in. How's that sound, Partner?")

"Lousy!"

("Get used to it,") the voice singsonged.

"Why bother? You won't be in there much longer. The doc'll see to that!"

("He won't find a thing, Steve.")

"We'll see."

The door to the medical complex swished open when Dalt touched the operating plate and he passed into a tiny waiting room.

"What can we do for you, Mr. Dalt?" the nurse-receptionist said. Dalt was a well-known figure about the ship by now.

He inclined his head toward the woman and pointed to the bald spot. "I want to see the doc about this. I'm going below tomorrow and I want to get this cleared up before I do. So if the doc's got a moment, I'd like to see him."

The nurse smiled. "Right away." At the moment, Dalt was a very important man. He was the only one on ship legally allowed on Kwashi. If he thought he needed a doctor, he'd have one.

A man in a traditional white medical coat poked his head through one of the three doors leading from the waiting room, in answer to the nurse's buzz.

"What is it, Lorraine?" he asked.

"Mr. Dalt would like to see you, Doctor."

He glanced at Dalt. "Of course. Come in, Mr. Dalt. I'm Dr. Graves." The doctor showed him into a small, book-and-microfilm-lined office. "Have a seat, will you? I'll be with you in a minute."

Graves exited by another door and Dalt was alone . . . almost.

("He has quite an extensive library here, doesn't he?") said the voice. Dalt glanced at the shelves and noticed printed texts that must have been holdovers from the doctor's student days and microfilm spools of the latest clinical developments. ("You would do me a great service by asking the doctor if you could borrow some of his more basic texts.")

"What for? I thought you knew all about me."

("I know quite a bit now, it's true, but I'm still learning and I'll need a vocabulary to explain things to you now and then.")

"Forget it. You're not going to be around that long."

Dr. Graves entered then. "Now. What seems to be the problem, Mr. Dalt?"

Dalt explained the incident in the cave. "Legend has it—and colonial experience seems to confirm it—that 'of every thousand struck down, nine hundred and ninety-nine will die.' I was floored by an alaret but I'm still kicking and I'd like to know why."

("I believe I've already explained that by luck of a random constitutional factor, your nervous system didn't reject me.")

Shut up! Dalt mentally snarled.

The doctor shrugged. "I don't see the problem. You're alive and all you've got to show for your encounter is a bald spot, and even that will disappear—it's bristly already. I can't tell you why you're alive because I don't know how these alarets kill their victims. As far as I know, no one's done any research on them. So why don't you just forget about it and stay out of caves."

"It's not that simple, Doc." Dalt spoke carefully. He'd have to phrase things just right; if he came right out and told the truth, he'd sound like a flaming schiz. "I have this feeling that something seeped into my scalp, maybe even into my head. I feel this thickness there." Dalt noticed the slightest narrowing of the doctor's gaze. "I'm not crazy," he said hurriedly. "You've got to admit that the alaret did something there—the bald spot proves it. Couldn't you make a few tests or something? Just to ease my mind."

The doctor nodded. He was satisfied that Dalt's fears had sufficient basis in reality, and the section-eight gleam left his eyes. He led Dalt into the adjoining room and placed a cubical helmetlike apparatus over his head. A click, a buzz, and the helmet was removed. Dr. Graves pulled out two small transparencies and shoved them into a viewer. The screen came to life with two views of the inside of Dalt's skull: a lateral and an anterior-posterior.

"Nothing to worry about," he said after a moment of study. "I scanned you for your own peace of mind. Take a look."

Dalt looked, even though he didn't know what he was looking for.

("I told you so,") said the voice. ("I'm thoroughly integrated with your nervous system.")

"Well, thanks for your trouble, Doc. I guess I've really got nothing to worry about," Dalt lied.

"Nothing at all. Just consider yourself lucky to be alive if those alarets are as deadly as you say."

("Ask him for the books!") the voice said.

I'm going to sleep as soon as I leave here. You won't get a chance to read them.

("You let me worry about that. Just get the books for me.")

Why should I do you any favors?

("Because I'll see to it that you have one difficult time of getting to sleep. I'll keep you repeating 'get the books, get the books, get the books' until you finally do it.")

I believe you would!

("You can count on it.")

"Doc," Dalt said, "would you mind lending me a few of your books?"

"Like what?"

"Oh, anatomy and physiology, to start."

Dr. Graves walked into the other room and took two large, frayed volumes from the shelves. "What do you want 'em for?"

"Nothing much," Dalt said, taking the books and tucking them under his arm. "Just want to look up a few things."

"Well, just don't forget where you got them. And don't let that incident with the alaret become an obsession with you," the doc said meaningfully.

Dalt smiled. "I've already banished it from my mind."

("That's a laugh!")

Ω

Dalt wasted no time in reaching his quarters after leaving the medical offices. He was on the bed before the door could slide back into the closed position. Putting the medical books on the night table, he buried his face in the pillow and immediately dropped off to sleep.

He awoke five hours later, feeling completely refreshed except for his eyes. They felt hot, burning.

("You may return those books anytime you wish,") the voice said.

"Lost interest already?" Dalt yawned, stretching as he lay on the bed.

("In a way, yes. I read them while you were asleep.")

"How the hell did you do that?"

("Quite simple, really. While your mind was sleeping, I used your eyes and hands to read. I digested the information and stored it away in your brain. By the way, there's an awful lot of wasted space in the human brain. You're not living up to anywhere near your potential, Steve. Neither is any other member of your race, I gather.")

"What right have you got to pull something like that with my body?" Dalt said angrily. He sat up and rubbed his eyes.

("*Our* body, you mean.")

Dalt ignored that. "No wonder my eyes are burning! I've been reading when I could have been—*should* have been—sleeping!"

("Don't get excited. You got your sleep and I built up my vocabulary. You're fully rested, so what's your complaint? By the way, I can now tell you how I entered your head. I seeped into your pores and then into your scalp capillaries, which I followed into your parietal emissary veins. These flow through the parietal foramina in your skull and empty into the superior sagittal sinus. From there it was easy to infiltrate your central nervous system.")

Dalt opened his mouth to say that he really didn't care, when he realized that he understood exactly what the voice was saying. He had a clear picture of the described path floating through his mind.

"How come I know what you're talking about? I seem to understand but I don't remember ever hearing those terms before . . . and then again, I do. It's weird."

("It must seem rather odd,") the voice concurred. ("What has happened is that I've made my new knowledge available to you. The result is you experience the fruits of the learning process without having gone through it. You know facts without remembering having learned them.")

"Well," Dalt said, rising to his feet, "at least you're not a complete parasite."

("I resent that! We're partners . . . a symbiosis!")

"I suppose you may come in handy now and then," Dalt sighed.

("I already have.")

"What's that supposed to mean?"

("I found a small neoplasm in your lung—middle lobe on the right. It might well have become malignant.")

"Then let's get back to the doc before it metastasizes!" Dalt said, and idly realized that a few hours ago he would have been worrying about "spread" rather than "metastasis."

("There's no need to worry, Steve. I killed it off.")

"How'd you do that?"

("I just worked through your vascular system and selectively cut off the blood supply to that particular group of cells.")

"Well, thanks, Partner."

("No thanks necessary, I assure you. I did it for my own good as well as yours—I don't relish the idea of walking around in a cancer-ridden body any more than you do!")

Dalt removed his serf clothing in silence. The enormity of what had happened in that cave on Kwashi struck him now with full force. He had a built-in medical watchdog who would keep everything running smoothly. He smiled grimly as he donned ship clothes and suspended from his neck the glowing prismatic gem that he had first worn as Racso and had continued to wear after his cultural-survey assignment on Kwashi had been terminated. He'd have his health but he'd lost his privacy forever. He wondered if it was worth it.

("One other thing, Steve,") said the voice. ("I've accelerated the growth of your hair in the bald spot to maximum.")

Dalt put up a hand and felt a thick fuzz where before there had been only bare scalp. "Hey! You're right! It's really coming in!" He went to the mirror to take a look "Oh, no!"

("Sorry about that, Steve. I couldn't see it so I wasn't aware there had been a color change. I'm afraid there's nothing I can do about that.")

Dalt stared in dismay at the patch of silvery gray in the center of his otherwise inky hair. "I look like a freak!"

("You can always dye it.")

Dalt made a disgusted noise.

("I have a few questions, Steve,") the voice said in a hasty attempt to change the subject.

"What about?"

("About why you're going down to that planet tomorrow.")

"I'm going because I was once a member of the Federation cultural-survey team on Kwashi and because the Star Ways Corporation lost an experimental pilot brain down there. They got permission from the Federation to retrieve the brain only on the condition that a cultural-survey man does the actual retrieving."

("That's not what I meant. I want to know what's so important about the brain, just how much of a brain it actually is, and so on.")

"There's an easy way to find out," Dalt said, heading for the door. "We'll just go to the ship's library."

The library was near the hub of the ship and completely

computer-operated. Dalt closed himself away in one of the tiny viewer booths and pushed his ID card into the awaited slot.

The flat, dull tones of the computer's voice came from a hidden speaker.

"What do you wish, Mr. Dalt?"

"I might as well go to the route: Let me see everything on the brain project."

Four microspools slid down a tiny chute and landed in the receptacle in front of Dalt. "I'm sorry, Mr. Dalt," said the computer, "but this is all your present status allows you to see."

("That should be enough, Steve. Feed them into the viewer.")

The story that unraveled from the spools was one of biologic and economic daring. Star Ways was fast achieving what amounted to a monopoly of the interstellar-warp-unit market and from there was expanding to peri-stellar drive. But unlike the typical established corporation, SW was pouring money into basic research. One of the prime areas of research was the development of a use for cultured human neural tissue. And James Barre had found a use that held great economic potential.

The prime expense of interstellar commercial travel, whether freight or passenger, was the crew. Good spacers were a select lot and hard to come by; running a ship took a lot of them. There had been many attempts to replace crews with computers but these had invariably failed due either to mass/volume problems or overwhelming maintenance costs. Barre's development of an "artificial" brain—by that he meant structured in vitro—seemed to hold an answer, at least for cargo ships.

After much trial and error with life-support systems and control linkages, a working prototype had finally been developed. A few short hops had been tried with a full crew standing by, and the results had been more than anyone had hoped for. So the prototype was prepared for a long interstellar journey with five scheduled stops—with cargo holds empty, of course. The run had gone quite well until the ship got into the Kwashi area. A single technician had been sent along to insure that nothing went too far awry, and, according to his story, he was sitting in his quarters when the ship suddenly came out of warp with the emergency/abandon ship signals blaring. He wasted no time in getting to a lifeboat and ejecting. The ship made a beeline for Kwashi and disappeared, presumably in a crash. That had been eight months ago.

No more information was available without special clearance.

"Well, that was a waste of time," Dalt said.

"Are you addressing me, Mr. Dalt?" the computer asked.

"No."

("There certainly wasn't much new information there,") the voice agreed.

Dalt pulled his card from the slot, thereby cutting the computer off from this particular viewer booth, before answering. Otherwise it would keep butting in.

"The theories now stand at either malfunction or foul play."

("Why foul play?")

"The spacers' guild, for one," Dalt said, standing. "Competing companies, for another. But since it crashed on a restricted splinter world, I favor the malfunction theory." As he stepped from the booth he glanced at the chronometer on the wall: 1900 hours ship-time. Jean would be waiting.

Ω

The cafeteria was nearly deserted when he arrived with Jean and the pair found an isolated table in a far corner.

"I really don't think you should dye your hair at all," Jean was saying as they placed their trays on the table and sat down. "I think that gray patch looks cute in a distinguished sort of way . . . or do I mean distinguished in a cute sort of way?"

Dalt took the ribbing in good-natured silence.

"Steve!" she said suddenly. "How come you're eating with your left hand? I've never seen you do that before."

Dalt looked down. His fork was firmly grasped in his left hand. "That's strange," he said. "I didn't even realize it."

("I integrated a few circuits, so to speak, while you were asleep,") the voice said. ("It seemed rather ridiculous to favor one limb over another. You're now ambidextrous.")

Thanks for telling me, Partner!

("Sorry. I forgot.")

Dalt switched the fork to his right hand and Jean switched the topic of conversation.

"You know, Steve," she said, "you've never told me why you quit the cultural-survey group."

Dalt paused before answering. After the fall of Metep VII, last in a long line of self-styled "Emperors of the Outworlds," a new independent spirit gave rise to a loose organization of worlds called simply the Federation.

"As you know," he said finally, "the Federation has a long-range plan of bringing splinter worlds—willing ones, that is—back into the fold. But it was found that an appalling number had regressed into barbarism. So the cultural surveys were started to evaluate splinter worlds and decide which could be trusted with modern technology. There was another rule which I didn't fully appreciate back then but have come to believe in since, and that's where the trouble began."

"What rule was that?"

"It's not put down anywhere in so many words, but it runs to the effect that if a splinter-world culture had started developing on a path at variance with the rest of humanity, it is to be left alone."

"Sounds like they were making cultural test tubes out of some planets," Jean said.

"Exactly what I thought, but it never bothered me until I surveyed a planet that must, for now, remain nameless. The inhabitants had been developing a psi culture through selective breeding and were actually developing a tangential society. But they were being threatened by the non-psi majority. I pleaded for protective intervention and early admission to the Federation."

"And were turned down, I bet," Jean said.

Dalt nodded. "Right. And I might have gone along if I hadn't become emotionally involved with the psis. That was the first rule I broke. Then I found myself in the middle of a crisis situation that pushed me over the edge. I took decisive action on my own, and then resigned."

"Before you were fired."

"Right again. I broke half a book's worth of rules on that planet. But I can see the Fed's reasoning now. They knew the psi culture wasn't mature enough to withstand exposure to interstellar civilization. They were afraid it would be swallowed up and lose its unique qualities. They wanted to give it another few centuries in isolation before opening it up. And they were right in theory. But they weren't on that planet. I was. And I knew if things kept on the way they were going, the psi-folk would be wiped out in less than a generation. So I . . . did something to make sure that didn't happen."

"No hard feelings then?"

"Not on my part. I've come to see that there's a very definite philosophy behind everything the Federation does. It not only wants to preserve human diversity, it wants to see it stretched to the limit. Man was an almost completely homogenized species before he began colonizing the stars; interstellar travel arrived just in time. Old Earth is still a good example of what I mean; long ago the Eastern and Western Alliances fused—something no one ever thought would happen—and Earth is just one big faceless, self-perpetuating bureaucracy. The populace is equally faceless.

"But the man who left for the stars—he's another creature altogether! Once he got away from the press of other people, once he stopped seeing what everybody else saw, hearing what everybody else heard, he began to become an individual again and to strike out in directions of his own choosing. The splinter groups carried this out to an extreme and many failed. But a few survived and the Federation wants to let the successful ones go as far as they can, both for their own sake and for the sake of all mankind. Who knows? *Homo superior* may one day be born on a splinter world."

They took their time strolling back to Dalt's quarters. Once inside, Dalt glanced in the mirror and ran his hand through the gray patch in his hair. "It's still there," he muttered in mock disappointment.

He turned back to Jean and she was already more than half undressed. "You weren't gone all that long, Steve," she said in a low voice, "but I missed you—really missed you."

It was mutual.

III

She was gone when he awakened the next morning but a little note on the night table wished him good luck.

("You should have prepared me for such a sensory jolt,") said the voice. ("I was taken quite by surprise last night.")

"Oh, it's you again," Dalt groaned. "I pushed you completely out of my mind last night, otherwise I'd have been impotent, no doubt."

("I hooked into your sensory input—very stimulating.")

Dalt experienced helpless annoyance. He would have to get used to his partner's presence at the most intimate moments, but how many people could make love knowing that there's a peeping tom at the window with a completely unobstructed view?

("What are we going to do now?")

"Pard," Dalt drawled, "we're gonna git ready to go below." He went to the closet and pulled from it a worn leather jerkin and a breastplate marked with an empty red circle, the mark of the mercenary. Stiff leather breeches followed and broadsword and metal helm completed the picture. He then dyed his hair for Racso's sake.

"One more thing," he said, and reached up to the far end

of the closet shelf. His hand returned clutching an ornate dagger. "This is something new in Racso's armament."

("A dagger?")

"Not just a dagger. It's—"

("Oh, yes. It's also a blaster.")

"How did you know?"

("We're partners, Steve. What you know, I know. I even know why you had it made.")

"I'm listening."

("Because you're afraid you're not as fast as you used to be. You think your muscles may not have quite the tone they used to have when you first posed as Racso. And you're not willing to die looking for an artificial brain.")

"You seem to think you know me pretty well."

("I do. Skin to skin, birth to now. You're the only son of a fairly well-to-do couple on Friendly, had an average childhood and an undistinguished academic career—but you passed the empathy test with high marks and were accepted into the Federation cultural-survey service. You don't speak to your parents anymore. They've never forgiven their baby for running off to go hopping from splinter world to splinter world. You cut yourself off from your home-world but made friends in CS; now you're cut off from CS. You're not a loner by nature but you've adapted. In fact, you have a tremendous capacity to adapt as long as your own personal code of ethics and honor isn't violated—you're very strict about that.")

Dalt sighed. "No secrets anymore, I guess."

("Not from me, at least.")

Ω

Dalt planned the time of his arrival in Bendelema Duchy for predawn. He concealed the shuttle and was on the road as the sky began to lighten. Walking with a light saddle slung over his shoulder, he marveled at the full ripe fields of grains and greens on either side of him. Agriculture had always been a hit-or-miss affair on Kwashi and famines were not uncommon, but it looked as if there would be no famines in Bendelema this year. Even the serfs looked well fed.

"What do you think, pard?" Dalt asked.

("Well, Kwashi hasn't got much of a tilt on its axis. They seem to be on their way to the second bumper crop of the year.")

"With the available farming methods, that's unheard of . . . I almost starved here once myself."

("I know that, but I have no explanation for these plump serfs.")

The road made a turn around a small wooded area and the Bendelema keep came into view.

"I see their architecture hasn't improved since I left. The keep still looks like a pile of rocks."

("I wonder why so many retrograde splinter worlds turn to feudalism?") Pard said as they approached the stone structure.

"There are only theories. Could be that feudalism is, in essence, the law of the jungle. When these colonists first land, education of the children has to take a back seat to putting food on the table. That's their first mistake and a tragic one, because once they let technology slide, they're on a downhill spiral. Usually by the third generation you have a pretty low technological level; the stops are out, the equalizers are gone, and the toughs take over.

"The philosophy of feudalism is one of muscle: Mine is what I can take and hold. It's ordered barbarism. That's why feudal worlds such as Kwashi have to be kept out of the Federation—can you imagine a bunch of those yahoos in command of an interstellar dread-naught? No one's got the time or the money to reeducate them, so they just have to be left alone to work out their own little industrial revolution and so forth. When they're ready, the Fed will give them the option of joining up."

"Ho, mercenary!" someone hailed from the keep gate. "What do you seek in Bendelema?"

"Have I changed that much, Farri?" Dalt answered.

The guard peered at him intensely from the wall, then his face brightened. "Racso! Enter and be welcome! The Duke has need of men of your mettle."

Farri, a swarthy trooper who had gained a few pounds and a few scars since their last meeting, greeted him as he passed through the open gate. "Where's your mount, Racso?" He grinned. "You were never one to walk when you could ride."

"Broke its leg in a ditch more miles back than I care to remember. Had to kill it . . . good steed, too."

"That's a shame. But the Duke'll see that you get a new one."

Dalt's audience with the Duke was disturbingly brief. The lord of the keep had not been as enthusiastic as expected. Dalt couldn't decide whether to put the man's reticence down to distraction with other matters or to suspicion. His son Anthon was a different matter, however. He was truly glad to see Racso.

"Come," he said after mutual greetings were over. "We'll put you in the room next to mine upstairs."

"For a mercenary?"

"For my teacher!" Anthon had filled out since Dalt had seen him last. He had spent many hours with the lad, passing on the tricks of the blade he had learned in his own training days. "I've used your training well, Racso!"

"I hope you didn't stop learning when I left," Dalt said.

"Come down to the sparring field and you'll see that I've not been lax in your absence. I'm a match for you now."

Ω

He was more than a match. What he lacked in skill and subtlety he made up with sheer ferocity. Dalt was several times hard-pressed to defend himself, but in the general stroke-and-parry, give-and-take exercises of the practice session he studied Anthon. The lad was still the same as he had remembered him, on the surface: bold, confident, the Duke's only legitimate son and heir to Bendelema, yet there was a new undercurrent. Anthon had always been brutish and a trifle cruel, perfect qualities for a future feudal lord, but there was now an added note of desperation. Dalt hadn't noticed it before and could think of no reason for its presence now. Anthon's position was secure—what was driving him?

After the workout, Dalt immersed himself in a huge tub of water, a habit that had earned him the reputation of being a little bit odd the last time around, and then retired to his quarters, where he promptly fell asleep. The morning's long walk carrying the saddle, followed by the vigorous sword-play with Anthon, had drained him.

He awoke feeling stiff and sore.

("I hope those aching muscles cause you sufficient misery.")

"Why do you say that, Pard?" Dalt asked as he kneaded the muscles in his sword arm.

("Because you weren't ready for a workout like that. The clumsy practicing you did on the ship didn't prepare you for someone like Anthon. It's all right if you want to make yourself sore, but don't forget I feel it, too!")

"Well, just cut off pain sensations. You can do it, can't you?"

("Yes, but that's almost as unpleasant as the aching itself.")

"You'll just have to suffer along with me then. And by the way, you've been awful quiet today. What's up?"

("I've been observing, comparing your past impressions of Bendelema keep with what we see now. Either you're a rotten observer or something's going on here . . . something suspicious or something secret or I don't know what.")

"What do you mean by 'rotten observer'?"

("I mean that either your past observations were inaccurate or Bendelema has changed.")

"In what way?"

("I'm not quite sure as yet, but I should know before long. I'm a far more astute observer than you—")

Dalt threw his hands up with a groan. "Not only do I have a live-in busy-body, but an arrogant one to boot!"

There was a knock on the door.

"Come in," Dalt said.

The door opened and Anthon entered. He glanced about the room. "You're alone? I thought I heard you talking—"

"A bad habit of mine of late," Dalt explained hastily. "I think out loud."

Anthon shrugged. "The evening meal will soon be served and I've ordered a place set for you at my father's table. Come."

As he followed the younger man down a narrow flight of roughhewn steps, Dalt caught the heavy, unmistakable scent of Kwashi wine.

A tall, cadaverous man inclined his head as they passed into the dining hall. "Hello, Strench," Dalt said with a smile. "Still the majordomo, I see."

"As long as His Lordship allows," Strench replied.

The Duke himself entered not far behind them and all present remained standing until His Lordship was seated. Dalt found himself near the head of the table and guessed by the ruffled appearance of a few of the court advisers that they had been pushed a little farther from the seat of power than they liked.

"I must thank His Lordship for the honor of allowing a mercenary to sup at his table," Dalt said after a court official had made the customary toast to Bendelema and the Duke's longevity.

"Nonsense, Racso," the Duke replied. "You served me well against Tependia and you've always taken a wholesome interest in my son. You know you will always find welcome in Bendelema."

Dalt inclined his head.

("Why are you bowing and scraping to this slob?")

Shut up, Pard! It's all part of the act.

("But don't you realize how many serfs this barbarian oppresses?")

Shut up, self-righteous parasite!

("Symbiote!")

Dalt rose to his feet and lifted his wine cup. "On the subject of your son, I would like to make a toast to the future Duke of Bendelema: Anthon."

With a sudden animal-like cry, Anthon shot to his feet and hurled his cup to the stone floor. Without a word of explanation, he stormed from the room.

The other diners were as puzzled as Dalt. "Perhaps I said the wrong thing. . . ."

"I don't know what it could have been," the Duke said, his eyes on the red splotch of spilled wine that seeped across the stones. "But Anthon has been acting rather strange of late."

Dalt sat down and raised his cup to his lips.

("I wouldn't quaff too deeply of that beverage, my sharp-tongued partner.")

And why not? Dalt thought, casually resting his lips on the brim.

("Because I think there's something in your wine that's not in any of the others' and I think we should be careful.")

What makes you suspicious?

("I told you your powers of observation needed sharpening.")

Never mind that! Explain!

("All right. I noticed that your cup was already filled when it was put before you; everyone else's was poured from that brass pitcher.")

The doesn't sound good, Dalt agreed. He started to put the cup down.

("Don't do that! Just wet your lips with a tiny amount and I think I might be able to analyze it by its effect. A small amount shouldn't cause any real harm.")

Dalt did so and waited.

("Well, at least they don't mean you any serious harm,") Pard said finally. ("Not yet.")

What is it?

("An alkaloid, probably from some local root.")

What's it supposed to do to me?

("Put you out of the picture for the rest of the night.")

Dalt pondered this. *I wonder what for?*

("I haven't the faintest. But while they're all still distracted by Anthon's departure, I suggest you pour your wine out on the floor immediately. It will mix with Anthon's and no one will be the wiser. You may then proceed to amaze these yokels with your continuing consciousness.")

I have a better idea, Dalt thought as he poured the wine along the outside of his boot so that it would strike the floor in a smooth silent flow instead of a noisy splash. *I'll wait a few minutes and then pass out. Maybe that way we'll find out what they've got in mind.*

("Sounds risky.")

Nevertheless, that's what we'll do.

Dalt decided to make the most of the time he had left before passing out. "You know," he said, feigning a deep swallow of wine, "I saw a bright light streak across the sky last night. It fell to the earth far beyond the horizon. I've heard tales lately of such a light coming to rest in this region, some even say it landed on Bendelema itself. Is this true or merely the mutterings of vassals in their cups?"

The table chatter ceased abruptly. So did all eating and drinking. Every face at the table stared in Dalt's direction.

"Why do you ask this, Racso?" the Duke said. The curtain of suspicion which had seemed to vanish at the beginning of the meal had again been drawn closed between Racso and the Duke.

Dalt decided it was time for his exit. "My only interest, Your Lordship, is in the idle tales I've heard. I . . ." He half rose from his seat and put a hand across his eyes. "I . . ." Carefully, he allowed himself to slide to the floor.

"Carry him upstairs," said the Duke.

"Why don't we put an end to his meddling now, Your Lordship," suggested one of the advisers.

"Because he's a friend of Anthon's and he may well mean us no harm. We will know tomorrow."

With little delicacy and even less regard for his physical well-being, Dalt was carried up to his room and unceremoniously dumped on the bed. The heavy sound of the hardwood door slamming shut was followed by the click of a key in the lock.

Dalt sprang up and checked the door. The key had been taken from the inside and left in the lock after being turned.

("So much for that bright idea,") Pard commented caustically.

"None of your remarks, if you please."

("What do we do, now that we're confined to quarters for the rest of the night?")

"What else?" Dalt said. He kicked off his boots, removed breastplate, jerkin, and breeches, and hopped into bed.

The door was unlocked the next morning and Dalt made his way downstairs as unobtrusively as possible. Strench's cell-like quarters were just off the kitchen, if memory served . . . yes, there it was. And Strench was nowhere about.

("What do you think you're doing?")

I'm doing my best to make sure we don't get stuck up there in that room again tonight. His gaze came to rest on the large board where Strench kept all the duplicate keys for the locks of the keep.

("I begin to understand.")

Slow this morning, aren't you?

Dalt took the duplicate key to his room off its hook and replaced it with another, similar key from another part of the board. Strench might realize at some time during the day that a key was missing, but he'd be looking for the wrong one.

Dalt ran into the majordomo moments later.

"His Lordship wishes to see you, Racso," he said stiffly.

"Where is he?"

"On the North Wall."

("This could be a critical moment.")

"Why do you say that, Pard?" Dalt muttered.

("Remember last night, after you pulled your dramatic collapsing act? The Duke said something about finding out about you today.")

"And you think this could be it?"

"Could be. I'm not sure, of course, but I'm glad you have that dagger in your belt.")

The Duke was alone on the wall and greeted Dalt/Racso as warmly as his aloof manner would permit after the latter apologized for "drinking too much" the night before.

"I'm afraid I have a small confession to make," the Duke said.

"Yes, Your Lordship?"

"I suspected you of treachery when you first arrived." He held up a gloved hand as Dalt opened his mouth to reply. "Don't protest your innocence. I've just heard from a spy in the Tependian court and he says you have not set foot in Tependia since your mysterious disappearance years ago."

Dalt hung his head. "I am grieved, M'Lord."

"Can you blame me, Racso? Everyone knows that you hire out to the highest bidder, and Tependia has taken an inordinate interest in what goes on in Bendelema lately, even to the extent of sending raiding parties into our territory to carry off some of my vassals."

"Why would they want to do that?"

The Duke puffed up with pride. "Because Bendelema has become a land of plenty. As you know, that last harvest was plentiful everywhere, and, as usual, the present crop is stunted everywhere . . . except in Bendelema." Dalt didn't know that but he nodded anyway. So only Bendelema was having a second bumper crop—that was interesting.

"I suppose you have learned some new farming methods and Tependia wants to steal them," Dalt suggested.

"That and more." The Duke nodded. "We also have new storage methods and new planting methods. When the next famine comes, we shall overcome Tependia not with swords and firebrands, but with food! The starving Tependians will leave their lord and Bendelema will extend its boundaries!"

Dalt was tempted to say that if the Tependians were snatching up vassals and stealing Bendelema's secrets, there just might not be another famine. But the Duke was dreaming of empire and it is not always wise for a mere mercenary to interrupt a duke's dreams of empire. Dalt remained silent as the Duke stared at the horizon he soon hoped to own.

The rest of the day was spent in idle search of rumors and by the dinner hour Dalt was sure of one thing: The ship had crashed or landed in the clearing he had inspected a few days before. More than that was known, but the Bendelema locals were keeping it to themselves—*yes, I saw the light come down; no, I saw nothing else.*

Anthon again offered him the head table and Dalt accepted. When the Duke was toasted, Dalt took only a tiny sip.

What's the verdict, Pard?

("Same as last night.")

I wonder what this is all about. They don't drug me at lunch or breakfast—why only at dinner?

("Tonight we'll try to find out.")

Since there was no outburst from Anthon this time, Dalt was hard put to find a way to get rid of his drugged wine. He finally decided to feign a collapse again and spill his cup in the process, hoping to hide the fact that he had taken only a few drops.

After slumping forward on the table, he listened intently.

"How long is this to go on, Father? How can we drug him every night without arousing his suspicions?" It was Anthon's voice.

"As long as you insist on quartering him here instead of with the other men-at-arms!" the Duke replied angrily. "We cannot have him wandering about during the nightly services. He's an outsider and must not learn of the godling!"

Anthon's voice was sulky. "Very well . . . I'll have him move out to the barracks tomorrow."

"I'm sorry, Anthon," the Duke said in a milder tone. "I know he's a friend of yours, but the godling must come before a mercenary."

("I have a pretty good idea of the nature of this godling,") Pard said as Dalt/Racso was carried upstairs.

The brain? I was thinking that, too. But how would the brain communicate with these people? The proto-type wasn't set up for it.

("Why do you drag in communication? Isn't it enough that it came from heaven?")

No. The brain doesn't look godlike in the least. It would have to communicate with the locals before they'd deify it. Otherwise, the crash of the ship would be just another fireside tale for the children.

In a rerun of the previous night's events, Dalt was dumped on his bed and the door was locked from the outside. He waited a few long minutes until everything was silent beyond the door, then he poked the duplicate key into the lock. The original was pushed out on the other side and landed on the stone floor with a night-marishly loud *clang*. But no other sounds followed, so Dalt twisted his own key and slinked down the hall to the stairway that overlooked the dining area.

Empty. The plates hadn't even been cleared away.

"Now where'd everybody go?" Dalt muttered.

("Quiet! Hear those voices?")

Dalt moved down the stairs, listening. A muted chanting seemed to fill the chamber. A narrow door stood open to his left and the chanting grew louder as he approached it.

This is it . . . they must have gone through here.

The passage within, hewn from earth and rock, led downward and Dalt followed it. Widely spaced torches sputtered flickering light against the rough walls and the chanting grew louder as he moved.

Can you make out what they're saying?

("Something about the sacred objects, half of which must be placed in communion with the sun one day and the other half placed in communion with the sun the next day . . . a continuous cycle.")

The chant suddenly ended.

("It appears the litany is over. We had better go back.")

No, we're hiding right here. The brain is no doubt in there and I want to get back to civilization as soon as possible.

Dalt crouched in a shadowed sulcus in the wall and watched as the procession passed, the Duke in the lead, carrying some cloth-covered objects held out before him, Anthon sullenly following. The court advisers plucked the torches from the walls as they moved, but Dalt noticed that light still bled from the unexplored end of the passage. He sidled along the wall toward it after the others had passed.

He was totally unprepared for the sight that greeted his eyes as he entered the terminal alcove.

It was surreal. The vaulted subterranean chamber was strewn with the wreckage of the lost cargo ship. Huge pieces of twisted metal lay stacked against the walls; small pieces hung suspended from the ceiling. And foremost and center, nearly indistinguishable from the other junk, sat the silvery life-support apparatus of the brain, as high as a man and twice as broad.

And atop that—the brain, a ball of neural tissue floating in a nutrient bath within a crystalline globe.

("You can't hear him, can you?") Pard said.

"Him? Him who?"

("The brain—pictures itself as a him—did manage to communicate with the locals. You were right about that.")

"What are you talking about?"

("It's telepathic, Steve, and my presence in your brain seems to have blocked your reception. I sensed a few impulses back in the passage but I wasn't sure until it greeted us.")

"What's it saying?"

("The obvious: It wants to know who we are and what we want.") There was a short pause. ("Oh, oh! I just told it that we're here to take it back to SW and it let out a telepathic emergency call—a loud one. Don't be surprised if we have company in a few minutes.")

"Great! Now what do we do?" Dalt fingered the dagger in his belt as he pondered the situation. It was already too late to run and he didn't want to have to blast his way out. His eyes rested on the globe.

"Correct me if I'm wrong, Pard, but I seem to remember something about the globe being removable."

("Yes, it can be separated from the life-support system for about two hours with no serious harm to the brain.")

"That's just about all we'd need to get it back to the mothership and hooked up to another unit."

("He's quite afraid, Steve,") Pard said as Dalt began to disconnect the globe. ("By the way, I've figured out that little litany we just heard: The sacred objects that are daily put in 'communion with the sun' are solar batteries. Half are charged one day, half the next. That's how he keeps himself going.")

Dalt had just finished stoppering the globe's exchange ports when the Duke and his retinue arrived in a noisy, disorganized clatter.

"Racso!" the Duke cried on sight of him. "So you've betrayed us after all!"

"I'm sorry," Dalt said, "but this belongs to someone else."

Anthon lunged to the front. "Treacherous scum! And I called you friend!" As the youth's hand reached for his sword hilt, Dalt raised the globe.

"Stay your hand, Anthon! If any of you try to bar my way, I'll smash this globe and your godling with it!" The Duke blanched and laid a restraining hand on his son's shoulder. "I didn't come here with the idea of stealing something from you, but steal it I must. I regret the necessity." Dalt wasn't lying. He felt, justifiably, that he had betrayed a trust and it didn't sit well with him, but he kept reminding himself that the brain belonged to SW and he was only returning it to them.

("I hope your threat holds them,") Pard said. ("If they consider the possibilities, they'll realize that if they jump you, they'll lose their godling; but if they let you go, they lose it anyway.")

At the moment Anthon voiced this same conclusion, but his father restrained him. "Let him take the godling, my son. It has aided us with its wisdom, the least we can do is guarantee it safe passage."

Dalt grabbed one of the retainers. "You run ahead and ready

me a horse—a good one!" He watched him go, then slowly followed the passage back to the dining area. The Duke and his group remained behind in the alcove.

"I wonder what kind of plot they're hatching against me now," Dalt whispered. "Imagine! All the time I spent here never guessing they were telepaths!"

("They're not, Steve.")

"Then how do they communicate with this thing?" he said, glancing at the globe under his arm.

("The brain is an exceptionally strong sender and receiver, that's the secret. These folk are no more telepathic than anyone else.")

Dalt was relieved to find the horse waiting and the gate open. The larger of Kwashi's two moons was well above the horizon and Dalt took the most direct route to his hidden shuttlecraft.

("Just a minute, Steve,") Pard said as Dalt dismounted near the ship's hiding place. ("We seem to have a moral dilemma on our hands.")

"What's that?" Pard had been silent during the entire trip.

("I've been talking to the brain and I think it's become a little more than just a piloting device.")

"Possibly. It crashed, discovered it was telepathic, and tried to make the best of the situation. We're returning it. What's the dilemma?"

("It didn't crash. It sounded the alarm to get rid of the technician and brought the ship down on purpose. And it doesn't want to go back.")

"Well, it hasn't got much choice in the matter. It was made by SW and that's where it's going."

("Steve, it's *pleading* with us!")

"Pleading?"

("Yes. Look, you're still thinking of this thing as a bunch of neurons put together to pilot a ship, but it's developed into something more than that. It's now a *being*, and a thinking, reasoning, volitional one at that! It's no longer a biomechanism, it's an intelligent creature!")

"So you're a philosopher now, is that it?"

("Tell me, Steve. What's Barre going to do when he gets his hands on it?")

Dalt didn't want to answer that one.

("He's no doubt going to dissect it, isn't he?")

"He might not . . . not after he learns it's intelligent."

("Then let's suppose Barre doesn't dissect him—I mean *it* . . . no, I mean *him*. Never mind. If Barre allows it to live, the rest of its life will be spent as an experimental subject. Is that right? Are we justified in delivering it up for that?")

Dalt didn't answer.

("It's not causing any harm. As a matter of fact, it may well help put Kwashi on a quicker road back to civilization. It wants no power. It memorized the ship's library before it crashed and it was extremely happy down there in the alcove, doling out information about fertilizers and crop rotation and so forth and having its batteries charged every day.")

"I'm touched," Dalt muttered sarcastically.

("Joke if you will, but I don't take this lightly.")

"Do you have to be so self-righteous?"

("I'll say no more. You can leave the globe here and the brain will be able to telepathically contact the keep and they'll come out and get it.")

"And what do I tell Clarkson?"

("Simply tell him the truth, up to the final act, and then say that the globe was smashed at the keep when they tried to jump you and you barely escaped with your life.")

"That may kill the brain project, you know. Retrieval of the brain is vital to its continuance."

("That may be so, but it's a risk we'll have to take. If, however, your report states that the brain we were after had developed a consciousness and self-preservation tendencies, a lot of academic interest will surely be generated and research will go on, one way or the other.")

Much to his dismay, Dalt found himself agreeing with Pard, teetering on the brink of gently placing the globe in the grass and walking away, saying to hell with SW.

("It's still pleading with us, Steve. Like a child.")

"All right, dammit!"

Cursing himself for a sucker and a softy, Dalt walked a safe distance from the shuttlecraft and put down the globe.

"But there's a few things we've got to do before we leave here."

("Like what?")

"Like filling in our little friend here on some of the basics of feudal culture, something that I'm sure was not contained in his ship's library."

("He'll learn from experience.")

"That's what I'm afraid of. Without a clear understanding of

Kwashi's feudalism, his aid to Bendelema might well unbalance the whole social structure. An overly prosperous duchy is either overcome by jealous, greedy neighbors, or it uses its prosperity to build an army and pursue a plan of conquest. Either course could prove fatal to the brain and further hinder Kwashi's chances for social and technological rehabilitation."

("So what's your plan?")

"A simple one: You'll take all I know about Kwashi and feudalism and feed it to the brain. And you can stress the necessity of finding a means for wider dissemination of its knowledge, such as telepathically dropping bits of information into the heads of passing merchants, minstrels, and vagabonds. If this prosperity can be spread out over a wide area, there'll be less chance of social upheaval. All of Kwashi will benefit in the long run."

Pard complied and began the feeding process. The brain had a voracious appetite for information and the process was soon completed. As Dalt rose to his feet, he heard a rustling in the bushes. Looking up, he saw Anthon striding toward him with a bared sword.

"I've decided to return the godling," Dalt stammered lamely.

Anthon stopped. "I don't want the filthy thing! As a matter of fact, I intend to smash it as soon as I finish with you!" There was a look of incredible hatred in his eyes, the look of a young man who has discovered that his friend and admired instructor is a treacherous thief.

"But the godling has seen to it that no one in Bendelema will ever again go hungry!" Dalt said. "Why destroy it?"

"Because it has also seen to it that no one in the court of Bendelema will ever look up to me as Duke!"

"They look up to your father. Why not you in your turn?"

"They look up to my father out of habit!" he snarled. "But it is the godling who is the source of authority in Bendelema! And when my father is gone, I shall be nothing but a puppet."

Dalt now understood Anthon's moodiness: The brain threatened his position.

"So you followed me not in spite of my threat to smash the godling but because of it!"

Anthon nodded and began advancing again. "I also have a score to settle with you, Racso! I couldn't allow you to betray my trust and the trust of my father and go *unpunished!*" With the last word he aimed a vicious chop at Dalt, who ducked, spun, and dodged out of the way. He had not been wearing his sword when he left his room back at the keep, and consequently did not have it with him now. But he had the dagger.

Anthon laughed at the sight of the tiny blade. "Think you can stop me with that?"

If you only knew! Dalt thought. He didn't want to use the blaster, however. He understood Anthon's feelings. If there were only some way he could stun him and make his escape.

Anthon attacked ferociously now and Dalt was forced to back-peddle. His foot caught on a stone and as he fell he instinctively threw his free hand out for balance. The ensuing events seemed to occur in slow motion. He felt a jarring, crushing, cutting, agonizing pain in his left wrist and saw Anthon's blade bite through it. The hand flew off as if with a life of its own, and a pulsing stream of red shot into the air. Dalt's right hand, too, seemed to take on a life of its own as it reversed the dagger, pointed the butt of the hilt at Anthon, and pressed the hidden stud. An energy bolt, blinding in the darkness, struck him in the chest and he went down without a sound.

Dalt grabbed his forearm. "My hand!" he screamed in agony and horror.

("Give me control!") Pard said urgently.

"My hand!" was all Dalt could say.

(*"Give me control!"*)

Dalt was jolted by this. He relaxed for a second and suddenly found himself an observer in his own body. His right hand dropped the dagger and cupped itself firmly over the bleeding stump, the thumb and fingers digging into the flesh of his forearm, searching for pressure points on the arteries.

His legs straightened as he rose to his feet and calmly walked toward the concealed shuttlecraft. His elbows parted the bushes and jabbed the plate that operated the door to the outer lock.

("I'm glad you didn't lock this up yesterday,") Pard said as the port swung open. There was a first-aid emergency kit inside for situations such as this. The pinky of his right hand was spared from its pressure duty to flip open the lid of the kit and then a container of stat-gel. The right hand suddenly released its grasp and, amid a splatter of blood, the stump of his left arm was forcefully shoved into the gel and held there.

("That should stop the bleeding.") The gel had an immediate clotting effect on any blood that came into contact with it. The thrombus formed would be firm and tough.

Rising, Dalt discovered that his body was his own again. He stumbled outside, weak and disoriented.

"You saved my life, Pard," he mumbled finally. "When I looked at that stump with the blood shooting out, I couldn't move."

("I saved *our* life, Steve.")

He walked over to where Anthon lay with a smoking hole where his chest had been. "I wished to avoid that. It wasn't really fair, you know. He only had a sword. . . ." Dalt was not quite himself yet. The events of the last minute had not yet been absorbed.

("Fair, hell! What does 'fair' mean when someone's trying to kill you?")

But Dalt didn't seem to hear. He began searching the ground. "My hand! Where's my hand? If we bring it back maybe they can replace it!"

("Not a chance, Steve. Necrosis will be in full swing by the time we get to the mothership.")

Dalt sat down. The situation was finally sinking in. "Oh, well," he said resignedly. "They're doing wonderful things with prosthetics these days."

("Prosthetics! We'll grow a *new* one!")

Dalt paused before answering. "A new hand?"

("Of course! You've still got deposits of omni-potential mesenchymal cells here and there in your body. I'll just have them transported to the stump, and with me guiding the process there'll be no problem to rebuilding the hand. It's really too bad you humans have no conscious control over the physiology of your bodies. With the proper direction, the human body is capable of almost anything.")

"You mean I'll have my hand back? Good as new?"

("Good as new. But at the moment I suggest we get into the ship and depart. The brain has called the Duke and it might be a good thing if we weren't here when he arrived.")

"You know," Dalt said as he entered the shuttle-craft and let the port swing to a close behind him, "with your watching over my body, I could live to a ripe old age."

("All I have to do is keep up with the degenerative changes and you'll live forever.")

Dalt stopped in midstride. "Forever?"

("Of course. The old natives of this planet knew it when they made up that warning for their children: 'Of every thousand struck down, nine hundred and ninety-nine will die.' The obvious conclusion is that the thousandth victim will *not* die.")

"Ever?"

("Well, there's not much I can do if you catch an energy bolt in the chest like Anthon back there. But otherwise, you won't die of old age—I'll see to that. You won't even get old, for that matter.")

The immensity of what Pard was saying suddenly struck Dalt with full force. "In other words," he breathed, "I'm immortal."

("I'd prefer a different pronoun: *We* are immortal.")

"I don't believe it."

("I don't care what you believe. I'm going to keep you alive for a long, long time, Steve, because while *you* live, *I* live, and I've grown very fond of living.")

Dalt did not move, did not reply.

("Well, what are you waiting for? There's a whole galaxy of worlds out there just waiting to be seen and experienced and I'm getting damn sick of this one!")

Dalt smiled. "What's the hurry?"

There was a pause, then: ("You've got a point there, Steve. There's really no hurry at all. We've got all the time in the world. Literally.")

sand struck down, nine hundred and ninety-nine will die. The obvious conclusion is that the thousandth victim will not die.")

"Ever?"

("Well, there's not much I can do if you catch an energy bolt in the chest like Acting back there. But otherwise, you won't die of old age—I'll see to that. You won't even get old, for that matter.")

The immensity of what Fred was saying suddenly struck Dalt with full force. "In other words," he breathed, "I'm immortal."

("I'd prefer a different pronoun: We are immortal.")

"I don't believe it."

("I don't care what you believe. I'm going to keep you alive for a long, long time, Steve, because while you live, I live, and I've grown very fond of living.")

Dalt did not move, did not reply.

("Well, what are you waiting for? There's a whole galaxy of worlds out there just waiting to be seen and experienced and I'm getting damn sick of this one!")

Dalt smiled. "What's the hurry?"

There was a pause, then: ("You've got a point there, Steve. There's really no hurry at all. We've got all the time in the world. Literally.")

HEALER II

(age 218)

Heal Thy Neighbor

It is difficult in these times to appreciate the devastating effect of "the horrors." It was not a plague in the true sense: it struck singly, randomly, wantonly. It jumped between planets, from one end of Occupied Space to the other, closing off the minds of victim after victim. To date we remain ignorant of the nature of the malady. An effective prophylaxis was never devised. And there was only one known cure—a man called The Healer.

The Healer made his initial public appearance at the Chesney Institute for Psychophysiologic Disorders on Largo IV under the auspices of the Interstellar Medical Corps. Intense investigative reporting by the vid services at the time revealed that a man of similar appearance (and there could have been only one then) was seen frequently about the IMC research center on Tolive.

IMC, however, has been steadfastly and frustratingly recalcitrant about releasing any information concerning its relationship with The Healer, saying only that they gave him "logistical support" as he went from planet to planet. As to whether they discovered his talent, developed his talent, or actually imbued him with his remarkable psionic powers, only IMC knows.

from *The Healer: Man & Myth*
by Emmerz Fent

IV

The man strolls slowly along one of Chesney's wide thoroughfares, enjoying the sun. His view of the street ahead of him is suddenly blotted out by the vision of a huge, contorted face leering horribly at him. For an instant he thinks he can feel the brush of its breath on his face. Then it is gone.

He stops and blinks. Nothing like this has ever happened to him before. He tentatively scrapes a foot forward to start walking again and kicks up a cloud of—

—dust. An arid wasteland surrounds him and the sun regards him cruelly, reddening and blistering his skin. And when he feels that his blood is about to boil, the sky is suddenly darkened by the wings of a huge featherless bird which circles twice and then dives in his direction at a speed which will certainly smash them both. Closer, the cavernous beaked mouth is open and hungry. Closer, until he is—

—back on the street. The man leans against the comforting solidity of a nearby building. He is bathed in sweat and his respiration is ragged, gulping. He is afraid . . . must find a doctor. He pushes away from the building and—

—falls into a black void. But it is not a peaceful blackness. There's hunger there. He falls, tumbling in eternity. A light below. As he falls nearer, the light takes shape . . . an albino worm, blind, fanged and miles long, awaits him with gaping jaws.

A scream is torn from him, yet there is no sound.

And still he falls.

V

Pard was playing games again. The shuttle from Tarvodet had docked against the orbiting liner and as the passengers were making the transfer, he attempted to psionically influence their choice of seats.

("The guy in blue is going to sit in the third recess on the left.")

Are you reading him? Dalt asked.

("No, nudging him.")

You never give up, do you? You've been trying to work this trick for as long as I can remember.

("Yeah, but this time I think I've got it down. Watch.")

Dalt watched as the man in blue suddenly stopped before the third recess on the left, hesitated, then entered and seated himself.

"Well, congratulations," Dalt whispered aloud.

("Thank you, sir. Now watch the teenager sit in the same recess.")

The lanky young man in question ambled by the third recess on the left without so much as a glance and settled himself in the fifth on the right.

("Damn!")

What happened?

("Ah, the kid probably had his mind already made up that he wanted to sit there . . . probably does a lot of traveling and likes that seat.")

Possible. It's also possible that the guy in blue does a lot of traveling, too, and that he just so happens to like to sit in the third recess on the left.

("Cynicism doesn't become you, Steve.")

Well, it's hard to be an engenue after a couple of centuries with you.

("Then let me explain. You see, I can't make a person part his hair on the left if he prefers it parted on the right. However, if he doesn't give a damn where it's parted, I can probably get him to do it my way.")

A slim, blond beauty in an opalescent clingsuit strolled through the port.

("Okay, where should we make her sit?")

I don't care.

("Oh, yes you do. Your heart rate just increased four beats per minute and your groin is tingling.")

I'll admit she's attractive—

("She's more than that. She bears a remarkable resemblance to Jean, doesn't she?")

I really hadn't noticed.

("Come now, Steve. You know you can't lie to me. You saw the likeness immediately . . . you've never forgotten that woman.")

And he probably never would. It was over 140 standard years since he'd left her. What started as a casual shipboard romance during the Kwashi expedition had stretched into an incredible idyll. She accepted him completely, though it had puzzled her that he'd refused disability compensation for the loss of his left hand on Kwashi. Her puzzlement was short-lived, however, and was soon replaced by astonishment when it became evident that her lover's hand was growing back. She'd heard of alien creatures who could regenerate limbs and there was talk that the Interstellar Medical Corps was experimenting with induced regeneration, but this was spontaneous!

And if the fact that the hand was regenerating was not bizarre enough, the manner in which it regenerated bordered on the surreal. No finger buds appeared; no initial primative structures heralded the reconstruction of the severed hand. Instead, the wrist was repaired first, then the thenar and hypothenar eminences and the palm started to appear. The palm and the five metacarpals were completed before work was begun on the thumb phalanges; and the thumb, nail and all, was completed before the fingers were started. It was similar to watching a building being constructed floor by floor but with every floor completely furnished before the next one above is started. It took four standard months.

Jean accepted that—was glad, in fact, that her man had been made whole again. And then Dalt explained to her that he was no longer entirely human, that a new factor had been added, had entered through that patch of silver hair on the top of his head. He was a dual entity: one brain but two minds, and that second mind was conscious down to the cellular level.

And Jean accepted that. She might not have if it weren't for the hand which had grown back where the old one had been sliced off. No question about it: the hand was there—discolored, yes, but there nonetheless. And since that was true, then whatever else Dalt told her might also be true. So she accepted it. He was her man and she loved him and that was enough . . .

. . . until the years began to show and she watched her hair begin to thin and her skin begin to dry. The youth treatments were new then and only minimally effective. Yet all the while the man she loved remained in his prime, appearing to be not a day older than when they had met. This she could not accept. And so slowly her love began to thin, began to dry, began to crumble into resentment. And from there it was not far to desperate hatred.

So Dalt left Jean—for her sake, for the sake of her sanity. And never returned.

("I think I'll have her sit right here next to you.")

Don't bother.

("I think I should bother. You've avoided a close male-female relationship ever since you left Jean. I don't think that's—")

I really don't care what you think. Just don't play matchmaker!

("Nevertheless . . .")

The girl paused by Dalt's shoulder. Her voice was liquid. "Saving that seat for anyone?"

Dalt sighed resignedly. "No." He watched her as she settled herself across from him. She certainly did justice to the clingsuit: slim enough to keep the suit from bulging in the wrong places, full enough to fill it out and make it live up to its name. He idly wondered how Jean would have looked in one and then quickly cut off that train of thought.

"My name's Ellen Lettre."

"Steven Dalt," he replied with a mechanical nod.

A pause then: "Where're you from, Steve?"

"Derby." Another pause, this one slightly more awkward than the first.

("Have mercy on the girl! She's just trying to make friendly conversation. Just because she looks like Jean is no reason to treat her as if she's got Nolevatol Rot!")

You're right, he thought, then spoke. "I was doing some microbial research at the university there."

She smiled and that was nice to see. "Really? That means you were connected with the bioscience department. I took Dr. Chamler's course there last year."

"Ah! The Chemistry of Schizophrenia. A classic course. Are you in psychochem?"

She nodded. "Coming back from a little field trip right now, as a matter of fact. But I don't remember seeing you around the bioscience department."

"I sort of kept pretty much to myself—very involved in the work." And this was true. Dalt and Pard had developed a joint interest in the myriad microbial lifeforms being found on the explorable planets of the human sector of the galaxy. Some of the metabolic pathways and enzyme systems were incredible and the "laws" of biological science were constantly being revamped. Alien microbiology had become a huge field requiring years to make a beginning and decades to make a dent. Dalt and Pard had made notable contributions and published a number of respected papers.

"Dalt . . . Dalt," the girl was saying. "Yes, I believe I did hear your name mentioned around the department a few times. Funny, I'd have thought you'd be older than you are."

So would his fellow members of the bioscience department if he hadn't quit when he did. Men who had looked his age when he first came to the university were now becoming large in the waist and gray in the hair and it was time to move. Already two colleagues had asked him where he was taking his youth treatments. Fortunately, IMC Central had offered him an important research fellowship in antimicrobial therapy and he had accepted eagerly.

"You on a sabbatical from Derby?" she was asking.

"No, I quit. I'm on my way to Tolive now."

"Oh, then you're going to be working for the Interstellar Medical Corps."

"How did you know?"

"Tolive is the main research-and-development headquarters for IMC. Any scientist is assumed to be working for the group if he's headed for Tolive."

"I don't consider myself a scientist, really. Just a vagabond student of sorts, going from place to place and picking up what I can." So far, Dalt and his partner had served as an engineer on a peristellar freighter, a prospector on Tandem, a chispen fisher on Gelc, and so on, in a leisurely but determined search for knowledge and experience that spanned the human sector of the galaxy.

"Well, I'm certain you'll pick up a lot with IMC."

"You've worked for them?"

"I'm head of a psychiatric unit. My spesh is really behavior mod, but I'm trying to develop an overview of the entire field; that's why I took Chamler's course."

Dalt nodded. "Tell me something, Ellen—"

"El—"

"Okay, then: El. What's IMC like to work for? I must confess that I'm taking this job rather blindly; the offer came and I accepted with only minimal research."

"I wouldn't work anywhere else," she stated flatly, and Dalt believed her. "IMC has gathered some of the finest minds in the human galaxy together for one purpose: knowledge."

"Knowledge for knowledge's sake has never had that much appeal for me; and frankly, that's not quite the image I'd been given about IMC. It has a rather mercenary reputation in academic circles."

"The practical scientist and the practicing physician have limited regard for the opinions of most academicians. And I'm no exception. The IMC was started with private funds—loans, not grants—by a group of rather adventurous physicians who—"

"It was a sort of emergency squad, wasn't it?"

"At first, yes. There was always a plague of some sort somewhere and the group hopped from place to place on a fee-for-service basis. Mostly, they could render only supportive care; the pathogens and toxins encountered on the distressed planets had already been found resistant to current therapeutic measures and there was not much the group could do on such short notice, other than lend a helping hand. they came up with some innovations which they patented, but it became clear that much basic research was needed. So they set up a permanent base on Tolive and started digging."

"With quite a bit of success, I believe. IMC is reputedly wealthy—extremely so."

"Nobody's starving, I can say that. IMC pays well in hopes of attracting the best minds. It offers an incredible array of research resources and gives the individual a good share of the profits from his marketable discoveries. As a matter of fact, we've just leased to Teblinko Pharmaceuticals rights for production of the antitoxin for the famous Nolevatol Rot."

Dalt was impressed. The Nolevatol Rot was the scourge of the interstellar traveler. Superficially, it resembled a mild case of tinea and was self-limiting; however, the fungus produced a neurotoxin with invariably fatal central-nervous-system effects. It was highly contagious and curable only by early discovery and immediate excision of the affected area of skin . . . until now.

"That product alone would finance the entire operation of IMC, I imagine."

El shook her head. "Not a chance. I can see you have no idea of the scope of the group. For every trail that pays off, a thousand are followed to a dead end. And they all cost money. One of our most costly fiascos was Nathan Sebitow."

"Yes, I'd heard he'd quit."

"He was *asked* to quit. He may be the galaxy's greatest biophysicist but he's dangerous—complete disregard of safety precautions for both himself and his fellow workers. IMC gave him countless warnings but he ignored them all. He was working with some fairly dangerous radiation and so finally his funds were cut off."

"Well, it didn't take him long to find a new home, I imagine."

"No, Kamedon offered him everything he needed to continue his work within days after he supposedly 'quit' IMC."

"Kamedon . . . that's the model planet the Restructurists are pouring so much money into."

She nodded. "And Nathan Sebitow is quite a feather in its cap. He should come up with something very exciting—I just hope he doesn't kill anybody with that hard radiation he's fooling around with." She paused, then, "But getting back to the question of knowledge for knowledge's sake: I find the concept unappealing, too. IMC, however, works on the assumption that all knowledge—at least scientific knowledge—will eventually work its way into some scheme of practical value. Existence consists of intra- and extracorporeal phenomena; the more we know about those two groups, the more effective our efforts will be when we wish to remedy certain interactions between them which prove to be detrimental to a given human."

"Spoken like a true behaviorist," Dalt said with a laugh.

"Sorry." She flushed. "I do get carried away now and again. Anyway, you see the distinction I was trying to make."

"I see and agree. It's good to know that I'm not headed for an oversized ivory tower. But why Tolive? I mean, I've—"

"Tolive was chosen for its political and economic climate: a non-coercive government and a large, young work force. The presence of IMC and the ensuing prosperity have stabilized both the government—and I use that term only because you're an outsider—and the economy."

"But I've heard stories about Tolive."

"You mean that it's run by a group of sadists and fascists and anarchists and whatever other unpleasant terms you can dig up, and that if it weren't for the presence of the IMC the planet would quickly degenerate into a hell-hole, right?"

"Well, not quite so bluntly put, perhaps, but that's the impression I've been given. No specific horror stories, just vague warnings. Any of it true?"

"Don't ask me. I was born there and I'm prejudiced. But guess who else was born there, and I think you'll know what's behind the smear campaign."

Dalt pondered a moment, baffled. Pard, with his absolute recall, came to the rescue. ("Peter LaNague was born on Tolive.")

"LaNague!" Dalt blurted in surprise. "Of course!"

El raised her eyebrows. "Good for you. Not too many people remember that fact."

"But you're implying that someone is trying to smear LaNague by smearing his homeworld. That's ridiculous. Who would want to smear the author of the Federation Charter?"

"Why, the people who are trying to alter that charter: the Restructurists, of course. Tolive has been pretty much the way it is today for centuries, long before LaNague's birth and long since his death. Only since the Restructurist movement gained momentum have the rumors and whispers started. It's the beginning of a long-range campaign; you watch—it'll get dirtier. The idea is to smear LaNague's background and thus taint his ideas, thereby casting doubt upon the integrity of his lifework: the Federation Charter."

"You must be mistaken. Besides, lies can easily be exposed."

"Lies, yes. But not rumors and inference. We of Tolive have a rather unique way of viewing existence, a view that can easily be twisted and distorted into something repulsive."

"If you're trying to worry me, you're doing an excellent job. You'd better tell me what I've gotten myself into."

Her smile was frosty. "Nobody twisted your arm, I assume? You're on your way to Tolive of your own free choice, and I think you should learn about it firsthand. And speaking of hands . . ."

Dalt noticed her gaze directed at his left hand. "Oh, you've noticed the color."

"It's hard to miss."

He examined the hand, pronating and supinating it slowly as he raised it from his lap; a yellow hand, deepening to gold in the nail beds and somewhat mottled in the palms. At the wrist, normal flesh tone resumed along a sharp line of demarcation. Anthon's sword had been sharp and had cut clean.

"I had a chemical accident a few years back which left my hand permanently stained."

El's brow furrowed as she considered this.

("Careful, Steve,") Pard warned. ("This gal's connected with the medical profession and may not fall for that old story.")

"That can easily be remedied," El said after a pause. "I know a few cosmetic surgeons on Tolive—"

Dalt shook his head and cut her off. "Thanks, no. I leave it this color to remind me to be more careful in the future. I could have been killed."

("Go on! Persist in your stubbornness! For almost two centuries now you've refused to allow me to correct that unsightly pigmentation. It was my fault, I admit. I'd never overseen the reconstruction of an appendage before and I—")

I know, I know! You made an error in the melanin deposition. We've been over this more times than I care to remember.

("And I can correct it if you'll just let me! You know I can't stand the thought of our having one yellow hand. It grates on me.")

That's because you're an obsessive-compulsive personality.

("Hah! That's merely a term used by slobs to denigrate perfectionists!")

El was now eyeing the gray patch of hair on the top of his head. "Is that, too, the result of an accident?"

"A terrible accident." He nodded gravely.

("No fair! I can't defend myself!")

She leaned back and appraised him. "A golden hand, a crown of silver hair, and a rather large flamestone hanging from your neck—you cut quite a figure, Steven Dalt." El was frankly interested.

Dalt fingered the jewel at his throat and pretended not to notice. "This little rock is a memento of a previous and far more hazardous form of employment. I keep it for sentimental reasons only."

"You have lots of color for a microbiologist," she was saying, and her smile was very warm now, "and I think you'll make a few waves at IMC."

A few days later they sat in the lounge of the orbit station and watched Tolive swirl below them as they sipped drinks and waited for the shuttle to arrive. A portly man in a blue jumper drifted by and paused to share the view with them.

"Beautiful, isn't it?" he said, and they replied with nods. "I don't know what it is, but every time I get in front of a view like this, I feel so insignificant. Don't you?"

El ignored the question and posed one of her own. "You aren't from Tolive, are you?" It was actually a statement.

"No, I'm on my way to Neeka. Have to lay over in orbit here to make a connecting jump. Never been down there," he said, nodding at the globe below. "But how come you sound so sure?"

"Because no one from 'down there' would ever say what you said," El replied, and promptly lost interest in the conversation. The portly man paused, shrugged, and then drifted off.

"What was that all about?" Dalt asked. "What did he say that was so un-Tolivian?"

"As I told you before, we have a different way of looking at things. The human race developed on a tiny planet a good many light-years away and devised a technology that allows us to sit in orbit above a once-alien planet and comfortably sip intoxicants while awaiting a ship to take us down. As a member of that race, I assure you, I feel anything but insignificant."

Dalt glanced after the man who had initiated the discussion and noticed him stagger as he walked away. He widened his stance as if to steady himself and stood blinking at nothing, beads of sweat dropping from his face and darkening the blue of his jumper. Suddenly he spun with outstretched arms, and with a face contorted with horror, began to scream incoherently.

El bolted from her seat without a word and dug a microsyringe from her hip pouch as she strode toward the man, who had by now collapsed into a blubbering, whimpering puddle of fear. She placed the ovid device on the skin on the lateral aspect of his neck and squeezed.

"He'll quiet down in a minute," she told a concerned steward as he rushed up. "Send him down to IMC Central on the next shuttle for emergency admission to Section Blue." The steward nodded obediently, relieved that someone seemed to feel that things were under control. And sure enough, by the time two fellow workers had arrived, the portly man was quiet, although still racked with sobs.

"What the hell happened to him?" Dalt asked over El's shoulder as the man was carried to a berth in the rear.

"A bad case of the horrors," she replied.

"No, I'm serious."

"So am I. It's been happening all over the human sector of the galaxy, just like that: men, women, all ages; they go into an acute, unremitting psychotic state. They are biochemically normal and usually have unremarkable premorbid medical histories. They've been popping up for the past decade in a completely random fashion and there doesn't seem to be a damn thing we can do about them," she said with a set jaw, and it was obvious that she resented being helpless in any situation, especially a medical one.

Dalt gazed at El and felt the heaviness begin. She was a remarkable woman, very intelligent, very opinionated, and so very much like Jean in appearance; but she was also very mortal. Dalt had resisted the relationship she was obviously trying to initiate and every time he weakened he merely had to recall Jean's hate-contorted face when he had deserted her.

I think we ought to get out of microbiology, he told Pard as his eyes lingered on El.

("And into what?")

How about life prolongation?

("Not that again!")

Yes! Only this time we'll be working at IMC Central with some of the greatest scientific minds in the galaxy.

("The greatest minds in the galaxy have always worked on that problem, and every 'major breakthrough' and 'new hope' has turned out to be a dead end. Human cells reach a certain level of specialization and then lose their ability to reproduce. Under optimum conditions, a century is all they'll last; after that the DNA gets sloppy and consequently the RNA gets even sloppier. What follows is enzyme breakdown, toxic overload, and finally death. Why this happens, no one knows—and that includes me, since my consciousness doesn't reach to the molecular level—and from recent literature, it doesn't seem likely that anyone'll know in the near future.")

But we have a unique contribution to make—

("You think I haven't investigated it on my own, if not for any other reason than to provide you with a human companion of some permanence? It's no fun, you know, when you go into those periods of black despair.")

I guess not. He paused. *I think one's on its way.*

("I know. The metabolic warning flags are already up. Look: why not take up with this woman? You both find each other attractive and I think it will be good for you.")

Will it be good for me when she grows into a bitter old woman while I stay young?

("What makes you think she'll want you around that long?") Pard jibed.

Dalt had no answer for that one.

Ω

The shuttle trip was uneventful and when El offered to drive him from the spaceport to his hotel, Dalt reluctantly accepted. His feelings were in a turmoil, wanting to be simultaneously as close to and as far from this woman as possible. So to keep the conversation safe and light, he made a comment about the lack of flitters in the air.

"We're still pretty much in the ground-car stage, although one of the car factories is reportedly gearing for flitter production. It'll be nice to get one at a reasonable price; the only ones on Tolive now were shipped via interstellar freight and *that* is expensive!"

She pulled her car alongside a booth outside the spaceport perimeter, fished out a card, and stuck it into a slot. The card disappeared for a second or two and then the booth spit it out. El retrieved it, sealed her bubble, and pulled away.

"What was that all about?"

"Toll."

Dalt was incredulous. "You mean you actually have toll roads on this planet?"

She nodded. "But not for long . . . not if we get a good supply of flitters."

"Even so, the roads belong to everybody—"

"No, they belong to those who built them."

"But taxes—"

"You think roads should be built with tax money?" El asked with a penetrating glance. "I use this road maybe once or twice a year; why should I pay anything for it the rest of the time? A group of men got together and built this road and they charge me every time I use it. What's wrong with that?"

"Nothing, except you've got to fork over money every time you make a turn."

"Not necessarily. Members of a given community usually get together and pool their money for local streets, build them, and leave them at that; and business areas provide roads gratis for the obvious reason. As a matter of fact, a couple of our big corporations have built roads and donated them to the public—the roads are, of course, named after the companies and thus act as continuous publicity agents."

"Sounds like a lot of trouble to me. It'd be a lot simpler if you just made everyone ante up and—"

"Not on this planet it wouldn't be. You don't *make* Tolivians do anything. It would take a physical threat to make me pay for a road that I'll never use. And we tend to frown on the use of physical force here."

"A pacifist society, huh?"

"Pacifist may not be—" she began, and then swerved sharply to make an exit ramp. "Sorry," she said with a quick, wry grin. "I forgot I was dropping you off at the hotel."

Dalt let the conversation lapse and stared out his side of the bubble at the Tolivian landscape. Nothing remarkable there: a few squat trees resembling conifers scattered in clumps here and there around the plain, coarse grass, a mountain range rising in the distance.

"Not exactly a lush garden-world," he muttered after a while.

"No, this is the arid zone. Tolive's axis has little deviation relative to its primary, and its orbit is only mildly ellipsoid. So whatever the weather is wherever you happen to be, that's probably what it'll be like for most of the year. Most of our agriculture is in the northern hemisphere; industry keeps pretty much to the south and usually within short call of the spaceports."

"You sound like a chamber-of-commerce report," Dalt remarked with a smile.

"I'm proud of my world." El did not smile.

Suddenly, there was a city crouched on the road ahead, waiting for them. Dalt had spent too much time on Derby of late and had become accustomed to cities with soaring profiles. And that's how the cities on his homeworld of Friendly had been. But this pancake of one- and two-story buildings was apparently the Tolivian idea of a city.

SPOONERVILLE said a sign in Interworld characters. POP: 78,000. They sped by rows of gaily colored houses, most standing alone, some interconnected. And then there were warehouses and shops and restaurants and such. The hotel stood out among its neighboring buildings, stretching a full four stories into the air.

"Not exactly the Centauri Hilton," Dalt remarked as the car jolted to a halt before the front entrance.

"Tolive doesn't have much to offer in the way of tourism. This place obviously serves Spoonerville's needs, 'cause if there was much of an overflow somebody'd have built another." She paused, caught his eyes, and held them. "I've got a lovely little place out on the plain that'll accommodate two very nicely, and the sunsets are incredible."

Dalt tried to smile. He liked this woman, and the invitation, which promised more than sunsets, was his for the taking. "Thanks, El. I'd like to take you up on that offer sometime, but not now. I'll try to see you at IMC tomorrow after my meeting with Dr. Webst."

"Okay." She sighed as he stepped out of the car. "Good luck." Without another word she sealed the bubble and was off.

("You know what they say about hell and fury and scorned women,") Pard remarked.

Yeah, I know, but I don't think she's like that ... got too good a head on her shoulders to react so primitively.

Dalt's reserved room was ready for him and his luggage was expected to arrive momentarily from the spaceport. He walked over to the window which had been left opaque, flipped a switch, and made the entire outer wall transparent. It was 18.75 in a twenty-seven-hour day—that would take some getting used to after years of living with Derby's twenty-two-hour day—and the sunset was an orange explosion behind the hills. It probably looked even better from El's place on the plains.

("But you turned her down,") Pard said, catching the thought. ("Well, what are we going to do with ourselves tonight? Shall we go out and see what the members of this throbbing metropolis do to entertain themselves?")

Dalt squatted down by the window with his back against the wall. "I think I'll just stay here and watch for a while. Why don't you just go away," he muttered aloud.

("I can't very well leave . . .")

"You know what I mean!"

("Yes, I know what you mean. We go through this every time we have to uproot ourselves because your associates start giving you funny looks. You start mooning over Jean—")

"I do *not* moon over her!"

("Call it what you will, you mope around like a Lentemian crench that's lost its calf. But it's really not Jean. She's got nothing to do with these mood swings; she's dead and gone and you've long since accepted that. What's really bothering you is your own immortality. You refuse to let people know that you will not grow old with the years as they do—")

"I don't want to be a freak and I don't want that kind of notoriety. Before you know it, someone will come looking for the 'secret' of my longevity and will stop at nothing to get it. I can do very well without that, thank you."

("Fine. Those are good reasons, excellent reasons for wanting to pass yourself off as a mortal among mortals. That's the only way we'll ever really get to do what we want to do. But that's only on the surface. Inside you must come to grips with the fact that you cannot *live* as a mortal. You haven't the luxury of ascribing an infinite span to a relationship, as do many mortals, for 'the end of time' to them is the same as the end of life, which is all too finite. In your case, however, 'the end of time' may occur with you there watching it. So, until you can find yourself another immortal as a companion, you'll just have to be satisfied with relatively short-term relationships and cease acting so resentful of the fact that you won't be dying in a few decades like all your friends.")

"Sometimes I wish I *could* die."

("Now, we both know that you don't mean that, and even if you were sincere, I wouldn't allow it.")

Go away, Pard!

("I'm gone.")

And he was. With Pard tucked away in some far corner of his brain—probably working on some obscure philosophical problem or remote mathematical abstraction—Dalt was finally alone.

Alone. That was the key to these periodic black depressions. He was all right once he had established an identity on a new world, made a few friends, and put himself to work on whatever it was he wanted to do at that particular time in his life. He could thus delude himself into a sense of belonging that lasted a few decades, and then it began to happen: the curious stares, the probing questions. Soon he'd find himself on an interstellar liner again, between worlds, between lives. The sense of rootlessness would begin to weigh heavily upon him.

Culturally, too, he was an outsider. There was no interstellar human culture as yet to speak of; each planet was developing its own traditions and becoming proud of them. No one could really feel at home on any world except one's own, and so the faux pas of an off-worlder was well tolerated in the hope of receiving the same consideration after a similar blunder on his homeworld. Dalt was thus unconcerned about any anachronisms in his behavior, and with the bits and pieces he was taking with him from every world he lived on, he was fast becoming the only representative of a true interstellar human culture.

Which meant that no world was actually *home*—only on interstellar liners did he feel even the slightest hint of belonging. Even Friendly, his birth world, had treated him as an off-worlder, and only with great difficulty did he manage to find a trace or two of the familiar in his own hometown during a recent and very discouraging sentimental journey.

Pard was right, of course. He was almost always right. Dalt couldn't have it both ways, couldn't be an immortal and retain a mortal's scope. He'd have to broaden his view of existence and learn to think on a grander scale. He was still a man and would have to live among other men, but he would have to develop an immortal's perspective in regard to time, something he had as yet been unable and/or unwilling to do. Time set him apart from other men and had to be reckoned with. Until now he had been living a lot of little lives, one after the other, separate, distinct. Yet they were all his, and he had to find a way to fuse them into a single entity. He'd work on it. No hurry . . . there was plenty of time—

There was that word again. He wondered when he would end. Of *if* he would end. Would the moment ever come when he'd want to stop living? And would he be allowed to do so? Pard's earlier statement had made him uneasy. They shared a body and thus an existence, as the result of an accident. What if one partner decided he wanted out? It would never be Pard—his intellectual appetite was insatiable. No, if anyone would ever want to call it quits, it would be Dalt. And Pard would forbid it. Such a situation appeared ludicrous on the surface but might very well come to be, millennia hence. How would they resolve it? Would Pard find a way to grant Dalt's wish by somehow strangling his mind, thereby granting his death wish—for in Pard's philosophy, the mind is life and life is the mind—and leaving Pard as sole tenant of the body?

Dalt shuddered. Pard's ethics would, of course, prevent him from doing such a thing unless Dalt absolutely demanded it. But still it was hardly a comforting thought. Even in the dark fog of depression that enveloped him tonight, Dalt realized that he loved life and living very much. Planning to make the most of tomorrow and every subsequent tomorrow, he drifted off to sleep as the second of Tolive's three moons bobbed above the horizon.

VI

A somewhat harried Steven Dalt managed to arrive at the administrative offices of IMC in time for his 09.5 appointment with Dr. Webst. His back ached as he took a seat in the waiting room, and he realized he was hungry.

A bad morning so far—if this was any indication of how the rest of the day was going to be, he decided he'd be better off returning to the hotel, crawling into bed, and spending it in the fetal position. He'd awakened late and cramped in that corner by the window, with his baggage sitting inside the door. He'd had to rummage through it to find a presentable outfit and then rush down to the lobby and find a taxi to take him to the IMC administration building. He did not want to keep Dr. Webst waiting. Dalt seemed to be placing greater and greater importance on punctuality lately. Perhaps, he mused, the more aware he became of his own timelessness, the more conscious he became of the value of another man's time.

("Well, what'll it be?") Pard asked suddenly.

Welcome back.

("I should be saying that to you. Once again: What'll it be?")

What are you talking about?

("Us. Are we sticking with the microbes or do we go into gerontology or what?")

I'm not sure. Maybe we won't stay here at all. They hired us for antimicrobial research and may not want us for anything else. But I think I've had enough of microbes for now.

("I must agree. But what shall we try next?")

I haven't given it too much thought yet—

("Well, get thinking. We'll be seeing Dr. Webst in a moment and we'd better have something to tell him.")

Why don't we just improvise?

Pard seemed to hesitate, then, ("Okay, but let's be as honest as possible with him, 'cause we start getting paid as of this morning.")

So, a few credits won't break IMC.

("It would be unethical to accept payment for nothing.")

Your rigidity wears on me after a while, Pard.

("Value received for value given—don't forget it.")

Okay, okay, okay.

The door to Dr. Webst's office dilated and a tall, fair young man with an aquiline profile stepped through. He glanced at Dalt, who was the room's only occupant, paused, then walked over and extended his hand. "Dr. Dalt?"

"The 'Dalt' part is correct, but I have no doctorate." Actually, this was untrue; he held two doctorates in separate fields but both had been granted a number of lives ago."

"*Mister* Dalt, then. I'm Dr. Webst." They performed the ancient human ritual known as the handshake and Dalt liked Webst's firm grip.

"I thought you'd be older, Doctor," Dalt said as they entered Webst's sparsely appointed office.

Webst smiled. "That's funny . . . I was expecting an older man, too. That paper you published a year ago on Dasein II fever and the multiple pathogens involved was a brilliant piece of work; there was an aura of age and experience about it."

"Are you in infectious diseases?" Dalt asked quickly, anxious to change the subject.

"No, psych is my field."

"Really? I made part of the trip from Derby in the company of Ellen Lettre. Know her?"

"Of course. Our department has high hopes for Dr. Lettre—an extremely intelligent woman." He paused at his desk and flashed a rapid series of memos across his viewer. "Before I forget, I got a note from personnel about your forms. Most of them are incomplete and they'd like to see you sometime today."

Dalt nodded. "Okay, I'll see if I can make it this afternoon." This was often a problem—personal history. He had changed his name a couple of times but preferred to be known as Steven Dalt. Usually he went from one field of endeavor to another totally unrelated to the first and thus obviated the need for references; he would start at the bottom as he had at the university on Derby, and with Pard as his partner, it wouldn't be long before the higher-ups realized they had a boy genius among them. Or, he'd go into a risky field such as chispen fishing on Gelc, where the only requirement for employment was the guts to go out on the nets . . . and no questions asked.

As for the IMC personnel department—he had paid a records official on Derby a handsome bribe to rig some documents to make him appear to be a native of the planet. He'd been purposely vague and careless with the IMC applications in order to stall off any inquiries until all was ready. All he could do now was hope.

"Question," Dalt said. Webst looked up. "Why a psychiatrist to meet me rather than someone from the microbiology department?"

"Protocol, I guess. Dr. Hyne is head of the micro department but he's on vacation. It's customary to have an important new man—and you fall into that category—welcomed by a departmental head. And I'm head of psych."

"I see," Dalt nodded. "But when do I—"

Webst's phone buzzed. "Yes?" The word activated the screen and a technician's face appeared.

"*Private message, Doctor.*"

Webst picked up the earpiece and swung the screen face away from Dalt. "Go ahead." He listened, nodded, said, "I'll be right over," and hung up.

"Have you had breakfast yet?" he asked Dalt, whose headshake left little doubt about the current state of his stomach. "Okay, why don't you make yourself at home at that table behind you and punch in an order. I've got to go check out some equipment—should only take me a few minutes. Relax and enjoy the meal; we have an excellent commissary and the local hens lay delicious eggs." He gave a short wave and was gone.

("May the god of empty stomachs bless and keep him!") Pard remarked as Dalt punched in an order. ("No dinner last night and no breakfast this morning—very careless.")

Dalt waited hungrily. *Couldn't be helped.*

("I like Webst,") Pard said as a steaming tray popped out of a slot in the wall. ("He seems rather unpretentious and it would be easy for a young man in such a high position to be otherwise.")

I didn't notice either way. Dalt began to eat with gusto.

("That's the nice part—he doesn't make a show of his unpretentiousness. It seemed very natural for him to personally bring you in from the waiting room, didn't it? But think: Most departmental heads would prefer to have the receptionist open the door and let you come to them. This man made an effort to make you feel at home.")

Maybe he just hasn't been a head long enough and doesn't know how to act like one.

("I have a feeling, Steve, that Dr. Webst is at the top of his field and knows it and can act any way he damn well pleases.")

Webst returned then, appearing preoccupied. He went directly to his desk, seated himself, and stared at Dalt for a long moment with a puzzled expression playing over his face.

"What's the matter?" Dalt asked, finally.

"Hmmm?" He shook himself. "Oh, nothing. A technical problem . . . I think." He paused. "Tell you what: Everybody over in microbiology is rather tied up today—why don't you come with me over to psychiatry and I'll show you around. I know you're anxious to get to see micro—"

("Not really,") Pard interjected.

"—but at least this way you can start to get a feel for IMC."

Dalt shrugged. "Fine with me. Lead the way."

Webst seemed very pleased with Dalt's acquiescence and ushered him out a rear door to a small carport.

("He's lying to us, Steve.")

I had that feeling, too. You think we're in trouble?

("I doubt it. He's such a terrible liar, it's unlikely that he's had much practice at it. He just wants to get us over to the psych department, so let's play along and see what he has in mind. This just may lead to a chance to get out of microbes and into another field. Can you dredge up any interest in mental illness?")

Not a particularly overwhelming amount.

("Well, start asking questions anyway. Show a little interest!")

Yessir!

"—nice weather, so I think we'll take the scenic tour," Webst was saying. "When it rains, which isn't that often, we have a tunnel system you can use. A dome was planned initially but the weather proved to be so uniform that no one could justify the expense."

The small ground car glided out over the path and the combination of warm sunlight, a cool breeze through the open cab, and a full belly threatened to put Dalt to sleep. At a leisurely pace they passed formations of low buildings, clean and graceful, with intricate gardens scattered among them.

("Questions, Steve,") Pard prompted.

Right. "Tell me, Doctor—if I may be so bold—what sort of astronomical sum did IMC have to pay for such a huge tract of land so close to the center of town?"

Webst smiled. "You forget that IMC was here before you and I were born—"

("Speak for yourself, sir.")

"—and the town was only a village at the time Central was started. Spoonerville, in fact, grew up around IMC."

"Well, it's beautiful, I must say."

"Thank you. We're proud of it."

Dalt drank in a passing garden, then asked, "What's going on in psychiatry these days? I thought mental illness was virtually a thing of the past. You have the enzymes and—"

"The enzymes only *control* schizophrenia—much the same as insulin controlled diabetics before beta-cell grafts. There's no cure as yet and I don't foresee one for quite some time." His voice lapsed unconsciously into a lecture tone. "Everyone thought a cure was imminent when Schimmelpenninck isolated the enzyme-substrate chains in the limbic system of the brain. But that was only the beginning. Different types and degrees of schizophrenia occur with breaks at different loci along the chains but environmental history appears to be equally important."

Webst paused as the car rounded a corner and had to wait for an automatic gate to slide open. Then they were in an octagonal courtyard with people scattered here and there, in groups or alone, talking or soaking up the sun.

"These are our ambulatory patients," he replied to Dalt's questioning glance. "We give them as much freedom as possible, but we also try to keep them from wandering off. They're all harmless and they're all here voluntarily." He cleared his throat. "But where was I? . . . Oh, yes. So it all boils down to a delicate balance between chemistry, intellect, and environment. If the individual has learned how to handle stress, he can often minimize the psychotic effects of a major break in the enzyme chains. If he hasn't, however, even a minor break at the terminus of a chain can throw his mind off the deep end."

He gave a short laugh. "But we still really don't know what we're talking about when we say *mind*. We can improve its function and grasp of reality with our drugs and teaching techniques, but it remains a construct that defies quantitative analysis."

He guided the vehicle into a slot next to a large blue building and stepped out. "And then, of course, there are the chemonegative psychotics—all their enzyme chains seem to be intact but they are completely divorced from reality. Victims of the so-called 'horrors.' They're the one's we're working on here in Big Blue, where we keep our intractable patients," Webst said as he passed his hand over a plate set in the doorframe. Silently, the first of the double doors slid open and waited for them to enter, and it was not until the first was completely secure in its closed position that the second began to move.

"Are they dangerous in here?" Dalt asked uneasily.

"Only to themselves. These patients are totally cut off from reality and anything could happen to them if they got loose."

"But what's wrong with them? I saw a man go into one of these fits on the orbit station."

Webst twisted his mouth to the side. "Unfortunately, these aren't 'fits' that come and go. The victim gets hit with whatever it is that hits him, screams hysterically, and spends the rest of his life—at least we assume so, although the first recorded case was only ten years ago—cut off from the rest of the world. Cases are popping up on every planet in the Federation. It's even rumored that the Tarks are having problems with it. We need a breakthrough."

Webst paused, then said, "Let's look in here." He opened a door marked 12 and allowed Dalt to precede him into the room. It was a nicely appointed affair with a bed, two chairs, and indirect lighting. And it was empty, or at least Dalt thought it was until Webst directed his attention to a corner behind one of the chairs. A young girl of no more than eighteen years crouched there in a shivering state of abject terror.

"First name, Sally," Webst intoned. "We dubbed her that. Last name: Ragna—that's the planet on which she was found. A typical 'horrors' case: We've had her for one and a half standard years and we haven't been able to put even a chink into that wall of terror."

Webst went to a plate in the wall by the door and waved

his hand across it. "This is Dr. Webst. I'm in room twelve with Mr. Dalt."

"Thank you, Doctor," said a male voice. *"Would you mind stepping down the hall a minute?"*

"Not at all," he replied, and turned to Dalt. "Why don't you stay here and try to talk to Sally while I see what they want. She's perfectly harmless, wouldn't—couldn't—hurt anyone or anything, and that's the crux of her problem. We've normalized her enzymes and have tried every psychotropic agent known to break her shell, with no results. We've even gone so far as to reinstitute the ancient methods of electroconvulsive therapy and insulin shock." He sighed. "Nothing. So try to talk to her and see what we're up against."

With Webst gone, Dalt turned his attention to the girl.

("Pitiful, isn't it?") Pard said.

Dalt did not reply. He was staring at a girl who must have been attractive once; her face now wore a ravaged, hunted expression that had caused seemingly permanent furrows in her skin; her eyes, when not squeezed shut, were opened wide and darting in all directions. Her arms were clasped around her knees, which were drawn up to her chest, and her hands gripped each other with white-knuckled intensity.

This could be very interesting, Dalt told Pard at last.

("It certainly could. I think it could also be interesting to know what Dr. Webst is up to. He was obviously stalling for time when he left us here.")

Maybe he wants us for his department.

("Highly unlikely. To the best of his knowledge, we are eminently unqualified in this field.")

"Hello, Sally," Dalt said.

No reaction.

"Do you hear me, Sally?"

No reaction.

He waved his hand before her eyes.

No reaction.

He clapped his hands loudly and without warning by her left ear.

No reaction.

He put his hands on her shoulders and shook her gently but firmly.

No reaction. Not an extra blink, not a change in expression, not a sound, not the slightest hint of voluntary movement.

Dalt rose to his feet and turned to find Dr. Webst standing in the doorway staring at him.

"Something wrong, Doctor?" Again, he wore the preoccupied, puzzled expression that did not seem to be at home on his face.

"I don't think so," he replied slowly. "Something may be very right, as a matter of fact. But I'll have to look into it a little more." He looked frustrated. "Would you mind going over to personnel for now and straightening out your papers while I try to straighten out a few things over here? I know what you're thinking . . . but IMC is really much better organized than I've demonstrated it to be. It's just that we've had some strange occurrences this morning that I'll explain to you later. For the moment, however, I'm going to be tied up."

Dalt had no desire to talk to the personnel department. On an impulse, he asked, "Is Ellen around?"

Webst brightened immediately. "Dr. Lettre? Yes, she's in the next building." He guided Dalt back to the entrance and pointed to a red building on the other side of the garden, perhaps twenty meters away. "Her office is right inside the far door. I'm sure she'll be glad to show you around her section, and I'll contact you there later." He passed his hand over the doorplate and the inner door began to move.

("Nice security system,") Pard said as they strolled past the lolling patients. ("The intercoms and the doorlocks are all cued to the palms of authorized personnel. Patients stay where you put them.")

Unless of course someone gets violent and decides that the quickest way to freedom is to cut off someone's authorized hand and waltz right out of the complex.

("Your sense of humor eludes me at times . . . but let's get to more-pressing matters.")

Such as?

("Such as Webst. At first he lied to get us over to the psychiatry units; now he seems anxious to get rid of us and made up some lame excuses to do so. I'd very much like to know what he's up to.")

Maybe he's just inefficient and disorganized.

("I assure you, Steve, that man is anything but inefficient. He's obviously puzzled by something and we seem to be implicated.")

He did, however, promise to explain it all to us later.

("Correct. Hopefully, he'll keep that promise.")

The door Webst had pointed out opened easily at Dalt's touch and did not lock after him. He concluded that there must not be any patients quartered in this area of the building. On a door to his left was a brass plate engraved DR. ELLEN H. LETTRE. He knocked.

"Come in," said a familiar voice. El looked almost as beautiful in a gray smock as she had in her clingsuit aboard ship.

"Hasn't that dictation come through yet?" she asked without looking up. "It's been almost ten minutes."

"I'm sure it'll be along soon," Dalt said.

El's head snapped up and she gave him a smile that he didn't feel he deserved after his cool treatment of her the night before. "How'd you get here?" she asked brightly.

"Dr. Webst showed me the way."

"You know him?"

"Since this morning."

"Oh? I thought you were going to be with the microbi—"

Dalt held up his hand. "It's a long story which I don't fully understand myself, but I'm here and you said you'd show me around your unit someday. So?"

"Okay. I was about to take a break anyway." She took him on a leisurely tour of her wing of the building where various behaviorist principles were being put to work on the rehabilitation of schizophrenics who had successfully responded to medical management. Dalt's stomach was starting to rumble again as they returned to her office.

"Can I buy you lunch?"

"You sure you want to get that involved?" she said with a side-long glance.

"Okay," Dalt laughed, "I deserved that. But how about it? You've got to eat somewhere."

She smiled. "I'd love to have you buy me lunch, but first I've got to catch up on a few things—that 'break' I just took was well over an hour long." She thought for a minute. "There's a place on the square—"

"You actually have a town square?" Dalt exclaimed.

"It's a tradition on Tolive; just about every town has one. The town square is one of the very few instances of common ownership on the planet. It is used for public discussion and . . . uh . . . other matters of public concern."

"Sounds like a quaint locale for a restaurant. Should be nice."

"It is. Why don't you meet me there at 13.0. You can familiarize yourself with the square and maybe catch a little of the flavor of Tolive." The square was near the IMC complex and she told him how to get there, then called an orderly to drive him out of the maze of buildings to the front entrance.

A cool breeze offset the warmth of the sun as he walked and when he compared the vaguely remembered cab trip of the morning to the route El had given him, he realized that his hotel was right off the square. He scrutinized his fellow pedestrians in an effort to discern a fashion trend but couldn't find one. Men wore everything from briefs to business jumpers; women could be seen in everything from saris through clingsuits to near-nude.

Shops began to proliferate along the street and Dalt sensed he was nearing the square. A sign caught his eye: LIN'S LIT in large letters, and below, at about a quarter of the size above, For the Discerning Viewer.

("There's plenty of time before your lunch date. Let's see what they sell on Tolive—you can learn a lot about a culture's intellectual climate from its literature.")

All right. Let's see.

They should have been prepared for what was inside by the card on the door: "Please be advised that the material sold within is considered by certain people to be obscene—you might be one of those people."

Inside they found a huge collection of photos, holos, telestories, vid cassettes, etc., most devoted to sexual activity. Categories ranged from human & human, through human & alien animal, to human & alien plant. And then the material took a sick turn.

I'm leaving, Dalt told Pard.

("Wait a minute. It's just starting to get interesting.")

Not for me. I've had enough.

("Immortals aren't supposed to be squeamish.")

Well, it'll be a couple more centuries before I can stomach some of this junk. So much for Tolive's cultural climate!

And out they went to the street again. Half a block on, they came to the square, which was actually round. It was more like a huge traffic circle with the circumference rimmed by shops and small business offices; inside the circle was a park with grass and trees and amusement areas for children. A large white structure was set at its hub; from Dalt's vantage point it appeared to be some sort of monument or oversized art object in the ancient abstract mode.

He wandered into a clothing store and was tempted to make some purchases until he remembered that he had no credit on Tolive as yet, so he contented himself with watching others do the buying. He watched a grossly overweight woman step onto a fitting platform, punch in a style, fabric weight and color code, and then wait for the measuring sensors to rise out of the floor. A *beep* announced that her order was being processed and she stepped down and took a seat by the wall to wait for the piece she had ordered to be custommade to her specifications.

A neighboring shop sold pharmaceuticals and Dalt browsed through aimlessly until he heard a fellow shopper ask for five hundred-milligram doses of Zemmelar, the trade name for a powerful hallucinogenic narcotic.

"You sure you know what you're getting into?" the man behind the counter asked.

The customer nodded. "I use it regularly."

The counterman sighed, took the customer's credit slips, and punched out the order. Five cylindrical packages popped onto the counter. "You're on your own," he told the man who pocketed the order and hurried away.

Glancing at Dalt, the counterman burst out laughing, then held up his hand as Dalt turned to leave. "I'm sorry, sir, but by the expression on your face a moment ago, you must be an off-worlder."

"What's that supposed to mean?"

"It means that you think you just witnessed a very bold illegal transaction."

"Well, didn't I? That drug is reserved for terminal cases, is it not?"

"That's what it was developed for," the man replied. "Supposed to block out all bodily sensations and accentuate the patient's most pleasant fantasies. When I'm ready to go, I hope somebody will have the good sense to shoot some of it into me."

"But that man said he uses it regularly."

"Yeah. He's an addict, I guess. Probably new in town . . . never seen him before."

"But that drug is illegal!"

"That's how I know you're an off-worlder. You see—there are no illegal drugs on Tolive."

"That can't be true!"

"I assure you, sir, it is. Anything in particular you'd like to order?"

"No," Dalt said, turning slowly and walking away. "Nothing, thanks."

This place will take some getting used to, he told Pard as they crossed the street to the park and took a seat on the grass beneath one of the native conifers.

("Yes. Apparently they do not have the usual taboos that most of humanity carried with it from Earth during the splinter-world period.")

I think I like some of those taboos. Some of the stuff in that first shop was positively degrading. And as for making it possible for anybody with a few credits to become a Zem addict . . . I don't like it.

("But you must admit that this appears to be a rather genteel populace. Despite the lack of a few taboos traditional to human culture, they all seem quite civilized so far. Admit it.")

All right, I admit it.

Dalt glanced across the park and noticed that there were a number of people on the white monument. Letters, illegible from this distance, had been illuminated on a dark patch near the monument's apex. As he watched, a cylinder arose from the platform and extended what appeared to be a stiff, single-jointed appendage with some sort of thong streaming from the end. A shirtless young man was brought to the platform. There was some milling around, and then his arms were fastened to an abutment.

The one-armed machine began to whip him across his bare back.

VII

"Finish that drink before we talk," El said.

"There's really not much to talk about," Dalt replied curtly. "I'm getting off this planet as soon as I can find a ship to take me."

They drank in silence amid the clatter and chatter of a busy restaurant, and Dalt's thoughts were irresistibly drawn back to that incredible scene in the park just as he himself had been irresistibly drawn across the grass for a closer look, to try to find some evidence that it was all a hoax. But the man's cries of pain and the rising welts on his back left little doubt. No one else in the park appeared to take much notice; some paused to look at the sign that overhung the tableau, then idly strolled on.

Dalt, too, looked at the sign:

A. Nelso
Accused of theft of
private ground car on
9-6.
Convicted of same on
9-20. Appeal denied.
Sentence of public
punishment to 0.6 Gomler
units to be administered
on 9-24.

The whipping stopped and the sign flashed blank. The man was released from the pillory and helped from the platform. Dalt was trying to decide whether the tears in the youth's eyes were from pain or humiliation, when a young, auburn-haired woman of about thirty years ascended the platform. She wore a harness of sorts that covered her breasts and abdomen but left her back exposed. As attendants locked her to the pillory, the sign came to life again:

> H. T. Hammet
> *Accused* of theft of
> miniature vid set from
> retail store on 9-8.
> *Convicted* of same on
> 9-22. Appeal denied.
> *Sentence* of public
> punishment to 0.2 Gomler
> units to be administered
> on 9-24.

The cylinder raised the lash, swung its arm, and the woman winced and bit her lower lip. Dalt spun and lurched away.

("Barbaric!") Pard said when they had crossed the street and were back among the storefronts.

What? No remarks about being squeamish?

("Holograms of deviant sexual behavior posed for by volunteers are quite different from public floggings. How can supposedly civilized people allow such stone-age brutality to go on?")

I don't know and I don't care. Tolive has just lost a prospective citizen.

A familiar figure suddenly caught his eye. It was El.

"Hi!" she said breathlessly. "Sorry I'm late."

"I didn't notice," he said coldly. "I was too busy watching that atavistic display in the park."

She grabbed his arm. "C'mon. Let's eat."

"I assure you, I'm not hungry."

"Then at least have a drink and we'll talk." She tugged on his arm.

("Might as well, Steve. I'd be interested in hearing how she's going to defend public floggings.")

Noting a restaurant sign behind him, Dalt shrugged and started for the entrance.

"Not there," El said. "They lost their sticker last week. We'll go to Logue's—it's about a quarter-way around."

El made no attempt at conversation as she led him around to the restaurant she wanted. During the walk, Dalt allowed his eyes to stray toward the park only once. Not a word was spoken between them until they were seated inside with drinks before them. Logue's modest furnishings and low lighting were offset by its extravagant employment of human waiters.

It was not until the waiter had brought Dalt his second drink that he finally broke the silence.

"You wanted me to see those floggings, didn't you," he said, holding her eyes. "That's what you meant about catching 'a little of the flavor of Tolive.' Well, I caught more than a little, I caught a bellyful!"

Maddeningly patient, El sipped her drink, then said, "Just what did you see that so offended you?"

"I saw floggings!" Dalt sputtered. "Public floggings! The kind of thing that had been abandoned on Earth long before we ever left there!"

"Would you prefer *private* floggings?" There was a trace of a smile about her mouth.

"I would prefer no floggings, and I don't appreciate your sense of humor. I got a look at that woman's face and she was in pain."

"You seem especially concerned over the fact that women as well as men were pilloried today."

"Maybe I'm just old-fashioned, but I don't like to see a woman beaten like that."

El eyed him over her glass. "There are a lot of old-fashioned things about you . . . do you know that you lapse into an archaic speech pattern when you get excited?" She shook herself abruptly. "But we'll go into that another time; right now I want to explore your high-handed attitude toward women."

"Please—" Dalt began, but she pushed on.

"I happen to be as mature, as responsible, as rational as any man I know, and if I commit a crime, I want you to assume that I knew exactly what I was doing. I'd take anything less as a personal insult."

"Okay. Let's not get sidetracked on that age-old debate. The subject at hand is corporal punishment in a public place."

"Was the flogging being done for sport?" El asked. "Were people standing around and cheering?"

"The answers are 'no' and 'no'—and don't start playing Socrates with me."

El persisted. "Did the lash slice deeply into their backs? Were they bleeding? Were they screaming with pain?"

"Stop the questions! No, they weren't screaming and they weren't bleeding, but they were most definitely in pain!"

"Why was this being done to these people?"

Dalt glared at her calm face for a long moment. "Why are you doing this?"

"Because I have this feeling that you're going to be very important to IMC and I didn't want you to quietly slip away after you read the Contract."

"The IMC contract? I read that and there's nothing—"

"Not that one. The Tolive Contract."

"I don't understand," Dalt said with a quick shake of his head.

"I didn't think you would. I mean," she added quickly, "that Dr. Webst was very excited about something this morning and I figured he never gave you your copy or explained anything about it."

"Well, you're right on that account. I haven't the vaguest idea of what you're talking about."

"Okay, then I'll take it upon myself to give you an outline of what you can expect from Tolive and what Tolive expects from you. The Contract sounds rather cold and terrible unless you know the background of the planet and understand the rationale for some of the clauses."

"I don't think you should waste your breath."

"Yes, you do. You're interested now, though you won't admit it."

Dalt sighed reluctantly. "I admit it. But I can't think of anything you can say that'll make public floggings look good."

"Just listen." She finished her drink and signaled for another. "Like most of the Federation member planets, Tolive was once a splinter world. It was settled by a very large group of anarchists who left Earth as one of the first splinter colonies. They bore no resemblance to the bearded, bomb-throwing stereotype from the old days of Earth, nor to the modern-day Broohnins. They merely held that no man has the right to rule another. A noble philosophy, wouldn't you say?"

Dalt gave a noncommittal shrug.

"Good. Like most anarchists of their day, however, they were anti-institutionalists. This eventually caused some major problems. They wanted no government at all: no police, no courts, no jails, no public works. Everything was to be handled by private firms. It took a couple of generations to set things up, and it worked quite well . . . at first. Then the private police forces got out of hand; they'd band together and take over a town and try to set up some sort of neofeudal state. Other police forces had to be hired to come in and roust them out, and there'd be a lot of bloodshed and property destruction." She paused briefly as the waiter brought a fresh drink and El recommended that they order the vegetable platter.

"So," she continued, "after this happened a few too many times, we—my ancestors, that is—decided that something had to be done to deal with the barbarians in our midst. After much debate, it was finally decided to create a bare minimum of public institutions: police, judiciary, penal, and administration."

"No legislature?"

"No. They balked at creating posts for men who like to make rules to control other men; the very concept of a legislature was suspect—and still is, as far as I'm concerned. I mean, what kind of a man is it who wants to spend his life making plans and rules to alter or channel lives other than his own? There's a basic flaw in that kind of man."

"It's not so much a desire to rule," Dalt said. "With many it's merely a desire to be at the center of things, to be in on the big decisions."

"And those decisions mean power. They feel they are far better suited to make decisions about your life than you are. An ancient Earthman said it best: 'In every generation there are those who want to rule well—but they mean to rule. They promise to be good masters—but they mean to be masters.' His name was Daniel Webster."

"Never heard of him. But tell me: how can you have a judiciary if you have no law?"

"Oh, there's law—just no legislature. The minimum necessary legal code was formulated and incorporated into the Contract. Local police apprehend those who break the Contract and local judges determine to what extent it has been broken. The penal authority carries out the sentence, which is either public flogging or imprisonment."

"What?" Dalt said mockingly. "No public executions?"

El found no amusement in his attitude. "We don't kill people—someone just may be innocent."

"But you flog them! A person could die on that pillory!"

"That pillory is actually a highly sophisticated physiological monitor that measures physical pain in Gomler units. The judge decides how many Gomler units should be administered and the machine decides when that level has been reached relative to the individual in the pillory. If there are any signs of danger, the sentence is immediately terminated." They paused as the waiter placed the cold vegetable platters before them.

"He goes to prison then, I guess," Dalt said, eagerly biting into a mushroom-shaped tomato. Delicious.

"No. If he's undergone that much stress, he's considered a paid-up customer. Only our violent criminals go to jail."

Dalt looked bewildered. "Let me get this straight: Nonviolent criminals receive corporal punishment while violent criminals are merely locked away? That's a ridiculous paradox!"

"Not really. Is it better to take a young man such as the car thief out there today and lock him up with armed robbers, killers, and kidnapers? Why force a sneak thief to consort with barbarians and learn how to commit bigger and better crimes? We decided to break that old cycle. We prefer to put him through a little physical pain and a lot of public humiliation for a few minutes, and then let him go. His life is his own again, with no pieces missing. Our system is apparently working because our crime rate is incredibly low compared to other planets. Not out of fear, either, but because we've broken the crime-imprisonment-crime-imprisonment cycle. Recidivism is extremely low here!"

"But your violent criminals are merely sent to prison?"

"Right, but they're not allowed to consort with one another. The prison has historically acted as a nexus for the criminal subculture and so we decided to dodge that pitfall. We make no attempt at rehabilitation—that's the individual's job. The purpose of the prison on Tolive is to isolate the violent criminal from peaceful citizens and to punish him by temporarily or permanently depriving him of his freedom. He has a choice of either solitary confinement or of being blocked and put to work on a farm."

Dalt's eyes were wide. "A work farm! This sounds like the Dark Ages!"

"It's preferable to reconditioning him into a socially acceptable little robot, as is done on other, more 'enlightened' planets. We don't believe in tampering with a man's mind against his will; if he requests a mind block to make subjective time move more quickly, that's his decision."

"But work farms!"

"They have to help earn their keep some way. A blocked prisoner has almost no volition; consequently, the farm overhead is low. He's put to work at simple agrarian tasks that are better done by machine, but this manages to defray some of the cost of housing and clothing him. When the block is finally removed—as is done once a year to give him the option of remaining blocked or returning to solitary—he is usually in better physical condition than when he started. However, there's a piece of his life missing and he knows it . . . and he doesn't soon forget. Of course, he may never request a block if he wishes to press his case before the court—but he spends his time in solitary, away from other criminals."

"Seems awful harsh," Dalt muttered with a slow shake of his head.

El shrugged. "They're harsh men. They've used physical force or the threat of it to get what they want and we don't take kindly to that on Tolive. We insist that all relationships be devoid of physical coercion. We are totally free and therefore totally responsible for our actions—and we hold each other very close to that responsibility. It's in the Contract."

"But who is this Contract with?"

("It's 'whom,'") Pard interjected.

Silence!

"Tolive," El replied.

"You mean the Tolivian government?"

"No, the planet itself. We declared our planet a person, just as corporations were declared legal entities many centuries ago."

"But why the planet?"

"For the sake of immutability. In brief: All humans of sound mind must sign the Contract within six months of their twentieth birthday—an arbitrary age; they can sign beforehand if they wish—or on their arrival on the planet. The Contract affirms the signer's right to pursue his own goals without interference from the government or other individuals. In return for a sum not to exceed more than five per cent of his annual income, this right will be protected by the agents of the planet—the police, courts, et cetera. But if the signer should inject physical coercion or the threat of it into any relationship, he must submit to the customary punishment, which we've already discussed. The Contract cannot be changed by future generations, thus we safeguard human rights from the tamperings of the fools, do-gooders, and powermongers who have destroyed every free society that has ever dared to rear its head along the course of human history."

Dalt paused. "It all sounds so noble, yet you make a dangerous drug like Zemmelar freely available and you have stores that sell the most prurient, sick material I've ever seen."

"It's sold because there are people who want to buy it," El replied with another shrug. "If a signer wants to pollute his body with chemicals in order to visit an artificial Nirvana, that's his business. The drugs are available at competitive prices, so he doesn't have to steal to feed his habit; and he either learns how to handle his craving or he takes a cure, or he winds up dead from an overdose. And as for prurience, I suppose you stopped in at Lin's—he's our local pornographer. All I'll say about that is that I'm not for telling another individual how to enjoy himself . . . but didn't you hunt up any other lit shops? There's a big one on the square that sells nothing but classics: from *The Republic* to *No Treason* to *The Rigrod Chronicles*, from Aristotle to Hugo to Heinlein to Borjay. And down on BenTucker Drive is a shop specializing in new Tolivian works. But you never bothered to look for them."

"The scene in the park cut short my window shopping," Dalt replied tersely. They ate in silence for a moment and Pard took the opportunity to intrude.

("What're you thinking?")

I'm thinking that I don't know what to think.

("Well, in the meantime, ask her about that tax.")

Good idea! Dalt swallowed a mouthful and cleared his throat. "How do you justify a tax in a voluntary society?"

"It's in the Contract. A ceiling of five per cent was put on it because if a government spends much more than that, it's doing more than it should."

"But you don't even have any government to speak of; how does it spend even that much?"

"Federation dues, mostly: We have no army so we have to depend on the Fed Patrol for protection from external threat. The rest of the expenses go to the police, judiciary, and so on. We've never reached five per cent, by the way."

"So it's not a completely voluntary society, then," Dalt stated.

"Signing the Contract is voluntary, and that's what counts." She ran her napkin across her mouth. "And now I've got to run. Finish your meal and take your time and think about what we've discussed. If you want to stay, Webst will probably be waiting back at the complex. And don't worry about the bill . . . it's on me today." She leaned over, brushed her lips against his cheek, and was gone before Dalt could say a word.

("Quite an exit,") Pard said with admiration.

Quite a woman, Dalt replied, and went back to eating.

("Still ready to take the first shuttle out of here?")

I don't know. Everything seems to fit together in some weirdly logical way.

("Nothing weird about it at all. It works on the principle that humans will act responsibly if you hold them responsible for their actions. I find it rather interesting and want to spend some time here; and unless you want to start the fiercest argument of our partnership, you'll agree.")

Okay. We'll stay.

("No argument?")

None. I want to get to know El a little—a lot!—better.

("Glad to hear it.")

And the funny thing is: the more time I spend with her, the less she reminds me of Jean.

("That's because she's really nothing at all like Jean; she's far more mature, far more intelligent. As a matter of fact, Ellen Lettre is one of the more fascinating things on this fascinating planet.")

Dalt's lack of response as he cleared his plate was tacit agreement. On the way out, his eye was caught by a golden seal on the door. It read: "Premises, kitchen, and food quality graded Class I by Nauch & Co., Inc." The date of the most recent inspection was posted below.

("I guess that's the Tolivian equivalent of a department of public health,") Pard said. ("Only this Nauch is probably a private company that works on a subscription basis. When you think about—")

Pard paused as a ground car whined to a halt before the restaurant and Dr. Webst leaped out. He looked relieved at the sight of Dalt.

"Glad I found you," he said as he approached. "I met Dr. Lettre back at the complex and asked her when you were coming back; she said she wasn't sure if you were coming back at all."

"That was a possibility."

"Well, look, I don't know what this is all about, but you must come back to the complex with me immediately."

Dalt stiffened. "You're not trying to make an order out of that, I hope."

"No, of course not. It's just that I've made some startling discoveries about you that may have great medical significance. I've double-checked everything."

"What are you talking about?" Dalt had a sudden uneasy feeling.

Webst grabbed Dalt's arm and guided him toward the car. "I'm babbling, I know, but I'll explain everything on the way over to the complex." He paused in midstride. "Then again, maybe it's you who should do the explaining."

"Me?" Dalt was genuinely puzzled.

"Yes. Just who or what are you, Mr. Dalt?"

VIII

"This is my psi pattern," Webst said, pointing to an irregular red line undulating across the viewscreen in his office. "It shows the low level of activity found in the average human—nothing special about my psi abilities. Now, when we focus the detector on you, look what happens." He touched a panel and two green lines appeared on the screen. The one at the lower end was very similar to Webst's and occasionally superimposed itself on it at certain points.

"That's what I expected from you: another normal pattern. And I got it . . . but what the hell is that?" He was pointing to the large, smoothly flowing sine-wave configuration in the upper part of the screen. "We have tried this out on thousands of individuals and I have never once seen a pattern that even vaguely approximates that, neither in configuration nor in amplitude.

"Whatever it is," Webst continued as he blanked the screen, "it seems to like you, 'cause it goes where you go. At first I thought it was a malfunction, that's why I brought you over to Big Blue, where we have another model. But the same pattern appeared as soon as you walked into the building—and disappeared as soon as you left. So, what have you got to say for yourself, Mr. Dalt?"

Dalt shrugged with convincing bafflement. "I really don't know what to say." Which was true. His mind raced in an attempt to give Webst, obviously an expert in psionics, a plausible but fictitious explanation. The machine in question was a fairly recent development of IMC research—it detected levels of psionic capacity, even in the nascent stage, and was planned for interplanetary marketing to the psi schools which were springing up on every planet. The current thrust of Webst's research was in the field of psionics and psychotherapy, so he took the liberty of screening for psi ability everyone who entered his office. He felt he had hit pay dirt with Dalt.

"You mean to say that you've never had any inkling of psi ability?" Webst asked. Dalt shook his head. "Well then, are there any blank spots in your memory . . . do you ever find yourself somewhere and can't recall how you got there?"

"What are you driving at?"

"I'm looking for a dissociative reaction or a second personality—something, anything, to explain that second level of activity. I don't want to alarm you," he said gently, "but you're only allowed one: one mind, one psi level. The only conclusion I can draw is that you either have two minds or the most unusual single mind in the galaxy.

("He was right the first time.")

I know, but what do we do?

("Play dumb, of course. We wanted to get out of microbiology and into psych—this may be our chance.")

Dalt mulled this over. Finally, "This is all very interesting, Dr. Webst, but quite meaningless as far as my professional life is concerned." *That should put the conversation on the track we want.*

"That's what I'd like to discuss with you," Webst replied. "If I can get a release from Dr. Hyne, would you be interested in spending some time with my department assisting us with some experiments?"

"Just what kind of experiments?"

Webst came around his desk to stand before Dalt. "I've been trying to find a use for psionics in psychotherapy. We are daily trying to probe the minds of these so-called horrors cases in an effort to find out why they don't respond to conventional therapy. I have no doubt that it's the path of the future—all we need is the right technology and the right psi talents.

"Remember Sally Ragna? The girl who hides in the corner and no known psychotherapy can reach? That's the kind of patient I'm after. We've developed an instrument to magnify psi powers, and right now a man with one per cent of your aptitude is trying to get a look inside her mind." Webst suddenly stiffened and his eyes burned into Dalt. "Right now! Would you come over to Big Blue right now and give it a try? All I want you to do is take a quick look—just go in and out, no more!"

("This is our chance,") Pard urged. ("Take it!") He was obviously anxious to give it a try.

"All right," said Dalt, who had a few reservations lurking in the back of his mind. "Might as well give it a try and see if anything at all can be done."

In Big Blue they seated him before Sally Ragna, who wasn't cringing now, due to heavy sedation. The psi booster Webst had mentioned, a gleaming silver disk, was slung above them.

This is a waste of time, Dalt told Pard.

("I don't think so. I've learned one thing, anyway: That machine of Webst's isn't worth a damn—I'm not getting a bit of boost from it. But I don't think I'll need it. I've made a few probes using the same technique I played with on the liner and I'm meeting with very little resistance. I'm sure I can get in. One thing, though . . . I'm going to have to take you with me.")

I don't know if I like that.

("It's necessary, I'm afraid. I'll need every ounce of reserve function to stay oriented once I get in there, and I may even have to draw on your meager psi power.")

Dalt hesitated. The thought of confronting madness on its own ground was deeply frightening. His stomach lurched as he replied, *Okay, let's do it. But be careful!*

("I'm frightened too, friend.")

The thought flashed across Dalt's mind that he had never before considered the possibility of Pard being frightened of anything. Concerned, yes . . . but frightened—

The thought disappeared as his view of Sally Ragna and the room around them swirled away and he entered the place where Sally was spending her life:

/countless scintillating pinpoints of light that somehow gave off no illumination poured into treelike shapes/a sky of violet shot through with crimson flashes that throw shadows in para-

doxical directions/an overall dimness that half obscures living fungus forms that crawl and leap and hang from the pointillistic trees/

/moving forward now/

/past a cube of water with schools of fish each made of two opposing tails swimming forever in stasis/mountains crumble to the right/breach-born ahead is a similar range/which disappears as they step off a sudden precipice and float through a dank forest and are surrounded by peering, glowing, unblinking yellow eyes/

/descent/

/to a desert road stretching emptily and limitlessly ahead/and suddenly a town has sprung up around them, its buildings built at impossible angles/a stick man walks up and smiles as his form fills out and then swells, bloats, and ruptures, spewing mounds of writhing maggots upon the ground/the face and body begin to dissolve but the mouth remains, growing larger and nearer/it opens to show its double rows of curved teeth/ and growing still larger it moves upon them, enveloping them, closing upon them with a SNAP/

Dalt next found himself on the floor with Webst and a technician bending over him. But it was Pard who awakened him.

("Get up, Steve! Now! We've got to go back in there as soon as possible!")

Dalt rose slowly to his feet and brushed his palms. "I'm all right," he told Webst. "Just slipped out of the chair." And to Pard: *You must be kidding!*

("I assure you, I am not. That was a jolting experience, and if we don't go back immediately, we'll probably build up a reflex resistance that will keep us out in the future.")

That's fine with me.

("But we can do something for this girl; I'm sure of it.")

Dalt waved Webst and his technician away. "I'm going to try again," he muttered, and repositioned himself before the girl. *Okay, Pard. I'm trusting you.*

/and then they were in a green-fogged bog as ochre hands reached up for them from the rank marsh grasses to try to pull them into the quicksand/

/the sun suddenly appeared overhead but was quickly muffled by the fog/it persisted, however, and slowly the fog began to thin and burn away/

/the land tilted then and the marsh began to drain/the rank

grasses began to wither and die in the sun/slowly a green carpet of neatly trimmed grass unrolled about them, covering and smothering the ever-clutching hands/

/a giant, spheroid boulder rolled in from the horizon at dazzling speed and threatened to overrun them until a chasm yawned suddenly before it and swallowed it/

/dark things crept toward them from all sides, trailing dusk behind them, but a high, smooth, safe wall suddenly encircled them and sunlight prevailed/

Dalt was suddenly back in the room again with Sally Ragna, only this time he was seated on the chair instead of the floor.

("We'll leave her in that sanctuary by herself for a few minutes while I get the lay of the land here.")

You made all those changes, then?

("Yes, and it was easier than I thought it would be. I met a lot of resistance at first when I tried to bring the sun out, but once I accomplished that, I seemed to be in full control. There were a couple of attempts to get at her again, but they were easily repulsed.")

What now?

("Now that we've made her comfortable in her sylvan nunnery—which is as unreal as the horror show she's lived in all these years, but completely unthreatening—we'll bring her back to reality.")

Ah, but what is reality?

("Please, Steve. I haven't time for such a sophomoric question. Just go along with me, and for a working definition we'll just say that reality is what trips you up when you walk around with your eyes closed. But no more talk . . . now comes the hard part. Up until now we've been seeing what she sees; the task at hand is to reverse that situation. Here goes.")

They were back in again and apparently Pard's benign reconstruction had held—and had been improved upon; the wall had been removed and a smooth grassy sward stretched to the far horizon. Pard set up a bare green panel to the left; three more panels appeared and boxed them in . . . a lighted ceiling finished the job. An odd piece of metallic machinery overhung them, and there, just a short distance before them, sat a man with a golden hand and a flamestone slung at his throat, whose dark hair was interrupted by a patch of silver at the crown.

A sudden blurring and they were looking at Sally again. Only this time she was looking back—and smiling. As tears slid down her cheeks, the smile faded and she collapsed into unconsciousness.

IX

"You've done something," Webst said later at the office after Sally had been examined and returned to her bed, "something beneficial. Can't be sure just yet, but I can smell it! Did you see her smile at you? She's never smiled before. Never!"

Webst's enthusiasm whirled past Dalt without the slightest effect. He was tired, tired as he'd never been before. There was a vague feeling of dissociation, too; he'd visited the mind of another and had returned home to find himself subtly altered by the experience.

"Well, I certainly hope I didn't go through all that for nothing."

"I'm sure you didn't," said a voice behind him. He turned to see El walking across the room. "She's sleeping now," she said, sliding easily into a chair, "and without a hypnotic. You've gotten through to her, no question about it."

Webst leaned forward on his desk. "But just what is it you've done?" he asked intently. "What did you see in there?"

Dalt opened his mouth to protest, to put off all explanations and descriptions until tomorrow, but Pard cut him off.

("Tell them something. They're hungry for information.")

How can I describe all . . . that?

("Try. Just skim the details.")

Dalt gave a halting summary of what they had seen and done, then:

"In conclusion, it's my contention that the girl's underlying lesion was not organic but conceptual. Her sense of reality was completely aberrant, but as to how this came to be, I do not know." He hesitated and El thought she saw him shudder ever so slightly. "For a moment I got the feeling that I was working against something . . . something dark and very alien, just over the horizon. At one point I thought I actually touched it, or it reached for me, or—" He shook himself. "I don't know. Maybe it was part of her fantasy complex. Anyway, what matters is that she was a very sick girl and I think I've helped her."

"I take it, then," Webst said, "that we can assume that these acute, unremitting, chemonegative schizophrenics are actually only conceptually deranged. Okay, I'll buy that. But *why* are they deranged?"

Dalt remembered the dark thing he had sensed in Sally's mind and the word "imposed" rushed into his thoughts, but he pushed it away. "Can't help you there as yet. But let's get her back on her feet and worry about why it happened later on. Chemotherapy was no good because her enzyme chains are normal; and psychotherapy has been useless because, as far this patient was concerned, the psychotherapist didn't exist. Apparently, only a strong psionic thrust and subsequent reconstruction of the fantasy world is of any value. And by the way, her mind was extremely easy to enter. Perhaps in erecting an impenetrable barrier against reality, it left itself completely open to psionics."

El and Webst were virtually glowing with the exhilaration of discovery. "This is incredible!" Webst declared. "A whole new direction in psychotherapy! Mr. Dalt, I don't know how we can repay you!"

("Tell him what he can pay you.")

We can't take money for helping that poor girl!

("He's going to ask you to do it again . . . and again. That was no sylvan picnic in there—it's risky business. I won't allow us to enter another mind unless we're compensated for it. Value given for value received, remember?")

That's crass.

("That's life. Something that costs nothing is usually worth the price.")

That's trite.

("But true. Quote him a figure.")

Dalt thought for a moment, then said, "I'll require a fee for Sally . . . and any others you want me to try." He named a sum.

"That sounds reasonable." Webst nodded. "I won't dicker with you."

El's face reflected amusement tinged with amazement. "You're full of surprises, aren't you?"

Webst smiled too. "He's welcome to every credit we can spare if he can bring those horrors patients around. We'll even try to get a bigger budget. I'll talk to Dr. Hyne and have you transferred to this department; meanwhile, there's an ethical question you should consider. You are in effect performing an experimental procedure on mentally incompetent patients who are incapable of giving their consent."

"What about their guardians?"

"These patients have no guardians, no identity. And a guardian would be irrelevant as far as the ethical question is concerned—that is up to you. In the physician role, you've got to decide whether an experimental procedure—or even an established procedure—will have a greater chance of benefiting the patient than doing harm to him, and whether the possible benefits are worth the risk. And the patient must come first; not humanity, not science, but the *patient*. Only you can decide."

"I made that decision before I invaded Sally," Dalt replied with a touch of acid. "The gains were mutual: I would learn something, she would, hopefully, receive therapeutic value. The risks, as far as I could foresee, would all be mine."

Webst considered this. "Mr. Dalt," he said finally, "I think you and I are going to get along just fine." He extended his hand and Dalt grasped it firmly.

El came to his side and hooked her arm around his. "Welcome to the department," she said with a half smile tugging at the corners of her mouth. "This is quite a turnaround from the man who swore a few hours ago that he was taking the next shuttle out."

"I haven't forgotten that episode, believe me. I can't quite accept the code you Tolivians live by as yet, but I think I'd like to stick around and see if it works as well as you say it does."

The viewphone had beeped again while they were talking. Webst took the call, then suddenly headed for the door. "That was Big Blue—Sally just woke up and asked for a drink of water!" Nothing more needed to be said; El and Dalt immediately fell in behind him as he made his way to the carport.

The last sanguine rays of the sun slipping into the plaza found the ambulatory patients clustered in hushed, muttering knots. And all eyes suddenly became riveted on the car that held Webst, Dalt, and El as it pulled up beside Big Blue. An elderly woman broke away from a small group and came forward, squinting at the trio in the waning light.

"It's him!" she cried hoarsely as she reached the car. "He's got the silver patch of hair, the flamestone, and the golden hand that heals!" She clutched the back of Dalt's suit as he turned away. "Touch me with your healing hand!" she cried. "My mind is sick and only you can help me! Please! I'm not as sick as Sally was!"

"No, wait!" Dalt said, whirling and shrinking away. "It doesn't work that way!"

But the woman seemed not to hear him, repeating, "Heal me! Heal me!" And over her shoulder he could see the other patients in the plaza crowding forward.

Webst was suddenly at his side, his face close, his eyes shining in the fading darkness. "Go ahead," he whispered excitedly, "touch her. You don't have to do anything else, just reach out that left hand and lay it on her head."

Dalt hesitated; then, feeling foolish, pressed the heel of his palm against her forehead. The woman covered her face at his touch and scurried away, muttering, "Thank you, thank you," through her hands.

With that, it was as if a dam had burst. The patients were suddenly swirling all around him and Dalt found himself engulfed by a torrent of outstretched hands and cries of, "Heal me! Heal me! Heal me! Heal me!" He was pushed, pulled, his clothes and limbs were plucked at, and it was only with great difficulty that El and Webst managed to squeeze him through the press of supplicants and into the quiet of Big Blue.

"Now you know why he's at the top of his profession," El said softly, nodding her head toward Webst as she pressed a drink into Dalt's hand, a hand that even now, in the security of Big Blue, betrayed a slight but unmistakable tremor. The experience in the plaza had unnerved him—the hands, the voices, reaching and crying for him in the twilight, seeking relief from the psychological and physiological afflictions burdening them; the incident, though only moments past, was becoming increasingly surreal in retrospect.

He shook himself and took a deep gulp of the drink. "I don't follow."

"The way he sized up the situation immediately as mass hysteria and put it to good use: the enormity of placebo effect in medicine has never been fully appreciated, even to this day. There were a lot of chronically ill patients in that plaza who had heard of a man who performed a miraculous cure and they all wanted a piece of that miracle for themselves."

"But how did they find out?"

El laughed. "The grapevine through these wards could challenge a subspace laser for speed of transmission!"

Webst flicked off the viewphone from which he had been receiving a number of hurried reports, and turned to them, grinning. "Well, the blind see, the deaf hear, and the lame walk," he announced, then burst out laughing at the horrified expression on Dalt's face. "No, nothing as dramatic as that, I'm afraid, but we have had a few remarkable symptomatic remissions."

"Not because of me!" Dalt snapped, his tone betraying annoyance. "I didn't do a thing—those people only think I did."

"*Exactly!* You didn't cure them per se, but you did act as a catalyst through which the minds of those people could gain some leverage on their bodies."

"So I'm a faith-healer, in other words."

"Out in the plaza, you were—and still are, now more than ever. We have a rare opportunity here to study the phenomenon of the psychosomatic cure, something which fascinates the student of behavior more than anything else. It's the power of the mind over the body in action . . . we know almost nothing of the dynamics of the relationship."

("I could tell them a few things about that,") Pard muttered.

You've said quite enough tonight, friend.

"And you're a perfect focal point," Webst added. "You have a genuine healing ability in a certain area, and this along with an undeniably unique appearance evidently works to give you an almost messianic aura in susceptible minds."

("Defensively worded in the best scientific tradition.")

Webst continued in lowered tones, talking to himself more than to anyone else. "You know, I don't see why the same phenomenon couldn't be duplicated on any other planet in the human system, and on a much larger scale. Every planet has its share of horrors cases and they're all looking for a way to handle them. If we limit the amount of information we release—such as keeping your identity a secret—the inevitable magnification that occurs with word-of-mouth transmission will have you raising the dead by the time you finish your work here. And by then every human planet will be clamoring for your services. And while you're reconstructing sick minds, Dr. Lettre and I will be carefully observing the epiphenomena."

"Meaning the psychosomatic cures?"

El nodded, getting caught up in Webst's vision. "Right. And it would be good for Tolive, too. He-Who-Heals-Minds—pardon the dramatic phrasing—will come from Tolive, and that should counteract some of the smears being spread around."

"How does that sound, Mr. Dalt . . . or should I say, 'Healer'?"

What do you think?

("Sounds absolutely wonderful to me, as long as we don't start to believe what people will be saying about us.")

"Interesting," Dalt replied slowly, "very interesting. But why don't we see how things go here on Tolive before we start star-hopping." He had a lot of adjustments to make, physically and intellectually, if he was going to spend any time here.

"Right!" Webst said, and headed back to the viewphone. "And I'm sure it's been a long day for you. I'll have the plaza cleared and you can return to your hotel as soon as you like."

"That's not the place I had in mind," Dalt muttered to El, "but I guess the sunset's long gone by now out there on the plain."

El shrugged warmly. "The sunrise is just as good."

Three:
Middle Phase

HEALER III

(age 291)

Hide Thyself

The Healer's advent coincided with a period of political turmoil within the Federation. The Restructurist movement was agitating with steadily increasing influence for a more active role by the Federation in planetary and interplanetary affairs. This attitude directly contradicted the laissez-faire orientation of the organization's charter.

His departure from human affairs occurred as political friction was reaching its peak and was as abrupt as his arrival. Certain scholars claim that he was killed in a liner crash off Tarvodet, and there is some evidence to support this.

His more fanatical followers, however, insist that he is immortal and was driven from his calling by political forces. Their former premise is obviously ridiculous, but the latter may well have some basis in fact.

from *The Healer: Man & Myth*
by Emmerz Fent

INTERLUDE:

A Soliloquy for Two

Can't you do anything?

("I've already tried . . . a number of times. And failed.")

I didn't know that. Why didn't you tell me?

("I know how much she means to you, so I made the attempts on my own. The most recent was yesterday. When you entered her body, I entered her mind—that seems to be her most vulnerable moment.")

And?

("The cells won't respond. I'm unable to exert any influence over the components of another body. They simply will not respond.")

Oh.

A long pause, then an audible sigh.

All things must pass, eh?

("Except us.")

Yeah. Except us.

Ω

The Healer, the most recognizable figure in the human galaxy, stood gloved, cloaked, cowled, and unrecognized amid the small group of mourners as the woman's body was tenderly placed within the machine that would reduce it to its component elements. He felt no need for tears. She had lived her life to the fullest, the latter half of it at his side. And when the youth treatments had finally become ineffective and she'd begun to notice a certain blurring on the perimeters of her intellectual function, she ended her life, calmly and quietly, to insure that she'd be remembered by her lover as the proud woman she had always been, not the lesser person she might become. And only The Healer, her lover, knew how she had died.

The wrinkled little man next to him suspected, of course. And approved. They and the others watched in silence as the machine swallowed her body, and all drank deeply of the air about them as it became filled with her molecules, each witness trying to incorporate into himself a tiny part of a cherished friend.

The old man looked at his companion, who had never deigned to show a year's worth of aging in all the time he had known him—at least not on the surface. But there had been strain and fatigue growing behind the eyes during the past few years. A half century of sickness and deformity of mind and body, outstretched hands and blank eyes lay behind him and possibly endless years of the same awaited him.

"You look weary, my friend."

"I am." The others began to drift away. "It all seems so futile. For every mind I open, two more are reported newly closed. The pressure continually mounts—'come to us'—'no, come to us, we need you more!' Everywhere I go I'm preceded by arguments, threats, and bribes between vying clinics and planets. I seem to have become a commodity."

The old man nodded with understanding. "Where to now?"

"Into private practice of some sort, I suppose. I've stayed with IMC this long only because of you . . . and her. As a matter of fact, a certain sector representative is waiting for me now. DeBloise is the name."

"A Restructurist. Be careful."

"I will." The Healer smiled. "But I'll hear what he has to say. Stay well, friend," he said and walked away.

The wrinkled man gazed wistfully after him. "Ah, if only I had your talent for that."

Ω

Sector Representative DeBloise had for some time considered himself quite an important man, yet it took him a few minutes to adjust to the presence of the individual seated calmly across the desk from him, a man of unmistakable appearance who had gained almost mythical stature in the past few decades: The Healer.

"In brief, sir," DeBloise said with the very best of his public smiles, "we of the Restructurist movement wish to encourage you to come to our worlds. You seem to have made a habit of avoiding us in the past."

"That's because I worked through the IMC network in which the Restructurist worlds refuse to participate . . . something to do with the corps' support of the LaNague charter, I'm told."

"That's part of it." The smile became more ingratiating as he said, "Politics seems to work its way into everything, doesn't it. But that's irrelevant now, since it was the news that you'd no longer be with IMC that brought me here to Tolive. I want you to come to Jebinose; our Bureau of Medicine and Research will pay all your fees."

"I'm sorry," The Healer said slowly, "but I deal only with patients, not with governments."

"Well, if you mean to come to Jebinose and practice independently of the Bureau, I'm afraid we couldn't allow that. You see, we've set very high and very rigid standards for the practice of medicine on our planet and I'm afraid allowing you such license, despite your reputation, would set a bad precedent."

"If a patient wishes my services, he or his guardian should be free to engage them. Why should some bureau have anything to say in the matter?"

"What you ask is impossible," DeBloise said with a shake of his head. "Our people must be protected from being duped by frauds."

The Healer's smile was rueful as he rose to his feet. "That is quite evident. And thus Jebinose is not for me."

DeBloise's face suddenly hardened, the smile forgotten. "It's quite evident to me, *Healer*"—he spat the word—"that you've spent too much time among these barbaric Tolivians. All right, play your game: but I think you should know that a change is in the wind and that we shall soon be running the entire Federation *our* way. And when we do, we'll see to it that every planet gets its fair share of your services!"

"Perhaps there will be no Healer, then," came the quiet reply.

"Don't try to bluff me!" DeBloise laughed. "I know your type. You glory in the adulation that greets you everywhere you go. It's more addicting than Zemmelar." There was a trace of envy in his voice. "But Restructurists are not so easily awed. You are a man—a uniquely talented one, yes, but still just one man—and when the tide turns for us, you will join in the current or be swept under."

The Healer's eyes blazed but his voice was calm. "Thank you, Mr. DeBloise. You have just clarified a problem and prompted a decision that has been growing increasingly troublesome over the past decade or so." He turned and strode from the room.

Nearly two and a half centuries passed before The Healer was seen again.

Wheels Within Wheels

In the light of what we know today, it is difficult to imagine how the Restructurist movement engendered any popular support at all. But it did. Whole sectors at one time declared themselves "Restructurist" and agitated for what they called reform legislation.

But "reform" was a gross misnomer: the Restructurist hierarchy was composed of first-order reactionaries, economic royalists who were avowed enemies of the free market. Their political philosophy had been thrown out by the LaNague revolution and the Federation charter kept it out. But they hung on, cloaking their ambitions in feigned social concern, mouthing humanitarian slogans as they maneuvered to exert control over interstellar trade.

from STARS FOR SALE:
An Economic History of Occupied Space
by EMMERZ FENT

PROLOGUE

The room was a special one, situated in the far corner of a building on the outskirts of the Federation complex. The Continuing Fund for the Restructuring of the Federation had leased it more than twenty standard years before and had footed the bill for all the extensive and expensive renovations.

The windows had been removed and the openings filled in and sealed. The wall spaces had been filled with a heavy mixture of synthestone and lined with a micromesh grid which, when activated, would distort not only the vibrations in the walls themselves but any electronic transmissions down to but not including the subspace level as well. The grid encapsulized the room and door, ensuring that an external amplifier attempting to monitor voices within the room would pick up only an indecipherable garble of sounds and no more. A psi-shield had been added as a final touch. Nothing within, short of a subspace transmitter, could beam a message out, and even the most compact s-s set in existence couldn't hide there.

Especially here. The walls, floor, and ceiling were completely bare and the lamps were self-powered floor models. All the furniture was made of the transparent crystal polymer that had been so popular two decades before. There was no hiding place in the room for any sort of monitoring device and any attempt to insert one into the wall would disrupt the micromesh and set off a malfunction signal. It was the "safe room" reserved for special meetings of the upper echelon of the Restructurist movement. Elson deBloise had called for such a meeting today.

Douglas Habel entered first. He was the grand old man of the movement, now in semi-retirement. He avoided the head seat with some effort—that belonged to Elson now—and situated himself along the far side of the conference table.

Philo Barth came in soon after. Paunchy, ribald, a seemingly supercilious individual, he was firmly entrenched as a Federation representative from his sector.

" 'Lo, Doug," he said, and fell heavily into a chair. He and Habel discussed in low, casual tones the upcoming hiatus during which all the representatives would return to their respective homeworlds.

Doyl Catera entered next, a scowl on his face. He was young, an up-and-coming bright star in the Restructurist firmament, but his moods were mercurial . . . and he despised the "safe room." Nodding to the other two, he threw himself into a chair and waited in moody silence.

Before long, Elson deBloise made his entrance, carefully timed for last. He had a heavy build, dark brown hair graying just the right amount at the temples, and a presence that reeked of self-assurance.

DeBloise slid the door shut behind him and pressed a button at its center which would mesh it with the grid woven around the rest of the room. Without hesitation, he then took the seat at the head of the table and extracted a small noteplate from his pocket.

"Well," he said affably, "we all know why we're here, I guess."

"Not why we're *here*, no," Catera said with biting precision.

DeBloise maintained a friendly tone. "Doug, Philo, and I are well aware of your objections to the security precautions in this room, Doyl, but we feel they're necessary evils."

"Especially at this point of the game, Doyl," Habel said. "We're on Fed Central and this planet is run by the pro-charter forces. And while I must admit that during my long career they have, as a group, respected our security, there are others outside the political community who have no such scruples. I have reliable information that someone has been keeping close watch on our movements lately, especially yours, Els. I don't know who's behind the surveillance as yet, but at this stage of our plan, I must emphasize that we cannot be too careful. Is that clear, Doyl?"

"All right." Catera's tone was resigned. "I'll go along with the security charade for now. Let's get on with our business and get it over with."

"I'm all for that," Barth muttered. "The subject is money, I believe."

"Isn't it always?" deBloise replied. He had remained carefully aloof from the preceding exchange, maintaining a pose of lofty equanimity. He despised Catera for his reckless maverick tendencies and, although he rarely admitted it even to himself, for his potential threat to deBloise's position as standard bearer of the movement. But nearly three decades in active political life had taught him to hide his personal feelings well.

"The sector treasurers are raising a bit of a fuss about the amount," Barth said. "They can't imagine what kind of project could possibly require such a sum."

"You all stuck to the agreed-upon pitch, I hope," deBloise said with an eye toward Catera.

Catera held his gaze. "Of course. We told them it was for a penetrating investigation into the way the LaNague Charter is failing many of the Federation planets. It was stretching the truth to the limits of endurance, but I suppose we can ultimately defend our sales pitch if the plan goes awry."

"Have no fear of that," deBloise assured him. "But the money—are the treasuries going to come through with what we need?"

Barth nodded. "They'll come through, but reluctantly. If it hadn't been for Doug's little speech, they'd still be holding out."

Habel beamed. He had recorded a short, stirring message for the representatives to carry with them to the sector committees. In it he had exhorted all committed Restructurists to rise to the challenge of the day; to free the monies that would allow the Restructurist leadership to gather the necessary information to open the eyes of the Federation Assembly and turn it around.

"It was a good speech, even if I say so myself."

"It was," deBloise agreed, "and it seems to have worked, which is of primary importance. Now we can finally set the plan into motion."

"I still have my reservations, Elson," Catera said, and the other occupants in the room held their breath. Catera's sector was one of the richest and they were counting on it for a large share of the money. If he held back . . .

"How could you possibly object to the plan, Doyl?" Habel said with all the fatherliness he could muster.

"It's a moral question, actually. Do we have the right to play political games with a technological innovation of this magnitude? It has the capacity to revolutionize interstellar travel and could eventually make all planets neighbors."

"We're not playing games, Doyl," deBloise replied with passion. "What we intend to do will move us closer to the goals of the movement. An opportunity like this presents itself once in a lifetime—once in a millennium! If properly handled, it can bring all our efforts to fruition. And if we don't seize it now and use it to our advantage, then we don't deserve to call ourselves Restructurists!"

"But I've been to Dil. I've—"

DeBloise held up a hand. "We've agreed to mention no names at any time. We all know who you're talking about and we all know where he lives."

"Then you all know that he's an unstable personality! His device could be lost to us forever!"

"Don't worry about that," Barth said. "When we're in power he'll have to give it up. No individual quirks will stand in our way—we'll see to that."

Catera frowned and shook his head. "I still don't like it."

"You'd better like it!" deBloise hissed. He was on his feet and speaking through clenched teeth. Whether there was genuine concern on Catera's part or just the start of a power play, deBloise could not be sure. But he intended to get a commitment here and now. "The movement is a little over a hundred years old now and we've made considerable gains in that time. It started as a handful of discontented representatives and now entire sectors think of themselves as Restructurist. But we've become stagnant and we all know it. Oh, we make grand gestures and sweeping generalizations in public, but our point of view seems to have peaked. Some of our analysts even see the start of a downswing on the marginally committed planets."

He paused to let this sink in. "Our speeches no longer cause even a ripple in the Assembly and we introduce amendments to the charter that are knocked down time after time. Our constituents are going to start wondering if we really know what we're doing and it may not be too long before we find others sitting in our seats in the Assembly unless we do something now!"

A prolonged silence followed as Catera gazed at his shoes through the transparent tabletop. Finally: "I'll see to it that the funds I control are deposited in the account tomorrow," he said in a low voice.

"Thank you, Doyl," deBloise replied in a conciliatory tone as he seated himself again. "How much can we count on?"

Catera shrugged. "Don't know exactly. It's in mixed currencies, of course. I think the total will come to about half a million Federation credits after conversion."

"Excellent! Philo?"

And they went on totaling the contributions, completely unaware that the entire meeting was being recorded.

The course of public events is often shaped by seemingly unlikely individuals occupying seemingly marginal positions. As for the present state of Occupied Space, a good part of the credit or blame—depending on your philosophical viewpoint—probably belongs to the members of a single family, the name of which is no doubt totally unfamiliar to you unless you're involved in interstellar trade. The family name? Finch.

from STARS FOR SALE:
An Economic History of Occupied Space
by EMMERZ FENT

I

OLD PETE

"Ah, how I'd love to wring that man's neck!" Old Pete said to the air.

He lay stretched out on the sand listening to the recording as Ragna's G2 Primary beat down on him from a distance of approximately 156 million kilometers. He was eighty-one years old but neither looked nor felt it. His legs were scrawny, true—"chicken legs," he called them—and the skin was loose at his neck and wrinkled around his eyes, with the frontal areas of his scalp sporting nowhere near the amount of hair they had of old; but when he walked he moved briskly and lightly with swinging arms and a straight spine.

He loved the sun. Loved to sit in it, bake in it, broil in it. His graying hair had been bleached white by that sun and his skin was a tough, dark brown that accentuated the brown of his eyes. Minute collections of pale, flaky skin dotted his extended forehead. Actinic keratosis, a doctor had told him . . . or something like that. From too much sun, especially through Ragna's relatively thin ozone layer. Can lead to skin cancer, the doctor had said. Be smart. Use this lotion. It'll dissolve the keratoses. And start using this sun-screen lotion daily. Either that or stay in the shade.

Old Pete did neither. If the keratotic areas took a malignant turn, well, they had a lotion for that, too. Until then he'd enjoy his sun to the fullest.

And it was his sun. At least the part of it that shone down upon this particular island. The Kel Sea stretched away in all directions to an unbroken horizon where it merged with the lighter blue of the sky. The island was an oblong patch of sand and rock about a kilometer long and half that distance across, supporting a single house, some scattered scruffy trees, and little else. But it belonged to Peter Paxton and to him alone. He had purchased it shortly after leaving IBA and rarely left it. A luxury flitter was moored on the roof of the house for those occasions when he did.

So he lay supine on the beach, seeing red as the sun trans-illuminated his eyelids, and listened to a recording of other men's voices. His right hand held a printed transcript but he preferred to hear the original. There were nuances of inflection and tone not reproducible on paper that were as important to him as the content of the words themselves.

Nor did he need the transcript to tell him who was speaking at any particular moment. He'd never met the men on the recording but was as familiar with their voices as he was with his own. Old Pete had been keeping tabs on the Restructurist hierarchy at sporadic intervals for a number of years now, but his surveillance had increased in intensity with the news not too long ago that something special and oh-so-secret was afoot in the inner circle. He was determined to find out what it was.

As the recording came to a close, he sat up with a grunt.

"Poor Doyl Catera—almost got himself in trouble there for a moment. His sense of ethics made a serious attempt to break through to the surface. Almost made it, too. Then deBloise brought up elections and the threat of being replaced in the Assembly—the things that really matter to a politico—and ethics went plunging into the pit again. Ah, well," he sighed. "To be expected, I suppose."

The visitor to the island sat impassively on the other side of the player. Old Pete looked at him.

"What do you make of all this, Andy?" he asked.

Andrew Tella shrugged. He was short, dark, and still carried himself in a manner that hinted at his former years of rigid training in the Federation Defense Force. He didn't want to express an opinion. He was an operative. His job was to gather information and he did his job well. His client, Old Pete, had just mentioned ethics and Tella did not like to discuss ethics. Not that the subject itself made him uncomfortable, it was just that his code of ethics was somewhat different from most other people's. He had no compunction about prying into matters others wanted to keep secret. Events occurred, facts existed. They belonged to those who could discover them and ferret them out. That was the part that kept him in this business: the process of discovery. And even that became a humdrum affair at times . . . finding out what a client's wife or business associates or competitors were planning or doing. Then someone like this Peter Paxton came along and it was a whole new game. A man with no political connections who wanted to know the secret goings on of some of the biggest names in Federation politics. Here was a challenge, and a profitable one to boot.

Receiving no verbal reply, Old Pete went on. "You did a good job. Actually got a recording device into their security conference room. How'd you manage that?"

"It wasn't all that difficult," Tella replied with a self-satisfied grin. "They have all these elaborate security precautions—the distorter grid, the guard, that trite transparent furniture. But they don't scan the people coming into the room. I simply planted a recorder in the heel of Catera's left shoe the night before the meeting and retrieved it two days later. You just heard the results."

Old Pete laughed and looked toward the horizon. "I'd give anything to stick this under deBloise's nose and play it for him. But unfortunately that's out of the question. I've got to let them go blithely on their way thinking it's all still a big secret." He paused. "You know, that's the second time we've heard them mention Dil. I think it's about time you took a little trip to that planet to see if you can find out what's so important to them there."

"That might not be the most practical approach," Tella replied. "I could waste a lot of time on Dil before I learned a thing. The Federation Office of Patents and Copyrights would be a better starting point. We are, after all, looking for what was called a 'technological innovation,' and only a raving madman would fail to register something like that before marketing it. And I happen to have a few contacts in that office."

"I suppose that's true," Pete agreed with a nod. "Tell me: you ever do any industrial espionage?"

Tella hesitated, then: "A few times, when I was starting out. That's where I got my contacts at the Office of P&C. Never was very good at it, though."

Old Pete raised an eyebrow at this and Tella caught it. "I don't consider myself a thief," he said defensively. "I dig up information that other people would rather keep hidden but I do not steal the products of another man's mind. That's why I joined up with Larry. He feels the same way."

Old Pete lifted his hands with an amused look on his face. "Did I question your ethics?"

"Your expression did."

"You're too touchy. I knew all about you and Larry Easly before I hired you. Research, you know. I was looking for undercover operatives who took their work and their reputations seriously and you two fit the bill. Now get to Fed Central or Dil or wherever you feel you've got to go and find out what you can about this device deBloise and his rats are meddling with."

Somewhat mollified, Andy Tella nodded and reached over to the player set between them. He held a small box over the top of the set, pressed a button, and a tiny silvery sphere popped out to be magnetically scooped into the box, which then closed with a snap. He rose to his feet.

"You've got resources, Mr. Paxton," he said, letting his eyes roam over the house and island, "but you're going to need more than you've got if you figure on putting a kink or two into their plans."

"What makes you think I want to interfere at all? How do you know this isn't all just idle curiosity to fill an aging man's final hours?"

Tella grinned. "Who're you trying to con? You mentioned research before. That's *my* field. You think I'd snoop around Fed Central for you before checking out who you are, where you've been, and how you got there? In your whole life, as far as I can tell, you've never done a single thing without an ultimate purpose in mind. And this isn't just politics for you—you've got a personal stake here, but that's your business. I'm merely warning you: you're dealing with some pretty powerful characters here. You're going to need help, Mr. Paxton."

Old Pete resumed his supine position on the sand and closed his eyes. "I'm all too well aware of that. But for the time being, let's see if we can find out exactly what they're up to." Without opening his eyes, he waved a hand in Tella's direction. "Get in touch when you have something."

The receding sound of Tella's footsteps vibrated through the hot sand to the back of Old Pete's skull as he lay there and considered his options. Things were beginning to come to a head. He would have to start setting the stage for a countermove now or risk being caught off guard when the time for action arrived.

And that meant he would have to go back to IBA.

A flood of memories swirled around him. Interstellar Business Advisors . . . he and Joe Finch had founded the company on a shoestring more than half a century before. Fifty-four years ago to be exact. Hard to believe that much time had passed. Then again, when he considered all they had accomplished in that period, it seemed a wonder they'd had enough time at all.

It had begun on Earth when a very young Peter Paxton received word from Joseph Finch, editor and publisher of Finch House Books, that his manuscript on the theory and practice of business on an interstellar scale had been accepted. And Mr. Finch wanted to meet with him personally.

The meeting still remained fine-etched in his mind: Joe Finch slouching behind his cluttered desk, fixing him now and again with those penetrating eyes, and telling him how his book was going to revolutionize interstellar trade. And imagine! Written by a man who had never even weekended on the moon! They spent the afternoon in the office. Joe Finch's range of interests and knowledge was impressive. He was an omnivore with an insatiable appetite for information. He spoke at length on the fine points of the latest attempts to mine the neutron stars, then switched to an impromptu dissertation on the reasons for the most recent additions to Earth's list of extinct flora and fauna. He gave a technical explanation of his own experimental techniques in holographic photography and then expounded on his perdurably unorthodox view of Earth's current fiscal and political situation. And through it all ran an invisible thread of logic that somehow strung everything into a cohesive whole.

They talked for hours in the office and then went to Finch's house, where he lived alone except for his giant pet antbear.

The rest of the night was spent in the living room, talking and drinking Joe Finch's horde of natural scotch whiskey until they both passed out in their chairs.

Never in his life among the teeming homogenized masses of Earth had Pete met such a forceful personality. That night was the beginning of a close friendship. So close, that when Joe fled Earth after incurring the wrath of the planet's chief administrator, Peter Paxton, his book yet unpublished, went with him. The antbear came along, too.

They ran to Ragna, rented an office, and decided to put Pete's book into practice rather than publish it. Obtaining a business loan on Ragna was no easy matter in those days, but they swung it and announced the opening of Interstellar Business Advisors—a big name on a little door.

Soon they began advising. A few small-time independent traders with timorous plans for growth or consolidation were the first clients. Pete plugged the type of product, the demographics, the population projections, political vagaries, et cetera, of the sectors in question into his theoretical programs and ran them through a computer on rented time. The computer results were then run through Joe Finch, who processed them with his indefinable combination of intuition and marketing experience, and a strategy was formed.

Success was slow in coming. The efficacy of an IBA program was never immediately apparent. The final proof was, as ever, in the marketplace, and that took time. But Joe and Pete chose their clients carefully, weeding out the fantasists and quick-credit artists from the serious entrepreneurs, and after six or seven standard years word got around the trade lanes that those two fellows in that little office on Ragna really knew what they were doing.

The fitful trickle of inquiries soon swelled to a steady stream and IBA began renting more space and hiring ancillary personnel. Each of the partners had found himself a mate by then. Joe became the father of Joseph Finch, Jr., and life was good.

The company continued to expand, and after two standard decades it held advisory accounts with a large number of the mainstay firms in interstellar trade, many of which would not make a move into a new market without first checking with Joe and Pete. But the accounts the partners liked most were the small, marginal ones that involved innovative products and processes, the speculation jobs that taxed their ingenuity to the limit. The big, prestigious accounts kept them solvent, the speculatory ones kept them interested. They charged a flat fee for service to the former and arranged a percentage of the adjusted gross over a variable period of time for the latter.

Time passed.

They grew rich. And as news of the Earthside exploits that drove Joe from the mother planet filtered through to the out-worlds, he became a celebrity of sorts on Ragna. A psychological malady known as "the horrors" was sweeping across the planets and a few IBA staff members were struck down. Pete's childless marriage broke up. A man calling himself The Healer appeared out of Tolive saying he could cure the horrors, and apparently he could. IBA contracted the construction of its own office building and began renting space to other businesses.

They had bizarre experiences, like the time Joe and Pete were almost swindled out of a fortune by an accelerated clone of Occupied Space's most famous financier. The clone had to be destroyed, of course—the Clone Laws on almost all planets dictated that—which was a shame because they had both found him charming.

They had near-tragedy when Joe, Jr., was almost killed by a radiation leak at a construction site shortly after he joined the firm. He was only eighteen at the time and managed to pull through.

And they had joy with the arrival of Josephine Finch, augmenting Junior and his wife after five years of marriage—a little late by out-world standards, but worth the wait to all concerned.

Then tragedy struck full force. Joe's flitter had a power failure while he, his wife, and daughter-in-law were two kilometers in the air.

Things were thrown into disarray for a while. Joe had been talking of retiring in the next few months when his seventy-fifth year coincided with IBA's thirty-fifth, but no one had taken that too seriously. Everyone fully expected to see him in his office every morning long after he had officially retired. Now he was gone and IBA would never be the same.

Everyone, including Pete, looked to Joe's son to fill the void, but Junior balked. For reasons apparent only to himself, he left Ragna with no particular destination in mind and was never seen or heard from again until his body was found a year later in an alley in a backwater town on Jebinose with a Vanek ceremonial knife in his heart.

Junior had placed control of his stock with Pete and his

death left Pete in complete control of IBA. But Old Pete—it was at about that time that the "Old" became an integral part of his name—wanted no part of it. He appointed a board of directors with himself as chairman and made it a point not to attend any of the meetings. This went on for a number of years. The directors adapted to the company and kept it going at an adequate pace, although not with the spirit and verve of the original, and became entrenched in the process. Old Pete never noticed. He had taken up a new hobby—politico-watching, he called it—which occupied most of his time. His purposes were his own, his methods were the best money could buy. The hobby seemed to satisfy the sense of political mischief he had inherited from Joe.

The status quo might have remained undisturbed indefinitely had not an attractive and rather hostile nineteen-year-old girl walked into his office one day and demanded control of her father's stock in IBA. Josephine Finch had come of age.

Old Pete gave her the stock without hesitation. As Junior's only descendant, she had a right to it. She went on to request temporary proxy power of *his* stock and, for his own reasons, he gave it to her. And that's when Josephine Finch began to turn IBA upside down. The outcome was a flurry of resignations from the board of directors and the forced retirement of Old Pete himself.

Retirement afforded him more time to devote to his politico-watching and now he had stumbled onto something that threatened all of interstellar trade. He didn't know just what was being planned, but if the Restructurists were talking in units of a half-million Fed credits, it was big . . . very big. And if it was good for the Restructurists, it was bad for him—bad for IBA, bad for the companies he had counseled over the years, bad for all the freedoms that had made his life so worth while.

Tella was right. This was too big for him. He was going to need help and the only place he could go to was IBA. He didn't relish the thought. There remained quite a residue of ill feeling between Jo and him, all of it on her side. He had been surprised and hurt by the forced retirement, especially after letting her use his stock against the board of directors, but he had not fought it. He had been seriously considering dropping his nominally active role in the company for some time but had never got around to doing anything about it. The forced retirement made up his mind for him and he left quietly for the Kel Sea island he had purchased shortly after Junior's death.

No, he bore no ill feelings—the girl reminded him too much of Junior for that—but he wished he could say the same for Jo. He couldn't understand her. There had been an undercurrent of hostility in all her relations with him, and for no apparent reason.

Old Pete sighed resignedly and rose to his knees, then to his feet. He hated to leave the island. Even more, he hated the thought of facing that fiery little girl again. Because seeing her always brought back memories of Joe, Jr.

And remembering Junior always made Old Pete a little sad.

II

JUNIOR

The two men gazed at the bustle of the spaceport below them.

"But where are you going?" the older one asked. He appeared genuinely concerned.

Joe Finch, Jr., shrugged. "Really haven't decided yet. Probably into the outer sectors."

"But the company—"

"It's only for a year, Pete, and I'm sure IBA won't miss me. If anyone can take care of things, it's you. I haven't contributed much since Dad's death anyway."

"But you just can't drop everything and take off like this," Paxton protested. "What about Josephine?"

Junior put his hand on Paxton's shoulder. They were close—Junior had called him "Uncle Pete" as a kid—and Paxton now and then tended to take on a fatherly attitude, especially since the death of Joe, Sr. "Look. Jo's ten now. I've tried to be a mother and a father to her for the three years since the accident. She's perhaps overly attached to me at this point, but she'll survive a year without me. I'm thirty-three and I've got to get away for a while or I won't be much of anything to anybody. Especially to me."

"I know what's going on inside that head of yours," Paxton said gravely, "so don't take this wrong . . . but can't you climb a mountain or something?"

Junior laughed. "I've no desire to be a mountain hanger. I . . . I just don't feel part of IBA, that's all. It's not my company. It's yours and Dad's. I had nothing to do with its founding or growth. It's just being handed to me."

"But the company has a lot of growing to do," Paxton said. "You could be a big part of that. In fact, IBA's future will ultimately depend on you, you know. If you run out on it now, there's no telling what—"

"IBA's present momentum," Junior interjected, "will easily carry it another decade with little help from anyone. I've got no qualms about taking out a year to go somewhere."

"And do what?"

"I dunno . . . something." He extended his hand. "Good-by, Pete. I'll contact you when I get where I'm going."

Peter Paxton watched the slouching figure amble off in the direction of one of the shuttle ramps, a man in the shadow of his father, the only son of Joe Finch trying to prove to himself that he was worthy of the title. It was distressing to see him wander off like this, but Paxton had to admire him for having the guts to do it. After all, it was only for a year. Maybe he could find himself in that time, or do something to put him at ease with himself. He wouldn't be much use around the company in his present state anyway.

So both men parted convinced that it was for the best and only for a year; neither realized that one would be dead before that year was up.

Ω

Junior didn't know exactly why he picked Jebinose. Maybe he had heard about its minor racial problem once and the memory had lingered in his subconscious, waiting for the opportune moment to push him in the planet's direction. Maybe he was drawn to situations in flux. Jebinose was in minor flux.

The planet's background was a minor blot on the early history of man's interstellar colonization. In the old days of the splinter colonies, exploration teams were sent out in all directions to find Earth-class planets. At that time the Earth government was offering a free ride to a suitable planet to any dissident group that desired an opportunity to realize its own idea of a perfect society. The policy served many purposes: it disseminated Terrans in a rough globe of space with Earth holding a vague central position; it allowed humanity to start dehomogenizing itself by cutting divergent parts off from the whole and letting them develop on their own; it took enormous pressure off the Earth bureaucracy—the real reason for the plan's inception—by forming an exit route for the malcontents and free-thinkers on the planet.

A lot of planets were needed and this put considerable pressure on the exploration teams. Sometimes they became careless. A major criterion for colonizable classification was the absence of an "intelligent" native species. No one was quite sure of just exactly what was meant by "intelligent," but tool-making was the accepted rule of thumb for dividing the thinkers from the non-thinkers. There were countless long, ponderous discussions on the wisdom of using a single criterion to determine a race's position on the intellectual scale but those discussions took place on Earth. The actual decisions were left up to the explorer crews; and as far as they were concerned, tool-making was it.

The Jebinose blunder, however, had nothing to do with interpretation of the rules. The planet was given an "M" classification (Earth-type, suitable for settling) after the most cursory of examinations. The colonists were indeed surprised when they discovered that they were sharing the planet with a tribe of primitive humanoids.

No one knows too much about the early colonial history of Jebinose. The splinter group that landed there was composed of third-rate syndicalists and was conspicuous only by reason of its particular ineptitude at the task of colonization. But for the Vanek, not a single member would have survived the first winter.

The Vanek are an alien enigma. They are quiet, humble, peaceful, fatalistic. Few in number, they are intensely devoted to a rather vague religion which bids them to welcome all newcomers to the fold. Their civilization had reached an agrarian plateau and they were quite willing to let it remain there.

Humanoid with blue-gray skin and long, spindly arms, they found it easy to befriend the colonists. It was not long before the Vanek had completely swallowed them up.

The cross-breeding phenomenon between human and Vanek has yet to be explained. There are many theories but no single one has received general acceptance. No matter . . . it worked. The Jebinose colony, as in the case of many other splinter colonies, was completely forgotten until the new Federation tried to order the chaos of the omnidirectional human migration. By the time it was rediscovered, human and Vanek genes had been pooled into a homogeneous mixture.

Much heated debate ensued. Some argued that since the original colony had been completely absorbed, resettlement would, in effect, be interference with an alien culture. Others argued that the Vanek were now part human and thus had a right to Terran technology . . . and besides, Jebinose was favorably situated in regard to an emerging trade route that had great potential.

Jebinose was resettled. The emerging trade route, however, failed to live up to its potential. The planet had an initial spurt of growth in its population as spaceports were constructed and cities grew up around them. Then the population stabilized into a slower, steadier growth pattern and some of the hardier citizens moved to the hinterlands where the Vanek lived and technology was at a low level. Jebinose was typical of many middle level planets: modern cities and relatively primitive outlands; not a backwater planet, but hardly in the thick of interplanetary affairs.

The Vanek tribes were scattered over the planet, mostly in the agricultural areas. It was through one of these that Junior wandered. He was tall and wiry with a good amount of muscle on a light frame. The unruly sandy hair that covered the tops of his ears and curled at his neck was his mother's; the long straight nose, blue eyes and sure movements were his father's. His face was fair, open, likable, ready to accept the universe on its own terms until he found good reason to change it. Although there was no physical abnormality, his shoulders were perpetually hunched; he'd been told all his life to straighten his back but he never did.

His wandering eventually brought him to the town of Danzer. It was a tiny place, the town center consisting of eight wooden buildings, a general store/restaurant among them. A few rugged-looking ground cars rolled up and down the dirt street that ran through the middle of town. On each side of the street ran a raised wooden boardwalk. Junior found a shady spot on the south side, unslung his backpack, and sat down.

He had been walking for days and was bone weary. A cool breeze helped evaporate the sweat beading his face as he put his head back against a post and closed his eyes. And to think he had considered himself in good physical condition. That was rough terrain out there! Those gentle rolling hills that looked so beautiful from a distance were sheer torture on the upside, especially with an extra tenth of a G to work against. He could have rented a flitter or a ground car; could have bought one outright. But he hadn't wanted to do it that way. Now he wondered if that had been such a wise idea.

He reopened his eyes as the last drop of sweat dried and noticed a middle-aged man staring at him from across the street. The man continued to stare for a short while longer, then he stepped off the boardwalk and crossed over to Junior for a closer look.

"You're new around here, aren't you?" he asked in provincial tones and stuck out his right hand. "I'm Marvin Heber and I like to know everyone in Danzer."

Junior shook that proffered hand—it was lightly callused; not a field worker's hand. "My name's Junior Finch and, yes, I'm new around here. Very new."

Heber sat down beside him and tipped back the brim of the cap he was wearing. His face was a weathered ruddy brown up to the hatband line about two centimeters above his eyebrows. At that point the skin abruptly turned white. He was gaunt and about average height. Some of his teeth were missing—a sight Junior was not at all used to—and it appeared he had neglected to apply a depilatory cream that morning. Hardly an arresting figure of a man, this Marvin Heber, but something in the quick, searching eyes told Junior that this man was quite a bit more than he seemed.

"Just moving in, huh?"

"No. Moving through, actually. I've been wandering around the region just to see what I can see."

"See anything interesting?" The man was nosy and did not make the slightest attempt to hide it. Junior decided to be as oblique as possible.

"Lot of virgin land left around here," he replied.

Heber nodded and eyed the newcomer. "If you want to settle, I'm sure we can help you find a place."

"Who's *we*?" It was Junior's turn to ask a question.

"Me, really. I was using the plural in the editorial sense." Now Junior was certain this man was more than he seemed.

He fumbled for something to say next and was getting nowhere when the approach of an odd-looking figure changed the course of the conversation. An elderly, spindle-armed beggar in a dusty robe came up to him and asked for alms. His skin was bluish gray and his black hair was pulled back from a high forehead and wound into a single braid that was slung in front of his left shoulder.

Junior fished in a pocket, came up with a few small coins, and dropped them into the earthen bowl extended in his direction.

"Wheels within wheels, *bendreth*," the beggar said in high, nasal tones, and then continued his journey down the street.

"That was a Vanek, right?" Junior asked as he watched the figure recede. "I hear they're common in this region but that's the first one I've seen close up since I arrived."

"As a group they keep pretty much to themselves and only come into town to buy supplies now and then. There's always a beggar or two about, however."

Junior made no reply, hoping his silence would draw Heber out.

"They spend most of their time on their reservation—"

"They're confined to a reservation?"

"Confined is hardly the word, my young friend. Before the Federation would allow resettlement of this planet, the Vanek leaders were approached and asked if they objected. Their reply: 'Wheels within wheels, *bendreth*.' When asked to choose whatever areas they would like reserved—without limit, mind you—for their exclusive use, they replied, 'Wheels within wheels, *bendreth*.' So their nomadic patterns were observed and mapped out and everywhere they wandered was reserved for their exclusive use." He grunted. "Waste of good land if you ask me."

"Why do you say that?"

"They don't wander any more. And there aren't all that many of them. Never was. Their total population peaked at about a hundred thousand planet-wide about fifty standard years ago. They've leveled off at about ninety thousand now. Looks like they'll stay there, too."

"Why'd they stop wandering?"

"Don't have to any more. All they've got to do is sit around meditating and carving their little statues."

"Eh?"

"That's right. Little statues. But you won't see any around

here. Some company in the city buys them up as fast as the Vanek can turn them out and sells them as curios all over Occupied Space. 'Handmade by alien half-breeds' believe the ads run."

"You know," Junior said, straightening up, "I think I've seen one or two in gift shops." He had a vague memory of oddly grained wood, carved into intricate and bizarre landscapes and tableaux. He also remembered the price tags.

"Then you realize why the Vanek have no financial worries."

"Why do they beg, then?"

Heber shrugged. "It's somehow mixed up with their religion, which no one really understands. Mostly it's the old Vanek who do the begging; I guess they get religious in their dotage just like a lot of humans. You heard him say, 'Wheels within wheels' after you gave him some coins, didn't you?"

"Yeah," Junior replied with a nod. "Then he said, '*bendreth*,' or something like that."

"*Bendreth* is the Vanek equivalent of 'sir' or 'madam.' They say that to just about everybody. 'Wheels within wheels,' however, has something to do with their religion. According to tradition, a wise old Vanek philosopher with an unpronounceable name came up with the theory that the universe was a conglomeration of wheels: wheels within wheels within wheels within wheels."

"Wasn't too far wrong, was he?"

"No, I guess not. Anyway, he managed to tie everything—and I mean everything—into the workings of these wheels. Got to the point where the only answer or comment he could make about anything was 'Wheels within wheels.' It's a pretty fatalistic philosophy. They believe that everything works out in the end so they rarely take any decisive action. They figure the wheels will turn full circle and even things up without their help."

He paused for a breath, puffing out his cheeks as he exhaled it. "Did you notice the cracks in the begging bowl, by the way?"

Junior nodded. "Looked like it had been broken and then glued back together again."

"That's part of the religion, too. You see, that old philosopher went to a banquet once—this was in the ancient days when the Vanek were a rather lusty and barbaric race—and the chief of this particular tribe sought to question him on his philosophy. Of course, the only answer he could get was 'Wheels within wheels, *bendreth.*' This annoyed him but he contained his anger until they all sat down at the eating table. During the meal it is said that the old philosopher uttered his favorite phrase over 250 times. Finally, the chief could take no more and broke a heavy earthen salad bowl over the old man's head, killing him. So now all Vanek beggars carry an earthen salad bowl that they have broken and then repaired as a sign that the philosopher did not die in vain."

Junior shook his head in wonder. "Sound like strange folk. How do the local Terrans get along with them?"

Heber shot him a sidelong glance, then answered. "I guess 'get along' is about the only way you could put it," he admitted. "There's no animosity between the two groups but there's certainly no friendship either. The Vanek are not easy people to warm up to. They float in and out of town and have no effect on the rest of us. Some of the city folks have been making noises about Terrans discriminating against the Vanek and I suppose there are plenty of instances where it happens, but it's a passive thing. When you come down to it, most Terrans around here just don't have any respect for the Vanek because the Vanek don't care about respect and consequently do nothing to engender it.

"And it's not racial antagonism as many outsiders might think." Again, the sidelong glance at Junior. "The fact that the Vanek are partially alien has nothing to do with it. That's a minor difference. It's other differences that cause problems."

"Like what?" Junior asked on cue.

"For one thing, there's no first person singular pronoun in the Vanek language. Some of the early anthropologists at one time thought this was a sign of group consciousness, but that was disproved. It's just that they don't think of themselves as individuals. They're all one on the Great Wheel. It makes it hard for Terrans to relate to them as individuals and thus it's hard to respect them as individuals.

"And there's more. The people around here are hard workers. They sweat their guts out trying to get a living out of the ground, and here are these skinny Vanek sitting around all day whittling wood and making a fortune. The local Terrans don't consider that an honest day's work."

"So it comes right back to lack of respect again," Junior observed.

"Right! But try to convince the legislators in the capital about that! They're getting together some sort of a bill to combat the so-called discrimination against the Vanek and it looks like it'll pass, too. But no law's going to make a Terran respect a Vanek and that's where the problem lies."

He kicked a stone out into the middle of the street. It was a gesture of disgust. "Damn fools in the capital probably don't even know what a Vanek looks like! Just trying to make political names for themselves."

"Well," Junior began, "equality—"

"Lip-service equality!" came the angry reply. "A forced equality that might well cause resentment on the part of the Terran locals. I don't want to see that. No, Mr. . . . Finch, wasn't it?" Junior nodded. "No, Mr. Finch. If equality's going to come to Danzer and other places like it, it's gotta come from the locals, not from the capital!"

Junior made no comment. The man had a good point—an obvious one to Junior—but Junior couldn't decide whether it was sincerely meant or just an excuse to oppose some legislation that happened to interfere with his racial prejudices. He noted that Heber made no alternative proposals.

Heber glanced at the sun. "Well, time for me to get back to work," he said.

"And just what is it you do, if I may ask?"

"I'm the government in town, you might say—mayor, sheriff, judge, notary, and so on." He smiled. "Nice to have met you, Mr. Finch. Hope you enjoy your stay around here."

"Nice to have met *you*, Mr. Heber," Junior replied. And he meant it . . . with only a few reservations. Heber was an outwardly pleasant and garrulous type but Junior wondered why he had taken so much time to explain the Terran-Vanek situation to him. Politics, maybe. If enough outsiders could be turned against the pending anti-discrimination bill, maybe it wouldn't pass. Whatever his reasons, Heber had been highly informative.

Junior forced himself to his feet and walked across the street to the general store. A land-rover passed close behind him as he crossed. Ground transportation was the rule here, probably because flitters were too expensive to buy, run, and service. Heber was right about the hard work involved in living off the land on Jebinose, and the rewards were minimal. The farm lands, for all intents and purposes, were economically depressed. That would help explain a part of the poor Terran-Vanek relations: the local Terrans were in control as far as numbers and technology were concerned, and they owned all the businesses; but the Vanek held a superior economic position solely through the sale of their carvings. The situation was tailor-made to generate resentment.

Junior found himself indifferent to the conflict. It was unfortunate, no doubt, that there had to be friction between the two races, but if these Vanek were as fatalistic as Heber said, then why bother with them?

He approached the general store building. The foodstuffs and supplies piled out front in their shiny, colorful plastic or alloy containers struck an odd contrast to the weather-beaten wood of the store. All the buildings of Danzer were handmade of local wood. Prefab probably cost too much.

A hand-lettered sign proclaiming that Bill Jeffers was the proprietor hung over the doorway and Junior's nostrils were assailed by a barrage of odors as he passed under it. Everything from frying food to fertilizer vied for the attention of his olfactory nerve.

His pupils were still adjusting to the diminished light of the store interior when Junior bumped into someone just inside the door. Straining his eyes and blinking, he saw that it was a young Vanek.

"Sorry," he muttered to the robed figure. "Can't see too well in here just yet." He continued on his way to the main counter in the rear, unaware of the intense gaze he was receiving from the Vanek.

"Yes, sir!" said the burly bear of a man behind the counter. His two huge hands were resting palms down on the countertop and his teeth showed white as he smiled through an unruly black beard. "What can I do for you?"

"I'd like something to eat. What's on the menu?"

The big man winked. "You must be new around here. You don't get *a* meal here, you get *the* meal: local beef, local potatoes, and local greens."

"All right then," Junior said with a shrug. "Serve me up an order of *the* meal."

"Fine. I'm Bill Jeffers, by the way," he said, wiping his right hand on the plaid of his shirt and then jabbing in it Junior's direction.

Junior shook hands and introduced himself.

"Staying around here long, Mr. Finch?" Jeffers asked.

Junior shook his head. "I doubt it. Just wandering around the area." These rurals, he thought. Nosy. Always the unabashed questions about who you were and how long you were staying.

Junior was used to people obtaining this sort of information in a more indirect way.

Jeffers nodded at Junior, then looked past him. "What'll it be?"

"The meal, *bendreth*," said a high-pitched, sibilant voice behind him. He turned and found himself facing the Vanek he had accidentally jostled on his way in.

"Hello," he said with a nod.

"Good day, *bendreth*," replied the Vanek. He had a slight frame, smooth grayish skin with a hint of blue in it, and piercing black eyes. There was an indigo birthmark to the left of midline on his forehead.

"How are you today?" Junior asked in a lame effort to make conversation. Despite his years with IBA and its myriad contacts throughout Occupied Space, he had never been face to face with an alien. Although most of the Vanek were thought to carry traces of human genetic material, they were, in every other sense, true aliens. And here was one now, standing next to him, ordering lunch. He wanted desperately to strike up a conversation, but finding a common ground for discussion was no easy matter.

"We are mostly well," came the reply. Junior noted the plural pronoun and remembered what Heber had told him. It was gauche to bring it up, but it might help to open a conversation.

"I've heard that the Vanek always use the word 'we' in the place of 'I,' " he said, cringing and feeling like an obnoxious tourist. "Why's that?"

"It is the way we are," came the impassive reply. "Our teachers tell us that we are all one on the Great Wheel. Maybe that is so. We do not know. All we know is that we have always spoken thus and no doubt we always shall. There is no Vanek word for the single man."

"That's too bad," Junior said with obvious sincerity, and then instantly regretted it.

"And why do you say that, *bendreth*?" The Vanek was showing some interest now and Junior realized that he would have to come up with a tactful yet honest answer.

"Well, I was always raised to believe that a race progresses through the actions of individuals. The progress of the Vanek, in my estimation, has been terribly slow. I mean, from what I can gather, you've gone nowhere in the past few centuries. Maybe that's the result of having the word 'I' absent from your functional vocabulary. I hope I haven't offended you by what I've just said."

The Vanek eyed him narrowly. "You needn't apologize for speaking what you think. You may—" His words were cut short by the arrival of the meals: steaming mounds of food on wooden slabs. Each paid for his portion in Jebinose script and Junior expected the Vanek to follow him to one of the small tables situated in the corner to their left. Instead, the alien turned and walked toward the door.

"Where're you going?"

"Outside. To eat."

"It's too hot out there. We'll sit at one of these tables."

The Vanek hesitated and glanced around. The store was empty and Jeffers had disappeared into the back. Wordlessly, he followed Junior to a table.

Both were hungry and, once seated, began to eat. After rapidly swallowing two mouthfuls, Junior spoke around a third. "Now, what were you about to say?"

The Vanek looked across the table at him and chewed thoughtfully. "You may be right. Once we might have said that we have progressed as far as we desire. But that doesn't hold true any more. We Vanek have shown ourselves quite willing to accept and utilize the benefits of a civilization technologically far superior to our own. So perhaps it has not been by desire that our culture has been stagnated. Still, there is more to culture than technology. There is—"

"*Hey*!" came a shout from the rear of the store. "What's he doing over there?" Junior looked past the Vanek and saw Jeffers standing behind the counter, glaring in his direction.

Without looking around, the Vanek picked up his slab and walked out the door. Junior watched in stunned silence.

"What was that all about?" he asked. "I was talking to him!"

"We don't allow any Vaneks to eat in here," Jeffers told him in a more subdued tone.

"Why the hell not?"

"Because we don't, that's why!"

Junior could feel himself getting angry. He put a lid on it but it wasn't easy. "That's a damn humiliating thing to do to somebody, you know."

"Maybe so. But we still don't allow any Vaneks to eat in this store."

"And just who are the 'we' you're referring to?"

"Me!" said Jeffers as he came around from behind the

counter and approached Junior's table. He moved with surprising grace for a man of his size. "It's my place and I've got a right to call the shots in my own place!"

"Nobody's saying you don't, only . . . only you could show a little respect for his dignity. Just a little!"

"He's a half-breed!"

"Then how about half the respect you'd accord a Terran? How's that sound?"

Jeffers' eyes narrowed. "Are you one of those meddlers from the capital?"

"No," Junior said, dropping his fork into his mashed potatoes and lifting his slab. "I only arrived on the planet a few weeks ago."

"Then you're not even from Jebinose!" Jeffers laughed. "You're a foreigner!"

"Aren't we all," Junior said over his shoulder as he walked out the door.

Ω

The Vanek was seated on the boardwalk outside the store, calmly finishing his meal. Junior sat down beside him and put his own slab aside. He was choked with what he recognized as self-righteous anger and couldn't eat. It was a strange sensation, rage. He had never experienced it before. He'd had his angry moments in the past, of course, but he'd never run across anything like this in the three-odd decades of his tranquil and relatively sheltered life. This was pure, self-righteous, frustrated rage. And he knew it could be dangerous. He breathed deeply and tried to cool himself back to rationality.

"Is it always that way?" he asked finally.

The Vanek nodded, "Yes, but it is his store."

"I know it's his store," Junior said, "and I certainly appreciate his right to run it as he wishes—more than you know—but what he did to you is wrong."

"It is the prevailing attitude."

"It's a humiliating attitude, a total lack of respect for whatever personal dignity you might possess." There was that word again: respect. Heber had said that the local Terrans had none of it for the Vanek. And maybe they had no reason to respect these introspective, timid creatures, but . . .

. . . thought patterns developed after years at IBA whirled, then clicked into place, and Junior suddenly realized that of all the Terrans in Danzer, Bill Jeffers owed the Vanek the most consideration.

"But we're going to change that attitude, at least in one mind."

The Vanek threw him a questioning glance—the similarity in facial expressions between the two races struck Junior at that moment. Either they had always responded alike or the Vanek had learned to mimic the Terrans. Interesting . . . but he let the thought go. He had other things on his mind.

"You're going to take me to your tribe or camp or whatever it is," Junior said, "and we're going to figure out a way to put some pressure on Mr. Jeffers."

The pressure of which he was speaking was the economic kind, of course. Economic pressure was a household word as far as the Finch family was concerned.

The Vanek sighed. "Whatever your plan is, it won't work. The elders will never agree to do anything that might influence the course of the Great Wheel. They'll reject whatever you suggest without even hearing you out."

"I have a feeling they'll agree. Besides, I have no intention of asking them to do anything; I'm going to ask them *not* to do something."

The Vanek gave him another puzzled look, then shrugged. "Follow me, then. I'll take you to the elders. But you have been warned: it's futile."

Junior didn't think so. He had found something unexpected in the attitude of the young Vanek—whose name, he learned as they walked, was pronounced something like *Rmrl*. He'd read it in the flick of his gaze, the twist of his mouth, and realized that for all his detached air, for all his outward indifference, this particular Vanek was keenly aware of the discrimination he faced daily in the Terran town. Junior had seen through the carefully woven façade and knew that something could be done, must be done, and that he could do it.

III

JO

Dark brown skin and eyes against a casual white jumper and short white hair: Old Pete was a gaunt study in contrasts, moving with such ease and familiarity through the upper-level corridors of IBA that the receptionist in the hall hesitated to accost him. But when he passed her desk on his way to the inner executive offices, she felt compelled to speak.

"May I help you, sir?" she asked politely.

"Yes." He turned toward her and smiled. "Is The Lady in at the moment?"

She answered his question with another. "Do you have an appointment?" Her desktop was lit with the electronic equivalent of a daybook and an ornate marker was poised to check off his name.

"No, I'm afraid not. You see—"

"I'm very sorry." The finality in her tone was underscored by the abrupt dimming of her desktop. "Miss Finch can see no one without an appointment." The daybook read-out was her ultimate weapon and she was skilled at using it to control the flow of traffic in and out of the executive suites.

The old man rested a gnarled hand on the desktop and leaned toward her. "Listen, dearie," he said in a low but forceful tone, "you just tell her Old Pete is here. We'll worry about appointments later."

The receptionist hesitated. The name "Old Pete" sounded vaguely familiar. She tapped her marker once, twice, then shrugged and touched a stud on the desktop.

A feminine voice said, "Yes, Marge," from out of the air.

"Someone named Old Pete demands to see you, Miss Finch."

"Is this some sort of joke?" the voice asked.

"I really couldn't say," the receptionist answered nervously.

"Send him in."

She rose to show him the way but the old man waved her back to her seat and strode toward an ornate door made of solid Maratek firewood that rippled with shifting waves of color. The name *Josephine Finch* was carved in the wood at eye level, its color shifts out of sync with the rest of the door.

Old Pete? thought the woman within. What was he doing at IBA? He was supposed to be in the Kel Sea, out of her sight and out of her mind. She dropped a spool of memos onto the cluttered desk before her. After taking an all-too-rare long weekend, work had accumulated to the point where she'd have to go non-stop for two days to make up for the extra day off. Project reports, financial reports, feasibility studies, new proposals—a half-meter stack had awaited her return. The interstellar business community, at least that portion of it connected with IBA, had apparently waited until she'd left the office three days ago before unloading all its backed-up paperwork.

At times like this she idly wished she had an accelerated clone to share the work load. But as it stood now with the Clone Laws, she'd go to jail and the clone would be destroyed if anyone ever caught on.

A clone would be especially nice right now, just to deal with Old Pete. But he was here and there was no avoiding a meeting with him. It wasn't going to be pleasant, but she'd have to do it herself.

The door opened without a knock and there he stood. He'd changed. His skin was darker and his hair was whiter than she'd ever seen it. Over all, his appearance was more wizened, but the changes went deeper than that. Jo had always thought of Old Pete as the perfect example of a high-pressure executive—his movements had always been abrupt, rapid, decisive, his speech terse and interruptive. He appeared much more at ease now. There was new flow to his movements and speech.

He had changed, but the feelings he engendered in her had not. The old distrust and hostility rekindled within her at the sight of him.

For a heartbeat or two after coming through the door, the old man stood with his eyes fixed on her, his mouth half open, frozen in the instant before speech. Abruptly, he appeared to reassert control over himself and arranged his features into familiar lines.

"Hello, Jo," he said softly, closing the door behind him. "You're looking well."

And she was. A few pounds in the right places had matured her figure since the last time the two of them had faced each other. She was wearing a clingsuit—blue, to match her eyes—and she wore it well; in the past she had been too thin by most outworld standards, but the extra weight on her light frame brought her close to optimum. Her dark hair, its normal sandy color permanently altered years before to a shade closely matching her late grandfather's, was parted in the middle, curving downward into a gentle frame for her oval face, and then cut off sharply below the ears. Between the straight line of her nose and a softly rounded chin, her lips would have appeared fuller had they not now been compressed by irritation.

"You're not looking so bad yourself," she replied stiffly. "Island life seems to be agreeing with you. How've you been?" She really didn't care.

"Can't complain."

The amenities went on for a few more minutes with Jo doing her best to be as pleasant as possible. Old Pete's return irritated her. IBA was running smoothly now, and all because of her. What did he want here anyway? She resented anyone from the old days intruding on IBA. It was her company now—the Finch flair had been restored and IBA was reasserting its claim to pre-eminence in its field.

Old Pete. Of all the people from the past, he was the last she wished to see at her door. And he must know that. She'd made no secret of it when he was forcefully retired; and even now, years later, she could feel the hostility radiating from her despite her calm and cordial demeanor.

Old Pete was glancing around the room. A figure standing in a far corner caught his eye and he whirled. "*Joe*! Good—" Then he realized he was looking at a hologram. "That's one of the most lifelike holos I've ever seen," he said with obvious relief as he moved around to view it from different angles. "For a moment I actually thought . . ."

"The founder's portrait has to go somewhere," Jo said.

"*Co*-founder, you mean."

Jo hesitated, then backed down. He was right and it would serve no purpose to get petty with him. "The *late* co-founder," she finally replied, then made an attempt to bring the conversation toward the bottom line. "What brings you back?"

Frowning, he eased himself into a chair across from Jo's desk and stared at her. "I don't know how to put this, exactly. In a way, I'm here to ask IBA to help me, the Federation, and IBA." His mouth twisted into a wry smile. "Sounds kind of convoluted, doesn't it?"

"Sounds like you're hedging," Jo replied without returning the smile.

Old Pete's laugh was genuine. "Just like your grandfather! Okay, I *am* hedging, but only because I've got to somehow convey to you a convincing version of a vague concept formed from speculation based on incomplete and/or secondhand information."

"What is it, then?" she snapped, then reminded herself to show restraint and have patience. He was, after all, an old man.

"I've uncovered a plot against the Federation charter."

Jo let the statement hang in the air, waiting for more. But her visitor outwaited her.

Finally, "What's that got to do with IBA?" she asked grudgingly.

"Everything. The charter severely limits the activities of the Federation; it restricts it from meddling in planetary affairs and from interfering in interplanetary trade. For the past couple of centuries it has bound the planets tightly together while managing to stymie the bureaucrats at every turn. But there's a delicate balance there, easily upset. If the charter should be changed or, worse yet, thrown out somehow, the politicos at Fed Central who are so inclined will have free rein to indulge their whims."

Jo shrugged. "So what? That doesn't affect IBA. We have

absolutely no connection with anyone in the Federation. We don't even have a connection in the Ragna Co-operative. So how can any political machinations be of any consequence to us?"

"If the charter goes, so does the free market," he told her.

A drawn-out, very dubious, "Ohhhh?" was her only reply.

Old Pete grunted. "Jo, what do you know about the Restructurist movement?"

"It's a political group that wants to make some changes in the Federation," she replied. "DeBloise is their current leader, I believe. Beyond that, I don't know much about them. Nor do I care much about them or any other political group."

"You'd better start learning. To say they want to 'make some changes in the Federation' is to put it lightly . . . turn it inside out is more like it! The Fed was designed to keep the lid on interplanetary affairs: mediate some disputes, promote a little harmony while simultaneously maintaining a low level of constructive discord, and quashing the violent plans of some of the more acquisitive planetary regimes. But that's not enough for the Restructurists. True to their name, they want to restructure the entire organization . . . turn it into some sort of social and economic equalizer that'll regulate trade in free space and even get involved in the internal affairs of some of the planets."

Jo remained unconcerned. "They'll never get anywhere. From what I understand, the Fed charter is defensively worded in such a way as to make it impossible for anyone to get around it."

"You forget: there's an emergency clause that allows for a temporary increase in the scope of Federation activity should it or its planets be threatened. Peter LaNague, who designed the charter, disowned it after that clause was attached over his protests."

"I'm aware of all that," Jo said with a forced patience. The conversation seemed to have veered off its original course . . . or had it? In spite of the pile of work spread out before her, she felt compelled to follow Old Pete's train of thought through to its finish. "And it seems every time I catch a vidcast, there's a news item about another attempt to invoke the security clause in the Fed charter. And every time it's voted down. Even if they do succeed in invoking it, so what? It's only temporary."

"That's where you're wrong, Jo," he said gravely. "If you look at the history of old Earth, you'll find that very seldom, if ever, is any increase in governmental power temporary. The emergency clause is probably the key to Restructurist control: once they invoke it they'll have their foot in the door and the Federation will never be the same again. I don't want to see that happen, Jo. Your grandfather and I were able to make IBA a going concern because of the Fed's hands-off policy toward any voluntary transactions. It's my personal belief that we Terrans have come as far as we have in the last couple of centuries because of that policy. I don't want to see it changed. I don't want to see the Federation regress toward empire—it arose from the ashes of another empire—but I see it looming in the future if the Restructurists have their way."

"But they won't," Jo stated.

"I wouldn't be too sure of that. Many of those Restructurists may seem like starry-eyed idealists, but a good number are crafty plotters with power as their goal. And Elson deBloise is the worst of the bunch. He's an ambitious man—a mere planetary delegate ten years ago, he's now a sector representative—and this plot, whatever it is, centers around him and his circle. I've made a connection between deBloise and an as yet unnamed man on Dil. The man is some sort of physicist, probably, and if deBloise thinks he can be of use, then both he and the Federation had better be on guard!"

Jo was struck by the old man's vehemence. "Why not go directly to the Federation if you think something dirty is up?"

"Because I don't have a shred of tangible evidence. I would look like a nut and deBloise would have plenty of time to cover his tracks. Frankly, I'd rather not even involve the Fed. It's not set up to deal with deBloise's type. I'd much prefer to handle everything behind the scenes and avoid any open involvement with the politicos. To do that I need IBA's contacts."

"It's always been a company policy to stay out of politics," Jo said after a moment of silence. "It's one of our by-laws, as a matter of fact."

Old Pete's face creased into a smile. "I know. I wrote it."

"Then why the sudden change of heart?"

"No change of heart, really. I still don't think business should have any connection with government. It's dangerous and it's usually sneaky. When a businessman and a politician get together, certain things are bound to occur." He ticked the points off on the fingers of his left hand. "The businessman is usually one who's found that he hasn't quite got what it takes to make it in the free market, so he will try to persuade the government to use its coercive power to help him gain an advantage over his competitors: a special sanction, an import quota, a right of way, et cetera. The politician will find that if he complies he will grow richer in power and/or material wealth. The colluding business will aim for a monopoly over a particular market while the politician will aim in turn for further extension of political influence into the marketplace by controlling that monopoly. They both wind up winners. The losers: everybody else.

"So I still say, government should have no influence in the economy and business should have no influence in government. And that's the way it's been under the LaNague Charter. You don't see any lobbyists at Fed Central because the Federation has denied itself any and all economic power. Nobody's getting any special favors and I want to keep it that way. And the only way for me to do that is to meet a few politicos head-on."

Jo drummed her fingers on the desk and studied the old man. His concern was genuine. And despite the conspiratorial overtones of his suspicions, Jo had an uneasy feeling that he could be right. The Restructurists had been rather quiet of late. Maybe something was brewing after all.

But a secret plot to trigger the emergency clause of the Federation charter? Unlikely. But then again . . . Old Pete had never been known to be prone to hysteria, nor to paranoia. He was getting on in years, true, but not that far on. He and her grandfather had possessed two of the shrewdest minds in the interstellar market in their day and she sensed that Pete's was still sharp. If he thought there was something in the wind that threatened IBA, then it might be wise to give him the benefit of the doubt.

Jo withheld complete acceptance. She'd help, even if it meant continued close contact with Pete, but she'd keep an eye on him. If he was wrong and his suspicions had no basis in fact, then little was lost except some time and personal aggravation. If he happened to be right, however . . . well, IBA was her home and her family. Anything that threatened it, threatened her.

"I've always found conspiracy theories titillating," she said after a long pause, "though rarely verifiable. But if it's in IBA's interest, I'll do what I can."

Old Pete's body relaxed visibly as he heard this. "Good! You can help me dig. I've already got someone checking out this fellow on Dil. We'll have to keep a watch on all the Restructurist eminentoes to see if anything else is about to break."

Jo nodded. "I can see to that. I'll also send someone of my own to Dil to see what can be uncovered there." She rose to her feet, anxious to end the meeting. "In the meantime . . ."

Old Pete sat where he was and held up his hand. "Not so fast."

"What's the matter?"

"If we're going to be working together on this thing," he said, "let's get one thing settled: Why do you hate me?"

Jo's voice rose half an octave. "I don't hate you."

"Yes, you do. And I'd like an explanation. You owe me that much, at least."

She wondered at times if she owed him anything; then at other times she felt she owed him everything. But always, when she thought of him, old hatreds rose to the surface. She hesitated.

"I'm waiting," Old Pete said patiently.

Jo shook herself and made ready the reply that was as unpleasant for her to say as it was going to be for Old Pete to hear.

"If it hadn't been for you," she said slowly and distinctly, "my father would be alive today."

Old Pete's face registered the expression she had expected: shock. And something more . . . he was hurt, too.

After a long pause, he spoke in a low voice. "How could you think such a thing?"

"Because it's true! You probably talked him into that sabbatical of his. And if you didn't talk him into it, you could have talked him out of it. But however it was, you got control of his stock and sent him off to be killed!"

Old Pete suddenly looked all of his eighty-one years. A lot of things were suddenly very clear to him.

"You *must* believe that Junior insisted on leaving . . . I did my best to dissuade him, but you can't talk a Finch out of anything once he's got his mind set on it. He thrust the stock on me for safekeeping until his return—he only planned to be away a year."

"But he never returned and it all turned out very nicely for you, didn't it?"

"You're not thinking very clearly, little girl," Old Pete said as anger began to absorb the hurt. "Think! What did I do with that stock? Did I set myself up as all-powerful ruler of the IBA complex? Did I remake the company in my own image? Did I milk it dry? No! No to all of them! I set up a board of directors to run things for me because I'd lost interest in the whole affair. Joe dead, and then Junior dead . . . all within four years . . ." His voice softened again. "I just didn't feel like going on with any of it any more."

In the long silence that followed, Jo was almost tempted to believe him. His hurt at what she had said seemed so real. But she couldn't accept it. Not yet. There was something locked away in Old Pete, something he would never let her see. She had no idea what it was or what it concerned, but it was there. She sensed it. And she couldn't let the old hatreds go. She had to have someone to blame for losing a second parent by the time she was eleven years old, for the years spent with an indifferent uncle and a preoccupied aunt.

"Well," she faltered, "someone made him leave. Someone got him out of the picture."

"Yes, and that someone was Junior himself."

Jo's voice broke. "Then he was a fool!"

"You can't understand why he left, can you?" Old Pete said softly, as if seeing Jo for the first time. "And I think I know the reason. Since you were in your teens you've known what you wanted and you had to work to get it. You had to confront me, then the board of directors, and then you had to prove yourself to the interstellar traders."

He rose and began to pace the room. "It was different, however, for Junior . . . perhaps we shouldn't have called him that but it got to be a necessity when he and his father were working together. You'd say 'Joe' and they'd both say 'What?' But anyway, it was different for him. He grew up in your grandfather's shadow; he was Joe Finch's son and everything was cut out for him. He had a prefab future in IBA and most sons would have slipped right into the mold.

"But not Junior. IBA was a golden apple waiting to be plucked and he walked away. Oh, he hung on and gave it a try for a couple of years after his father's death, but it just wasn't for him. At least not yet. He didn't feel he'd earned it. It was no accomplishment for him to take over IBA. He balked!" Old Pete snorted. "That Finch blood, I guess."

"And you couldn't change his mind?"

He shook his head. "No. Tried up to the last day. He said good-by not knowing where he was going; I said good-by figuring to see him again in a year or so. You know the rest."

"What there is to know, yes." Jo slumped in her chair. "I'm sorry, but I don't care to talk about this any more."

Old Pete ignored her. "You know, I just realized what's missing in this office: a picture of Junior. Jo, you really shouldn't reserve all your ancestral reverence for your grandfather."

"Please," Jo said, "not now. I'll have someone show you to the guest suite."

"Quite all right," came the smiling reply. "I know exactly where it is—I helped design this building, don't forget." He turned at the door. "A nice little holo of your father would go very well on the desk there. Think about it. Junior was really quite a fellow in his own way. And you're closer to him than you'll ever know."

Jo remained in her chair after he had gone. It was a long time before she was able to get back to her work.

IV

JUNIOR

The Vanek village was an odd place, almost humorous in its incongruities. Sitting in front of their smooth-domed mud huts, the Vanek women, almost identical to the men in appearance, prepared the coming meal or mended clothes; the men whittled their statuettes and tableaux as they had no doubt done for centuries; the children romped as all children have romped for eons. A timeless scene at first glance. Then one noticed that the pump over the well in the center of the village was of Terran design and powered by solar batteries. A closer look and one noticed that fine strands of insulated wire ran from hut to hut. And filtering through the primitive background noise of the village in its natural surroundings was the hum of a modern generator. The Vanek had looked upon electric lighting and had seen that it was good . . . at least in this particular village.

Rmrl left Junior standing by an odd-looking contraption while he went to confer with the elders. It was a series of intricately carved gearlike wheels suspended on axles set at crazy angles. Junior touched one of the smaller wheels and it began to rotate; he gave it a push to move it faster and suddenly all the wheels were turning. The rates and angles were all different, but all were turning.

He returned his attention to Rmrl, who was approaching a large hut that stood apart from the others. The mud on the walls had been etched with countless, intricate gyrating designs.

The young Vanek was met at the door by a wizened figure. As their conversation grew animated, other figures appeared in the doorway. Fingers pointed, hands gestured back and forth, a confusion of high-pitched voices drifted toward Junior as he watched with interest. Finally, Rmrl turned away. The door closed behind him.

"They do not wish to listen," he said with an expressionless face as he returned to Junior's side. "I'm sorry, *bendreth*."

"There's hardly any need to apologize to me," Junior grunted. "I'm not the one on the dirty end of the stick."

"Pardon, *bendreth*?"

"Nothing. Just an expression." He watched the rotating wheels and pondered the situation. His first inclination was to drop the whole matter and continue his hike through the region. If they were content with the situation, then let it be. He had always despised people who thought they knew what was best for others, and feared that he might be falling prey to that very same attitude in regard to the Vanek.

If they don't want my help, then why should I even bother? They could be right . . . bringing things to a head may not be the best answer. And if they don't want to move, why should I push them?

Then he caught the expression on Rmrl's face—the tiniest glimmer of unhoped-for hope had been doused. It was well hidden, but it was there.

Junior found himself striding toward the Elder Hut.

"*Bendreth*!" Rmrl cried. "Come back! It will do no good! They will refuse to listen!" Ignoring him, Junior pushed through the door and entered the hut.

It was dark inside, the only illumination coming from a single dusty incandescent bulb, primitive in design and low in wattage, hanging lonely and naked from the ceiling. There was a dank, musty odor, but what he could see was reasonably clean.

Seven scrawny, robed figures started up from the floor at

Junior's precipitous entrance. He noted their frightened expressions and quickly held out his empty palms.

"I mean you no harm. I only wish to speak to you." Rmrl came up behind him and stood in the doorway, watching.

"We know what you wish to say," replied one of the elders, the most wizened of the lot. "You wish us to take action to influence the Great Wheel. We will not. It is forbidden and it is unnecessary. The Great Wheel has a wisdom of its own, indecipherable in mortal terms, and brings all things 'round in good time. We will do nothing to alter its course, *bendreth*."

"But I'm not going to ask you to *do* anything," Junior said quickly. "I want you to try and *not* do something."

The seven muttered among themselves at this. *If this is what you have to go through to get anything moving in this place,* Junior thought, *small wonder they still live in mud huts!*

The same elder turned to him again. He was apparently the chief or something. "We have decided that under those circumstances it would not be unorthodox to listen to you, *bendreth*."

Junior shot a quick glance at Rmrl and then seated himself on the hard-packed earth of the floor. The elders did likewise. It was as he had expected: the elders, and probably most other Vanek, were dogmatists. Not doing something, according to the letter of their creed, was quite different from doing something.

"What we are dealing with here," Junior began, "is really a very simple problem. On one hand we have Bill Jeffers, a man who is quite willing to sell you food, clothing, and fuel for your generator, but is loath to let you eat in the store where you buy all these things. Now is neither the time nor the place to make a moral judgment on the rightness or wrongness of this policy. He owns his store and what he wants to do with it is his business. It's just a fact we have to deal with.

"Just as it is a fact that you Vanek do not like this policy."

The elders glanced warily at each other as Junior said this, but he hurried on with his speech.

"It is another fact that you Vanek make up a good part of Jeffers' business. You earn your money, and where and how you spend it is *your* business. You have something Jeffers wants—money. And in return for spending your money in his store you would like to be treated with the same respect he accords his Terran customers."

The chief elder opened his mouth to speak but Junior cut him off: "Don't deny it. You hide it well, but it gnaws at you."

The old Vanek hesitated, then gave him an almost imperceptible nod. This pushy Terran had suddenly risen in the elders' collective estimation.

"Okay. Now, the next step is to bring this point home to Jeffers. To accomplish this, all you've got to do is stay away from his store until he gets the message that unless he bends a little, his gross income from now on will be a lot less than what he's used to. And don't worry about him getting the message; he's a businessman and you'll be speaking his language."

The elders stared at Junior in openmouthed wonder. They had little knowledge of the economic forces at work around them. The general store was a tremendous convenience to them. No longer did they have to till the fields in the hot sun, no longer did the fullness of their bellies depend on the success of the harvest. Let the Great Wheel bring whatever weather it may, as long as the Terran curio dealers bought the statuettes and carvings, the Vanek would never go hungry.

So, since the day of its construction, the general store had been looked upon as a boon from the Great Wheel. But now this Terran was revealing that their relationship with the proprietor of the store was one of interdependence. It was all so obvious! Why hadn't they seen it before?

"You are very wise, *bendreth*," the chief elder said.

"Hardly. It's all common sense. What's your decision on the matter?"

Muttering and mumbling, the elders grouped into a knot on the far side of the hut. A few seemed to be opposed to the idea—it would influence the Great Wheel. Others contended that they had managed without Jeffers and his store in the past and certainly it would not be unorthodox to get along without him now. The latter argument prevailed.

The chief elder turned to Junior. "We have agreed to your plan, *bendreth*. The word shall be passed to our brother Vanek in this region that we no longer buy from Jeffers." He hesitated. "We still find it hard to believe that such action on our part will have any effect."

"Don't worry," Junior reassured him. "He takes you all for granted now; but he'll change his tune once the receipts start to dwindle. You'll all suddenly become very important to Bill Jeffers. Wait and see."

The elder nodded absently, still not quite believing. The meek had been told they had power, yet they were unsure of its use, unsure that it really existed.

Junior left the hut in high spirits. It was all so simple when you used your head. In a few days Jeffers would start to wonder why he hadn't seen any Vanek around his store lately. He would get his answer and the choice would be his. Junior had little doubt as to what that choice would be.

He felt good inside. He was doing something worthwhile and doing it on his own. No one was paving the way for him. He was breaking his own ground.

The sun was down behind the trees as he unrolled his sleeping bag in the middle of a small clearing somewhere between the Vanek village and Danzer. He'd sleep well tonight, better than he had in many years.

Ω

Dawn broke chilly and damp. Reaching into his sack, Junior brought out a container of breakfast rations and activated the heating strip. Two minutes later he was downing a hot meal.

The sun was up and chasing the ground fog as he moved toward Danzer at a brisk pace. His plan was to go to town and hang around Jeffers' store to watch how things developed as the day wore on. And should the shopkeeper begin to wonder where all the Vanek were keeping themselves, Junior would be sure to offer his opinion.

Yes, he was thinking, *today ought to prove very interesting.*

Jeffers was on a short ladder, stocking one of the shelves, when Junior walked in.

"G'morning, Finch," he said with a glance over his shoulder. Junior was surprised that he remembered his name. "Cooled off from yesterday?"

"Entirely."

"Good. Looking for breakfast?"

"Had some already out in the field. But I'll take some coffee if you've got it."

Jeffers smiled as he poured two cups at the counter. "Ever had Jebinose coffee before?"

Junior shook his head.

"Then this one's on the house. Our coffee takes some getting used to and you may not want to finish your first cup."

Junior hesitantly nodded his thanks. Try as he might, he could not work up a personal dislike for Jeffers. He sampled the coffee; it had a strong, bitter-sour taste to it and Jeffers' grin broadened as he watched Junior add a few spoonfuls of sugar. He tried it again and it was a little more palatable now.

After a pause, Junior asked, "Just what is it you have against the Vanek, Bill? It's none of my business, I know, but I'm interested."

"You're right about it being none of your business," Jeffers said curtly, then shrugged. "But I'll tell you this much: I don't have anything in particular against them. It's just that they strike me as weird. They get on my nerves with all that talk about wheels and such and, frankly, I just don't like to have them sitting around."

Junior nodded absently. Jeffers was rationalizing and they both knew it.

"What time do they usually start showing up here?" he asked.

"They're usually my first customers of the day."

"But not today, eh?" Junior remarked confidently.

"You didn't beat them in, if that's what you mean. Two of them left just a few minutes before you arrived . . . bought some food." He stared at Junior curiously. "Something wrong?"

"No, nothing," was the hasty reply. Junior had visibly started at the news but recovered quickly. However, he doubted his ability to hide his surprise and dismay much longer. "Thanks for the coffee, Bill. I'll probably stop back in later on."

"Anytime," he heard Jeffers say as he walked out to the street.

Danzer was fully awake by now. All the shops—they totaled four counting the general store—were open and some of the farmers were driving up and down the street in heavy-duty lorries, some loaded with hay or feed, others with livestock. A pair of locals gave him a friendly nod as they brushed by him on their way into Jeffers' store.

Junior's eyes roamed the street for the robe of a Vanek. He spotted one hurrying up the boardwalk toward him so he advanced to meet him. It was Rmrl.

"At last we have found you, *bendreth*," the young Vanek said breathlessly. He scrutinized Junior's face closely. "I see you already know what we have come to tell you."

Junior gave a confirming nod. "I know. But what I want to know is *why*? Did the elders go back on their word?"

"No. They kept their word. They told the villagers not to buy from Jeffers but they complained far into the night. The elders held firm for a while but finally had to yield to the pressure."

"I don't understand."

"Our people . . . they *want* to buy from Jeffers. They do not want to deprive him of their business."

"Why not?"

"Wheels within wheels, *bendreth*."

"Doesn't what happens to them in that store matter to them?" Junior was totally baffled.

Rmrl shrugged and Junior thought he noticed a trace of resentment in the gesture.

"And you, Rmrl? How do you feel about it all?"

"Wheels within wheels," he repeated and walked away.

Junior was about to go after him but a voice made him turn.

"Bit off a little more than you could chew, Mr. Finch?"

It was Heber.

"What's that supposed to mean?" he asked the older man, who was leaning in the doorway of his office as he watched the offworlder.

"It means that I happened to overhear your conversation with Rmrl. I suppose I could have closed the door, but knowing what's going on in this town is part of my job." For a few fleeting seconds his eyes locked with Junior's, then: "Come inside a minute, Mr. Finch—please."

"Why?" Frustration and bafflement were edging him into a hostile and suspicious mood.

"Well, for one thing, I think I may be able to explain to you why your little plan failed. At least I'll be able to give you something more than 'wheels within wheels.'"

Interested, Junior grudgingly complied. Heber's office was small and tight-fitting, most of the room being taken up by filing cabinets and a huge desk handmade from local wood. A Vanek carving, unmistakable in its style, of a Jebinose species of fowl in a natural woodland setting was prominently displayed on a corner shelf.

"I thought you said there were no Vanek carvings left around here," Junior remarked as he caught sight of the object.

"I meant there were none for sale. That one's a personal gift from one of the elders."

Junior showed his surprise. "A gift?"

"Sure. I have pretty good relations with the Vanek myself. I rather like them. They're quiet, peaceful, and they mind their own business: an all-too-rare quality these days."

"I get the point."

Heber smiled. "There's an ancient saying about 'if the shoe fits . . .' But I wasn't necessarily referring to you, Mr. Finch.

In fact, I have no objections whatsoever to your scheme against Jeffers—except, perhaps, to its over-all ineptness."

Again Junior's face registered surprise.

"Since our little chat yesterday, you've been convinced that I'm some sort of a bigot, eh? You've probably got this whole town pegged as being full of bigots, too. It's not, I assure you. We have our share, but let me warn you: overgeneralization can be a serious error on the part of someone trying to institute a few changes."

Junior mulled this over. "Could be I owe you an apology—"

"But you're not ready to say so for sure yet. Just as well. I wouldn't want to hear it anyway." He ran his fingers through a shock of graying hair and indicated a rickety chair. "Let me tell you why your attempt at a boycott failed."

"I'm waiting," Junior said after seating himself. Sunlight was pouring through the dirty front window and illuminating the cloud of dust motes swirling in the air before him. There was a timeless air about the tiny office, as if it had always been there and always would. Junior found his suspicions and hostilities beginning to fade.

Heber cleared his throat as he took his place behind the desk. "Seems to me you overlooked one major fact: Bill Jeffers owns the only general store within thirty kilometers. His closest competitor is old Vince Peck over in Zarico. So to put it simply: if the Vanek don't get their supplies at Jeffers' place, they don't get any supplies. And if they can't get supplies, they don't eat."

"I find that hard to believe," Junior said. "The Vanek were here long before Bill Jeffers arrived with his store. How did they eat then?"

"They lived off the land. They combined farming and nomadism—instead of rotating crops, they rotated the tribe from one field to the next every year. It wasn't easy, but they managed."

"That's what I figured. And if they managed before, they can manage again."

Heber gazed at him. "Have you any idea what it's like to farm this soil? Terran technology has been strained to the limit to bring in a good crop every year. I don't know how the Vanek ever got by. But the point is this: with the arrival of Jeffers and his store, and the discovery that the income from their statues will buy them all the food they can eat, the Vanek gave up farming. And I don't blame them for not wanting to go back to it. It was a full-time, back-breaking job to get their fields to produce. Now they can fill their bellies by doing what they used to do for recreation: carve little statues."

"They could still go back to it if they had to," Junior persisted.

"I suppose they could, but not immediately. The fields are all overgrown now and . . . and there's the very nature of the race. They're a quiet, introverted, contemplative folk. The excess of spare time they enjoy now is perfectly suited to them. They cherish it."

Heber paused and shook his head. "I'm sure they'd like to sit at one of Jeffers' tables and eat their meal inside just like the Terrans, but the price you're asking them to pay is too great."

Junior leaned back and stared at nothing in particular. It was very probable that Heber was right about the Vanek.

"Then I may just have to feed them out of my own pocket until Jeffers softens up," he said suddenly.

"That would take a pile of money," Heber said with narrowed eyes. "You'd have to ship the food in from someplace else. You got that kind of money, Mr. Finch?"

"I've got it."

There was something in Junior's offhanded affirmation that convinced Heber that the younger man had more than a nodding acquaintance with large sums of money.

"Well, if you're that rich, why don't you start your own general store at the other end of town. You could operate at a loss. Or better still, why not buy Jeffers out? Hell! Just go out and buy the whole town of Danzer!"

Heber straightened some papers on his desk as he let this sink in, then, "Somehow, I don't think you'd find that very satisfying, Mr. Finch. Because somehow I sense that there's more to your actions than a desire to put a stop to a little discrimination at the general store."

Junior tried to hide his discomfort with a shrug. His prior suspicions had been confirmed—under Marvin Heber's slow, rough-cut exterior was an acutely perceptive mind.

"And I wouldn't find that very satisfying, either," Heber continued. "Certain ends of my own would be served by seeing you win this one, but not with a big bankroll. If a victory here in Danzer is going to mean anything to you, to me, or to the Vanek, it must be won with the raw materials at hand. Do you see what I mean?"

Junior nodded slowly. It was obvious what winning this

would mean to the Vanek and he was well aware of what it would mean to him. As to Marvin Heber's stake in the affair—he had a vague idea of where he fit in but still couldn't pin the man down. Yet that was of tertiary importance at the moment. His task now was to devise a way to let the Vanek boycott Jeffers' store without making them sacrifice all the conveniences to which they'd become so attached. His brow furrowed, then he jerked upright in his seat.

"Of course! The Vanek have their own income . . . why couldn't they use it to start a general store of their own? A temporary co-op of some sort that they could operate themselves until Jeffers comes around?"

Heber laughed. "The Vanek as shopkeepers? Ridiculous! A Vanek co-op would fall apart in a week. Their minds just aren't geared to inventories, balance sheets, and so on. And besides, it's not on the Great Wheel. You'd just be wasting your time. And remember, you haven't got much of that."

"Why not?"

"That government anti-discrimination bill—it comes up for a vote in less than two months. Some people who're supposed to know what they're talking about say it will pass, too. So you'd better think of something that'll get the job done *your* way, or the butt-ins from the capital will come in and do it *their* way." He punctuated the remark by spitting in the corner.

Junior stood up. "I'll come up with something." He was now sure he knew the reason for Heber's support. He started out but turned as he reached the door. "Thanks, Mr. Heber."

"It's Marvin," he said as he rested his feet on the desk. "And we'll see who thanks who when this thing's over."

Ω

The skim milk sky of pre-dawn found Junior on the road west out of Danzer. A small flock of black-feathered birds darted above him like a sprinkle of iron filings on its way to a magnet as he stopped for a rest at the halfway point to Zarico. It was a long trip to make on foot but he had no other means of transportation, and the general store there offered him the only possible hope of a solution.

The sun was high when he first caught sight of Zarico and his initial feelings of *déjà vu* were heightened as he entered the town. It was as if he had traveled in a tremendous circle and wound up back in Danzer. Peck's general store was of the same design as Jeffers' and it, too, offered a hot lunch.

"Are you busy at the moment, Mr. Peck?" Junior asked as the grizzled old man laid a steaming plateful of stew before him. The store was deserted, and now was as good a time as any to sound him out.

"Not at the moment," Peck replied amiably. "Why?"

"Like to discuss something with you."

"Business?"

"Maybe."

"Find yourself a table and I'll join you in a minute." He disappeared into the back. When he returned, he was carrying an earthen jug and two glasses. Seating himself across from Junior, he filled both glasses about halfway and pushed one across the table. "Nothing like a glass of wine at midday, I always say. Go ahead—try it. It's my own."

Junior did so. The crystal clear fluid was light, dry, surprisingly good. "Very nice. My name's Finch, by the way." Peck nodded and they clinked glasses.

"Well, now," Peck said after a long swallow. "What can I do for you, Mr. Finch?"

"I'd like to talk to you about the Vanek."

"Vanek? We don't have any Vaneks around here. Oh, one or two may pass through now and again, but if you want to know about Vaneks, you'd best go to Danzer."

"I know all I want to know about them," Junior said—which wasn't true. "What I want to know right now is how you feel about them."

Peck finished his glass and refilled it, this time to the brim. "They're all right, I guess. I'm not crazy about their spooky looks but I don't see enough of them to care much one way or the other." He noticed Junior's empty glass so he poured him some more, then drained and refilled his own glass once again.

"Would you mind very much if they bought their supplies here?"

"Hell, no! I'll sell to anyone who's got the money to buy!"

"How about lunch?"

"Sure." He drained his third glass of wine. "Sell them breakfast and even dinner if there's enough of them wanting it."

"Would you let them sit here and eat just as I'm doing?"

Peck paused in mid-pour at this thought, then sloshed the glass full.

"I don't know about that. Vaneks and Terrans don't usually eat together in these parts. Might hurt my business."

"I doubt it. Where else is anybody in Zarico going to go? To Danzer?"

Peck nodded slowly. "I see what you mean."

"And even if you did lose a few customers, I'm going to bring you one Vanek for every Terran customer you've got!" Junior smiled as Peck took a wide-eyed swallow. "That's right. I can double your present business if you'll let the Vanek eat lunch here in the store."

"How're y'gonna get 'em here?" The wine was starting to take effect.

"You must have something around here you use for transportation."

"Sure. I got an ol' lorry out back. It's a wheeled job but it gets around."

"Good. If you let me use that every day, I'll be able to double your profits."

Peck shook his head. "No-no. Won't work. Cause trouble."

"Why?" Junior asked, deciding that now was the time to get aggressive. "Is Bill Jeffers a friend of yours or something?"

"Never met him."

"Then let me give it a try!"

"No. People aroun' here won' like it."

Junior pounded his fist on the table with a ferocity that made the now half-empty wine jug jump. "Who owns this store, anyway?" he shouted. "You gonna let other people tell you how to run your own store?"

Peck straightened his spine and slammed his own fist on the table. "Hell no!"

"Good!" Junior said. He grabbed the jug and filled both glasses to the brim. "Give me a week, and if I can't double your profits in that time, then we'll call the whole thing off."

"I'll drink to that!" said Peck.

Ω

The plan worked well for the first week—profits were not quite doubled but the increase was significant—and Peck extended the trial period. Twice a day, early morning and early afternoon, Junior would squeeze a dozen hesitant Danzer Vanek into the lorry, then ferry them to Zarico. He would return the first group at noon and the second later in the afternoon, then return the lorry to Zarico, where he'd spend the night. Peck had set up living quarters for him in the back of the store.

Things went quite smoothly until the end of the second week. It was twilight and Junior was about to enter the lorry for the trip back to Zarico when someone grabbed his arms from behind and pinned them there. Then he was spun around. Before his eyes could focus on his assailants, a fist was driven into his abdomen and then into his face. This procedure was repeated until Junior lost consciousness. The last thing he remembered was being dragged along the ground, then nothing.

V

OLD PETE

It was nearly a week after their first meeting and Old Pete was in good spirits as he entered Jo's office suite. He had renewed a few old acquaintances around town and had allowed the deBloise matter to slip toward the back of his mind. Jo looked up from her desk as he entered. There was a here-he-is-again sourness in her expression but he didn't let it bother him. She was learning to tolerate his presence—she didn't enjoy it, but put up with it as a necessary and temporary evil.

"You know," he told her, "I just saw a fellow walking down the hall with a rat perched on his shoulder. You taking animal acts under your wing, too?"

"That's no act, and that was no ordinary rat. That man—name's Sam Orzechowski—has managed to tame *rattus interstellus*—"

"Don't try and tell me that was a space rat! Those things can't be trained. If that were a real space rat, it would've swallowed the guy's ear long ago!"

"I checked his background and I can assure you he's all he says he is. Now I have to find some commercial use for the rats. But that's not why I called you here. We've got some information on what's going on with deBloise and Dil."

Old Pete took a seat. "What've you found?"

"Don't know just yet. I put one of the best investigators in the business on the job. He called to say that he's got some interesting news."

"But he didn't say what it was?"

"He never says anything of interest when there's the possibility that the wrong ears might hear it." Something in her voice told Old Pete that there might be more than a professional relationship between Jo and this investigator.

"When does he arrive?" he asked.

"He doesn't," Jo replied with a quick shake of her head. "He never comes to this building. IBA uses his services on a regular basis and frequent visits would give away the relationship. We meet him in a few hours in the casino."

"That's hardly what I'd call a secluded meeting place. It's crowded day and night."

"It's really an excellent place for exchanging information, if you lay the proper groundwork. I make it a practice to visit the casino once a week and he stops in whenever he's in town. That way, no one thinks it strange when we run into each other now and then—especially since we're both avid pokochess players."

"Really? So am I. And I haven't had a good game with another human in a long time; playing against a machine keeps you sharp but somehow lacks something when you win."

"It must get lonely on that island."

"Only once or twice a year do I crave the company of others; but I'm never alone—I have me. Fortunately, I'm not one of those people who, when left alone, is faced with the unpleasant realization that there's really no one there."

The conversation ranged over various topics without direction until Jo brought it around to one of the trouble spots in her mind.

"Did IBA do any investigating into my father's death?"

Old Pete nodded slowly. "Yes. On two occasions. Neither came up with anything useful. It seems that the head man around the town—I think his name was Heber, or Hever, or something like that—anyway, he seemed to have a genuine regard for Junior and made sure that our people had access to everything they needed for the investigation. He had done a pretty thorough job himself before word even got back to IBA that Junior was dead."

"Those aliens murdered him then?"

"That's what all the evidence says. I still can't quite believe it, though. They've got a special marker for his grave and the vid recording of his funeral that was brought back—"

"I know. I've seen it."

"Then you know that they practically thought of him as a demigod. It makes no sense."

"But you left his body there. Why? Not that I have any morbid need to see my father's remains interred on Ragna; I'm just curious as to why you didn't bring them back."

Old Pete shrugged. "Because his body belonged in that Vanek graveyard more than anywhere else."

Jo made no reply. She made a mental note to look up the copy of her father's autopsy report, then her thoughts slipped back to the day her aunt told her that her daddy wouldn't be coming back; that he'd had an accident on a faraway planet and had died. She remembered trying to hold back the anguish and fear and loss by smothering it with denial, but that didn't work. It was true, she knew. Jo cried then, harder and longer than she had ever cried before. Her aunt held her for a long time, now and then joining her in tears. She was never that close to her aunt again. She could not really remember ever crying again since then, either.

Bringing herself back to the present with a start, she rose to her feet. "Time to go. I'll drive."

As the flitter rose from the IBA roof, Old Pete sought to keep the conversation away from Junior.

"I happened to see some of the figures on the currency exchange you started. Not exactly what IBA was intended for, but very impressive."

"Quite the contrary," she said, relishing the chance to correct him. "It's a natural outgrowth of the company's activities. In the course of investigating new markets for clients, we have to keep tabs on the political and economic climates. The monetary policies of local governments are of prime importance, as you well know, so we began indexing rates of inflation, growth of the money supplies, et cetera, for each trade sector. I used some of that data to do a little personal currency speculation a few years ago and did quite well. If a novice like me could make a nice percentage with IBA's index, I figured a currency expert working full time on it could open a new service to our clients. So we hired a couple and we're doing all right."

"You keep much of your own money in that fund?"

Jo shook her head. "I only participate on occasions when I can make a short term gain. If they tell me the Nolevetol *krona* is overvalued, I'll sell them short; if the Derby pound is undervalued, I'll buy a few bundles and wait. Otherwise my money sits in a vault as Tolivian certificates of deposit."

Old Pete nodded approval and said no more. His savings had also been converted to Tolivian CD's long ago. The banks of Tolive were considered an anachronism in many financial circles because they insisted on backing their currency 100 per cent with precious metals. The only coins they issued were 0.999 fine gold or silver, and a "certificate of deposit" meant just that: a given amount of gold or silver was on deposit at that particular bank and was payable on demand. The nominal government of Tolive had only one law concerning monetary policy: all currency must be fully backed by a precious metal; any deviation from that policy was considered fraud and punishable by public flogging.

Old Pete liked the idea of hard money, always had. So did Jo. Apparently she had more in common with him than she cared to admit—

—or with Junior. He was more used to her appearance now. At first sight of her last week, even with her hair darkened toward black, Jo had looked so much like Junior that he had been struck dumb for a moment. But the similarities went beyond mere physical appearance. There was an ambiance about her that reeked of Junior. Anyone who had known the man well would see it in her. He had, of course, expected that, but not to such a degree.

There were differences, too, which were equally startling.

So like Junior, he thought, *and yet so unlike him. I really shouldn't be surprised. After all, their developmental environments were so different. And don't forget the opposing sexual orientation . . .*

As his thoughts began to wander into forbidden ground, he was called back to the present by the sound of Jo's voice.

"There it is," she said, and banked the flitter to the right. "By the way, if you like filet of chispen, they've got a restaurant in the casino that does a superb job on it."

The casino glowed below them like a luminescent fish of prey lurking on an inky sea bottom. Alighting from the flitter onto the roof, they were greeted by an elaborately costumed doorman to whom Jo was obviously a familiar figure. He bowed them through the arched entrance.

The casino consisted of five large rooms arranged in a circular fashion. The elevators from the roof deposited you in the hub and from there you were given free choice as to the manner in which you wished to lose money. Jo headed directly for the pokochess parlor. This was her favorite game, a game of chance and skill in which each player was "dealt" a king, three pawns, and five more pieces randomly chosen from the twelve remaining possibilities. The two players could bet as each new piece was dealt and were allowed to raise the ante whenever a piece was taken during the course of the game.

Pokochess was not too popular with the casino because the house could make a profit only when a guest played one of the house professionals. But the game was the current rage on Ragna and a pokochess parlor in the casino proved to be a good draw. Patrons could use the house tables for a small hourly fee.

Jo stopped at the entrance to the pokochess section and ran her gaze over the room. It came to rest on a nondescript man in his middle thirties sitting alone at a table in a far corner of the room. A shorter, darker man had just left his side and was headed in the direction of the bar.

"There he is," Jo said, a smile lighting her face. She started forward but Old Pete grabbed her elbow.

"That's the man you have working for you?" he asked in a startled tone.

"Yes—Larry Easly. Why?"

Old Pete broke into a laugh. "Because that fellow moving away from him has been working for *me*—and he's Easly's partner!"

"Really?" They started to make their way toward the corner where Easly sat. "Small galaxy, isn't it?"

Old Pete nodded. "Wheels within wheels, *bendreth*."

"What's that mean?"

"Oh, just an old, old expression that means pretty much what you want it to mean." He threw her a sidelong glance. "You mean you've never heard it before?"

"Doesn't sound familiar . . . where'd it originate?"

"Never mind." He didn't want to bring *that* up again.

Easly spotted them then, rose from his seat, and came forward. He and Jo clasped hands briefly, formally, but their eyes locked and held on after the hands had parted. Had he wished it, Larry Easly could have been a distinguished-looking man, but the nature of his work demanded that he downplay any striking features. So he made certain that his posture and the cut of his clothes hid his muscular build, that his complexion and the cut of his dark blond hair invited anonymity.

There was a certain squinting quality about Easly's hazel eyes, almost as if the light hurt them. But Old Pete noted that they were constantly roving under cover of that squint, missing nothing.

Larry Easly extended his hand. "We meet at last, Mr. Paxton."

"I knew we would eventually," Old Pete said, "but this is quite a surprise."

Andrew Tella returned then with a drink-laden waiter in tow. After shaking hands with Old Pete and being introduced to Jo, he handed out drinks—scotch to the former, a glass of cold Moselle to the latter—and they all sat down around a pokochess table.

"You can't be as surprised as Andy and I were when we discovered we'd both been requested to investigate the same thing," Easly said with a trace of a smile. His features were soft, gentle-looking, not at all what Old Pete had expected. "But we guessed what had happened and, since Andy got the assignment first, he had the honor of completing it."

Andy Tella cleared his throat and straightened up in his chair. "Since you're both here to learn of the mysterious doings on Dil, I'll get right to them—and believe me, they make some story."

Easly nodded in agreement as he ignited the end of a torpedo-shaped cigar, but said nothing. Clouds of blue-white smoke encircled his head for a brief instant before being drawn away by the ventilation system.

"First step," Tella began, "was to go to the Fed patent office, use a few contacts, and find out if there's been much activity in the way of new patents from Dil. Answer: yes. A spatial engineer by the name of Denver Haas has recently developed something he calls a 'warp gate' and is ready to go into production. I managed to get a quick look at his file—made a copy of it, naturally"—the briefest of smiles here—"and Larry and I went over it."

Easly picked up the story here. "You must understand, of course, that neither Andy nor I have much of a grounding in physics and those papers were pretty damn technical. We couldn't go around asking experts to decipher them for us because we weren't supposed to have a copy. So we bought some text tapes and came up with a rough idea of what this 'warp gate' is."

"Let's lay some groundwork first," Tella said, and turned to Jo and Old Pete. "Do you know how the warp unit on the average interstellar ship works?"

Jo shrugged. "It creates some kind of field that allows the ship to leave real space and enter subspace where it can take exaggerated advantage of the normal curvature of space."

"Very nicely put," Tella said with an approving nod. "I've been studying this stuff for the past week and I never could have capsulized it so well. But you've got just about everything there. The warp drive lets you travel under the curve of space; the higher the degree of warp, the longer the jump. That 'some kind of field' is important here, because it determines the degree of warp. Warp fields are a poor imitation of the field around a black hole; Haas has gone a step further. He has managed to link a pair of quantum black holes and generate one helluva warp field between them."

"I knew it!" Old Pete slapped the table. "When I heard fifty years ago that they'd found a way to lock up quantum holes in a stasis field, I said someday somebody's going to find a commercial use for those things! And sure enough, somebody has!"

Jo was pensive. "So he's turned things around, eh? Instead of generating the warp from inside the ship, he generates it externally and lets the ship pass through—for a fee, I assume."

"I suppose so," Tella replied. "Either that or a company buys a gate and uses it exclusively for its own craft. They're going to be hellishly expensive, though. Finding quantum holes isn't too hard, but locking them up in a stasis field small enough to make the holes useful and large enough to prevent anything from accidentally entering their event horizons is pretty tricky. But that's not the whole story. Wait'll you hear this: Denver Haas is rumored to be working on modifications that will theoretically allow his warp gate to operate *inside* a planet's gravity well!"

There was stunned silence at Old Pete and Jo's end of the table. The major drawback to the current on-board warp unit was its inability to generate a stable warp field in the presence of any appreciable gravitational influence, whether stellar or planetary in origin. This necessitated the use of peristellar drive tubes to travel past the point of critical influence for a given planet circling a given star. And this type of travel, despite the use of a proton-proton drive in tubes lined with Leason crystals, was maddeningly slow. But if all that could be eliminated, if all you had to do was shuttle up to the ship, board, and then flash through an orbiting warp gate . . .

"If that's truly possible," Old Pete said in an awe-tinged voice, "then man will be able to begin his golden age as an interstellar race."

Easly and Tella glanced at each other and the latter said, "I never looked at it that way, but—"

"But nothing!" the old man retorted. "The first interstellar trips took decades; the perfection of the warp field made them a matter of days, weeks, or months, depending on where you were coming from and where you were going. We are now talking about *hours!* Hours between the stars! Think of what that will mean for trade!"

"The thing is, Mr. Paxton," Easly said patiently, "that this guy Haas hasn't perfected those modifications yet."

"He must have if he's going into production as Andy said."

Easly shook his head. "He's going to market with a prototype that can only operate beyond the critical point in the gravity well."

For the second time that evening, there was dead silence at that particular pokochess table. Jo finally broke it.

"You must be mistaken, Larry."

"I assure you I'm not."

"But it simply doesn't make sense. He'll be trying to market a rather expensive device that offers no real advantage over the on-board warp unit."

"Oh, it has advantages," Easly replied. "The gates generate an extremely high-degree warp, high enough so a ship can travel from gate to gate in a single jump. No more jumping in and out of warp, checking co-ordinates, then jumping again. You just follow a subspace beam from one gate to another."

"Not enough!" Jo said. "The big expense in interstellar travel is time, and the Haas gate that takes days to get to saves no time. The warp jumps are inconvenient, but they add little appreciable time to the trip. If Haas can eliminate the trip out past—and back from—the critical point in the gravity well, he'll have revolutionized interstellar travel; if not, then he's only invented an expensive toy."

"Expensive to his backers, you mean," Old Pete added.

"That, too," Jo agreed with a nod. "Star Ways will see to it that he doesn't sell too many gates."

"How can they do that?" Tella asked. "And why?"

Jo signaled the waiter for another round of drinks before answering. "Star Ways is known as the biggest corporation in human history, right? It's a conglomerate with subsidiaries in every sector of Terran space. Everybody knows that. But what is the basis for its growth to its present size?"

Comprehension suddenly dawned in Tella's face. "Of course! The on-board warp unit!"

"Right. The warp gate is an eventual threat to the product that forms the economic basis for the conglomerate. Star Ways is not going to let anything hurt its warp unit sales if it can help it. It will cut prices to the bone until Haas has to fold."

"The Haas warp gate," Old Pete summarized, "is doomed if it goes to market in its present form. It might have a chance if there were no competition from the conventional warp unit sector—some of the trade fleets might decide to invest in gates as their present onboard units depreciated—but it would be a very slow seller. If someone asked me whether or not to venture any money on Mr. Haas, my answer would be a definite *no*!"

He halted discreetly as the waiter arrived with the fresh drinks, and resumed when the four of them were alone again. "But the question still remains: what's the connection between Haas and deBloise? There's no doubt in my mind now that Doyl Catera was talking about the warp gate when he referred to a technological innovation that could make all planets neighbors. But why is it so important to the Restructurists? What do they hope to get out of it?"

"Well," Easly said after carefully weighing and assessing the facts and opinions that had crisscrossed the table since they had seated themselves, "certainly not a return on their investment."

"You mean deBloise and his crew are backing Haas?" Old Pete sputtered, almost choking on a sip of scotch.

"One hundred per cent. But apparently they don't want anyone to know. They've gone to an awful lot of trouble—three or four dummy investment groups, I'm told—to keep their names out of it. Haas probably doesn't even know they're involved. They've done an excellent job, according to my informant; no one could ever prove conclusively that there was a connection between Denver Haas and the Restructurist big shots . . . and my informant says he'll deny any knowledge of the whole affair if I try to use him as a source."

"Sounds sinister," Jo mused with a glance at Old Pete. "Your conspiracy theory sounds more and more plausible every minute. But the rationale behind the whole thing completely eludes me at the moment."

"I may not know the means," Old Pete offered, "but I know the end: the end of the free market."

Jo wrinkled up her nose in a frankly skeptical grimace.

"You look like you just got a whiff of week-old chispen innards," Old Pete said.

"It's just that it's such an absurd idea. I mean, how can you have commerce without a free market?"

"It can be done. It's not easy, but it can be done. Traders can always find a way. They're the most resourceful members of the species. If a government tries to destroy a free market, as it is often wont to do, by controlling the supply of certain commodities or restricting the free movement of goods, traders and buyers will always manage to get together some way. If the free market is declared void by the government, they make their own. Only then it's known as a 'black' market."

Old Pete paused as he noted the puzzled expressions around him. "I forgot. Your economic education in the outworlds is still very naïve. You lack my advantage of growing up on Earth. I'm all too familiar with things such as excise taxes, trade bureaus, commerce commissions, sales taxes—"

"Sales taxes! What are they?" Tella asked with an amused smile.

"That's a new one on you, is it? You've heard of the income tax, of course. Most outworlds have it in some form or another. That's the way the politicos get your money as it enters your pocket. And when they've taxed that to the limit the populace will tolerate, they go to work on finding ways to get a piece of what's left of your money as it comes *out* of your pocket. That's called a sales tax: you pay a tribute to the current regime every time you buy something."

Jo shook her head in disbelief. "I find it incredible that any population would put up with such abuse. There'd be rioting in the streets here on Ragna if anyone tried to foist that kind of nonsense on us!"

"Don't count on it. As that famous Earth philosopher Muniz put it a long time ago: 'The masses are asses.' And while I don't subscribe to such a cynical, elitist point of view, I fear he may have been right. I never cease to be amazed at what people will put up with if it's presented to them in a pretty package. These tax schemes are always preceded by a propaganda blitz or by a financial crisis that has been either manufactured or caused by the bureaucracy itself. The 'public good' is stressed and before you know it, the public has allowed someone else to slip his hand into its pocket. As time goes on, little by little the state manages to funnel more and more money through its myriad bureaus and eventually the politicians are running the entire economy."

Jo was still dubious. "Who in his or her right mind would allow politicians to make economic policy? Most of them are small-town lawyers who got involved in planetary politics and wound up in the Federation Assembly. They've had a year or so of economic theory in their undergraduate education, usually from a single text tape, and that's the extent of their qualifications in the field of economics. How can they possibly have the gall to want to plan the course of an economy that affects the lives of billions of people?"

"They not only have the gall for it; they will claw and scramble over each other in a mad rush to see who can do more of it."

"Okay. Granted, such men exist and some of them are probably in the Federation Assembly. But I'm sure they're outnumbered."

"I'm going to tell you Paxton's first law," Old Pete said, raising his index finger: "Never trust anyone who runs for office."

"Maybe it's time someone paid a visit to Mr. Haas and got some firsthand information," Easly suggested, getting back to business.

"Good idea, Larry," Jo began. "Why don't you—"

Old Pete interrupted. "I think Jo and I should go see Mr. Haas ourselves. We'll go as representatives of IBA; he's got a product and we want to help him market it. That's our business. What could be more natural?"

Tella and Easly agreed that it was a reasonable approach, but Jo objected.

"Sorry, can't go. Too much work to do."

"You can get away for a while," Old Pete said. "IBA won't fall apart without you. And think of the impact on Mr. Haas when the head of IBA pays a personal visit to his humble abode. Why . . . I'm sure he'll fall all over himself telling us everything we want to know!"

Everyone laughed and Jo reluctantly agreed to accompany Old Pete to Dil. She hated interstellar travel, hated the wave of nausea that hit her every time the ship came in and out of warp. But Dil wasn't that far away and IBA employed a first-rate jump engineer for its executive craft. He could probably make the trip in two jumps and that wouldn't be too bad. She'd bring along some data spools just so the trip wouldn't be a total loss.

The conversation turned to other matters and Old Pete leaned back with a smile on his face and sighed with relief.

VI

JUNIOR

Someone splashed water into his face. It was Heber. His expression was grim as he helped Junior to his feet.

"I was afraid something like this would happen."

"You were, huh? Why didn't you let me in on it?" Junior glanced around as he tried to piece together his whereabouts. He last remembered standing over by the lorry. He had been beaten, then dragged away from it . . . about half a dozen locals stood around him now . . . acrid smoke filled the air . . .

"The lorry!" he cried, and looked past Heber's shoulder. The vehicle was still smoking, though covered with a thick coat of hissing foam.

"Two of Zel Namer's boys did it," Heber told him. "They'd been drinking a bit too much, started feeling mean, and things got out of hand. We've got them locked up for now. I'm just glad they had the sense to drag you far enough from the lorry so's you wouldn't be hurt by the blast."

Junior nodded and gingerly felt his swollen face. "So am I."

The lorry had been parked about one hundred meters from the town center. The locals must have heard the explosion and come running with fire-fighting equipment. His eyes came to rest on a familiar figure: Bill Jeffers stood off to the side, a spent extinguisher dangling from his hand. He sensed Junior's scrutiny and turned.

"I want you to know that I had nothing to do with this, Finch," he said. "Even if you *are* doing your damnedest to put me out of business."

"You know something, Bill," Junior said in a low voice, "I believe you. And the last thing I want to do is put you out of business. All I want you to do is change a few of your policies."

"You're trying to get me to feed a bunch of half-breeds in my store!"

"I'm not forcing you to do anything," Junior said, maintaining a calm, reasoned tone for the benefit of the other locals nearby who were all ears. "Whatever you decide, the choice will be yours and yours alone. I'm just making it more profitable for you to see things my way."

Jeffers fumbled for an answer. Failing to find a suitable one, he wheeled and stalked away.

"Well, whether it's force or not really doesn't matter much now," said Heber, glancing after Jeffers. "Without that lorry, the game is up."

Junior nodded slowly, grimly. "I guess it is. Peck will never jeopardize another one, and I can't say I blame him."

"Maybe something can be worked out," Heber said. His eyes were fixed on the horizon.

"Like what?"

He shrugged. "I'm not sure, yet. But we can always hope, can't we?"

"Guess so. But hope by itself has a notoriously poor efficiency record."

Heber laughed. "Agreed. And since it doesn't look like you're going to make it back to Zarico, you'll need a place to spend the night. C'mon back to the office and I'll fix you up with a cot."

They walked back to the town in silence. Once in the office, Heber reached down between the side of the desk and the wall and pulled out a folding cot.

"I keep this here for times when it gets too hot upstairs."

"You mean you don't have a temperature regulator?" Junior asked.

Heber snorted. "The human race may be able to travel between the stars but there's no temperature regulator in this building, or in any other building in Danzer. You've got to get it into your head, Mr. Finch, that people out here are just scraping by. You may see a flitter truck now and again but don't mistake it for affluence—it's a necessity for some farmers. We live here at just about the same level as pre-space man back on old Earth. It's a different story in the capital, of course; but Danzer and Copia might as well be on different planets. And speaking of Copia, I've got a call to make."

"Where to?"

"You'll find out. But for now, why don't you just lie down on that cot and get some sleep. Things may look better in the morning."

Junior doubted that but nodded agreement. When Heber was gone, he lay back on the cot and put his hands behind his head, planning to stay awake until Heber's return. He was asleep in minutes.

Ω

Someone was shaking him and he opened his eyes. The morning sun was turning from orange to yellow and was streaming through the window into the office.

"Wake up!" Heber was saying. "I've got a vid reporter from the capital waiting to meet you."

Junior jerked upright in the cot. "A vid reporter? Is that who you called in Copia last night?"

Heber nodded. "Yes! And did he jump when I told him what had happened. He seems to think it will make a big story. Wants to meet you right away."

"Damn!" Junior said as he rubbed his eyes and rose to his feet. "Why'd you have to go and do that? You should have asked me about it first."

"What's the matter? I thought you'd be happy."

"Not about a vid reporter, I'm not. They bring nothing but trouble."

"Trouble's already here, I'm afraid," Heber said gravely. "A quick look in the mirror will remind you of that." Junior gingerly touched his swollen, discolored left cheek as Heber continued. "Maybe the knowledge that the vid's got an eye on the town will prevent any follow-ups to last night's incident."

Junior considered this a moment, then shrugged. "Maybe you're right, but I doubt it. Where is he?"

"Right outside. C'mon."

As Junior stepped from the office he saw a compact man in a bright, clean, tailored suit; he was immediately struck by the incongruity of such apparel in the Danzer setting. As the reporter caught sight of him, he snatched up his recording plate and held it out at arm's length. Junior suddenly realized that he must look like hell—his hair uncombed, his bruised face unwashed and unshaven, his clothes slept in.

"Mr. Finch?" said the reporter. "I'm Kevin Lutt from JVS. I'd like to ask you a question or two if I may."

"Sure," Junior said with ill-concealed disinterest. "What do you want to know?"

"Well, first of all, I'd like to get a look at the lorry that was burned."

Junior shrugged. "Follow me." He turned to Heber. "I'll meet you back here later."

Walking ahead as the vid man recorded the scenery, Junior felt ill at ease. He did not relish being probed and questioned about his involvement with the Vanek. It was really no one else's business but his own, but Heber seemed to think an interview would help . . . and things couldn't get much worse, anyway.

When they reached the charred remains of the lorry, Junior stood back and watched as the vid reporter set the scene for an interview. He scanned the wreck, then turned his recorder plate on Junior.

"How does it feel to have so narrowly escaped death, Mr. Finch?" he asked.

"It was no narrow escape. I was dragged a good distance from the lorry before it was fired. No one tried to kill me, just scare me a little."

Lutt tried another tack. "Just what are your reasons for getting involved in this?"

Junior merely shrugged and said, "Wheels within wheels." He didn't like Lutt and he was feeling more and more uncooperative by the minute. The big outside world was threatening to push its way into Danzer and the little town could be ruined in the process. And it would all be his fault.

"Did you know there's legislation pending in the capital that pertains directly to such blatant bigotry as this?"

"Heard something to that effect."

"Then why do you feel it necessary to risk your life to do something that the legislature will do for you in a short time?"

"First of all, Mr. Lutt, let me repeat that my life has not yet been in danger, and most likely will not be. And as for your question: I have never depended on any legislation to do anything whatsoever *for* me. As a matter of fact, it usually winds up doing something *to* me."

Lutt brushed this off. "You're facing a violent, bigoted town, Mr. Finch. The events of last night prove that. Aren't you just a little afraid?"

Junior almost lost control on that one. In typical journalese, Lutt was lumping Heber and all those like him in with the likes of the Namer boys.

"Get lost, Lutt," he snarled and turned away. He was about to start walking back toward town when a movement in the brush caught his eye.

In a slow procession, the Vanek were coming. As he stood and watched them approach, he noted that Lutt had repositioned himself with his recorder plate held high. When the entire group had assembled itself in a semi-circle around Junior, the chief elder stepped forward and raised his hand. As one, the forty-odd Vanek bowed low and held the position as the elder presented Junior with a begging bowl and a detailed carving of a Jebinose fruit tree in full bloom.

"They'll never believe this at home," Lutt muttered breathlessly, recording the scene from different angles.

"Now cut that out!" Junior yelled at the Vanek.

"But, *bendreth*," said the elder, "we wish to pay you honor. You have been harmed on our behalf. This has never happened before and—"

"And nothing!" Junior interrupted. "The whole idea of this little campaign was to get you to assert yourselves and demand the dignity and respect you deserve. I turn around and the next thing I know you're bowing and scraping. Cut it out and stand erect!"

"But you don't understand, *bendreth*," said the elder.

"I think I do," Junior said softly, "and I'll treasure these gifts for as long as I live, but let's forget about gratitude and all that for now. Our main concern at the moment is a replacement for the lorry. Until we can get one, you'll just have to hold out. Borrow from each other, share what food you have until we can get some transportation. Whatever you do, hold to the plan until you hear from me."

The elder nodded and started to bow, but caught himself. "Yes, *bendreth.*"

"And don't bow to anyone—ever." He gave a quick wave and started for the town. Lutt trotted up behind him.

"Mr. Finch, you've just made me a famous man. If I don't get the journalism award for this recording, no one will. I'll never be able to repay you for this."

Junior increased his stride and kept his face averted as he replied. The simple unabashed gratitude in the little Vanek ceremony had moved him more than he cared to admit. As he hurried toward town clutching the bowl and the statue, one under each arm, his eyes were filled with tears.

"You can get lost," he told Lutt.

Ω

Heber smiled and shook his head as Junior gave him a quick rundown of what had happened.

"You can't blame them, really," he said. "Every once in a while a Terran will go out of his way for a Vanek, but you're the first one they've ever known to take a beating on their behalf. You'll probably rate a spot on one of the major spokes of the Great Wheel when they tell their grandchildren about you." He paused, then, "How'd you get on with Lutt?"

"Not too well, I'm afraid. How would you feel if you were tired, dirty, grubby, and hungry, and some fast-talking reporter was sticking his recorder plate in your face and asking a lot of stupid questions?"

"Not too much like being friendly, I suppose," Heber admitted.

"And even under the best of conditions I doubt if you'd have liked the timbre of his questions."

Heber shrugged. "I expect some smug generalizations to come out of this, but publicity—even unfair publicity—may save you from another beating."

Junior rubbed his tender jaw. "I'm all for that."

Ω

Heber entered his office the next morning with a news sheet clutched in his hand. Junior was just finishing off a breakfast ration pack.

"Here—read this! It's fresh from the capital."

"Where'd you get it?"

"About half a dozen reporters came in this morning. One of

them gave it to me." Heber beamed. "We're all over the front page!"

It was true. The first sheet of the vid service's printed counterpart was devoted entirely to the doings in Danzer. As Junior skimmed the story under Lutt's by-line, he saw himself portrayed as a mysterious, closemouthed crusader against bigotry. And in the middle of the front page was a large photo of the Vanek kneeling in homage to him.

"This is incredible! Lutt has played me up like some sort of fictional vid hero!"

"There's not much else doing on Jebinose, I guess, and you seem to make good copy."

Junior dropped the sheet on the desk in disgust and went to the window. "Where are they now?"

"If I said they were out back, where would you go?"

"Out front!"

"Well, don't worry too much now. They're well occupied down the street at the moment with Bill Jeffers. Probably asking him some very pointed questions."

"Oh no!" Junior went to the door and peered out. He could see Jeffers standing in the doorway of his store, surrounded by reporters.

"What's the matter?" Heber asked.

"Does Jeffers have a short temper?"

"He gets hot pretty fast, yes."

"Then I'd better get down there," he said, and was out the door.

As he hurried down the street, he noted that Jeffers was posed in the stance of a cornered animal, his face red, his eyes bright, his muscles coiled to spring. Junior broke into a loping run. It could well be the intention of one of the reporters to provoke the storekeeper into violence—something to make good vid viewing. It wouldn't help the Vanek cause to have the media make a fool of Jeffers and portray him as a violence-prone imbecile; it would only serve to double his obstinance.

"Well, well! 'The Crusader Against Bigotry' has arrived!" Jeffers called and waved a news sheet in the air as he caught sight of Junior approaching.

The reporters immediately forgot Jeffers and turned on Junior with a flurry of questions.

"I'll talk to you later," he said, elbowing his way by them. "Right now I have something to discuss with Mr. Jeffers."

An overweight reporter in a bright green jumper blocked his

path. "We have some questions to ask you first, Mr. Finch." He thrust his recorder plate in Junior's face.

"No you don't," was the tight-lipped reply.

The recorder plate clicked on as the reporter started his interview, oblivious to whatever else Junior had in mind. "Now, first off, just where are you from? Rumor has it that you're an offworlder and I think you should divulge your—"

Without warning, Junior slapped the recorder plate out of the man's hand, grabbed two fistfuls of the shiny fabric of his suit, and shoved him off the boardwalk. Hearing a recorder click into operation behind him, he whirled, snatched the plate, ripped it from the extended hand, and hurled it, too, into the street.

"Now, I said I'd like to speak to Mr. Jeffers. So if you don't mind, wait across the street until I'm finished. It's a private conversation."

"Our viewers have a right—" someone began.

"Look! If you want any kind of an interview at all, you'll wait over there!"

This threat had real meaning for them. They'd had little time with Jeffers and much of that had been stony silence. If there was anything to be gleaned from this long hot trip out to the sticks, it would be in an interview with this Finch character. Slowly, reluctantly, they drifted across to the other side of the street, muttering that they'd rather be off-planet somewhere tracking down the rumor that The Healer was coming to this sector next.

"You should be careful," Jeffers said, watching Junior curiously. "You'll ruin your image."

"I couldn't do that if I tried," he replied with a rueful smile, "just as you couldn't improve yours. They've cast us in our roles and we're locked into them. I'm the hero, you're the villain. My obnoxious behavior just now will be written off in their minds as a personality quirk. If you had acted the same way, it would have demonstrated a basic flaw in your character and people all over the planet would have seen it tonight."

Jeffers made no reply but continued his curious stare.

"Anyway, I guess you can figure out why I'm here, Bill," Junior said finally. "I want to ask you to give in and let's get things back on an even keel around here."

But Jeffers' mind was occupied with something else. "I just can't figure you out, Finch," he muttered, shaking his head in wonder. "Just can't figure you out." Still shaking his head, he turned and disappeared into the darkness within his store.

Junior started to follow, then changed his mind and headed back toward Heber's office, ignoring the waiting reporters. Halfway there, he was stopped by a familiar voice calling him from the street.

"*Bendreth* Finch!" It was Rmrl and he was waving from the cab of a shiny new flitterbus. The vehicle pulled to the curb and Rmrl and a Terran emerged.

"Mr. Finch?" the Terran asked, extending his hand. "I represent a flitter dealer in the capital. Last night we received an anonymous check in full payment for one flitterbus to be delivered to you in Danzer today."

"There's no such thing as an anonymous check," Junior replied as he gauged the size of the bus. It could easily hold thirty or thirty-five Vanek.

"Well, the check wasn't exactly anonymous, but the donor wishes to remain so. I can tell you this, however," he said in a confidential tone, "he's one of the more influential traders on the planet."

Heber, who missed little of what transpired on the street, had come out of his office to see what was going on and heard the last part of the conversation.

"You mean it's free? Free and clear? No strings?"

The flitter dealer nodded. "The donor has reasons of his own, I suppose, but he has asked for no conditions."

Heber slapped Junior on the back. "See! I told you the publicity would do us some good."

"Can't argue with you," Junior said. He turned to the man from the capital. "What can I say? I accept . . . and 'thank you' to whoever donated it."

"Just sign the receipt and it's yours."

Junior signed and turned to Rmrl. "Let's start the shuttle right now." But the Vanek was already halfway into the cab.

Ω

Vince Peck was not particularly overjoyed to see Junior again, even if he did bring along a busload of blue-skinned customers with him. But after Junior promised him the new bus as a replacement for the burned-out lorry, the shopkeeper became more tractable. He even made so bold as to offer Junior a salary.

"Yeah," he said, "receipts have been way up since you

started shipping in these Vaneks, so I guess it's only fair I should pay you a little something. How's ten credits Jebscript a day sound?"

Junior shrugged. "Sounds okay to me. I'm worth twice that, but you're giving me room and board. And I'd prefer something harder than Jebscript—like Tolivian ags—but that would be inconvenient in this neck of the woods. So we'll call it a deal. We'll count today as my first paying workday. Okay?"

Peck's mouth hung open.

"Why so surprised? Did you think I'd refuse?"

"Frankly, yes. I always thought you do-gooder types weren't interested in money."

"Never considered myself much of a do-gooder, Mr. Peck. Always been fairly interested in money, though. And we have a saying in my family: 'Something for nothing breeds contempt.' If I did all this driving for free, you just might take me for granted. And I wouldn't want that to happen." He regarded his new employer with amusement. "I'm glad you brought it up yourself—saved me the trouble of asking you."

Ω

"You wished to speak to me?"

"Yes, sir."

"Well, have a seat."

"Thank you, sir."

"Now, what's on your mind?"

"I understand you have a problem in Danzer, sir."

"You understand nothing of the sort. I have no problem in Danzer or anywhere else."

"If you say so, sir. However, I can take care of that problem very tidily."

"I'm very sorry, but I have no problems to speak of. And if I did, I'm certainly capable of handling them myself. Good day to you."

"As you wish, sir. But here is my number. I can remedy the problem without any evidence that it was remedied. Remember that: no evidence."

Ω

It was sunset. The day's run finished, Junior sat in Marvin Heber's office and savored the evening breeze as it came through the open door and cooled the perspiration on his face.

"Remember when I asked you about a temp regulator a

while back?" He and Heber had become close friends since the lorry-burning incident. The older man nodded.

"Well, I've been thinking. It has its advantages—all-around comfort and all that—but if this little office were regulated, I wouldn't be sitting in this breeze and getting all these fresh smells brought to me for absolutely nothing."

Junior was feeling mellow and very much at peace with himself. "It's really amazing, you know," he rambled, gesturing at the brightening stars. "Out there we've got everything from professional telepaths to genetic architects, and so many people are completely unaware that places such as Danzer exist. And there must be so many Danzers, where people get on with outdated technology and wouldn't have it any other way. I think I'm really glad I came here."

There was a knock on the doorjamb and a young man with an attaché case stood silhouetted in the waning light. "They told me I could find Mr. Finch here."

"That's me."

The man entered. "I'm Carl Tayes and I'd like to speak to you for a moment, if I may."

"Not another reporter, I hope."

"No, not at all. I represent a number of legislators in the capital."

Heber pushed a chair over to the newcomer with his foot. "Sit down."

"Thank you," Tayes said and did so. He placed the attaché case on his lap and opened it. "You've become quite a figure in the last few weeks, Mr. Finch. In that time, you've aroused more planetwide interest in the Vanek Problem than the entire legislature has been able to do in the past few years. But the battle is far from over. Passage of the Vanek Equality Act is not yet assured. To be frank: support is drying up."

"What's this have to do with me?"

"Just this: we would like you to address a few key groups in the capital and urge them to support the bill."

"Not interested," Junior said flatly.

"But you must!"

"I must nothing!" Junior said vehemently and rose from his seat. "What I'm doing here is contrary to everything in that bill! Can't you see that? If I'm successful here, I'll have proved your Vanek Equality Act to be as superfluous as the men who conceived it!"

Heber listened with interest. He was suddenly seeing a different side of Junior Finch and it answered a few lingering questions.

Tayes was framing a reply when Bill Jeffers burst into the office. He held a pair of ledgers high over his head, then slammed them down on Heber's desk.

"Dammit, Finch!" he roared. "I'm licked. I've just been going over my books and I can't last another day! I give! Bring back my Vaneks!"

"What about eating lunch inside with everybody else?" Junior asked, trying desperately to mute his elation.

"I don't care if they hang from the rafters by their toes and eat lunch! Just bring 'em back!"

"Then they'll be there tomorrow." He stuck out his hand. "No hard feelings, I hope."

Jeffers grasped the hand firmly. "No, and I can't figure out why. If you'd been a different sort of guy, I'd've closed up before I gave in. But you, Finch . . . I don't know what it is, but somehow I don't mind losing to you."

"Lose? What did you lose?"

Jeffers brow furrowed, then he smiled. "You know, you're right!" He started to laugh and Junior joined him. There was mirth to the sound, but also the tone of immense tension released and dissipating.

Heber leaned over his desk and clapped both men on the shoulders. "This is wonderful!" he kept saying. "This is wonderful!" Then he, too, joined in the laughter.

"Let's go down to my place for something to drink," Jeffers said finally. "I think I need a good drunk!"

"Good idea," Junior said. "Only I'm buying."

"Coming, Marv?" Jeffers asked.

"Right behind you." Heber glanced at the government man, who had been noticeably silent. "Care to join us?"

Tayes shook his head abruptly and snapped his attaché case shut. "No, thank you. I've got to get back to the capital immediately." He rose and hurried off into the dusk.

The other three headed for the store. Walking between the lanky Heber and the mountainous Jeffers, Junior Finch felt like a man reborn. For perhaps the first time in his adult life, he truly felt like a Finch.

Ω

"Ah! So it's you. I've been expecting your call. I knew you'd need me."

"Never mind that! Can you . . . remedy the situation as you said in my office? With no evidence of . . . anything?"

"Yes."

"Can you do it tonight?"

"Where?"

"Danzer, of course!"

"Yes, that can be arranged. But first there's the matter of compensation for my efforts."

"That's no problem. If you can remedy the situation in the proper way, you will be amply compensated."

"Very well. I'll leave immediately. One thing first, however—I must be absolutely sure of this: we are talking about this Junior Finch character, are we not?"

"I thought that would be obvious. Tell me . . . just what is it you're going to do?"

"You'll know by tomorrow morning."

Ω

Many hours and many quarts of local squeezings later, the party was interrupted by the opening of the front door to the store. A small, sallow man with a receding hairline stepped inside and looked at the three celebrants.

"Private party!" Jeffers roared. "Store's closed. Come back tomorrow."

"Very well," the little man said with a faint smile. Junior noted that the stranger's gaze seemed to rest on him for a moment and he shuddered. He couldn't identify what it was exactly, considering his near-stuporous condition, but there was something cold and very unpleasant in that man's dark eyes. He left without another word, however, and Junior went back to drinking.

"Gentlemen," Junior said, struggling to his feet an hour later, "I'm calling it a night."

"Siddown!" Jeffers said. "There's plenny left."

Junior regarded him with genuine fondness. Throughout the entire episode he had been unable to work up any real dislike for Jeffers. The big man was naturally straightforward and honest . . . just that one blind spot in his character.

"No, Bill. I'm going back to the office to sleep this off. I'm really tight and I'm not used to it. See you both tomorrow."

Heber and Jeffers waved good-by and continued drinking.

Ω

At dawn the next morning, a farmer pulled up outside Jeffers' store and was heading for the door when he noticed something in the shadows of the alley next to the building. He walked over to investigate. Junior Finch lay in the dust, a Vanek ceremonial dagger neatly inserted in his heart.

By late afternoon most of the planet had been informed of the incident and Heber found himself besieged by an army of reporters in his office. It was hot, it was muggy, there was no air to be had in that little room, and he felt sick and wished everyone would just go away. He'd grown very fond of that young man in the few weeks he'd known him, and now he was dead.

"The medical report has just come in," he said in a trembling voice that suddenly quieted the babble-filled office, "and it clears the man you were all very quick to suspect." He paused and spoke with studied deliberateness: *"The time of death has been fixed and I can vouch for Mr. Jeffers at that time.* Is that quite clear?" There was a murmured response, a reluctant acceptance of the fact.

"Now, about the knife. It's utterly ridiculous, of course, to suspect the Vanek. Disregard the fact that there were no human fingerprints or skin cells on the weapon . . . that can be easily managed with a lightweight glove. For even if the Vanek were capable of such an act, Junior Finch would have been the last person on Jebinose they would have harmed. So, we must look for a Terran murderer. It seems to me—"

The crowd of reporters parted as a young Vanek pushed his way through. Heber recognized Rmrl.

"We have come for the knife, *bendreth.*"

"I'm sorry, my friend, but I must keep it for a while . . . evidence, you know."

Rmrl paused, then: "We have come for the body, too. It is to be buried with our ancestors."

"I suppose that can be arranged when the remains are returned from the capital. There's no one else on the planet to claim it and nobody knows where he came from." As the Vanek turned to go, Heber asked, "Do you have any idea who stole the knife, Rmrl?"

"Stole? It was not stolen."

"Then how was it used against him?"

The Vanek's face twisted into a grimace that could only be interpreted as grief. "We killed him, *bendreth*!"

"I refuse to believe that!" Heber gasped as pandemonium broke loose in the little room.

"It is true."

"But what possible reason could you give for such an act?"

"It is written on the Great Wheel," Rmrl blurted, and pushed his way out.

It took Heber a while to restore order to the office, but when it was finally quiet enough for him to speak: "I refuse for a moment to believe that a Vanek plunged a dagger into Junior Finch's heart! They loved that man. No, there's a Terran at work here and he's holding something over the Vanek to make them take the blame." He came out from behind his desk, suddenly looking very old and tired. "Now all of you please get out of here. I've had enough of this for one day."

The reporters filed out slowly, wondering where to go next. One hung back until only he and Heber were in the doorway. He was young and had said little during the afternoon.

"But I thought Vanek never lie," he whispered.

Heber's expression was a mixture of emotional pain and bafflement, with a touch of fear on the edges. "They don't," he said, and closed the door.

Ω

Junior was buried by the Vanek the next day with full rites and honors, a ceremony previously accorded to only the wisest and most beloved of their own race.

Marvin Heber and a number of operatives from the capital made a thorough investigation of the incident but could find no evidence that would lead them to the killer.

And as is so often the case, Junior Finch was mourned and praised by many, understood by only a few. His ghost was tearfully, skillfully, and ruthlessly invoked to obtain enough votes to pass the Vanek Equality Act, the very piece of legislation his efforts had proved unnecessary.

VII

JO

The trip to Dil took two jumps and six standard days, and really wasn't too bad physically. Emotionally, however, it was wearing. Old Pete was her only company and Jo found it impossible to generate any warmth for the man. She had done her best to get out of the trip—had even hoped that Haas would refuse to see them. No such luck. He was delighted to give them an appointment.

The shipboard time did, however, give her a chance to study her old nemesis, and she found him more puzzling than ever. He was maneuvering her toward something. Pretending to allow her to take the lead, he was actually calling all the plays. But what was the final destination?

And what was his stake in all this? He was out of the company and probably running out of years. Why was he out between the stars with her now?

The pieces didn't fit into a picture that made any sense to

her. Everything Old Pete had done had been for her benefit. Why then did she feel she couldn't trust him? Why did she always feel he was hiding something? And he was. Despite countless protestations to the contrary, she knew he was guarding something from her.

Her father's autopsy report was another thing that bothered her. It was incomplete: a whole section was blank. Nothing of any pertinence was missing—the cause of death, a myocardial laceration by a Vanek ceremonial knife, was incontestable—but the blank area gnawed at her. Old Pete had obtained the report but couldn't explain the lapse. Jo would find out sooner or later, though. It wasn't her way to let things ride. Just as it hadn't been her way to sit back and passively collect the annuity from her father's IBA stock.

Jo couldn't remember exactly when she decided to put a Finch back into IBA—somewhere in her mid-teens, she guessed—but it soon grew to be an obsession with her. She studied the history of the company, its solid successes, its more notorious gambles. She grew to be an authority on its workings, maneuverings, and strategies. After tracking down all the printed and unprinted stories of Joe Finch's Earthside and outworld exploits, Jo became infatuated with her grandfather. She was only seven when his flitter crashed, and had vague memories of a very tall man who always had a present or two concealed on his person. And the more she learned about him, the more he grew in stature. By the time she was ready to make her move on IBA, Joe Finch was a giant in her mind.

Old Pete was another matter, however. She knew that IBA had used his theories as a base and probably would not have existed at all without him. He was an integral part of the company's history. She admired him for that, but no amount of admiration could offset the deep conviction that he was responsible for her father's absence. She would need his help, however, if IBA was to have a Finch in charge again.

Surprisingly, Old Pete had gone along with her. After a long conversation during which he quizzed her on the theoretical and practical aspects of IBA's operations, and was suitably impressed, he not only returned her father's stock to her, but gave her proxy power over his own to use as she saw fit when she faced the board of directors. The gesture seemed as out of character then as it did now, but Jo hadn't argued.

The board of directors—seven hard-nosed, tough-minded business professionals; over two centuries of experience in the constant give-and-take of the interstellar markets seated around a conference table, smiling politely and condescendingly as she rose to address them.

The mood around the table was tinged with amusement when she began but had undergone a startling metamorphosis by the time she was finished. The smiles were gone, replaced by expressions of anger, shock, and resentment.

Never would she forget that day. She had been frightened and shaking before beginning her speech, and was bathed in perspiration at its finish. Five of the directors tendered their resignations on the spot in an obvious attempt to frighten her into backing down. She called their bluff, and within three weeks the two remaining directors had joined the others. The official reason for the resignations of all seven directors was that the handwriting was on the wall: IBA was on its way to becoming a family company again and this would mean the institution of despotic control over the board. This, being contrary to their concept of the position of the board of directors in the company hierarchy, left them no alternative but to resign.

Privately, they told their friends that they had no intentions of taking orders from a green kid. Especially a green *female* kid.

That had been the deciding factor, Jo knew: her sex. Those men would not work for a woman. It was a matter of pride for them, but the problem went deeper. They had no confidence in a woman's ability to run a company of IBA's complexity.

Strangely enough, Old Pete did not seem to share that view, probably because he was an Earthie. And Earthies, despite all their crowding, their decadence, their bureaucracy-strangled lives, considered males and females equal. In the colonial days, outworlders had held that view, too. Men and women had made the trip out to the stars as equals, had made landfall as equals, and had started the colonies as equals. After a while, however, things changed . . . especially on the splinter worlds. With little or no contact with the mother planet, the level of technology slipped and the embryo initiators and fetal maintenance units were often among the first pieces of hardware to fall into disrepair.

Children—lots of them—were a vital necessity to the settlements if they were going to survive past the second or third generation, so . . . the colonists returned to the old-fashioned kind of fetal maintenance unit, and the technicians, navigators, and engineers who happened to be female were soon relegated to the roles of baby-bearers and nest-keepers.

Now, centuries later, after the colonies had come into their own as the outworlds, banding together under the Metep Imperium at first, and now under the Federation banner, the attitude remained: a woman's place was in the home.

Jo couldn't—wouldn't—accept that. But her rejection of the prevailing attitudes toward women was not a conscious struggle, nor a crusade. She carried no banners and nailed no theses to the door. After taking over IBA, she was approached by numerous groups pushing for male-female parity but she eschewed them all—partly because she didn't have time and partly because she couldn't really grasp the problem. As far as she could see, women wound up in secondary roles because they accepted them. It would have been easy for her to live off the proceeds of her stock in IBA, but she hadn't been able to accept that. She felt she had a right to lead the company and lead it she would. If anyone objected, he'd better have a good reason or get out of the way. Jo had often been called shortsighted and selfish for this, but her invariable reply was, Excuse me, I've got work to do.

In interstellar trade circles, it was almost unthinkable that a woman should head a major corporation. It had never really occurred to Jo's mind that a woman should not do so. And that was the major difference between Josephine Finch and her contemporaries: others spent their time shouting about woman's equality to man; Jo spent hers proving it.

Ω

Word came back that the ship was about to enter orbit, so Jo and Old Pete got their things together and prepared to make the transfer to the shuttle. Dil's name was not well known among the inhabited worlds; it was an industrious little planet but had little in the way of natural beauty and no political notoriety.

Not too far from Dil's main spaceport was the warehouse Denver Haas called home, a large ramshackle affair with a high fence around the perimeter. The most vital and innovative aspects of his warp gate were now protected by Federation patents, but Haas was involved in further refinements and so security remained tight. Jo and Old Pete had to be cleared twice before they were allowed to enter the building.

Haas was obviously not out to impress anyone. The inside

of the building was as dingy as the outside and a lone, harried receptionist-secretary occupied the single desk within the cluttered foyer.

Jo handed the girl a clearance pass. "Josephine Finch and Peter Paxton to see Mr. Haas," she said.

The girl took the pass without looking up, checked the appointment book, and nodded. Pressing a button, she said, "Finch and Paxton are here."

"Send them in!" replied a gruff voice.

The girl pointed to a nondescript door with a simple "Haas" printed on it. Jo knocked and entered with Old Pete trailing a few steps behind.

The office was an incredible clutter of filing cabinets, diagrams, blueprints, microstats, and miscellaneous notes and drawings on scraps of paper. Denver Haas, a stubby, feverish little man, was bent over his desk, reading and making notes, looking like a gnome king ensconced among his treasures. He glanced up as he heard the door close.

"Ah, Miss Finch and Mr. Paxton," he said, smiling tightly. "You've come. This is quite an honor, even if it is a waste of time for the three of us."

Only one empty chair sat before the desk. Haas rose, gathered some papers off another chair in a corner and threw them on the floor. Pushing the chair around to the front of the desk, he said to Jo, "Sit here," and indicated the other seat for Old Pete.

They did as they were bid and waited for the little man to regain his own seat. He was older than Jo had imagined, with gnarled hands, an unruly shock of graying hair, and, of all things, a beard. With all the permanent depilation techniques available, facial hair was an unusual sight.

"Well, just what is it you wanted to see me about?" he demanded abruptly. "As if I didn't know."

"Your warp gate," Jo stated with her customary directness.

"I thought that was it," Haas muttered, and shook his head. "I've paid a small fortune for what I was assured was the best available security, and here you walk in and talk about my warp gate like you just had it for lunch!"

"Word of something like that gets around," Jo assured him, "especially since this isn't exactly a one-man operation."

Haas's head snapped around. "What do you mean by that? This is my creation! Mine! From the first diagram to the working model—mine!"

"And financed entirely by you, of course."

"What do you know about my financing?" Haas asked in clipped tones.

"Not much. But outside financing causes outside talk, and I keep myself informed on any talk about innovative devices."

"I'll bet you do."

"It's my job. And because it's my job, I've traveled all the way from Ragna to try and convince you that you need IBA. Your device has good potential, but we can make sure you get the most out of it."

" 'Good potential,' you say?" he said mockingly with what he probably thought was a sly smile. "It has excellent—it has *astounding* potential! So what makes you think I need any help at all from IBA?"

"Because you're going to market too soon."

"That is a matter of opinion, Miss Finch."

"It's fact, I'm afraid. Your gate has the potential for use inside a planet's gravity well, but you haven't perfected that aspect yet, and it's that—"

Haas slammed his fist down on his desk and shot to his feet. "How do you know all this! How can you! It's all secret! No one's supposed to know!"

A thought drifted through Jo's mind, like a small winged thing banking off an updraft: *What a naïve little man.* But she refused to allow herself to be drawn from the matter at hand.

"When are you planning to introduce the gate on the market, Mr. Haas? Within one standard year, am I correct?"

Haas nodded, amazed that this young woman could know so much about his affairs.

"And when will the intra-gravity well capability be perfected?"

Haas seated himself again. "Five standards or so," he said hoarsely.

"Well, then. My advice is to wait. It will be extremely difficult to generate much interest in the gate as it stands. You must remember that every interstellar freighter currently in use is equipped with its own on-board warper. These ships have absolutely no use for a warp gate stationed at the critical point in the gravity well; it does little for them that they can't do themselves. The big companies might purchase a few for high traffic use along the major trade lanes, but the smaller companies are going to be hard-pressed to meet what I assume will be a very steep price. In brief, Mr. Hass: without the intra-gravity well capability, your warp gate will never get off the ground."

Haas snorted. "We've already considered all that and dismissed it. There will be an initial flood of orders, no question about it. And when that comes in, we'll be able to produce subsequent gates at reduced cost due to increased production scale." Clasping his hands behind his neck, he leaned back in his chair with a what-do-you-think-of-that? look on his face. "You see? We've taken everything into account."

"Have you? What about Star Ways?"

"What about it?"

"Competition. You don't—"

Haas's burst of harsh laughter cut Jo off. "Competition! The gate is unique! There is *no* competition."

"If you'd let me finish what I was about to say," Jo snapped with thinning patience, "you might learn something. You don't really think that SW is going to sit still and let you make its primary product obsolete, do you? It's going to cut its prices on the on-board warper and it's going to keep those prices down—way down—until you fold. And when you go out of business, SW will come along and lease the rights to the warp gate from you and sell it for you. The royalties you'll receive in return will net you enough money to buy a small planet, but your company will be gone." Her voice softened. "IBA can prevent that from happening. Or if not, we'll at least give that big conglomerate a battle the likes of which it's never seen."

"No," Haas said in an intense, low voice as he leaned forward and rested his arms on the desk. "That will never happen. Star Ways will never get the rights to the gate because I own them completely—*completely!* And I'll never sell or lease or rent or trade them. No matter what the price. It's not the money any more . . ." His eyes seemed to glaze, and though he was looking in Jo's direction, he wasn't seeing her. "It's something more than that. The warp gate is my life. I've worked on nothing else for as long as I can remember. Only recently have I been able to devote my full time to it, but it's always been with me. I've worked as an engineer, a designer, even a technician when times weren't so good, but I've always come home to the gate. It's part of me now. I would no sooner lease the gate to another company than I would lease my right arm to another man. The Haas Company will only lease the rights from me; and if the Haas Company can't sell the gate, no one else will. That I promise you."

There was silence in the room. Jo frowned and wondered if deBloise and his associates were aware of Haas's monomania. She could see nothing but financial ruin ahead.

Old Pete's thoughts ran along a different path. He'd been silent since they'd entered the room, watching and admiring the way Jo handled herself. He'd also been studying Haas and had been moved by the little man's disturbed and revealing statements. A little old man—younger than Pete, yes, but still old—with a dream. His body, and perhaps his mind, were becoming unreliable vehicles, but still he drove them toward that dream. A dream! For a person in his or her second or third decade it would be called a dream; for someone Denver Haas's age, it would no doubt be termed an obsession.

Old Pete finally broke the silence. "I wonder what your backers would say if they learned of your attitude."

"They know all about it," Haas replied. "I've always leveled with potential backers." A thin smile briefly straightened the habitual downward curve of his lips. "That's why backers have been a rare species for me. But these fellows—they're with me 100 per cent."

Jo was stunned by the statement. It didn't make sense. "They know, and they're still with you?"

Haas nodded.

"Would you mind telling us the names of your backers?" Old Pete asked.

"Not at all. Be glad to tell you if I knew, but I don't. Oh, I could tell you the names they gave me, but I know they're fronts. For some reason, they wish to remain anonymous—strange, but none of my concern, really. I've searched long and hard to find men with vision such as these. We're in complete accord and everything is legal, so I couldn't care less if they want to remain anonymous."

"They know you want to put the gate on the market as is?" Jo repeated, bafflement wrinkling her forehead.

"Know? They not only know, they've encouraged me to move as quickly as possible. They see no reason to let the gate languish in its present state when it could be earning a good return on their investment while I perfect the modifications." He rose. "And now I must get back to my work. But I do want to thank you both for stopping in: I've always had the utmost confidence in the gate, but you've managed to boost it even higher."

"That wasn't our intention, I assure you," Jo said.

"Well, that's the net effect, no matter what you intended. I was shocked at first by how much you knew about the gate, but then I realized that IBA has far-reaching contacts. The fact that you're interested enough in the gate to come this far in person in order to get in on the kill, that's proof enough for me that its success is guaranteed. Everybody knows that IBA rarely takes on losers."

Jo wanted to say that most of her clients were losers *before* seeking out IBA's help, but realized the futility of further talk. IBA could have done a lot for him, but under no circumstances could she work with a man like Denver Haas. Shrugging, she rose to her feet and turned toward the door.

"Oh, and there's one little factor you completely neglected in your assessment of the gate's chances on the market," Haas said in a gloating tone.

Jo threw him a questioning glance.

"Military contracts! You forgot all about the military possibilities of the gate! It's perfect for supply and personnel transport on a large scale!" He smiled expansively. "Yes, I don't think there'll be any problem in getting those initial orders. We'll just sit back and let them roll in."

"Good day, Mr. Haas," Jo said, continuing toward the door. "And good luck."

Old Pete followed her out, shaking his head sadly.

Ω

Preoccupied silence filled the rented flitter as they headed back to the spaceport. Neither of them noticed a man leave the Haas warehouse after them and enter his own flitter. He was not far behind when they docked their craft in the rental drop-off zone.

"Well," said Old Pete as they entered a lounge alcove to await seats on a shuttle up to their orbiting ship, "I certainly don't know what to make of it."

"I'm in a daze myself," Jo replied. "Especially after his parting shot: military contracts! The man's mad!"

"Obsessed, maybe. But not mad. At least not completely."

"But military contracts! The Federation Defense Force will, I'm sure, be glad to know that such a thing as the warp gate is available, but the prospects of a big order are nil."

"I doubt if the DF will buy a single unit."

"Why do people like Haas allow themselves to get involved in the business end of things?" Jo mused. "He's unquestionably a brilliant designer and theorist—the existence of the gate proves that—but he has no idea of the economic forces against him in the market. We could do a lot for him, you know. Right now I've got a good half-dozen ideas that could possibly get him through the first few years until he worked out the necessary modifications. But as it stands now, SW will wipe him out in no time and deBloise and his crew will lose all their money."

Old Pete grunted. "That's what bothers me: deBloise throwing away a fortune. I've never met that man, Josephine, but I know him . . . I know him as well as his mother, his father, and his wife know him. I probably know some things about him that even *he* doesn't know. And one thing's certain: he's not a fool. He's crafty, he covers all exits, and his involvement in this fiasco-to-be is totally out of character."

"Which leaves us with only one possible conclusion," Jo said, glancing at a man leaning against a wall outside the lounge area. It almost seemed as if he were watching them.

"I know," Old Pete replied in a breathy voice. "DeBloise knows something we don't know. And that bothers me."

Jo dismissed the watcher as just another bored traveler; this conspiracy talk must be getting to her. "What bothers me more is the thought that the warp gate could be lost to us. I mean, what if Haas's company folds and he really does decide to withhold the gate from sale or lease or whatever. That could be tragic."

Old Pete shrugged. "Tragic, yes. But he'd be perfectly within his rights. According to Andy, the patents are good for at least another couple of decades. The human race would just have to wait it out."

The signal for their shuttle flight flashed and they rode the belt out onto the field. The man who had been standing across from the lounge area went up to the observation deck and watched them enter the shuttle. Only after the craft was airborne did he go below.

He headed directly for the row of subspace transmission booths that are a feature at every spaceport. Entering the first booth, he sealed himself in, opaqued the glass, and began to transmit an urgent message to Fed Central.

VIII

DEBLOISE

The barroom was done entirely in wood, something you didn't see much any more on Fed Central. But this section of the club had originally been a tavern in the Imperium days and had been preserved in the original state. The bar itself was the same one patrons had leaned on nearly three centuries ago when the place had been called the White Hart, its solid *keerni* wood preserved under a clear, thick, high-gloss coating through which an idle drinker could still make out doodles and initials scratched into the original finish.

It belonged now to the Sentinal Club, the oldest, most respected, most exclusive club in the outworlds. Membership was strictly male, and restricted to those who had managed to achieve status in the financial, political, and artistic spheres. Elson deBloise reveled in such a rarefied atmosphere, felt a real sense of place and purpose here. He belonged here. There was no comparable establishment on his homeworld where a man of his breeding and wealthy heritage could be among his peers.

He was not among his peers at the moment, however. The hour was a shade early and he was alone at the bar, hunched over a delicate glassful of Derbian orchid wine. The green-tinged fluid was a little too sweet for his taste but was all the rage on Fed Central these days, so he ordered it whenever he was out. Had to keep up with the times, be as modern as the next man, if not more so. Talk about tomorrow, never about the old days.

Because nobody around here thought of the old days as good. LaNague had seen to that: his revolution had changed more than the power structure; it had reached into the hearts and minds of his contemporaries and caused a fundamental alteration in the way they viewed their society. Today, generations later, outworld thinking was still influenced by the lesson of that revolution. So a conservative image had to be avoided at all costs.

"Restructurist" was much preferred as a label. It was neutral in emotional tone and had a certain progressive ring to it. After all, that's what they intended to do—restructure the Federation. DeBloise smiled to himself. Restructure? They were going to turn it upside down and twist it around.

He continued to smile. It was fitting in a way that he should be sitting here in this converted tavern plotting the scrapping of the LaNague Charter. It was said that Peter LaNague and Den Broohnin had spent many an evening in this very room when it was called the White Hart as they conspired to bring down the Metep Imperium nearly three centuries ago.

And what a conspiracy that had been! Despite the fact that deBloise publicly minimized LaNague's contribution to the revolution, despite the fact that the Restructurist movement had for years been engaged in a clandestine campaign to discredit the bizarre society that had spawned LaNague, thereby discrediting the man himself, despite the fact that the man's ingenious wording of the charter had frustrated Restructurists for generations, he had to grant LaNague grudging admiration. His conspiracy had reached into every level of Imperial society, had stretched from the deepest galactic probe to Earth itself. Utterly masterful!

DeBloise felt he could be generous in his praise. After all, he was the engineer of a conspiracy of his own. True, it didn't have the breadth and depth of LaNague's, and its flashpoint would be nowhere near as brilliant and dramatic, but its outcome would eventually prove to be as crucial to the course of human history. The Haas warp gate provided the key. And when that key was turned, there would be furious protests in some quarters, but nothing that could not be soothed by promises that the invocation of the emergency clause in the charter was merely temporary. All would soon return to normal just as soon as we get this one little matter settled, they would say.

But things would never be the same again. A single instance of forceful intervention in the interstellar economy by the Federation was all that was necessary; thereafter, the power of the charter to restrain the Restructurists would be effectively broken. In a few standard years, the charter would be a revered but vestigial document and the Federation would be under complete Restructurist control.

He could almost picture himself on the high presidential dais after the next Assembly elections. He deserved that seat. He'd worked for it. It had taken many years of searching and planning to find the right issue—volatile enough to energize the Assembly, and yet still manageable as to timing and discretion concerning his involvement. Only he had seen the political potential of Haas's invention; only he had possessed the influence over his fellow Restructurists to convince them to go along with his plan.

Yes, he deserved the presidential seat. And he'd make good use of it once it was his. All economic activity—and thereby all *human* activity—within the Federation would come under his supervision. Bringing the larger corporations and trade services to heel would be no easy matter but it could be done. First he'd start singling out oddball planets like Flint and Tolive and bring them into line through trade sanctions—they'd never willingly accept a Restructurist-dominated Federation. The corporations would naturally protest since they didn't like anyone to close a market to them. When they did, he'd bring the full weight of a bolstered Federation Defense Force against them. And when they tried to bribe him—as he knew they eventually must—he would righteously expose them as the money-grubbing leeches they were.

And soon . . . soon humanity would shape itself into a cohesive unit, soon there would be true harmony and equality among the planets, each sharing in the bounties of the others. Soon there would begin a new Golden Age for humanity, a Golden Age designed and administered by Elson deBloise.

LaNague had had an opportunity to take a similar course three centuries ago; he'd held the outworlds in the palm of his hand but had refused to grasp them. Instead, he presented them with his charter and hurled them free. Such an act remained far beyond deBloise's comprehension. The human race needed someone to guide it and oversee its course. The great mass of humanity had no thought of destiny. Too many individuals expended their energies in chase of puny, short-sighted goals. They all needed direction and deBloise was convinced he could provide it.

There would, of course, be those who'd insist on choosing their own course and the rest of humanity be damned. There would always be self-styled individuals who'd selfishly insist on pursuing their own personal values. These would have to be discouraged or weeded out from the vast body of the human race.

He'd also have to contend with that other breed of nay-sayer: the ones who could point to history and say that economies and societies controlled from the top have never succeeded; that the impetus for a society must come from within, not from above.

But he knew that no society in history had ever had a man such as Elson deBloise at its helm. Where others had failed, he could succeed.

A few years ago such thoughts would have been idle fantasies, but now the actual means to achieve them was in his grasp. It was all so exhilarating, almost intoxicating, that even the prospect of today's departure for his homeworld couldn't take the edge off his mood. He checked the chronometer on the wall: he had another hour to kill before his orbital shuttle left the spaceport.

He flagged the bored bartender and indicated his need for a refill. The man dutifully complied and then returned to the far end of the bar. He had tried in the past to strike up a friendly conversation with deBloise—the Sentinal Club paid him well to add the human touch to bar service—but had been rudely ignored each time. So now he kept his distance from Mr. deBloise. And deBloise in turn studied his fingernails as the glass was filled; if he'd been interested in socializing with the likes of the bartender, he would have had his drinks out at the spaceport bar.

He really didn't need the extra drink—he'd already had two before leaving Anni's—but decided to have it anyway. The next few days would be spent aboard a Federation liner. The passenger list would contain the names of many elite and no doubt interesting people, some of whom would surely be from his homeworld. And thus he'd be dutybound to play his role of Elson deBloise, sector representative and leader of the Restructurist movement, to the hilt.

The role became trying after a while. That's when he would miss Anni. She was an excellent mistress, socially and sexually skilled—he could let down his guard with her. Yes, he'd miss her the most. Not sexually, however. With the final stages of the Haas plan fast approaching, he'd found himself unable to perform without the use of drugs. The plan dominated his thoughts every hour of the day, sapping his strength and sorely trying his patience.

He smiled again, wondering what the reaction would be if it became generally known that he kept a mistress on Fed Central. A respected sector representative . . . and a family man, too! It was a common practice in the Assembly and no one paid it too much mind in the cosmopolitan atmosphere here. But it would be difficult for those provincial clods at home to swallow; they were all firm believers in faithful monogamy, or at least pretended to be. If it came out, someone would no doubt try to score some political points with it on the local level, and his home life would be disrupted for a while; he'd deny it all, of course, and before too long it would all be forgotten. Voters have always had short memories.

No, there wasn't much he could do short of a violent crime or a public obscenity that would significantly erode his support among the yokels back home. He had led the sector into the Restructurist fold with promises of economic rebirth; they expected him to deliver on those promises . . . someday. Until then, he was the local boy who'd made good and they would follow him anywhere.

But there were always dues to pay. His wife and children remained at home; he wanted it that way. There was, after all, the children's education to think of—it wouldn't do to have them hopping back and forth between worlds—and besides, his wife would help to keep his presence felt on the homeworld when he was off on Federation business. Still, he had to return on a regular basis. The yokels expected it. He had to be seen among them, had to appear at certain local functions, had to play ombudsman for the sector.

And it was all such a bore, really, listening to their petty complaints and trivial problems when there were so very many much more important things that required his attention . . . like the Haas plan. But, *noblesse oblige.*

There was another reason he disliked going home: a little man named Cando Proska. By the Core, how that monster of a human being frightened him! And as sure as Fed Central circled its primary, he'd be calling at the deBloise office with a new demand. But enough of that! Such thoughts were disturbing.

Another glance at the chronometer showed that it was time to go. He pulled a rectangular disk from his pocket, tapped in a code, and his secretary's face appeared. After telling her to send a flitter to the Sentinal Club to take him to the spaceport, he was about to blank the screen when he noticed that she seemed to be disturbed.

"Something wrong, Jenna?" he asked.

She shrugged. "One of the girls on the second floor came down with the horrors at lunch."

DeBloise muttered his condolences and faded her out. The horrors—he'd almost forgotten about that. The plague of random insanity that had started before he was born and continued to this day was something that everyone in Occupied Space had learned to live with, but it was something that was rarely forgotten. New cases popped up daily on every planet. Yet the Haas plan had pushed it almost entirely from his mind.

He rose to his feet and quickly downed the rest of the wine. The juxtaposition of Haas and the horrors in his thoughts was unsettling. What if Haas got hit by the horrors? The whole plan would have to be scuttled. Worse yet: what if he himself were struck down?

He didn't dare think about that too much, especially since The Healer, the only man thus far able to do anything about the horrors, had seemingly vanished a few years ago. And as each succeeding year passed, deBloise became more firmly convinced that he had been responsible for precipitating The Healer's disappearance.

It had happened on Tolive. DeBloise had traveled all the way to IMC headquarters to talk to the man, to convince him gently to see things in a light more favorable to Restructurism, and had wound up threatening him. The Healer had only smiled—an icy smile that deBloise remembered vividly to this day—and departed. No one had seen or heard from him since. He was probably dead, but there was still this nagging suspicion . . .

A light flashed above the bar, indicating that someone had a flitter waiting, and deBloise hurried to the roof as if to escape thoughts of the horrors and enigmatic men who could not be bullied or cajoled into line. Thank the Core there weren't too many of those around.

As he took his seat, the flitter driver handed him a coded message disk. He tapped in a combination that only he and a few of his closest associates knew, and five lines of print began to glow on the black surface. The words would remain lit for fifteen seconds, then would be automatically and permanently erased. There could be no recall.

The lines read:

Haas had two visitors today
Young female named Josephine Finch
Older man unidentified as yet
Both from IBA
Any instructions?

T.

There had obviously been a leak, but that was not what occupied deBloise's mind at that moment. It was the name Finch. It seemed to mean something to him . . . and then it came, rushing out of the past.

Of course. Finch. How could he have forgotten?

An uneasy feeling settled over him and he couldn't shake it off.

Finch.

There couldn't be any connection, could there? Of course not. It was just a coincidence. Just an awful coincidence.

IX

EASLY

Easly ran the fingers of his right hand up and down the middle of Jo's bare back and wondered idly how she continued to have such a disconcerting effect on him.

Not when they were out in public, of course. Then everything was always cool and professional. They both had their roles and played them well—*lived* them well. She was mistress of a respected business advisory firm; he was master of an information-gathering service. They'd meet now and then for a game or two of pokochess and, if time permitted, perhaps a light meal afterward. They were two self-sufficient and self-reliant individuals who enjoyed each other's company on occasion, but otherwise led separate personal lives. That was in public. And he could handle that easily enough.

But when they were alone, especially like this—in bed, skin to skin, tangled limbs and breathless afterglow, communicating in the tiniest whispers, barely moving their lips and eyes—at times like these he found himself totally bewildered at the emotional bond that had grown between them. He'd never known a woman like Jo.

And he'd never expected to become emotionally involved with a client. But, then, virtually all of his clients had been male until Jo.

Until Jo. So many things these days seemed to start and end with that phrase.

It seemed like only just the other day that he'd received her message requesting a meeting about a possible assignment. He had hesitated then at the thought of taking her on as a client. He had never dealt with a woman on those terms, and if her last name had been anything other than Finch, he might well have turned her down.

He was glad he hadn't, for he'd found her delightful. Expecting a staid, middle-aged matron, he discovered instead a bright, vivacious creature who could sparkle with the best of them and yet had a laser-quick mind, strong opinions, and unquestionable integrity. Before long, he found himself looking forward to their meetings, not just for the intriguing assignments that often developed, but for the stimulus he derived from her company. He would search for ways to increase the frequency of their meetings, and to prolong them once they were together.

Eventually, they met for other than business reasons and quickly graduated to the sexual intimacy of lovers. Here, again, Jo surprised him. For one so cool and seemingly detached across a pokochess board or a dinner table, she exhibited a passion and a lack of inhibition between the sheets that to this day continued to leave him gasping.

An enigma, this woman. Easly couldn't decide whether she was a core of steel with a woman's exterior, or a vulnerable little girl hiding behind a metallic patina. Sometimes she seemed one, sometimes the other. He was forever off balance, but delightfully so.

One thing was certain: this woman was a friend. She was a companion; she complemented him, rounded him off, made him feel somehow more complete when he was with her than when he was not. Especially at a time like this when they had each other totally to themselves.

She was a *friend,* and he wasn't used to having friends who were women. Until Jo.

He had told Jo that once, and she'd haughtily called him a

typical product of the outworlds. On the surface, he resented being called typically anything, but inwardly he was forced to admit she was right. His view of women had been typically and rigidly stereotyped: they were frail, lovable creatures, good for homekeeping and bed-warming, requiring affection, protection, and occasionally a good swift kick; their capacity for original thought and practical behavior in the outside world was strictly limited.

He'd never verbalized these concepts, of course; he owed himself credit for that. But he also had to admit to being surprised whenever a woman exhibited prowess in any field of endeavor outside the home, thus eminently qualifying him for the title, "Typical Product of the Outworlds." Until Jo.

In the past his relationships with women had been fleeting and superficial. Intentionally so. Women were for huddling with, for satisfying mutually urgent physical needs, but not for spending serious time with. There were more important, more intriguing, more demanding things calling him.

Until Jo.

Easly knew he would never be the center of her life; nor she the center of his, for that matter. They each had "the business" as the major recipient of his or her attentions. It was a subject that had never come up in discussion and probably never would. It was understood. Neither of them was the type of person who lived for other people.

Yet they were close—as close as each could be to another person. But despite that emotional proximity, Easly was aware that there was an important part of Jo closed off to him. Somewhere within her psyche he sensed a hot, high-pressure core of . . . what? Something raging and ravenous there, locked away from the world and, perhaps, even from Jo herself. There were times in the too few nights they could spend together when he'd awaken and find her rigid beside him. She'd be asleep, her eyes closed, but her teeth would be clenched, her hands would be squeezing his arm, and every muscle in her body would be straining as if against some invisible force. Then she would suddenly relax and a thin film of cool perspiration would sheen her skin.

"What's your secret?" he whispered to her.

"Mmmh?" Jo lifted her head and opened her eyes.

He shook her playfully. "What dark mystery is enshrouded within you? C'mon . . . tell me!"

She rolled onto her back and threw her right forearm across

her eyes. She was naked, quite unself-consciously so. "*Sacre bleu! Tu es foul*" she moaned, lapsing into Old French, the second language of Ragna.

After a moment or two of silence, she uncovered her eyes and rose up on one elbow. "You're really serious, aren't you?"

Easly nodded, holding her eyes with his.

"Some nerve!" she snapped. "You've never even told me what planet you were born on, and don't tell me Ragna 'cause I know you weren't born here."

"How can you be so sure?"

"You don't speak French."

"Maybe I just pretend I don't."

"Maybe you pretend a lot of things, Larry. Maybe that isn't really your name. But before you try your deductive powers on me, better do a little talking about yourself!"

Sitting up, Easly leaned his shoulders against the headboard and reached for a cigar. He favored the dry-cured type, toasted crisp in the ancient Dutch method. He picked a torpedo shape out of a recess in the wall behind him, squeezed the tip to ignite it, and was soon puffing away. Regarding the white ash, he said, "Nice aroma. Reminds me of a story. Want to hear it?"

"I'm ready to settle for anything by now," Jo replied sharply. "Stop fooling with that foul-smelling roll of dried leaves and start talking."

"Soon as I get comfortable." He drew his legs into the lotus position and leaned back, puffing leisurely on the cigar. "Can't do this in that float bed of yours," he remarked. Easly used to have a deluxe, anti-gravity float bed with laminar air flow and all the other accessories. But he'd found himself walking every morning with a stiff back.

"Okay. Where shall I begin? How about the name of the planet on which the story takes place?"

"Good start!" came the sarcastic reply.

"The planet is Knorr and the story concerns a love triangle of sorts. The woman's name was Marcy Blake and the man's was Edwin—Eddy—Jackson—typical names for Knorr since most of the original colonists there were of English extraction. Marcy was young, beautiful, and had inherited a personal fortune of a couple of million Knorran pounds. She was unattached, too; which might seem strange, considering her appearance and wealth. But anyone who knew her personally did not think it strange at all: besides being of borderline intelligence, Marcy's personality was totally obnoxious. She was an incredibly boring woman whose voice and manner always managed to set people's teeth on edge.

"Eddy Jackson was as handsome as Marcy was beautiful, as crafty as she was stupid, and as poor as she was rich."

Jo interrupted: "And so he decided to marry her, have her killed, and inherit her fortune. What else is new?"

"Just have a little patience, my dear. You're jumping way ahead of me. Eddy toyed with the idea of marrying her but never quite had the courage to take the plunge—which will give you an idea of what Marcy's personality was like. He did keep company with her now and then, however, just to keep his options open. And he noticed that she made a few visits to the neurosurgical center in Knorr's capital city. A little bribe here, a little bribe there, and he learned that Marcy had a unique, idiopathic degenerative disease of the central nervous system. The prognosis was death in two years or so.

"*Then* he decided to marry her, especially since Knorr's common law provided certain advantages in the area of survivor's rights. Eddy figured he could put up with anything for two years, after which he would be a bereaved but wealthy widower.

"So he figured. But marriage seemed to have a beneficial effect on Marcy's condition. Two years passed. Then three. By the time their fifth anniversary rolled around, Eddy was near the breaking point. Marcy had controlled the purse strings for those five years, keeping Eddy on a strict allowance, and talking, talking, talking. He finally confronted her physicians, who informed him that the disease seemed to have undergone a spontaneous remission. If her progress continued at its current rate, she would probably have a normal lifespan."

"That's when he decided to kill her," Jo stated confidently, but Easly shook his head.

"No. That's when he decided to leave her, money or not. He took what money he had saved out of his allowance and traveled to the city to see what kind of luck he'd have in the casinos. He was sure he could parley his winnings into a good-sized stake, and then he'd say good-by to Marcy.

"Naturally, he lost every cent and had to return home in disgrace. And then, a miracle—or what seemed like one. Eddy entered the house and noted the faintest aroma of cigar smoke; it was particularly strong in the bedroom. Cigar smoke! Neither he nor Marcy smoked at all, and few of their friends did since tobacco wasn't plentiful on Knorr. He asked Marcy if anyone had stopped by over the weekend and she very innocently said no . . . *too* innocently, he thought.

"Eddy was flabbergasted. Incredible as it seemed, Marcy was cheating on him! Infidelity, as I'm sure you know, is the rule rather than the exception on the Sol system planets. But on outworlds like Knorr, it remains scandalous. Not that he cared—it was just a question of *whom.* The *why* of it was conceivable: she was undeniably attractive and, he supposed, bearable in small doses.

"He decided to learn the identity of her lover and even went so far as to tip a rookie flitter-patrol cop to watch the house and see who came and went when Eddy wasn't there. He planned to threaten Marcy with exposure and disgrace once he had his proof, and allow her to buy his silence with a nice chunk of her fortune.

"But the patrolman reported nothing: no visitors to the Jackson home. Eddy's allowance wouldn't cover the expense of a detective, so he resigned himself to the unhappy conclusion that Marcy's affair must have been a one-time thing—after a single intimate meeting, Marcy's lover had probably come to know her well enough to know that he didn't want to know her any more."

Easly paused to blow some smoke rings, then he turned to Jo. "*That's* when he decided to kill her."

She yawned. " 'Sabout time."

"His plan was very tight, very simple, and very workable. He borrowed a gambling buddy's flitter, made a copy of the by-pass key (Knorran flitters use a thumbprint for ignition, but everyone keeps a by-pass key in case someone else has to drive it), and arranged to have this buddy meet him in the city for a night at the tables. At one point during the evening, he intended to excuse himself from the room, run for the casino roof, and roar off in his friend's flitter. With his running lights out, he'd land in the dark back yard of his home, go inside, kill Marcy, grab some valuables, then race back to the casino. He'd have an alibi: he was at the casino all night; the roof attendant would truthfully say that the Jackson flitter never left its dock; and the crime was obviously a robbery-homicide.

"Not a perfect plan, but as I said: tight, simple, workable."

"But it obviously didn't work," Jo said. "Otherwise you wouldn't be telling me all about it."

"Right. But it almost worked. He came in the house and

grabbed a vibe-knife from the kitchen and called for Marcy. She was on the upper level and asked him why he was home so early. As he rode the float-chute up, he said he got bored with the games and decided to come home. She was wearing only a filmy robe and her back was to him as he walked into the bedroom. Without hesitation, he spun her around and plunged the vibe-knife into the middle of her chest. Its oscillating edges sliced through cloth, skin, bone, cartilage and heart muscle without the slightest difficulty; and Marcy Jackson, *nee* Blake, died with a strangled, gurgling sound.

"It was probably just then that Eddy noted an odor in the room; and his olfactory sense was probably just about to label it for him when he heard a voice behind him.

" 'You killed her!' it said in a shocked whisper.

"Eddy spun around to see the rookie cop—the one he had tipped to keep an eye on the place—emerging from behind a drape. He was half-dressed; there was a half-smoked cigar in his left hand, and a blaster pistol in his right. The last thing Eddy saw before he died was a searing white light at the tip of the blaster barrel."

"Cute," Jo said in an unenthusiastic tone. "But hardly original. Especially that part about hiding behind the drape."

"Where would you have hidden in his place?"

Jo shrugged. "Whatever happened to this rookie?"

"He got in a lot of trouble. At first he tried to tell his superiors that he'd heard Marcy scream and went in to investigate, but soon the history of his detours into the Jackson home whenever Eddy was out and things on the beat got slow came to light, and he finally told the whole story."

Jo suddenly became interested in the rookie. She sat up and faced Easly. "What'd they do to this cigar-smoking character?"

"Oh, not much. A trial would have been an embarrassment to the force; and, they rationalized, even though he shouldn't have been in the Jackson home at all, he *was* on duty at the time he blasted the murderer. The conundrum was finally resolved when it was decided that the best thing the rookie could do was resign from the force and set up future residence on a planet other than Knorr. Which is just what he did."

"Tell me something," Jo said. "Why is it you named only two of the characters in the triangle? Why does the rookie remain nameless?"

"His name isn't important, just the fact that he was a young, inexperienced rookie who foolishly allowed himself to get involved in a compromising situation."

"How come you know so much about him?"

Easly puffed on his cigar: "Professional interest."

"And where is this rookie now?"

"Speaking of professional interest," Easly said with a quick cough, simultaneously shifting his body position and the subject of conversation, "how're you getting along with Old Pete?"

"Why do you ask?"

"You don't trust him—I can tell."

"You're right. And as days go by, I trust him less and less. Remember that autopsy report on my father I told you about—the one with the blank area?"

Easly nodded. "Sure."

"Well, I contacted the Jebinose Bureau of Records and their copy is incomplete, too."

"Maybe it's just a clerical error. Things like that do happen, you know. There wasn't anything of consequence missing, right?"

"No. Just the analysis of the urogenital system. But I checked the company records and found vouchers for Old Pete's trip to Jebinose after the murder. He was there about the time the report was filed. And when he tells me he can't explain that blank area, I don't believe him. I have this feeling he's hiding something."

Easly chewed on the end of his cigar for a moment, then: "Tell you what—since you got nowhere with Haas, why don't I send someone to Jebinose to investigate deBloise's background. And while he's there he can check into this autopsy report."

Jo bolted upright in the bed. "Jebinose? What has deBloise got to do with Jebinose?"

"It's his homeworld."

"Jebinose?" She pressed her palms against her temples. "I knew he represented that sector, but I never realized that was his homeworld!"

"I thought everybody knew that."

"I've never had much interest in where politicos come from, who they are, or what games they play." She lowered her hands and turned narrowed eyes upon Easly. "Until now. Larry, I want you to go to Jebinose yourself. Dig into deBloise's past for whatever you can find. And while you're there, dig up whatever you can on the death of one Joseph Finch, Jr."

Josephine Finch had just become personally involved in Old Pete's conspiracy theory.

X

JO

Jo sat behind her desk and thought about rats. Or tried to. She had just completed a short meeting with Sam Orzechowski, the man with the trained space rats, and had informed him that she'd only found partial backing for him. He'd seemed disappointed but was willing to keep on waiting. He had no choice, really: IBA was the first company to take him seriously since he had come up with his rat control method years ago. But Jo felt she should have been able to do more for him by now . . . if only this warp gate affair would get out of her mind and let her get back to work.

She expected Old Pete momentarily. He'd said he wanted to see her—something about planning the next step. He was so persistent on deBloise! She had tried to drop the subject and let it go as a foolish gamble on the politician's part, but Old Pete wouldn't let her. And even if he had, the problem would have stayed with her.

It was that damn recording from the Restructurists' conference room. It raised too many questions that wouldn't let the problem go away. Besides . . . deBloise was from Jebinose.

Old Pete strolled in. "What's new?" he asked, sliding into a chair. He always said that, even if he'd seen you only a few hours before. It was his way of saying hello.

"Nothing," she said curtly. That incomplete autopsy report still bothered her.

"I was afraid you'd say that. Looks like we don't know much more now than we did at the start."

"Not true," Jo replied. "We now know who Haas is and we know that he's developed something that will eventually revolutionize interstellar travel. We also know that Elson deBloise and the Restructurist inner circle have placed a huge sum behind Haas and the warp gate."

Old Pete's smile was grim. "And we can be certain that the motives behind their actions are purely political. In my years of study of deBloise's life, I've yet to find any action on his part that was not designed to further his political career and increase his political power. His mind is homed in on one goal and he allows nothing to sway him from pursuit of it. Nothing!"

"That leaves us with the obvious conclusion that there's a political plot connected with the Haas warp gate."

"Which is right back where we started," he grunted.

"But the way they're going about it, they must know that the gate will be driven off the market before Haas can perfect the improvements that will make it economically viable."

"And if Haas means what he says—and I believe he's absolutely sincere about withdrawing the gate permanently from the market if it fails commercially—we'll have lost the greatest boon to interstellar travel since the original warp field was developed back on old Earth."

Jo leaned forward and rested her chin on folded hands. "You know, I have this horrible suspicion that they *want* the gate to be a commercial failure, that they know Haas will withdraw it from the market then, and it will be lost to us until the patents run out or somebody else figures out a different way to get the same result."

"I can't see the sense in that at all."

"Why else would they be encouraging Haas to rush the gate to market?"

"Don't know. Maybe there *is* something to that remark about military contracts. Maybe deBloise has cooked up something with one or two of the higher-ups in the Fed Defense Force."

"A military coup?"

"No." Old Pete sighed. "That's patently ridiculous, I know. But the military could be involved just the same."

Jo shook her head slowly, confidently. "The military's not involved."

"I suppose you're right," he admitted. "The gate could be of tremendous value in a war, but there is no war. I mean, who're we going to fight? The Tarks?"

"You never know." Her tone was serious.

"Don't be silly, Jo," he laughed. "We may not be on the best terms with the Tarks—as a matter of fact, we've *never* been on good terms with those scoundrels—but there's no such thing as a war in sight, despite the wails of the more panicky members of the Fed Assembly. And don't go thinking of the Tarks as a potential market for the gate, either. They'll buy one as a model, then pirate the design and build their own. The Tarks are a blind alley, I'm afraid."

"Perhaps you're right. Anyway, on the deBloise end, I sent Larry to Jebinose to do some direct investigation on him. And while he's there, I told him to look into my father's death."

She watched Old Pete's face closely for a reaction. She saw surprise and . . . was it fear?

"Why Jebinose?" he said, the words coming in a rush. "I thought you'd send him to Fed Central. That's where all deBloise's machinations take place."

"Maybe he's more careless at home."

Old Pete suddenly seemed anxious to leave the room. "Let me know the very instant he turns anything up."

"Oh, you can count on that," Jo replied in a low voice as the door closed behind him. She'd never seen Old Pete so upset. What secret lay dormant on Jebinose that he feared disturbing?

Never mind that now. Larry would find out. Right now another part of her brain was screaming for attention. Something Old Pete had said before had closed a circuit . . . something about a war with the Tarks when they were talking about Haas and his—

She leaped to her feet and began to pace the floor. She knew deBloise's plan. All the pieces that hadn't seemed to fit had suddenly fallen together. And the Tarks were the key. Old Pete's reference to them had brought a vast conspiratorial vista into sharp focus and Jo was struck by the genius and delicacy and deviousness of what she saw. She was terrified, too.

The entire interstellar free market was threatened.

She pressed a stud on her desktop. "Find Bill Grange—tell him to drop whatever he's doing and get up to my office immediately!"

The market. To some people it was the place where stocks and bonds were traded; to others it was the local food store. But these formed only a minuscule part of the market. For the market was life itself, and the free market was free life, the active expression of volitional existence. It was billions of billions of daily transactions: the purchase of a loaf of bread, the selling of an asteroid mining firm along with all its equipment and planetoid leases; every interaction and transaction—be it social, moral, or monetary—between every sentient being in Occupied Space added to its endless flux and flow.

The free market was neither good nor evil, selfish nor generous, moral nor immoral. It was the place where rational minds met for a free exchange of goods, services, ideas. It played no favorites and bore no grudges. It had its own ecology, regulated by the inexorable laws of supply and demand, which were in turn determined by the day-to-day activities of every intelligent creature who interacted with another intelligent creature. If demand for a species of product or service dried up, that species became extinct. When new demands arose, new species sprung into being to satisfy them.

The market's urge toward a balanced ecology was indomitable. It could be warped, skewed, stretched, contracted, puffed up, and deflated by those who wanted to control it, and thereby control its participants; but not for too long. It always sought and found its own level. And if manipulators—invariably governmental—prevented it from finding its true level for too long, a great mass of people suffered when it finally burst through the dams erected against it.

LaNague had taught the outworlds that bitter lesson. But three hundred years had passed since then and it was quite possible that history was ready to set the stage for a repeat performance. The Restructurists were fortunate to have a remarkable man such as Elson deBloise at their head in their drive for control of the Federation and, from there, control of the market.

But the market had Josephine Finch. The market was inviolate as far as she was concerned. It was an integral part of human existence, especially Jo's existence. Her professional life was spent in taking the pulse and prognosticating the course of the market and she would do her best to see that no one meddled with it.

Right now, the only way she could see to put a stop to deBloise was to cripple Star Ways, the biggest interstellar conglomerate in Occupied Space. Hardly a realistic option, but it was all she had.

Bill Grange was IBA's resident expert on Star Ways and his knowledge would be a critical factor in Jo's plan. Of course, it would save her an intolerably large amount of time and effort if she could go up to someone in charge of Star Ways and tell him that a monstrous political plot was afoot and that his company was going to be used as a scapegoat. But you couldn't do that with a conglomerate, you couldn't deal person-to-person with it. So Jo would have to *induce* co-operation from Star Ways; she'd have to jab at it, stab at it, slice away at its appendages until it was forced to do her bidding. And she'd relish every minute of it.

For there was no love lost between Josephine Finch and the interstellar conglomerates. They disturbed her sense of fair play. It was not that they broke any of the rules of the free market—they sold to those who wanted to buy and bought from those who wished to sell. But there was something about them that . . . offended her.

The conglomerates were faceless monoliths. Nobody seemed to be in charge. There were boards of directors and committees all composed of people; they hired and directed the work of other people; products were turned out which were sold to still other people. Human beings were intimately involved in every function of the conglomerates, yet the final result was a structure devoid of all human qualities. It became a blind, impersonal leviathan lumbering through the market, obliterating anything that got in its way—not through technical skill or marketing expertise, but through sheer size.

And it was not size itself that Jo found offensive, although that was part of the problem. Despite the fact that people made all the decisions for them, their huge size prevented their humanity from showing through. Smaller companies each seemed to have their own personality. Conglomerates strode through the market, the testing ground for all human endeavor, like giant automatons.

Yes, they were huge, and their size and diversification inured them and insulated them from immediate changes in the market. But no insulation is perfect. The conglomerates were not invincible. If a subsidiary company was ailing, there was a great financial pool from which it could draw. But there were limits to any pool. And if more than one subsidiary were in trouble . . .

Leviathan could be wounded and caused to retreat if attacked at multiple vulnerable sites.

Jo only hoped that Star Ways had a few vulnerable sites.

The door opened and Bill Grange walked through. He was tall, gaunt, graying, fifty-four years old—he liked to say that he and IBA had been born the same year. He had been with the firm nearly a decade when Joe, Sr., died and had stayed on through all the turmoil that followed. He had been neither for nor against Josephine when she took over IBA; all he wanted was someone in charge who could get the company going again. If she could do it, he was all for her. If she loused it up, he'd walk. As it stood now, there wasn't much he wouldn't do for Josephine Finch.

"Something wrong, Jo? The message sounded urgent."

"I need some information on Star Ways," she said, taking her place behind the desk again, "and I need it now."

Grange visibly relaxed at this statement and took a seat. He probably knew more about Star Ways than many of its board members. He knew it from dealing with it on a daily basis in the current market, and he knew it from a historical perspective. The conglomerate was centuries old, born in a small company on old Earth celled Helene Technical, which happened to develop the first commercial interstellar warp unit. The old name was quickly scrapped for the more picturesque Star Ways, and the new company severed its ties with Earth, relocating on the planet Tarvodet—a tiny world but one that afforded mammoth tax advantages.

It became a huge, successful corporation. Through imaginative marketing, tricky financial maneuvers, and the old tried and true business practice of hiring the best and making it worth their while to stay on, SW moved into other fields, buying up subsidiary companies and becoming the first interstellar conglomerate. Other conglomerates had developed since, but Star Ways Corporation was still the largest.

"What do you want to know? I could talk all day."

"I'm sure you could. But I want to know where, in light of

what's going on in the current market, SW can be hurt. *If* it can be hurt at all."

Grange's eyebrows lifted. "Hurt Star Ways, eh? Not so hard these days as it might have been when you arrived on the scene."

"Oh, really?"

"Yeh. SW's mortgaged to the hilt and overextended in all quarters. It needs some new blood on those boards, and when the financial reports come out"—he chuckled—"there'll be a lot of screaming from the stockholders."

"I wasn't aware of this."

"It's not public knowledge yet, but that's what our informants tell us. And I've seen it coming for years. But don't worry. Star Ways will pull through just fine—minus some dead wood at the top, however."

Jo mulled this over. It was encouraging. "Give me some specific weak points."

"I can think of three right off the top of my head: General Trades, Stardrive, and Teblinko. General Trades has always generated a lot of income on luxury items, but has lately run into hordes of competitors and lost part of its share of the market.

"Stardrive is a different story. That's their tube drive subsidiary—SW's oldest subsidiary, as a matter of fact. When they picked that up, they were able to outfit ships for both interstellar and peristellar travel—that's when they really started to grow. Stardrive, Inc., has always had competitors, but lately a little company by the name of Fairleigh Tubes has been giving it a real run for its money." He grinned. "Does that name sound familiar?"

Jo nodded and returned his smile. "Certainly does." Fairleigh Tubes was an IBA account.

"Then we come to Teblinko Corporation, the pharmaceutical firm Star Ways acquired a few years back—that's been a real problem lately. They had to pour a lot of money into it to get it moving, and it's only now just starting to pay off. Once Teblinko starts consolidating its gains, it'll be less crucial to SW's over-all profit picture; but right now it's touch and go.

"If you're still looking for more cases, I can—"

Jo held up her hand. "That'll do for now, I think." She paused. "Teblinko's biggest competitor is Opsal Pharmaceuticals, right?"

Grange nodded. "We did some work for them in the past."

"How come they're not with us now?"

"Don't need us. They're doing fine, so we put them in the inactive file." He grinned again. "But with the way Teblinko is moving up, I expect to be hearing from them soon."

Jo nodded absently, making mental notes.

"What's this all about, if I might ask?"

Jo considered bringing Grange in on it, then vetoed the idea. If she told him what deBloise was planning, he'd think she was paranoid; and if she explained what she wanted to do to Star Ways, he'd be fully convinced that she had crossed the line into overt schizophrenia. No, better keep it to herself.

"Just working out a theoretical problem," she told him. "And you've been a big help. Can I call on you again if I need some more information?"

"Of course," Grange replied, taking the hint and rising. He was too canny to be fooled by Jo's lame explanation—you weren't told to drop everything and get up to the head office because of a theoretical problem—but he was sure he'd be filled in on all the details if and when he came to be involved.

He turned at the door. "It occurs to me that you might not have a certain factor in your theoretical problem, a factor that has the potential to put Fairleigh way ahead of Stardrive: the Rako deal. If that ever comes through—"

Jo's eyes widened. "Rako! Of course! You know, I'd forgotten all about that! Thanks, Bill."

When he was gone, Jo ordered the complete files on Fairleigh Tubes and Opsal Pharmaceuticals. She also asked the company computer the same questions she had asked Bill Grange. The print-out arrived and agreed with Grange that General Trades and Teblinko were the weak links in SW's chain of subsidiaries. But Stardrive, the subsidiary Grange had emphasized, was conspicuous by its absence.

Jo wasn't surprised. Bill Grange approached the market with an intuitive sense that could not be programmed into any machine, no matter how sophisticated.

The records department informed her that the Fairleigh and Opsal files were now keyed to her viewer and she could activate them anytime during the next two hours. This was part of the IBA security routine. Client files were available only to authorized personnel on specific request and only for a strictly limited time period. Most contained sensitive and confidential information that would be invaluable to a competitor.

Current information on Opsal was scanty. It was a reputable

firm with a long-standing history of high quality pharmaceutical production. Teblinko was coming up in the field and pushing Opsal, but the older company was maintaining its lead by virtue of its superior distribution system.

Not much help there.

She moved on to Fairleigh. The peristellar drive tube market was a stable one. The proton-proton drive had remained the best real-space propulsion method for centuries and the Leason crystal had remained the only practical lining for the drive tubes for an equal amount of time. Emmett Leason, an extraterrestrial geologist, first identified the crystal on one of the three tiny moons of Tandem. When he could not determine the melting point of the crystal by conventional means, he knew he had something.

Someone eventually devised a means of coating the inner surface of a proton-proton drive tube with the crystals and found that the new lining prevented the tube from vaporizing as had all the previous prototypes. An experimental means of transportation suddenly became the norm.

Leason crystals became a hot item among prospectors but it was soon discovered that natural deposits were rare. While these were being mined down to bare rock, the laboratory boys were hard at work developing a synthetic substitute. They were successful, but the man-made crystals were hellishly expensive.

And that was how the drive tube market stood. The patents on the synthetic process were long defunct and anyone who wanted to make Leason crystals was welcome to do so. But that didn't make the process any cheaper. As the human race expanded and colonized more new worlds, the demand for p-p tubes grew steadily, and more and more companies entered the market. Still, no one was able to reduce significantly the cost factor in synthesizing the crystals, so they remained the major contributor to the tubes' high price tag. It was thus the dream of every company to stumble upon a mother lode planet of natural crystals.

Fairleigh had found such a planet: Rako. But there was a hitch. As a matter of fact, there were a number of hitches.

One of them was the Tarkan Empire.

Jo frowned. The Tarks were popping up more and more lately. There would no doubt be a clash someday—a big one. But not in the near future. The Tarkan Empire was ruthless and active and probably took the loose, formless structure of the Federation as a sign of weakness. One day it would overstep its boundaries to test the Federation's mettle. The empire's economy was rigidly controlled and centralized and such economies needed periodic armed conflicts to rejuvenate themselves. Free markets tended toward the other extreme: wars meant killing, and killing meant a reduction in the overall total of available customers.

She activated her intercom. "Get hold of Mr. Balaam at Fairleigh for me."

The smiling, distinguished face of Harold Balaam soon filled her vid screen. He had held the president's seat of the drive tube company, which kept its main office there on Ragna, for the past decade. He and Jo enjoyed an excellent working relationship.

After the usual amenities, Jo asked, "How's the Rako situation going, Hal?"

The smile faded. "Don't ask. It's costing us a fortune and we're getting nowhere. I'm afraid I'm going to be forced to pull the team if we don't start getting some results soon."

"Anything in particular holding you up?"

"Yes. The Rakoans themselves." He gave her a brief summary of the situation.

"Sounds like you need a public relations man out there."

Balaam grunted. "Know of a PR company that has any experience with degenerate aliens?"

"Not exactly," Jo laughed, "but if I can have an authorization from you, I may be able to send somebody out there who can help."

Balaam considered this for a few seconds, then nodded. "I think we can commission a trouble shooter through you. You haven't steered us wrong yet . . . and if you come through on this, you can name your fee."

"The usual contingency percentage will be fine. Just beam the authorization over as soon as possible and I'll get right to work on it."

When the screen was blank, Jo leaned back in her chair. She needed someone to send to Rako immediately, someone with good judgment, a quick mind, and the ability to improvise. That was Larry. But he was on Jebinose and so she'd have to settle for whoever was next in line. Perhaps "settle" wasn't fair. Larry had the utmost confidence in Andy and that should be sufficient endorsement for anyone.

She hoped he was available. She was going to send him out to the far edge of the human sector of the galaxy.

XI

DEBLOISE

It was a corner office, and when the windows were set at maximum transparency the view was impressive. Copia, the capital city of Jebinose, was a showcase for the planet. The average outworld could claim one large city and it was usually located near its major—and sometimes only—spaceport. Into this city was poured all the technical skills and available funds the inhabitants could muster. Some cynics denounced the efforts as hypocritical window dressing, but to most inhabitants of the planet it was very important to put on a pretty face for visitors, important to leave an impression of prosperity and well-being.

Copia was designed to leave such an impression. The rest of Jebinose might be economically and culturally backward, but Copia had a medical center, a psi-school, a university, a museum of Vanek artifacts, and a huge sports arena.

DeBloise's office overlooked the northern quarter of Copia;

its outer corner pointed toward the graceful spire that marked the university campus. Delicate violet and yellow-striped tendrils of Nolevetol *deng* grass intertwined across the floor, forming a thick, soft, living rug. Exotic plants climbed three corners of the room; a huge desk, its entire top surface made of solid Maratek firewood, filled the fourth.

DeBloise sat behind that desk. Holographs of his wife and two children were prominently arrayed before him, but his eyes were on the latest in the morning's long procession of visitors and supplicants.

Henro Winterman, a leader of one of the sector's larger merchant combines, didn't fit deBloise's image of a merchant. Merchants should be porcine and endomorphic; this one was lean and lupine. And vaguely arrogant. But his pompous air carried a wheedling undertone. Winterman's group and others like it had formed a strong pro-deBloise base in the sector's business community. They had helped significantly in elevating him to initial prominence in interstellar politics, but he had gone on from there without their help. And at this point Winterman was not too sure of his footing with the man who was now so closely identified with the Restructurist movement.

"It seems that my associates are growing just a little bit impatient, sir," he said with the perfect blend of impudence and deference. "We've actively backed you for a good number of years now and we don't seem to be getting anywhere. The sector continues to wallow in an economic slump and, very frankly, sir, none of us is getting any younger."

"So?" deBloise said with raised eyebrows and a completely neutral tone. Certain economic considerations had been implied when they had offered their support for his initial campaign to go to the Federation as a Restructurist. Somewhat less than two standard decades had passed since then and apparently some of the merchants thought the bill was past due. It irritated deBloise to the point of fury that Winterman should have the audacity to approach him in this manner, but he checked himself and limited his reply to the noncommittal monosyllable. The time had not yet come when he could loose his rage on Winterman, but that time was coming . . . it was coming. Until it arrived, he could not allow anything to erode his power base.

"Well," Winterman said slowly when it became obvious that deBloise was waiting to hear more, "my associates and I are quite concerned about the indigenous economic integrity of our sector."

DeBloise had to smile at that: *Indigenous economic integrity.* What an ingenious phrase! It meant nothing, really, but was infinitely malleable. DeBloise had used a number of similar phrases and catchwords on his way up; they were indispensable to the political process when it was necessary to create an issue.

Interpreting the smile as encouragement, Winterman hurried on. "We know the Restructurist movement is sympathetic to our goal of eliminating outside commercial interests from the sector, and we know it's just a matter of time before the movement achieves dominance in the Fed Assembly and gives us the backing we need . . . but there *is* a bit of an economic lag in the sector and we were wondering how long—"

"Not too much longer, Henro," deBloise said with hearty confidence and one of his best public smiles. But beneath the smile he was snarling. He saw the merchant as a filthy, greedy, money-grubbing parasite and knew exactly what he and the other members of the merchant combine meant by the "indigenous economic integrity of the sector": they wanted a monopoly on all trade in and out of the sector. None of the members was skilled or talented enough to achieve that goal either as an individual or as part of a collective. So they were looking for a little Federation muscle to help them. But the LaNague Charter prohibited any and all interference in the economy by the Federation. Thus their support of deBloise and Restructurism. Strange bedfellows, indeed.

Speaking continuously as he moved, he rose and expertly guided Winterman out of the office. With his hand on the man's shoulder, he assured him of his deep sympathy and concern for his predicament and of his firm intention to do all he could for him just as soon as the Movement made some headway toward changing the charter. He also made a point of reminding him that if that day was ever to come, it would require the continued support of such model citizens as Henro Winterman and his fellow merchants.

DeBloise glanced questioningly at his receptionist as the waiting room door slipped closed behind Winterman.

"You're ahead of schedule, sir," she said, knowing what was on his mind. "That reporter isn't due until ten-point-five."

He nodded and returned to his inner office. A mirthless smile warped his lips as he waited for the chair to adjust to his posture in a semi-reclining position. It never ceased to amaze him how much a part greed played in politics. That, at least, was something he was well insulated against, thank the Core. The deBloise name had been synonymous with wealth on Jebinose for generations; his personal fortune was more than he could hope to spend in two lifetimes.

No, Elson deBloise had more important concerns than money, but that didn't mean he would renege on his promise to use whatever power he achieved after the Haas plan came to fruition to aid Winterman's crowd. He'd be delighted to help them gain a stranglehold on trade in the sector, absolutely delighted.

And soon, as Restructurist control of the Federation increased—as it inevitably must after they achieved their beachhead—the Jebinose trade cartel and others like it would find themselves under direct supervision of the newly restructured Federation. The *real* power over the human sector of Occupied Space would then be where it belonged—with the new Fed president, Elson deBloise.

Money as an incentive? Never! Then what was his incentive? DeBloise's mind had developed numerous diversionary tactics to deal with that question. Most of them were quite ingenious. But every once in a while his defenses collapsed and the inescapable truth leaked through: rich and influential men entered politics for one reason . . . power. Lower class nobodies became politicos with the power motive in mind, too, but it was often diluted by a drive for prestige and the financial advantages that so often attend the acquisition of public office. Being moneyed and respected at the start, however, left only power as a goal.

The quest for dominion over other men's lives was not necessarily an evil thing if, after achieving that dominion, it was used toward certain beneficial ends. DeBloise had repeated this to himself so many times that by now he actually believed it, and the thought that a good many people might not share his vision for the human race did not bother him in the least. He would override their opinions and in the end they would see that it was all for their own good.

As his mind reflexively skittered away from any in-depth analysis of the moral implications of his life's work, his eyes came to rest on the holographs of his wife and children on the desktop.

His daughter was on the left: a pretty brunette with some wild tendencies. These were presently being curbed—he wanted no bad publicity involving his family.

Rhona, his wife, was in the middle. She too was a brunette, although she weighed more now than she did in the holo. Their offspring had been limited to two—one of each sex—at deBloise's insistence; it made for a perfectly balanced family portrait. Rhona had been the eldest daughter of another rich Jebinose family, and two fortunes, as well as two people, had been united at their wedding. They were husband and wife now in name only, however. They slept in separate quarters at night and led separate lives by day; only on public record and in the public eye were they married. Both seemed content with the situation as it was.

He had never loved Rhona. At one time he thought he might someday grow to love her, but as his rise in politics began to accelerate, the discrepancies between the public deBloise and the private Elson widened. And he found that he preferred the role of the public deBloise, a role he could not play with any conviction in Rhona's presence. She'd known him since adolescence, knew all his fears, fantasies, and idiosyncrasies. In her eyes, he would never be the wonderful man who was the public deBloise, and so he avoided her.

The homely face of his son, Elson III, filled the third and final holo. He was proud of Els—just fourteen, president of his class and active in the Young Restructurists Club. He encouraged his son in these activities, for he'd found them invaluable in his own youth. Through being a class officer and the head of committees, you learned how to handle people, how to get them involved in projects, how to get them to work for you.

His son would start at the university next year, and that brought back a swarm of memories for deBloise. He had never planned on going into politics, aiming rather for a long life devoted to being very idle and very rich. Something during his years of higher education had sparked him, however. He didn't remember exactly what it was . . . perhaps some of those Restructurist-oriented professors who were so openly critical of the Federation, spending entire class periods in an overt attempt to sway developing minds toward their point of view. Perhaps young Elson deBloise had sensed a path to power within the philosophy of political interventionism.

He entered the political sphere soon after graduation, not as a Restructurist, however. Restructurism was irrelevant then as a philosophy in lower-echelon politics on Jebinose. His name and his position made him welcome in the inner circles of the local machine where he quickly identified the movers and the shakers. He made the right connections, spoke up for the right causes at key affairs, and finally gained enough leverage to be nominated to the Jebinose Senate.

Even as he made his maiden speech before that august body, he was planning the moves that would take him to Fed Central. Jebinose was not yet in the Restructurist fold, was not in any fold, for that matter. The planet was situated near some of the major trade lanes, yet did little trading. There was little there to interest anyone: no drugs, technological hardware, or chemicals—just those damn Vanek artifacts, and a single shipload could handle a year's output.

So, traders rarely stopped at Jebinose. It was a fact of life. But coupled with the current slow, steady decline of the planet's economy, that fact of life held great potential as a political issue of interstellar scale. To transform it into such an issue would require some fancy footwork and what his advisers referred to as "the old reverse."

This is how it would work: It was obvious to anyone vaguely familiar with Jebinose and elementary economics that major traders didn't stop there because it had a simple agrarian economy with nothing to trade. To make an important political issue of that, you merely inverted the situation: Jebinose had a poor, simple agrarian economy because the traders refused to stop there; if the traders could be made to stop and deal with Jebinose, the planet would undergo an industrial and economic boom. And that's why Jebinose needs a Restructurist working for her at Federation Central!

You couldn't spring this on the populace *de novo*, of course. You had to spend a few years laying the groundwork in the media, dropping phrases like "functional trade sanction" whenever asked about the Jebinose economy, and continuing to utilize the phrase until it was picked up by others. After it had been repeated often enough, it would be accepted as matter-of-fact truth. And if they could accept that amorphous phrase, then they would have no trouble swallowing "the old reverse."

Used properly, that would be the issue to launch him into interstellar politics. But until the foundation had been properly laid, he must cast around for local issues to keep himself prominently displayed before the public.

And that was when some minor public official suggested that there was too much discrimination against the Vanek in the rural areas where they lived. DeBloise and the other Restructurists in the Jebinose Senate jumped on the idea and the Vanek Equality Act was soon making its way through the legislature. Elson deBloise, more than anyone else, had staked his political future on that bill. He toured the entire planetary surface speaking on it. If it passed, he would instantly become the fair-haired boy of Jebinose politics and would immediately introduce his manufactured trade issue in a bid for the Jebinose seat at the Federation Assembly. If it hit a snag, it would set his timetable back five, perhaps ten years.

It hit a snag.

And that's when Cando Proska introduced himself.

"That reporter is here, sir," said his receptionist's voice from out of the air.

DeBloise shook himself back to the present and assumed a more upright posture.

"Send him in."

A nondescript man of average build with dark blond hair and eyes that seemed to be bothered by the bright, natural light of the office strolled through the door and extended his hand.

"Good day to you, sir. I'm Lawrence Easly from the Risden Interstellar News Service and it's an honor to meet you."

XII

EASLY

Easly's credentials as a news service reporter were the best money could buy. It was a useful identity, allowing him to roam and ask embarrassing questions. It secured him an interview with deBloise himself within the span of one local day—it was difficult for any politico to turn down free exposure in the interstellar news media.

He had done all the research he could on the way out from Ragna, and now he had the rest of the day on his hands. Danzer wasn't too far away, so he rented a small flitter for a quick run to the little town. Jo had told him about her father's murder there and he just wanted to have a look . . for her sake.

And for his own. Easly had approached the Junior Finch aspect of the Jebinose trip as he would a typical missing person case. His routine in such was to learn all he could about the individual in question before starting the leg work; he liked to feel as if he knew the quarry before initiating the search. In Junior's case he had found that unsettlingly easy.

Old holovid recordings in the Finch family library were the starting point. There weren't many. None of the Finches was crazy about sitting still for cameras, it seemed. He did manage to find one, a long one, recorded at what must have been a family outing shortly before the death of Jo's grandparents in the flitter crash. The viewing globe filled with woods, grassy knolls, a pond, and for a short while, Junior Finch sitting under a tree with a five- or six-year-old Josephine perched on his lap. They were posing and the family resemblance was striking, especially since Jo's hair had been lighter then.

But Easly's eyes had drawn away from the child who had grown to be his lover and come to rest on Junior. He felt as if he were looking at a slightly distorted reflection of the adult Josephine, recognizing parallels that went beyond build, facial features, complexion. There was a whole constellation of intangible similarities pouring out of the globe: the relentless energy forever pushing to find new channels, the undefined urgency that so typified Jo's character as he knew her today was there below Junior's surface even in the midst of pastoral tranquility.

But not until the camera had panned to the right, placing Junior on the periphery of the visual field, did the uncanny similarity between Jo and her father strike him full force. Junior stood leaning against a tree, staring at nothing, his arms folded, his mind obviously light-years away from the family picnic. It startled Easly because he'd caught Jo hundreds—thousands!—of times staring off into space that same way, steeped in the same private world.

There were other recordings, and on the trip to Jebinose Easly had studied them, watching Junior's every move. He found something immensely appealing in the man's quiet intensity and became increasingly involved in him . . . fascinated, infatuated, haunted by the shade of a man he had never met, yet felt he had known most of his life. It bothered him.

The tragic course of Junior's life saddened him, and annoyed him as well. What made a grown man drop a top position with a respected firm like IBA, a firm presented with interesting, challenging problems on a daily basis, and travel to a place like Jebinose?

He smiled as a thought came to him: probably the same thing that made a nineteen-year-old girl forsake a life of ease and luxury to singlehandedly challenge the IBA board of directors and outworld conventions as well. He then realized why he felt so close to Junior Finch: Josephine, for all the adulation and admiration she lavished on the memory of her grandfather, had grown into the image of his son.

And now he was gliding toward the death-place of that son, her father. She had given him three names: Bill Jeffers, Marvin Heber, and a Vanek named Rmrl, or something like that. The first would be easy to find if he still ran the store.

He missed Danzer on the first pass, but circled around and followed a dirt road back into the center of the tiny town. Jeffers' name was still on the sign above the general store, so he made that his first stop.

Jeffers wasn't there at the moment, but a clean-shaven, heavy-set young man who professed to be his son asked if he could help.

"I'm looking for a Marvin Heber," Easly said. "Know where I can find him?"

"He's dead. Died sometime last spring."

"Oh, I'm sorry to hear that."

"You a friend of his?"

"Not really. A friend of a relative of an old friend of his—you know what I mean." Young Jeffers nodded. "I was supposed to stop in and say hello and see how he was. Oh, well . . ."

He strolled out onto the boardwalk. It was hot and dry outside and a gust of wind blew some dust into his face. He sneezed twice. Hard to believe people still lived like this.

He still had some time left to check out this Rmrl. Jo had told him that the Vanek tribe had set up a vigil of sorts on the spot in the alley next to Jeffers' store; it was the one place where he could always be sure of finding a Vanek, no matter what the time of day.

Today was no exception. Easly rounded the corner of the store and there, cross-legged in the center of a crude circle of stones, humming and jiggling the coins in his cracked earthen bowl, sat a lone Vanek beggar.

"Wheels within wheels, *bendreth,*" he intoned as Easly approached the circle.

"Sure," Easly replied, stopping with his shoes a few centimeters from the stones. "Can I speak with you a minute?"

"Speak, *bendreth.*"

He squatted and looked at the beggar. Pupils dilated from a long watch in the shade of the alley gazed out at him from beneath hooded eyelids but appeared to be focused on something other than Easly, something neither of them could see. The blue-tinted skin of the face was wrinkled and dusty. This was one of the older Vanek.

"I want to know about Junior Finch," Easly said in a low voice, after glancing around to be sure that he and the beggar were alone in the alley.

The Vanek's mouth curled into a poor imitation of a human smile. "He was our friend."

"But he was killed."

The smile remained. "Wheels within wheels, *bendreth.*"

"But who killed him?"

"We did."

"But why?"

"He was our friend."

Easly was getting annoyed. "But why would you kill a man you say was your friend?"

"He was different."

"How was he different?"

"Wheels within wheels, *bendreth.*"

"That doesn't tell me a damn thing!" Easly said, his voice rising. "You've said you killed him. Just tell me why."

"He was our friend."

"But no one kills somebody because he's a friend!"

"Wheels within wheels, *bendreth.*"

Easly made a guttural sound and rose quickly to his feet. If he thought the beggar was deliberately trying to be evasive, he would have understood that and accepted it. But this was apparently the way the Vanek mind worked.

Or was it?

"Do you know Rmrl?" he asked abruptly.

The Vanek's pupils contracted noticeably, and for an instant he actually looked *at* Easly rather than through him.

"We all know Rmrl," he replied.

"Where is he at the moment?"

"Among us." The eyes resumed their indeterminate gaze.

"How can I find him?"

"Wheels within wheels, *bendreth,*" the beggar said, and jiggled his alms bowl.

Easly growled and strode away without leaving any coins. How could he hope to glean any coherent information from a member of a half-breed alien race that killed he man who tried to help it, then made a shrine of sorts out of the place where they murdered him? The whole trip had been a waste of time. He hadn't even enjoyed the scenery.

He spent the early part of the next morning gearing himself up for his meeting with deBloise. This was the prelude to his investigative work: getting a feel for the man. And for that he needed personal contact. His object was to find out anything at all that might be useful against him—anything. Jo seemed to be playing for keeps on this one.

He arrived at Sector Representative deBloise's plush home-world offices a little early and watched the receptionist until she motioned him into the next room.

DeBloise stood and waited for him behind his desk. He had a bigger build than Larry had expected—probably muscular once, now tending slightly toward puffiness—but the dark hair and the graying temples were familiar, as was the cordial smile fixed on the face. Easly reflexively disregarded the comfortable, friendly exterior; his research had shown beyond a doubt that there was a core of diamond-hard ambition hiding underneath.

"Well, Mr. Easly," deBloise said after they shook hands, "what do you think of our fine planet so far?"

"Very nice," Easly lied as he took the indicated seat.

"Good. How can I help you?"

"The Risden Service is doing a series of reports on human-alien relations, and the most intimate such relationship, of course, exists here on Jebinose with the Vanek."

DeBloise nodded. "It must be remembered that the Vanek are not totally alien; they are a mix of human and alien. But I can see why they would be of prime interest in such a series. Where do I fit in, however?"

"You were one of the principal sponsors of the Vanek Equality Act, were you not?" DeBloise inclined his head. "Well then, that makes you a principal figure in modern Terran-Vanek relations, and your files would be of invaluable assistance to me. Might I have access to them?"

DeBloise considered this; there was extraordinary potential here for a massive amount of good press. "I could give you selective access. I'm sure you understand that I couldn't possibly open all my files to you."

"Of course. Whatever you think best. Now, there's also another important figure in Terran-Vanek relations: Joseph Finch, Jr., I believe."

There was a barely perceptible cooling of deBloise's attitude at the mention of Junior's name. "I'm afraid I didn't know him at all. Never met him."

"But that was quite an impassioned speech you made about him on behalf of the Equality Act after his death. I heard a recording . . . very moving, even after seventeen years."

"Thank you," deBloise replied with a bland smile. "But one didn't have to know him personally to be moved by his death. I knew what he was trying to do: he was trying to bring equality to those less fortunate than he; he was trying to bestow a little dignity on the Vanek; he was going out on a limb for a fellow rational being. I understood him perfectly, and I'm willing to wager that if he were alive today he'd be very active in the Restructurist movement."

Easly nearly choked, but managed to keep a straight, attentive expression. "What about the Equality Act, sir? Would it have passed without Mr. Finch's death?"

"Definitely. Not with such resounding unanimity, perhaps, but it would have passed. It was an idea whose time had come. That bill, by the way, was pending before Finch came to Jebinose."

"And on the reputation you earned with the passage of the Equality Act, you went on to successfully run for a planetary representative seat at Fed Central, is that correct?"

DeBloise paused and scrutinized his interviewer. "Are we talking about human-alien relations or my political career?"

"The two are somewhat intertwined, don't you think?"

"Somewhat." This writer, Easly, had a manner about him that deBloise did not care for . . . made him feel as if he were under a microscope. He'd have to run a check on the man before he let him anywhere near his files.

The intercom chimed and waited to be recognized. "I thought I told you not to disturb me for the next few minutes," deBloise said.

"I'm sorry, sir," the receptionist said, "but Mr. Proska is here and wishes to see you immediately."

The casual observer would have noticed nothing. But Larry Easly's training enabled him to pick up certain cues immediately. His attention became riveted on deBloise.

The man was terrified. At the mention of the name "Proska," his entire body had become rigid; there was the slightest blanching of the skin, the slightest tightening of the mouth. To a trained observer, Elson deBloise was transmitting acute fear. His voice, however, was remarkably calm when he spoke.

"Tell him I'll see him in a moment," he said to the air, then turned back to Easly. "I'm very sorry, but some urgent business has just come up and I'm afraid we'll have to cut this interview short. I'm leaving for Fed Central in a few days but will probably return within a standard month. Please check with my secretary and make another appointment."

"But your files—" Easly began.

"We can attend to that next month." DeBloise rose. "But right now, you must excuse me."

Easly muttered a thank-you and made his exit. He was bitterly disappointed—those files were crucial to his investigation. As he reentered the waiting room, he saw only one occupant besides the receptionist. A small, sallow, balding man sat with his hands on his knees, and rose as Easly left the inner office. Easly was about to classify him as a timid nonentity until he caught a glimpse of the man's eyes as he passed. There was not a hint of timidity—nor love nor fear nor hatred nor mercy, for that matter—to be found there.

This was undoubtedly the Mr. Proska who struck such fear into the heart of the powerful, secure, influential Sector Representative Elson deBloise. It was suddenly very obvious to Easly that Mr. Proska had some sort of hold over deBloise; finding out just what that was might prove to be quite useful.

"Excuse me," he said to the receptionist after the door to the inner office had closed behind Proska. "Wasn't that Harold Proska?"

The receptionist smiled. "No, that was *Cando* Proska. Perhaps you know his brother."

"Does he have a brother?"

"I couldn't say." She shrugged. "I believe he's an old friend of Mr. deBloise's. He stops in now and then. But I really don't know a thing about him."

"I must be thinking of someone else," he said, and sauntered out of the waiting room.

An old friend, eh? he thought as he walked across the hall and stepped into the downchute. He fell at the rate of one kilometer per hour until he passed the "Ground Floor" sign, then grabbed the handles and pulled himself out of the chute and into the lobby. *No old friend of mine ever scared me like that!*

Pondering his next move as he stepped out into the late morning sunlight, Easly suddenly remembered that he was on a Restructurist world. And all worlds within the Restructurist fold had a policy of maintaining what they called a Data Center, a centralized bank where vital, identifiable statistics of all natives and permanent residents were kept on file. The information stored usually included date of birth, place of birth, parents' names, education, employment record, present location, and so on.

Easly flagged a flittercab and headed for Copia's municipal complex. He idly wished that all planets had Data Centers—it would certainly make things easier for someone in his line of work—but then banished the thought when he realized his own vital statistics would be listed.

The Data Centers were a natural outgrowth of Restructurist philosophy, which viewed humanity as a mass and approached it as such. As a result, the government on a Restructurist world was highly centralized and geared its actions toward what it decided were the common denominators of the collective. To determine those common denominators—to "better serve the public interest," as it was wont to put it—the government had to know all about the public in question.

Thus the Data Centers. And since all men were brothers, all should have access to the data. This was the Restructurist version of a truly "open society."

Individuals like Larry Easly and Josephine Finch and Old Pete posed a thorny problem for Restructurist theory, however: sometimes consciously, most often unconsciously, they refused to accept the common denominator for themselves and persisted in sticking their heads above the level of the crowd. They thought brotherhood was a nice idea but they didn't think it could be institutionalized. And they never ceased to be amazed at the amount of garbage other people would swallow if the sugar coating were laid on thick enough.

The flittercab dropped him off before a complex of Neo-Gothic abstract buildings that housed the municipal offices of Copia. From there it was no problem finding the Data Center. Slipping into an empty booth, he punched in the name Cando Proska. If the little man had been born on Jebinose, his name would definitely be listed. If he were an immigrant, there was still a good chance to locate him here.

A single identity number flashed on the screen. Easly punched it in and hoped for the best.

PROSKA, Cando Lot 149, Hastingsville
Male

Age: 44 Jebinose years
Height: 1.58 M
Weight: 68.2 Kg
Parents: Carter & Dori Proska
Both deceased.
Developmental environment: SW sector, Copia
Religion: none
Political affiliation: none
Marital status: unattached.
Offspring: none
Education history: Copia psi-school, age 5–10
Copia secondary, age 11–16
Employment history: Clerk, Jebinose Bureau of Standards, age 19–27 (voluntary termination)
Current employment status: none

There could be little question that this was the man: height, age, weight, it all seemed to fit. He noted with interest the fact that Proska had dropped out of psi-school at age ten. That was certainly unusual because there's no such thing as losing a psi-talent—you're born with it and it stays with you the rest of your life. The purpose of a psi-school is to hone and develop a native talent; therefore you have to be able to demonstrate psionic ability before being accepted into such a school.

And you didn't quit. People with psi-talents were always in demand; even those with the most mediocre abilities were assured a good income for the rest of their lives. Proska had been a student there for five years, which meant he had some psionic talent. Why did he drop out?

And why hadn't he put the talent to use? He had spent eight years at the bottom rung in a government office that even in the best of times was notable only for its nuisance value. Then he quit again. No employment for the last seventeen years. Also strange.

Not much information, but Easly was satisfied with it as a starting point. And as a little extra bonus, something had clicked in the back of his mind as he was reviewing the information; he couldn't place it right now—his brain often made correlations without immediately informing him—but he knew from experience not to push it. Sooner or later it would come to the surface.

He decided that a quick look at Proska's living quarters was in order and wrote down the address. It was a calm, sunny day so he rented an open flitter and took it up to a high hover level where he could put the vehicle in a holding pattern and consult the directory. The autopilot code number for the aerial co-ordinates of Lot 149, Hastingsville, was F278924B. Easly punched it in, set the speed at slow cruise, and leaned back to enjoy the ride.

It took longer than he anticipated. Instead of heading him toward inner Copia, the autopilot took him northeast and outward. He had originally expected to find himself over one of the poorer areas of the city, but now he was entering a suburb.

The flitter stopped and hovered over a sprawling mansion located in the center of an obviously well-to-do neighborhood. He allowed the flitter to lose altitude so he could get a better look. The house consisted of four octagonal buildings connected in an irregular line and built at varying levels. The landscaping had been extensive: the rest of the lot was covered with an intricate pattern of color-co-ordinated shrubbery. A "149" on the landing platform confirmed the address.

Not bad for a man who hasn't worked in seventeen years, Easly thought. *Not bad at all.*

As her dropped lower, a number of bright red lights began to flash from the roof and landing pad, a warning that clearance was required from below before he would be allowed to land. Easly veered off and followed the fenced perimeter of the property all the way around. His trained eye picked up traces that indicated the presence of a very effective and very expensive automated security system.

He was about to make another pass over the house when his peripheral vision caught sight of a moving object to his left: another flitter was approaching. He gave the guide stick a nudge and moved off in the opposite direction at an unhurried pace. The other craft seemed to hesitate in the air, then landed at Proska's residence. There were two men inside—he was almost positive they were deBloise and Proska—and they did not leave the vehicle right away.

Cursing himself for his carelessness in renting an open flitter, he picked up speed and altitude and set a course in the general direction of Copia. Of course, he did have an excuse or two: he had made the erroneous assumption that Proska would be living at a low socio-economic level, and that his home would be somewhere in the capital city where an extra flitter in the air would go completely unnoticed.

But Hastingsville was not in Copia; it was in an exurban area where his hovering craft was like a vagrant leaf in a well-kept swimming pool. If deBloise had recognized him, then Easly's cover was most certainly in jeopardy. His policy in any situation such as this was to assume the worst. That being the case, the wisest thing he could do at this point was to get off-planet immediately.

But there was one more thing he had to check before leaving. He looked up the aerial co-ordinate code number for the psi-school in Copia, punched it in, and sat back to review what he knew so far as the autopilot took over.

Proska was blackmailing deBloise. That much was obvious. Easly had no idea what the lever was, but it had to be a big one. Proska had no doubt squeezed the mansion and a generous annuity out of deBloise's personal fortune in return for his silence. But there was more going on besides simple blackmail. DeBloise was in actual physical terror of the little man.

The reason for that could, perhaps, be found at the psi-school.

The flitter stopped over an imposing, windowless, cuboid structure. Easly landed and walked inside. He waited until someone who looked like a student strolled by.

"Excuse me," he asked a boy who looked to be about ten standard years of age. "Who's the dean?"

"Why, Dr. Isaacs, of course."

"How long's he been dean?"

The boy shrugged. "How should I know? Check the plaque over there. You should be able to figure it out from that."

Easly approached the indicated wall where a silvery metal plaque listed all the deans and their period of tenure since the school's founding. A man named Jacob Howell had been dean thirty-four years ago. That was the man he wanted.

The vidphone directory gave him the address and phone code of a *Howell, Jacob,* who lived in Copia. Easly went to a booth, punched in the code, and waited. The face of a thin, elderly man lit up the screen after the third chime.

"I'm sorry to bother you, sir," Easly said, "but are you the Dr. Jacob Howell who used to be dean of the psi-school?"

"One and the same," the old man said with a smile. "What can I do for you?"

He held up his bogus identity card. "I'm doing a series of articles on psi-schools for the Risden News Service. The piece I'm currently working on concerns psi-school dropouts, and I understand there was a dropout when you were dean. Now, I was wondering if you could tell me—"

"Why, of course!" Howell beamed. "I'll be glad to help. Come right over and we'll talk about it."

"I really haven't got too much time left on Jebinose," Easly protested. "If you could just answer—"

"I'll be home all day," the man said, smiling. "You can drop by anytime." With that, he cut the connection.

Easly debated his next move. Howell obviously wanted to get him over to his home. Why? Was he lonely? Or didn't he want to discuss anything over the phone? Or was there another reason?

He decided to go. There were a few unanswered questions here that would nag him incessantly if he did not make at least one attempt to answer them.

Ω

"Ah! So you decided to come after all!" Jacob Howell said as he opened the door to his modest apartment. It was immaculate. The walls were studded with plaques, degrees, and testimonials; the furnishings were simple and functional. A holo of a middle-aged woman was affixed to the wall above the vid screen.

A quick glance around and Easly had a capsule description of the man: a retired academic, a widower, somewhat compulsive in his habits, lonely. He welcomed Easly warmly. Any company, even that of strangers, was better than sitting alone.

"Please have a seat and let me get you a cool drink," Howell said.

Easly demurred and tried to get to the point. "There was a student named—"

"No names, please," Dr. Howell said, raising both hands before him. "I was dean of the psi-school for nearly forty years and only one child dropped out. I will discuss the matter with you freely, but without the use of a name."

Definitely compulsive, Easly thought.

"I assure you the article will not name names, but I do need to know some specifics."

"Of course. Well, I've been going over the incident in my mind since your call. It's not something one would easily forget. Nasty business, that."

"What do you mean?"

"Well, little Can—" He stopped short. "I mean, the boy

we're discussing got into an argument with another little fellow—it was in the telekinesis lab, I think—and the other boy died right there on the spot. It was a shocking incident. The boy you're interested in—let's call him 'Master X,' shall we?—apparently blamed himself and refused to set foot inside the school again."

"What did the other boy die of?"

Howell shrugged. "We never found out. His parents were from the farm region and were devout members of the Heavenly Bliss sect—we had a lot of them on Jebinose, you know—and they refused to allow an autopsy. It's part of the Heavenly Bliss canon that the human body not be willfully mutilated, neither before birth, during life, nor after death."

"There are plenty of non-invasive methods of determining the cause of a death."

"These were employed, of course, and nothing beyond a previously known congenital heart defect was uncovered. That was assumed to be the cause of death. It was probably the excitement of his argument with Master X that triggered it, and of course one couldn't lay any blame on the little fellow. But you couldn't convince *him* of that, however. He considered himself responsible and never wanted to come back."

"Congenital heart defect?" Easly's tone was dubious. "That's ancient history. Nobody walks around with something like that any more."

"He does when his parents refuse to consent to surgery . . . mutilation, you know. If the same thing happened today, there would be an autopsy, Heavenly Bliss sect or not. But we weren't as well organized then as we are now. I wish we could have insisted on an autopsy, then little Master X would have been spared such a burden of guilt. I seem to remember that he showed promise. Such a shame."

"Would you happen to know what he's doing nowadays?" Easly asked.

Howell shook his head. "No, I never kept track of him. To be perfectly frank with you, I tried to forget the whole matter as soon as possible."

Easly digested what Howell had told him for a few minutes, then rose. "Thank you for your time, Dr. Howell. You've been most helpful."

"You mustn't leave yet!" Howell said, leaping to his feet. "There's a lot more I can tell you about psi-schools. I can prepare an early supper and fill you in on many operational details that may prove very useful as background material."

"Some other time, perhaps," Easly said, reaching for the door. "I'm on a very tight schedule now, really."

"Stay and have a drink, at least."

Easly begged off and slipped out the door. As he walked down the hall he could feel the lonely old man's eyes on his back. He felt guilty. All Dr. Howell wanted in return for his information was a little companionship. But companionship meant time, and time was something in short supply at the moment.

The sum total of Larry Easly's instincts and training was prodding him to leave Jebinose immediately, but he shrugged it off. He was hooked now and couldn't run out just yet. He had the tantalizing feeling that all the pieces were here and that a nice coherent picture would be formed if he could arrange them in the proper light. He started laying them out for examination.

DeBloise was terrified of Proska; Proska was a psionic talent of some sort. Those two could be accepted as fact.

Now for a little extrapolation: A little boy at psi-school had died during an argument with Proska and Proska had refused to return to the school because of guilt. Why so much guilt? Unless he *knew* he had killed the other boy!

Could Cando Proska kill with his mind? Was that why he inspired such fear in deBloise? Was it that plus some very sensitive knowledge that had enabled him to extort a house and probably a yearly income from deBloise for the last seventeen years?

Seventeen years . . . the Vanek Equality Act had passed almost seventeen years ago—

The subconscious correlation his mind had made back at the Data Center suddenly bobbed to the surface: Junior Finch was murdered on this planet seventeen years ago!

There were too many seventeens involved here to be written off as mere coincidence: deBloise's political career took a sharp upward turn seventeen years ago with the passage of the Vanek Equality Act; Junior Finch was murdered while working among the Vanek seventeen years ago; Cando Proska, a man who might have the ability to kill with his mind, stopped working for a living seventeen years ago and started blackmailing deBloise.

It all fit!

No, it didn't. The Vanek killed Junior . . . they admitted it openly. And Vanek never lie. Or did they? It was also generally conceded that Junior's death merely increased the margin by which deBloise's pet Equality Act was passed. So deBloise had nothing to gain from Junior's death. Or had he?

By the time he reached the roof, he knew where he was going. Not to the spaceport . . . he had just two more stops to make before the spaceport: The first, his hotel room; the second, Danzer.

Ω

It was dark by the time he reached Danzer and there was a different Vanek sitting cross-legged inside the circle this time. A small flame sputtered before him and cast a wan glow on his features. This one was younger—middle-aged, Easly guessed—with a spot of dark blue pigmentation on his forehead. This Vanek would no doubt be as informative as the last one, but Easly had secured a small vial of gas from his hotel room, something to give him a conversational edge over the Vanek.

"Wheels within wheels, *bendreth,*" the beggar greeted him.

"Wheels within wheels, yourself," Easly muttered as he squatted before him.

"Have you come again to meditate on our friend, Junior Finch?"

Easly started. "How did you know I was here before?"

"We know many things."

"I'll bet you do. Right now I'd like to meditate on someone else. His name is Cando Proska. Know him?"

The beggar's eyes remained impassive. "We know Mr. Proska, but we do not fear his power."

The directness of the response surprised him. "What power?"

"The Great Wheel imparts many powers in its turning. Mr. Proska possesses an unusual one."

"Yes, but just what is his power?"

The beggar shrugged. "Wheels within wheels, *bendreth.*"

Here we go again, Easly thought, and reached for a cigar. But there was a subtle difference here. Yesterday's beggar had an air of tranquility about him; he had sensed an innate passivity about that one. Today's beggar was something else entirely. Outwardly, he looked like a quiet, removed, contemplative sort. But Easly sensed that this was a thin veneer under which churned a very purposeful being. There was power here, and determination. This creature was not at all like a Vanek should be.

He took his time lighting the cigar. By the time the tip was glowing a bright red, both he and the beggar were enveloped in a cloud of strong-smelling smoke. This was the effect he desired, for he had removed the small gas vial along with the cigar and now had it palmed against his thigh and pointing toward the Vanek. A flick of his index finger opened the cork and the colorless contents streamed out.

Easly held his breath and waited for the vial to empty. It contained a powerful cortical inhibitor that worked as a highly effective tongue-loosener on humans. The gas, kelamine, was not entirely odorless, however, thus the improvised smoke screen. He had taken a considerable risk by traveling with kelamine. It was illegal on most planets—Jebinose included—and mere possession could result in imprisonment. There were no physical or mental aftereffects, but its use was classified as "chemical assault."

A vial was kept hidden in his luggage at all times for use in extreme circumstances. This was such a circumstance. He could only hope that the half-breed Vanek nervous system was human enough to respond to the gas.

When the vial was empty, he slipped it back into his pocket and allowed himself to breath again.

"What is Proska's power?" he asked again.

"Wheels within wheels, *bendreth*," came the standard reply.

Easly cursed softly and was about to get to his feet when he noticed the beggar begin to sway.

"I am dizzy, *bendreth*. I fear it is the smoke you make."

"Very sorry," Easly said with the slightest trace of a smile. A mild dizziness was the drug's only side effect. He ground the cigar out in the dirt.

"Perhaps you misunderstood my question," he said carefully. "I want to know what *kind* of power Mr. Proska possesses."

"It is a power of the mind," the Vanek said, and put a finger to his forehead.

Now we're getting somewhere!

Ω

It was fully an hour later when Easly returned to his flitter and took to the air. Even with the help of the kelamine, it had been hard work to pull any concrete information out of the Vanek; their minds work in such a circumspect manner that he almost had to start thinking like one before he could get the answers he wanted.

But Easly had his answers now and his new-found knowledge made him set a course for the spaceport at full throttle. His luggage was still at the hotel, and as far as he was concerned, it could stay there. There was only one thing he wanted now and that was to get off Jebinose.

His expression was grim as he dropped the flitter off on the rental platform and went to secure a seat on the next shuttle up. The mystery of Junior Finch's death and Proska's diabolical psi-talent had been cleared up. He shuddered at the thought of running into Proska now. The little man was no mere psi-killer as Easly had originally suspected. No, what Cando Proska could do to a man was much worse.

Larry Easly was frightened. He had faced danger before—in fact, at one point during an investigation last year, someone's bodyguard had placed the business end of a blaster over his left eye and threatened to pull the trigger—but it had never affected him like this. This was different. This was an unseen danger that could strike anywhere, at anytime, without the slightest warning. And there was no possible way to defend himself against it.

He didn't know the range of Proska's power. Did it require a certain proximity to its target to be effective, or could he just sit in a room somewhere and strike out at will? Every shadowy corner posed a threat now. His palms were clammy, his stomach felt as if something cold and sharp was clawing at it, and the skin on the nape of his neck crawled and tingled.

He was almost giddy with relief when the read-out at the reservation desk told him he had a seat on the next orbital shuttle leaving in one quarter of a standard hour.

On his way to the shuttle dock, he passed the subspace communication area and thought it might be a good idea to get a message off to Jo . . . just in case something happened to him.

He entered one of the large, transparent booths, closed the door behind him, and seated himself at the console. The locus computer informed him that it was midday at the IBA offices on Ragna. Not that it mattered: the subspace laser was the fastest means of communication yet developed, but it was still a one-way affair. Delay between transmission and reception could range from minutes to hours. And Easly was not waiting around for a reply anyway. The message would be automatically recorded at IBA and Jo would replay it at her convenience.

Easly noted the vid receptor before him and realized he was in a deluxe booth that sent a combined video and aural message. He shrugged and tapped in the IBA locus. All he wanted to do was get the message off, then get up to the shuttle dock. The extra expense was the least of his worries. A red light went on and he slipped his credit ID disk into a slot. The disk popped out and the light turned green. A two-minute transmission had begun.

Ω

Jo was surprised to learn that she had a subspace call from Larry. He would only contact her like this under emergency conditions, so she ordered an immediate replay on her office vid screen. She started to smile as his face appeared, then remembered that he could neither see nor hear her. His voice was stern:

"This is a personal and confidential message for Josephine Finch—her eyes only. Please record the following without monitoring." He waited a few seconds, then his tone softened.

"I'll have to make this quick, Jo, and more cryptic than my usual since I don't know who else will see this before it gets to you. First off, as to your close relative's end, it's not at all what it seemed to be. The man you sent me here to investigate may well be intimately involved. And there's a wild card: a psi-talent who . . . who . . ."

Jo saw Larry's face go slack as his voice faltered. He swayed in front of the screen, fighting to keep his balance. Utterly helpless, Jo had to sit and watch in horror as his eyes rolled up into his head and he sank from view.

Picture transmission was not interrupted, however, and Jo anxiously watched the passers-by, hoping that one of them would glance in and realize that something was wrong with Larry. One man did stop and peer through the glass. he was short, sallow, and balding. His hard little eyes seemed to rest on the spot where Larry had fallen but he registered no surprise, made no move to help.

He merely smiled and turned away.

XIII

TELLA

Andy Tella had a strict personal rule against taking blind assignments. He not only insisted on knowing the immediate objective but the final one as well. This attitude had ultimately led to his failure as a Defense Force trooper: he hadn't been able to muster the reflexive obedience required to function successfully in a military unit.

He was bending his rule somewhat for the current assignment, however. The immediate objective was quite clear: secure the export contract for the Rakoan Leason crystals; do it in accordance with Federation conventions on relations with alien races . . . but do it. The ultimate objective remained vague, and that bothered him.

His first impulse had been to turn the assignment down. He knew nothing about dealing with aliens, knew nothing about Leason crystals other than the fact that they were used to line drive tubes and were extremely valuable, and had no desire to increase his knowledge in either area. But the request had come from Josephine Finch and she said the job was important and of a highly sensitive nature. It pertained to the deBloise caper, but she wouldn't say just how.

On faith alone, he had accepted the assignment and was now a passenger aboard IBA's own interstellar cruiser as it slowed into orbit around a cloud-streaked, brown and blue ball called Rako. The days on ship had been spent in encephalo-augmented study of everything known about the planet and the humanoids who inhabited it. Rako was a water-oxygen world circling an F3 star situated along the mutual expansion border of the Terran Federation and the Tarkan Empire. It had been discovered six and a half standard years previously by a Fairleigh Tubes exploration team on a follow-up mission after spectrographic analysis of its primary suggested the possibility of deposits of natural Leason crystals. They found them—huge fields of them.

They found something else, too. The planet was inhabited. They came upon evidence of intelligent life long before they found the Rakoans, however. Dead cities—dank, decaying, alloy and polymer corpses, some almost completely overgrown with vegetation—dotted the planet, indicating a sophisticated level of technology at one time. But no natives. It was initially suspected that a plague or biological catastrophe had wiped them out and the members of the exploration team breathed a sigh of relief—intelligent life forms on Rako would complicate matters by preventing them from claiming the planet for Fairleigh.

They decided to take a look at one final derelict city that appeared less overgrown than most of the others from the air. And that's where they found the last of the Rakoans. Besides their height—some of the adults were almost three meters tall—the most outstanding feature of the otherwise humanoid mammals was their thick, horny epidermal layer, which was constantly flaking off. They had three fingers and an opposing thumb, wide-set eyes, and a shapeless nose that drooped down over a lipless mouth equipped with short, flat, block-like teeth—a sure sign of a vegetarian.

And they were dying.

Not from disease, but from a birth rate that produced one healthy child for every twenty-three adults of the previous generation. The result was a very steep geometric regression in the planet's population—from an estimated five billion to roughly thirty thousand, most of them gathered in this single city.

That was one complication for the Fairleigh team. Then the Tarks arrived, claiming they had discovered the planet previously and were only now getting around to mining it. That was a transparent lie. The Tarks had long ago pirated the process for synthesizing Leason crystals and would have immediately begun stripping Rako of its natural deposits—with or without native permission—if they had been the first there.

The Federation stepped in then. It reminded the Tarkan Empire of the expansion treaty it had signed with the Fed nearly two standard centuries before. One of the major articles of the treaty outlined the accepted procedures for dealing with worlds inhabited by intelligent creatures. Since Rako fell into this class, the question of who discovered it first was irrelevant. The Empire and Fairleigh Tubes would have to make competing offers for a trade contract with the Rakoans, with the strong proviso that consent from the Rakoans be *informed* consent.

The Federation made it clear to the Tarks that it was quite willing to enter into armed conflict to protect the interests of Fairleigh and the Rakoans. Fairleigh, in turn, was advised to abide strictly by the conventions or Fed protection would be withdrawn from the company—not only on Rako, but throughout Occupied Space.

So the Terrans, the Tarks, and the leader of the Rakoan remnant got down to dealing. And that's where the third complication arose.

The Rakoans wanted more than money and technology in return for their crystals. They wanted a future for their race.

Ω

"I suppose you're well on your way to a solution by now, eh, Doc?" Tella said, fully aware that the answer would be negative.

He sipped a cup of hot tea as he sat across a table from Avery Chornock, the head of the research team on Rako. Chornock had disliked him on sight, and Tella sensed this. But he chose to ignore it, preferring to play the part of the brash, young, bonus-hungry company trouble shooter to the hilt. For that's how Chornock had labeled and pigeonholed him after reading his authorization from the Fairleigh home office.

"We're nowhere near a solution, Mr. Company Man," the

lank, aging scientist rumbled. "And under present conditions, it's highly unlikely we'll *ever* get near one."

"What more could you want? You've got a full research team of your own choice here; you've got a subspace link to the Derby University computer, which is packed with every available scrap of information on human and non-human reproduction; and you've got an open-ended budget for any hardware you should need."

"Not enough!"

Tella considered this. If Dr. Avery Chornock, the number one expert on alien embryology and reproduction in the Federation, was at an impasse, what could he contribute?

"What more do you need?"

"I need to be back in my lab at Derby U. investigating live Rakoan subjects. We've done all the cadaver work we need and I've exhausted the possibilities of field work on live subjects. I need to get a few males and females back to my lab for definitive studies and then I might—I said, *might*, mind you—be able to come up with something."

"None of the Rakoans will volunteer, I take it?"

Chornock nodded. "That is correct."

"Maybe they're scared of you."

"No. These people aren't scared of much. It's got something to do with their religion." He made a disgusted noise. "They'll all be extinct in a few generations and all because of some imbecilic superstition!"

One of the lab technicians stuck his head through the door. His expression was anxious.

"Vim is here."

Chornock twisted abruptly in his seat. "Are you trying to be funny or something?"

"Of course not!" the technician replied in an offended tone.

"Well, don't just stand there. Send him in immediately!"

The head disappeared and a Tarkan male entered a few seconds later. Tella had seen holos of them before, and had seen them on the vid, but this was the first time he had ever viewed a Tark in the flesh. There was quite a difference: the doglike face with its short snout and sharp yellow incisors was the same, as were the stubby-fingered hands, the barrel chest and the short, dark, bristly fur; but no vid recording or holo had ever managed to convey the sheer brute strength that seemed to ripple under the creature's exterior . . . nor the pungent odor that surrounded it like a cloud. It stood close to two meters tall and weighed 100 kilos easily.

A second Tark entered and stayed slightly behind and to the right of the first.

"Please have a seat, Dr. Vim," Chornock said, rising.

The Tark to the rear made some growling noises and the first Tark replied in kind. Then the second Tark spoke to Chornock in oddly guttural, but grammatically perfect Instel.

"No time, I'm afraid. I've been recalled."

"Oh no! This is terrible! Why?"

Again, the growling exchange between the two aliens. It was now obvious to Tella that the first Tark was Vim and that he didn't speak the Terran interstellar language. The translator turned back to Chornock.

"Too expensive, it seems. My superiors have interpreted our lack of progress as a sign that this race is doomed. They have decided to wait until its final members die off. Then there will be no need to make arrangements to pay these primitives for the crystals."

"Do you agree?"

"I do not see much hope for a solution under these conditions," The translator said after another exchange. He paused while Vim said some more, then continued. "Before I leave, may I say that it has been a privilege to share the same soil with you. I would have much desired to work at your side in this matter, but that was forbidden, as you know. I look forward to seeing more translations of your excellent papers. Good-by."

With that, the pair of aliens turned and left.

Chornock sat in silence for a few long moments. "A decent fellow, Vim. I know he's deeply disappointed."

"Didn't show it," Tella remarked.

"Tarks cannot afford to show displeasure with their superiors' decisions; from what I understand, such behavior tends to shorten their lifespan—if you catch my drift. But he's disappointed. The Rakoans pose quite a challenge. We could clone out new ones, of course, but their leader says that's an unacceptable solution. He wants true, natural biological reproduction re-established on a scale that will ensure the future of the race. I can't blame him, but I'm afraid I can't help him either."

"They're sterile?" Tella asked. Chornock had lost some of his hostility as he talked about the Rakoans; he was almost likable.

"Sterility would be much easier to deal with. No, there are

plenty of active gametes in both sexes—they just won't combine as they should. But I'm sure Vim's also disappointed about leaving the *bassa* behind."

"What's that?"

"A very fascinating grain rust with curious antibiotic activity: when an extract of the rust is ingested in sufficient quantity, it irreversibly incorporates itself into the metabolic pathways of any and all the bacteria in the body within one standard day."

"So?"

"So, when the extract is withdrawn, the bacteria die. The patient must be immediately reinoculated with his own enteric organisms, but the Rakoans seem to have the technique perfected. There doesn't seem to be any evidence of resistance, either."

"What about host metabolic pathways? Don't they get changed?"

"Apparently not—probably because the nucleoproteins of a larger animal don't replicate at anywhere near the rate of a bacterium's, so there just isn't time for the rust extract to insinuate itself into the metabolism. But I suppose if one made a steady diet of the rust . . ." he let the thought trail off.

Tella used this opportunity to make his exit. He rose. "Well, time for me to get to work."

"And just what kind of work might that be, Mr. Company Man?" Chornock asked, his surliness coming to the fore again.

"Convincing these aliens to send a few volunteers back to Derby with you, for one thing. Who can take me to them?"

"I'll let Sergeant Prather take you over—just to make sure you don't try anything foolish. You'll probably find him in the courtyard behind this building."

Ω

Prather was running his daily check on the a-g combat unit that stood in a sheltered corner of the courtyard. It towered a full four meters in height and, once inside, a seasoned trooper could clear a forest, level a city, or hide at the bottom of a lake for a month. Prather was the Federation Defense Force representative on Rako. A cruiserful of troopers waited in orbit. Just in case.

The sergeant was preoccupied and ignored Tella's request for a tour around the city. But Tella knew how to break through the soldier's barrier of military professionalism.

"Doesn't look like they've changed the unit much since I was in the Force."

Prather's glossy shaved head snapped up. "You were in the Force? When?" Tella was suddenly a real person to Prather.

"Eight standards ago. Infantry, like you. Used to be pretty damn good in one of these things."

"Howcum you're out?"

Tella shrugged. "Didn't get along too well with the brass. You know how it is."

"Yeah," Prather agreed with a nod. "They get to some people more than others. But you say you used to operate a unit like this?"

"Almost like it; this must be a newer model." Tella stepped back and looked at the combat suit. It was squatter than the one he'd trained in, and looked lighter. Except for the prominent Federation star-in-the-ohm insignia, the unit's surface was a dull black from the anti-gravity plates in the feet to the observation dome on the shoulders, but only because it wasn't activated. In action it could assume any color scheme for instant camouflage.

"It's the latest. Easy maintenance, for which I'm glad at the moment. With the Tarks calling it quits on the research, there's no telling what they might try."

"You don't really think they'd try anything against Chornock and his crew, do you?"

"They wouldn't dare! They know we're fully armed up there," he said, jerking a thumb at the sky, "and they know I'm down here with my unit. We made sure they knew about that—although we were careful to hide the unit from the natives; they might not understand that this monstrosity is here for their protection. What I do worry about is the Tarks trying some sneaky way of wiping out the Rakoans so they won't have to wait for them to die of natural causes."

Tella was at once sickened and amazed at the simple, direct logic of such a solution. And if the Tarks were only one half as ruthless as their reputation, ways and means had no doubt long been formulated to bring about such an end.

"Well, I'm sorry, Sergeant," Tella said, turning away, "but I've got to get over to the Rakoan section of the city. And if you won't take me, I'll just have to find my own way."

"Now just wait a minute there . . . Andy, isn't it?" Tella nodded. "My first name's Bentham—Ben—and I don't see why I can't take a few minutes out to show an ex-trooper around the city. Give me a few minutes to get this lubricant off my hands and we'll be on our way."

Ω

It was Tella's first good look at the city. The Rakoans obviously had a thing for spires—every building he saw tapered to a graceful point. And there was a strange quality to the streets in the way they twisted and turned and interconnected around the buildings; almost as if the buildings had been set down wherever the constructor's fancy indicated, and the roads put in later as a sort of afterthought. The small, open flitter did not have to make many turns before Tella was hopelessly lost.

"You know where you're going, Ben?"

"Sure. I make the trip every day to keep an eye on the natives and make sure the Tarks aren't up to anything. You'll know we're there when we get there."

Tella puzzled over that last remark until they rounded the corner of the next building. There, in a clearing, stood a building without a spire. It was a low dome, remarkably crude in comparison to the other architecture of the city, and around it stood a circle of Rakoans, male and female, shoulder to shoulder.

"What's going on?"

"That's the temple of Vashtu, the ancient god of Rako. At any time of the day or night you can find five hundred and twelve natives standing around it as a guard. Why that particular number?" he asked, anticipating Tella. "If you remember that the Rakoans have four digits on each hand, it's no surprise that their number system has a root of eight."

Prather let the flitter glide toward an ungainly old Rakoan who was strolling toward the temple carrying a long wooden staff.

"That's Mintab, the leader of what's left of the natives. If you want to talk to someone, it might as well be him. He's the mouthpiece; his people make all their decisions as a group. And don't try to pull anything over on him—he's a sly old bird."

Mintab spotted the flitter and stood waiting as Prather grounded it; he joined the two humans as they debarked. It was an unholy trio standing there beside the vehicle: the tall, shaggy-skinned, floppy-nosed Rakoan, the short, dark, stocky Tella, and the glossy-scalped Prather.

The trooper introduced Tella as the-man-who-wants-to-buy-the-rocks. Although he addressed Mintab in the Rakoan tongue, Tella's crash encephalo-augmented course in the language during the trip out allowed him to understand what was being said. Speaking Rakoan, however, was a different matter—there were many nasal intonations that were impossible to reproduce without practice—but he could manage to make himself understood if he kept it short and chose his words carefully.

"The furry ones have left," Mintab said, turning his gaze on Tella. "When will your people remove your doctor?"

"Soon," Tella replied in halting Rakoan. "No answer here. Must take some people away for answer."

"I have tried to convince my people of this but they will not listen." He glanced over to the encircled dome. "Don't judge us too harshly. Our manner of living was not always so primitive. Our dead cities tell you that. We once flew through the air and talked across the oceans. But there are no longer enough of us to maintain that level of technology. As our numbers collapsed, so did our means of production, and thereafter we ran out of precision parts. We are now reduced to this."

"But why won't your people co-operate?" Tella asked.

Mintab started for the dome. "Come. You will see."

The circle of Rakoans parted for the trio as Mintab led them into the crude structure.

"You are entering the temple of Vashtu, Giver of Light and God to us, his chosen race," he said. "Before you is his shrine."

In the center of the gloomy temple stood a huge statue; a good seven or eight meters in height, it was hand-carved out of a jadelike stone and showed one creature standing over the slumped form of another.

"It looks . . . old," Tella remarked lamely. The lighting, the postures, and the sheer size of the work gave it an eerie power.

"It is ancient. We do not know when it was carved, but throughout our recorded history it has been the focus for my race's religion . . . now more than ever. It depicts Vashtu triumphant over the fallen M'lorna, God of Evil and Darkness."

Tella moved closer. Vashtu was Rakoanoid with a sunburst for a face; he held a staff with a huge scarlet gem affixed to the end. The creature at his feet was indistinct, however.

"I can't see M'lorna."

Mintab motioned him toward the doorway where the light was slightly better. A carving on the wall showed a biped creature with a huge single eye where the head should be, and pincerlike hands. Its body was covered with alternating green and yellow stripes.

"That is M'lorna."

"But I still . . . do not understand . . . why your people will not help us help them."

"It was in this very place," Mintab said, "that Vashtu defeated M'lorna in the days when our world was new. But M'lorna was proud and swore that he would return and destroy the temple of Vashtu. The great Vashtu gave my people the mission of defending the temple when M'lorna returns.

"Generations ago, when our cities teemed with healthy millions, we forgot Vashtu and turned our minds and hearts to other matters. We left the temple unguarded. And for this dereliction, Vashtu has allowed our numbers to decrease. Soon there will not be enough of us to adequately guard the temple. And then M'lorna will come and destroy the temple at his leisure. When that happens, we will have failed Vashtu and he will cast our spirits adrift among the stars."

"But . . ." Tella searched for the phrasing and couldn't find it. But Mintab seemed to know what he wanted to say.

"None will leave the planet. A race that was once ruled by reason is again enslaved to superstition: They fear the day of the Dark One is near and feel they must be here. I have tried to tell them that Vashtu will understand that they left Rako for the good of the race, so that it might go on protecting the temple. But they insist it will be taken as a sign of further desertion of our sacred trust." The alien paused; then, "I would leave myself but I am beyond the age when I would be of use."

Tella could not read Rakoan expressions, posture, or vocal tone, but there was a very definite air of hopelessness about Mintab as they walked back into the waning sunlight.

He and Prather were halfway back to the Terran camp at the edge of the city when the idea struck him. It was daring, even by his own standards, and would either land him the crystal contract or land him in a Federation prison. He decided to check with Jo first.

On landing, he went directly to the communications setup and sent a carefully worded vocal message to Jo on Ragna. It went out via subspace laser and he decided to spend a little more time with Prather while waiting for a reply. He had given no details about what he planned to do, but had hinted that it was legally risky; he had also mentioned the antibiotic properties of the *bassa* and wanted to know if she could find a use for it.

Prather was back at work on his combat unit when Tella found him. "Do they still have manual controls on the camouflage?" he asked the trooper. "I used to pull some fancy tricks when I was in the force."

Prather nodded and showed him the controls. There hadn't been any significant changes in the past few years; the console still had a familiar feel. Tella activated the skin, then adjusted the tint and pattern controls. Prather stepped back and began to laugh as the combat unit lit up like a red and white barber pole.

"Where'd you learn to do a thing like that, Andy?"

"This is just one of the many things that endeared me to my superiors during my four years in the force. Whenever I got bored I'd figure out a new way to dress up my unit. Even figured out a few pornographic ones if you're interested."

The communications operator came out then, saying he had a brief message from Ragna for Mr. Tella. Andy took the player and listened to the recording of Jo's reply. Her voice was clear but sounded strained:

"Andy, I'm rushing off to Jebinose. Your success on Rako may be more crucial now than even before, especially if what you say about this bassa *is true. As of now, you not only represent Fairleigh Tubes, but Opsal Pharmaceuticals as well, and can make tentative arrangements for them should the Rakoans decide to sell* bassa. *If you're successful, notify the interstellar news services without delay. Good luck."*

Tella handed the player back to the operator, then climbed back into the combat unit. "Tell me if this reminds you of anything, Ben."

He made some adjustments on the console, then closed the observation bubble over his head. The body, arms, and legs of the unit began to glow in green and yellow stripes while the observation bubble took on a brilliant blue-white color with a large black spot in the middle.

Prather's voice came through the earphones: "You know, Andy, that looks a lot like that god of Evil over in the temple. Whatsisname . . . ?"

"M'lorna," Tella whispered and activated the anti-grav plates.

Ω

There wasn't much light left, but he didn't think he'd get lost. After all, he had no intention of trying to follow the streets. He climbed for altitude and headed in the general direction of the dome. It was easy to spot from the air and he circled around in order to approach it from the far side.

It was dark where he landed at the edge of the park, but infra-red lenses and image intensifiers gave him a day-bright picture on his screen.

Let's make this short but sweet, he thought, and started the unit on a slow walk toward the dome.

He was almost halfway there before one of the natives spotted the towering and all-too-familiar figure shambling out of the darkness. There was an instant of panic, then a great shout went up as the guardians quickly formed a barrier between M'lorna and the temple of Vashtu. Rakoans of every description—male, female, crippled, and infirm—poured onto the clearing from all sides to reinforce the living wall before the Dark One. Tella watched Mintab scurry inside the temple, then activated one of the lasers.

A beam of green light lanced out and scored a groove along the outer wall of the dome to his right, then arced over the doorway and grooved the left wall of the dome. And then M'lorna was among the Rakoans.

They smashed, bashed, slashed at him with fists, feet, rocks, clubs, and knives to no avail. Their proud defiance faded as they saw the God of Evil and Darkness wade inexorably through their ranks like a farmer through a grainfield. M'lorna was at the entrance to the temple of Vashtu, his Ancient enemy, and nothing could stop him.

But before the Dark One could enter, a struggling, staggering Mintab emerged, holding high the jewel-tipped staff that had rested in the hands of Vashtu in the shrine. M'lorna halted abruptly and, as Mintab moved forward with the staff, gave ground. Then, before the eyes of the assembled faithful of Vashtu, the God of Evil and Darkness rose slowly, silently, and disappeared into the blackened sky.

Ω

"You're under arrest, Tella!" said Prather as Tella extricated himself from the unit. The sergeant's face was scarlet, and he held a gravity cuff under one arm.

"What's the charge?"

"How does assault on an alien population sound for a start?"

"What makes you say I assaulted anyone?" Tella knew he was in trouble but was not going to allow himself to be trapped into any admissions.

Prather smirked. "I monitored your screens from the moment you left. I saw every move you made; even made a recording of it. You're in trouble, friend. You're going up to the cruiser for safe-keeping, and from there you're going to Fed Central to face charges."

"But first he's going to make an abject apology to Mintab and the Rakoan people for desecrating their shrine!" said Chornock as he stormed into the courtyard. "He has completely destroyed whatever good will I've managed to build up with these people and I demand that he make an apology before he leaves!"

After a lengthy debate, Prather reluctantly agreed to ferry Chornock and Tella over to the Rakoan section of the city, but the trip proved unnecessary: Mintab was waiting for them by the flitter.

"My people will now go with the doctor to his homeland," he said without preamble. He stood tall and impassive in the dark, but his respiratory rate seemed to be more rapid than usual.

"But . . ." Chornock stammered.

"My people are celebrating now. They have successfully defended their temple and deserve to congratulate themselves. In the morning, however, we shall begin to make arrangements with this man to trade for the stones." He indicated Tella.

"I'm afraid Mr. Tella will not be here in the morning," Prather said.

"We will deal with no one else," Mintab shot back. It was a statement of fact.

Chornock and Prather glanced at each other, then shrugged. "Very well. He will be here in the morning."

"And *bassa*?" Tella asked, feeling relief flood through him; he was off the hook. "Will you trade *bassa*?"

"Of course. What we shall ask in return is continued work toward assuring the future of our race." His eyes bored into Tella's. "With help, my people will surely be here to protect the temple on the day M'lorna *really* comes."

Tella suddenly felt as if someone had rammed a fist into his solar plexus. "Excuse me," he said in his native tongue as he backed away from the alien. "I've got a number of very important subspace calls to make."

XIV

JO

Traveling in a state of mental and emotional anesthesia, Jo barely remembered the trip between Ragna and Jebinose. One shock had followed another and it was only after the commercial liner she had boarded had gone into orbit around her destination that she began taking notice of her surroundings again.

Immediately after seeing Larry collapse during his subspace call, she had placed a call of her own to the spaceport on Jebinose. The administrator there informed her that an unidentified man had been rushed to Copia Hospital—alive but unconscious. Her next call was a message to the hospital stating that the man from the spaceport was to be given all necessary care and that all bills would be paid in full through a given account number at a sector bank.

Then came the next shock: after deciding to go to Jebinose herself and to take Old Pete with her—she didn't want him out of her sight—she discovered that he had departed for Jebinose days before. There could no longer be any doubt in her mind that Old Pete was involved in her father's death . . . and perhaps involved in whatever had happened to Larry.

Jebinose twirled below her now, looking like any other innocent, Earth-class planet. But Jebinose was different. Jebinose had killed her father and injured her lover. Jo was reluctant to board the waiting downward shuttle. She feared the planet.

Thoughts of her father tumbled into her head; sharp, clear memories that time couldn't blur. There had existed an indescribable bond between them that had been intensified after her mother's death to the point where at times she almost thought she knew what her father was thinking. She hadn't understood then why he had left her with her aunt and uncle and gone off to another planet. It had crushed her. She couldn't fully understand it now, but at least she could accept it. Her acceptance in no way, however, diminished the inner tension between the love she still felt for her father and the residual anger and resentment at what she considered a callous desertion.

She looked again at the planet outside the viewport and felt a pressure within her. She wanted to strike out at something, someone, anything. She was like a dying giant star that had collapsed in on its iron core and was waiting to go supernova. But she held on. You couldn't hate a planet. There was a human hidden somewhere on Jebinose who was responsible for what happened to Larry. She knew what he looked like—she had replayed the recording of Larry's subspace call over and over on the way out from Ragna until that balding head, sallow skin, and pair of merciless eyes were seared upon her memory. She fingered the tiny blaster in her hip pouch. She would find him . . .

She would find Old Pete, too. And what an explosive confrontation that would be. It was all his fault, really. If he had only stayed on his island in the Kel Sea, if he had only stayed out of her life, if he had only kept his suspicions to himself, she and Larry would probably be at the casino now playing a round or two of pokochess.

True, his suspicions had not been unfounded—there was most certainly a plot against the Federation and he deserved credit for recognizing it long before anyone else. But that could not absolve him from whatever he was covering up on the planet below.

The steward was signaling her that it was time to board the shuttle. With a deep breath and clenched fists, she turned from the viewport and walked toward the lock.

Ω

The spaceport outside Copia doubled as a port for intra-atmospheric travel as well and was jammed with people at this hour. Jo felt very much alone despite the crowd eddying about her. She didn't even have her own name to lean on—she was traveling under an assumed identity and had paid for her ticket in cash on the chance that someone might be looking for a traveler named Finch or one from IBA.

As she stepped out of a dropchute from the upper level, Jo saw her first Vanek, unmistakable in his dusty robe with his blue-tinted skin and braided black hair. He sat silent and cross-legged with his back against a column in the middle of the wide, crowded, ground-floor mall. His left hand was folded inside his robe and his right held a cracked begging bowl in his lap. A few coins gleamed dully from the bowl. Passers-by took little notice of him and the Vanek, in turn, seemed oblivious to the activity around him. His hooded eyes were apparently fixed on something within.

Jo stopped and stared at the beggar momentarily. So here was one of the half-breeds who had killed her father. Perhaps the very one. Looked harmless enough.

With a quick shake of her head and shoulders—almost as if she felt a chill—she started walking. There were too many things to do before warp lag caught up with her to waste time sight-seeing. She passed within arm's length of the Vanek without another glance—she certainly wasn't going to give him anything for his bowl—and didn't notice his eyes snap open and follow her as she moved away. She was about to round a corner when she heard a crash behind her.

Startled, she turned to see the Vanek beggar on his feet, statue still, staring at her with wide dark eyes. His earthen bowl was shattered on the floor, some of the coins still rolling away on end in random directions. The travelers passing through the mall slowed their comings and goings to watch the tableau.

Then the Vanek moved toward Jo, his step faltering, hesitant. Drawing to within a half meter of her, he stopped.

"It's you!" His voice was a hoarse, high-pitched whisper.

He reached out a spindly arm and touched her hand. Jo recoiled from the dry, parchment touch.

"It is truly you! The Wheel has turned full circle!"

He whirled abruptly and hurried away.

When he was out of sight, Jo shrugged uncomfortably and continued on her way. The momentary spectators around her did the same. Soon, only two small boys remained at the scene, picking spilled coins from among the shards of the forgotten begging bowl.

Ω

She found a public vidphone booth and called Copia Hospital. The Vanek incident moments earlier lingered in her mind. There was an eerie quality about the whole thing. He seemed to recognize her. Could he have somehow perceived the relationship between her and Junior Finch? She shrugged again. Who knew what went on inside a Vanek head anyway?

A middle-aged woman in traditional medical white appeared on the screen. "Copia Hospital," she said.

"I'd like some information on a patient named Lawrence Easly," Jo told her. "He was admitted as an emergency three nights ago."

"I'm sorry, but that is considered privileged information and not for release. If you wish, you may contact the patient's physician directly—"

"I was given to understand," Jo cut in, "that he was alive three days ago. Can you tell me that much?"

"I can tell you that he is stable and that's about all," the woman said, sensing Jo's concern. "Does that help any?"

"Yes, it does," Jo replied, obviously relieved. That meant he was holding his own.

A sign on the wall outside the vidphone area glowed "Subspace Calls" and she followed the blinking arrow. The booths were located halfway down a long, low mezzanine that ran between the mall and the service area. Jo stood and surveyed the six deluxe booths. All were identical and it would have been virtually impossible to identify the booth she sought had she not noticed the tool cart sitting outside the furthest one.

A closer look revealed a man in coveralls crouching on the floor of the booth, peering through an inspection port.

Playing a hunch, Jo opened the door. "Find out what hurt that guy yet?" she asked.

The serviceman looked up. "Nothing in here hurt anybody, lady. Everything's in top shape." His attitude was defensive.

"I've got a few questions about these booths—" Jo began.

"Look, lady," he said with some annoyance, "I'm not supposed to say anything. If you've got questions, go ask them down at the main office. Addams Leasing—it's in the directory."

"Okay. I'll do just that."

She rented a flitter, punched in the code number of the company's main office, and sat lost in thought while Copia passed unnoticed beneath her. It stopped automatically above her destination and she brought it down for a landing on the roof.

Inside, a lean, hawkish man awaited her behind a counter. "May I help you?" he said in unctuous tones as she approached.

"Yes. I'd like some information on your subspace call booths."

A sign on the counter identified the man as Alvin Mirr and he brightened visibly. "Ah! You wish to lease some?"

"No, I just want to ask somebody a few questions."

Mr. Mirr's attitude cooled abruptly. "Oh. In that case, you can find all you want to know in this." He brusquely flipped a pamphlet across the counter at her and started to turn away.

"Listen, you!" Jo flared, flinging the pamphlet back in his face. "One of my employees—who happened to be in excellent health until he stepped into one of your booths—has spent the last three days in the local hospital, and whether or not you find yourselves up to your ears in a lawsuit may very well depend on the answers I get here today!"

Mr. Mirr suddenly became very accommodating. "You must be referring to that unfortunate incident out at the spaceport. We're terribly sorry about that, of course, but I can assure you unequivocally that our callbooths are absolutely accident-proof. Especially our deluxe models—they're shielded in every way with the finest insulation. Why, we even have a psi-shield on each and every one. We haven't overlooked a thing. And something else I should—"

"Wait! Stop!" Jo said, interrupting the torrent of explanations. "Did you say the callbooths have psi-shields?"

"The deluxe models, yes," he nodded. "For the utmost in privacy. The caller can even opaque the glass to guard against lip-readers if he so desires."

"But why a psi-shield?"

"Some very important and sensitive communiqués regarding high-level business and political matters go out from those booths. Our customers want to know that every effort to ensure their discretion has been made. They want to know that even a telepath can't eavesdrop on them."

Jo considered this for a moment. "Does it work in both directions?" she asked after a pause.

"I don't under—" Mirr began, a puzzled expression flickering across his face. Then, "Oh, I see what you mean. Yes, the psi-shield is non-directional: there's a damper effect on either side of the booth wall."

"Thank you!" Jo said and turned and headed for the roof.

Next stop was Copia Hospital. She punched in the number and thought about psi-shields. Before collapsing, Larry had mentioned a "wild card," a psi-talent who was somehow involved—involved with her father or involved with deBloise, he never said. Then there was that horrible little man who looked into the booth after Larry went down. She wondered ... maybe Larry was supposed to die in that booth and maybe the psi-shield saved his life.

But that would mean she was dealing with a psi-killer and such people were not supposed to exist. Of course, the psi-killers lurking about Occupied Space would certainly like everyone to think so. There had never been a confirmed case, but Jo was sure that somewhere there was a psi who could kill with his mind ... in all of humanity's trillions on all the inhabited planets, there should be at least one—more than one.

One thing she knew: Larry uncovered something here, something potentially damaging to deBloise or his plans. There was even an intimation of deBloise's involvement in her father's death in that foreshortened call. But how could that be?

Unless Old Pete was the link.

The flitter slowed and hovered. Copia Hospital waited below.

Ω

Jo had never been inside a hospital before and she did not find the experience a pleasant one. It was as if the big building existed apart from the rest of society, isolated in its own time and space. There was a subculture here consisting of the physically ill and those who cared for them. Nothing else seemed to matter.

A nurse guided her to Larry's private room where she happened to catch his doctor on afternoon rounds. Most of the medical care as well as most of the scut work in the hospital could have been handled by machines at greater speed and at much less expense. But the fully automated hospital had been tried long ago . . . and found wanting. Patients simply didn't do well in them. There appeared to be significant psychophysiological benefit to be derived from personalized care by another human being, rather than a machine. And so the physical presence of the attending physician at intervals, and the ever-present nursing staff, remained an integral and indispensable part of the hospital routine.

"At first we thought he was another case of the horrors," the doctor said. He was a heavy-set, swarthy man who spoke in clipped tones and wasted neither time nor words. "But we have ways of testing for the horrors, and this is definitely something else."

Jo was surprised at Larry's appearance—he looked so healthy. He lay quietly in the bed, breathing easily, a calm, untroubled expression on his face. He looked for all the world like a man taking an afternoon nap. But no one could wake him.

"The horrors," the doctor was saying, "is an unwillingness to respond to any external stimuli. The conscious and subconscious portions of the brain receive the stimuli but block response as part of the pathological process. Mr. Easly's problem is different: he seems to be suffering from complete deafferentation."

"You'll have to explain that term, Doctor." Jo was listening attentively but her eyes had not moved from Larry's face.

"Well, it means that all—and I mean *all*—external stimuli are being blocked from his conscious mind. For a crude analogy, think of a computer with all its inputs disconnected."

"And what could cause something like that?"

"Can't say. Was he a stable personality? We could be dealing with a psychotic state, you know."

"He was about as stable as they come," Jo said, glancing at the doctor. "Could this . . . deafferentation, as you call it, be some sort of defense mechanism?"

The doctor's smile was condescending. "Highly unlikely. And if it were, it isn't a very good one. It's like sticking your head in the sand: it doesn't do much for the rest of the body."

"It does if someone's aiming at your head," Jo muttered. She caught a puzzled glare from the doctor and changed the subject. "How long before he comes out of it?"

"Impossible to say at this point—tomorrow, a week, a year, I don't know. But he will come out of it."

"You're sure?"

"As sure as I can be with no past experience in this kind of thing. Our tests this morning showed a slight decrease in the level of deafferentation; we repeated them just before you came in, and if those show a further decrease, we'll be able to estimate the rate of improvement and give you a prognosis." So saying, he turned and left the room.

Jo returned her attention to Larry and the sensation of an impending internal explosion returned, more forcefully than ever this time. Larry should not be like this—he was such a strong, capable man, it was obscene to see him lying in a comatose state, utterly helpless. And there was nothing she could do to help him.

She grasped the top rung of the guardrail at the side of the bed and squeezed until her knuckles turned white and emitted little popping sounds of protest. She wanted to scream in utter frustration but held back. She would save it for the time when she caught up with the man who did this.

Eventually, she made herself relax with slow, deep breaths. She released the guardrail and slowly paced the room with her arms folded across her chest. She was almost herself again by the time the doctor returned.

"He's making excellent progress," he said in a matter-of-fact tone. "Should be out of it in six or eight hours if he continues his present rate of reafferentation."

Jo's heart leaped. "How will he be when he wakes up?"

The doctor shrugged. "How can I say? Anything I tell you will be pure guesswork. He could be alert and well rested, like a man awakening from a good night's sleep, or he could be irreversibly psychotic. We'll have to wait and see."

The nurses were changing shifts then and the new head nurse came in as the doctor was leaving.

"Sorry," she said, "but visiting hours are over."

"Not for me," Jo said. There was something in her tone that made the head nurse hesitate. She glanced at the doctor.

"Let her stay," he said. "It's a private room and she won't be disturbing anybody."

The nurse shrugged. "As long as you chart it as done by your authority, it makes little difference to me."

When they were gone, she dropped into a chair, then flipped a switch and watched as part of the outer wall became transparent. The sun was setting in gory splendor and she closed her eyes and let its bloody dying light warm her face until it was out of sight behind the neighboring buildings. A noise behind her made her turn.

The door was opening and through it passed a procession of five cloaked and hooded figures. The last to enter closed the door behind him and then all pulled back their hoods at once to reveal blue-gray skin, high-domed foreheads, and long black hair in a single braid.

Vanek!

Jo rose to her feet as the first visitor approached her. He appeared to be identical in features to the other four except for a spot of darker blue pigment to the left of center on his forehead. Although there was nothing menacing in their actions, Jo felt uneasy . . . these were the creatures who freely admitted murdering her father.

"What do you want?" she asked and cursed her voice for the way it quavered on the last word.

The one who appeared to be the leader stopped before her and bowed at the waist. His four companions did likewise. Holding this position, they began a sonorous chant in the old Vanek tongue. There was a queer melodic quality to the sound that Jo found oddly soothing. As they held the final note, they resumed an erect posture.

The leader then withdrew his hands from beneath his robe. The right held a cracked earthen bowl, the left a delicate carving of a fruit tree in bloom.

"These belong to you," he said in a sibilant voice. Jo could not read his expression clearly. There was deep respect there, but it was overlaid with a mixture of awe and vindication.

She took the gifts and tried to speak, but found she could not. She knew they had originally been given to her father and holding them in her hands suddenly made her feel close to him again.

"The evil one is near," the leader said. "But he will not harm you again. I will see to that."

" 'Evil one!' " she said abruptly, finding her voice at last. "Who is he? Where can I find him?"

"Wheels within wheels, *bendreth*," was the answer. Then the five Vanek pulled their hoods up and filed out the door without another word. Dazed by the entire incident, Jo simply stood in the middle of the room and watched them leave. With the click of the closing door, however, she shook herself and hurried after them.

The hall was deserted. A nurse rounded the corner and Jo stopped her. "Where did those Vanek go?" she asked.

The nurse cocked her head. "Vanek?"

"Yes, five of them were in Lawrence Easly's room just now."

"My dear," she said with a short laugh, "I've spent half my life working in this hospital and I've never seen *one* Vanek in these halls, let alone five! They have their own medicine." Her brow furrowed momentarily. "Come to think of it, though, there *have* been an awful lot of them outside the hospital lately. I guess they could sneak in, but I don't know why they'd want to."

"But what about the room monitor?" Jo had noticed a vid receptor plate high on the wall opposite the foot to Larry's bed. "Didn't anyone see them on the screen?"

"We only monitor the patient's bed with that," was the terse reply. "Now if you don't mind, I've got work to do."

Jo nodded absently and returned to the room. She placed the bowl and statue on the night table and pulled a chair up next to the bed. This was where she would spend the night. She was tired, but somehow she doubted she would be able to sleep.

XV

DEBLOISE

Elson deBloise tapped in Proska's vidphone code and waited. He was calling from a public booth. In all the too-many dreadful years of his association with Proska, this was only the second time he had ever called him, and he was not going to entrust the ensuing conversation to his office phone. After the events of the past few days, there was no telling who might be listening in on that.

He waited for Proska's face to appear. How he hated and feared that little monster. How he wished he had never oozed into his office that day—was it really seventeen years ago?—and offered to put Finch out of the picture without force or violence. If only he hadn't—

The screen lit up with Proska's grim, pinched features.

"Well, well!" the little man said with genuine surprise. "What have we here? An eminent sector representative calling me on my humble vidphone! Such an honor!"

"Never mind the feeble attempts at humor—it doesn't become you. And there's nothing humorous behind this call."

"Well?"

"I've got an errand for you," deBloise said and watched carefully for Proska's reaction. He was going to cherish this—after seventeen years of catering to the monster's every whim, at last he had a demand for *him*.

But Proska remained impassive, only the slightest flicker of his dark-eyed gaze revealing anything untoward in the conversation. He waited in silence until deBloise was forced to go on.

"You failed. The booth was psi-shielded, and a source at the hospital informs me that the investigator you were supposed to eliminate will regain consciousness before morning."

"Investigator? I thought you told me he was some sort of a reporter."

"That's what I thought. That's what customs thought. His identification was completely phony. I had a few of my contacts check with the Risden Service and they never heard of him. The name he used, however, was legitimate: he is Lawrence Easly, a private investigator who does a lot of work in the business sector."

"Business? Why would he be checking up on you?"

"I don't know. I didn't say he was exclusively an industrial spy. Besides, I've been aware that I've been under some sort of surveillance for a number of years now and perhaps he's been behind it."

"But to what end?"

"Very possibly he works for someone with political ambitions who's preparing for the day when he meets me head-on and wants to store up a little dirt in advance."

"A potential blackmailer, then."

"Yes. Competition for you."

Proska's smile was not a nice thing to see. "No one could know what I know, could they, Elson? Or if they did know, they couldn't prove it like I can."

"That doesn't matter right now! If I'm exposed . . . if even a hint of what happened in Danzer should leak out, I'll be ruined. And that'll mean the end of your meal ticket. So I expect you to go over to the hospital and finish the job!"

"Dear Elson, how you've changed! I remember the horror and revulsion you expressed the first time I demonstrated my little specialty to you. And now you actually want me to use it twice on the same man!"

Proska's mocking observation stunned deBloise and his mind suddenly leaped back seventeen years to the day a lowly civil servant stood in his office—smaller and more sedate than the one he occupied these days—and told him he could "take care of the problem in Danzer." DeBloise had summarily dismissed the man, but the memory of his eyes and his expression when he spoke remained with him.

And when Tayes returned from Danzer a few days later with the news that Jeffers had capitulated and that the Vanek Equality Act would be as good as dead once word got out, deBloise knew he had to act immediately if he was to save anything. He contacted the little man and sent him to Danzer.

The next morning, all of Jebinose was shaken by the news that the man who had been pushing the Vanek cause in Danzer was dead. And that the Vanek had confessed—as a group—to his murder. So it was a natural reaction for deBloise to laugh in Proska's face when he showed up that afternoon demanding "compensation" for his services.

Proska did something to him then . . . something horrible . . . a little taste of his "specialty," as he liked to call it. And then he took him to the oldest, most run-down part of Copia, picked out a besotted derelict, and showed deBloise what happened when Cando Proska loosed the full force of his power on a man.

But that wasn't the end of the show. Next stop was Proska's dim little flat where deBloise watched in horror as a vid recording showed him telling Proska to put an end to Junior Finch's meddling in Danzer. He was watching a copy. The original would be released to the public should any mishap, even slightly suspicious, befall Proska.

Cando Proska had been bleeding him ever since. And the thought of what Proska could do to him, politically and personally, had haunted him ever since, waking him in the night sweating, panting, and clawing at the air.

"I never realized then what you intended to do," he said hoarsely, snapping himself back to the present, "or what you could do."

"Would it have made any difference?" Proska sneered. "Finch showed the VEA to be a useless political charade. I saw that coming; that's why I came to you. Because once he succeeded, support for your Vanek Equality Act would have evaporated. And if the VEA went down, so would you! You remember how you looked on that recording—you were ready to do anything. Anything!" His tone of voice suddenly became very businesslike. "Speaking of the recording, it now resides on Fed Central, addressed to the Federation ethics committee."

DeBloise's face blanched and his voice shook. "Proska, I'd like to—"

"I know what you'd like to do, that's why the recording is where it is."

DeBloise struggled for control and finally regained it. After a long pause, he said, "Are you going to finish the job?"

"Certainly. But I need a way to get into the hospital without attracting too much attention. I require a certain proximity, you know."

"That can be arranged. I'll have my source at the hospital contact you. I'm leaving for Fed Central tonight. I hope everything is settled before my ship has made its first jump."

"Don't worry. I'll take care of everything."

XVI

JO

Jo was dozing lightly in a chair when the new head nurse came in during the changeover to the third shift and startled her to wakefulness.

"Sorry if I surprised you, dear," she said with a warm smile. "Just making my rounds." She was older than most of the other nurses and seemed to have all her moves down to an almost unconscious routine. She checked the vital-signs contacts and gave Larry a long, careful look. Apparently satisfied, she smiled and nodded to Jo, then left.

The door was opened again a few moments later by a middle-aged orderly. He was short, sallow-skinned, and balding. He seemed unduly surprised to see Jo sitting by the bed. "I'm sorry, miss," he said in a low voice, "but I'm going to prepare the patient for some final tests and you'll have to step out for a few minutes."

Jo shot to her feet and started to reach for her pouch, then changed her mind. "What? Must I?"

"I'm sorry . . . hospital rules."

"All right," she said resignedly, and started for the door, swaying slightly with fatigue. When she passed behind the orderly, however, her whole demeanor changed. Her right hand shot into her hip pouch and pulled out a small but very deadly blaster. She had it pointed at the orderly's head and was squeezing the trigger when his peripheral vision caught the movement. He turned—

—and Jo had no body. At least that's the way it seemed. All tactile and proprioceptive impulses from her extremities and torso had been cut off. She was a head floating in the room. It was a sickening sensation. She could still use all her facial muscles and could move her eyes. Could she speak? She was afraid to try, afraid she'd only be able to scream. And she didn't want to do that, not in front of this . . . creature.

"Not a fair play at all," he said mockingly. Jo's arm was still extended in front of her, the blaster still in her hand. He reached out casually and took it from her grasp. "Why would you want to blow a poor orderly's head off?"

Jo took a deep breath. At least she thought she did; there was no sensation of her chest expanding. She wasn't sure she could keep herself from gibbering with fear, but she would try to speak.

"I . . ." Her throat seemed to be closing; she swallowed and tried again. "I wanted to keep you from finishing what you started the other night."

Eyes wide, the little man moved closer. "How do you know about that?"

"I was on the receiving end of the subspace call he was making when he collapsed. You walked up, looked in, and walked away. I knew you were responsible."

"So," he said slowly, glancing between Jo and Easly, "it seems I made *two* mistakes the other night. Not only did I forget about the psi-shields on those booths, but I walked into the field of the visual pickup. I'm either getting old or I'm getting careless." He held up the blaster. "Tell me, would you have really used this on the back of my head?"

Jo tried to nod, but her neck muscles wouldn't respond. "Without the slightest hesitation." Her right arm remained extended with her hand a few tantalizing centimeters from the blaster, but she could not reach for it. The arm would not respond! It was as if it no longer belonged to her. She gave up trying and hunted for ways to keep the man talking. Maybe the head nurse would come back . . .

"Can you think of a better way to handle a psi-killer?" she added.

"Is that what you think I am?" he said with an amused leer. "A psi-killer? How quaint!"

"Aren't you?"

"My dear, to compare my capabilities to those of a psi-killer is to compare the transmitting power of a subspace laser to an ancient crystal radio."

Right then and there, Jo knew she was dealing with a monstrous ego.

"What can you do that's so special?"

His eyes danced as he looked at her, and suddenly she was—

—nowhere. There was blackness, a total absence of light. There was silence, a total absence of sound. There was a total negation of sensation: she did not soar, she did not float, she did not fall. The blackness had no depth, nor did it press in on her. There were no dimensions: no time, no depth, no length or width—she couldn't even call herself a locus. She was nowhere and there was no way out. She began to panic. There were no reference points. If only she could find something to latch onto, to focus her mind on, she'd be able to hold her sanity. But there was nothing but nothingness. Her panic doubled. Then doubled again. Before too long it would overwhelm her consciousness and she'd be irretrievably insane. She—

—was back in the hospital, a head floating in the room.

"Like it?" he asked, still smiling and watching her closely. "That's my specialty and that's how you'll spend the rest of your life. But first, some answers, please. We know this man is a detective—did you hire him?"

It was a while before Jo could speak. She was totally unnerved. She'd say anything to delay being sent back into nowhere, but right now she couldn't speak. He waited patiently. Finally:

"Yes. I hired him years ago to see what he could get on Elson deBloise." She would lie, but slowly and carefully.

"Why deBloise?"

"I represent a number of pro-Charter groups who think the Restructurists are getting too powerful. They want leverage against deBloise."

"Ah! Political blackmail!"

"The name of the game. But we never expected to run into

anything like you," she added, trying to maneuver the conversation back around to what was undoubtedly the man's favorite subject: himself.

He bit. "And you never will! Even if you should walk out of this room and live for another thousand years, you will never meet another like Cando Proska! I was ten years old when I first found out I could hurt someone with my mind. I killed a boy that day. The knowledge of what I had done, and could still do, nearly destroyed me then. But no one believed I was responsible."

Although his eyes remained fixed in Jo's direction, he was no longer seeing her. "I never tried to use my power again, never had another contact with psionics until I was eighteen. I was walking through one of the seedier sections of our fair city one night when a young man about my age pointed a blaster in my face and demanded money." He paused and smiled. "I killed him. It was so simple: I just wished him dead and he dropped to the pavement.

"Suddenly, I was a different person!" he said, his eyes focusing on Jo again. He was relishing the telling of his story—he had the power of life and death over anyone he chose, but no one knew it. He could not gloat in public and he desperately craved an audience.

"I began experimenting. I used the flotsam and jetsam of the city—the zemmelar zombies, the winos, the petty thieves, people no one would miss. I didn't understand my power then, and I still don't, but I know what I can do. I can shock a person into brief unconsciousness, or kill him instantaneously. Or"—again a pause, again a smile—"I can throw him into permanent limbo: not only complete deafferentation, as they call it, but complete de-*ef*ferentation as well. No neurological impulses can enter or leave the conscious mind. It is the most horrifying experience imaginable. You just had a taste of it and can appreciate how long your sanity would last under those conditions."

He began to pace the room. "I bided my time doing bureaucratic drudge work until I could find a way to make my special talents pay off. My patience was rewarded when I found I could help out Elson deBloise by working my little specialty on a troublemaker in a town called Danzer. If you were a native you'd have heard of the man—Junior Finch."

Had Proska been watching Jo at that moment, he would have realized that he had struck a nerve. Jo closed her eyes and clamped her teeth down on her lower lip. All fear was suddenly gone, replaced by a mind-numbing coldness. But in the center of that coldness was a small flame, growing ever brighter and hotter. The sensation of an impending explosion was returning, building inexorably.

"I've heard of him," she managed to gasp after the slightest hesitation. "But I thought the Vanek killed him."

"Oh, they did!" Proska said with a laugh. "They said they did and the Vanek never lie. Perhaps you'll appreciate the story. The man, Finch, was posing a real threat to deBloise's political career. We came to an agreement: In return for certain financial considerations, I would take Finch out of the picture. I went to Danzer that night, waited for him to leave a little celebration he was having, and then intercepted him in an alley. He had been drinking, yet even in an alcoholic haze he gave me more resistance than all my previous experimental subjects combined. But I succeeded, as I always do. He was little more than a drooling vegetable when I left him, an apparent victim of a very severe case of the horrors. And that was the turning point of my life."

Jo was sick and nearly blind with fury at this point, but utterly helpless to do anything. Her voice was almost a sob. "But the knife . . . the Vanek knife."

"Ah!" he said, too enraptured by his own narrative to notice Jo's tortured expression. "That was the final and perfect touch! One of Finch's Vanek friends apparently happened on him in the alley and somehow realized what had been done to him—they have much greater depth of perception than pure Terrans. A knife in the heart is a true act of friendship to someone I've put into limbo. The death worked out very well for deBloise—his legislation passed with great fanfare and his political future was set. He gave me a little trouble by crediting the Vanek with ending Finch's interference, but I gave him firsthand experience in the range of my power, and he suddenly became quite agreeable. As an insurance policy, I have proof of his first-degree involvement in Finch's death ready to go to the Federation ethics committee should anything suspicious happen to me. All in all, my life is quite comfortable nowadays as a result of our arrangement."

He moved close to Jo now, his face inches from hers. "But so much for history. My hold over deBloise is weakened if anyone else knows what I know. Therefore, it is my sad duty to see to it that you and your detective friend never know anything again."

The room dimmed but did not disappear. Jo was ready for him this time and held on to reality with every fiber of her consciousness. Her mind was being fueled by a most formidable force: hate.

Proska's voice seemed to come from far away. "You put up a good defense," he said with amusement. "The last one to give me this much of a fight was Finch."

"Maybe it runs in the family," Jo heard herself say.

"What do you mean?" His tone was puzzled and the onslaught against her mind slackened ever so slightly. She screamed:

"JUNIOR FINCH WAS MY FATHER!"

The emotional bomb that had been building within Jo detonated then, and the force of the explosion coursed along the psionic channel that Proska had opened between them. It was an awesome thrust: the grief, the anger, the repressed self-pity that had accumulated within Jo since the death of her father had at last found an object. It merged with the fresh rage and fury sparked by Proska's cold-blooded recounting of the destruction of her father's mind, and lashed out with one savage, berserk assault.

Proska reeled backward and slammed his palms over his eyes. His mouth opened to scream but no sound came forth as he toppled to the floor and lay flat on his back, unconscious.

Jo suddenly was aware of her body again. Her arms, legs, and torso were hers once more, but the legs wouldn't support her. Her knees buckled and she hit the floor. Consciousness began to slip away, but before it was completely gone, she saw a hooded, blue-skinned head poke inside the door and peer about the room.

Ω

When Jo next opened her eyes, she found herself looking into the face of the night nurse. It took a few heartbeats to orient herself, then she looked across the floor to where she had last seen Proska. He was gone. So was her blaster.

"Where is he?" she asked, raising herself to a crouching position.

"Where is who?"

"That man! The one who was on the floor over there!"

The nurse smiled. "I'm afraid you might be just a little bit overtired, dear. You should take better care of yourself. You might have been lying on the floor here half the night if Mr. Easly hadn't buzzed."

"Larry!" Jo cried, leaping to her feet.

Larry Easly lay quietly in bed, his hands folded on his chest, a tired smile on his face. "Hi, Jo," he said.

Relief and reaction flooded through Jo as she crossed to the side of his bed and grasped both his hands. There were tears on her cheeks . . . for the second time in seventeen years, she cried. It was a joy to see Larry conscious again, to see life in his eyes and hear his voice. But there was something else . . . mingling in the relief was a curious, unfamiliar lightness of spirit, as if she had been purged of all doubt and grief and fear. She felt reborn, released from the past.

. . . Except for Old Pete. There was still that reckoning to come.

"I'll leave you two alone a minute," the nurse said, "then he's got to go to neuro for retesting." She closed the door behind her.

"I'm okay, Jo," Larry said in a faint voice. "Just weak. So weak, it was all I could do to press the buzzer when I came to and saw you lying on the floor."

Jo's head snapped up. "Did you see anyone else on the floor?"

"No. Who do you mean?"

"Proska."

Larry's eyes widened. "You know about him?"

"He was here! He tried to do to me what he did to my father and almost did to you." She hesitated. "Were you in . . . limbo all this time?"

"No," he said, shaking his head vigorously. "But I know what you mean. A Vanek explained to me what Proska could do. No, I was unconscious. I don't remember a thing between the booth and this room. But where is he?"

"I don't know. Something happened when he tried to do whatever it is he does, and we both collapsed. He was on the floor last time I saw him." She glanced at the wall clock. "And that was two hours ago!"

"Well, I've only been conscious for about a quarter hour and he wasn't here when I came to." He tried to lift his head but the effort was too much. "That means he's free. Jo, we've got to get off Jebinose. Proska is the most dangerous man alive! I can't walk yet, but I'll go on a stretcher!"

The nurse returned then. "Time to go. The neuro crew's waiting for you."

"The only place I'm going is deep space!" Larry said with what little vehemence he could muster.

Ignoring him, the nurse flipped open the top of a small console at the foot of the bed. "You're going to neuro. Doctor's orders. Besides, you're too weak to go anywhere else." She tapped in a three-digit combination, then closed the console cover.

The bed began to roll toward the door and Larry looked around helplessly. "Jo?"

"It's okay," she said. "I'll wait for you here." She was not looking at Larry anymore. Her eyes were riveted on a dark figure standing in the shadows out in the hall.

When the bed had disappeared down the hallway to the left with the nurse in tow, Jo went and sat in the chair by the window.

Old Pete entered. Jo's blaster was in his right hand and he crossed the room and laid it on the night table beside her. "You won't be needing this," he said.

"You sure?" Jo's voice was flat, hard. Her eyes were on the wall.

"Proska is dead. He will probably be found shortly after sunrise in the park across the street. His hands and feet have been tied to a tree; the top of his skull has been removed and his brain has been smashed at his feet."

Jo looked at Old Pete's face and saw in it a sense of infinite satisfaction. "You?"

He shook his head. "No. The Vanek. They removed him shortly after he passed out here and then Rmrl came to my hotel room. He returned your blaster and led me out to view their handiwork."

"But I thought the Vanek never took any initiative—never acted on their own or anyone's behalf."

"They don't. Or at least they didn't until now." He took a deep breath and shivered. "For beginners, they sure don't fool around."

"How do the Vanek know you?"

"I met Rmrl seventeen years ago when I was looking into Junior's death."

"Is he the one with the blue spot on his forehead?"

Old Pete nodded. "He's the one who delivered the *coup de grâce* on your father and he's been waiting in silence all those years for the Great Wheel to turn full circle and exact its vengeance on Proska. Your arrival prompted him into action. He was no longer a typical Vanek after his close association with Junior Finch, and when word of your arrival spread among the Vanek—"

"How did they know who I was?"

He avoided Jo's eyes. "They . . . knew. And Rmrl was determined to prevent the same thing that happened to Junior from happening to you. So he and a few of his friends decided to take Proska out of the picture permanently. He had to die . . . there was no other way to handle him."

"I hope they catch up to deBloise, too!"

"They have no quarrel with him."

"They should—Proska told me that he went after my father at deBloise's direction."

Old Pete's voice was a whisper. "Then it's true!"

"What . . . ?"

"It's true! DeBloise is involved. I've had that feeling in my gut for seventeen years and could never prove a thing! That's why I've kept such close surveillance on him all this time!"

"And what about Proska?"

"Never knew he existed until this morning when Rmrl told me all about him and showed me his remains."

There was a long silence. When Jo finally broke it, her voice was low but carried a sharp edge.

"Do you really expect me to believe that?"

"It's true."

She rose slowly to her feet and faced him. She wanted to believe it. She wanted everything over and done with and settled so she could get on with her life. But there were still too many dark areas concerning the old man.

She spoke the question that had hovered unasked between them since Old Pete entered the room.

"Why are you here?"

"On Jebinose? I came to see if I could help Larry. After all, I've been here before and—"

"*Lie!* You came here to cover something up—or to make sure it stayed covered. What is it?"

"Nothing!" He spoke the word without conviction, as if he knew he would not be believed.

"Another lie! The only connection between you and Jebinose is my father—and he's dead. You're somehow involved in that and I want to know how!"

"Never! I'd never do anything to hurt Junior. How can you say that?"

"The Vanek told me, 'He will not harm you again.' Did he mean you?"

"No! He meant Proska!"

"Impossible! Proska didn't even know I existed until tonight. How could he hurt me 'again'?"

Old Pete blanched and said nothing.

Turning to the night table, Jo picked up the blaster and pointed it at the old man's head.

"Tell me now or I swear by all I believe in I'll burn a hole in you! What was your involvement in my father's death?"

Her eyes told him that she was not bluffing. She had tasted vengeance tonight and was not going to stop until all accounts were settled. Old Pete began to tremble. He found a seat by the far wall and slowly lowered himself into it. Looking up, he held Jo's angry glare and spoke in a dry, cracked whisper.

"Junior Finch isn't dead and he wasn't your father."

The words lay on the air like dead fish on a stagnant pond. Finally, Jo shook her head as if to clear it.

"What are you saying?" She was nearly insane with rage. "Do you think you can get yourself out of this by concocting some wild—"

"It's true! Junior Finch was completely sterile as a result of the radiation leak that almost killed him when he was eighteen. He didn't produce a single gamete from then on. The histology report on the genitournary system in the autopsy reconfirmed this, and I paid an ungodly sum to have that part wiped."

Jo's finger tightened on the blaster trigger. "But you said he isn't dead! How can you have an autopsy report on a man who isn't dead?"

Old Pete held up his hands. He was tired, defeated, and more than a little frightened by what he saw in Jo's eyes. "Just let me continue. When your grandfather found out Junior was sterile, he was crushed. It meant there'd be no Finch beyond Junior to carry IBA into the future. That was important to him. He set great store by family—didn't start one till late in life, but once he had one, it became the prime focus of his life. Junior was one child, IBA another. He wanted them both to go on forever. Me, I couldn't care less."

"Get to the point."

"I am: your grandfather—a most persuasive man—talked Junior and his wife into cloning a child from Junior. I helped them arrange it." He paused. Then, regretfully: "*You* are that child."

"But I'm female. Junior Finch was male." The blaster did not waver. "A clone is an exact genetic duplicate."

"Surely you know that a female can be cloned from a male. All that needs to be done is to discard the 'y' chromosome and duplicate the already existing 'x.' That's basic genetics. They decided on a female clone to head off any possible future suspicions. A male would grow up to look *exactly* like its donor, and if anyone ever raised the question, it would only take a simple chromosome test to put Junior in jail and you in a molecular dissociation chamber. There are laws against clones, remember? A female was safer."

Jo lowered the blaster. She believed him. The same instinct that had told her he was lying before, now told her that Old Pete was telling the truth. And it fit. It explained a number of things, especially the awe she seemed to inspire in the Vanek—they had recognized her for what she was.

Jo was inspiring a little awe in herself right now. She should be reeling, numb, crushed, shattered. But she wasn't. She felt strangely aloof from the revelation, as if Old Pete were talking about someone else.

"I've kept this from you all along," he was saying. "I never wanted you to know. When I went, I was going to take it with me since Junior's death left me the only one alive who knew. Even the technicians who did the cloning never knew whose cells they were working with."

"Why would you keep that from me?"

"Because I didn't see any purpose being served by telling you that you're not a real person under the law. I didn't know how you'd react to being a clone . . . that knowledge could destroy someone. Don't you see? Junior Finch isn't dead. He's you—and you're Junior Finch."

Jo answered without hesitation, her voice tranquil and full of confidence. "No. I'm *Josephine* Finch. I always have been and always will be. Junior Finch lies buried out there. Josephine Finch will go on living as she always has—as Josephine Finch."

It was a declaration of identity that brought Old Pete to his feet and made his face light with relief. Jo's sense of self had brought her through. She knew who she was and intended to remain who she was, no matter what her origins. He stepped toward her, falteringly, until he stood before her. Placing his arms on her shoulders, he said, "I'm proud of you . . . Josephine."

She dropped the blaster and hugged him. She wanted to speak, wanted to tell him how glad she was that his only crime was trying to protect her, but her larynx was frozen. She could only squeeze his thin old body very hard.

Old Pete understood and held her until his arms ached. Then he pushed her to arm's length. "Can we be friends now?"

Jo nodded, smiled, then began to laugh. Old Pete joined her and only the return of Larry and his bed prevented them from breaking into tears.

"What's so funny?" he asked. His voice sounded stronger than before. "And what are you doing here, Pete?"

Jo waited until the bed had moved back into its old position, then sat on it next to Larry.

"He came to see if we needed any help," she said with a smile.

"Well, we do. We've got to put some distance between Proska and us!"

"No," she said. "He's dead. The Vanek killed him." She then went on to tell Larry and Old Pete about Proska's blackmail scheme against deBloise.

"What a totally vile, amoral character!" Old Pete said when she was finished.

"Almost as bad as deBloise," Jo replied coldly. "He sent Proska to Danzer, then used my dead father's name to further his filthy career." She realized she still thought of Junior Finch as her father, and no doubt always would. And someday, she would explain it all to Larry. But now was certainly not the time.

"But, Jo," Larry said. "A Vanek committed the actual murder."

"He did the right thing." Her voice was soft now. "I'd want the same for myself . . . you don't know what it was like. The Vanek did the right thing for Proska, too. But the deBloise account stays open."

"He's not even on Jebinose," Old Pete said. "Left for Fed Central yesterday. I heard it on the vid while I was getting dressed earlier."

"DeBloise is finished already," Larry said. "At least he is if what Proska told you about the recording is true."

"It's true. There was no reason for him to lie to me. He said the original would go to the Federation ethics committee if 'anything suspicious' happened to him. When the news of his death is released, I'm sure the person to whom he entrusted the recording will find the circumstances sufficiently suspicious to warrant its forwarding to the committee." Her smile was grim. "It should arrive within the next standard day. And that should put an end to deBloise's career."

"Well, that's fine," Old Pete observed testily, "and it's well deserved, and it's about time. But it doesn't do anything for the purpose for which we all became involved in this mess. What's there to keep the rest of the Restructurists from carrying through with the Haas plan, whatever it is?"

"That may not be a problem any more," Jo said, her smile brightening. "I'll know for sure after I make a single call."

She went to the vidphone by the bed and asked to be connected with the Jebinose brokerage house, galactic stocks division.

"At this hour of the morning?" Larry asked.

Old Pete explained: "The Galactic Board never closes, Larry; and on a sparsely populated planet like Jebinose, there's usually only one office dealing with galactic stocks. So, to take orders from all over the planet, they have to stay open 'round the clock. The younger brokers usually get stuck with the night watch."

"But what's all this got to do with deBloise and Haas?"

"I haven't the faintest idea," Old Pete said with a shrug.

"You will," Jo said as she waited for a connection. "I'll explain it all just as soon as I get a few quotes."

A youngish male face appeared on the screen. "Galactic stocks division," he muttered wearily.

"Good morning," Jo said with as much pleasantness as she could muster. "I've decided to buy stock in a couple of companies and would like to know the current selling price."

"Surely. Which ones are you interested in?"

"Fairleigh and Opsal."

The broker's hand had been reaching for the computer terminal built into his desktop with the intention of punching in the company names. Jo's words arrested the motion. He smiled wanly. "You and everybody else."

"What do you mean?"

"I mean that it seems like half of Occupied Space wants to buy shares in those two companies. I've been trying to beam in a bid all night and I can't even get through!"

"Why the sudden interest?"

"It started as an unsubstantiated report by one of the news services that Fairleigh had tapped a lode of natural Leason crystals and that Opsal would soon be coming out with the most revolutionary antibiotic since penicillin. When the companies confirmed, the Galactic Board began to go crazy. Everybody wants to get in on the ground floor. Let's face it, Fairleigh will be able to cut its production costs by a half—it's going to have the peristellar drive field pretty much to itself for a while. And Opsal's new product is going to make hundreds of other antibiotics obsolete."

"May I leave a buy order with you?"

"Yes," he sighed, "but I don't think I'll be able to do anything for you until the stocks split—which I expect to happen before the end of the trading day."

"How about Teblinko?"

"Down. Way down."

"And Stardrive?"

"Same story. A lot of people are trying to dump their Stardrive and Teblinko for Fairleigh and Opsal. As a matter of fact, the whole Star Ways family is being hurt by this. Now, how many shares did you want to—"

"Thank you," Jo interjected with a pleased smile. "You've been most helpful." She abruptly broke the connection and the broker's startled visage faded from the screen.

"What was that all about?" Larry asked.

Old Pete shook his head in admiration. "My boy, you've just seen the largest conglomerate in Occupied Space knocked on its ear! And your lady friend here is the one responsible for the whole thing!"

"I had a lot of help from Andy . . . couldn't have done it without him, in fact."

Larry struggled to a sitting position. "Now wait a minute! Why does everybody seem to know what's going on here except me? And how did Andy get involved?"

Jo slipped into the chair next to the vidphone. "I said I'd explain, so let's start with the Restructurists. The main thrust of all their activities and all their rhetoric is to get the Federation into the free market and start exercising some controls on the interstellar economy—that's where real power lies. But the LaNague Charter prevents the Federation from doing anything of the sort. So, the Restructurists must find a way to nullify the charter, and the only way to do that is to activate the emergency clause."

"If you remember your Federation history, Larry," Old Pete added, "that's the clause that temporarily voids the entire charter and thus all the limits on the Federation as a government. LaNague disowned it, even though it was designed to be activated only in times of threat to the Fed and its member planets; he wanted no emergency powers at all and fought tooth and nail against the clause. But he was ignored and it was tacked on against his protests."

"I vaguely remember learning something about that once," Larry said, "but it's not exactly recent history."

"Maybe not," Jo replied, "but it's very important history to the Restructurists. They've had their eyes on the emergency clause for a long time—it's the one weak spot in the charter. And this time they figured they'd found the way to get to it. The Haas warp gate was going to be the trigger to activate the emergency clause."

She leaned forward and alternated her gaze between Larry and Old Pete. "Now comes the tricky part. DeBloise and his circle were pouring enormous amounts of money into the warp gate and pushing Haas to market it prematurely—*before* the final improvements which would have made it a truly revolutionary product. No intelligent investor would do such a thing; it was financial suicide. And since deBloise is anything but a fool, I could interpret the situation only one way: the Restructurists wanted the gate to be a tremendous commercial failure.

"Why would they want to do that? It baffled me until two things clicked: Haas's statement about military contracts and Old Pete's joking reference to the Tarks. That's when I knew what deBloise was up to."

"I think I'm beginning to see," said Old Pete with a slow smile.

"I'm not!" Larry snapped. "What have Tarks and warp gates got to do with the Federation charter?"

"The Tarks are on their way to becoming a big problem," Jo explained. "There are numerous areas of conflict between Terran and Tarkan interests, and the list lengthens each year. Keeping that in mind, and considering the potential military uses of the gate in a wartime situation, you can see what a perfect lever it could be against the emergency clause.

"Let me give you the scenario as I believe it was planned. DeBloise and the other Restructurists involved were going to push the gate onto the market prematurely and wait for the inevitable: Star Ways would drop the price on *its* warp unit and suck off most of Haas's potential customers. When the Haas company collapsed, SW would make a nice offer to lease production rights to the gate—an offer that would make Haas richer than he'd ever dreamed. But Denver Haas, like a spoiled child, would take his ball and go home.

"That's when the deBloise circle would leap into action. They'd rush before the various defense committees and claim that continued sale and development of the warp gate was an essential preparation against the inevitable day when the Federation clashes violently with the Tarkan Empire. They'd claim that unregulated competition was depriving the Federation of the gate and would demand invocation of the emergency clause in order to intervene against SW and save the gate.

"It would be difficult to oppose them if they managed to generate enough fear. Not only would they be screaming 'security,' but they'd be painting the emotional picture of a huge conglomerate destroying a tiny company and the entire Federation suffering as a result of it. I'm sure they'd have got some sort of economic control out of it."

"And that would have been the beginning of the end," Old Pete said.

"Right. So I took aim at the one variable they figured to be a constant—Star Ways. Conglomerates are less susceptible to changes in the market, but they're by no means immune. With Andy Tella's help, I was able to put a few dents in two of SW's major subsidiaries. There's no way it can wage a successful price war against Haas now."

"That's all fine and good," Larry mused, "but without you the gate *would* have been lost. That doesn't say much for the free market."

"It says that the market deplores stupidity!" Old Pete replied in a loud voice. "It would be damn stupid for anyone to push the gate onto the market before the final refinements were perfected. Anyone with the idea of profiting from an investment would have waited. You forget—deBloise *wanted* the gate to flop; his profit was to be political, not financial.

"But enough of this talk. It's all worked out for the best. The Federation charter is safe, the warp gate will be on the market when we need it, and a certain murderer has received a long-delayed sentence. I think we should celebrate!"

"Not yet," Jo said, her facial muscles tightening and her eyes going crystalline. "Not until I've personally seen Elson deBloise thrown out of the Federation."

"You're not going without me!" Old Pete said.

EPILOGUE

They arrived at Fed Central just in time. The ethnics committee had not delayed a moment after receiving Proska's package of damning proof. Its members confronted deBloise with the evidence that he was directly responsible for the murder of another man in order to further his own political career.

DeBloise, of course, denied everything, calling it a plot instigated by the various anti-Restructurist factions within the Federation. The ethics committee was unmoved and decided that the evidence would be presented to the entire General Council at its next session. DeBloise asked, and was granted, permission to address the Council before the charges and evidence were presented.

Jo and Old Pete arrived in time to catch the tail end of his speech:

". . . that this is not government! We have tried to demonstrate this fact to you, but all in vain. We have tried for years, for centuries, to open your eyes, but you refuse to see. You refuse to see the chaos of the non-system of non-government in which you dwell. We have tried to bring order to this near-anarchy but you have repeatedly refused it.

"And now . . ." He let those two words hang in the air. He was using his considerable oratory talents to the fullest, knowing his performance was being recorded, knowing it would be played and replayed on vid news all over Occupied Space.

"And now you have stooped to smearing my reputation! Do you really believe that the other progressive members of this body would accept the trumped-up charges against me as true? They are not fools! They recognize a cynical plot when they see one! We have caucused for days, we of the Restructurist movement, and after much soul searching and heated debate, after innumerable subspace messages to the planets we represent, a decision has been reached."

Again, he paused for full effect, then:

"The worlds that stand shoulder-to-shoulder in the Restructurist movement have decided that they can no longer be a party to this insane chaos you call a Federation!

"Be it known," he said into the rising tumult from the floor, "that we are seceding from the Federation—seceding from anarchy into order. Travel in the trade lanes through our sectors is here now restricted to ships of those companies that seek and receive prior approval from the new Restructurist Union. Unauthorized craft infringing upon our territories will be seized. We shall fire on sight at any craft bearing the emblem of the LaNague Federation. From this day on, we govern our own!"

With a dramatic swirl of his cape, Elson deBloise descended from the podium and strode down the central isle of the General Council assembly hall. As he moved, other Restructurists, Philo Barth and Doyl Catera among them, rose and followed him. The rest of the Council watched in stunned silence.

Jo and Old Pete were standing by the main door to the assembly hall as deBloise passed. He glanced at Jo as he strode by but paid her no more attention than he did *any* other spectator. With the collapse of Teblinko and Star Drive on the stock exchange, his scheme to use the Haas gate against the Federation charter was voided; and with the delivery of Proska's blackmail package to the ethics committee, his personal freedom, as well as his public career, were about to suffer a similar fate. A Restructurist-Federation charter split was the only way to salvage anything.

And so he passed within a half-meter of Josephine Finch, never realizing that this tame-looking female had blasted all his plans, all his lifetime dreams of power to ruins. She was just another tourist and his glance flicked away as he went by.

A vid reporter was scrambling around the antechamber to

the assembly hall looking for reactions to this startling, historic announcement. He spied Jo and Old Pete and approached at a trot.

"Pardon me," he said breathlessly, "but I'd like to know what you think about the Restructurist secession." He pointed the vid recorder plate at Old Pete. "Do you think there's a chance of war?"

"Hardly," Old Pete replied slowly. "It's a bold move, all right—certainly a surprising one—but to talk of 'war' is a little melodramatic. Oh, I'm sure there'll be skirmishes over resource planets, and these will no doubt be referred to as 'battles,' but I foresee nothing on a large scale."

"Yes. Well, uh . . . thank you, sir," the reporter said, obviously displeased. Calm, rational answers were of no value to a good vid newscast—they slowed up the pace. He turned to Jo in the hope of finding a little feminine hysteria.

"How about you, miss? Do you think there was really a plot to assassinate Elson deBloise's character?"

Jo's mouth twisted mischievously. "Wheels within wheels, *bendreth*," she said in a solemn tone.

Then she linked her arm with Old Pete's and together they walked toward the exit, laughing.

It is given that the Tarkan Empire would never have initiated the Terran-Tarkan War if it had not been tempted by the inflamed rhetoric and spectacle of a civil war between the Federation and the Restructurist Union.

It is also given that the Restructurist secession from the Federation was precipitated when serious criminal charges were brought against Elson deBloise, the movement's most prominent member at that time. Restructurist apologists today say that the charges were false and never proven; other students of the period think otherwise. Both camps, however, agree on this: after the secession, the packet of evidence against deBloise was forwarded to Jebinose but mysteriously disappeared on the way.

One thing is certain: the contents of that packet significantly altered the course of human history.

from STARS FOR SALE:
An Economic History of Occupied Space
by EMMERZ FENT

HEALER IV

(age 505)

Find Thy Progeny

Not long after the disappearance of The Healer, the so-called deBloise scandal came to the fore. The subsequent Restructurist walk-out led to the Federation-Restructurist civil war ("war" is hardly a fitting term for those sporadic skirmishes) which was eventually transformed into a full-scale interracial war when the Tarks decided to interfere. It was during the height of the Terro-Tarkan conflict that the immortality myth of The Healer was born.

Oblivious to the wars, the horrors continued to appear at a steady rate and the psychosciences had gained little ground against the malady. For that reason, perhaps, a man with a stunning resemblance to The Healer appeared and began to cure the horrors with an efficacy that rivaled that of the original. Thus an historical figure became a legend.

Who he was and why he chose to appear at that particular moment remains a mystery.

from *The Healer: Man & Myth*
by Emmerz Fent

HEALER IV

(age 505)

Find Thy Progeny

Not long after the disappearance of The Healer, the so-called deBlock Scandal came to the fore. The subsequent Hearings that led to the Federation-Restructurist civil war ("war" is hardly a fitting term for those sporadic skirmishes) which was eventually transformed into a full-scale interstellar war when the Tarks decided to interfere. It was during the height of the Tarko-Terran conflict that the imaginatively myth of The Healer was born.

Of Fact, as the wars, the horrors continued to appear at a steady rate and the psychosomatics had gained little ground against the malady. For that reason, perhaps, a man with a startling resemblance to The Healer appeared and began to cure the horrors with an efficacy that rivaled that of the original. Thus an historical figure became a legend.

Who he was and why he chose to appear at that particular moment remains a mystery.

from The Healer: Man & Myth
by Emmerich Frant

I

Dalt locked the flitter into the roof cradle, released the controls, and slumped into the seat.

("There. Don't you feel better now?") Pard asked.

"No," Dalt replied aloud. "I feel tired. I just want to go to bed."

("You'll thank me in the morning. Your mental outlook will be better, and you won't even be stiff because I've been putting you through isometrics in your sleep every night.")

"No wonder I wake up tired in the morning!"

("Mental fatigue, Steve. *Mental*. We've both gotten too involved in this project and the strain is starting to tell.")

"Thanks a lot," he muttered as he slid from the cab and shuffled to the door. "The centuries have not dulled your talent for stating the obvious."

And it was obvious. After The Healer episode, Dalt and Pard had shifted interests from the life sciences to the physical sciences and pursued their studies amid the Federation-Restructurist war without ever noticing it. That muddled conflict had been about ready to die out after a century or so, due to lack of interest, when a new force injected itself into the picture. The Tarks, in an attempt at subterfuge as clumsy as their previous attempts at diplomacy, declared an unilateral alliance with the Restructurist coalition and promptly attacked a number of Federation bases along a disputed stretch of expansion border. Divide and conquer is a time-tested ploy, but the Tarks neglected to consider the racial variable. Humans have little compunction about killing each other over real or imagined differences, but there is an archetypical repugnance at the thought of an alien race taking such a liberty. And so the Feds and Restructurists promptly united and declared *jihad* on the Tarkan Empire.

Naturally, weapons research blossomed and physicists became very popular. Dalt's papers on field theory engendered numerous research offers from companies anxious to enter the weapons market. The Tarkan force shield was allowing their ships to penetrate deep into Terran territory with few losses, and thus became a prime target for big companies like Star Ways, whose offer Dalt accepted.

The grind of high-pressure research, however, was beginning to take its toll on Dalt; and Pard, ever the physiopsychological watchdog, had finally prevailed in convincing Dalt to shorten his workday and spend a few hours on the exercise courts.

Wearily, Dalt tapped out the proper code on the entry plate and the door slid open. Even now, drained as he was in body and mind, he realized that his thoughts were starting to drift toward the field-negation problem back at Star Ways labs. He was about to try to shift his train of thought when a baritone voice did it for him.

"Do you often talk to yourself, Mr. Cheserak? Or should I call you Mr. Dalt? Or would you prefer Mr. Storgen?" The voice came from a dark, muscular man who had made himself comfortable in one of the living-room chairs; he was pointing a blaster at the center of Dalt's chest. "Or how about Mr. Quet?" he continued with a self-assured smile, and Dalt noticed two other men, partly in shadow, standing behind him. "Come now! Don't just stand there. Come in and sit down. After all, this *is* your home."

Eyeing the weapon that followed his every move, Dalt chose a chair opposite the intruders. "What do you want?"

"Why, your secret, of course. We thought you'd be out longer and had hardly begun our search of the premises when we heard your flitter hit the dock. Very rude of you to interrupt us."

Dalt shook his head grimly at the thought of humans conspiring against their own race. "Tell your Tark friends that we're no closer to piercing their force shields than we were when the war started."

The dark man laughed with genuine amusement. "No, my friend, I assure you that our sympathies concerning the Terro-Tarkan war are totally orthodox. Your work at Star Ways is of no interest to us."

"Then what do you want?" he repeated, his eyes darting to the other two figures, one a huge, steadfast hulk, the other slight and fidgety. All three, like Dalt, wore the baggy coversuits with matching peaked skullcaps currently in fashion in this end of the human part of the galaxy. "I keep my money in a bank, so—"

"Yes, I know," the seated man interrupted. "I know which bank and I know exactly how much. And I also have a list of all the other accounts you have spread among the planets of this sector."

"How in the name of—"

The stranger held up his free hand and smiled. "None of us has been properly introduced. What shall we call you, sir? Which of your many aliases do you prefer?"

Dalt hesitated, then said, "Dalt," grudgingly.

"Excellent! Now, Mr. Dalt, allow me to introduce Mr. Hinter"—indicating the hulk—"and Mr. Giff"—the fidget. "I am Aaron Kanlos and up until two standard years ago I was a mere president of an Interstellar Brotherhood of Computer Technicians local on Ragna. Then one of our troubleshooters working for the Tellalung Banking Combine came to me with an interesting anomaly and my life changed. I became a man with a mission: to find you."

As Dalt sat in silence, denying Kanlos the satisfaction of being told to go on, Pard said, ("I don't like the way he said that.")

"I was told," Kanlos finally went on, "that a man named Marten Quet had deposited a check from Interstellar Business Advisers in an account he had just opened. The IBA check cleared but the man didn't." Again he looked to Dalt for a reaction. Finding a blank stare, he continued:

"The computer, it seems, was insisting that this Mr. Quet was really a certain Mr. Galdemar and duly filed an anomaly slip which one of our technicians picked up. These matters are routine on a planet such as Ragna, which is a center for intrigue in the interstellar business community; keeping a number of accounts under different names is the rule rather than the exception in those circles. So, the usual override code was fed in, but the machine still would not accept the anomaly. After running a negative check for malfunction, the technician ordered a full printout on the two accounts." Kanlos smiled at this. "That's illegal, of course, but his curiosity was piqued. The pique became astonishment when he read the listings, and so naturally he brought the problem to his superior."

("I'm sure he did!") Pard interjected, ("Some of these computer-union bosses have a tidy little blackmail business on the side.")

Be quiet! Dalt hissed mentally.

"There were amazing similarities," Kanlos was saying. "Even in the handwriting, although one was right-handed and the other obviously left-handed. Secondly, their fingerprints were very much alike, one being merely a distortion of the other. Both were very crude methods of deception. Nothing unusual there. The retinal prints were, of course, identical; that was why the computer had filed an anomaly. So why was the technician so excited? And why had the computer ignored the override code? As I said, multiple accounts are hardly unusual." Kanlos paused for dramatic effect, then: "The answer was to be found in the opening dates of the accounts. Mr. Quet's account was only a few days old . . . Mr. Galdemar's had been opened two hundred years ago!

"I was skeptical at first, at least until I did some research on retinal prints and found that two identical sets cannot exist. Even clones have variations in the vessels of the eyegrounds. So, I was faced with two possibilities: either two men generations apart possessed identical retinal patterns, or one man has been alive much longer than any man should be. The former would be a mere scientific curiosity; the latter would be of monumental importance."

Dalt shrugged. "The former possibility is certainly more likely than the latter."

"Playing coy, eh?" Kanlos smiled. "Well, let me finish my tale so you'll fully appreciate the efforts that brought me to your home. Oh, it wasn't easy, my friend, but I knew there was a man roaming this galaxy who was well over two hundred years old and I was determined to find him. I sent out copies of the Quet/Galdemar retinal prints to all the other locals in our union, asking them to see if they could find accounts with matching patterns. It took time, but then the reports began to trickle back—different accounts on different planets with different names and fingerprints, but always the same retinal pattern. There was also a huge trust fund—a truly staggering amount of credits—on the planet Myrna in the name of Cilo Storgen, who also happens to have the Quet/Galdemar pattern.

"You may be interested to know that the earliest record found was that of a man known simply as 'Dalt,' who had funds transferred from an account on Tolive to a bank on Neeka about two and a quarter centuries ago. Unfortunately, we have no local on Tolive, so we couldn't backtrack from there. The most recent record was, of course, the one on Ragna belonging to Mr. Galdemar. He left the planet and disappeared, it seems. However, shortly after his disappearance, a Mr. Cheserak—who had the same retinal prints as Mr. Galdemar and all of the others, I might add—opened an account here on Meltrin. According to the bank, Mr. Cheserak lives here . . . alone." Kanlos's smile took on a malicious twist. "Care to comment on this, Mr. Dalt?"

Dalt was outwardly silent but an internal dispute was rapidly coming to a boil.

Congratulations, mastermind!

("Don't go putting the blame on me!") Pard countered. ("If you'll just think back, you'll remember that I told you—")

You told me—guaranteed me, in fact—that nobody'd ever connect all those accounts. As it turns out, you might as well have left a trail of interstellar beacons!

("Well, I just didn't think it was necessary to go to the trouble of changing our retinal print. Not that it would have been difficult—neovascularization of the retina is no problem—but I thought changing names and fingerprints would be enough. Multiple accounts are necessary due to shifting economic situations, and I contend that no one would have caught on if you hadn't insisted on opening that account on Ragna. I warned you that we already had an account there, but you ignored me.")

Dalt gave a mental snort. *I ignored you only because you're usually so overcautious. I was under the mistaken impression that you could handle a simple little deception, but—*

The sound of Kanlos's voice brought the argument to a halt. "I'm waiting for a reply, Mr. Dalt. My research shows that you've been around for two and a half centuries. Any comment?"

"Yes." Dalt sighed. "Your research is inaccurate."

"Oh, really?" Kanlos's eyebrows lifted. "Please point out my error, if you can."

Dalt spat out the words with reluctant regret. "I'm twice that age."

Kanlos half started out of his chair. "Then it's true!" His voice was hoarse. "Five centuries . . . incredible!"

Dalt shrugged with annoyance. "So what?"

"What do you mean, 'so what?' You've found the secret of immortality, trite as that phrase may be, and I've found you. You appear to be about thirty-five years old, so I assume that's when you began using whatever it is you use. I'm forty now and don't intend to get any older. Am I getting through to you, Mr. Dalt?"

Dalt nodded. "Loud and clear." To Pard: *Okay, what do I tell him?*

("How about the truth? That'll be just about as useful to him as any fantastic tale we can concoct on the spur of the moment.")

Good idea. Dalt cleared his throat. "If one wishes to become immortal, Mr. Kanlos, one need only take a trip to the planet Kwashi and enter a cave there. Before long, a sluglike creature will drop off the cave ceiling onto your head; cells from the slug will invade your brain and set up an autonomous symbiotic mind with consciousness down to the cellular level. In its own self-interest, this mind will keep you from aging or even getting sick. There is a slight drawback, however: Legend on the planet Kwashi has it that only one in a thousand will survive the ordeal. I happen to be one who did."

"I don't consider this a joking matter," Kanlos said with an angry frown.

"Neither do I!" Dalt replied, his eyes cold as he rose to his feet. "Now I think I've wasted just about enough time with this charade. Put your blaster away and get out of my house! I keep no money here and no elixirs of immortality or whatever it is you hope to find. So take your two—"

"That will be enough, Mr. Dalt!" Kanlos shouted. He gestured to Hinter. "Put the cuff on him!"

The big man lumbered forward carrying a sack in his right hand. From it he withdrew a metal globe with a shiny cobalt surface that was interrupted only by an oval aperture. Dalt's hands were inserted there as Giff came forward with a key. The aperture tightened around Dalt's wrists as the key was turned and the sphere suddenly became stationary in space. Dalt tried to pull it toward him but it wouldn't budge, nor could he push it away. It moved freely, however, along a vertical axis.

("A gravity cuff,") Pard remarked. ("I've read about them but never expected to be locked into one.")

What does it do?

("Keeps you in one spot. It's favored by many law-enforcement agencies. When activated, it locks onto an axis through the planet's center of gravity. Motion along that axis is unrestricted, but that's it; you can't go anywhere else. This seems to be an old unit. The newer ones are supposedly much smaller.")

In other words, we're stuck.

("Right.")

". . . and so that ought to keep you safe and sound while we search the premises," Kanlos was saying, his veneer of civility restored. "But just to make sure that nothing happens to you," he smiled, "Mr. Giff will stay with you."

"You won't find anything," Dalt said doggedly, "because there isn't anything to find."

Kanlos eyed him shrewdly. "Oh, we'll find something, all right. And don't think I was taken in by your claim of being five hundred years old. You're two hundred fifty and that's about it—but that's longer than any man should live. I traced you back to Tolive, which happens to be the main research center of the Interstellar Medical Corps. I don't think it's a coincidence that the trail ends there. Something was done to you there and I intend to find out what."

"I tell you, nothing was—"

Kanlos held up a hand. "Enough! The matter is too important to bandy words about. I've spent two years and a lot of money looking for you and I intend to make that investment pay off. Your secret is worth untold wealth and hundreds of years of life to the man who controls it. If we find no evidence of what we're looking for on the premises, we'll come back to you, Mr. Dalt. I deplore physical violence and shall refrain from using it until I have no other choice. Mr. Hinter here does not share my repugnance for violence. If our search of the lower levels is fruitless, *he* will deal with you." So saying, he turned and led Hinter below.

Giff watched them go, then strode quickly to Dalt's side. He made a hurried check of the gravcuff, seemed satisfied, then stole off to one of the darker corners of the room. Seating himself on the floor, he reached into his pocket and removed a silvery disk; with his left hand he pushed back his skullcap and parted the hair atop his head. The disk was attached here as Giff leaned back against the wall and closed his eyes. Soon, a vague smile began to play around his lips.

("A button-head!") Pard exclaimed.

Looks that way. This is a real high-class crew we're mixed up with. Look at him! Must be one of those sexual recordings.

Giff had begun to writhe on the floor, his legs twisting, flexing, and extending with pleasure.

("I'm surprised you don't blame yourself for it.")

I do, in a way—

("Knew it!")

—even if it is a perversion of the circuitry we devised for electronic learning.

("Not quite true. If you remember, Tyrrell's motives for modifying the circuits from cognitive to sensory were quite noble. He—")

I know all about it, Pard. . . .

The learning circuit and its sensory variation both had noble beginnings. The original, on which Dalt's patent had only recently expired, had been intended for use by scientists, physicians, and technicians to help them keep abreast of the developments in their sub-or sub-sub-specialties. With the vast amount of research and experimentation taking place across the human sector of the galaxy it was not humanly possible to keep up to date and still find time to put your knowledge to practical use. Dalt's (and Pard's) circuitry supplied the major breakthrough in transmitting information to the cognitive centers of the brain at a rapid rate.

Numerous variations and refinements followed, but Dr. Rico Tyrrell was the first to perfect the sensory mode of transmission. He used it in a drug rehabilitation program to duplicate the sensory effects of addictive drugs, thus weaning his patients psychologically off drugs after their physiological dependence was gone. The idea was quickly pirated, of course, and cassettes were soon available with sensory recordings of fantastic sexual experiences of all varieties.

Giff was whimpering now and flopping around on the floor.

("He's got to be a far-gone button-head to have to tune in at a time like this . . . and right in front of a stranger, at that.")

I understand some of those cassettes are as addictive as Zemmelar and chronic users become impotent in real sexual contexts.

("How come we've never tried one?")

Dalt gave a mental sniff. *I've never felt the need. And when the time comes that I need my head wired so I can get a little—*

There was a groan in the corner: Giff had reached the peak of the recording. His body was arched so that only his palms, his heels, and the back of his skull were in contact with the floor. His teeth were clamped on his lower lip to keep him from crying out. Suddenly he slumped to the floor, limp and panting.

That must be quite a cassette!

("Most likely one of those new numbers that combines simultaneous male and female orgasms—the ultimate in sexual sensation.")

And that's all it is: sensation. There's no emotion involved.

("Right. Superonanism.") Pard paused as they watched their sated guard. ("Do you see what's hanging from his neck?")

Yeah. A flamestone. So?

("So it looks exactly like yours—a cheap imitation, no doubt, but the resemblance is remarkable. Ask him about it.")

Dalt shrugged with disinterest, then noticed Giff stirring. "Are you quite finished?"

The man groggily lifted his slight frame into a sitting position. "I disgust you, don't I," he stated with a low voice, keeping his eyes averted to the floor as he disconnected the cassette from his scalp.

"Not really," Dalt replied, and sincerity was evident in his voice. A few centuries ago he would have been shocked, but he had learned in the interim to view humanity from a more aloof vantage point—a frame of mind he had consciously striven for since his days as The Healer. It had been difficult to maintain at first, but as the years slid by, that frame of mind had become a natural and necessary component of his psyche.

He didn't despise Giff, nor did he pity him. Giff was merely one expression of the myriad possibilities open to human existence.

Dalt moved the gravcuffs downward and seated himself crosslegged on the floor. When Giff had stowed the cassette in a sealed compartment in his overalls, Dalt said, "That's quite a gem you have tied around your neck. Where'd you steal it?"

The fidgety man's eyes flashed uncharacteristically. "It's mine! It may not be real but it's mine. My father gave one to all his children, just as his own mother gave one to him." He held out the stone and gazed at its inner glow.

"Hm!" Dalt grunted. "Looks just like mine."

Giff rose to his feet and approached Dalt. "So you're a Son of The Healer, too?"

"Wha'?"

"The stone . . . it's a replica of the one The Healer wore centuries ago. All Children of The Healer wear one." He was standing over Dalt now and as he reached for the cord around his neck, Dalt idly considered ramming the gravcuff upward into Giff's face.

("That won't work,") Pard warned. ("Even if you did manage to knock him unconscious, what good would it do us? Just play along; I want to hear more about these Children of The Healer.")

So Dalt allowed Giff to inspect his flamestone as he sat motionless. "I'm no Son of The Healer. As a matter of fact, I wasn't aware that The Healer ever had children."

Giff let go of Dalt's gem and let it dangle from its cord again. "Just a figure of speech. We call ourselves his children great-great-great-*grand*children would be more accurate—because none of us would have been born if it hadn't been for him."

Dalt gave him a blank stare and Giff replied in an exasperated tone, "I'm a descendant of one of the people he cured a couple of hundred years ago. She was a victim of the horrors. And if The Healer hadn't come along and straightened her out, she'd have been institutionalized for all her life; her two sons would never have been born, would never have had children of their own, and so on."

("And you wouldn't be here standing guard over us, idiot!") Pard muttered.

"The first generation of Children of The Healer," Giff went on, "was a social club of sorts, but the group soon became too large and too spread out. We have no organization now, just people who keep his name alive through their families and wear these imitation flamestones. The horrors still strikes everywhere and some say The Healer will return."

"You believe that?" Dalt asked.

Giff shrugged. "I'd like to." His eyes studied Dalt's flamestone. "Your's is real, isn't it?"

Dalt hesitated for an instant, engaged in a lightning conference. *Should I tell him?*

("I think it's our only chance. It certainly won't worsen our situation.")

Neither Pard nor Dalt was afraid of physical violence or

torture. With Pard in control of all physical systems, Dalt would feel no pain and could at any time assume a deathlike state with a skin temperature cooled by intense vasoconstriction and cardiopulmonary activity slowed to minimal level.

Yeah. And I'd much prefer getting out of these cuffs and turning a few tables to rolling over and playing dead.

("That would gall me, too. Okay—play it to the hilt.")

"It's real, all right," Dalt told Giff. "It's the original."

Giff's mouth twisted with skepticism. "And I'm president of the Federation."

Dalt rose to his feet, lifting the gravcuff with him. "Your boss is looking for a man who's been alive for two or three centuries, isn't he? Well, I'm the man."

"We know that."

"I'm a man who never sickens, never ages . . . now what kind of a healer would The Healer be if he couldn't heal himself. After all, death is merely the culmination of a number of degenerative disease processes."

Giff mulled this over, accepting the logic but resisting the conclusion. "What about the patch of silver hair and the golden hand?"

"Pull this skullcap off and take a look. Then get some liquor from the cabinet over there and rub it on my left wrist.

After a full minute's hesitation, wherein doubt struggled in the mire of the afterglow of the cassette, Giff accepted the challenge and cautiously pulled the skullcap from Dalt's head. "Nothing! What are you trying—"

"Look at the roots," Dalt told him. "You don't think I can walk around with that patch undyed, do you?"

Giff looked. The roots in an oval patch at the top of Dalt's head were a silvery gray. He jumped away from Dalt as if stung, then walked slowly round him, examining him as if he were an exhibit in a museum. Without a word, he went to the cabinet Dalt had indicated before and drew from it a flask of clear orange fluid.

"I . . . I'm almost afraid to try this," he stammered, opening the container as he approached. He poised the bottle over Dalt's wrists where they were inserted into the gravcuff, hesitated, then took a deep breath and poured the liquor. Most of it splashed on the floor but a sufficient amount reached the target.

"Now rub," Dalt told him.

Without looking up, Giff tucked the flask under his arm and

began to massage the fluid into the skin of Dalt's left wrist and forearm. The liquor suddenly became cloudy and flesh-colored. Giff took a fold of his coveralls and wiped the solution away. From a sharp line of demarcation at the wrist on down over the back of the hand, the skin was a deep, golden yellow.

"You *are* The Healer!" he hissed, his eyes meeting Dalt's squarely for the first time. "Forgive me! I'll open the cuff right now." In his frantic haste to retrieve the key from his coveralls, Giff allowed the liquor flask to slip from beneath his arm and it smashed on the floor.

"Hey! That was real glass!" Dalt said.

Giff ignored the crash and the protest. The key was in his hand and he was inserting it into its slot. The pressure around Dalt's wrists was suddenly eased and as he pulled his hands free, Giff caught the now-deactivated cuff.

"Forgive me," he repeated, shaking his head and fixing his eyes on the floor. "If I'd had any idea that you might be The Healer, I would've had nothing to do with this, I swear! Forgive—"

"Okay! Okay! I forgive you!" Dalt said hurriedly. "Now, do you have a blaster?"

Giff nodded eagerly, reached inside his coveralls, and handed over a small hand model, cheap but effective at close range.

"Good. Now all we've got to do—"

"Hey!" someone yelled from the other side of the room. "What's going on?"

Dalt spun on reflex, his blaster raised. It was Hinter and he had his own blaster ready. There was a flash, then Dalt felt a searing pain as the beam from Hinter's weapon burned a hole through his chest two centimeters to the left of his sternum. As his knees buckled, everything went black and silent.

II

Rushing to the upper level at the sound of Giff's howl, Kanlos came upon a strange tableau: the prisoner—Dalt, or whatever his name was—was lying on his back with the front of his shirt soaked with blood and a neat round hole in his chest . . . very dead. Giff kneeled over him, sobbing and clutching the empty gravcuff to his abdomen; Hinter stood mutely to the side, blaster in hand.

"You fool!" he screamed, white-faced with rage. "How could you be so stupid!"

Hinter took an involuntary step backward. "He had a blaster! I don't care how valuable a guy is, when he points a blaster in my direction, I shoot!"

Kanlos strode toward the body. "How'd he get a blaster?"

Hinter shrugged. "I heard something break up here and came to investigate. He was out of the cuff and holding the blaster when I came in."

"Explain," he said, nudging the sobbing Giff with his foot.

"He was The Healer!"

"Don't be ridiculous!"

"He was! He proved it to me."

Kanlos considered this. "Well, maybe so. We traced him

back to Tolive and that's where The Healer first appeared. It all fits. But why did you let him loose?"

"Because I am a Son of The Healer!" Giff whispered. "And now I've helped kill him!"

Kanlos made a disgusted face. "Idiots! I'm surrounded by fools and incompetents! Now we may never find out how they kept him alive this long." He sighed with exasperation. "All right. We've still got a few rooms left to search."

Hinter turned to follow Kanlos. "What about him?" he said, indicating Giff.

"Useless button-head. Forget him."

They went below, leaving Giff crouched over the body of The Healer.

III

("C'mon. Wake up!")

Wha' happen?

("Hinter burned a hole right through your heart, my friend.")

Then how come I'm still alive?

("Because the auxiliary heart I constructed in your pelvis a couple of hundred years ago has finally come in handy.")

I never knew about that.

("I never told you. You know how you get when I start making improvements.")

I'll never object again. But what prompted you to build a second heart?

("I've always been impressed by what happened to Anthon when you blasted a hole in his chest, and it occurred to me that it just wasn't safe to have the entire circulatory system dependent on a single pump. So I attached the auxiliary organ to the abdominal aorta, grew a few bypass valves, and let it sit there . . . just in case.")

I repeat: I'll never object again.

("Good. I've got a few ideas about the mineral composition of your bones that I—")

Later. What do we do now?

("We send the button-head home, then we take care of those two below. But no exertion; we're working on only one lung.")

How about waiting for them with the blaster?

("No. Better idea: Remember the sights we came across in the minds of all those people with the horrors?")

I've never quite been able to forget.

("Neither have I, and I believe I can recreate enough of them to fill this house with a concentrated dose of the horrors . . . concentrated enough to insure that those two never bother us or anyone else again.")

Okay, but let's get rid of Giff.

IV

Without warning, the body in front of Giff suddenly rolled over and achieved a sitting position. "Stop that blubbering and get out of here," it told him.

Giff's mouth hung open as he looked at the obviously alive and alert man before him with the gory front and the hole in his chest where his heart should be. He looked torn between the urge to laugh with joy and scream with horror. He resolved the conflict by vomiting.

When his stomach had finally emptied itself, he was told to go to the roof, take the emergency chute down to the ground, and keep on going.

"Do not," the body emphasized, "repeat: do not dally around the grounds if you value your sanity."

"But how . . ." he began.

"No questions. If you don't leave now I won't be responsible for what happens to you."

Without another word but with many a backward glance, Giff headed for the roof. At last look, he saw the body climb unsteadily to its feet and walk toward one of the chairs.

Dalt sank into a chair and shook his head. "Dizzy!" he muttered.

("Yeah. It's a long way from the pelvis to the brain. Also,

there's some spasm in the aortic arch that I'm having trouble controlling. But we'll be all right.")

I'll have to trust you on that. When do we start with the horrors?

("Now. I'll block you out because I'm not sure that even you can take this dose.")

I was hoping you'd say that, Dalt thought with relief, and watched everything fade into formless grayness.

And from the bloody, punctured body slumped in the chair there began to radiate evil, terror, horror. A malignant trickle at first, then a steady stream, then a gushing torrent.

The men below stopped their search and began to scream.

V

Dalt finished inspecting the lower rooms and was fully satisfied that the two gurgling, drooling, blank-eyed creatures that had once been Kanlos and Hinter were no longer a threat to his life and his secret. He walked outside into the cool night air in a vain attempt to soothe his laboring right lung and noticed a form slumped in the bushes.

It was Giff. From the contorted position of his body it was evident that he had fallen from the roof and broken his neck.

"Looks like this Son of The Healer couldn't follow directions," Dalt said. "Must've waited up on the roof and then went crazy when the horrors began and ran over the edge."

("Lot's son.")

"What's that supposed to mean?"

("Nothing. Just a distorted reference to an episode in an ancient religious book,") Pard said, then switched the subject. ("You know, it's amazing that there's actually a cult of Healer-followers awaiting his return.")

"Not really so amazing. We made quite an impression . . . and left a lot undone."

("Not because we wanted to. There was outside interference.")

"Right. But that won't bother us now, with the war going on."

("You want to go back to it, don't you?")

"Yes, and so do you."

("Guess you're right. I'd like to learn to probe a little deeper this time. And maybe find out whoever or whatever's behind the horrors.")

"You've hinted at that before. Care to explain?"

("That's all it is, I'm afraid: a hint . . . a glimpse of something moving behind the scenes. I've no theory, no evidence. Just a gnawing suspicion.")

"Sounds a little farfetched to me."

("We'll see. But first we'll have to heal up this hole in the chest, get the original heart working again—if I may quote you: 'What kind of a healer would The Healer be if he couldn't heal himself!'—and try to think up some dramatic way for The Healer to reappear.")

After a quick change of clothes, they went to the roof and steered their flitter into the night, leaving it to the Meltrin authorities to puzzle out two babbling idiots, a broken button-head, and a respected physicist named Cheserak who had vanished without a trace.

They blamed it on the Tarks, of course.

FOUR:
LATE PHASE

HEALER V

(age 1231)

Heal Thy Nation

The horrors persisted at varying levels of virulence for well over a millennium and during that period certain individuals with the requisite stigmata of flamestone, snowy patch of hair, and golden hand, purporting to be The Healer, appeared at erratic intervals. The efforts of these impostors were somehow uniformly successful in causing remissions of the malady. And although this was vigorously dismissed as placebo effect by most medical authorities (with the notable exception of IMC, which, for some unaccountable reason, refused to challenge the impostors), the explanation fell on deaf ears. The Children of The Healer would have none of it. Rational explanations were meaningless to them.

And so the cult grew, inexorably. It crossed planetary, commonwealth, and even racial barriers (we have already discussed the exploits among the Lentemians and among the Tarks during the postwar period), spreading in all directions until . . . the horrors stopped.

As suddenly and as inexplicably as the phenomenon had begun, the horrors came to a halt. No new cases have been reported for the last two centuries and the cult of The Healer is apparently languishing, kept alive only by the fact that various individuals in Healer regalia have been spotted on vid recordings in public places here and there about the planets. (The only consistency noted in regard to these sightings is that, when interviewed later, no one in these scenes could ever remember seeing a man who looked like The Healer.)

The Children of The Healer say that he awaits the day when we shall need him again.

We shall see.

from *The Healer: Man & Myth*
by Emmerz Fent

I

Federation Central: first-adjutant's office, Federation Defense Force.

Ros Petrical paced the room. He was fair, wiry, and prided himself on his appearance of physical fitness. But he wasn't trying to impress the other occupant of his office. That was Bilxer, an old friend and the Federation currency coordinator, who had been passing the time of day when the report came in. Bilxer's department was responsible for tabulating and reporting—for a fee, of course—the fluctuations in the relative values of the member planets' currencies There had, however, been a distinct and progressive loss of interest in the exchange rates through recent generations of currency coordinators, and consequently Bilxer found himself with a surfeit of time on his hands.

Petrical, until very recently, could hardly complain about being overworked during his tenure as first adjutant. At the moment, however, he wished he had studied finance rather than military science. Then he would be stretched out on the recliner like Bilxer, watching someone else pace the floor.

"Well, there goes the Tark theory," Bilxer said from his repose. "Not that anyone ever truly believed they were behind the incidents in the first place."

"Incidents! That's a nice way of dismissing cold, calculated slaughter!"

Bilxer shrugged off Petrical's outburst as semantic nitpicking. "That leaves the Broohnins."

"Impossible!" Petrical said, flicking the air with his hand. He was agitated, knew it, and cursed himself for showing it. "You heard the report. The survivors in that Tark village—"

"Oh, they're leaving survivors now?" Bilxer interjected. "Must be mellowing."

Petrical glared at his guest and wondered how they had ever become friends. He was talking about the deaths of thousands of rational creatures and Bilxer seemed to assign it no more importance than a minor devaluation of the Tark erd.

Something evil was afoot among the planets. For no apparent reason, people were being slaughtered at random intervals in random locations at an alarming rate. The first incidents had been trifling—trifling, at least, on an interstellar scale. A man burned here, a family destroyed there, isolated settlements annihilated to a man; then the graduation to villages and towns. It was then that reports began to filter into Fed Central and questions were asked. Petrical had painstakingly traced the slaughters, reported and unreported, back over seven decades. He had found no answers but had come up with a number of questions, the most puzzling of which was this: If the marauders wanted to wipe out a village or a settlement, why didn't they do it from the atmosphere? A single small peristellar craft could leave a charred hole where a village had been with little or no danger to the attackers. Instead, they arrived on-planet and did their work with antipersonnel weapons.

It didn't make sense . . . unless terror was part of the object. The attack teams had been very efficient—they had never left a witness. Until now.

"The survivors," Petrical continued in clipped tones, "described the marauders as vacuum-suited humanoids—no facial features noted—appearing out of nowhere amid extremely bizarre atmospheric conditions, and then methodically slaughtering every living thing in sight. Their means of escape? They run toward a certain point and vanish. Granted, the Broohnins are unbalanced as far as ideology goes, but this just isn't their style. And besides, they don't have the technology for such a feat."

"Somebody does."

Petrical stopped pacing. "Yeah, somebody does. And whatever they've got must utilize some entirely new physical principle." He stepped behind his desk and slumped into the seat. His expression was gloomy as he spoke. "The Tarks are demanding an emergency meeting of the General Council."

"Well, it's up to you to advise the director to call one. Do you dare?"

"I don't have much choice. I should have pushed for it some time ago, but I held off, waiting for these slaughters to take on a pattern. As yet, they haven't. But now that the Tarks have been hit, I'm up against the wall."

Bilxer rose and ambled toward the door. "It's fairly commonly accepted that the Federation is dead, a thing of the past. A nice noisy emergency session could lay that idea to rest."

"I'm afraid," Petrical sighed, "that the response to this emergency call will only confirm a terminal diagnosis."

II

Josif Lenda inventoried the room as he awaited Mr. Mordirak's appearance. The high, vaulted ceiling merged at its edges with row upon row of sealed shelves containing, of all things, books. Must be worth a fortune. And the artifacts: an ornately carved desk with three matching plush chairs, stuffed animals and reptiles from a dozen worlds staring out from corners and walls, interspersed with replicas of incredibly ancient weapons for individual combat . . . maybe they weren't replicas. The room was windowless with dusky indirect lighting and Lenda had that feeling that he had somehow been transported into the dim past.

In spite of—and no doubt because of—his almost pathological reclusiveness, Mr. Mordirak was probably Clutch's best-known citizen. A man of purportedly incredible wealth, he lived in a mansion that appeared to have been ripped out of Earth's preflight days and placed here upon a dizzy pinnacle of stone amid the planet's badlands. As far as anyone could tell, he rarely left his aerie, and when he did so, he demonstrated a remarkable phobia for image recorders of any type.

Lenda felt a twinge of apprehension as he heard a sound on the other side of the pair of wooden doors behind the desk. He desperately needed the aid of a man of Mordirak's stature, but Mordirak had remained studiously aloof from human affairs since the day, nearly a half century ago, when he had suddenly appeared on Clutch. Rumors had flashed then that he had bought the planet. That was highly unlikely, but there grew up about the man an aura of power and wealth that persisted to this day. All Lenda needed was one public word of support from Mordirak and his plans for a seat in the Federation Assembly would be assured.

And so the apprehension. Mordirak never granted interviews, yet he had granted Lenda one. Could he be interested? Or was he toying with him?

The doors opened and a dark-haired, sturdy-looking man of approximately Lenda's age entered. He seated himself smoothly at the desk and locked eyes with the man across from him.

"Why does a nice young man like you want to represent Clutch at the Federation Assembly, Mr. Lenda?"

"I thought I was to see Mr. Mordirak personally," Lenda blurted, and regretted his words as he said them.

"You are," was the reply.

Despite that fact that he had expected him to be older, had expected a more imposing appearance, Lenda had recognized this man as Mordirak from the moment he'd entered the room. The man's voice was young in tone but held echoes of someone long familiar with authority; his demeanor alone had beamed the message to his subconscious instantly, yet the challenge had escaped of its own accord.

"Apologies," he sputtered. "I've never seen an image of you."

"No problem," Mordirak assured him. "Now, how about an answer to that question?"

Lenda shrugged off the inexplicable sensation of inadequacy that this man's presence seemed to thrust upon him and spoke. "I want to be planetary representative because Clutch is a member of the Federation and should have a say in the Assembly. No one here seems to think the Fed is important. I do."

"The Federation is dead," Mordirak stated flatly.

"I beg to differ, sir. Dying, yes. But not dead."

"There has not been a single application for membership in well over three centuries, and more than half of the old members can't stir up enough interest in their populations to send planetary reps, let alone sector reps. I call that *dead*."

"Well, then," Lenda said, jutting out his jaw, "it must be revived."

Mordirak grunted. "What do you want of me?"

"Your support, as I'm sure you are well aware."
"I am politically powerless."
"So am I. But I am also virtually unknown to the populace, which is not true in your case. I need the votes of more than fifty percent of the qualified citizens of Clutch to send me to Fed Central. To get those votes, all I require is your endorsement."
"You can't get them on your own?"
Lenda sighed. "Last election, I was the only candidate in the running and not even half the qualified population bothered to vote. The Federation Charter does not recognize representatives supported by less than half their constituents."
Mordirak's sudden smile seemed ill-fitted to his face. "Doesn't that tell you something, Mr. Lenda?"
"Yes! It tells me that I need someone who will get them out of their air recliners and over to their vid sets to tap in a simple 'yes' or 'no' during the hour that the polls are open next month!"
"And you think I'm that man?"
"Your name is magic on this planet, Mr. Mordirak. If Clutch's famous recluse thinks representation is important enough to warrant endorsement of a candidate, then the voters will think it important enough to warrant their opinion."
"I'm afraid I can't endorse you," Mordirak said, and his tone held an unmistakable tone of finality.
Lenda tried valiantly to hide his frustration. "Well, if not me, then somebody else. Anyone . . . just to get things moving."
"Sorry, Mr. Lenda, but I've never had much to do with politics and politicians, and I don't intend to begin now." He rose and started to turn.
"Dammit, Mordirak!" Lenda cried, leaping to his feet. "The human race is going to hell! We're degenerating into rabble! A group here doing this, a faction there doing that, out-of-touch, smug, indifferent! We've become a bunch of fragments with a common genetic background as our only link. I don't like what I see happening and I want to do something about it!"
"You have passion, Mr. Lenda," Mordirak said with a touch of approval. "But just what is it you think you can do?"
"I . . . I don't know as yet," he replied, cooling rapidly. "First I have to get to Fed Central and work from there—from the inside out. The Federation in its prime was a noble organiza-

tion with a noble record. I hate to think of it dying of attrition. All the work of men like LaNague and—"

"LaNague . . ." Mordirak murmured as his face softened momentarily. "I came of age on his home planet."

"So you're a Tolivian," Lenda said with a sudden nod of understanding. "That would explain your disinterest in politics."

"That's a part of it, yes. LaNague was born on Tolive and is still held in high regard there. And I hold a number of late Tolivians in high regard."

For the first time during their meeting, Lenda felt as if he was talking to a fellow human being. The initial void between them had diminished appreciably and he pressed to take advantage of the proximity. "I visited Fed Central not too long ago. It would break LaNague's heart if he could see—"

"That tactic won't work," Mordirak snapped, and the void reasserted itself.

"Sorry. It's just that I'm at a loss as to what to do."

"I can see that. You're frustrated. You want desperately to be elected but can't even find an election in which to run."

"That's unfair."

"Is it? Why then do you want to go to the seat of power? 'Born to rule,' perhaps?"

Lenda was silent. He resented the insinuation but it struck a resonance within the bowels of his mind. He had often questioned his political motives and had never been entirely satisfied with the answers. But he refused to accept the portrait Mordirak was painting for him.

"Not to rule," he replied. "If that were my drive, I'd rejoice at the downfall of the Federation. No one ever went to Fed Central to rule unless he was a Restructurist." He paused and averted his eyes. "I'm a romantic, I guess. I've spent most of my adult life studying the Federation and know the way it was in the days before the war. I've seen the old vid recordings of the great debates and decisions. In all sincerity, if you knew the Federation as I know it, and could see it now, you would weep."

Mordirak remained unmoved.

"And there's another thing," Lenda pressed. "These slaughters, these senseless attacks on random planets, are accelerating. The atrocities are absolutely barbaric in themselves, but I fear the final outcome will be much worse. If the Federation cannot make an adequate response, I foresee the Terran race—

in fact, this entire arm of the galaxy—entering a long and perhaps endless period of interstellar feudalism!"

Mordirak's gaze did not flicker. "What is that to me?"

Lenda sagged visibly but made a final attempt to reach him. "Come to Fed Central with me . . . see the decay for yourself."

"If you wish," Mordirak said. "Perhaps next year."

"Next year!" Lenda was astounded at his own inability to convey any sense of urgency to the man. "Next year will be too late! The General Council is in emergency session right now."

Mordirak shrugged. "Today, then. We'll take my tourer."

Ω

In a fog of bewilderment at the turn of events and at Mordirak's total lack of a sense of time, Lenda allowed himself to be led down the dim halls and into the crystalline mountaintop sunlight. They boarded a sporty flitter, lifted, then plunged through the tenuous layer of clouds below on a direct course for the coast. No words were spoken as they set down on the beach and entered a cab in the down-chute of the submarine tube. Their momentum grew slowly until the angle steepened and they shot off the continental shelf toward the bottom of the undersea cavern that held the largest of Clutch's three Haas gates.

The Haas gates had revolutionized interstellar travel a millennium before by allowing ships to enter warp within a star's gravity well. For the first half of their existence, the gates had been placed in interplanetary space. Attempts at operation within a planet's atmosphere had met with tragic results until someone decided to try a deep-pressure method on the ocean floor. It worked. The pressure cushioned the displacement effects and peristellar and interstellar travel was rerevolutionized by eliminating escape-velocity requirements. The orbital gate, however, remained an obvious necessity for incoming craft, since contact with anything other than vacuum at the velocities obtained during warp drive would prove uniformly disastrous.

Lenda said nothing as they entered the sleek tourer, and Mordirak appeared disinclined to break the uncomfortable silence, seemed oblivious to it, in fact. But after the craft had been trundled toward the bronze-hued pillars that represented the gate and had shuddered into warp in the field generated between them, Lenda felt compelled to speak.

"If I may be so bold to ask, Mr. Mordirak, what moved you to change your mind and travel to Fed Central?"

Mordirak, the only other occupant of the tourer's passenger compartment, did not seem to realize he had been spoken to. Lenda waited for what he considered a reasonable period of time and was about to rephrase his question when Mordirak replied.

"I have a horrid fascination for the process of government. I am repulsed by all that it implies and yet I am drawn to discussions and treatises on it. You say the Federation is dying. I want to see for myself." He then leaned back in the seat and closed his eyes.

Further attempts at conversation proved fruitless and Lenda finally resigned himself to silence for the rest of the trip.

After flashing through the Fed Central gate and setting up orbit around the planet, Lenda was unpleasantly surprised at the short wait for seats on the down-shuttle. He muttered his apprehensions.

"The Fed must be in even worse shape than I'd imagined. The call for an emergency session should have crammed the orbits with incoming representatives and the shuttles should be running far behind."

Mordirak nodded absently, lost in his own thoughts.

Ω

"From your impassioned description," Mordirak said as they strolled through the deserted, polished corridors of the Assembly Complex, "I half expected to see littered streets and cracked walls."

"Oh, there's decay all right. The cracks are there but they're metaphysical. These halls should be crowded with reporters and onlookers. As it is . . ." His voice trailed off as he caught sight of a dejected-looking figure farther down the corridor. "I think I know that man," he said. "Mr. Petrical!"

The man looked up but gave no sign of recognition. "No interviews now, I'm afraid."

Lenda continued his approach and extended his hand. "Josif Lenda. We met last year during my clerkship."

Petrical smiled vaguely and murmured, "Of course." After being introduced to Mordirak, who responded with a barely perceptible nod, he turned to Lenda with a grim expression. "You still sure you want to be a representative?"

"More than ever," he replied. Then, with a glance up and

down the deserted corridor, "I only hope there's something left of the Federation by the time I manage to get elected."

Petrical nodded. "That's a very real consideration. Let me show you something." He led them through a door at the far side of the corridor into an enclosed gallery overlooking the huge expanse of the General Council assembly hall. A high podium with six seats was set at the far end of the room. Five of the seats were empty. The lower podium in front of it was designated for sector representatives, and only seven of the forty seats were occupied. The immense floor section belonged to the planetary reps and was virtually deserted. A few lonely figures stood about idly or sat in dejected postures.

"Behold the emergency meeting of the General Council of the Federation of Planets!" Petrical intoned in a voice edged with disgust. "Hear the spirited debates, the clashing opinions!"

There followed a long silence during which the three men looked down upon the tableau, their individual reactions reflected in their faces. Petrical's jaw was thrust forward as his eyes squinted in frustrated anger. Lenda appeared crushed and there was perhaps a trace more fluid in his eyes than necessary for lubrication alone. Mordirak's face was set in its usual mask and only for the briefest instant did a smile twitch at the corners of his mouth.

Finally, Lenda whispered, "It's over, isn't it," and it was a statement, not a question. "Now we begin the long slide into barbarism."

"Oh, it's not really that bad," Petrical began with forced heartiness which faded rapidly as his eyes met Lenda's. There was no sense playing word games with this young man. He knew. "The slide has already begun," he said abruptly. "This just . . ." he waved his hand at the all-but-deserted assembly hall, "just makes it official."

Lenda turned to Mordirak. "I'm sorry I asked you here. I'm sorry I bothered you at all today."

Mordirak looked up from the scene below. "I think it's quite interesting."

"Is that all you can say?" Lenda rasped through his teeth. He felt sudden rage clutching at his throat. This man was untouchable! "You're witnessing not only the end of the organization that for fifteen hundred years has guided our race into a peaceful interstellar civilization, but the probable downfall of that very civilization as well! And all you can say is it's 'interesting'?"

Mordirak was unperturbed. "Quite interesting. But I've seen enough, I think. Can I offer you transportation back to Clutch?"

"No, thank you," he replied disdainfully. "I'll make my own accommodations."

Mordirak nodded and left the gallery.

"Who was that?" Petrical asked. He knew only the man's name, but fully shared Lenda's antipathy.

Lenda turned back toward the assembly room. "No one."

III

As he stepped through the lock from the shuttle to his tourer, Dalt considered the strange inner glee that suffused him at the thought of the Federation's downfall. He had seen it coming for a long time but had paid it little heed. In fact, it had been quite some time since he had given much heed at all to the affairs of his fellow humans. Physically disguising himself from them had been a prime concern at one time, but now even that wasn't necessary—a projected psi image of whomever he wished to appear to be proved sufficient in most cases. (Of course, he had to avoid image recorders of any sort, since they were impervious to psi influence.) Humanity might as well be another race, for all the contact he had with it; the symbol of the human interstellar culture, the Federation, was dying and he could not dredge up a mote of regret for it.

And yet, he should feel something for its passing. Five hundred, even two hundred years ago his reactions might have been different. But he had been someone else then and the Fed had been a viable organization. Now, he was Mordirak and the Fed was on its deathbed.

The decline, he supposed, had begun with the termination of the Terro-Tarkan war, a monstrous, seemingly endless conflict. The war had not gone well for the Terrans at first. The monolithic Tarkan Empire had mounted huge assault forces which wrought havoc with deep incursions into the Terran sphere of influence. But the monolithism that gave the Tarks their initial advantage proved in the long run to be their downfall. Their empire had long studied the loose, disorganized, eccentric structure of the Fed and had read weakness. But when early victory was denied them and both sides dug in for a long siege, the diversification of humanity, long fostered by the LaNague Charter, began to tell.

Technological breakthroughs in weaponry eventually pierced the infamous Tarkan screens and the Emperor of the Tarks found his palace planet ringed with Terran dread-naughts. He was the seventh descendant of the emperor who had started the war, and, true to Tarkan tradition, he allowed the upper-echelon nobles assembled around him to blast him and his family to ashes before surrender. Thus honorably ending—in Tarkan terms—the royal line.

With victory, there followed the expected jubilant celebration. Half a millennium of war had ended and the Federation had proved itself resilient and effective. There were scars, yes. The toll of life from the many generations involved had reached into the billions and there were planets on both sides left virtually uninhabitable. But the losses were not in resources alone. The conflict had drained something from the Terrans.

As the flush of victory faded, humanity began to withdraw into itself. The trend was imperceptible at first, but it gradually became apparent to the watchers and chroniclers of the Terran race that expansion had stopped. Exploratory probes along the galactic perimeter and into the core were postponed, indefinitely. Extension of the boundaries of Occupied Space slowed to a crawl.

Man had learned to warp space and had jubilantly leaped from star to star. He had made mistakes, had learned from them, and had continued to move on—until the Terro-Tarkan war. The outward urge had been stung then and had retreated. Humanity turned inward. An unvoiced, unconscious directive set the race to tending its own gardens. The Tarks had been pacified; had, in fact, been incorporated into the Federation and given second-class representation. They were no longer a threat.

But what about farther out? Perhaps there was another belligerent race out there. Perhaps another war was in the wings.

Back off, the directive seemed to say. Sit tight for a while and consolidate.

But consolidation never occurred, at least not on a productive scale. By the end of the war, the Terrans and their allies were linked by a comprehensive network of Haas gates and were more accessible to one another than ever before. Had the Federation been in the hands of opportunists at that time, a new imperium could have been launched. But the opposite had occurred: Federation officials, true to the Charter, resisted the urge to use the post-war period to extend their franchise over the member planets. They urged, rather, a return to normalcy and worked to reverse the centrist tendencies that all wars bring on.

They were too successful. As requested, the planets loosened their ties with the Federation, but then went on to form their own enclaves, alliances, and commonwealths, bound together by mutual trade and protection agreements. They huddled in their sectors and for all intents and purposes forgot the Federation.

It was this subdividing, coupled with the atrophy of the outward urge, that caused the political scientists the most concern. They foresaw increasing estrangement between the planetary enclaves and, subsequently, open hostility. Without the Federation acting as a focus for the drives and ambitions of the race, they were predicting a sort of interstellar feudalism. From there the race would go one of two ways; complete consolidation under the most aggressive enclave and a return to empire much like the Metep Imperium in the pre-Federation days, or complete breakdown of interstellar intercourse, resulting in barbarism and stagnation.

Dalt was not sure whether he accepted the doomsayers' theories. One thing was certain, however: The Federation was no longer a focus for much of anything anymore.

With the image of the near-deserted General Council assembly hall dancing in his head, he tried to doze. But a voice as familiar by now as the tone of his own thoughts intruded on his mind.

("Turning and turning in the widening gyre/The falcon cannot hear the falconer;/Things fall apart, the center cannot hold;/mere anarchy is loosed upon the world/. . . the best lose all conviction.")

Don't bother me.

("You don't like poetry, Dalt? That's from one of my favorites of the ancient poets. Appropriate, don't you think?")

I really couldn't care.

("You should. It could apply to your personal situation as well as that of your race.")

Begone, parasite!

("I'm beginning to wish that were possible. You worry me lately. Your personality is disintegrating.")

Spare me your trite analyses.

("I'm quite serious about this. Look at what you've become: a recluse, an eccentric divorced from contact with other beings, living in an automated gothic mansion and surrounding himself with old weapons and death trophies, brooding and miserable. My concern is genuine, though hardly altruistic.")

Dalt didn't answer. Pard had a knack for cutting directly to the core of a matter and this time the resultant exposure was none too pleasant. He had long been plagued by a gnawing fear that his personality was deteriorating. He didn't like what he had become but seemed unable to do anything about it. When and where had the change begun? When had occasional boredom become crushing ennui? When had other people become other things? Even sex no longer distracted him, although he was as potent as ever. Emotional attachments that had once been an easy, natural part of his being had become elusive, then impossible. Perhaps the fact that all such relationships in the past had been terminated by death had something to do with it.

Pard, of course, had no such problems. He did not communicate directly with the world and had never existed in a mortal frame of reference. From the instant he had gained sentience in Dalt's brain, death had been a mere possibility, never an inevitability. Pard had no need of companionship except for occasional chats with Dalt concerning their dwindling mutual concerns, and found abstract cogitations quite enthralling. Dalt envied him for that.

Why, he wondered in a tangent, did he always refer to Pard in the male gender? Why not "it"? Better yet, why not "her"? He was wedded to this thing in his head till death did them part.

("Don't blame your extended lifespan for your present condition,") said the ever-present thoughtrider. ("You're mistaking inertia for ennui. You haven't exhausted your possibilities; in fact, you've hardly dented them. You adapted well for a full millennium. It's only in the last one hundred fifty years or so that you've begun to crack.")

Right again, Dalt thought. Perhaps it had been the end of the horrors that had precipitated the present situation. In retrospect, The Healer episodes, for all the strain they subjected him to, had been high points while they lasted—crests between shallow troughs. Now he felt becalmed at sea, surrounded by featureless horizons.

("You should be vitally interested in what is happening to your race, because you, unlike those around you today, will be there when civilization deteriorates into feudalism. But nothing moves you. The rough beast of barbarism is rattling the cage of civilization and all you can do is stifle a yawn.")

You certainly are in a poetic mood today. But barbarians, like the poor, are always with us.

("Granted. But they aren't in charge—at least they haven't been to date. Tell me: Would you like to see a Federation modeled on the Kwashi culture?")

Dalt found that a jolting vision but replied instead, *I wish you were back on Kwashi!* He instantly regretted the remark. It was childish and unworthy of him and further confirmed the deterioration of his mental state.

("If I'd stayed there, you'd be over a thousand years dead by now.")

"Maybe I'd be happier!" he retorted angrily. There was a tearing sound to his right as the armrest of his recliner ripped loose in his hand.

How'd I do this? he asked.

("What?")

How'd I tear this loose with my bare hand?

("Oh, that. Well, I made some changes a while back in the way the actin and myocin filaments in your striated muscle handle ATP. Human muscle is hardly optimum in that respect. Your maximum muscle tension is far above normal now. Of course, after doing that, I had to strengthen the cross-bridges between the filaments, reinforce the tendinous origins and insertions of the muscles, and then toughen up the joint capsules. It also seemed wise to increase the epidermal keratin to prevent . . .")

Pard paused as Dalt carelessly flipped the ruined armrest onto the cabin floor. In the old days Pard would have received a lecture on the possible dangers of meddling with his host's physiology. Now Dalt didn't seem to care.

("You seriously worry me, Dalt. Making yourself miserable . . . it's unpleasant, but your emotional life is your own affair. I must warn you, however: If you take any action that threatens our physical life, I'll take steps to preserve it—with or without your consent.")

Go away, parasite, Dalt thought sulkily, *and let me nap.*

("I resent your inference. I've more than earned my keep in this relationship. It becomes a perplexing question as to who is really the parasite at this point.")

Dalt made no reply.

Ω

Dalt awoke with Clutch looming larger and larger below him as the tourer eased through the atmosphere toward the sea. Amid clouds of steam it plunged into the water and then bobbed to the surface to rest on its belly. A pilot craft surfaced beside it, locked onto the hull, and, as the tourer took on water for ballast, guided it below the surface to its berth on the bottom.

The tube car deposited him on the beach a short time later and he strolled slowly in the general direction of his flitter. The sun had already completed about a third of its arc across the sky and the air lay warm and quiet and mistily opaque over the coast. Bathers and sunsoakers were out in force.

He paused to watch a little sun-browned, towheaded boy digging in the sand. For how many ages had little boys done that? He knew he must have done the same during his boyhood on Friendly. How long ago was that? Twelve hundred years? It seemed like twelve thousand. He felt as if he had never been young.

He wondered idly if he had made a mistake in refusing to have children and knew immediately that he hadn't. Watching the women he had loved grow old and die had been hard enough; watching his children do the same would have been more than he could have tolerated.

Pard intruded again, this time with a definite tone of urgency. ("Something's happening!")

What're you talking about?

("Don't know for sure, but there's a mammoth psi force suddenly operating nearby.")

A slight breeze began to stir and Dalt glanced up from the boy as he heard excited voices down by the water. The mist in the air was starting to move, being drawn to a point about a meter from the water's edge., A gray, vortical disk appeared, coin-sized at first, then persistently larger. As it grew in size, the breeze graduated to a wind. By the time the disk reached a diameter equal to a man's height, it was sucking in mist and spray at gale force.

Curious, the little boy stood up and began to walk toward the disk, but Dalt put a hand on his shoulder and gently pulled him back.

"Into your sand hole, little man," he told him. "I don't like the looks of this."

The boy's blue eyes looked up at him questioningly but something in Dalt's tone made him turn and crawl back into his excavation.

Dalt returned his attention to the disk. Something about it raised his hackles and he squatted on his haunches to see what would develop. It had stopped growing now and a number of people, bracing themselves against the draw of the gale, formed a semi-circular cluster around it at a respectful distance.

Then, as if passing through a solid wall, a vacuum-suited figure with a blazing jetpack on its back materialized and hit the sand at a dead run. Carrying what appeared to be an energy rifle, it swerved to the right and dropped to one knee. A second figure appeared then, and as it swerved to the left, the first turned off its jetpack, raised its rifle, and started firing into the crowd. The second soon joined it and the semicircle of observers broke into fleeing, terrified fragments. A steady stream of invaders began to pour onto the beach, fanning out and firing on the run with murderous accuracy.

Dalt had instinctively flattened onto the sand at the sight of the first invader, and he now watched in horror as the people who had only moments before been bathing in the sun and the sea became blasted bodies littering the sand. Panic reigned as scantily clad figures screamed and scrambled to escape. The marauders, bulky, faceless, and deadly in their vacsuits, pursued their prey with remorseless efficiency. Their ranks were forty or fifty strong now and as one ran in his direction, Dalt realized that he was witnessing and would no doubt soon be a victim of one of the mindless slaughters Lenda had been telling him about.

He sensed movement on his right and turned to see the little boy sprinting across the sand, yelling for his mother. Dalt opened his mouth to tell him to get down, but the approaching invader spotted the fleeing figure and raised his weapon.

Dalt found himself on his feet and racing toward the invader. With the high quality of marksmanship exhibited by the marauders so far, he knew he had scant hope of saving the boy. But he had to try. Something, either concern for a young life or for his own, or a combination of both, made him run. His feet churned up furious puffs of sand as they fought for traction, but he could not gain the momentum he needed. The invader's weapon buzzed quietly and out of the corner of his eye Dalt saw the boy convulse in mid-stride and go down.

The thought of self-preservation was suddenly submerged in a red tide of rage. Dalt wanted to live, yes. But more than that, right now he wanted to kill. If his pumping feet could get him there in time, the memory of the torn armrest on his tourer told him what he could do. The invader gave a visible start—though no facial expression could be seen through the opaque faceplate—as he caught sight of Dalt racing toward him. He began to swing the blaster around but too late. Dalt pushed the weapon aside, grabbed two fistfuls of the vacsuit fabric over the chest, and pulled. There was a ripping sound, a whiff of fetid air, and then Dalt's hands were inside the suit. They traveled up to the throat and encircled the neck. A dull *snap* followed and the invader went limp.

Extricating his hands, Dalt pushed the body to the ground with one and snatched the falling blaster with the other. After a brief inspection: *How do you work this thing?* There was no trigger.

Beside him, the body of the slain invader suddenly flared with a brief, intolerable, incandescent flash, then oily smoke began to rise from the torn suit.

"What the—" Dalt began out loud, but Pard cut him off.

("A good way to hide your planet of origin. But never mind that. Try that little button on the side of the stock and try it quickly. I believe you've drawn some unwanted attention to yourself.")

Dalt glanced around and saw one of the invaders staring at him, momentarily stunned with amazement. Then he began to raise his weapon into the firing position.

Suddenly everything slowed, as if under water.

What's going on?

("I've accelerated your mind's rate of perception to give you a much-needed edge over the energy bolt that's about to come our way.")

The blaster had inched up to the invader's shoulder by now and Dalt dove to his left. He seemed to float gracefully, gently through the air. But there was nothing gentle about his impact with the ground. He grunted, rolled, pointed his blaster in the general direction of the invader, and pressed the button three times in rapid succession.

One of the energy bolts must have found its mark. The invader threw up his arms in a slow, wide arc and drifted toward the sand to rest on his back.

Then, as movements resumed their normal cadence, the body flared and belched smoke like the one before it. Dalt noted that he now occupied a position behind the advancing line of marauders.

Maybe you'd better keep up the speed on the perception, He told Pard.

("I can only do it in bursts. The neurons can't maintain the necessary metabolic rate for more than a minute or two.")

Dalt settled himself in the prone position, shouldered the weapon, and found that the button fit under his thumb with only a little stretching.

Let's even up the odds a little while we can. Without the slightest hesitation or remorse, he sighted on the unsuspecting backs of the invaders as they went on with their slaughter of the remaining bathers. As the invaders fell one by one to the silent bolts of energy from Dalt's weapon, the skills he had learned as a game hunter on the lesser-settled planets of Occupied Space came back to him: Hit the stragglers and the ones on the perifery, then move inward. A full dozen of their comrades lay dead and smoking on the sand before the main body of the force realized that all was not going according to plan.

A figure in the center of the rank looked around and, noticing that his detail was unaccountably shrinking in size, signaled to the others. They began to turn their attention from the bathers before them to seek out the unexpected threat from the rear. Pard accelerated perception again and then Dalt's weapon began to take a merciless toll of the force. He was constantly moving and sighting the strange blaster, getting the feel of it and becoming more deadly with every bolt he fired. As soon as an invader raised his weapon in his direction, he would shift, sight, and fire, shift-sight-fire, shift-sight-fire. If the muscles of his fingers, arms, and shoulders could have responded at the speed of his perception, he would have killed them all by now. As it was, he had cut their number in half. The assault had been effectively crippled and it wouldn't take many more casualties before it would fall apart completely.

As Dalt sighted on the figure he took to be the leader, his vision suddenly blurred and vertigo washed over him. The wave receded briefly, then pounded down upon him again with greater force. He felt a presence, totally malignant, totally alien . . . and yet somehow oddly familiar.

Then came an indescribable wrenching sensation and he felt for an instant as if he were looking at the entire universe from both within and without. Then he saw and felt nothing.

Ω

He awoke with sand in his eyes and nostrils and the murmur of the sea and human voices in his ears. Rising to his knees, he brushed the particles from his face with an unsteady hand and opened his eyes.

A small knot of people encircled him, its number growing steadily. The circle widened as he gained his feet. All eyes were fixed upon him, and mixed among the hushed mutterings of the voices, the word "Healer" was repeated time and again. It was suddenly obvious that his psi cover must have cut off while he was unconscious.

Dalt felt something in his right hand: the stolen weapon. He loosened his grip and let it fall to the sand. As he resumed the interrupted trek to his flitter, the crowd parted and left him a wide path obstructed only by the bodies of fallen bathers and the remains of the invaders he had killed.

He surveyed the scene as he walked. The assault had apparently been broken: the attackers were gone, their vortical gateway from who-knows-where had closed. The still-smoldering ashes of the invaders who had not escaped gave him a primitive sense of satisfaction.

That'll teach 'em.

The crowd followed him to his flitter at a respectful distance and stood gazing upward as he piloted the craft above the mist and toward the mountains. Reaction began to set in and his hands were shaking when he reached the aerie. Gaining the study, Dalt poured himself a generous dose of the thin, murky Lentemian liquor he had acquired a taste for in the last century or so. He usually diluted it, but took it straight now and it burned delightfully all the way down.

Sitting alone in the darkness with his feet on the desk, Dalt became aware of a strange sensation. No, it wasn't the liquor. It was something else . . . something unpleasant. He put the glass down and returned his feet to the floor as he recognized the feeling.

He was alone.

Pard? he called mentally, awaiting the familiar reply. None came.

He was on his feet now and using his voice. "Pard!"

The emptiness that followed was more than a lack of response. There was a void within.

Pard was gone. Pard the father, Pard the son, Pard the wife and mother, Pard the mentor, the confidant, the companion, the preserver, the watchdog, Pard the friend, Pard . . . was gone.

The sudden shattering sensation of being alone for the first time in over a millennium was augmented by the awareness that without Pard he was no longer immortal. The weight of the centuries he had lived became crushing as Dalt realized that once again his days could be numbered.

His voice rose to a scream.

"Pard!"

IV

Three sullen days passed, during which Dalt's aerie was besieged by a legion of news-service reporters vying for an interview. The Healer had returned and everyone wanted an exclusive. Foreseeing this, Dalt had hired a security force to keep them all away. Finally word came that a Federation official and a local politico named Lenda were requesting an audience, claiming they were acquaintances. Should they be allowed in?

Dalt nodded to the face on the screen and switched off the set. *What do they want?* he wondered. If it was a return of The Healer, they were out of luck. Without Pard he had no special psionic powers; he was just another man, and a strange-looking one at that.

It really didn't matter what they wanted. Dalt, strangely enough, wanted some company. For three days he had sulked in the windowless study, and an unaccustomed yearning for sunlight, fresh air, and other human beings had grown within him.

The door to the study opened and Lenda entered with Petrical following. Wonder and awe were evident on the former's face as he remembered the last time he'd been in this room. He had sat across the desk from another man then—at least it had seemed like another man. Now, a thousand-year legend sat before him. The white patch of hair atop his head and the golden hand—only the flamestone was missing—accentuated an image known to every being in Occupied Space. Petrical seemed less impressed but his manner was reserved.

"Nice to see you two gentlemen again," Dalt said with pointed cordiality, fixing his eyes on Lenda. "Please sit down."

They did so with the awkward movements of outlanders in a strange temple. Neither spoke.

"Well?" Dalt said finally. Four or more days ago he would have waited indefinitely, enjoying their discomfiture at the long silence. Now he was possessed of a sense of urgency. Minutes were precious again.

Petrical gained his voice first but fumbled with titles. "Mr. Mordirak . . . Healer . . ."

"Dalt will do nicely."

"Mr. Dalt, then." Petrical smiled with relief. "There's one question I must ask you, for my own sake if not for humanity's: Are you really The Healer?"

Dalt paused, considering his answer. Then, "Does it really matter?"

Furrows appeared on Petrical's brow but Lenda straightened in his chair with sudden comprehension.

"No, it doesn't." He glanced at Petrical. "At least not for practical purposes. By now most of Occupied Space considers him The Healer and that's all that matters. Look what happened: A lone man, outnumbered fifty to one, turns back a murderous assault on helpless bathers. And that man happens to look exactly like The Healer. The incident has proven more than enough for the Children of The Healer and I believe it is quite enough for me."

"But how could you be The—" Petrical blurted, but Dalt stopped him with an upraised hand.

"That is not open for discussion."

Petrical shrugged. "All right. We'll accept it as our basic premise and work from there."

"To where?"

"That will be entirely up to you, Mr. Dalt," Lenda said.

"Yes. Entirely." Petrical nodded, taking the lead. "You may or may not be aware of what has been taking place during the last three standard days. Federation Central has been bombarded with requests for information on the Clutch incident from all corners of Occupied Space. The isolated slaughters which until three days ago had been of interest only to the victim planets—and even in those cases of only passing interest—are fast becoming a major concern. Why? Because the Children of The Healer, a group that has previously been of mere sociological interest because of its origin and its sheer size—and long thought defunct—has undergone a tremendous resurgence and is applying political pressure for the first time in its history."

Dalt frowned. "I never knew they were still around in any number."

"Apparently the group never died out; it just became less visible. But they've been among us all along, keeping to themselves, growing and passing along the article of faith that The Healer would one day return in time of crisis and they should be ready to aid him by whatever means necessary."

"I'm gratified," Dalt said quickly, "but please get to the point."

"That *is* the point," Lenda said. "People in and around Fed Central have recognized these assaults as the first harbinger of interstellar barbarism. They see a real threat to our civilization but have been powerless to do anything about it—as you well know. They could no longer find a common thread among the planets. But the thread was there all along: your followers. The Children of The Healer form an infrastructure that cuts across all boundaries. All that was needed was some sort of incident—'sign,' if you will—to activate them, and you provided it down there on the beach. You, as The Healer, took a stand against the butchery of these assaults, and that suddenly makes opposition to them a cause for your followers."

"They're working themselves up to a frenzy," Petrical added, "but totally lack direction. I sent representatives from the Federation Defense Force with offers of cooperation, but they were uniformly rebuffed."

"That leaves me, I suppose," Dalt said.

Petrical sighed. "Yes. Just say the word and we can turn a rabble into a devoted, multicentric defense force."

"Blasterfodder, you mean."

"Not at all. The civilians have been blasterfodder for these assaults to date. They're the ones being slaughtered and they're the ones we want to protect."

"Why don't they just protect themselves?" Dalt asked.

"First off, they're not set up for it. Secondly, the assaults take place in such a limited area when they hit that there's a prevailing attitude of 'it can't happen here.' That will eventually change if the number of assaults continues to rise at its present rate, but by then it may be too late. The biggest obstacle to organizing resistance remains our inability to name the enemy."

"Weren't there any clues left down on the beach?"

Petrical shook his head. "Nothing. The bodies were completely incinerated. All we know about the marauders is that they're carbon-cycle beings and either human or markedly humanoid. The weapons they carried had a lot of alien features about them, but that could be intentional." He grunted. "A bizarre transport system, strange weapons, and bodies that self-destruct . . . someone's trying awfully hard to make this look like the work of some new alien race. But I don't buy it. Not yet."

Dalt shifted in his chair. "And what do you expect me to do about all this?"

"Say a few words to the leaders of the planetary Healer sects," Petrical replied. "We can bring them here or to Fed Central or wherever you'd like. All we have to tell them is they'll see The Healer in person and they'll come running."

"And what's in all this for you?"

"Unity. We can perhaps go a step further beyond a coordinated defense. Perhaps we can bind the planets together again, start a little harmony amid the discord."

"And inject a little life into the Federation again," Lenda added.

Dalt turned on him, a touch of the old cynicism in his voice. "That would make you the man of the hour, wouldn't it?"

Lenda reddened. "If you harbor any doubts about my motives which might prevent you from acting, I will withdraw myself completely from the picture."

Dalt was beginning to see Josif Lenda in a new light. Perhaps this errant politician had the makings of a statesman. The two species were often confused, although the former traditionally far outnumbered the latter. He smiled grimly. "I don't think that will be necessary."

Lenda looked relieved but Petrical frowned. "Somehow I don't find your tone encouraging."

Dalt hesitated. He didn't want to turn them down too abruptly but he had no intention of allowing himself to become involved in another conflict like the Terro-Tarkan war, which this might well escalate to in the near future. He still had a number of good years left—in normal human terms—but to a man who had become accustomed to thinking in terms of centuries, it seemed a terribly short number. He knew that should the coming struggle last only half as long as the T-T war, any contribution he made, no matter how exalted the expectations of the two men before him, would be minuscule. And besides, he had things to do. Just what those things were he had yet to decide, but the remaining years belonged to him alone and he intended to be miserly with them, milking them for every drop of life they held.

"I'll think about it," he told them, "and give you my decision in a few days."

Lenda's lips compressed but he said nothing. Petrical gave out a resigned sigh and rose. "I suppose we'll just have to wait, then."

"Right," Dalt said, rising. "One of the security men will show you out."

As the dejected pair exited, Dalt was left alone to face a chaotic jumble of thoughts and emotions. He paced the room in oppressive solitude. He felt guilty and didn't know why. It was his life, wasn't it? He hadn't wanted to be a messiah; it had been manufactured for him. He'd only wanted to perform a service. Why should he now be burdened with the past when the future seemed so incredibly short?

His thoughts turned to Pard, as they had incessantly for the past three days. It was obvious now that their two minds had been in tandem far too long; the sudden severing of the bond was proving devastating. He did not feel whole without Pard—he was a gelding, an amputee.

He felt anger now—inwardly at his own confusion, outwardly at . . . what? At whatever had killed Pard. Someone or something had taken a part of him down on that beach. The mind with which he had shared twelve hundred years of existence, shared like no other two minds had ever shared, had been snuffed out. The anger felt good. He fueled it: Whoever or whatever it was that had killed Pard would have to pay; such an act could not be allowed to pass without retribution.

He leaped to the vidcom and pressed the code for the guard station. "Have those two men left the property yet?" he demanded.

The security chief informed him that they were at the gate now.

"Send them back."

Ω

"The pattern of these attacks is either inapparent at this time," Petrical was saying, "or there simply is no pattern." He was in his element now, briefing the leaders of the planetary sects of the Children of The Healer.

Dalt watched the meeting on a vid panel in the quarters that had been set up for him on Fed Central. As The Healer, he had appeared before the group a few minutes ago, speaking briefly into the awed silence that had filled the room upon his arrival. It continued to amaze him that no one questioned his identity. His resemblance to the millions and millions of holos of The Healer in homes throughout Occupied Space was, of course, perfect. But that could be achieved by anyone willing to sink some money into reconstructive work. No . . . there was more to it than appearance. They seemed to sense that he was the genuine article. More importantly, they *wanted* him to be The Healer. Their multigenerational vigil had been vindicated by his return.

A few words from The Healer emphasizing the importance of organized resistance to the assaults and endorsing cooperation with the Federation had been sufficient. Petrical would take it from there.

The plan was basically simple and would probably prove inadequate. But it was a start. The Children of The Healer would form a nucleus for planetary militia forces which would be on day-and-night standby. At the first sighting of a vortex, or as soon as it was known that there was an attack in progress, they were to be notified and would mobilize immediately. Unless a local or planetary government objected, representatives from the Federation Defense Force would be sent out to school them in tactics. The main thrust of this would be to teach the first group on the scene how to cut the invaders off from their passage until other groups could arrive and a full counteroffensive could be undertaken.

The Children of The Healer would become minutemen, a concept of defense that had been lost in the days of interstellar conflict.

The sect leaders would leave by the end of the day. After that it would be a waiting game.

Ω

"I just got word that you were back," Petrical said as he entered Dalt's quarters. His features showed a mixture of relief and annoyance at the sight of Dalt. "You're free, of course, to come and go as you please, but I wish you'd let someone know before you disappear like that again. Nine days without a word . . . we were getting worried."

"I had a few private sources of information to check out," Dalt said, "and I had to do it in person."

"What did you learn?"

Dalt threw himself into a lounger. "Nothing. No one even has a hint of who or what's behind all this. Anything new at this end?"

"Some good news, some not so good," Petrical replied, finding himself a seat. "We've had reports of four assaults in the past eight days. The first two occurred on planets which had not yet set up battle-ready militia units. The third"—his face broke into a smile—"occurred in a recreational area on Flint!"

Dalt began to laugh. "Oh, I'd have given anything to be there! What happened?" Flint was an independent planet, a former splinter world on which virtually every inhabitant was armed and ready to do battle.

"Well, we don't have much hard information—you know how the Flinters are about snoopers—but all reports indicate that the assault force was completely wiped out." He shook his head in grudging admiration. "You know, I've always thought that everyone on Flint was a little crazy, but I'll bet it's quite some time before they're bothered with one of these assaults again."

"What about the minutemen?" Dalt asked. "Have they seen any action?"

Petrical nodded. "Yesterday, on Aladdin. A vortex was reported only a hundred kilometers away from a fledgling unit. They didn't do too well. They forgot all their tactical training. Granted, it wasn't much, but they might as well have had none at all for the way they conducted the counterattack. They forgot all about cutting off the escape route; just charged in like crazy men. A lot of them were killed, but they did manage to abort the attack."

"First blood," Dalt said. "It's a start."

"Yes, it is," Petrical agreed. He glanced up as Lenda hurried into the room but kept on speaking. "And as the militia groups proliferate I think we can contain these attacks and eventually render them ineffective. When that happens, we'll just have to wait and see what response our unknown assailants make to our countermeasures."

"They've already made it," Lenda said in a breathless voice.

"Neeka was just hit simultaneously in four different areas! The militia groups didn't know which way to go. The attacks were all in greater force than previous ones and the carnage is reported as incredible." He paused for reaction and found it in the grim, silent visages of the two men facing him. "There was an unusual incident, however," he continued. "One of the minutemen drove a lorry flitter into the vortex."

Dalt shook his head sadly. "I guess our side has its suicidal elements, too."

"Why do you say that?" Lenda asked.

"Because the passage obviously has either low or no pressure on the other side of the opening. It appears to be a vortex because the pressure differential sucks in atmosphere wherever it opens. The attackers don't wear jetpacks and vacsuits just to hide their identity. I'm sure they *must* wear them to survive transit through the passage."

Petrical nodded in agreement. "We've assumed that from the beginning, and have told the men to keep their distance from the vortex. That fool's bodily fluids probably started to boil as soon as he crossed the threshold."

"But it's indicative of the dedication of these groups that they all want to try the same stunt now," Lenda said. "They want to carry the battle to the enemy."

"A counterattack on the enemy's home position would be the answer to many problems," Petrical mused, "but where is their home? Until we find out, we're just going to have to use the forces we've got to play a holding game." He glanced across the room. "Any ideas, Mr. Dalt?"

"Yes. A couple of obvious ones, and one perhaps not so obvious. First, we must definitely discourage the minutemen from entering the passage. Next, we've got to expand the militia groups. These attacks are escalating rapidly. Rather than random incidents, they're now occurring with a murderous regularity that worries me. This whole affair could be bigger and more sinister than anyone—and that includes the two of you—has yet appreciated."

"I'm ahead of you on that last point," Petrical said with a satisfied air. "Before coming in here I issued another call for an emergency session of the General Council, and this time I think the response will be different. Your followers have been agitating for action on all the planets and have generated real concern. As a result, the Federation has received a steady stream of applications for reinstatement. In fact, there are loads of fresh new representatives on their way to Fed Central right now."

This was not news to Lenda, who kept his eyes on Dalt. "What's your 'not so obvious' idea?"

"Drone flitters equipped with reconnaissance and signal gear," he replied. "They've given us a tunnel right to their jump-off point. Why don't we use it against them? The flitters can send out a continual subspace beam and we can set up an all-points directional watch to see where they end up."

Petrical jumped to his feet. "Of course! We can place a drone with each militia group and it can send it through during a counterattack. We'll keep sending them through until we've pinpointed their position. And when we know where to find them . . ." He paused. "Well, they've got a lot of lives to answer for."

"Why can't we just send an attack force through?" Lenda asked.

"Because we wouldn't know where we'd be sending them," Petrical replied. "We don't know a thing about this vortical passage. We assume it to be a subspace tunnel, but we don't know. If it is, then we're dealing with a technology that dwarfs anything we have. Any man who got through to the other end—and that's a big 'if' in itself—would probably be killed before he had a chance to look around. No. Unmanned craft first."

Lenda persisted. "How about sending a planetary bomb through?"

"Those have been outlawed by convention, haven't they?" Dalt said.

Petrical gazed at the floor. "A few still exist." He glanced up. "They're in deep-space hidey holes, of course. But a planetary bomb is out of the question. We'd have to manufacture a lot more of them, one for every planet involved, and they'd have to be armed and trundled to the assault scene by inexperienced personnel. A tragedy of ghastly proportions would be inevitable. We'll stick with Mr. Dalt's idea."

The two men left hurriedly, leaving Dalt alone with a feeling of satisfaction. It was gratifying to have his idea accepted so enthusiastically, an idea that was totally his. He had relied too much on Pard's computer-speed analyses in recent centuries. It felt good to give birth to an idea again. The lines between his own mental processes and Pard's had often blurred and it had at times been difficult to discern where an idea had originated.

With the thought of Pard, a familiar presence seemed to waft through the room and touch him.

"Pard?" he called aloud, but the sensation was gone. An old memory and nothing more.

Pard, he thought as he clenched his golden hand into a fist before his eyes. *What did they do to you, old friend?*

V

There was an awful wrenching sensation, at once numbing and excruciatingly painful, and then Pard's awareness expanded at a cataclysmic rate. The beach was left behind, as were Clutch and its star, then the entire Milky Way, then all the galaxies.

He had been cut free from Dalt. He had no photoreceptors, yet he could see; he had no vibratory senses, and yet he could hear. He was now pure, unhindered awareness. He soared giddily, immaterially. Spatial relationships were suddenly meaningless and he was everywhere. The universe was his . . .

. . . or was it?

He felt a strain . . . subtle at first but steadily growing more pronounced . . . a stretching of the fibers of his consciousness . . . thoughts were becoming fuzzy . . . he was becoming disoriented. The tension of cosmic awareness was rapidly becoming unbearable as the infinite scope and variety of reality threatened to crush him. All the worlds, all the lifeforms, and all the vast empty spaces in between pressed upon him with a force that threatened sudden and irrevocable madness. He had to focus down . . .

focus down . . .

focus down . . .

He was on the beach again. Dalt lay sprawled on the sand,

alive but unconscious. Pard watched as the marauders made a hasty retreat toward their hole in space. The question of their identity still piqued his curiosity and he decided to find out where they were going. Why not? Dalt was safe and he was gloriously free to follow his whims to the ends of existence.

He hesitated. The bond that had united their minds for twelve centuries was broken . . . but other bonds remained. It would be strange, not having Dalt around. He found the indecision irritating and steeled himself to go.

("Goodbye, Steve,") Pard finally said to the inert form he had suddenly outgrown. ("No regrets, I hope.") His awareness shifted toward the closing vortex. Like a transformed chrysalis departing its cocoon, he left Dalt behind.

Within the vortex he found the deadly silence of complete vacuum and recognized the two-dimensional grayness of subspace. The attackers activated their propulsion units and seemed to know where they were going. Pard followed.

Abruptly, they passed into real space again, onto a beach not unlike the one on Clutch. There was no mist here, however. The air was dry and clear under a blazing sun that Pard classed roughly as GO. There were other differences: The dunes had been fused and were filled with machinery for kilometers in either direction up and down the coast, and more was under construction.

He turned his attention to the inhabitants of the beach. As the remnant of the assault force landed on the beach, each member stripped off his or her vacsuit and bowed toward a mass of rock on the sea's horizon.

They were most definitely not human, nor did they belong to any race Pard had ever seen. He allowed his awareness to expand to locate his position relative to Occupied Space. The discovery was startling.

He was in the far arm of the Milky Way, beyond the range of even the deepest human probe, sixty thousand light-years away from the edge of Occupied Space. And yet the attackers had traversed the distance with little more than a jet-assisted flying leap into subspace. The ability to extend a warp to such a seemingly impossible degree, from atmosphere to atmosphere with pinpoint accuracy, indicated a level of technological sophistication that was frightening.

He focused down again and allowed his awareness to drift through the worlds of these beings. They were oxygen breathers and humanoid with major and minor differences. On the minor side was the lack of a nose, which was replaced by a single oblong, vertical olfactory orifice. A major variation was the presence of two accessory appendages originating from each axilla. These were obviously vestigial, being supported internally by cartilage and equipped with only minute amounts of atrophic muscle. Both sexes—another minor variation here was the placement of male gonads within the pelvis—adorned the appendages with paints and jewelry.

After observing a small, hivelike community for a number of local days, he concluded that from all outward appearances, this was a quiet and contented race. They laughed, cried, loved, hated, fought, cheated, stole, bought, sold, produced, and consumed. The children played, the young adults courted and eventually married—the race was strictly monogamous—had more children, took care of them, and were in turn cared for when age made them feeble.

A seemingly docile people. Why were they crossing an entire galaxy to slaughter and maim a race that didn't even know they existed?

Pard searched on, focusing on world after world. He found their culture to be oppressively uniform despite the fact that it spanned an area greater than that of the Federation and the old Tarkan Empire combined. He came upon the ruins of three other intelligent races they had contacted. These races had not been assimilated, had not been subjugated, had not been enslaved. They had been annihilated. Every last genetic trace had been obliterated. Pard recoiled at the incongruous racial ferocity of these creatures and searched on for a reason.

The most consistent feature of the culture was the ubiquitous representation of the visage of a member of their own race. A holo of it was present in every room of every hive and a large bust occupied a traditional corner of the main room. There were huge bas-reliefs protruding from the sides of buildings and carved heads overhanging the intersections of major thoroughfares. The doorways to the temples in which one fifth of every day was spent in obeisant worship were formed in the shape of the face. The faithful entered through the mouth.

And there in the temples, perhaps, was a clue to the mysterious ferocity of this race. The rituals were intricate and laborious but the message came through: "We are the chosen ones. All others offend the sight of the Divine One."

Pard expanded again and refocused on the mother world, his port of entry, the planet from which the attacks were launched. He noted that there was now a much larger contingent of troops on the beach: they were bivouacked in half a dozen separate areas.

Multiple attacks? he wondered. Or a single massive one? He realized he had lost all track of time and his thoughts strayed to Steve. Was he all right or had he been caught in another attack? It was highly unlikely but still a possibility.

He vacillated between investigating that revered mound of rock in the sea and checking on Dalt. The former was a curiosity; the latter, he realized, would soon become a compulsion.

Had he possessed lungs and vocal cords, he would have sighed as he expanded to encompass the entire Milky Way; he then allowed a peculiar homing instinct to guide him to Steven Dalt, who was sitting alone in a small room on Fed Central.

He watched him for a few moments, noting that he seemed to be in good health and good spirits. Then Dalt suddenly sat erect. "Pard?" he called. He had somehow sensed his presence and Pard knew it was time to leave again.

Back on the alien mother world, he concentrated on his previous target—the island. It was immediately evident that this was not a natural formation but an artifact cut out of the mainland and set upon a ridge on the ocean floor. The island was a single huge fortress-temple shaped in the form of what he now knew to be the face of the race's goddess; the structures upon it formed the features of the face. An altogether cyclopean feat of engineering.

He allowed his awareness to flow down wide, high-ceilinged corridors tended by guards armed with bows and spears—an insane contrast to the troops gathered on the mainland. The corridors were etched with the history of the race and its godhead. In an instant, Pard knew all of the goddess's past, knew what she had been to humanity and what she had planned for it. He knew her. Even had a name for her. They had met . . . thousands of times.

He sank deep into the structure and came across banks of sophisticated energy dampers—that explained the primitive weapons on the guards. Rising to sea level again, he found himself within a tight-walled maze and decided to see where it led.

He finally found her at the very heart of the edifice, in a tiny room at the end of the maze. Her body was pale, corpulent, and made only minimal voluntary movements. But she was clean and well cared for—a small army of attendants saw to that.

She was old, nearly as old as mankind itself. A genetic freak with a cellular consciousness much like Pard had possessed when in Steve's body, which had kept her physically alive and functioning over the ages. Unlike Dalt/Pard, however, the goddess had only one consciousness, but that was a prodigious one, incorporating psionic powers of tremendous range through which she had dominated her race for much of its existence, shaping its goals and fueling its drives until they had merged and became one with her will.

Unfortunately, the goddess had been a full-blown psychotic for the past three thousand years.

She hated and feared anything that might question her divine supremacy. That was why three other races had already perished. She even distrusted her own worshipers, had made them move her ancient temple out to sea and insisted that her guards don the garb and accouterments of the days of her girlhood.

Pard was aghast at the scope of the tragedy before him. Here was a race that had color and variety in its past. Now, however, through the combination of a psionically augmented religion and a philosophy of racial supremacy, it had been turned into a hive of obedient drones with their lives and culture centered around their goddess-queen. Any independent minds born into the race were quickly culled out once they betrayed their unorthodox tendencies. The reasoning was obvious: The will of the goddess was more than the law of the land—it was divine in origin. To question was heresy; to transgress was sacrilege. The result was a corrupt version of natural selection on an intellectual level. The docile mind that found comfort in orthodoxy survived and thrived, while the reasoner, the questioner, the wavemaker, the rebel, the iconoclast, and the skeptic became endangered species.

As Pard watched her, the goddess lifted her head and opened her eyes. A line about "a gaze blank and pitiless as the sun" went through his mind. She sensed his scrutiny. Her psi abilities made her aware of his presence, tenuous as it was.

She threw a thought at him. It was garbled, colored with rage, couched in madness, but the context could be approximated as:

You again! I thought I had destroyed you!

Enjoying her impotent anger, Pard wished he had the power to send a laugh pealing through the chamber to further arouse her paranoia. As it was, he'd have to be content with observing her thrashing movements as she tried to pinpoint his location.

Pard's awareness began to expand gradually and he soon found himself around as well as within the temple. He tried to focus down again but was unable to do so. He continued to expand at an accelerated rate. He was encircling the planet now.

For the first time since he had awakened to sentience in Dalt's brain, Pard knew fear. He was out of control. Soon his consciousness would be expanded and attenuated to the near-infinite limits he had experienced immediately after being jolted from Steve's body—permanently. And he knew that would be the end of him. His mind would never be able to adjust to it; his intelligence would crumble. He'd end up a nonsentient life force drifting through eternity. It had long been theorized that consciousness could not exist without a material base. He had proven that it could—but not for long. He had to set up another base. He tried desperately to enter the mind of one of the goddess's subjects but found it closed to him. The same with the lower lifeforms.

All minds were closed to him . . . except perhaps one. . . .

He headed for home.

VI

Dalt awoke with a start and bolted upright in bed.

("Hello, Steve.")

A cascade of conflicting emotions ran over him: joy and relief at knowing Pard was alive and at feeling whole again, anger at the nonchalance of his return. But he bottled all emotions and asked, *What happened? Where've you been?*

Pard gave him a brief but complete account in the visual, auditory, and interpretive mélange possible only with mind-to-mind communication. When it was over, it almost seemed to Dalt that Pard had never been gone. There were a few subtle differences, however.

Do you realize that you called me "Steve"? You've been addressing me by my surname for the last century or so.

("You seem more like the old Steve.")

I am. Immortality can become a burden at times, but facing the alternative for a while is a sobering experience.

("I know,") Pard replied, remembering the panic that had gripped him before he had managed to regain the compact security of Dalt's mind. They were now welded together—permanently.

"But back to the matter at hand," Dalt said aloud. "You and I now know what's behind these assaults. The question that bothers me most is: Why us? I mean, if she wants to send her troops out to kill, surely there are other races closer to her than sixty thousand light-years."

("Perhaps the human mind is especially sensitive to her, I don't know. Who can explain a deranged mind? And believe me, this one is deranged! She's blatantly paranoid with xenophobia, delusions of grandeur, and all the trappings. Steve, this creature actually believes she is divine! It's not a pose with her. And as far as her race is concerned, she is god."

"Pity the atheist in a culture like that."

("There are none! How can there be? When these beings speak of their deity, they're not referring to an abstraction or an ephemeral being. Their goddess is incarnate! And she's with them everywhere! She can maintain a continuous contact with her race—it's not control or anything like that, but a hint of *presence*. She has powers none of them possess *and she doesn't die!* She was with them when they were planet-bound, she was with them when they made their first leap into space. She has guided them throughout their entire recorded history. It's not a simple thing to say 'no' to all that.")

"All right, so she's divine as far as they're concerned, but how can she change an entire race into an army of berserk killers? She must have some sort of mind control."

("I can see you have no historical perspective on the power of religion. Human history is riddled with atrocities performed in the names of supposedly benign gods whose only manifestations were in books and tradition. This creature is not merely a force behind her culture . . . she *is* her culture. Her followers attack and slaughter because it is divine will.")

Dalt sighed. "Looks like we're really up against the wall. We were planning to send probes through the passages to try to locate the star system where the assaults originate so we could launch a counteroffensive. Now it makes no difference. Sixty thousand light-years is an incomprehensible distance in human terms. If there was just some way we could get to her, maybe we could give her a nice concentrated dose of the horrors. That'd shake her up."

("I'm afraid not, Steve. You see, this creature is the source of the horrors.")

Dalt sat in stunned silence, then: "You always hinted that the horrors might be more than just a psychological disorder."

("You must admit, I'm rarely wrong.")

"Yes, rarely wrong," Dalt replied tersely. "And frequently insufferable. But again: Why?"

("As I mentioned before, the human mind appears to be extraordinarily sensitive to her powers. She can reach across an entire galaxy and touch one of them. I believe she's been doing that for ages. At first she may only have been able to leave a vague impression. Long ago she was probably probing this arm of the galaxy and left an image within a fertile mind that started the murderous Kali cult in ancient India. Its members worshiped a many-armed goddess of death that bears a striking resemblance to our enemy. So for all practical purposes, we might as well call her Kali, since her given name is a mish-mash of consonants.")

"Whatever happened to the cult?"

("Died out. Perhaps she went back to concentrating on her own race, which was probably moving into space at about that time, and no doubt soon became busy with the task of annihilating the other races they encountered along the way.

("Then came a hiatus and her attention returned to us. Her powers had grown since last contact and although she was still unable to control a human mind, she found she could inundate it with such a flood of terror that the individual would withdraw completely from reality.")

"The horrors, in other words."

("Right. She kept this up, biding her time until her race could devise a means of bridging the gap between the two races. They did. The apparatus occupies the space of a small town and is psionically activated. You know the rest of the story.")

"Yeah," Dalt replied, "and I can see what's coming, too. She's toying with us, isn't she? Playing a game of fear and terror, nibbling at us until we turn against each other. Humiliation, demoralization—they're dirty weapons."

("But not her final goal, I fear. Eventually she'll tire of the game and just wipe us out. And with ease! All she has to do is open the passage, slip through a short-timed planetary bomb, close the passage, and wait for the bang.")

"In two standard days," Dalt said in a shocked whisper, "she could destroy every inhabited planet in Occupied Space!"

("Probably wouldn't even take her that long. But we've quite a while to go before it comes to that. She's in no hurry. She'll probably chip away at us for a few centuries before delivering the coup de grace.") Pard went silent for a while. ("Which reminds me: I saw a major assault force gathered on the beach. If she really wanted to strike a demoralizing blow . . .")

"You don't think she'll hit Fed Central, do you?"

("With a second chance at interstellar unity almost within reach, can you think of a better target?")

"No, I can't," Dalt replied pensively. The thought of alien berserkers charging through the streets was not a pleasant one. "There must be a way to strike back."

("I'm sure there is. We just haven't thought of it yet. Sleep on it.")

Good idea. See you in the morning.

Morning brought Lenda with news that some of the flitter-probes were outfitted and ready. He invited Dalt to take a look at them. Lacking both the heart to tell Lenda that the probes were a futile gesture and anything better to do, he agreed to go along.

Arriving at a hangar atop one of the lesser buildings in the complex, he saw five drones completed and a sixth in the final stages. They looked like standard models except for the data-gathering instruments afixed to the hulls.

"They look like they've been sealed for pressurization," Dalt noted.

Lenda nodded. "Some of the sensors require it."

("I know what you're thinking!") Pard said.

Tell me.

("You want to equip these flitters with blaster cannon and attack Kali's island, don't you? Forget it! There are so many energy dampers in that temple that a blaster wouldn't even warm her skin if you could get near her. And you wouldn't. Her guards would cut you to ribbons.")

Maybe there's a way around that. He turned to Lenda. "Have Petrical meet me here. I have an errand to run but I'll be back shortly."

Lenda gave him a puzzled look as he walked away.

Dalt headed for the street. *Throw the Mordirak image around me. I don't want to be mobbed out there.*

("Done. Now tell me where we're going.")

Not far. He stepped outside and onto the local belt of the moving strol-lane. The streets were crowded. The new incoming representatives had brought their staffs and families and there were tourists constantly arriving to see the first General Council of the new Federation. He let the strol-lane carry him for a few minutes, then debarked before a blank-fronted store with only a simple hand-printed sign over the door: WEAPONS.

Stepping through the filter field that screened the entrance, he was faced with an impressive array of death-dealing instruments. They gleamed from the racks and cases; they were sleek and sinister and beautiful and deadly.

"May I help you, sir?" asked a little man with squinty eyes.

"Where are your combustion weapons?"

"Ah!" he said, rubbing his palms together. "A sportsman or a collector?"

"Both."

"This way, please." He led them to the rear of the shop and placed himself behind a counter. "Now, then. Where does your interest lie? Handguns? Rifles? Shotguns? Automatics?"

"The last two."

"I beg your pardon?"

"I want an autoshotgun," Dalt said tersely. "Double-barreled with continuous feed."

"I'm afraid we only have one model along that line."

"I know. Ibizan makes it."

The man nodded and searched under the counter. He pulled out a shiny black case, placed it before him, and opened it.

Dalt inspected it briefly. "That's it. You have waist canisters for the feed?"

"Of course. The Ibizan is nonejecting, so you'll have to use disintegrating cases, you know."

"I know. Now. I want you to take this down to the workshop and cut the barrel off"—he drew a line with his finger—"right about here."

"Sir, you must be joking!" the little man said with visible shock, his eyes widening and losing their perpetual squint. But he could see by Dalt's expression that no joke was intended. He spoke petulantly. "I'm afraid I must see proof of credit before I deface such a fine weapon."

Dalt fished out a thin alloy disk and handed it over. The gunsmith pressed the disk into a notch in the counter and the image of Mordirak appeared in the hologram box beside it, accompanied by the number 1. Mordirak had first-class credit anywhere in Occupied Space.

With a sigh, the man handed back the disk, hefted the weapon, and took it into the enclosed workshop section.

("Your knowledge of weaponry is impressive.")

A holdover from my game-hunting days. Remember them?

("I remember disapproving of them.")

Well, combustion weapons are still in demand by "sportsmen" who find their sense of masculinity cheated by the lack of recoil in energy weapons.

("And just what is this Ibizan supposed to do for you?")

You'll see.

The gunsmith reappeared with the foreshortened weapon.

"You have a target range, I presume," Dalt said.

"Yes. On the lower level."

"Good. Fill the feeder with number-eight end-over-end cylindrical shot and we'll try her out."

The man winced but complied.

The target range was elaborate and currently set up with moving, bounding models of Kamedon deer. Sensors within the models rated the marksman's performance on a flashing screen at the firing line that could read "Miss," "Kill," "Wounded," and variations. The firing line was cleared as Dalt hooked the feed canister to his waist and fed the string of shells into the chambers. Flicking the safety off, he held the weapon against his chest with the barrels pointing downrange and began walking.

"Left barrel," he said, and pulled the trigger. The Ibizan jerked in his hands; the cannonlike roar was swallowed by the sound dampers but the muzzle flash was a good twenty centimeters in length, and one of the leaping targets was torn in half. "Right barrel," was faintly heard, with similar results. Then a flip of a switch and, "Automatic." The prolonged roar that issued from the rapidly alternating barrels taxed the sound dampers to their limit and when the noise stopped, every target hung in tatters. The indicator screen flashed solid red on and off in confusion.

"What could you possibly want to hunt with a weapon like that?" the little gunsmith asked, glancing from Dalt to the Ibizan to the ruined range.

A smug but irresistible reply came to mind.

"God."

Ω

"You wanted to see me about something?" Petrical asked.

"Yes. I have good reason to believe—please don't ask me why—that the next assault will be a big one and will be directed against Fed Central itself. I want you to outfit these flitters with heavy-duty blasters and pick some of your best marksmen to man five of them. I'll take the sixth."

An amused expression crept over Petrical's face. "And just what do you plan to do with them?"

"We're going through the passage when it opens up," Dalt replied. "Maybe we can end these attacks once and for all."

Amusement was abruptly replaced by consternation. "Oh no, you're not! You're too valuable to risk on a suicide mission!"

"Unfortunately, I'm the only one who can do what must be done," Dalt said with a glare, "and since when do you dictate what I may and may not do."

But Petrical had been involved in too many verbal brawls on the floor of the General Council to be easily intimidated, even by The Healer. "I'll tell you what I *will* do, and that's have no part in helping you get yourself killed!"

"Mr. Petrical," Dalt said in a low voice, "do I have to outfit my own flitter and go through alone?"

Petrical opened his mouth for a quick reply and then closed it. He knew when he was outflanked. With the new General Council arriving for the emergency session, all that was needed to bring the walls tumbling down upon his head was news that he had let The Healer take the war to the enemy alone—with no backup from the Federation Defense Force.

"But the probes were your idea. . . ."

"The probes have been rendered obsolete by new information. The only solution is to go through."

"Well then, let me send a bigger force."

"No." Dalt shook his head. "If these six flitters can't do the job, then six hundred wouldn't make any difference."

"All right." Petrical grunted with exasperation. "I'll get the armorers down here and start asking for volunteers."

Dalt's smile was genuine. "Thanks. And don't delay—we may not have much time. Oh, and have an alarm system set up here in the hangar to notify us the minute a vortex is sighted. We'll live in and around the flitters until the attack comes. I'll brief your men on what to expect and what to do."

Petrical nodded with obvious reluctance.

Ω

("Why haven't I been consulted on any of this?") Pard asked indignantly as Dalt returned to his quarters.

Because I already know your answer.

("I'm sure you do. It's all insanity and I want no part of it!")

You don't have much choice.

("Be reasonable!")

Pard, this is something we must do.

("Why?") The voice in his head was angry. ("To live up to your legend?")

In a way, yes. You and I are the only ones who can beat her.

("You're sure of that?")

Aren't you? Pard did not reply and Dalt felt a sudden chill. *Answer me: Are you afraid of this Kali creature?*

("Yes.")

Why should you be? You defeated her at every turn when we were battling the horrors.

("That was different. There was no direct contact there. We were merely fighting the residue of her influence, a sort of resonating circuit of afterimages. We've only come into direct contact with her once . . . on the beach on Clutch. And you know what happened there.")

Yeah, Dalt replied slowly. *We were blasted apart.*

("Exactly. This creature's psi powers are immense. She's keyed her whole existence toward developing them because her dominion over her race springs from them. I estimate she had a four-thousand-year head start on us. All the defense precautions around her island temple—the energy dampers, the guards with their ridiculous costumes and ancient weapons—would not stand up against a single mercenary soldier in regulation battle gear. They're trappings required by her paranoia. The real defense system of that temple is in her mind. She can psionically fry any brain in her star system that threatens her. Short of an automated Federation dread-naught turning her entire planet to ash—and we have no way of getting one within half a galaxy of her—she's virtually impregnable.")

Pard paused for effect, then: ("You still want to go after her?")

Dalt hesitated, but only briefly. *Yes.*

("Insanity!") Pard exploded. ("Sheer, undiluted, raving insanity! Usually I can follow your reasoning, but this is one big blur. Is there some sort of racial urge involved? Do you feel you owe it to humanity to go down fighting? Is this a noble gesture or what?")

I don't know, exactly.

("You're right, you don't know! You owe your race nothing! You've given it far more than its given you. Your primary responsibility is to yourself. Sacrificing your—*our*—life is a meaningless gesture!")

It's not meaningless. And if we succeed, it won't be a sacrifice.

("We have about as much chance of defeating her as we have of growing flowers on a neutron star. I forbid it!")

You can't. You owe it.

("To whom?")

To me. This is my life and my body. You've augmented it, improved it, and extended it, true, but you've shared equally in the benefits. It remains my life and you've shared it. I'm asking for an accounting.

Pard waited a long time before giving his reply. ("Very well, then. We'll go.") There was a definite edge on the thought. ("But neither of us should make any long-range plans.")

Ω

With the flitters armed, the volunteers briefed, and the practice runs made, Dalt and his crew settled down for an uneasy vigil.

Think we'll have a long wait? Dalt asked.

("I doubt it. The Kalians looked almost set to go when I saw them.")

Well, at least we'll get enough sleep. If there's been any consistency at all in the attacks, it's been their occurrence in daylight hours.

("That may not be the case this time. If my guess is right and they are aiming for Fed Central, their tactics might be different. For all we know, they may just want to set up a device to destroy the Federation Complex.")

Dalt groaned softly. *That would be a crippling coup.*

("Nonsense! The Federation is more than a few buildings. It's a concept . . . and idea.")

It's also an organization; and if there's one thing we need now, it's organization. There's a nucleus of a new Federation growing over at the General Council at this moment. Destroy that and organized resistance will be completely unraveled.

("Perhaps not.")

The Kalians are united wholeheartedly behind their goddess. Who've we got?

("The Healer, of course.")

At this point, if the Federation Complex is destroyed, so is The Healer. Dalt glanced up at the alarm terminal with its howlers and flashers ready to go. *I just hope that thing goes off in time for us to get through the passage.*

("If it goes off, it will probably do so because you set it off.")

What's that supposed to mean?

("The passage is psionically activated and directed by Kali, remember? If a psi force of that magnitude appears anywhere on Fed Central, I'll know about it—immediately.")

"Oh," Dalt muttered aloud. "Well, let's hope it's soon, then. This waiting is nerve-wracking."

("I'll be quite happy if they never show up.")

"We've already been through that!"

"Pardon me, sir," said a trooper passing within earshot.

"What is it?" Dalt asked.

The trooper looked flustered. "I thought you spoke to me."

"Huh? Oh, no." Dalt smiled weakly. "Just thinking out loud."

"Yessir." He nodded and walked on by with a quick backward glance.

("He thinks you may be crazy,") Pard needled. ("So do I, but for entirely different reasons.")

Quiet and let me sleep.

Ω

Their vigil was not a long one. Before dawn on the second day, Dalt suddenly found himself wide awake, his sympathetic nervous system vibrating with alarm.

("Hit the button,") Pard said reluctantly. ("They're here.")

Where?

("About two kilometers away. I'll lead everyone there.")

Fastening the Ibizan feeder belt to his waist as he ran, Dalt activated the alarm and the twenty marksmen were blared and strobed to wakefulness.

The sergeant in charge of the detail trotted up to Dalt. "Where we going?"

Dalt withheld a shrug and said, "Just follow me."

With the activation of the alarm, the hangar roof irised open and the six armed and pressurized flitters were airborne in less than a minute. Pard guided Dalt high above the Federation Complex.

("Now drop and bank off to the left of that building that looks like an inverted pyramind.")

"That's where they are?" Dalt exclaimed.

("Yes. Right in the heart of the complex.")

"From tens of thousands of light-years away . . how can they be so accurate?"

("Not 'they'—*she*. Kali directs the passage.")

With their running lights out, the flitters sank between two smooth-walled buildings until they hovered only a few meters above the pavement.

("It's at the far end of the alley.")

Dalt shook his head in grudging respect. "Pinpoint accuracy."

("And strategically brilliant. There's almost no room to maneuver against them here. I warned you she was a formidable opponent—still want to go through with this?")

Dalt wished he could frame a recklessly courageous reply but none was forthcoming. Instead, he activated the search beams on the front of the flitter and illuminated a chilling sight: The invaders were pouring from their hole in space like angry insects from a hive.

As the flitters came under immediate fire, Dalt gunned his craft to full throttle and it leaped ahead on a collision course with the oncoming horde. Invaders were knocked over or butted aside as he rammed into them. He noted that the flitters behind him were returning fire as they ran—

—and then all was gray, toneless, flat and silent as they passed through the vortex and into subspace. Dalt felt a brief rush of vertigo as he lost his horizon in the featureless void but managed to hold a steady course past surprised and wildly gesticulating invaders on their way to Fed Central.

("Keep her steady for just a little longer and we'll be there.")

Pard had no sooner given this encouragement than the craft burst into sunlight, bowling over more invaders in the process. Without a backward glance, Dalt kept the throttle at full and pulled for altitude toward the sea.

("See the island?")

"Straight ahead."

("Right. Keep going.")

"I just hope the sergeant remembered to tell Petrical where the breakthrough was before he went through."

("Don't worry about that. The sergeant's a seasoned trooper. We've got bigger problems ahead.")

The following flitters were through now and were busily engaged in strafing the Kalian encampments on the shore. Their mission was to cripple the attack on Fed Central and prevent any countermove against Dalt as he headed for the island.

("Veer toward the south side,") Pard told him.

"Which way is south?"

("Left.")

They were near enough now to make out gross details of the temple.

"Where do I land?"

("You don't. At least not yet. See that large opening there? Fly right into it.")

"Doesn't look very big."

("If you could thread that vortex, you can thread that corridor.")

The guardians of the fortress-temple were waiting for them at the entrance with arrows nocked, bows drawn, and spears at the ready.

("Slow up and hit them with the blasters,") Pard directed.

That seemed too brutal to Dalt. "I'll just ride right through them. They're only armed with sharpened sticks."

("I'll remind you of that when they swarm over us from behind and spit your body like a piece of meat. Compassion dulls your memory. Have you forgotten the bathers on Clutch? Or that little boy?")

Enough! Dalt filled his lungs and pressed the newly installed weapons button on the console. The blasters hummed but the guards remained undaunted and uninjured.

"What's wrong?"

("Nothing, except the energy dampers are more powerful than I expected. We may not even get near Kali.")

"Oh, we'll get there, all right." Dalt gunned his craft to top speed again as he dropped the keel to a half meter above the stone steps. Spears and arrows clattered ineffectively off the hull and enclosed cabin but the guards held their ground until Dalt was almost upon them. Then they broke formation. The quick dove for the sides and most escaped uunharmed. The slower ones were hurled in all directions by the prow of the onrushing craft.

Then darkness. At Pard's prompting, Dalt's pupils dilated immediately to full aperture and details were suddenly visible in the dimly lit corridor. The historical frescoes Pard had seen on his previous visit blurred by on either side. Ahead, the corridor funneled down to a low narrow archway.

"I don't think I can make that," Dalt said.

("I don't think so, either. But you can probably use it to hamper pursuit a bit.")

"I was thinking the same thing." He abruptly slowed the craft and let it glide into the opening until both sides crunched against stone. "That oughta do it." The side hatch was flush against the side of the arch, so he broke pressure by lowering the foreward windshield. Cool, damp, musty air filtered into the cabin, carrying a tang of salt and a touch of mildew.

He fed the first round from the canister into the sawed-off Ibizan and climbed out onto the deck. As he slid to the floor, something clattered against the hull close by and an instant later he felt an impact and a grating pain in the right side of his back. Spinning on his heel, he sensed something whiz over his head as he flipped the Ibizan to auto and fired a short burst in an arc.

Four Kalians in a doorway to his right were spun and thrown around by the ferocious spray of shot, then lay still.

What hit me? The pain was gone from his back.

("An arrow. It glanced off the eighth rib on the right and is now imbedded in the intercostal muscle. A poor shot—hit you on an angle and didn't make it through the pleura. I've put a sensory block on the area.")

Good. Which way now?

("Through that doorway. And hurry!")

As Dalt crossed the threshold into a small chamber, another arrow caught him in the left thigh. Again, he opened up the Ibizan and sprayed the room. He took a few of his own ricocheting pellets in the chest, but the seven Kalians lying in wait for him had taken most of them.

("Keep going!") There was more than a trace of urgency in the directive.

He managed to run, although his left leg dragged somewhat due to the arrow's mechanical impediment of muscle action. But he felt no pain from this wound either. As he left the bloody anteroom and entered another corridor, his vision suddenly blurred and his equilibrium wavered.

What was that?

("The same knockout punch that separated us on Clutch. Only this time I was ready for it. Now the going gets tough—the lady has decided to step in.")

Dalt started to run forward again but glanced down and found himself at the edge of a yawning pit. Something large and hungry thrashed and splashed in the inky darkness below.

"Where'd that come from?" he whispered hoarsely.

("From Kali's mind. It's not real—keep going.")

You sure?

("Positive . . I think.")

Oh, great! Dalt gritted his teeth and began to run. To his immense relief, his feet struck solid ground, even though he seemed to be running on air.

White tentacles, slime-coated and as thick as his thighs, sprang out from the walls and reached for him. He halted again.

Same thing?

("I hope so. You're only seeing a small fraction of what I'm seeing. I'm screening most of it. And so far she's only toying with us. I'll bet she's holding back until—")

A spear scaled off the wall to his right, forestalling further discussion. As Dalt turned with the Ibizan at the ready, an arrow plunged into the fleshy fossa below his left clavicle. The guards from the entrance to the temple had found a way around the flitter and were now charging down the corridor in pursuit. With a flash that lit up the area and a roar that was deafening in those narrow confines, the Ibizan scythed through the onrushing ranks, leaving many dead and the rest disabled, but not before Dalt had taken another arrow below the right costal margin. Fluid that looked to be a mixture of green, yellow, and red began to drip along the shaft.

How many of these things can I take? I'm beginning to look like a Neekan spine worm!

("A lot more. But not too many more like that last one. It pierced the hepatic duct and you're losing bile. Blood, too. I can't do too much to control the bleeding from the venous sinusoids in the liver. But we'll be all right as long as no arrows lodge in any of the larger joints or sever a major motor axon bundle, either of which would severely hamper mobility. The one under your clavicle was a close call; just missed the brachial plexus. Another centimeter higher and you'd have lost the use of your . . .")

The words seemed to fade out.

"Pard?" Dalt said.

(". . . run!") The thought was strained, taut. ("She's hitting us with *everything* now. . . .") Fade out again. Then, ("I'll tell you where to turn!")

Dalt ran with all the speed he could muster, limping with his left leg and studiously trying to avoid contact between the narrow walls and the shafts protruding from his body. The corridor became a maze with turns every few meters. At each intersection he would hear a faint ("left") or ("right") in his mind. And as minutes passed, the voice became progressively weaker until it was barely distinguishable among his own thoughts.

("Please hurry!") Pard urged faintly and Dalt realized that he must be taking a terrible beating—in twelve hundred years Pard had never said "please."

("Two more left turns and you're there . . . don't hesitate . . . start firing as soon as you make the last turn. . . .")

Dalt nodded in the murk and double-checked the automatic setting, fully intending to do just that. But when the moment came, when he made the final turn, he hesitated for a heartbeat, just long enough to see what he would be shooting at.

She lay there, propped up on cushions and smiling at him. El. Somehow it didn't seem at all incongruous that she should be there. Her death nearly a millennium ago had all been a bad dream. But he had awakened now and this was Tolive, not some insane planet on the far side of the galaxy.

He stepped toward her and was about to let the Ibizan slip from his fingers when every neuron in his body was jolted with a single message:

"Fire!"

His finger tightened on the trigger reflexively and El exploded in a shower of red. He was suddenly back in reality and he held the roaring, swerving, bucking weapon on target until the feed canister was empty.

The echoes faded, and finally, silence.

There was not too much left of Kali. Dalt only glanced at the remains, turned, and retched. As he gasped for air and wiped clammy beads of sweat from his upper lip, he asked Pard, *No chance of regeneration, is there?*

No answer.

"Pard?" he called aloud, and underwent an alarming instant of déjà vu. But this time he knew Pard was still there—an indefinable sense signaled his presence. Pard was injured, weakened, scarred, and had retreated to a far corner of Dalt's brain. But he was still there.

Without daring a backward glance, he tucked the Ibizan into the crook of his right arm, its barrel aligned with the arrow protruding from his liver, and reentered the maze. He was concerned at first with finding his way out, until he noticed drops of a familiar muddy fluid on the floor in the dim light. He had left a trail of blood and bile as it oozed from his liver, along the arrow shaft and onto the floor.

With only a few wrong turns, he managed to extricate himself from the maze and limp back to the flitter. There he was confronted with another problem.

A large group of Kali's guards stood clustered around the craft. Dalt's immediate reaction was to shift the Ibizan and reach for the trigger. A gesture as futile as it was unnecesary: the weapon was empty, and at sight of him, the guards threw down their arms and prostrated themselves face down on the ground before him.

They know she's dead, he thought. *Somehow, they know.* He hesitated only a moment, then stepped gingerly between the worshipers and their dead brethren who had attacked him earlier.

He had a difficult moment entering the flitter when the arrows protruding from the front and back of his chest caught on the window opening. The problem was resolved when he snapped off the shaft of the arrow under the clavicle a handsbreadth away from his skin.

Situating himself again at the console, he first replaced the empty feeder canister with a fresh one—just in case—and activated the instruments before him. The vid screen to his right immediately lit up with the sergeant's face. Dalt made a quick adjustment of the transmitting lens to limit focus to his face.

"Healer!" the sergeant exclaimed with obvious relief. "You're all right?"

"Fine," Dalt replied. "How are things over there?"

The sergeant grinned. "It was rough going for a while—couple of the flitters took a beating and one's down. But just when things were starting to look really bad, the opposition folded . . . just threw down their weapons and went into fits on the beach . . . ignored us completely. Some of them dove into the ocean and started swimming toward the island. The rest are just moping aimlessly along the water's edge."

"Everything's secure, then?" Dalt asked. The flitter's engine was humming now. He pulled the guide stick into reverse and upped the power. The craft vibrated as it tried to disengage from the doorway. With a grating screech, the flitter came free and caromed off the port wall before Dalt could throttle down and stabilize. The corridor was too narrow here to make a full turn, so he resigned himself to gliding part of the way out in reverse.

The sergeant said something but Dalt missed it and asked him to repeat. "I said, there's a couple of my men burned but they should do all right if we get back."

With his head turned over his left shoulder and two fingers on the guide stick, Dalt was concentrating fully on piloting the flitter in reverse. It was not until he reached the point where the corridor widened to its fullest expanse that the "if" broke through.

"What do you mean, 'if?" he asked, throwing the gears into neutral and hitting the button that would automatically guide the flitter in a 180-degree turn on its own axis.

"The gate or passage or warp or whatever you want to call it—it's closed," he replied. "How're we going to get home?"

Dalt felt a tightness in his throat but put on a brave face. "Just sit tight till I get there. Out."

"Right," the sergeant said, instantly reassured. He was convinced The Healer could do anything. "Out." The vid plate went black.

Dalt put the problem of crossing the sixty thousand light-years that separated his little group from the rest of humanity out of his mind and concentrated on the patch of light ahead of him. The return had been too easy so far. He could not help but expect some sort of reprisal, and his head pivoted continuously as he gained momentum toward the end of the corridor and daylight.

But no countermove was in the offing. As Dalt shot from the darkness into the open air, he saw the steps leading to the temple entrance blanketed with prostrate Kalians. Most eyes stayed earthward, but here and there a head was raised as he soared over the crowd and headed for the mainland. He could not read individual expressions but there was a terrible sense of loss in their postures and movements. The ones who looked after him seemed to be saying, "You've killed our godhead and now disdain to take her place, leaving us with nothing."

Dalt felt sudden pity for the Kalians. Their entire culture had been twisted, corrupted, and debased by a single being. And now that being was no more. Utter chaos would follow. But from the rubble would rise a new, broader-based society, hopefully with a more benign god, or perhaps no god. Anything would be an improvement.

("Perhaps,") said a familiar voice, ("their new god will be

Kalianoid with a white patch of hair and a golden hand. And minstrels will sing of how he crossed the void, shrugged off their arrows and spears, and went on to overpower the all-powerful, to slay She-Who-Could-Not-Die.")

Gained your strength back, I see.

("Not quite. I may never fully recover from that ordeal. All debts are paid, I hope, because I will never risk my existence like that again.")

I sincerely hope such a situation will never arise again. And yes, all debts are paid in full.

("Good. And if you awaken in the middle of the night now and again with the sound of horrified screaming in your brain, don't worry. It'll be me remembering what I've just been through.")

That bad, eh?

("I'm amazed we survived—and that's all I'll say on the matter.")

Details of the coast were coming into view now, and below, Dalt spotted an occasional Kalian swimming desperately for the island.

You know about the warp generator? Dalt asked.

("Yes. As I told you before, Kali activated it psionically. She's dead now so it's quite logical that it should cease to function. I think I can activate it briefly. So call the sergeant and have him get his men into the air—we'll have to make this quick.")

Dalt did so, and found four of the five flitters, each overloaded with men from the disabled craft, hovering over the shore.

("Here goes,") Pard said. ("I can only hope that there was some sort of lock on the settings, because I haven't the faintest idea how to direct the passage. We could end up in the middle of a sun or somewhere off the galactic rim.")

Dalt said only, "Do it!" and pressurized the cabin.

Nothing happened for a while, then a gray disk appeared. It expanded gradually, evenly, and as soon as its diameter appeared sufficient to accommodate a flitter, Dalt threw the stick forward and plunged into the unknown.

VII

They seemed to drift in the two-dimensional grayness interminably. Then, as if passing through a curtain, they were in real space, in daylight, on Fed Central. And what appeared to be the entire Federation Defense Force clogged the alley before them and the air above them in full battle readiness. There was more lethal weaponry crammed into that little alley than was contained on many an entire planet. And it was all trained on Dalt.

Ever so gently, he guided his flitter to ground between incinerated Kalian bodies and sat quietly, waiting for the following craft to do the same. When the last came through, the vortex collapsed upon itself and disappeared.

("That's the end of that!") Pard said with relief. ("Unless the Kalian race develops another psi freak who can learn to operate it, the warp passage will never open again.")

Good. By the time we run into them again—a few millennia hence, no doubt—they should be quite a bit more tractable.

With the closing of the passage, the marksmen in the other craft opened all the hatches and tumbled out to the pavement. At the sight of their comrades, the battle-ready troops around them lowered their weapons and pandemonium broke out. The flitters were suddenly surrounded by cheering, waving soldiers.

Ros Petrical seemed to appear out of nowhere, riding a small, open grav platform. The milling troops made way for him as he landed beside Dalt's flitter.

Dalt opened the hatch and came out to meet him. His effect on the crowd was immediate. As his head appeared and the snowy patch of hair was recognized, a loud cheer arose; but when his body came into view, the cheer choked and died. There followed dead silence broken only by occasional murmurs of alarm.

"Pardon my appearance," Dalt said, glancing at the bloody shafts protruding from his body and tucking the Ibizan under his arm, "but I ran into a little resistance."

Petrical swallowed hard. "You really are The Healer!" he muttered.

"You mean to say you had your doubts?" Dalt asked with a wry smile as he stepped onto the platform.

Petrical shot the platform above the silent crowd. "Frankly, yes. I've always thought there was a chain of Healers . . . but I guess you're the real thing."

"Guess so. Where're we going?"

"Well, I had planned to take you to the Council session; they're waiting to hear from you in person." He glanced at the arrows. "But that can wait. I'm taking you to the infirmary."

Dalt laid a hand on his arm. "To the Council. I'm quite all right. After all," he said, quoting a line that was centuries old, " 'what kind of a healer would The Healer be if he couldn't heal himself?' "

Petrical shook his head in bafflement and banked toward the General Council hall.

A sequence of events similar to that which had occurred in the alley was repeated in the Council hall. The delegates and representatives had receive word that The Healer's mission had been successful and that he was on his way to address them personally. Many of the men and women in the chamber were members of The Healer cult and started cheering and chanting before he appeared. As in the alley, a great shout went up at first sight of him on the high dais, but this was instantly snuffed out when it became obvious that he was mortally wounded. But Dalt waved and smiled to reassure them and then the uproar resumed with renewed intensity.

Between horrified glances at Dalt's punctured body, the elderly president protem of the Council was trying to bring order to the meeting and was being completely ignored. The delegates and reps were in the aisles, shouting, waving, and hugging one another. Dalt spotted Lenda standing quietly amid the Clutch delegation. Their eyes met and Dalt nodded his congratulations. The nod was returned with a smile.

After a few minutes of the tumult, Dalt began to grow impatient. Switching the Ibizan to the single-shot mode, he handed it to the president pro tem.

"Use this as a gavel."

The old man took it with a knowing grin and aimed the weapon at the high ceiling. He let off four rounds in rapid succession. The acoustic material above absorbed the end-over-end shot with ease but was less successful in handling the accompanying roar. The crowd quieted abruptly.

"Now that I have your attention," he said with forced sternness, "please take your places."

The Council members laughed good-naturedly and complied.

"I've never seen or heard of a more vigorous, more vital, more rowdy bunch of representatives in my life!" Petrical whispered, his face flushed with excitement.

Dalt nodded and inwardly told Pard, *I feel pretty vigorous myself.*

("About time,") came the sardonic reply. ("It's been a couple of centuries since you've shown much life.")

The president pro tem was speaking. "We have before us a motion to install The Healer as chief executive of the Federation by acclaim. Now what I propose to do is . . ." Even with amplification at maximum, his voice was lost in the joyous chaos that was unleashed by the announcement.

Shrugging, the old man stepped back from the podium and decided to let the demonstration run its course. The pandemonium gradually took the form of a chant.

". . . HEALER! HEALER! HEALER ! . . ."

Pard became a demon voice in Dalt's mind. ("They're in the palm of your hand. Take command and you can direct the course of human history from now on.")

And be another Kali?

("Your influence wouldn't have to be malevolent. Look at them! Tarks, Lentemians, Humans! Think of all the great things you could lead them to!")

Dalt considered this as he watched the crowd and drank in its intoxicating chant:

". . . HEALER! HEALER! HEALER! . . ."

Thoughts of Tolive suddenly flashed before him. *You know my answer!*

("You're not even tempted?")

Not in the least. I can't remember when I last felt so alive, and I find there are many things I still want to do, many goals I still want to achieve. Power isn't one of them.

Pard's silence indicated approval. ("What will you tell them?") he asked finally.

Don't know, exactly. Something about holding to the LaNague Charter, about letting the Federation be the focus of their goals but never allowing those goals to originate here. Peace, freedom, love, friendship, happiness, prosperity, and other sundry political catch-words. But the big message will be a firm "No thanks!"

("You're sure now?") Pard taunted. ("You don't want to be acclaimed leader of the entire human race and a few others as well?")

I've got better things to do.

Epilogue

Kolko lounged by the fire and eyed the wagon that sat in darkness on the far side of the flames. His troupe of Thespelian gypsies had turned in early tonight in preparation for their arrival in Lanthus tomorrow. Kolko was hurt and angry—but only a little. Thalana had taken up with the new mentalist and wanted no part of him.

He was tempted to enter the darkened wagon and confront the two of them but had decided against it for a number of reasons. First off, he had no real emotional attachment to Thalana, nor she to him. His pride was in pain, not his heart. Secondly, a row over a love triangle would only cause needless dissension in the peaceful little company. And finally, it would mean facing up to the new mentalist, a thought he did not relish.

An imposing figure, this newest member of the troupe, with all of his skin dyed gold and his hair dyed silver . . . a melding of precious metals. And quite a talent. Kolko had seen mentalists come and go but could not figure out how this one pulled off his stunts.

A likable fellow, but distant. Hiding from his past, no doubt, but that hardly made him unique among the gypsies of Thespel. He would laugh with the group around the fire and could drink an incredible amount of wine without ever opening up. Always one step removed. And he had an odd habit of muttering to himself now and again, but nobody ever mentioned it to him . . . there was an air about the man that brooked no meddling with his personal affairs or habits.

So let him have Thalana. There would be other dancers joining the troupe along the way, probably better-looking than Thalana and better in the bedroll . . . although that would take some doing.

Let 'em be. Life was too good these days. Good wine, good company, good weather, good crowds of free-spending people in the towns.

He picked up an arthritic tree limb and stirred the coals, watching the sparks swirl gently upward to mingle with the pinpoint stars overhead.

Let 'em be.

An excerpt from MAN-KZIN WARS II, created by *Larry Niven*:

The Children's Hour

Chuut-Riit always enjoyed visiting the quarters of his male offspring.

"What will it be this time?" he wondered, as he passed the outer guards.

The household troopers drew claws before their eyes in salute, faceless in impact-armor and goggled helmets, the beam-rifles ready in their hands. He paced past the surveillance cameras, the detector pods, the death-casters and the mines; then past the inner guards at their consoles, humans raised in the household under the supervision of his personal retainers.

The retainers were males grown old in the Riit family's service. There had always been those willing to exchange the uncertain rewards of competition for a secure place, maintenance, and the odd female. Ordinary kzin were not to be trusted in so sensitive a position, of course, but these were families which had served the Riit clan for generation after generation. There was a natural culling effect; those too ambitious left for the Patriarchy's military and the slim chance of advancement, those too timid were not given opportunity to breed.

Perhaps a pity that such cannot be used outside the household, Chuut-Riit thought. Competition for rank was far too intense and personal for that, of course.

He walked past the modern sections, and into an area that was pure Old Kzin; maze-walls of reddish sandstone with twisted spines of wrought-iron on their tops, the tips glistening razor-edged. Fortress-architecture from a world older than this, more massive, colder and drier; from a planet harsh enough that a plains carnivore had changed its ways, put to different use an upright posture designed to place its head above savanna grass, grasping paws evolved to climb rock. Here the modern features were reclusive, hidden in wall and buttress. The door was a hammered slab graven with the faces of night-hunting beasts, between towers five times the height of a kzin. The air smelled of wet rock and the raked sand of the gardens.

Chuut-Riit put his hand on the black metal of the outer portal, stopped. His ears pivoted, and he blinked; out of the corner of his eye he saw a pair of tufted eyebrows glancing through the thick twisted metal on the rim of the ten-meter battlement. *Why, the little sthondats*, he thought affectionately. *They managed to put it together out of reach of the holo pickups.*

The adult put his hand to the door again, keying the locking sequence, then bounded backward four times his own length from a standing start. Even under the lighter gravity of Wunderland, it was a creditable feat. And necessary, for the massive panels rang and toppled as the rope-swung boulder slammed forward. The children had hung two cables from either tower, with the rock at the point of the V and a third rope to draw it back. As the doors bounced wide he saw the blade they had driven into the apex of the egg-shaped granite rock, long and barbed and polished to a wicked point.

Kittens, he thought. *Always going for the dramatic.* If that thing had struck him, or the doors under its impetus had, there would have been no need of a blade. *Watching too many historical adventure holos. "Errorowwww!"* he shrieked in mock-rage bounding through the shattered portal and into the interior court, halting atop the kzin-high boulder. A round dozen of his older sons were grouped behind the rock, standing in a defensive clump and glaring at him, the crackly scent of their excitement and fear made the fur bristle along his spine. He glared until they dropped their eyes, continued it until they went down on their stomachs, rubbed their chins along the ground and then rolled over for a symbolic exposure of the stomach.

"Congratulations," he said. "That was the closest you've gotten. Who was in charge?"

More guilty sidelong glances among the adolescent males crouching among their discarded pull-rope, and then a lanky youngster with platter-sized feet and hands came squatting-erect. His fur was in the proper flat posture, but the naked pink of his tail still twitched stiffly.

"I was," he said keeping his eyes formally down. "Honored Sire Chuut-Riit," he added, at the adult's warning rumble.

"Now, youngling, What did you learn from your first attempt?"

"That no one among us is your match, Honored Sire Chuut-Riit," the kitten said. Uneasy ripples went over the black-striped orange of his pelt.

"And what have you learned from this attempt?"

"That all of us together are no match for you, Honored Sire Chuut-Riit," the striped youth said.

"That we didn't locate all of the cameras," another muttered. "You idiot, Spotty." That to one of his siblings; they snarled at each other from their crouches, hissing past barred fangs and making striking motions with unsheathed claws.

"No, you did locate them all, cubs," Chuut-Riit said. "I presume you stole the ropes and tools from the workshop, prepared the boulder in the ravine in the next courtyard, then rushed to set it all up between the time I cleared the last gatehouse and my arrival?"

Uneasy nods. He held his ears and tail stiffly, letting his whiskers quiver slightly and holding in the rush of love and pride he felt, more delicious than milk heated with bourbon. *Look at them!* he thought. At the age when most young kzin were helpless prisoners of instinct and hormone, wasting their strength ripping each other up or making fruitless direct attacks on their sires, or demanding to be allowed to join the Patriarchy's service *at once* to win a Name and household of their own . . . *His* get had learned to *cooperate* and use their minds!

"Ah, Honored Sire Chuut-Riit, we set the ropes up beforehand, but made it look as if we were using them for tumbling practice," the one the others called Spotty said. Some of them glared at him, and the adult raised his hand again.

"No, no, I am *moderately* pleased." A pause. "You did not hope to take over my official position if you had disposed of me?"

"No, Honored Sire Chuut-Riit," the tall leader said. There had been a time when any kzin's holdings were the prize of the victor in a duel, and the dueling rules were interpreted more leniently for a young subadult. Everyone had a sentimental streak for a successful youngster; every male kzin remembered the intolerable stress of being physically mature but remaining under dominance as a child.

Still, these days affairs were handled in a more civilized manner. Only the Patriarchy could award military and political office. And this mass assassination attempt was . . . unorthodox, to say the least. Outside the rules more because of its rarity than because of formal disapproval. . . .

A vigorous toss of the head. "Oh, no, Honored Sire Chuut-Riit. We had an agreement to divide the private possessions. The lands and the, ah, females." Passing their own mothers to half-siblings, of course. "Then we wouldn't each have so much we'd get too many challenges, and we'd agreed to help each other against outsiders," the leader of the plot finished virtuously.

"Fatuous young scoundrels," Chuut-Riit said. His eyes narrowed dangerously. "You haven't been communicating outside the household, have you?" he snarled.

"Oh, *no*, Honored Sire Chuut-Riit!"

"Word of honor! May we die nameless if we should do such a thing!"

The adult nodded, satisfied that good family feeling had prevailed. "Well as I said, I am somewhat pleased. If you have been keeping up with your lessons. Is there anything you wish?"

"Fresh meat, Honored Sire Chuut-Riit," the spotted one said. The adult could have told him by the scent, of course, a kzin never forgot another's personal odor, that was one reason why names were less necessary among their species. "The reconstituted stuff from the dispensers is always . . . so . . . *quiet*."

Chuut-Riit hid his amusement. Young Heroes-to-be were always kept on an inadequate diet, to increase their aggressiveness. A matter for careful gauging, since too much hunger would drive them into mindless cannibalistic frenzy.

"And couldn't we have the human servants back? They were nice." Vigorous gestures of assent. Another added: "They told good stories. I miss my Clothilda-human."

"Silence!" Chuut-Riit roared. The youngsters flattened stomach and chin to the ground again. "Not until you can be trusted not to injure them; how many times do I have to tell you, it's dishonorable to attack household servants! Until you learn self-control, you will have to make do with machines."

This time all of them turned and glared at a mottled youngster in the rear of their group; there were half-healed scars over his head and shoulders. "It bared its *teeth* at me," he said sulkily. "All I did was swipe at it, how was I supposed to know it would die?" A chorus of rumbles, and this time several of the covert kicks and clawstrikes landed.

"Enough," Chuut-Riit said after a moment. *Good, they have even learned how to discipline each other as a unit.* "I will consider it, when all of you can pass a test on the interpretation of human expressions and body-language." He drew himself up. "In the meantime, within the next two eight-days, there will be a formal hunt and meeting in the Patriarch's Preserve; kzinti homeworld game, the best Earth animals, and even some feral-human outlaws, perhaps!"

He could smell their excitement increase, a mane-crinkling musky odor not unmixed with the sour whiff of fear. Such a hunt was not without danger for adolescents, being a good opportunity for hostile adults to cull a few of a hated rival's offspring with no possibility of blame. *They will be in less danger than most*, Chuut-Riit thought judiciously. *In fact, they may run across a few of my subordinates' get and mob them. Good.*

"And if we do well, afterwards a feast and a visit to the Sterile Ones." That had them all quiveringly alert, their tails held rigid and tongues lolling; nonbearing females were kept as a rare privilege for Heroes whose accomplishments were not *quite* deserving of a mate of their own. Very rare for kits still in the household to be granted such, but Chuut-Riit thought it past time to admit that modern society demanded a prolonged adolescence. The day when a male kit could be given a spear, a knife, a rope and a bag of salt and kicked out the front gate at puberty were long gone. Those were the wild, wandering years in the old days, when survival challenges used up the superabundant energies. Now they must be spent learning history, technology, xenology, none of which burned off the gland-juices saturating flesh and brain.

He jumped down amid his sons, and they pressed around him, purring throatily with adoration and fear and respect;

his presence and the failure of their plot had reestablished his personal dominance unambiguously, and there was no danger from them for now. Chuut-Riit basked in their worship, feeling the rough caress of their tongues on his fur and scratching behind his ears. *Together*, he thought. *Together we will do wonders.*

From "The Children's Hour" by Jerry Pournelle & S.M. Stirling

---

FALLEN ANGELS

Two refugees from one of the last remaining orbital space stations are trapped on the North American icecap, and only science fiction fans can rescue them! Here's an excerpt from *Fallen Angels*, the bestselling new novel by Larry Niven, Jerry Pournelle, and Michael Flynn.

* * *

She opened the door on the first knock and stood out of the way. The wind was whipping the ground snow in swirling circles. Some of it blew in the door as Bob entered. She slammed the door behind him. The snow on the floor decided to wait a while before melting. "Okay. You're here," she snapped. "There's no fire and no place to sit. The bed's the only warm place and you know it. I didn't know you were this hard up. And, by the way, I don't have any company, thanks for asking." If Bob couldn't figure out from that speech that she was pissed, he'd never win the prize as Mr. Perception.

"I am that hard up," he said, moving closer. "Let's get it on."

"Say what?" Bob had never been one for subtle technique, but this was pushing it. She tried to step back but his hands gripped her arms. They were cold as ice, even through the housecoat. "Bob!" He pulled her to him and buried his face in her hair.

"It's not what you think," he whispered. "We don't have time for this, worse luck."

"Bob!"

"No, just bear with me. Let's go to your bedroom. I don't want you to freeze."

He led her to the back of the house and she slid under the covers without inviting him in. He lay on top, still wearing his thick leather coat. Whatever he had in mind, she realized, it wasn't sex. Not with her housecoat, the comforter and his greatcoat playing chaperone.

He kissed her hard and was whispering hoarsely in her ear before she had a chance to react. "Angels down. A scoopship. It crashed."

"Angels?" Was he crazy?

He kissed her neck. "Not so loud. I don't think the 'danes are listening, but why take chances? Angels. Spacemen. *Peace* and *Freedom*."

She'd been away too long. She'd never heard spacemen called *Angels*. And— "Crashed?" She kept it to a whisper. "Where?"

"Just over the border in North Dakota. Near Mapleton."

"Great Ghu, Bob. That's on the Ice!"

He whispered, "Yeah. But they're not too far in."

"How do you know about it?"

He snuggled closer and kissed her on the neck again. Maybe sex made a great cover for his visit, but she didn't think he had to lay it on so thick. "We know."

"We?"

"The Worldcon's in Minneapolis-St. Paul this year—"

The World Science Fiction Convention. "I got the invitation, but I didn't dare go. If anyone saw me—"

"—And it was just getting started when the call came down from *Freedom*. Sherrine, they couldn't have picked a better time or place to crash their scoopship. That's why I came to you. Your grandparents live near the crash site."

She wondered if there was a good time for crashing scoopships. "So?"

"We're going to rescue them."

"We? Who's we?"

"The Con Committee, some of the fans—"

"But why tell me, Bob? I'm fafiated. It's been years since I've dared associate with fen."

Too many years, she thought. She had discovered science fiction in childhood, at her neighborhood branch library. She still remembered that first book: *Star Man's Son*, by Andre Norton. Fors had been persecuted because he was different; but he nurtured a secret, a mutant power. Just the sort of hero to appeal to an ugly-duckling little girl who would not act like other little girls.

SF had opened a whole new world to her. A galaxy, a

universe of new worlds. While the other little girls had played with Barbie dolls, Sherrine played with Lummox and Poddy and Arkady and Susan Calvin. While they went to the malls, she went to Trantor and the Witch World. While they wondered what Look was In, she wondered about resource depletion and nuclear war and genetic engineering. Escape literature, they called it. She missed it terribly.

"There is always one moment in childhood," Graham Greene had written in *The Power and the Glory*, "when the door opens and lets the future in." For some people, that door never closed. She thought that Peter Pan had had the right idea all along.

"Why tell *you*? Sherrine, we want you with us. Your grandparents live near the crash site. They've got all sorts of gear we can borrow for the rescue."

"Me?" A tiny trickle of electric current ran up her spine. But . . . *Nah.* "Bob, I don't dare. If my bosses thought I was associating with fen, I'd lose my job."

He grinned. "Yeah. Me, too." And she saw that he had never considered that she might not go.

'Tis a Proud and Lonely Thing to Be a Fan, they used to say, laughing. It had become a *very* lonely thing. The Establishment had always been hard on science fiction. The government-funded Arts Councils would pass out tax money to write obscure poetry for "little" magazines, but not to write speculative fiction. "Sci-fi isn't literature." *That* wasn't censorship.

Perversely, people went on buying science fiction without grants. Writers even got rich without government funding. *They couldn't kill us that way!*

Then the Luddites and the Greens had come to power. She had watched science fiction books slowly disappear from the library shelves, beginning with the children's departments. (That wasn't censorship either. Libraries couldn't buy *every* book, now could they? So they bought "realistic" children's books funded by the National Endowment for the Arts, books about death and divorce, and really important things like being overweight or fitting in with the right school crowd.)

Then came paper shortages, and paper allocations. The science fiction sections in the chain stores grew smaller. ("You can't expect us to stock books that aren't selling." And they can't sell if you don't stock them.)

Fantasy wasn't hurt so bad. Fantasy was about wizards

and elves, and being kind to the Earth, and harmony with nature, all things the Greens loved. But science fiction was about science.

Science fiction wasn't exactly outlawed. There was still Freedom of Speech; still a Bill of Rights, even if it wasn't taught much in the schools—even if most kids graduated unable to read well enough to understand it. But a person could get into a lot of unofficial trouble for reading SF or for associating with known fen. She could lose her job, say. Not through government persecution—of course not—but because of "reduction in work force" or "poor job performance" or "uncooperative attitude" or "politically incorrect" or a hundred other phrases. And if the neighbors shunned her, and tradesmen wouldn't deal with her, and stores wouldn't give her credit, who could blame them? Science fiction involved science; and science was a conspiracy to pollute the environment, "to bring back technology."

Damn right! she thought savagely. We do conspire to bring back technology. Some of us are crazy enough to think that there are alternatives to freezing in the dark. *And some of us are even crazy enough to try to rescue marooned spacemen before they freeze, or disappear into protective custody.*

Which could be dangerous. The government might declare you mentally ill, and help you.

She shuddered at that thought. She pushed and rolled Bob aside. She sat up and pulled the comforter up tight around herself. "Do you know what it was that attracted me to science fiction?"

He raised himself on one elbow, blinked at her change of subject, and looked quickly around the room, as if suspecting bugs. "No, what?"

"Not Fandom. I was reading the true quill long before I knew about Fandom and cons and such. No, it was the feeling of hope."

"Hope?"

"Even in the most depressing dystopia, there's still the notion that the future is something we build. It doesn't just happen. You can't predict the future, but you can invent it. Build it. That is a hopeful idea, even when the building collapses."

Bob was silent for a moment. Then he nodded. "Yeah. Nobody's building the future anymore. 'We live in an Age of Limited Choices.' " He quoted the government line without cracking a smile. "Hell, you don't *take* choices off a list. You *make* choices and *add* them to the list. Speaking of which, have you made your choice?"

That electric tickle . . . "Are they even alive?"

"So far. I understand it was some kind of miracle that they landed at all. They're unconscious, but not hurt bad. They're hooked up to some sort of magical medical widgets and the Angels overhead are monitoring. But if we don't get them out soon, they'll freeze to death."

She bit her lip. "And you think we can reach them in time?"

Bob shrugged.

"You want me to risk my life on the Ice, defy the government and probably lose my job in a crazy, amateur effort to rescue two spacemen who might easily be dead by the time we reach them."

He scratched his beard. "Is that quixotic, or what?"

"Quixotic. Give me four minutes."